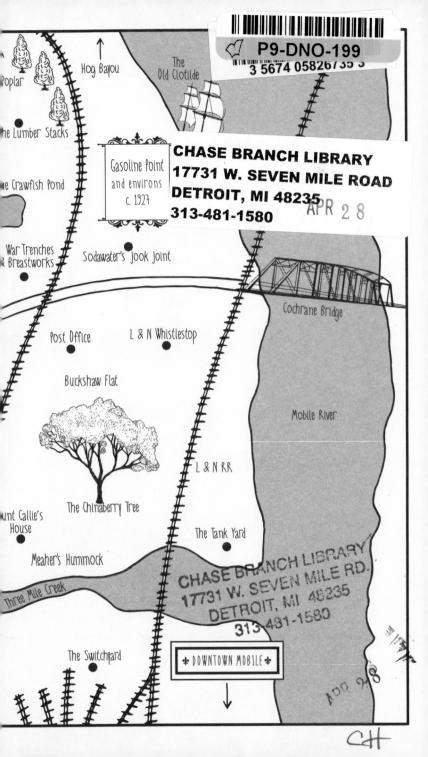

Hog Bayou

The Old Clotilde

Poplar

he Lumber Stacks

e Crawfish Pond

Gasoline Point
and environs
c. 1927

War Trenches
& Breastworks

Sodawater's Jook joint

Cochrane Bridge

Post Office

L & N Whistlestop

Buckshaw Flat

Mobile River

L & N RR

The Chinaberry Tree

unt Callie's
House

The Tank Yard

Meaher's Hummock

Three Mile Creek

The Switchyard

✦ DOWNTOWN MOBILE ✦

ALBERT MURRAY

ALBERT MURRAY

COLLECTED NOVELS & POEMS

Train Whistle Guitar
The Spyglass Tree
The Seven League Boots
The Magic Keys
Poems

Henry Louis Gates, Jr.
and Paul Devlin, *editors*

THE LIBRARY OF AMERICA

Published in the United States by Library of America.
Visit our website at www.loa.org.

The Spyglass Tree copyright © 1991 by Albert Murray.
The Seven League Boots copyright © 1995 by Albert Murray.
The Magic Keys copyright © 2005 by Albert Murray. Published by
arrangement with Vintage Anchor Publishing, an imprint of the
Knopf Doubleday Group, a division of Penguin Random House LLC.

Train Whistle Guitar copyright © 1974 by Albert Murray.
Conjugations and Reiterations copyright © 2001 by Albert Murray.
All other texts copyright © by Albert Murray.
Published by arrangement with the Albert Murray Trust and
The Wylie Agency LLC.

Endpaper by Donna G. Brown for Library of America.

This paper meets the requirements of
ANSI/NISO Z39.48–1992 (Permanence of Paper).

Distributed to the trade in the United States
by Penguin Random House Inc.
and in Canada by Penguin Random House Canada Ltd.

Library of Congress Control Number: 2017939511
ISBN 978–1–59853–561–7

First Printing
The Library of America—304

Manufactured in the United States of America

Albert Murray:
Collected Novels & Poems
is published with support from

Ford Foundation
Charlie Davidson
Crystal McCrary and Raymond J. McGuire
Jazz at Lincoln Center
Lewis and Kristin Jones
Sidney Offit
Douglas E. Schoen
&
The Administration, Faculty, Staff, and
Alumni of Tuskegee University in memory of
Dr. Benjamin Payton,
Fifth President of Tuskegee University, 1981–2010

Contents

TRAIN WHISTLE GUITAR

For Michele

THERE WAS a chinaberry tree in the front yard of that house in those days, and in early spring the showers outside that window always used to become pale green again. Then before long there would be chinaberry blossoms. Then it would be maytime and then junebugtime and no more school bell mornings until next September, and when you came out onto the front porch and it was fair there were chinaberry shadows on the swing and the rocking chair, and chinaberry shade all the way from the steps to the gate.

When you climbed up to the best place in the chinaberry tree and looked out across Gins Alley during that time of the year the kite pasture, through which you took the short cut to the post office, would be a meadow of dog fennels again. So there would also be jimson weeds as well as ragworts and rabbit tobacco along the curving roadside from the sweet gum corner to the pump shed, and pokesalad from there to the AT & N.

You couldn't see the post office flag from the chinaberry tree because it was down in Buckshaw Flat at the L & N whistlestop. You couldn't see the switch sidings for the sawmills along that part of Mobile River either, because all that was on the other side of the tank yard of the Gulf Refining Company. All you could see beyond the kite pasture were the telegraph poles and the sky above the pine ridge overlooking Chickasabogue Creek and Hog Bayou.

You couldn't see the blackberry slopes near the L & N Section Gang Quarters because first there were the honeysuckle thickets and then Skin Game Jungle where the best muscadine vines were and in which there were also some of the same owl tree holes you knew about from fireside ghost stories about treasures buried by the pirates and the Confederates.

Southeast of all of that was the L & N clearing, across which you could see the trains and beyond which you could also see that part of the river. Next on the horizon due south was Three Mile Crest, which blocked off Dodge Mill Bottom and that part of Three Mile Creek. So you couldn't see the waterfront either, nor any part of the downtown Mobile, Alabama skyline, not even with real binoculars.

Nor could you see One Mile Bridge beyond the treeline to the southwest. Nor the pecan orchard which you knew was due west looking out over the gate and the sunflowers and across the AT & N cut, which you couldn't see either. Nor African Baptist Hill. But between that neighborhood and the Chickasaw Highway was the Southern Railroad, whose night whistles you could sometimes hear as sometimes after midnight you could also hear the M & O, the GM & O and the GM & N en route to St. Louis, Missouri and Kansas City by way of Meridian, Mississippi.

All you could see due north up Dodge Mill Road beyond Buckshaw Corner and the crawfish pond that was once part of a Civil War artillery embankment was the sky above Bay Poplar Woods fading away into the marco polo blue horizon mist on the other side of which were such express train destinations as Birmingham, Alabama and Nashville, Tennessee, and Cincinnati, Ohio, and Detroit, Michigan, plus the snowbound Klondike of Canada plus the icebound tundras of Alaska plus the North Pole.

The Official name of that place (which is perhaps even more of a location in time than an intersection on a map) was Gasoline Point, Alabama, because that was what our post office address was, and it was also the name on the L & N timetable and the road map. But once upon a time it was also the briarpatch, which is why my nickname was then Scooter, and is also why the chinaberry tree (that was ever as tall as any fairy tale beanstalk) was, among other things, my spyglass tree.

I USED TO say *My name is also Jack the Rabbit because my home is in the briarpatch,* and Little Buddy (than whom there was never a better riddle buddy) used to say *Me my name is Jack the Rabbit also because my home is also in the also and also of the briarpatch because that is also where I was also bred and also born.* And when I also used to say *My name is also Jack the Bear* he always used to say *My home is also nowhere and also anywhere and also everywhere.*

Because the also and also of all of that was also the also plus also of so many of the twelve-bar twelve-string guitar riddles you got whether in idiomatic iambics or otherwise mostly from Lu-zana Cholly who was the one who used to walk his trochaic-sporty stomping-ground limp-walk picking and plucking and knuckle knocking and strumming (like an anapestic locomotive) while singsongsaying *Anywhere I hang my hat anywhere I prop my feet. Who could drink muddy water who could sleep in a hollow log.*

THE COLOR you almost always remember when you remember Little Buddy Marshall is sky-blue. Because that shimmering summer sunshine blueness in which neighborhood hens used to cackle while distant yard dogs used to bark and mosquito hawks used to flit and float along nearby barbwire fences, was a boy's color. Because such blueness also meant that it was whistling time and rambling time. And also baseball time. Because that silver bright midafternoon sky above outfields was the main thing Little Buddy Marshall and I were almost always most likely to be wishing for back in those days when we used to make up our own dirty verses for that old song about it ain't gonna rain no more no more.

But the shade of blue and blueness you always remember whenever and for whatever reason you remember Luzana Cholly is steel blue, which is also the clean, oil-smelling color of gunmetal and the gray-purple patina of freight train engines and railroad slag. Because in those days, that was a man's color (even as tobacco plus black coffee was a man's smell), and Luzana Cholly also carried a blue steel .32-20 on a .44 frame in his underarm holster. His face and hands were leather brown like dark rawhide. But blue steel is the color you always remember when you remember how his guitar used to sound.

Sometimes he used to smell like coffee plus Prince Albert cigarettes, which he rolled himself, and sometimes it was a White Owl Cigar, and sometimes it was Brown's Mule Chewing Tobacco. But when he was wearing slick starched wash-faded blue denim overalls plus tucked in jumper plus his black and white houndstooth-checked cap plus high top, glove-soft banker-style Stacy Adams, which was what he almost always traveled in, he also smelled like green oak steam. And when he was dressed up in his tailor-made black broadcloth boxback plus pegtop hickory-striped pants plus either a silk candy-striped or silk pongee shirt plus knitted tie and diamond stickpin plus an always brand new gingerly blocked black John B. Stetson hat because he was on his way somewhere either to gamble or to

6

play his guitar, what he smelled like was barbershop talcum and crisp new folding money.

I can remember being aware of Luzana Cholly all the way back there in the blue meshes of that wee winking blinking and nod web of bedtime story time when I couldn't yet follow the thread of the yarns I was to realize later on that somebody was forever spinning about something he had done, back when all of that was mainly grown folks talking among themselves by the fireside or on the swing porch as if you were not even there: saying Luzana and old Luzana and old Luze, and I didn't know what, to say nothing of where Louisiana was.

But I already knew who he himself was even then, and I could see him very clearly whenever they said his name because I still can't remember any point in time when I had not already seen him coming up that road from around the bend and down in the L & N railroad bottom. Nor can I remember when I had not yet heard him playing the blues on his guitar as if he were also an engineer telling tall tales on a train whistle, his left hand doing most of the talking including the laughing and signifying as well as the moaning and crying and even the whining, while his right hand thumped the wheels going somewhere.

Then there was also his notorious holler, the sound of which was always far away and long coming as if from somewhere way down under. Most of the time (but not always) it started low like it was going to be a moan or even a song, and then it jumped all the way to the very top of his voice and suddenly broke off. Then it came back, and this time it was already at the top. Then as often as not he would make three or four, or sometimes three followed by four, bark-like squalls and let it die away in the darkness (you remember it mostly as a nighttime sound); and Mama always used to say he was whooping and hollering like somebody back on the old plantations and back in the old turpentine woods, and one time Papa said maybe so but it was more like one of them old Luzana swamp hollers the Cajuns did in the shrimp bayous. But I myself always thought of it as being something else that was like a train, a bad express train saying Look out this me and here I come and I'm on my way one more time.

I knew that much about Luzana Cholly even before I was big enough to climb the chinaberry tree. Then finally I could climb all the way to the top, and I also knew how to box the compass; so I also knew what Louisiana was as well as where, or at least which way, it was from where I was.

At first he was somebody I used to see and hear playing the guitar when he was back in town once more. I hadn't yet found out very much about him. Nor was I ever to find out very much that can actually be documented. But it is as if I have always known that he was as rough and ready as rawhide and as hard and weather worthy as blue steel, and that he was always either going somewhere or coming back from somewhere and that he had the best walk in the world, barring none (until Stagolee Dupas (*fils*) came to town).

Anyway I had already learned to do my version of that walk and was doing the stew out of it long before Little Buddy Marshall first saw it, because he probably saw me doing it and asked me about it before he saw Luzana Cholly himself and that is probably how he found out about Luzana Cholly and rawhide and blue steel in the first place.

During that time before Little Buddy came was also when I was first called Mister. Miss Tee, who was the one I had always regarded as being without doubt the best of all Big Auntees, had always called me My Mister; and Mama had always called me Little Man and My Little Man and Mama's Little Man; but some time after Little Buddy Marshall came she used to drop the *Little* part off and that is how they started calling me Mister Man before my nickname became Scooter. But long before Little Buddy Marshall came I had been telling myself that Luzana Cholly was the Man I wanted to be like.

Then Little Buddy Marshall was there and it was as if time itself were sky-blue; and every day was for whistling secret signals and going somewhere to do something you had to have nerves as strong as rawhide to get away with. Luzana Cholly was the one we always used to try to do everything like in those days. Even when you were about to do something that had nothing whatsoever to do with anything you had ever heard about him, as often as not when your turn came you said Watch old Luze. Here come old Luze. This old Luze. If Luze can't ain't nobody can.

And then not only had we come to know as much as we did about what he was like when he was there in the flesh and blood, we also knew how to talk to him, because by that time he also knew who we were. Sometimes we would come upon him sitting somewhere by himself tuning and strumming his guitar and he would let us stay and listen as long as we wanted to, and sometimes he would sneak our names into some very well known ballad just to signify at us about something, and sometimes he would make up new ballads right on the spot just to tell us stories.

We found out that the best time to signify at him because you needed some spending change was when he was on his way to the Skin Game Jungles. (Also: as far as you could tell, gambling and playing the guitar and riding the rails to and from far away places were the only steady things he ever had done or ever would do, except during the time he was in the Army and the times he had been in jail—and not only had he been to jail and the county farm, he had done time in the penitentiary!)

We were supposed to bring him good luck by woofing at him when he was headed for a skin game. So most of the time we used to try to catch him late Saturday afternoon as he came across the oil road from Gins Alley coming from Miss Pauline Anderson's Cookshop. Sometimes he would have his guitar slung across his back even then, and that he was wearing his .32-20 in his underarm holster goes without saying.

Say now hey now Mister Luzana Cholly.

Mister Luzana Cholly one time.

(Watch out because here come old Luzana goddamn Cholly one more goddamn time and one goddamn time more and don't give a goddamn who the hell knows it.)

Mister Luzana Cholly all night long.

Yeah me, ain't nobody else but.

The one and only Mister Luzana Cholly from Bogaluzana bolly.

(Not because he was born and raised in Bogalusa, Louisiana; because he once told us he was bred and born in Alabama, and was brought up here and there to root hog or die poor. Somebody had started calling him Luzana because that was where he had just come back in town from when he made his first reputation as a twelve-string guitar player second to none, including Leadbelly. Then it also kept people from confusing him with Choctaw Cholly, who was part Indian and Chastang Cholly the Cajun.)

Got the world in a jug.
And the stopper in your hand.
Y'all tell em, 'cause I ain't got the heart.
A man among men.
And Lord God among women!
Well tell the dy ya.

He would be standing wide legged and laughing and holding a wad of Brown's Mule Chewing Tobacco in with his tongue at the same time. Then he skeet a spat of amber juice to one side like some clutch hitters do when they step up to the plate, and then he would wipe the back of his leathery hand across his mouth and squint his eyes the way some batters sight out at the pitcher's mound.

Tell the goddamn dyyyy ya! He leveled and aimed his finger and then jerked it up like a pistol firing and recoiling.

Can't tell no more though.

How come, little sooner, how the goddamn hell come?

B'cause money talks.

Well shut my mouth. Shut my big wide mouth and call me suitcase.

Ain't nobody can do that.

Not nobody that got to eat and sleep.

I knowed y'all could tell em. I always did know good and damn well y'all could tell em. And y'all done just told em.

But we ain't go'n tell no more.

We sure ain't.

Talk don't mean a thing in the world if you ain't got nothing to back it up with.

He would laugh again then and we would stand waiting because we knew he was going to run his hand deep down into his pocket and come up not with the two customary nickels but two quarters between his fingers. He would flick them into the air as if they were jacks and catch them again, one in each hand; and then he would close and cross his hand, making as if to look elsewhere, flip one to me and one to Little Buddy Marshall.

Now talk. But don't talk too loud and don't tell too much, and handle your money like the whitefolks does.

Mama used to say he was don't-carified, and Little Buddy Marshall used to call him hellfied Mister Goddamn hellfied Luzana ass-kicking Cholly; and he didn't mean hell-defying, or hell-fired either. Because you couldn't say he was hell-defying because you couldn't even say he ever really went for bad, not even when he was whooping that holler he was so notorious for. Perhaps that was *somewhat* hell-defying to some folks, but even so what it really meant as much as anything else was I don't give a goddamn if I *am* hell-defying, which is something nobody driven by hell fire ever had time to say.

As for going for bad, that was the last thing he needed to do, since everybody, black or white, who knew anything at all about him already knew that when he made a promise he meant if it's the last thing I do, if it's the last thing I'm able to do on this earth. Which everybody also knew meant if you cross me I'll kill you and pay for you, as much as it meant anything else. Because the idea of going to jail didn't scare him at all, and the idea of getting lynch-mobbed didn't faze him either. All I can remember him ever saying about that was: If they shoot at me they sure better not miss me they sure better get me that first time. Whitefolks used to say he was a crazy nigger, but what they really meant or should have meant was that he was confusing to them. Because if they knew him well enough to call him crazy they also had to know enough about him to realize that he wasn't foolhardy, or even careless, not even what they wanted to mean when they used to call somebody biggity. Somehow or other it was as if they respected him precisely because he didn't seem to care anything about them one way or the other. They certainly respected the fact that he wasn't going to take any foolishness off of them.

Gasoline Point folks also said he was crazy. But they meant their own meaning. Because when they said crazy they really meant something else, they meant exactly the same thing as when they called him a fool. At some point some time ago (probably when my favorite teacher was Miss Lexine Metcalf) I decided that what they were talking about was something like poetic madness, and that was their way of saying that he was forever doing something unheard of if not downright

outrageous, doing the hell out of it, and not only getting away
with whatever it was, but making you like it to boot. You could
tell that was the way they felt by the way they almost always
shook their heads laughing even as they said it, and sometimes
even before they said it: Old crazy Luzana Cholly can sure play
the fool out of that guitar. Old crazy Luzana Cholly is a guitar
playing fool and a card playing fool and a pistol packing fool
and a freight train snagging fool, and don't care who knows it.

I still cannot remember ever having heard anybody saying anything about Luzana Cholly's mother and father. Most of the
time you forgot all about that part of his existence just as most
people had probably long since forgotten whether they had
ever heard his family name. Nobody I know ever heard him use
it, and no sooner had you thought about it than you suddenly
realized that he didn't seem ever to have had or to have needed
any family at all. Nor did he seem to need a wife or steady
woman either. But that was because he was not yet ready to
quit the trail and settle down. Because he had lived with more
women from time to time and place to place than the average
man could or would even try to shake a stick at.

The more I think about all of that the more I realize that you
never could tell which part of what you heard about something
he had done had actually happened and which part somebody
else had probably made up. Nor did it ever really matter which
was which. Not to anybody I ever knew in Gasoline Point,
Alabama, in any case, to most of whom all you had to do was
mention his name and they were ready to believe any claim you
made for him, the more outrageously improbable the better.
All you had to do was say Luzana Cholly old Luzana Cholly
old Luze. All you had to do was see that sporty limp walk. Not
to mention his voice, which was as smoke-blue sounding as
the Philamayork-skyline-blue mist beyond blue steel railroad
bridges. Not to mention how he was forever turning guitar
strings into train whistles which were not only the once-upon-
a-time voices of storytellers but of all the voices saying what
was being said in the stories as well.

Not that I who have always been told that I was born to
be somebody did not always know on my deepest levels of

comprehension that the somebody-ness of Luzana Cholly was of its very nature nothing if not legendary. Which no doubt also has something to do with why I almost always used to feel so numb and strange when somebody other than kinfolks called out the name that Mama had given me and Miss Tee had taught me how to spell and write. I always jumped, even when I didn't move. And in school I wanted to hide, but you had to answer because it was the teacher calling the roll so I said Present and it didn't sound like myself at all. It was not until Uncle Jerome not so much nicknamed as ordained me Scooter that I could say That's me, that's who I am and what I am and what I do.

Anyway, such somehow has always been the nature of legends and legendary men (which probably exist to beget other legends and would-be legendary men in the first place) that every time Little Buddy Marshall and I used to do that sporty-blue limp-walk (which told the whole world that you were ready for something because at worst you had only been ever so slightly sprained and bruised by all the terrible situations you had been through) we were also reminding ourselves of the inevitability of the day when we too would have to grab ourselves an expert armful of lightning special L & N freight train rolling north by east to the steel blue castles and patent leather avenues of Philamayork, which was the lodestone center of the universe.

That is why we had started practicing freight train hopping on the tanks and boxcars in the switchyard as soon as we had gained enough leeway to sneak that far away from the neighborhood. That was the first big step, and you were already running a double risk (of being caught and of getting maimed for life at the very least) as soon as you started playing with something as forbidden as that, which was what they told you everything you had ever heard about old Peg Leg Nat to keep you from doing. Old Peg Leg Nat Carver, who had a head as bald and shiny as the nickelplated radiator of the Packard Straight Eight and who prided himself on being able to butt like a billy goat, and who now spent most of his time fishing and selling fresh fish and shrimp and crabs from the greenness of his palm frond covered wheelbarrow. Somebody was always reminding you of what had happened to him. Mama for instance, who could never pass up a chance to say Here come old Peg Leg Nat and a peg leg or something worse is just exactly what messing around with freight trains will get you. And she had had me scared for a while, but not for long. Because then Little Buddy Marshall and I found out that what had happened probably never would have happened if Old Nat, who was then known as old Butt Head Nat, had not been drunk and trying to show everybody how fancy he was. And anyway anybody could see that getting his leg cut off hadn't really stopped old Nat for good, since not only did he still do it again every time he got the itch to go somewhere, he also could still beat any two-legged man except Luzana Cholly himself snagging anything rolling through Gasoline Point.

———————

Then Little Buddy found out that Luzana Cholly himself was getting ready to leave town again soon and I myself found out which way he was going to be heading (but not where) and which day, so we also knew which train; and that was when we got everything together and started waiting.

Then at long last after all the boy blue dreaming and scheming and all the spyglass scanning it was that day and we were there in that place because it was time to take the next step. I was wearing my high top brogan shoes and I had on my corduroy pants and a sweater under my overalls with my jumper tucked in. I was also wearing my navy blue baseball cap and my rawhide wristband and I had my pitcher's glove folded fingers up in my left hip pocket. And Little Buddy was wearing and carrying the same amount of the very same traveling gear except for his thin first base pad instead of big thick Sears Roebuck catcher's mitt. Our other things plus something to eat were rolled up in our expertly tied blanket rolls so that we could maneuver with both arms free.

Little Buddy was also carrying Mister Big Buddy Marshall's pearl handled .38 Smith & Wesson. And our standard equipment for any trip outside that neighborhood in those days always included our all-purpose jackknives, which we had learned to snap open like a switchblade and could also flip like a Mexican dagger. Also, buckskin pioneers and wilderness scouts that we would always be, we had not forgotten hooks and twine to fish with. Nor were we ever to be caught in any root hog or die poor situation without our trusty old Y-stock (plus inner tube rubber plus shoe tongue leather) slingshots and a drawstring Bull Durham pouch of birdshot babbitt metal plus at least a handful of peewee sized gravel pebbles.

It was May but school was not out of session yet, so not only were we running away from home we were also playing hooky, for which the Truant Officer also known as the School Police could take you to Juvenile Court and have you detained and then sent to the Reformatory School. (Mt. Meigs and Wetumpka were where they used to send you in those days. No wonder I still remember them as being two of the ugliest place names in the whole state of Alabama. Not as ugly as Bay Minette, which I still remember as a prototype of all the rattlesnake nests of rawboned hawkeyed nigger-fearing lynch-happy peckerwoods I've ever seen or heard tell of. But ugly enough to offset most of the things you didn't like about grade school.)

It was hot even for that time of year, and with that many clothes on, we were already sweating. But you had to have them, and that was the best way to carry them. There was a thin breeze coming across the railroad from the river, the marsh and Polecat Bay, but the sun was so hot and bright that the rail tracks were shimmering under the wide open sky as if it were the middle of summer.

We were waiting in the thicket under the hill between where the Dodge Mill Road came down and where the oil yard switching spurs began, and from where we were you could see up and down the clearing as far as you needed to.

I have now forgotten how long we had to stay there waiting and watching the place from where we had seen Luzana Cholly come running across the right of way to the tracks so many times. But there was nothing you could do but wait then, as we knew he was doing, probably strumming his guitar and humming to himself.

Man, I wish it would hurry up and come on, Little Buddy said all of a sudden.

Man, me too, I probably said without even having to think about it.

Man, got to get to goddamn splitting, he said and I heard his fingers touching the package of cigarettes in his bib pocket.

We were sitting on the blanket rolls with our legs crossed Indian fire circle fashion. Then he was smoking another One Eleven, holding it the way we both used to do in those days, letting it dangle from the corner of your curled lips while tilting your head to one side with one eye watching and the other squinted, like a card sharper.

Boy, goddammit, you just watch me nail the sapsucker, he said.

Man, and you just watch me.

You could smell the mid-May woods up the slope behind us then, the late late dogwoods, the early honeysuckles, and the warm earth-plus-green smell of the pre-summer undergrowth. I can't remember which birds you used to hear during each season, not like I used to; but I do remember hearing a woodpecker somewhere on a dead hollow tree among all the other bird sounds that day because I also remember thinking that woodpeckers always sounded as if they were out in the open in the very brightest part of the sunshine.

Waiting and watching, you were also aware of how damp and cool the sandy soft ground was underneath you there in the gray and green shade; and you could smell that smell too, even as the Gulf Coast states breeze blew all of the maritime odors in to you from the river and the marshlands. Little Buddy finished his cigarette and flipped the stub out into the sunshine and then sat with his back against a sapling and sucked his teeth. I looked out across the railroad to where the gulls were circling over the reeds and the water.

You know something? Goddammit, when I come back here to this here little old granny-dodging burg, boy I'm going to be a goddamn man and a goddamn half, Little Buddy said, breaking the silence again.

As before, he was talking as much to himself as to me. But I said: And don't give a goddamn who knows it. Then he said:

Boy, Chicago. And I said: Man, Detroit. And he said: Man, St. Louis. And I said: And Kansas City. Then: Hey, Los Angeles. Hey, San Francisco. Hey, Denver, Colorado. Him calling one and me adding another until we had leapfrogged all the way back down to the Florida Coast Line, with him doing that old section gang chant: Say I don't know but I think I will make my home in Jacksonville (Hey big boy cain't you line em).

Then I was the one, because that is when I said: Hey, you know who the only other somebody else in the world I kinda wish was here to be going too? And little Buddy said: Old Cateye Gander. Me too. Old Big-toed Gander. Man, shit I reckon.

Man, old Gander Gallagher can steal lightning if he have to.

Man, who you telling?

Man, how about that time? You know that time getting them wheels for that go-cart. That time from Buckshaw.

Right on out from under that nightwatchman's nose, man.

And everybody know they got some peckerwoods down there subject to spray your ass with birdshot just for walking too close to that fence after dark.

Man, shit I reckon. And tell you you lucky it wasn't that other barrel, because that's the one with triple ought buckshot.

Hey man but old Luze though.

Man, you know you talking about somebody now.

Talking about somebody taking the cake.

Goddammit man, boy, just think. We going!

Me and you and old hard cutting Luze, buddy.

Boy, and then when we get back, I said that and I could see it. Coming back on that Pan American I would be carrying two leather suitcases, and have a money belt and an underarm holster for my special-made .38 Special. And I would be dressed in tailor-made clothes and handmade shoes from London, England by way of Philamayork.

Hey Lebo, I said, thinking about all that then. How long you think it might take us to get all fixed up to come back.

Man, shoot, I don't know and don't care.

You coming back when old Luze come back?

Man, I don't know. Just so we go. Man, me I just want to *go*.

I didn't say anything else then. Because I was trying to think about how it was actually going to be then. Because what I had been thinking about before was how I wanted it to be. I didn't say anything else because I was thinking about myself then. And then my stomach began to feel weak and I tried to think about something else. But I couldn't. Because what I suddenly remembered as soon as I closed my eyes that time was the barbershop and them talking about baseball and boxing and women and politics with the newspapers rattling and old King Oliver's band playing "Sugarfoot Stomp" on the Victrola in Papa Gumbo's cookshop next door, and I said I want to and I don't want to but I got to, then I won't have to anymore either and if I do I will be ready.

Then I looked over at Little Buddy again, who now was lying back against the tree with his hands behind his head and his eyes closed, whose legs were crossed, and who was resting as easy as some baseball players always seem able to do before gametime even with the band hot timing the music you always keep on hearing over and over when you lose. I wondered what he was really thinking. Did he really mean it when he said he didn't know and didn't even care? You couldn't tell what he was thinking, but if you knew him as well as I did it was easy enough to see that he was not about to back out now, no matter how he was feeling about it.

So I said to myself: Goddammit if Little Buddy Marshall can go goddammit I can too because goddammit ain't nothing he can do I cain't if I want to because he might be the expert catcher but I'm the ace pitcher and he can bat on both sides but I'm the all-round infield flash and I'm the prizefighter and I'm also the swimmer.

But what I found myself thinking about again then was Mama and Papa, and that was when I suddenly realized as never before how worried and bothered and puzzled they were going to be when it was not only that many hours after school but also after dark and I still was not back home yet. So that was also when I found myself thinking about Miss Tee again. Because she was the one whose house would be the very first place I was absolutely certain Mama would go looking for me, even before asking Mister Big Buddy about Little Buddy.

Hey, Lebo.
Hey, Skebo.
Skipping city.
Man, you tell em.
Getting further.
Man, ain't no lie.
Getting long gone.
Man, ain't no dooky.

Goddammit to hell, Little Buddy said then, why don't it come on?

Son-of-a-bitch, I said.

Goddamn granny-dodging son-of-a-bitching motherfucking motherfucker, he said lighting another One Eleven, come on here son-of-a-bitching motherfucking son-of-a-bitch.

I didn't say anything else because I didn't want him to say anything else. Then I was leaning back against my tree looking out across the sandy clearing at the sky beyond the railroad and the marsh territory again, where there were clean white pieces of clouds that looked like balled up sheets in a wash tub, and the sky itself was blue like rinse water with bluing in it; and I was thinking about Mama and Papa and Uncle Jerome and Miss Tee again, and I couldn't keep myself from hoping that it was all a dream.

That was when I heard the whistle blowing for Three Mile Creek Bridge and opened my eyes and saw Little Buddy already up and slinging his roll over his shoulder.

Hey, here that son-of-a-bitch come. Hey, come on, man.

I'm here, son, I said snatching my roll into place, Don't be worrying about me. I been ready.

The engine went by, and the whistle blew again, this time for the Chickasabogue, and we were running across the sandy crunch-spongy clearing. My ears were ringing then, and I was sweating, and my neck was hot and sticky and my pants felt as if the seat had been ripped away. There was nothing but the noise of the chugging and steaming and the smell of coal smoke, and we were running into it, and then we were climbing up the fill and running along the high bed of crosstie slag and cinders.

We were trotting along in reach of it then, that close to the um chuckchuck um chuckchuck um chuckchuckchuck, catching our breath and remembering to make sure to let at least one empty boxcar go by. Then when the next gondola came Little Buddy took the front end, and I grabbed the back. I hit the hotbox with my right foot and stepped onto the step and pulled up. The wind was in my ears then, but I knew all about that from all the practice I had had by that time. So I climbed on up the short ladder and got down on the inside, and there was old Little Buddy coming grinning back toward me.

Man, what did I tell you!

Man, did you see me lam into that sucker?

Boy, we low more nailed it.

Hey, I bet old Luze be kicking it any minute now.

Man, I'm talking about cold hanging it, man.

Boy, you know it, man, I said. But I was thinking I hope so, I hope old Luze didn't change his mind, I hope we don't have to start out all by ourselves.

Hey going, boy, Little Buddy said.

Man, I done told you!

We crawled up into the left front corner out of the wind, and there was nothing to do but wait again then. We knew that this was the northbound freight that always had to pull into the hole for Number Four once she was twelve miles out, and that was when we were supposed to get to the open boxcar.

So we got the cigarettes out and lit up, and there was nothing but the rumbling thunder-like noise the wide open gondola made then, plus the far away sound of the engine and the low rolling pony tail of gray smoke coming back. We were just sitting there then, and after we began to get used to the vibration, nothing at all was happening except being there. You couldn't even see the scenery going by.

You were just there in the hereness and nowness of that time then, and I don't think you ever really remember very much about being in situations like that except the way you felt, and all I can remember now about that part is the nothingness of doing nothing, and the feeling not of going but of being taken, as of being borne away on a bare barge or even on the bare back of a storybeast.

All you could see after we went through the smokey gray lattice-work of Chickasabogue Bridge was the now yellow blue sky and the bare floor and the sides of the heavy rumbling gondola, and the only other thing I have ever remembered is how I wished something would happen because I definitely did not want to be going anywhere at all then, and I already felt lost even though I knew good and well that I was not yet twelve miles from home. Because although Little Buddy Marshall and I had certainly been many times farther away and stayed longer, this already seemed to be farther and longer than all the other times together!

———————

Then finally you could tell it was beginning to slow down, and we stood up and started getting ready. Then it was stopping and we were ready and we climbed over the side and came down the ladder and struck out forward. We were still in the bayou country, and beyond the train-smell there was the sour-sweet snakey smell of the swampland. We were running on slag and cinders again then and with the train quiet and waiting for Number Four you could hear the double crunching of our brogans echoing through the waterlogged moss-draped cypresses.

Along there the L & N causeway embankment was almost as high as the telegraph lines, and the poles were black with a fresh coat of creosote and there were water lilies floating on the slimy green ditch that separated the railroad right of way from the edge of the swamp. Hot-collared and hustling to get to where we estimated the empty boxcar to be, we came pumping on. And then at last we saw it and could slow down and catch our breath.

And that was when we also saw that old Luzana Cholly himself was already there. We had been so busy trying to get there that we had forgotten all about him for the time being. Not only that but this was also the part that both of us had completely forgotten to think about all along. So we hadn't even thought about what we were going to say, not to mention what he was going to say.

And there he was now standing looking down at us from the open door with an unlighted cigarette in his hand. We had already stopped without even realizing it, and suddenly everything was so quiet that you could hear your heart pounding inside your head. It was as if the spot where you were had been shut off from everything else in the world. I for my part knew exactly what was going to happen then, and I was so embarrassed that I could have sunk into the ground, because I also thought: Now he's going to call us a name. Now he just might never have anything to do with us anymore.

We were standing there not so much waiting as frozen then, and he just let us stay there and feel like two wet puppies shivering, their tails tucked between their legs. Then he lit his cigarette and finally said something.

Oh no you don't oh no you don't neither. Because it ain't like that ain't like that ain't never been like that and ain't never going to be not if I can help it.

He said that as much to himself as to us, but at the same time he was shaking his head not only as if we couldn't understand him but also as if we couldn't even hear him.

Y'all know it ain't like this. I know y'all know good and well it *cain't* be nothing like *this.*

Neither one of us even moved an eye. Little Buddy didn't even dig his toe into the ground.

So this what y'all up to. Don't say a word. Don't you open your mouth.

I could have crawled into a hole. I could have sunk into a pond. I could have melted leaving only a greasy spot. I could have shriveled to nothing but an ash.

Just what y'all call y'allself doing? That's what I want to know. So tell me that. Just tell me that. Don't say a word. Don't you say one word. Don't you say a goddamn mumbling word to me. Neither one of you.

We weren't even about to make a sound.

What I got a good mind to do is whale the sawdust out of both you little crustbusters. That's what I ought to be doing right now instead of talking to somebody ain't got no better sense than that.

But he didn't move. He just stood where he was looking down.

Well, I'm a son-of-a-bitch. That's what I am. I'm a son-of-a-bitch. I'm a thick-headed son-of-a-bitch. Hell, I musta been deaf dumb and blind to boot not to know this. Goddamn!

That was all he said then, and then he jumped down and walked us to where the side spur for the southbound trains began, and all we did was sit there near the signal box and feel terrible until Number Four had come whistling by and was gone and we heard the next freight coming south. Then what he did when it finally got there was worse than any name he could ever have called us. He wouldn't let us hop it even though it was only a short haul and pickup local that was not much more than a switch engine with more cars than usual. He waited for it to slow down for the siding and then he picked me up (as they pick you up to put you in the saddle of a pony because you're not yet big enough to reach the stirrups from the ground on your own) and put me on the front end of the first gondola, and did the same thing to Little Buddy; and then he caught the next car and came forward to where we were.

So we came slow-poking it right back toward the Chick-asabogue and were back in Gasoline Point before the sawmill whistles even started blowing the hands back to work from noontime. I could hardly believe that so little time had passed. But then such is the difference between legendary time and actuality, which is to say, the time you remember and the time you measure.

We came on until the train all but stopped for Three Mile Creek Bridge, and then he hopped down and took Little Buddy off first and then me, and we followed him down the steep, stubble covered embankment and then to the place the hobos used under the bridge. He unslung the guitar and sat down and lit another cigarette and flipped the match stem into the water and watched it float away. Then he sat back and looked at us again, and then he motioned for us to sit down in front of him.

That was when we found out what we found out directly from Luzana Cholly himself about hitting the road, which he (like every fireside knee-pony uncle and shade tree uncle and tool shed uncle and barbershop uncle since Uncle Remus himself) said was a whole lot more than just a notion. He was talking in his regular matter-of-fact voice again then, so we knew he was not as exasperated with us as he had been. But as for myself I was still too scandalized to face him, and as for Little Buddy, he seldom if ever looked anybody straight in the eye anyway. Not that he was ever very likely to miss any move you made.

That time was also when Luzana Cholly told me and Little Buddy what he told us about the chain gang and the penitentiary: and as he talked, his voice uncle-calm and his facts first-hand and fresh from the getting-place, he kept reaching out every now and then to touch the guitar. But only as you stroke your pet or touch a charm, or as you finger a weapon or tool or your favorite piece of sports equipment. Because he did not play any tunes or even any chords, or make up any verse for us that day. But even so, to this day I remember what he said precisely as if it had actually been another song composed specifically for us.

Then, after he had asked us if it wasn't about time for two old roustabouts like us to eat something and the two of us had shared a can of sardines while he worked on a bite from his plug of Brown's Mule Chewing Tobacco, the main thing he wanted to talk about was going to school and learning to use your head like the smart, rich and powerful whitefolks, (nor did he or anybody else I can remember mean whitefolks in general. So far as I know the only white people he thought of as being smart were precisely those who were either rich and powerful or famous. The rest were peckerwoods, about whom you had to be careful not because they were smart but because so many of them were so mean and evil about not being smart and powerful and famous). He said the young generation was supposed to take what they were already born with and learn how to put it with everything the civil engineers and inventors and doctors and lawyers and bookkeepers had found out about the world and be the one to bring about the day the old folks had always been prophesying and praying for.

The three of us just sat looking across the water then. And then we heard the next northbound freight coming, and he stood up and got ready; and he said we could watch him but we better not try to follow him this time, and we promised, and we also promised to go to school the next morning.

So then we came back up the embankment, because the train was that close, and he stood looking at us, with the guitar slung across his back. Then he put his hands on our shoulders and looked straight down into our eyes, and you knew you had to look straight back into his, and we also knew that we were no longer supposed to be ashamed in front of him because of what we had done. He was not going to tell. And we were not going to let him down.

Make old Luze proud of you, he said then, and he was almost pleading. *Make old Luze glad to take his hat off to you some of these days. You going further than old Luze ever dreamed of. Old Luze ain't been nowhere. Old Luze don't know from nothing.*

And then the train was there and we watched him snag it and then he was waving goodbye.

*S*OMETIMES *I also used to call myself Jack the Nimble and Jack the Quick, and I also used to call the chinaberry tree my candlestick; and sometimes Little Buddy used to say I got your goddamn candlestick right here and also your goddamn hickory stick right here and also your goddamn greasy pole stick right here and also your goddamn totem pole stick right here and also your goddamn telegraph telephone tell-a-woman pole stick right here.*

But sometimes he also used to call his baseball bat his hickory stick, and that was when I used to say my right arm is my trickery stick. And so was my left jab. Because the also and also of Luzana Cholly (which was also to become at least in part the also and also of Stagolee Kid the piano player) was also the also and also of Jack Johnson who was by all accounts and all odds the nimblest footed quickest witted Jack of them all; who could spring six feet backwards and out of punching range from a standstill, who could salivate a Spanish fighting bull with a six-inch uppercut, whose eyes and hands were so sharp that he could reach out and snatch flies from mid-air without crushing them.

Which is why there was a cement sack punching bag hanging heavyweight-high from the lowest branch of the chinaberry tree, plus also a narrow circle that you were supposed to stand up and step into when Little Buddy said chingaling and stay there feinting and jabbing and bobbing and weaving and hooking and crossing and sneaking combinations from the minute he said ding until he said dong.

Because when the ku klux klan got mad and put on its white robes and started burning crosses just because somebody said bring me my coffee as black and strong as Jack Johnson and my scrambled eggs all beat up like poor old Jim Jeffries, I was the one they wanted to come and lynch. I was not as black or as big as Jack Johnson and I was never going to have all of my hair shaved off, but all the same as soon as I stepped into the prize ring I was the one who had set out from Galveston, Texas, not only to see the sights of the nation and seek my fortune wherever the chances were, but also to become the undisputed champion of the world. I was the one who had had to follow Tommy Burns all the way to

Sydney, Australia, to knock him out and bring back the golden belt. I was the one who was the scandal of San Francisco and Chicago and New York City. I was the talk of the town in London and the rage of Paris. And I had also fought Miura bulls in Spain and had even raced against Barney Oldfield at Sheepshead Bay, because after all I was as famous for my custombuilt sports cars as for my tailor-made suits and hand tooled shoes.

I had come up from the knockdown and broken off all of Stanley Ketchel's front teeth at the gums with one jam-pole right that time in Colma, California, not only because he was trying to doublecross me after I had agreed to take it easy for a twenty round exhibition, but also because that was my way of showing him that I knew that the newspapers were all set to declare him the undisputed champion if he would bring back old John L. Sullivan's color line, which I crossed every time I stepped into the workout circle around the punching bag.

——————

When what you were playing was baseball the chinaberry shade was the dugout and the front porch was the grandstand and the yard was the infield and the fence was the bleachers. For homeplate Little Buddy and I sometimes used a flattened out half-gallon syrup can that was only half the width of the regulation size. Sometimes all we had was a cord ball and sometimes we had a Nickel Rock but most of the time we had a used big league regulation ball from either Reach or Spalding. (You made the cord ball yourself. You could buy a Nickel Rock or Two-bit Rock or Fifty Cent Rock at Stranahan's Store. You could buy regulation balls at the Red Brick Drug Store, which was also where the Guidebook came from.)

Sometimes I used to fake with my glove like Joe Bowman when I was hesitating because there was a runner on first base, and sometimes I also used to snap my high drop like old Eddie Morgan from Chickasaw. My famous follow-through came from George Pipgras on the sports page of the Mobile Register *the year the New York Yankees won the World Series from the Pittsburgh Pirates in four straight games. But the only one you needed to be any time that you wanted to be the Jack Johnson of baseball was the same old long legged sleepy walking Elroy Augustus Gaither better known as Gus the Gator and Gator Gus who used to pitch in Chickasaw, in Whistler, in Davis Avenue Park, up in Plateau, down in Bayou La Batre and Moss Point or anywhere else anybody could get up enough money to hire him before he left Mobile for Kansas City and points north.*

Because (sports page pictures and cartoons or not) there was a time when I used to think that being a money ball pitcher like old Gus the Gator was what baseball was all about: because when that was what you were, as often as not, (unless somebody was able to get up enough money to hire you for the full nine innings) you didn't even come anywhere near any game—not even the Fourth of July game or the Labor Day game—before the sixth inning. Sometimes you didn't get there until the eighth, and sometimes you didn't go until somebody sent for you.

Then with the band playing "Sundown" or "Little White Lies" or "Precious Little Thing Called Love," as if it was pleading for help, you cruised up in your sporty roadster with the top down and the motor cadillacking and parked (sometimes near the grandstand, sometimes somewhere near third base and sometimes somewhere along the foul line beyond first) and sat half looking and half listening, with your left elbow on the steering wheel and your pitching arm around your honey brown finelegged frizzly headed woman for the day, while the money men from both sides took their turns and made their bids. Not that money was always what made the difference, because sometimes you let your girl choose the side (even as old Jack Johnson used to let his woman tell him to throw his knockout punch any time they got ready to go home and have some fried chicken. Some fried rabbit. Some barbecue with Brunswick stew. Some pickled eels. And then do some you-know-what).

Then depending on whether it was a park or a field, you went either to the clubhouse or to the thickets and put on your own personal togs, which sometimes, depending on the occasion, were only your cap, your jockstrap, your spikes with the brass toe plate and your notorious hand tailored Number Nine shirt, with your knife-edged hard finished pants turned up one turn. Then you came back and handed your sporty silk banded leghorn straw hat to your frizzly headed woman, who of course was also the one who held your warm-up sweater while you were out on the mound, and with that many of them already watching you instead of the game you stepped into the bullpen and started limbering up.

That was when somebody was bound to say: How do he feel do he feel like throwing that thing today? Somebody and somebody else and somebody else who had spent the whole week saying: Get Scooter. We got Scooter yet? We got to get up enough to bring old Scooter in there in the clutches. Somebody better get off your ass and get busy. Because if we mess around and don't, they sure in the hell will and goodbye. I'm telling you. When that cute brownskin rascal feel like chunking that thing, goodnight, fare thee the hell well and goodbye, and don't say I didn't tell you.

Then when you were warmed up enough to make Little Buddy's mitt echo so loud that the umpire had to hold up the game until you were ready to go in because most of the crowd was now watching the bullpen anyway, you knew very well all of the old signifying was going to begin again: Uhhhh-uh!

Yeahhh, look like he just might feel like chunking some ball today.

So, goodbye.

Uhhhh-uh!

Goodbye, sooner.

Kiss your money goodbye.

Goodbye, money. Hello, Monday morning.

Not that you always had enough to get them, and yourself out of the hole you were forever being called into. Because not even old Gator himself could do that every time; and he, after all, was the one who was supposed to be able to go out in the bottom of the ninth with a one run lead and make the first batter pop up to right, left or center; then after waving the outfielders to the sidelines and making the second man hit to first, second, shortstop or third, strike the last batter out with two balls, one called strike plus one of his mess-merizing curves followed by his special of specials the fadeaway.

Because all you had to do was be there to see that the main thing about old Gus the Gator was not how many games he saved and how much money he won but how good he always made you feel, win, lose or draw. Because afterwards everybody always said what everybody always said: Did you see him in there? Even when he had lost: Did you see old Gus in there after them rascals? Man, cain't nobody chunk that thing like the Gator.

BEING ALSO explorers and also discoverers and also wagon train scouts as well as sea pirates and cowboys among all the other things you had to be besides being also a schoolboy, Little Buddy Marshall and I knew very well that going through Chickasabogue Swamp was an expedition in itself. That was why he was not only wearing his mackinaw and his corduroys plus his mickey cochrane catcher's cap but was also carrying Mister Big Buddy's nickel-plated pearl handled .38 Smith and Wesson again. But the smoke-blue destination that day was the shipyards at Chickasaw Bend.

I was also equipped for emergency action. I was wearing my New York Yankee pitching cap and my heavy blue sweater (which was also a pitcher's warm-up sweater) and my Sears Roebuck twills and I was carrying Uncle Jerome's bowie knife. But the reason we were playing hooky was to see them working on the ships in the dry docks again. We planned to spend the whole day finding out about all that, with the cable winches grinding, the cranes swinging and the air hammers echoing like machine guns above the oil-black pier water lapping at the pilings and then we were going to come back along the AT & N and top the day off by crossing the nightmare trestle over Bay Poplar Gorge.

The first thing we did that morning was hide the books in the cache hole we used in Buckshaw mill yard. Then we laced on our marine store campaign leggings. Then we came on along the trail that sloped down into the first part of blue poplar woods, and by the time the last school bell rang we could hardly hear it, because we were already almost one third of the way to Chickasabogue Creek.

Squinting his eyes, and curling his lips, Little Buddy who was never going to be any more of a schoolboy than he was absolutely forced to be thumbed his nose and threw a dirty salute back over his shoulder in the direction from which the bell sound came and suddenly broke into old Luzana Cholly's sporty limp walk in spite of the fact that where we were was Indian territory.

Chickasaw, Chickasaw, he said, calling it out like the L & N porter we liked best in those days, Talking about Chickasaw.

But schoolboy that I already also was even then, as faint as the bell sound was, the minute I heard it I could also feel the way I always felt and see them lining up at the flagpole; and I couldn't keep myself from knowing exactly how long it would be before the Pledge of Allegiance and the high society march would be over and Miss Lexine Metcalf would be calling my name twice and looking up before marking me tardy.

Talking about Chickasaw, Little Buddy said and looked at me, and I pulled my cap all the way down square and looked straight ahead and walked rocking dicty with my shoulders rounded and my arms dangling as if I were moving along the aisle of a church and a train coach at the same time.

Oh will there be one, I said looking neither to the right nor the left.

Stand up, Little Buddy said, with his cap square too, Step down.

And give me your hand for Chickasaw Bend, Alabama, I said and held my arms out palms up and then let them fall.

Chickasaw Bend, Mobile County, Aladambama United Tits of a Milk Cow, one time, Little Buddy said.

Been long hearing tell of it.

And ain't but the one.

Oh but will there be one?

Oh stand up step up step down.

Oh whosoever will.

Let him come and give me your hand.

And give God your heart, brother.

One for Chickasaw.

I thank you, praise be, I thank you.

Two for Chickasaw Bend.

Amen Amen Amen Amen.

Hey, that's all right about your goddamn school, Little Buddy said. Hey, call us the goddamn school this time.

We got your goddamn school, I said. I got your goddamn school right here.

We followed the winding trail on down the thickly wooded slope and into the moss draped bottom, and when we came to the creek bank there was a launch putt-putting along out in the

channel towing a long raft of logs downstream toward Buckshaw's boom. The Chickasabogue was well over two hundred
yards wide at that point, and on the other side there was a cane
brake which stretched all the way out of sight to the L & N.

You couldn't see the L & N Bridge from the skiff boat landing where we were standing then, but we knew where it was
because it was also the gateway through which the Chickasabogue, which was really a tributary, flowed out into the Mobile
River which led down into Mobile Bay which spread out into
the Gulf of Mexico which was a part of the old Spanish Main
which was the beginning of the Seven Seas.

But the direction in which we were heading was upstream,
which was north meandering west, so, alert not only for water moccasins and salamanders but also for wild bo' hogs and
alligators we moved on into that part of the swamp; and it was
the up in the day part of the morning then, and beyond the
ferns and cypress trunks there was the water wrinkling in the
sunshine and the sky over the distant savannas and the bayou
country was clearing from smoke gray bundles of gauze to the
thin silky almost-summer blueness of midmorning.

The next traffic out in the channel was another launch going downstream with a log raft which was even longer than
the first, and not far behind was a tug with a string of empty
Tennessee Coal Iron Company barges. We padded softly on
having a good time just being where we wanted to be and
doing what we wanted to do with Chickasaw still to come.
Then the first tug heading upstream came into sight behind
us, and the barges behind it were loaded with rosin and tar,
and turpentine.

There was a blueness which went with the odor of caulk-
ing tar and turpentine and which was to twine and tarpaulin
what steel blue was to rawhide; and it went with Mobile because it was seaport blue, which was that infinite color of horizons beyond harbors and salt foam, that compass and spyglass
blue against which gulls circled and soared above red clanging
buoys, and against which international deck flags fluttered and
flapped during Mardi Gras while bilge green anchorage water
lapped dully at the barnacles and pilings along the piers.

Hey, you know something? Little Buddy said suddenly after
a while, I been thinking about seeing the world like we been

talking about and goddammit the thing I don't like about be-ing a sailor is they can't play baseball.

Man, that's the part I don't like either, I said, thinking about how we had always liked wearing pilot caps almost as much as baseball caps. But they can fight and swim.

So that was what I was thinking about when what happened happened this time, but before I could get to what I was go-ing to say about seeing the places on the map and the peo-ple I had read about in Geography, we came upon something which stopped everything. I don't remember even blinking but it happened so suddenly that it was as if I had just shut my eyes and opened them and found myself in another place on another day.

The moss shaded trail was making a wide detour away from the edge of the creek to skirt a shallow cypress backwater pond which was clogged with hyacinth pads, and I was on the look-out for water moccasins; but what I suddenly realized I was staring at was a human body.

I saw it first. Then Little Buddy looked and saw it, and we moved in close enough to be absolutely certain about what it was; and it was face down among the green and purple hy-acinths. It was floating but it moved only when the breeze made the entanglement of bladder-stemmed hyacinth leaves and backwater debris undulate.

Goddammit, Little Buddy whispered, I knew it.

I don't remember what I said.

I knew it, he said to himself, son-of-a-bitch if I didn't know it.

We were looking from the undergrowth of marsh ferns, reeds and calamus plants and there was the sweet/sour smell of the swamp, with the sunlight filtering through the cypress branches and even the thickest shade was sharp and clear. Little Buddy had drawn the pistol from his mackinaw but all he was doing was holding it in both hands and looking.

There was a musette bag floating off to one side; but I didn't see any fishing or hunting tackle, and you couldn't guess any-thing from what you could see of what he was wearing be-cause they were just ordinary everyday working clothes. He seemed to be a white man, but you couldn't really be certain about that either. All I could make out was that he was a dead man and he had pale skin and he had been dead long enough to be bloated.

Then I realized that one of the arms was missing and that part of the shoulder had been either torn or eaten away and I couldn't help remembering what I had always heard about gars and crabs ripping strips of flesh from drowned people; and I didn't want to have to see that happening too. But I didn't want to be the one to say let's go and I knew good and well that Little Buddy wasn't going to be the one either. So we both had to stay there, although I wasn't looking at it any more and neither was he, because I looked at him out of the corner of my eye and he wasn't looking at anything.

So I knew I had to figure out something, and I did, and I was watching him and when I saw him trying to steal a look at me, I jerked up as if I had just heard something behind us in the bushes somewhere, and we both started easing back and then I broke and ran, and I knew that he'd be right there running just as hard as I was, and he was.

We ran back the way we had been coming, and the farther we ran the more it seemed that I could still see it, and it seemed that I was smelling it too. The whole swamp seemed to smell like it, and when I had to step in a boggy place it seemed that I was stepping right into the soft dead body itself.

I was running and my neck was hot and my mouth began to taste like green brass, and then I was slowing down, but then it was as if I could see it squelching white, rotten, soggy and slimy like fish meat and I started running again, but I was too tired to run much more and I stopped and Little Buddy sat down on the log and I dropped down beside him.

Hell I ain't going to run no goddamn more, he said, still holding the pistol as if it were a toy.

Me neither, I said.

Goddamn if I run another goddamn step.

We were getting our breath back then, and I was trying to think of what to do next.

Did you hear something? Little Buddy said.

I thought I did, I said lying.

I thought I did, too, he said making us even.

What do you think happened to him?

I don't know. What you think?

I don't know, I said, But the first thing I thought about was bootlegging.

Me too, he said sucking his teeth three times and looking at the pistol as if none of it made any difference to him one way or the other.

Somebody could have shot him and pushed him overboard and he floated in there, I said.

Goddamn right, he said, he could have floated all the way from up in Hog Bayou.

If you already overboard and get shot the cramp will drown you, I said.

Don't care where the bullet hit you, he agreed, putting the pistol back inside his mackinaw and standing up. And I knew he was trying to think about something else because that was what I was also trying to do but I kept wondering how long it would be before somebody else came along as we had done.

Man, he said, suddenly, the goddamn coroner and the god-damn inquest, goddamn!

Man, but any more water lilies drift in there ain't going to be no inquest, I said.

Man, Goddamn, you know it too, he said. Man, God—damn!

So what you want to do now? I said.

You want to let's go on up to Chickasaw?

If you want to.

And cross the trestle going and coming.

If you do.

So we started back up the slope toward where we knew the AT & N was. That was the most direct route to Chickasaw anyway.

We came on back looking for the trail which would take us on out of the cypresses and up the hill and through the hicko-ries and chinquapins to the railroad. We were walking side by side and watching everything then. But as we turned up into the trail, he caught my arm and stopped.

Hey, listen.

I did, and heard footsteps.

Somebody coming!

We scrambled back into a thick clump of bushes and vines and waited, and then we heard them coming nearer, and then we saw them, and there were three of them, and we didn't know any of them. They came on by where we were, one walking in front and the two behind side by side, and two of them were carrying Winchesters.

We were squatting together in our hiding place not even breathing, and they went on down the trail toward the creek.

Peckerwoods, Little Buddy said under his breath. Goddamn peckerwoods.

I bet you they had something to do with it.

I bet so, too. Goddamn peckernose peckerwoods.

You want to let's follow them?

Goddammit, let's follow them goddamn razorback peckerwoods.

I knew he was going to say that, and I wanted to and I didn't want to, but I said all right and we did, and we kept close together in the bushes beside the trail and crept on back down toward the way they had gone.

But when we got to where we could see the creek again, we saw only one of them, and he was standing down by the edge of the water. We waited, watching, and then we saw the other two come paddling up in a rowboat.

They headed the boat into where the one on the bank was waiting and one of them handed him a pair of hip boots and the three of them were talking but we were not close enough to hear what they were saying. Then the one who had been waiting sat on the bank and pulled on the boots and stood and said something else, pointing up the creek, and the boat pulled away, and he was walking along the bank.

We stayed our distance and we could see him and see the two in the boat too, and he was searching along the bank and they were searching along the edge of the water.

I told you so, Little Buddy whispered.

They looking for something all right, I said.

Down in the boat one of them sat on the back end and paddled and the other one was half standing in the front, using his paddle to move the reeds and lilies.

They sure cain't miss him, I said low to Little Buddy.

Let's watch them do what they going to do.

They went on along the edge of the creek and we were following them, and then we knew that they were getting near where it was, and we stopped and waited. There was a strong breeze blowing from across the creek then but I was sweating and Little Buddy was too.

We saw the one on the bank turn in toward the trees, and we knew exactly where he was, and then we heard him whistle and the boat turned in there and was out of sight too.

They found it, Little Buddy whispered.

Come on.

We better get to a tree.

We scooted to the tree he pointed to and he climbed it and I was right there behind him, and then we were sitting hidden in the moss. You couldn't see them, yet, but we stayed there and waited, and there was no traffic in the channel at all.

I don't know how long we waited, but there was still no traffic, and after a while I saw the boat heading out again, and all three of them were in it. Two of them were rowing then, and the one who had been on the bank was sitting in the back and he was holding the dead man by one foot dragging him in the wake.

Goddamn, Little Buddy said. Look what them goddamn old pecks doing.

Then we realized that the dead man was naked. They had stripped all of his clothes off. They rowed out far enough to see up and down the creek, and then one of the ones rowing stopped and reached out and got what must have been the dead man's boots and knapsack and filled the boots with water and sank them and then tied the knapsack to something and sank that too.

Then they rowed on out into the channel still towing the floating dead man. They headed the boat up toward Chickasaw then, and turned the dead man loose and pulled away as fast as they could go.

We saw them pulling on away and saw the bloated dead man floating on down with the current going on toward the L & N Bridge. They pulled on out of sight, but we still could see the dead body and it looked like a floating sack. I looked back up the way the three men had gone and when I turned and looked at the body again it didn't look like anything but a piece of driftwood, and then it was nothing at all.

We got down out of the tree and started on back along the bank.

I bet you there's a goddamn motherfucking son-of-a-bitching whiskey still up in there somewhere, Little Buddy said. I bet you anything. I bet you a thousand dollars.

Me too, I said. Or maybe a transfer place.

I bet you that's where they gone right now.

Me too.

Goddamn old redneck peckerwood bootleggers.

We were coming on back, and the green and mossy woods were warm and quiet and the only sound was us and the breeze overhead in the trees.

What you want to do now? I said.

Let's cross that goddamn motherfucking son-of-a-bitching shitass trestle.

And if a freight comes, we'll swing down to the cross-beams and let it go over us.

Must have been some time ago.

Must have been.

With him puffed up that big.

I wonder how come they did.

I bet you he must have been spying or stealing or something.

I bet so too.

Do you think they been looking all this time while he was bloating up like that?

I don't know, I said. Maybe when he didn't turn up somewhere so somebody could find him they started looking.

I wonder why they shot him?

I don't know. Maybe because he was a revenue agent.

Maybe so, he said. Maybe he was trying to follow them and they faked him on up into one of the slews and waylaid his ass.

Man if he was a *Yankee* revenue agent them peckerwoods been watching his ass ever since he crossed the Mason-Dixie.

Man that's one thing about a peckerwood, he said. Some of them squint-eyed, nose-talking, bony-butt granny-dodgers don't back up off of nobody when it come to shooting a god-damn rifle and a shotgun.

But Little Buddy was thinking about something else then, because he was frowning to himself without knowing it, and I could tell he was gritting his teeth by the way his temples moved. That was something we both had picked up from

Sonny Crenshaw, who said it was something he did instead of chewing tobacco.

But that poor sappin somebody back there, he said suddenly. Suppose he was just out there fishing or something.

Man, I said, but bootleggers can tell when you really fishing or hunting.

Yeah but just suppose, he said. Just suppose he was only a stranger and it was night and all he was doing was wandering around lost.

We followed the trail on through the Chickasaw thickets and I knitted my brow and shook my head as if I were still trying to figure out something to say about what he had said. But I was thinking about something else then. Because I could still see the bloated corpse among the purple water lilies and the main thing was that someone was dead and gone and his body was nothing but something floating because he was dead and gone dead and gone dead and gone forever.

Then we saw the trestle. It stretched across the ugly bottom like a creosote dragon whose centipede's legs were so many knock-kneed telegraph pole stilts. Little Buddy stopped and took out the pistol. Then he aimed across his forearm and shot three stilts, and the sound went echoing up through Blue Poplar Hollow. Then I took it and shot three more. But there was the also and also of all that from then on even so.

IT was as if you had been born hearing and knowing about trains and train whistles, and the same was also true of sawmills and sawmill whistles. I already knew how to mark the parts of the day by sawmill whistles long before I learned to read time as such from the face of a clock.

Sometimes, probably having heard the earliest morning sawmill whistles in my sleep as you sometimes hear neighborhood roosters crowing for daybreak, I used to wake up and lie listening long enough to hear the first-shift hands passing by outside. That was when the daytime fireman relieved the night fireman, and it was also the time when you could hear the logging crews that came that way going to work on that part of Mobile River and Three Mile Creek. These were the putt-boat pilots and the raftmen, some of whom were also skiffboatmen. And there were also the boom men, who used to wear their turned down hip boots (which I also used to call magellan boots and isthmus of panama boots) to and from home, carrying their peavies and hook-and-jam poles angling across their shoulders as pike men did in story books and also as railroad crosstie cutters used to carry their crosscut saws and broadaxes to and from the timber woods.

It was the head day-shift fireman who always blew the next whistle, and that was when the main-shift hands would be coming by. So that was when what you heard passing was not only the log carriage experts like, say, old Sawmill Turner, for instance; but also the shed crews and the yard crews, including the timekeepers and tallymen. But I was usually asleep again by then, and when I woke up for good it would be time to get up and be ready before the first school bell rang.

It would be full daylight then, and by the time you finished breakfast, the first lumber trucks would be grinding their way up out of Sawdust Bottom. And when you heard the next gear shift, that meant they were finally up the hill and leveling off into our flat but somewhat sandy and rutty road to come whining by the gate. Then the next gear-stroke meant that they were ready to pick up speed to fade on away because they had turned onto Buckshaw Road, which was macadamized like Telegraph Road even before the Cochrane Bridge was built and they finally paved it with asphalt like the Chickasaw Highway and made it a part of US 90.

From September through the fall and winter and spring the next thing after the first lumber trucks was always the first school bell. So from then on it was as if you didn't really hear either the sawmills or train whistles (or even boat whistles) anymore until after three o'clock. Because during that part of every day except Saturday and Sunday, everything you did was part of the also and also that school bells and school bell times were all about. Such as singing in 70-degree Fahrenheit schoolroom unison: *Good morning to you good morning to you good morning dear teacher good morning to you.* With your scrubbed hands on the pencil tray desk for roll call and fingernail inspection, with your hair trimmed and combed and brushed and your head erect, your back straight, your shoulders square and your eyes on the exemplary pre-lesson neatness of the janitor-washed blackboard with its semi-permanent border design and theme of the month and motto of the month and chalk colored checkerboard calendar.

Good solo teacher talk morning dear children.

Good unison-pupil response-chant morning dear teacher. A very good morning from toothpaste smiles and rainbow ribbons and oilcloth book satchels and brown bag sandwich smells to you Miss So and Miss So and Miss So and So and Miss So-So and Miss So On and Miss So Forth to Miss Metcalf.

Then (when the first kitten mitten mornings of steaming breath and glittering wayside ponds were outside once more) also: *Old Jack Frost is a funny old fellow when the wind begins he begins to bellow. He bites little children on their nose. He bites little children on their toes. He makes little girls say Oh! Oh! Oh! And he makes little boys say Ouch! Ouch! Ouch! He makes little pointed-ats wring hands and blow fingers and say Oh! Oh! Oh! And he makes little nodded-and-smiled-ats shake fists and say Ouch! Ouch! Ouch! He makes little sugar and spice and everything nice girls say —! —! —! And he makes little frogs*

*and snails and puppydogtail boys (but not Scooter and not Little
Buddy Marshall and not old Cateye Gander Gallagher the Gallinipper) say ——! ——! ——!*

But sometimes (especially during afternoon quiet sessions)
you could still hear the syrup-green sawdust whine of the log
carriage even from that far away, and I could hardly wait to
get back home to my own play sawmill, which millwright that
I already was I had built complete with boom, rafts, conveyer
ramp, carriage, slab and sawdust pile, stacking yard, dry kiln
and planer shed, long before the time came to go to school
that first year. Because in the summertime in those days I almost always used to become a hard rolling sawmill man as
soon as Buckshaw whistle used to blow for high noon no matter what else I was supposed to be at the time. Because that
was when you could sit at the sawhorse table outside under
the chinaberry tree stripped to the waist like a stacking yard
hand, eating new corn and pole beans (or snap beans or string
beans) plus new red-skinned potatoes; or butterbeans plus
okra; or green (shelled) blackeye peas plus okra; or crowder
peas plus okra; along with the very thinnest of all shortening-
rich golden crusted corners of cornbread. Not to mention
the yellow-flecked mellowness of the home churned buttermilk of those days. Or the homemade lemonade or fresh
ice-tea. Especially when you could drink it from your very
own quart-size fruit jar not only as if you had been stacking
lumber all the morning but also as if all the good cooking in
your napkin-covered slat basket had been prepared by your
honey brown good-looking wife or woman, who had put on
her frilly starched baby doll gingham dress and brought it to
where she now sat beside you fanning away the flies in the
stacking yard shade.

But all of that was before Miss Lexine Metcalf, and her blue
and green and yellow globe revolving on its tilted axis with its
North and South Poles, and its Eastern and Western Hemi-
spheres, and its equator plus its Torrid and North Temperate
and South Temperate and Frigid Zones and its continents and
its oceans and seas and gulfs and great lakes and rivers and ba-
sins, and its mountain ranges and plains and deserts and oases,
and its islands and peninsulas and archipelagos and capes and
horns and straits.

Because from then on (what with her sandtable igloos and wigwams and thatched huts and mud huts and caravan tents and haciendas and chalets and chinese paper houses with lanterns; and what with her bulletin board costumes of many lands and her teacher's desk that could become the Roundtable from which armor-clad knights errant set forth to do battle with dragons and blackboard problems; what with her window box plants that could become Robin Hood's forest and what with her magic pointer that could change everyday Gasoline Point schoolgirls into Cinderellas and Sleeping Beauties and you into Prince Charming or Roland or Siegfried or Sinbad or Ulysses and your Buster Brown shoes or your Keds into Seven League Boots) I was to become a schoolboy above and beyond everything else, for all the absolutely indispensable times I was still to play hooky with Little Buddy Marshall.

What with Miss Lexine Metcalf with whose teacher-pronunciation my given name finally became the classroom equivalent not only of Scooter but also of the other nickname Mama used to call me which was Man which was to say Mama's Man which was to say Mama's Little Man which was to say Mama's Big Man; because Miss Lexine Metcalf was the one who also said it looking at you as if to let you know that she was also calling you what Miss Tee had always called you, which was her mister. *My Mister. Hello My Mister. This is My Mister. Show them My Mister.*

What with Miss Lexine Metcalf who came to be the one who was there in the classroom. But what also with Miss Tee, from whom had already come ABC blocks and ABC picture books and wax crayon coloring sets, and was the one for whom you learned your first numbers, and who was also the one who said: *This is My Mister who can write his name all by himself. Show them My Mister. This is My Mister who can do addition and subtraction all by himself. Show them My Mister. And show them how My Mister can also recite from the Reader all by himself. The cat said not I. The dog said not I. The little red hen said I will and she did. The little choo choo going up the hill said I think I can I think I can I thought I could I thought I could. Because it tried and it did.*

Sometimes a thin gray, ghost-whispering mid-winter drizzle would begin while you were still at school, and not only would it settle in for the rest of the mist-blurred, bungalow-huddled afternoon, but it would still be falling after dark as if it would continue throughout the night; and even as you realized that such was the easiest of all times to get your homework (even when it was arithmetic) done (no matter what kind of school-boy you were) you also knew as who hasn't always known that it was also and also the very best of all good times to be where grown folks were talking again, especially when there were the kind of people visiting who always came because there was somebody there from out of town and you could stay up listening beyond your usual time to be in bed.

Their cane bottom chairs and hide bottom chairs and rocking chairs plus stools always formed the same old family-cozy semi-circle before the huge open hearth, and from your place in the chimney corner you could see the play of the firelight against their faces and also watch their tale-time shadows moving against the newspaper wallpaper walls and the ceiling. Not even the best of all barbershops were ever to surpass the best of such nights at home.

They would be talking and rocking and smoking and sometimes drinking, and, aware of the roof sanding, tree-shivering night weather outside, I would be listening, and above us on the scalloped mantlepiece was the old fashioned pendulum clock, which was Papa's heirloom from that ancestral mansion of ante-bellum columns and gingham crisp kitchens in which his mulatto grandmother had herself been an inherited slave until Sherman's March to the Sea but which I still remember as the Mother Goose clock; because it ticked and tocked and ticked and tocked and tocked and struck not only the hours but also the quarter-hours with the soft clanging sound you remember when you remember fairy tale steeples and the rainbow colors of nursery rhyme cobwebs; because it hickory dickory docked and clocked like a brass spoon metronome above the steel blue syncopation of guitar string memories; because it hockey-tock rocked to jangle like such honky tonk piano mallets as echo midnight freight train distances beyond patch-quilt horizons and bedside windowpanes.

Sometimes it would be obvious enough that they were only telling the tallest tales and the most outrageous lies they could either remember or fabricate, and sometimes you could be every bit as certain that their primary purpose was to spell out as precisely as possible the incontestable facts and most reliable figures involved in the circumstance under consideration. But when you listened through the meshes of the Mother Goose clock you already knew long before you came to recognize any necessity to understand (not to mention explain) that no matter which one they said or even believed they were doing they were almost always doing it at least a little of both. (Because even as the Mother Goose clock was measuring the hours and minutes of ordinary days and nights and time tables its tic-toculation created that fabulous once upon a time spell under which you also knew that the Jacksonville of the section gang song for instance was really a make-believe place even though you could find it by moving your finger to the right from Pensacola and across Tallahassee on the map of Florida—just as you could find Kansas City by tracing left from St. Louis on the map of Missouri.)

Sometimes there would also be such winter-delicious things as papershell pecans and chinquapins and fresh roasted peanuts to pass around in Mama's pinestraw bowl-basket, and sometimes there was homemade blackberry wine or muscadine wine, and sometimes when it was really a very very special occasion Miss Alzenia Nettleton, who was once a cook in the Governor's Mansion, would either send or bring one of her mouth-melting sweet potato pones. Sometimes when it was blizzard weather there would be a big cast-iron pot of lye hominy (which is something I didn't learn to like until later on), and on some of the best nights the main reason everybody was there in the first place was that it was hog-killing-time weather and somebody had brought Mama the makings of a feast of chitterlings and/or middlings, but of course when that happened the best of the talking seldom if ever got started until the eating was almost over.

Uncle Jerome would always be there unless there was a fruit boat to be unloaded that night, clearing his throat even when he was not going to say anything, squinting his eyes and making a face and clearing again and swallowing and stretching and rolling his chin because he was a preacher. Because although he had been a longshoreman for the last twenty some odd years and a field hand for some thirty odd years before that, he was supposed to have the Call, although he had never been called by any congregation to be the pastor of any church.

Sometimes Mister Doc Donahue the Dock Hand would also be there. But they wouldn't be drinking just wine with him there. Because leather bellied stevedore that he was he always said that wine was for women and children and Christmas morning fruitcake, and he would get up and get the longshoreman's knapsack he always carried along with his cargo hook and bring out a brown crockery jug of corn whiskey, which always made Papa look over at Mama and get just about tickled to death. They would be passing it around, pouring against the light of the fire, and there would be that aroma then, which I always used to enjoy as much as the smell of warm cigar ashes and freshly opened Prince Albert tobacco cans.

They would talk on and on, and then (when somebody mentioned something about the weather itself and somebody else said Yeah but talking about some weather,) you could always tell you were going to hear about the great Juvember Storm again, and sometimes that would be what they spent the rest of the night telling about, each one telling it as he remembered it from where he was at the time, with Uncle Jerome telling his as if it all had been something happening in the Bible, although nobody, not even he, ever claimed that it had actually stormed for forty days and forty nights. But Uncle Jerome always pointed out that everything under the sun was in the Bible including automobiles, because old Ezekiel saw the wheel in the middle of the wheel, and what was an airship but a horseless chariot in the sky, and if somebody didn't cut in on him he would stand up and begin walking the floor and preaching another one of his sermons.

Everybody had his own way of telling about it, but no matter how many parts were added you always saw the main part the same way: rivers and creeks rising and overflowing the back country, washing houses off their foundations and sometimes completely away; bales of cotton and barrels of flour and molasses and cans of lard floating out of warehouses and scattering through the swamps; horses neighing and cows lowing and trying to swim but drowning because (so they used to say) their behinds sucked in so much water; people living in barns and hay lofts and paddling everywhere in skiff boats, people camping in lean-to tent cities in the hills like hobos. People camping on the bluffs like Indians, people camping on timber rafts like the early settlers; trains not running because not only were the tracks washed out but in some places whole spans of bridges had been swept loose. . . .

Then afterwards, there was the epidemic during which even more perished than during the storm itself. But all of that was always a part of the storm story also. And that was when Uncle Jerome always used to say God was warning sinners that He could do it again although He had promised that it would be the fire next time, and he would get up and start clearing his throat and making faces and walking the floor again and then he would go on to show you how even in the almighty act of bringing the flood again God had also brought the fire next time after all. Because what so many many people had suffered and died from was the FEVER, which meant that they were being consumed in a fire more terrible than brimstone! Mess around with mortal man born in sin and shaped in inequity but Gentlemen Sir don't you never start trying to mess with God.

But Papa, whose given name was Whit probably for Whitley but maybe for Whitney and so was sometimes called Papa Whit and sometimes Unka Whit, who had not been inside a church except to attend somebody's funeral since he was baptized thirty some odd years ago, would then take another swallow from his whiskey glass and wipe his mouth and wink at Mister Doc the Dock Hand and look over at Mama because he knew good and well she was going to be scandalized to mortification and say Amen God sure did work a mysterious way His wonders or His blessings or whichever it was to bestow because that was the same storm that had made more good paying jobs for our folks in that country than anything else till the war came.

What I always used to call Papa was Papoo and he used to call me his little gingerbrown papoose boy, which may have been why I called him Papoo in the first place. He himself was as white as any out and out white man I have ever seen in my life. And no wonder either, because not only was he said to be a whole lot more than just half white, it was also said quite accurately that he was acknowledged by most of his white blood relatives much more readily than he himself was ever willing to acknowledge any of them (except when it came to such legal matters as clearing titles to property inherited in common). I myself once overheard Mama telling Aunt Callie the Cat Callahan that the main reason we had moved down into Mobile County when the war boom came was to get away from Papa's white kinfolks in the country. And another time I heard her telling Miss Sadie Womack about how red Papa's ears used to turn when the white people back in the country used to see him driving her into town in the buckboard and pretend that they thought she was not his wife but only one of his black field hands.

Papa himself never talked about white people as such. But sometimes when they were talking about hard times, somebody would get him to tell about some of the things he had seen and done during those times when he had to go off somewhere and pass for white to get a job. That was something to hear about also, and one time when I was telling Little Buddy Marshall about it the next day, he said: Everybody say, don't care how much of his skin and his keen nose and his flat ass Mister Whit might have got from the whitefolks, he got his mother-wit from the getting place. That's how come you don't never catch nobody calling him no old shit-colored peckerwood behind his back.

There was also that time with that white man downtown by the marine store on Government Street. He and Papa knew each other and they were laughing and talking and I was having a good time looking in store windows, and I went looking all the way up to the sporting goods store, and when I came back they were talking about a job; and the man said something about something both of them had been doing somewhere, and that brought up something else, and I heard the man say Papa was a fool for being a durned ole niggie when he could be a wyat man. Hell Whit you as wyat as I am any durned day of the week be durned if you ain't, and Papa just shook his head and said You don't understand, Pete.

Midwinter nights around the fireplace was one of the times when Soldier Boy Crawford used to tell about crossing the Atlantic Ocean and about the mines and the torpedoes and the submarines, and then about the French places he had been to, and sometimes he would mix in a lot of French words with what he was saying such as bonjour come on tally voo and such as sand meal killing my trees easy to Paree and such as donay me unbootay cornyak silver plate and such as voo lay voo zig zig and so on, screwing up his face and narrowing his shoulders as well as his eyes and wiggling his fingers as if he were playing the words as notes on a musical instrument.

When you heard him talking about France in the barbershop he was usually telling either about the Argonne Forest or the Hindenburg Line or about French women whom he called frog women. But what he used to talk mostly about at the fireside was the kind of farming country they had over there, especially the wine making country. And he would also tell about the mountain country and the churches which he said had the finest bells and the keenest steeples and the prettiest windows in the world: Talking about some stain glass church windows y'all ain't seen no stain glass church windows y'all ain't seen no church statues and I ain't talking about no wood I'm talking about natural stone nine hundred years old.

What he used to tell about Paris at such times was mostly about the buildings and the streets with the cafes on the sidewalk and the parks and the cabarets, and that was also when he used to tell about eating horse meat, snails and frogs legs (but not about the pissoirs and the bidets and best of all the poules from whom came french kissing). He would always say Gay Paree was the best city in the world, and that was also when he would always say A man is a man over there and if somebody said as somebody as often as not did that a man ain't nothing but a man nowhere, you knew he was going to say Yeah but that ain't what *I'm* talking about, what I'm talking about is somewhere you can go anywhere you big enough to go and do anything you big enough to do and have yourself some of anything you got the money to pay for. That's what I'm talking about.

Soldier Boy Crawford, (who during blizzard weather also used to wear his woolen wraparound leggings along with his Army coat and overseas cap and who also had a steel helmet that looked like a wash basin but which he called his doughboy hat and who was said to have brought back a German Luger plus some hand grenades plus a bayonet, a musette bag and a gas mask too because he for one was never going to let them catch him with his pants down if he could help it) was the main one who used to tell me and Little Buddy Marshall about all of the things Luzana Cholly had done during the war. Because old Luze himself never did talk about any of that, not even when you asked him about it. Sometimes he used to say he was going to save it and tell us about it when we were old enough to understand it, and sometimes he would answer one or two questions about something, say, like how far Big Bertha could shoot, and how the Chau-Chau automatic rifle worked and things like that. But you could never get him to sit down and tell about the actual fighting like Soldier Boy Crawford did. Once you got Soldier Boy Crawford worked up he was subject to fight the whole war all over again.

The rain that was falling then would be crackling down on the shingles of the gabled roof of that house, and the fire in the hearth would sparkle as Papa poked it, and I would be in my same chair in my same place in the corner; and sometimes they would be telling about some of the same old notorious rounders and roustabouts that the guitar players and the piano players made up songs about. Especially if Mister Doc Donahue was there, because he was the one who could always remember something else about old John Henry, who went with blue steel sparks, and old John Hardy, who went with greased lightning. Once he held the floor all night just describing how old Stagolee shot and killed Billy Lyons, and what happened at that famous trial.

Mister Doc Donahue was also the one who used to tell about how old Robert Charles declared war on the city of New Orleans and fought the whole police force all by himself with his own special homemade bullets. But the best of all the old so-called outlaws he used to tell about was always the one from Alabama named Railroad Bill. Who was so mean when somebody crossed him and so tricky that most people believed that there was something supernatural about him. He was the one that no jail could hold overnight and no bloodhounds could track beyond a certain point. Because he worked a mojo on them that nobody ever heard of before or since. And the last time he broke jail, they had the best bloodhounds in the whole state there to track him. But the next morning they found them all tied together in a fence corner near the edge of the swamp, not even barking anymore, just whining, and when they got them untangled they were ruined forever, couldn't scent a polecat and wouldn't even run a rabbit; and nobody ever saw or came near hide nor hair of old Railroad Bill from that time on.

Naturally the whitefolks claimed they caught him and lynched him; but everybody knew better. The whitefolks were always claiming something like that. They claimed that they had caught old Pancho Villa and hung him for what he had done out in New Mexico; and they claimed that they had hemmed up old Robert Charles in a steeple and burned him alive; and they also claimed that Jessie Willard had salivated old Jack Johnson down in Havana that time! Well, they could go around bragging about how the great white hope had put the big black menace back in his place and proved white supremacy all they wanted to, but everybody knew that Jack Johnson who was married to a white woman had to trade his world championship in for his American citizenship, and thirty thousand dollars to get back in the USA and there was a picture in every barbershop which showed him letting himself be counted out, lying shading his eyes from the Cuban sun, lying with his legs propped like somebody lying on the front porch; and as for Jessie Willard, everybody knew he couldn't even stand up to Jack Dempsey, who was the same Jack Dempsey who brought back old John L. Sullivan's color line because he didn't ever intend to get caught in the same ring with the likes of Jack Johnson, Sam Langford or even somebody like Harry Wills, not even with a submachine gun. Everybody knew that.

The whitefolks claimed that they had finally caught up with old Railroad Bill at some crossroads store somewhere and had slipped up on him while he was sitting in the middle of the floor sopping molasses with his gun lying off to one side, and they swore that they had blown the back of his head off with a double barrel charge of triple-ought buckshot. But in the first place Railroad Bill didn't eat molasses, and in the second place he didn't have to break into any store to get something to eat. Because folks kept him in plenty of rations everywhere he went by putting out buckets of it in certain special places for him mostly along the Railroad which was what his name was all about; and in the third place he must have broken into more than fifty stores by that time and he just plain didn't rob a store in the broad open daylight, not and then sit down in the middle of the floor and eat right there; and in the fourth place there was at least a dozen other mobs in at least a dozen other places all claiming that they had been the ones who laid him low, each one of them telling a completely different tale about how and when and where it all happened. Some claimed that they had hung him upside down on the drawbridge and then riddled him and left what was left of him there for the buzzards. But they never settled on which bridge.

I didn't know very much about history then. Which was what all that about Uncle Walt and the bloodhounds was all about too. Because I knew even while it was happening that it wasn't just happening then. I didn't know very much about historical cause and effect then, but I knew enough to realize that when something happened it was a part of something that had been going on before, and I wasn't surprised at all that time when I was awakened in the middle of the night and got up and saw Uncle Walt sitting by the fire in Papa's clothes talking about how he had made his way through Tombigbee Swamp. He slept in Uncle Jerome's bed and Uncle Jerome slept on a pallet in front of the fireplace. They put ointment on the bruises and rubbed his joints down in Sloan's Liniment, and he slept all day the next day and all the day after that too, telling about it again the second night by the fire with his feet soaking in a tub of hot salt water, and I could see it all and I was in it too, and it was me running through the swamps, hearing them barking, coming, and it was me who swam across the creek and was running wet and freezing in the soggy shoes all the next day. Hungry and cold but not stopping even when I didn't hear them anymore, and not hopping a freight either, because they would be looking for you to do that. It was me who made my way because I knew that country like the Indians knew it, and I knew the swamps and the streams like the old keelboat men and I knew the towns and villages like a post rider, and then it was me who was long gone like a Natchez Trace bandit.

I saw Uncle Walt sitting there in the firelight not afraid but careful, talking about how he was going to make it across the Mason-Dixon, and I didn't really know anything at all about whatever it was he had done or hadn't done, and I still don't know what it was, but I knew that whatever it was it was trouble, and I said It's like once upon a time back then. Because that's what Mama always said, who knew it from her grandfather, who was Uncle Walt's grandfather too, who knew it from his father when there was no hope of foot rest this side of Canada, which was also called Canaan, which was the Promised Land, and I also knew that all of that was about something called the Underground Railroad, which ran from the House of Bondage to the land of Jubilo.

They were always talking about freedom and citizenship, and that was something else that Uncle Jerome used to start preaching about. He had all kinds of sermons ready for times like that. Sometimes he would be talking about children of Israel, and sometimes it would be the walls of Jericho, and sometimes it would be the big handwriting on the wall which was also the BIG HAND writing on the wall which was also the Big Hand writing on the WAR. That was when he used to say that the color of freedom was blue. The Union Army came dressed in blue. The big hand that signed the freedom papers signed them in blue ink which was also blood. The very sky itself was blue, limitless (*and gentlemen, sir, before I'd be a slave, I'll be buried in my grave*). *And I said My name is Jack the Rabbit and my home is in the briarpatch.*

Sometimes he would also say that the freedom road was a road through the wilderness and sometimes it wasn't any road at all because there never was any royal road to freedom for anybody (so don't you let nobody turn you round. And don't you let nobody know too much about your business either. And I said Call me Jack the Bear on my way somewhere).

Then it would be Education again. They didn't ever get tired of talking about that, the old folks telling about how they learned to spell and write back in the old days when they used to use slate tablets and the old Blueback Webster. The old days when they used to have to hold school whenever and wherever they could. Whenever they could spare the time from working the crops and wherever the teacher could find a place to shelter them. Whenever there was a teacher.

Then later on I was the one they meant when they said the young generation was the hope and glory. Because I had come that far in school by then; and sometimes it was Geography and sometimes it was History, and sometimes I had to tell about it, and sometimes I had to get the book and read it to them. Especially when it was about the Revolutionary War. Sometimes I had to read about Columbus too, and sometimes it would also be the explorers and the early settlers. But most of the time what they wanted to hear about was how the original thirteen colonies became the first thirteen states and who said what and who did what during that time and how the Constitution was made and who the first Presidents were and what they did.

That was also when I used to love to recite the Declaration of Independence, and the Gettysburg Address for them; and I could also recite the Preamble to the Constitution and part of the Emancipation Proclamation; and I could also quote from the famous speeches of Patrick Henry and James Otis and Citizen Tom Paine; and I knew all kinds of sayings from *Poor Richard's Almanac*.

That boy can just about preach that thing right now, Mister Jeff Jefferson said one night after I had recited the William Lloyd Garrison and Frederick Douglass parts from the National Negro History Week pageant.

That boy can talk straight out of the dictionary when he want to, Mister Big Martin said looking at me but talking to everybody.

It just do you good to hear that kind of talk.

Whitefolks need to hear some talk like that.

The whitefolks the very one said all that, Jeff.

What kind of whitefolks talking like that?

Histry-book whitefolks.

What kind of histry-book whitefolks?

Whitefolks in that same book that child reading.

I ain't never heard no whitefolks believing nothing like that in all of my born days.

Whitefolks printed that book, didn't they?

I don't care who printed that book, that's *freedom* talk.

Well, the histry book whitefolks got up the Constitution, didn't they?

Yeah, and there was some histry book blackfolks in there somewhere too, you can just about bet on that. There was a jet-black roustabout right in there with old Christopher Columbus, and the very first one to try to climb that bunker hill was a mean black son-of-a-gun from Boston. Ain't nothing never happened and wasn't some kind of a black hand mixed up in it somewhere. You just look at it close enough. The very first ones to come up with iron was them royal black Ethiopians.

You right about that, Mister Big Martin said, ain't nobody going to dispute you about that.

I know I'm right, Mister Jeff said, And I still say these whitefolks need to hear some of that kind of gospel. These ain't no histry book whitefolks around here and this ain't no histry. This ain't nothing but just a plain old everyday mess!

Trying to keep the black man down.

All whitefolks ain't like that, Phil.

Yeah, but them that is.

And some of us too, Jesus, Miss Minnie Ridley Stovall said, Lord the truth is the light, and some of us just ain't ready yet.

Amen, Mister Big Martin said.

Amen? Mister Phil Motley said. What you mean Amen?

That's what I want to know, Mister Jeff Jefferson said.

I mean the truth is the light just like Minnie say.

I done told you, Miss Minnie Ridley Stovall said.

Well ain't none of these peckerwoods around here ready for nothing neither, but just look at them. That's some truth for the light too.

Yeah but I still say some of us still ain't learned how to stick together yet.

Now Big'un, you know good and well that can get to be a horse of another color, Mister Doc Donahue said. I for one don't never intend to be sticking with any and everybody coming along because he say he one of us. You know better than that.

That's why I say *some* of us, Jesus, Miss Minnie Ridley Stovall said.

That's all right about all that, Mister Big Martin said. I'm talking about when you talking about going up against that stone wall. I want us to be ready. I'm talking about Stonewall Jackson. I'm talking about Jericho. That's what I'm talking about.

Well, we talking about the same thing then, Mister Phil Motley said.

That's all right about your Stonewall Jackson too, Mister Jeff Jefferson said, and your Vardaman and your Pitchfork Ben and all the rest of them. This child right here is getting old Stonewall Jackson's water ready.

They were all laughing then. Because everybody in Gasoline Point knew how Shorty Hollingsworth had met his waterloo and got the name Hot Water Shorty. His wife had come up behind him and dashed a pot of scalding lye water down the seat of his pants while he was sitting on the front steps cleaning his shotgun and bragging about what he was going to do if she didn't have his supper on the table in the next five minutes. He had yelled, dropped his shotgun and lit out across the barbwire fence and hadn't stopped until he was chin deep in Three Mile Creek. He had a new name from then on and he also had a new reputation: he could outrun a striped-assed ape.

Uncle Jerome said I was learning about verbs and adverbs and proverbs; and he preached his sermon on the dictionary that time, and he had his own special introduction to the principles of grammar: A noun is someone or something; a pronoun is anything or anybody; a verb is tells and does and is; an adverb is anyhow, anywhere, anytime; an adjective is number and nature; a preposition is relationship; and conjunction is membership; and interjection is the spirit of energy.

Then that time when Aunt Sue was visiting us from Atmore, old Mayfield Turner was there. Old Sawmill Turner, the log carriage expert, who Mama said had been trying to marry Aunt Sue for more than seventeen years, which meant that he had started before she married her first husband (she was visiting us because she had just separated from her fourth husband). Old Sawmill was wearing his blue pinstripe, tailor-made suit and his Edwin Clapp shoes and smelling like the barbershop and sitting cross-legged like Henry Ford; and every time he took a puff on his White Owl, he flashed his diamond ring like E. Berry Wall. Sometimes when they were talking about

him behind his back they used to give him names like John
D. Rockefeller Turner and J. P. Morgan Turner and Jay Gould
Turner because he also sported pearl gray kidskin gloves, and
he was always talking about stocks and bonds and worrying
about the National Debt.

I was reading about Valley Forge that night, and I knew he
was there just as I knew that Mister Lige and Miss Emma Tolliver and Bro Mark Simpkins and his wife, Miss Willeen were
all there, because they were always the first ones to come by to
see Aunt Sue when she was in town. But at first the only ones
that I was really conscious of were Miss Lula Crayton and Miss
Liza Jefferson, because every time I paused Miss Lula Crayton
kept saying Tribulation tribulation trials and tribulation, and
Miss Ida Jefferson would respond one time as if she were hearing some new gossip, and the next time as if I were reading
the Bible itself (saying Honey don't tell me, saying Lord have
mercy Jesus).

Then I happened to glance up and see old Sawmill again,
and he had stopped puffing on his cigar. He was leaning forward with his hand under his chin, his eyes closed, his lips moving, repeating everything I was reading, word for word. He
had forgotten all about Aunt Sue, for the time being at least.
I was reading about how the Redcoats were wining and dining and dancing warm in Philadelphia while the ragtag bobtail
Continental Army was starving and freezing in makeshift huts
and hovels, and about how General George Washington himself had to get out and personally whip slackers and stragglers
and would-be deserters back into the ranks with the flat of his
sword. All of which was what Give me liberty or give me death
really meant, which was why whenever you talked about following in the footsteps of our great American forefathers you
were also talking about the bloody tracks the half barefooted
troops left in the snow that fateful winter.

Everytime I glanced up I could see old Sawmill Turner still
leaning forward toward me, his lips still moving, the tip of his
cigar gone to ash. Then when I came to the end of the chapter
and closed the book, he stood up and stepped out; into the
center of the semi-circle as Uncle Jerome always did. I'm a
histry scholar myself, he said. I been a histry scholar ever since
I first saw all of them seals and emblems down at the post

office when I was a little boy back in Lowdnes County. Then he ran his hand down into his pocket and pulled out a fat roll of brand-new greenbacks, which he held against his chest like a deck of gambling cards. He peeled off a crisp one-dollar bill and held it up and said, Old George Washington is number one because he was first in war and first in peace and first in the hearts of his countrymen. He got it started.

And old Abe Lincoln. (*He held up a five-dollar bill.*) Came along later on and had to save the Union. Old Alexander Hamilton didn't get to be the President, but he was in there amongst them when they started talking about how they were going to handle the money, and here he is. (*He pulled off a ten-dollar bill.*) And here's old Tom Jefferson. (*Off came a twenty-dollar bill.*) Now he was a educated man and he knowed exactly what to do with his book learning. And then you come on up to old Ulysses S. Grant. (He held up a fifty-dollar bill without even pausing.) He was the one old Abe Lincoln himself had to send for when the going got tight, and later on they made him the eighteenth President.

He held up the fifty-dollar bill long enough for everybody to see that it really was a fifty-dollar bill and then he held up a hundred-dollar bill and said, Old Ben Franklin didn't ever even want to be the President. But old Ben Franklin left just as big a mark in histry as any of them. They didn't put him up there on no one-hundred-dollar bill for nothing. Old Ben Franklin was one of the smartest men they had back in them days, and everybody give him his due respect. Old Ben Franklin told them a lot of good points about how to put them clauses in the Constitution. He was just about the first one they thought about when they had to send somebody across the water to do some official business for the Government with them fast talking Frenchmen. And talking about being cunning, old Ben Franklin was the one that took a kite and a Cocola bottle and stole naked lightning.

He came and stood in front of my chair then. This boy is worth more than one hundred shares of gilt-edged preferred, and the good part about it is we all going to be drawing down interest on him. Then he handed me a five-dollar bill as crisp as the one he had held up before, and told me to buy myself a fountain pen; and he told Mama he was going to be the one to stake me to all the ink and paper I needed as long as I stayed in school. All I had to do was show him my report card.

All I could do was say thank you, and I said I would always do my best. And Miss Lula Crayton said Amen. And Miss Liza Jefferson said God bless the lamb and God bless you Mayfield Turner. Then before anybody else could say anything he excused himself and Aunt Sue walked him to the door and he put on his alpaca topcoat, his black Homburg hat and his Wall Street gloves and was gone.

All Mama could do was wipe her eyes, and all Papa could do was look at the floor and shake his head and smile. But Uncle Jerome was on his feet again, saying he was talking about the word made manifest for Manifest Destiny; and I knew he was going to take over where Sawmill Turner had left off and preach a whole sermon with me in it that night. And so did everybody else, and they were looking at me as if I really had become the Lamb or something. So I looked at the mantlepiece, and I heard the Mother Goose clock and outside there was the Valley Forge bitter wind in the turret-tall chinaberry tree.

WHEN YOU *looked out from the chinaberry tree southeast across the L & N clearing and that part of Mobile River and Polecat Bay you were also looking toward the Tensaw cane-brakes beyond which was the horizon blue territory of the Old Spanish Fort, about which there were fireside and swingporch tales that were also about the Old Spanish Trail.*

There was a time when I used to think it was called the Old Spanish Trail because of all the low hanging Spanish moss such as you saw from the picnic truck on the way to such shrimp and oyster and crab gumbo and baseball towns as Bayou La Batre and Pascagoula and Biloxi. So when they used to sit talking about the olden days when the explorers and pirates used to come ashore it was as if the Old Spanish Main had been so named because you had to bushwack your way through all that Spanish moss to get to the coast and see the Jolly Roger seadog schooner sails bounding suddenly into view from the foggy nina-pinta-santamaria gray Spanish distance beyond the horizon.

Once there had also been an Old French Fort. But that was now known as Twenty-Seven Mile Bluff. I had never been there, but I knew that it was supposed to be that many more miles farther up Mobile River so I also knew that it was something else you were sighting in the direction of when you swung your spy-glass around to the northeast and saw the sky falling away beyond Chickasabogue Swamp and Hog Bayou. It was not until later on in Miss Gale's Alabama History class that I was to find out that Twenty-Seven Mile Bluff was supposed to have been the site where the original French colonists had settled Mobile itself. That was when we were learning about how Mobile came to be known as the City of Five Flags, and that was also when I found out that the original name had been Fort St. Louis de la Mobile, because Mobile was the name of the Indians living on Twenty-Seven Mile Bluff before the first Frenchmen arrived with such weather-beaten cannons and wrought iron fountains and benches and gallery grillwork as you still saw in and around Bienville Square and up and down Dauphin and Royal and Conti, not to mention Government Street.

But I already knew something about the five flags before that because I had been seeing all of them fluttering and snapping above the downtown sidewalk decorations along the Mardi Gras parade route every year long before I was yet old enough to start to school. So I am almost certain that I had already heard Soldier Boy Crawford explaining which one was French and which was Spanish and which English long before I had ever heard of Miss Lexine Metcalf, to say nothing of Miss Gale. Because I can remember him coming to the soldier's position of attention and saluting as he named each one, but when he came to the Confederate flag he would always thumb his nose and slap his backside and call it the shit rag of the goddamn slavery time peckerwoods who fought against the Union because they wanted to keep the black man bound down in servitude under the white man.

I F YOU could have seen the L & N flagstop from the china-berry tree you could also have seen the Chickasabogue Bridge and the shallows where the gulls circled and dipped and swooped above what was left of the old *Clotilde*, which some people used to call the old Flotilla, and others the old Crow-tillie, but which I later came to realize had been the very same ship Unka JoJo the African had always been talking about when somebody asked him to tell once more about coming across the big water back in 'fifty-nine, which, I was to learn still later on, was one of the last if not the very last shipload of African captives (one hundred and sixteen) to be bootlegged directly into the continental limits of the United States before the outbreak of the War for Emancipation.

At first what I used to think Unka JoJo was talking about was the Journey of Jonah in the Belly of the Whale (what with him actually insisting over and over that that was how he came to be in Nineveh, even as so many others in church and out were forever declaring that we were all the Children of Israel on our way out of our sojourn of bondage in Egyptland). Be-cause as far as I was ever concerned at first, Unka JoJo the Af-rican was nothing, if not the most venerable local embodiment of all biblical prophets, apostles and disciples anyway. He wore the Afro-Chinese thin chin whiskers of a seer and sayer and wiseman, and I had no doubt whatsoever that his twisted ashy brown walking stick could become a snake, a burning bush, a divining rod, a lightning rod, or anything else he willed it to be anytime he threw it down and snapped his fingers and uttered the magic African biblical words.

Then there was also the even more obvious fact that as sexton of African Hill Baptist Church he was not only the one pulling the rope when you heard the African Hill Baptist bell tolling (as softly as if black crepe mourning veils were being hung out across the sky on a clothesline attached to a kite), he was also the one who kept the keys to the big French lace wrought iron gate to African Baptist Hill Graveyard and so was also the one who knew exactly which six-foot plot of earth would be allotted

to the next person to die. (Which was why when Little Buddy
Marshall and I used to mimic Unka JoJo's stick tapping, dicty-
rocking, one-step-drag-foot, catch-up shuffle walk we knew
very well indeed that we were flirting with bad luck, because
doing that you were not only getting pretty close to imitating
and thereby mocking the inevitable infirmities of old age which
you were supposed to have been born knowing better than to
do, but you were also just one step away from thumbing your
nose while somebody was praying or saying the Blessing, which
was the next worse thing to cutting a caper while the preacher
was saying ashes to ashes and dust to dust, something that only
the babylonian people in the voodoo town of New Orleans
were said to dare to do.

As for Unka JoJo being an African, at first I used to think
Africa was short for African Hill Neighborhood. So I used to
say: Okay, so they might have red clay hills and the Southern
Railroad and African Baptist, but in Gasoline Point we have
two creeks plus the river plus the L & N; and they can have
their fig trees and scuppernong arbors and plum thickets and
yard peas and gourd vines, and they can make all the elderberry
wine they want to, because we have all the best blackberry
slopes this side of Chickasaw plus almost all of the trees with
the best muscadine vines, so we make that kind of wine; and we
also live closer to the swamps and bayous and the whiskey stills,
which is why we have the best jook houses and the greatest
jook-house piano players in the world.

And when somebody from up there used to call us them
old sawmill quarters niggers, section gang niggers and foggy
bottom niggers who didn't come from anywhere but from
looking up a mule's ass back on the old plantations back in
slavery times, all I thought was that they were trying to get
even because we were also not only closer to all the best places
for hunting both land game and water game, but we also had a
baseball team that was in the same class as those from Chickasaw and Whistler and Maysville and Bayou La Batre and Biloxi.

It was not until I finally began to pay close enough attention during the New Year's Day ceremonies celebrating the
Emancipation Proclamation that I began to become aware of
the everyday flesh and blood geographical facts and historical circumstances that the old *Clotilde* had once been a part

and parcel of. But from then on you could also understand that there was indeed a fundamental similarity as well as an all-important difference between the Belly of the Whale and the Bowels of Middle Passage. Because back when I still used to think the Emancipation Commemoration Day speakers were saying not Abraham Lincoln but able hammer link gone and used to visualize the brawniest of plantation blacksmiths (with Arm & Hammer soda box muscles) cutting links of chain gang shackles with a cold chisel and a pig iron anvil, I also used to think the old *Clotilde* had once been a United Fruit Company boat on which Unka JoJo had come across the Gulf from somewhere in the Caribbean as had Blue Gum Silas the pigeon-toed West Indian (who was also known as Geechee Silas and as the Blue Gum Geechee because of the abba abba way he talked and because he was so crazy about rice like the abba abba talking Portugese or Portageechee sailors).

Anyway it was some time before I was to think any more about Unka JoJo being an African than about Blue Gum Geechee Silas the West Indian handyman or about Jake Hugh or JQ or Jacques Martinet the Creole fish and oyster peddler or about Chastang Cholly the Cajun nightwatchman or Chief Big Duck the Chickasaw Indian or Lil Duck the Choctaw Indian or Miss Queen Minnie Jo-Buck who was supposed to be a Black Creek Indian because she had coal black velvet-smooth skin and jet black glossy hair that came all the way down to her waist. Because as many times as I had tapped my imaginary walking stick and made my voice tremble mimicking the abba abba geechee talk of Unka JoJo saying All the time free in the old country, I still didn't realize that he was talking about coming all the way across the Atlantic Ocean from another continent and another hemisphere until I learned to use the globe for Miss Lexine Metcalf.

Then that day in the barbershop Papa Gumbo Willie McWorthy looked out and saw him coming hitch stepping along Buckshaw Road and said: Goddamn, deliver me from all that old dried-up-assed elephant hocky about how he used to be so goddamn free and equal back over somewhere in Africa. Like he supposed to be better than somebody because them old Rebs fired on Fort Sumter before the man had a chance to sell his ass off up the river to pick cotton on the plantation like our old folks used to have to do. Deliver me from all that old abba abba bullshit about them Hill niggers being some kind of pure-blooded Africans. Because if that ain't trying to play the dozens on everybody down here I sure would like to know what is.

He also said: Yeah, my daddy come from off of old Marster's old plantation, and my mammy used to belong to some white folks by the name of Shelby. Hell, wasn't but just six years between me myself and slavery times. My daddy used to say as far as he could figure and recollect he must have been born somewhere around eighteen and forty-one, and my mammy told me they told her they had papers to say she was born in 'forty-six. And I was born in 'seventy-one, six years after Surrender.

That was also the day when Soldier Boy Crawford said: You know what I tell them? This what I always tell them. I tell them don't make no goddamn difference to me. And I mean it. What the goddamn hell I care? You know what I tell them? The same thing I told them goddamn Germans. Fuck that shit. Let's go. Them som'iches over there talking about Nigger where your tail at. I said up your mama's ass, motherfucker, and this goddamn cold steel bayonet right here up yours. Because that's what I say. Don't make a goddamn bit of difference to me if my goddamn granddaddy was a goddamn tadpole, LET'S GO. Because I'm the som'ich right here ready to go up side your head. Don't care if my poor old grandmammy wasn't nothing but a stump hole, LET'S GO. And that's exactly the same thing I say when another one of them Hill Africans come trying to make out like his granddaddy used to be sitting on a solid gold diamond studded stool somewhere on the left-handed side of the Zulu River with his own niggers waiting on him. I say that's all right with me. LET'S GO. I say, Man, my old granddaddy was so dumb Old Marster wouldn't even trust him to pick cotton. I say Old Marster used to say the only thing my poor old granddaddy was good for was mixing cowshit and horseshit on the compost pile, so maybe that's how come I'm so full of bullshit. BUT THAT'S ALL RIGHT WITH ME, LET'S GO.

But sometimes he also used to like to tell about some of the Africans he had seen in France during the war. That was when he used to talk about how the Senegalese were never supposed

to unsheath their swords and daggers and even their bayonets
without drawing some human blood with them before putting
them back, so when they got faked into pulling them at the
wrong time they always had to cut themselves. To keep from
breaking the rule about always meaning business and never
woofing when it comes to weapons. And that was when he
also used to say that the Germans said they would stop using
gas warfare if France and Uncle Sam would promise to pull the
niggers and Africans out of the front lines and put them all in
the Quartermaster's and the Engineer's work battalions.

Now talking about somebody black, he said, Old Unka JoJo
supposed to be pure blood African, but that just go to show you
because he ain't all that black at all. Hell, he more rusty brown
than even chocolate colored. But, gentlemens, them goddamn
Sneegeleese sure enough black. And I'm talking about when
you so black you blue-black. But you want to know something
the blackest som'iches I ever seen in my life wasn't even no Africans at all. I seen some goddamn Hindu Indians blacker than
everybody up there on African Hill. Gentlemens, I seen some
goddamn Hindu Indians in Paris, France blacker than hair!

———————

Mama was not talking about us and the Africans that day when
she said what she said about not playing the dozens. She was
talking about Bubber Joe Davis and Stringbean Patterson,
who had just been arrested and taken to jail because they had
started out making jokes and signifying about each other's kinfolks and then had ended up shooting at each other. But, as
was almost always the case, what she said was also something
I was supposed to apply to myself when the time came (as it
did soon enough): Don't make a bit of difference in the world
where you come from you still got to do the best you can with
what you come here with. Don't care if it ain't nothing else
but just your health and strength, you better be thankful for
that instead of going around trying to make out like you born
with some kind of silver spoon in your mouth. Lord, I get so
sick and tired of folks got to always be up somewhere putting
on some kind of old airs for somebody to think they so much.
Anytime any of them come up playing you in some kind of

old dozens you just stay out of it. You just tell them I say the Christchild was born in a stall.

And laid in a manger, Uncle Jerome said coming in from the back room, and wrapped in swattling clothes. Don't take my word for it. Read the Bible. The Son of God was thuswise born and the son of man just better be glad to get here any way he can, considering he ain't nothing but clay except for the spirit, and considering except for the soul six foot of clay is exactly where he going to end up. Vanity of vanity all is vanity. That's what the Bible tells us. And it also say man born of a woman is but a few days and they are fraught full of trouble. So you tell them I say they ain't got no time to be playing no dozens. You tell them I say they better leave them dozens to God. Tell them I say God the one had TWELVE disciples and put TWELVE months in the year and marked TWELVE hours on the face of the clock. And why in the name of God do you think we count eggs by the dozens and not the five, ten, fifteen, twenties? Because the egg is the genesis and the revelation of life. Tell them I say if they just got to play some dozens go hunt some Easter Eggs. No, but they don't want nothing to do with something like that, because that's the CLEAN dozens and what they always subject to have on their dirty minds is the DIRTY dozens.

––––––––––

I don't remember that Miss Tee, who was the one who always came next after Mama and was already there long before Miss Lexine Metcalf, ever mentioned anything at all to me about the dozens as such. But then it was as if the only twelve that ever had any special significance for her in those days was the one that came after the Eleventh Grade. In any case so far as she was ever concerned there was no family name or ancestral bloodlines of identity and inheritance that was likely to stand you in much better stead than the also and also of the background you could create for yourself by always doing your best in school.

Which was also why once she was convinced that you had become a schoolboy above and beyond everything else, nothing she had or could come by was too good for you.

At first (when she was not yet Miss Tee but Auntee) she was mostly the one who always came to cuddle, kiss, and oopde-doopdedoodle you saying Some brown sugarboy lips and some sugarboy brownskin cheekbones and some brown sugarboy foreheadbone and some sugarboy brown right-hand knockout knucklebone and some left-hand knucklebone too. May your Anne Tee have some pretty please help herself to some of all this yum yum sugar and all this yum yum honey plus all this buster brownskin pudding and pie.

Then she was also the one who always used to come looking Where is my mister buster brownskin? as soon as she stepped inside the gate, smiling I Spy through her good fairy ring-fingers. Where in the world can he be this time Miss Melba? Oh I think I think I know I think I see guess who Miss Melba. But my how he just keeps on growing and growing so Miss Melba. This is isn't it the same Mister daredevil roustabout I had to look east of the woodpile and west of the hen nest to find last time Miss Melba, and east of the sunflowers west of the kitchen steps the time before that, and east of the east the time before that and west of the west the time before that and north of the north and south of the south the time before that and the time before that.

Then also more often than not: How would you like to may he Miss Melba come play awhile at my house this afternoon? Miss Melba says if you want to wouldn't you like to come visit your Miss Tee and see the new surprise something from the Sears and Roebuck Catalogue My Mister? To which I refuse to remember ever having said no. Not with all the storebought toys she always had both inside the house and out.

You couldn't see where she lived from the chinaberry tree, but as soon as you came to Miss Missie Mae Ferguson's cor-ner all you had to do was turn right and her house was the one with the whitewashed fence and flower garden and green latticework framing the swingporch. And there was also a screened-in back porch with a rocking horse, and in the back-yard there were two plowline swings and a seesaw and a play-shed that could become a play house, a play store, a play mill, a play school or anything else you wanted it to be.

Her husband was Mister Paul Miles Boykin, but he was not my uncle; not only because she was already my auntee before he came and married her, but also and mainly because I never did like him. I disliked his side-watchful eyes and shiny cowlicks and charlie chaplin mop of a mustache from the very outset, and then one day I also realized that the thing about his voice was that it almost always sounded as if he were trembling without knowing it because he could hardly keep himself from slapping you. That was long before the time he came home and saw me sitting on the back steps eating strawberries and cream and said: That's my money you eating, my young fellow. You don't ever call me your uncle but anytime you asking your Miss Auntee for something you asking Paul Miles Boykin too. When she given you them sailor boy clothes that's my money you wearing, and when you come around here, this my house I'm working and sweating to pay the whitefolks for, and all that's my money you playing with out there in that yard.

Which was also when Miss Tee said: He doesn't know a thing in the world about what's bothering you Mister Boykin. He's only an innocent child Mister Boykin. It's not his fault. If somebody did something wrong I'm the one. To which he said: I'm talking about my money. He also said: I'm talking about if he ain't too innocent to be always coming over here costing me money, he ain't too innocent to start learning a trade. If he was a child of mine I'd be learning him a trade by this time. When I was his age I wasn't setting around on somebody's steps eating no strawberries like money growing on trees. I was already pulling my own row. That's what I'm talking about.

Which is why the very next chance I got I said: What about me when you and Mister Paul Miles get your own little boy Miss Tee? And that was when she said she would always be my Miss Tee and if there were ever a new little boy he would be my cousin and I could always play like he was my little brother.

YOU ALWAYS used to know when it was Sunday morning again as soon as you woke up, because everything was always so still and quiet. Then instead of sawmills and lumber trucks and train whistles and switch engines there would be Sunday School bells, which in those days you could hear from churches as far away as Pine Hill Chapel, and which always used to sound as if they were sunshine blue and sunshine yellow even when you were listening through wind and rain.

Then it would be time for my Sunday morning bath before putting on my blue serge Sunday-go-to-meeting suit plus my Buster Brown kneestockings with my tongue-and-sidebuckle lowquarter Buster Brown Shoes plus my silk pongee shirt with my sailorboy bowtie plus my sailorboy blue flat-top hat. (That was when you used Palmolive instead of plain everyday washing soap, and you combed and brushed your hair using Pluko or Poro instead of plain everyday Vaseline, and when there was no Mum, you used to have to rub baking soda under your arms, and sometimes you also had to rub the shine off your nose and cheeks with Mama's chamois skin.)

Then it would be time for Sunday morning breakfast, and sometimes the main thing would be fresh pan sausage with flapjacks and molasses, and at other times it might be pork chops or fried chicken, and in season that was also when you got the best batter-fried oysters with grits and butter. But what I always remember first when I remember how it used to be when company was there for Sunday breakfast is smothered steak plus onion gravy with grits and with biscuits plus your choice of homemade blackberry jelly or peach jam or pear preserve or watermelon rind preserve. Along with all of which there was that special aroma of French Market chickory coffee which I didn't drink in those days but which I still remember when I remember Alabama Sunday mornings as I also remember barbershop cigar smoke when I remember how Saturday mornings used to be.

It was as if the big bells which used to ring for eleven o'clock services were there to hammer silver and gold for the stars and crowns the big choir used to sing about in heavenly host harmony above the stainedglass holiness of the organ. I used to think the pulpit was there because it was the same thing as the throne before which you were going to have to stand and give final testimony on Judgment Day (while all around you the whole world was becoming a lake of fire and brimstone into which the condemned would backslide).

There was also a time when I used to think Miss Sister Lucinda Wiggins was somebody who was not only trying to go to Heaven whole soul and body like the prophet Elijah, but was indeed over halfway there already, what with the way she always used to sit in the number one seat in the Amen Corner diagonally rocking in double time while fanning herself in half time. Saying: preach the word sir, tell them about it. And then saying: Lord have mercy Lord have mercy on my soul. In such a way as was always certain to move somebody to respond by breaking into one of the moans that she herself had made famous: Lord poor sin-ner in a hmmmmm aa hmmmmm. Lord the poor sinner innnn aaaaa hmmmmmmmmm aaaaa hmmmmmmmmm. And what with the way she would then say Yes Jesus yes Jesus yes Jesus yes Lord yes Jesus yes Lord yes Jesus yes Lord.

Sometimes she used to become so full of the Holy Ghost that she used to get up and strut up and down the aisle from the Amen Corner to the deacon's bench (stepping now in half time and fanning in double time) as if she could walk right on into a pillow of smoke and take the chariot to the Chancery on High. But most of the time it was as if she was there because it was her sacred duty to see to it that enough spirit was generated (between the Word and the worshippers) to make somebody else shout. Then when somebody like Miss Big Martha Sanford or Miss Edwina Henry used to start dancing and talking in unknown tongues it was also her duty to nod that it was time to calm them down or take them outside.

You used to have to be there in the midst of all of that (if not every Sunday at least every other Sunday), and sometimes the sermons used to be so full not only of ugly prophecies and warnings but also outright threats of devine vengeance on hyprocrites that when people all around you began stomping and clapping and shouting you couldn't tell whether they were doing so because they were being visited by the Holy Ghost or because being grownfolks and therefore accountable for their trespasses they were even more terrified of the dreadful wrath of God than you were (whose sins after all were still being charged against your parents).

Then when the pastor (who always struck me as being as much God's sheriff as God's shepherd) finally took his seat again, the entire congregation smelling not only of Palmolive soap (or Sweetheart soap or pine tar soap) but also of silk and satin and taffeta and jewelry and cologne and fur pieces and powder-puff bosoms, and of bay rum and talcum plus shoe polish and cigar fingers, used to ruffle-shuffle and stand in unison as if to rise shine and give God their glory by clapping and singing like soldiers of the Cross; and you knew it would not be but so much longer before you would be outside once more and on your way back home to find out what mischief the Katzenjammer Kids were getting into this time.

(Because you were not allowed to look at the Sunday-colored funnypapers in the *Mobile Register*—or the *New Orleans Times-Picayune* until you had first remembered the Sabbath day and kept it holy. But all the same Maggie and Jiggs like Mutt and Jeff and the Katzenjammer Kids used to be as much a part of Sunday as my Sunday School cards.)

Then it would be time for dinner with the Sunday table setting, and sometimes the main dish used to be baked hen with cornbread stuffing, and sometimes it was stewed chicken with dumplings, and sometimes it would be beef roast with brown gravy and mashed potatoes or pork roast with candied yams, and that was also when you had baked smoke-cured ham and potato salad that was almost as good as that which Miss Sister Lucinda Wiggins always made to sell on her church supper plates. And there would be side dishes of turnips and mustards which were more special than everyday collards plus tomatoes and cucumbers and red radishes, and for very very special occasions brown edged garden lettuce quick-smothered in olive oil and vinegar.

But the most special Sunday treat of all was ice cream. Not even those banquet festive times when you were permitted to help yourself to a hunk of jelly layer cake plus a slice of sweet potato pie plus a slice of coconut custard pie on the same serving were better than those Sundays on which by cracking the ice and turning the freezer you earned the right to scrape the dasher all by yourself. Unless there were so many for company that all had to be served at dinnertime, Mama always used to save one last smidgen until everybody got back after the Sunday night sermon, and then the only thing left over would be the wooden freezer bucket of melting ice on the dark summer gallery, plus the burlap-fuzzy aftertaste of ice cream salt as you fell off to sleep.

Then it would be Monday morning again, and I would hear Mama (who unlike Miss Sister Lucinda Wiggins was never one to make even the slightest display of her religious devotion in public) wake up saying what I always knew were her prayers and I would know that she was beginning another week by making thankful acknowledgement to a jealous but ever so merciful Heavenly Master that it was by His infinite and amazing Grace that creatures such as we in all our pitiful unworthiness were still spared to be here to be numbered among the living—which was the first Blessing, from which all other blessings flow.

Then, more often than not (because the chances were that you had dozed back off in the meantime) the next thing you heard would be her humming to herself in the kitchen; and what she would be humming was most likely to be either a prayer meeting hymn or an Amen Corner moan. In any case I don't remember Mama ever singing the actual words of any verses that early in the day.

But sometimes you might hear her mumbling something to herself precisely because she was praying again. And sometimes that was also when she used to talk as if to herself but really to the Maker, about the headlong and headstrong sinfulness of this day and time in this His world now so offensive to His majestical sight, who glory unto His holy name, had only to lift His little finger and wipe out all creation.

That was one way you could tell when she was either somewhat bothered or downright troubled about something. And sometimes she used to talk as if directly to God the Father (who sometimes listened from the low hanging clouds or from a sunbeam or perhaps even from a breeze against the windowpanes, and in His own good time answered—sometimes with raging thunder and lightning and sometimes with smiling flowers and bountiful fruit).

So Monday morning was also the time when you were most likely to hear Mama quoting from the Bible, saying: You said thus and so and thus and so Lord and I believe; and You said so forth and so on and I believe, because Father I do believe.

————————

Monday morning was also when Miss Sister Lucinda Wiggins used to wake up sometimes with so much leftover Sunday spirit and Holy Ghost that she had to tell the whole wide world about it. That was when you could sit in the chinaberry tree and see the smoke from her washpot in her backyard on the corner of Gins Alley and Cross Street and hear her moaning at the rub board as if for the benefit of the neighborhood at large. Then sometimes the next thing used to be Miss Libby Lee Tyler answering from her backyard at this end of Gins Alley; and the two of them would begin singing and humming back and forth at each other, and before long somebody else would join in (sometimes somebody like Miss Edwina Henry from as far away as half way to the AT & N on Cross Street) and sometimes by the time they were all ready to hang out their first batch of white pieces it was as if they were having a community wide Monday morning prayer meeting.

————————

Nothing makes me remember Miss Sister Lucinda Wiggins and Miss Libby Lee Tyler and all that so much as when two trumpet players begin trading blues choruses on an up-tempo dance arrangement, with the trombones and saxophones moaning and shouting in the background. Because that was also what I used to think about back when Little Buddy Marshall and I used to stand outside the Masonic Temple (or the Boon Men's Union Hall Ballroom) after a baseball game or a picnic listening to Sonny Tarver and Dewitt Ellis blowing back and forth at each other in Daddy Gladstone Giles' Excelsior Marching and Social Band.

Not that I didn't always know that the one thing you were never likely to hear Mama, Miss Sister Lucinda Wiggins or any other church folks humming, mumbling, to say nothing of singing, or even listening to at any time whatsoever back in those days was blues music. And no wonder either. Because according to every preacher or deacon who ever mentioned it the blues was the music of the Devil. When you said you had the blues (which was exactly the same as saying that the blues had you) that was only another way of saying that you were so possessed of sin that your soul was already churning in torment.

Because according to every preacher and Sunday School teacher I can remember, the reason you were not supposed to wake up with the blues was simple enough: once you were converted from the ways of sinfulness to the truth of the light you were supposed to have acquired soul salvation, which meant nothing if not precisely that you were saved not only from the fiery furnaces of the red Devil himself, but also from his ever busy imps the plain old everyday blue devils that bedeviled the world with the temptations of the flesh only to double right back and trouble your conscience to desolation and despair—which of course was, so far as church folks were concerned, all too obviously what singing the blues (by which they really meant crying the blues) was all about in the first place.

Not that you were not brought up in terms of all of that. But even so what I myself almost always used to think blues music was mostly about when I used to hear Luzana Cholly playing his notorious silver stringed gold fretted pearl studded guitar was not fire and brimstone but the blue steel train whistle blueness of the briarpatch (the habitat not only of the booger bear whose job was to frighten naughty children into obedience but also of that most grizzly and terrifying of all bears, the one who according to fireside and barbershop accounts put the mug on you, ripped out the seat of your pants and made you a tramp, ripped off the soles of your shoes, wiped out crops and caused famines, shut down mills and factories and caused panics).

Nor were all church folks always as hard set against blues music when it came to Luzana Cholly as most of their remarks would otherwise lead you to expect. Because on occasion even

Mama and Uncle Jerome used to forget. Because sometimes when he used to come strumming his way up out of the L & N bottom while we were all sitting on the front gallery in the summer twilight, Mama would be the very first one to say: There come old box-picking Luzana Cholly playing the fool out of that old thing like nobody else in the world. With never a word about him being on his way either to or from a skin game, or to a jook house. And Uncle Jerome would clear his throat and say: Old Luzana Cholly. Old Luzana Cholly out there amongst them. That's him all right. Here he come and ain't no two ways about it. Old Luzana Cholly. I done told you.

When it came to old frizzly headed, wicked walking, sneaky looking Stagolee Dupas (*fils*) however, and the kind of music he used to play on the piano, church folks used to call it the low-down dirty blues even when it was not. Because old Stagolee (who so far as Little Buddy Marshall and I were concerned was to honed steel and patent leather what old Luzana Cholly was to blue steel and rawhide) was liable to barrelhouse you right on out into the black alley in the simple process of vamping the chords to "Nearer My God to Thee."

Mister Stagolee Dupas (*fils*), or the Stagolee Kid was also called Stagolee the Son of Stagolee and Stagolee the Younger and Stagolee Junior and Son Stag and Kid Stag not because he was the son of the original Mister Bad Bad Stagolee (who was sometimes referred to as old Trigger Fingered Stagolee) but because he had followed in the footsteps of and probably even surpassed his father (who was a piano player famous for making up verses about the original Bad Man Stagolee, the notorious gambler who packed a stack barrel Forty-four). Sometimes when Stagolee the Son of Stagolee used to start adding some of his own new verses, he would keep on going until he had a verse for every key on the piano.

Mister Stagolee Dupas (*fils*) with his Creole pirate's mustache and his Creole bayou sideburns and his New Orleans sporting house patent leather shoes and his gambling den silk shirts. Not to mention the indescribably wicked way he had of winking at women without really winking at all, which was something he was almost as notorious for as for the way he also used to walk his left hand right on into the dirty dozens while keeping his own special til-the-cows-come-home tremolo going on and on with his right until (as somebody was forever repeating) the king of the signifying monkeys was subject to be out of tales to tell and out of breath to boot.

There were also long gone freight train whistles in the music he used to play years before anybody started calling that kind of blues boogie-woogie and he could also play wedding music and the church organ. But the only thing you were ever likely to hear any church folks mention him for was Saturday Night Music, which they also called Good Time Music, by which they meant the kind of nightlong blues-dragging, blues-rocking, blues-bumping, blues-jumping, blues-swinging, blues-shouting music for Saturday night honky tonk dances during which, according to them, somebody was forever getting stabbed or cutup or shotup and ending up either in the hospital or the graveyard, with somebody else either skipping city or going to jail and then on to the County Farm or the chain gang.

Because the word on him among most church folks was always the same: He had not only come from hell and was on his way back to there, but was indeed so obviously in league with the Devil that he had turned up in Gasoline Point precisely because he had been dispatched special delivery from the dins and dives of sin ridden New Orleans for the express purpose for providing all but irresistible wickedness for the weak and temptation for backsliders.

You could always count on somebody preaching another fire and brimstone sermon about the ungodly good time music in the houses of doom and iniquity whenever there had been another one of the sheriff's raids on the honky tonks, and the following Monday morning you could also count on hearing Miss Sister Lucinda Wiggins again. But what she used to tell the world when it was that kind of Monday morning was not about how the Comforter had come and brought joy joy joy to her soul, but about trouble in the land.

Sometimes when you heard somebody singing something other than church music over in Gins Alley on Monday morning it used to be Miss Honey Houston, whose house was next door to Miss Pauline's Cookshop, and who always used to begin with the same opening verse: Going to see Madame Ruth/Going to see Madame Catherine/Going to tell Madame Ruth/Going tell Madame Catherine (Got a world full of trouble/And sweet daddy so doggone mean).

But the one I remember above everybody else when I remember somebody who used to wake up on Monday morning and let the whole neighborhood know that she had another bad case of the blues, no matter what all the preachers and church folks in the state of Alabama said, is Miss Blue Eula Bacote who used to live at the other end of Gins Alley in the house with the yard that was mostly a flower garden and always used to wear high-heel patent leather pumps and spang-dangling 18-carat gold earrings with her almost-frizzly hair bobbed and poroed like a big city flapper, and used to have the best short plump brownskin strut you ever saw, even when she was too drunk to do anything except flash her jewel-studded Gay Paree cigarette holder.

The first thing she always used to do (after lighting a cigarette and making coffee) was wind up her Victrola and put on the latest record of Bessie Smith singing the blues. Then she would open all the doors and windows. And then she used to move all of the furniture out into the clean-swept part of the yard and string all of her hangers of coats, suits and frocks on the clothesline, and spread the mattress ticking and stuffing on the grass and drape all of her quilts and blankets on the fence. Then she used to get down on her knees with a scrubbing brush and a bucket of hot sudsy lye water and do all of the floors plus the porch and the steps.

Sometimes she used to play the same Bessie Smith record over and over and sometimes all you used to hear would be Bessie Smith and Ma Rainey. But most of the time she also used to like to listen to Mamie Smith and Trixie Smith and Ida Cox, all of whom she always went to see in person in the vaudeville every time they came to Mobile to play at the Pike Theatre out on Davis Avenue. And she was also the one who always used to buy every Jelly Roll Morton and King Oliver and Louis Armstrong record as soon as it came out. (So no wonder all of old Louis' highest trumpet runs always seem to come from beyond the roof tops of Gins Alley and to be aimed at me in the chinaberry tree.)

Then while the house was drying and airing out she always used to work on her flowers with the music still playing, and after that she used to sit in her rocking chair sometimes in the shade and sometimes in the sunshine still listening, but now also smoking and drinking black coffee (sometimes darning, sometimes making quilt patches, sometimes shelling peas or beans). But she herself never used to sing or even hum. All she ever used to do was hold her head to one side with her eyes closed and pat her feet and snap her fingers every now and then. The only words I can remember ever hearing her say while the music was playing were Hello central hello central hello central ring me Western Union. Which is what she also used to say on those Saturday nights when she used to sit all by herself in the corner of Sodawater's honky tonk getting high while Mister Mule Bacote, whose real name was Lemuel Bacote but who was also called Eula's Mule, was out in Skin Game Jungle.

Then by midday you wouldn't hear anything else, and if you went that way going to the post office you wouldn't see her anywhere either, so I always used to think she was probably taking a nap on a pallet in one of the empty rooms. Then by the middle of the afternoon, she always used to start putting everything back in place, and by time to begin supper it was as if she had finally gotten everything ready to make it through another week, and by the time Mister Lem the Mule, who was the number one raft towing expert for Buckshaw Mill, used to get back from the river it was always as if it all had been only another day.

According to most of the backfence and pumpshed mention, speculation and insinuation I used to hear, Miss Eula Bacote came to be the way she was because she was doomed to be forever childless and in love with a good man who was always gambling his hard earned wages away. But the first and foremost thing that comes to mind when I remember her now is how music used to sound on the old wind-up Gramophones of that time. Then what I always see again (along with her stylish clothes) is her yard with all the flowers plus the porch with the trellis and all the planting pots and boxes that used to make me think about Miss Tee every time I used to go through Gins Alley on my way to the kite pasture or the post office.

*T*HE MUSIC *I remember when I remember how Bea Ella Thornhill came to be known as Miss Red Ella is the special ragtime piano-roll version of the ever popular oldtime barroom ballad about what Frankie did to Johnny that Stagolee Dupas (fils) used to have to play again every time somebody else in Sodawater MacFadden's jook joint used to say Hey how about some more mean red evil for the old boll weevil.*

Because not only was the chain of events leading up to that particular bloody mess a story in itself, it was also one that almost everybody in Gasoline Point (including me and Little Buddy Marshall this time) knew or should have known verse by verse, chorus by chorus and therefore step by step already. And so also because for the next six or seven months following the funeral (to which Bea Ella came in handcuffs) and that trial (at which she was sentenced to serve a year and a day) it was as if the only thing left for anybody to do was go and get Stagolee Dupas (fils) to repeat that long since familiar tune at least four or five times every Saturday night.

———————

That day when Little Buddy Marshall and I heard the screaming and saw people running toward it from every direction and followed them on up into the alley off the crape myrtle lane behind Stranahan's store where we saw what had happened to Beau Beau Weaver neither of us was in the least surprised by what we heard from those who were standing there grunting and wagging their heads at each other as they waited for the sheriff and the coroner.

But then whenever anything which meant serious trouble of any kind whatsoever happened in Gasoline Point there was always somebody whose immediate reaction was to repeat the same old claim: I told you so. I told you so. I told you so. Even when what had occurred was obviously not only an accident but one which nobody in that part of the world at that time was likely either to have seen or even to have heard of before, somebody had to say it in one way or another: See there, what did I tell you? What else did you—could you or anybody else expect?

Even when it was some altogether natural phenomenon such as, say, a Gulf Coast gale ripping in from the river and Mobile Bay, you could be absolutely positive that somebody was somewhere shaking his head and grumbling as if anybody with any common sense at all should have been able to foresee and if not avert or avoid it at least be better prepared to withstand it.

You could also be every bit as certain that somebody was going to be explaining the fundamental cause along with the overall effect of whatever it was by citing the unimpeachable authority of the Bible. Nor was it at all unusual for somebody else to be pontificating about the natural as well as the human implications of it all with overtones suggestive not only of prophecy, but also of fortunetelling and even in not a few instances of conjuration.

As far as Little Buddy Marshall and I were concerned, however, almost all statements of that nature were likely to have much more to do with such foresight as is inevitably inherent in (and indeed is perhaps inseparable from) all accurate pragmatic insight than with any operation whatsoever—traditional or otherwise—of clairvoyance per se.

In this case the likelihood of a bloody mess had been mentioned more than once, to be sure—but so, as a matter of fact, had a number of other eventualities. But still and all, much more had been said about what had already come to pass in similar circumstances than about what was in store for the one at issue, whether sooner or later. Because what most people were really saying was I seen situations like this seen them time and again and ain't no telling what's going to happen!

Not that anyone we knew ever considered prediction, or perhaps better still, projection to be irrelevant. It was very much to the point indeed. For the moment involves anticipation as well as memory, and action itself is of its very nature nothing if not the most obvious commitment to the future. But if like me and Little Buddy you had been as profoundly conditioned by the twelve-string guitar insinuations of Luzana Cholly and the honky-tonk piano of Stagolee Dupas (*fils*) as by anything you had ever heard or overheard in church at school by the fireside or from any other listening post, you knew very well that anything, whether strange or ordinary, happening in Gasoline Point was, in the very nature of things, also part and parcel of the same old briarpatch, which was the same old blue steel network of endlessly engaging and frequently enraging mysteries and riddling ambiguities which encompass all the possibilities and determine all the probabilities in the world. But you also knew something else: no matter how accurate your historical data, no matter how impressive your statistics, the application of experience to flesh-and-blood behavior must always leave something to chance and circumstance.

But then the fact that Luzana Cholly and Stagolee Dupas (*fils*) were road-seasoned gamblers who were almost as notorious for being footloose ramblers as for playing music was as important to me and Little Buddy as anything else. Because after all if you had been bred and born in the briarpatch, and if like me and him you were enroute to Philamayork you had to be nimble by habit not only like Jack the Rabbit but also like Jack the Bear who could even be nowhere when necessary precisely because having been everywhere he knew when you were supposed to play drunk or even dead. Anyway, you were never supposed to take anything for granted.

Nor had we. And yet nobody, not even those who had always insisted irrevocably that anything under the sun could happen had included what was clearly the most decisive detail of all: Bea Ella Thornhill flashing a switchblade knife. Bea Ella Thornhill flashing a switchblade knife of her own. Bea Ella Thornhill flashing a switchblade knife which she herself had ordered COD from Sears Roebuck three weeks before. Nobody's conjectures had included anything like that at all. Not even after she had been given up as a lost ball in the high weeds.

On the other hand there was neither consternation nor even mild surprise at what had befallen Beau Beau Weaver, who was also known as Bo as in bo'hog and bo'weevil, whose name was Emmett James Scott Weaver but who sometimes bragged about being the weaverer, meaning spell weaver. Because although speculation about him may have been prudently vague, it had always been ominous. It had always included the possibility of violence because what people had expressed most concern about was not his integrity as was the case with Bea Ella Thornhill but his prospects for simple physical survival.

I myself knew that opinion about that had been negative (and unanimous) from the very outset. Because I could remember the day he arrived from the piney woods of Mississippi. I was the one who saw him when he got off the turpentine trailer at the AT & N crossing carrying a cardboard suitcase. I was the one who told him where the boarding house was.

Most people had registered serious misgivings about him as soon as they saw how he was dressed and the kind of airs he was putting on when he came breezing onto the block that first Saturday at twilight. And everything he said and did thereafter only substantiated their initial impressions. But as soon as the nature of his association with Bea Ella Thornhill became common knowledge, all speculations and conjectures began to seem like foregone conclusions.

So there was some justification for saying I told you so about what had happened to Beau Beau Weaver. But even as we stood there in the blood-stained green plus honeysuckle-yellow alleyway conceding that much, Little Buddy and I also remembered that beneath the consensus of open-ended forebodings we had always detected as much wishful thinking as understanding of the nature of consequence, inevitability or even of cause and effect. Because what most of them had been talking about had far less to do with the inscrutable than with their own theories about the wages of sin.

Because what had really been bothering people more than anything else was the fact that a schoolgirl like Bea Ella Thornhill who was every bit as good looking as Creola Calloway, for instance, but who had always been as sweet and well-mannered and *promising* as Creola Calloway was outrageous—had not only run away from her guardian—(and set up housekeeping with Beau Beau Weaver of all people) but had also hired herself out as a maid for white people as if she had never even been near a school—not to mention knowing how to record minutes and keep books. That was scandalous enough in itself but to top it off, all she did with the money she made was let him spend it on himself. That was certainly one reason they forgot about her even in the process of putting the bad mouth on him. It was as if the worst had happened to her already.

Most of what Little Buddy and I had learned about what people began calling Bea Ella's boll weevil epidemic situation had come from barbershop talk. But the very first time I had heard anything at all about it was not in the barbershop, but one day at the pump shed when Aunt Callie the Cat was talking to Miss Liza Jefferson about it. I was pumping wash water for Miss Liza Jefferson that day and Aunt Callie who was working in her front yard flower garden, came catting out to the fence in her unlaced man's brogans to give Miss Liza some cuttings from her famous rose trellis, and as usual they started swapping the news and Aunt Callie had the main items.

But Lord, she said as soon as they got through pretending that neither had heard any new gossip. Somebody did tell me Bea Ella Thornhill done taken up with that old low-down, good-looking nasty walking, sweet-smelling, grand rascal of a Bo Weaver or whatever his name is.

No she ain't neither, Miss Liza Jefferson said, shaking her head as if that would somehow keep it from having already happened.

That's what they tell me.

Aw you gone on now, Cat. You know good and well Bea Ella ain't done that. You know that child as well as I do.

If it's a lie it ain't mine, honey.

Well, I am speechless, honey, I'm just plain speechless. I just flat cain't open my mouth.

Lord, Beau Weaver, Jesus.

They tell me he a bo-weaver all right.

Mamie was telling me.

Mamie Taylor? Lord, Father in heaven, I ain't seen Mamie Taylor since I don't know when. When have I seen Mamie Taylor, Jesus?

Mamie say it happened right up there at that church supper the other night.

Up in Lula Crayton's yard. You know something? I plain forgot all about that until I suddenly got to wondering where everybody was, and it was too late to go then.

Mamie Taylor say he was there standing around looking just like he just stepped out of a bandbox as usual and after a while he sided up to that child's table and bought a plate of supper and stood there talking and eating and then he bought another one and ate that and stayed there laughing and talking, and stayed right on there and by that time he had her laughing and talking too, and when it come time to go they left together.

Now you know that gal ought to know better than that.

Lord, that grand rascal'll have that child so she don't know her head from her heels.

And after that I heard some others talking about it too, Miss Ida Thompson for instance, and Miss Millie Chapman; and every now and then Mama would be talking about it too; and I even heard Hot Water Shorty Hollingsworth telling Stagolee's Vyola that it was a pity and a shame that Bea Ella had been saving herself and her reputation all that time just to throw it all away for nothing on the likes of somebody who didn't stand for any more than Beau Weaver stood for.

But the main source of information that Little Buddy and I had about subjects like that and a number of other things as well in those days was Papa Gumbo Willie McWorthy's barbershop, because during that time, which was not long after old Jaycee Dickenson went to Kansas City, we didn't have to wait until we needed a haircut in order to be there. Because the new shoeshine expert who later on was going to become a chauffeur and a mechanic for Lem Buckshaw of Buckshaw Mill Company family and leave for Seattle, Washington was old Cateye Gander Gallagher whom everybody knew had always been our number one big buddy.

All you had to do was stop by as if you had come only because you wanted to watch old Cateye holding his head to one side like a drummer, skip popping a patent leather finish on somebody's Edwin Clapps. Not that you had anybody fooled. That was simply the way you had to do it. And when they started talking about something like, say, sporting houses such as those in New Orleans and San Francisco, or say the shysters, pimps and streetwalkers who hung out in Pig Alley which was in Paris, France, they were only pretending that they had forgotten that you were there listening because somebody had decided that it was time for you to start hearing about something like that.

Whenever that happened, as it did the day I heard old Soldierboy Crawford answering questions about such Parisian curiosities as pissoirs and bidets and then best of all, talking about getting paid to be in a smutty postcard show with three French women wearing frog stockings, somebody would also slip in something about the kind of diseases you had to know about but were not yet old enough to ask grown people about.

Everybody knew exactly what you were doing there, and all you were supposed to do was stay quiet and listen. And then finally somebody like old Davenport Davis, for instance, would turn and say, Boy you still here? Boy, you heard all that? Well if you cunning enough to get away with that I reckon, goddammit, you also clever enough to know you supposed to keep it to yourself. You go round repeating this stuff you ain't going to show nobody how much you know. All you going to do is show how much you don't know about when to keep your mouth shut.

Hell I'm satisfied he know that, Papa Gumbo Willie McWorthy, himself also said. And there was something about the way he winked when he said it that made me realize that Mama and Papa were no less satisfied because it was suddenly as plain as day to me that they were in on the whole thing too.

It was from the barbershop that I learned the all important differences between ordinary high yallers whose parents were high yallers, and brand new mulattoes. And it was also in the barbershop that I found out that Elmore Collins had left so suddenly for Los Angeles, California because there was no way in the world for the white people in Tucker's Quarters not to realize what had been going on between him and Miss Jessica Butterfield when one of them happened to be taking a shortcut through her peach orchard and saw him coming out of her backyard at 4:30 A.M. and her watching him from the backroom window.

Boy, Miss Jessica Butterfield don't count because she is one in a minnion. She can do anything she want to because she can buy every peckerwood in Tucker's Quarters. Buy them and bale them. Boy it's them others you got to worry about. Because just remember when they start looking at you they can holler rape if you don't and if you do you can be damn sure that's what they going holler if you get caught. And they'll know she lying and come after you just the same. Boy, Miss

Jessica Butterfield hid her sweet nigger out, give him his get-away money and walked down the middle of the goddamn street with a goddamn silk poker dot umbrella and don't even have to think about daring a single one of them bad-assed peckerwoods to even whisper. Boy that's one widow woman can lift her little pink ring finger and shut down half this town and starve every peckerwood in sight.

It was Papa Gumbo Willie McWorthy's barbershop and he was there most of the time but he was not a barber himself. He was an old Mississippi riverboat cook and he had also been a bartender in a San Francisco gambling den. Now he was a businessman and most of the time he sat at the cash register when he was not at the cookshop which he owned next door. He was called Papa because he had traveled so much and had seen and done so many things. But to this day I still don't know whether he was called Papa Gumbo because he knew so many Creole recipes or because his feet were as flat as gunboats.

The top barber at that time was Vanderbilt Coleman who had once been a pullman porter on the Southern Pacific. He was the one who was always talking about what was going on in the newspaper, and his Bible was the World Almanac. He always wore white Van Heusen shirts (some with collars and some without) and his tan shoes were the handmade kind that shine more and more like antique brass as the instep darkens.

The number one expert on big league baseball was Eddie Ashley who had a collection of Reach and Spalding guide books which went all the way back to 1913. The best checkers players were Decatur Callahan who was also a trombone player, and Chee Cholly Middleton who worked at Chickasaw dry docks and who was just as good when he came in as the money ball relief pitcher backing up old Stringbean Henderson as when he was playing third base.

But the one who almost always turned out to have most of the latest inside news about what was going on in Gasoline Point whenever the talk got around to the subject of men and women was Otis Smedley who in addition to being a jack leg carpenter and handyman was also the one who was always sought after by Baptist, Methodist and sanctified refreshment committees alike during picnics, camp meetings and association time because when it came to making barbecue and

Brunswick stew everybody agreed that nobody could touch him. Anyway, Otis Smedley was the one who knew most about what had been going on all along between Beau Beau Weaver and Bea Ella Thornhill.

I was not there the day he told about what happened that time when Beau Beau took her up to Miss Clementee Mayberry's boarding house. But old Gander Gallagher passed it on to me and Little Buddy when we saw him in Gins Alley after work that same night. Nobody really knew where Otis Smedley got his account from, but when he told it everybody believed it and they could only assume that he had heard it from Beau Beau Weaver himself.

Beau Beau had nice-talked her for three weeks and finally got her to go and she knew exactly what she was going for. But when she got there and it came time for to pull her clothes off she made him go into the closet and when she let him come back in she was standing not by the bed but in the middle of the room all wrapped up in the top sheet with her eyes closed as tight as she could get them and when he began unwinding it she started moaning and praying, saying Jesus forgive me, over and over.

Beau Beau's main hangout, the main place to look for him, was the poolroom, but he also used to come by the barbershop two or three times a week. The first thing he always did was have his shoes shined, and then he would stand primping before the mirror and if he decided that he didn't need his English brushback touched up he would help himself to the lotions and creams, whisk himself down and then flip Vanderbilt Coleman a two-bit tip.

Sometimes, of course, everybody would act is if he were not even there, let alone being noticed; to which he would respond by humming to himself and prancing around as if he were alone in his own private dressing room. Then he would hunch his sides with his elbows and breeze on out whistling through his teeth.

But as often as not somebody would start signifying at him about, say, where he was getting so many fancy clothes from and you could see that he was pleased because he really thought everybody in Gasoline Point was envious of him. He also assumed that everybody regarded him as being such a sweet man that women were climbing all over each other to get to him and to be sure that is what some few who didn't know any better actually did assume.

What those in the barbershop were really signifying about most of the time, however, was the rumor that the reason he didn't have to work in the daytime was not that so many women wanted to take care of him, since so far as anybody knew only Bea Ella Thornhill went that far, but because he worked at night delivering whiskey to the whitefolks' roadhouses for a white bootlegger from Leakesville, Mississippi. You could not tell that he ever suspected that part at all. Because all he would do was wink and grin and start signifying right back at them.

Ain't nothing to me, man.

Man who you stuffing?

I wouldn't stuff you, cousin.

What you putting down, sweet boy?

Tracks, daddy, just bird tracks. And that ain't many.

Just listen at him.

I ain't saying nothing, home boy.

Boy, all I can say is I just wish I had your line. That's all I can say.

Now just listen at him.

Just look at them dry goods all homes is wearing.

These just some of my working clothes, horse collar.

You hear him, Bander Bill?

I hear him.

And he ain't lying either.

Where you working nowadays, Beauboy Pretty?

Now watch out there now, pudding.

Boy they tell me you working all over this man's town, and I know what kind of work, too.

Now see there. Now there you go. That's the kind of old stuff you got to watch, sweetings.

Boy, if I had your hand, I'd throw mine in. That's all I say.

He would be standing his ever-so-cute pigeon-toed stand by the door then, smiling like he was almost blushing and sometimes he would be talking in a back-at-you woofing voice and sometimes he would be flashing his diamond ring with a cigarette in his hand and talking airish talk and getting it all mixed up, like saying *are* for *is* and *doesn't* for *don't* and *knew* for *knowed* and *came* for *come* and even adding words like *psychological* and *financial transaction*, and *incomprehensibility* and *ignorance personified*; and sometimes when he got ready to leave he would announce that he was regretfully making his departure from such an informational educational and inspirational but uneconomical vicinity and that he would recapitulate around that way again whenever his business permitted his absence to that recreational extent and degree.

Then through the plate glass window you could see him pausing outside by the barber's pole making sure that his hat was blocked long, the brim turned up Birmingham style. Then with his left shoulder hunched up and his left arm hanging loose he would move on off down the sidewalk toward Stranahan's block doing his wide tipping pigeon-toed walk about which Little Buddy who liked it even less than I did, used to say: Sheeet man, that ain't no goddamn mammy-hunching patent leather walk. Sheeet, look at that countryfied granny dodger. Think he so sporty and all he doing is looking like his goddamn feet killing him, like he got to pick them up and shake them and let his corns and bunions get some air everytime he take a goddamn step.

And even trying to get some of old Stagolee's slow dragging limp in it so somebody will think he got so many women they wearing him down. Sheeet, hell, goddamn, he just got the goddamn backache from handling all them whiskey jugs. Sheeet everybody know the only good-looking stuff he don't have to pay for is Bea Ella and she don't count. Sheeet, I bet you Creola wouldn't even look at that country-ass sapsucker—goddamn!

He had been in the barbershop that same morning. He had come in whistling to himself to let everybody know that he was in a hurry to get his primping done so he could be on his way to what was obviously a very special rendezvous. But as soon as he got to the mirror the signifying had begun with Chee Cholly Middleton and Decatur Callahan woofing back and forth at each other without even looking up from the checkerboard.

Man I can't help it. Man don't pay me no mind.

You hear him don't you Papa Gums. Remember this now.

Man I can't help it if some can and some can't. Man, some got it and some ain't.

Y'all hear him now.

Man you don't have to hear me. Man all you got to do is see me. See me coming raise your window high . . . see me leaving, hang your nappy nit-picking head and cry. I'm just passing by, man.

Well, me myself I'm just plain old everyday Cooter Callahan. Don't go to be no nighthawk and nothing like that. But that's all right. I'm still subject to touch you one of these times. Just don't let me put my finger on you in none of these alleys one night. Just be sure I don't walk right up and put my dog finger on you, horse collar.

You and Otis Smedley, huh.

Me and Otis Smedley? What about me and the law?

He had not been gone for more than an hour when we heard the first screams. Then we saw the people and then we were running to catch them, and what we found when we got there was him lying sprawled in nothing but his underwear and socks, cut to death.

Then we saw Bea Ella too. She was sitting on Miss Clementee's front steps with her hands in her lap as if they had already put the handcuffs on her. She was saying nothing, doing nothing and looking at nothing.

The first screams, it turned out, were those of Earlene Barlow, who had jumped out of the window with nothing on except her underskirt and struck off across toward Good Hope Baptist Church and the carline, running for everything she was worth. So by the time even the first of us got there she was probably somewhere over in Buckshaw Mill Quarters or half way to Blue Poplar Swamp.

Miss Clementee had been screaming too, but she had quieted down because she was the one who was there telling about it, saying: Lord Jesus, Bea Ella didn't say a mumbling word. Not a mumbling word. Beauboy and Earlene Barlow was there in that room and before anybody realized anything Bea Ella was already in the house and down the hall and bambing at the door where they was. That was when Earlene sailed out through the window.

That must have been when Miss Clementee herself started screaming because she said the next thing she saw was Bea Ella with the knife in her hand: And Lord, him trying to back away from her down the hall trying to soft-talk her then her swiping and stabbing at him with all her might. He was pleading with her then, but she still wasn't saying anything. She was not cursing and not crying, but she was not slacking up one bit either.

He was dodging and scrambling backwards all the time and she missed him all the way down the hall, but he got hung up in the screen door and that was where she stuck him the first time. That was when Miss Clementee started trying to call for somebody to come and help. But it was too late then. Because it was happening too fast then. Because he was staggering across the porch and down the steps and she was right after him, and all he could say was No baby, No baby, trying to ward her off with the hand he wasn't holding himself with.

She got him all hemmed up in the gate then, and it looked like she was going crazy cutting him, and by that time he couldn't help himself at all. And by the time the first people got there it was all over. He had finally torn himself out of the gate and started down the lane and had fallen right where he was now.

As for Bea Ella all she did then was drop the knife and stumble back to Miss Clementee's steps and sit there just staring out in front of her with her hands bloody and blood all up and down the front of her dress.

We were all there then, and I saw the rest of it myself, which was him lying there twisted and dead in the ragged shade of the honeysuckle lane, and her just sitting by herself on the boarding house steps waiting to give herself up to the law.

He must have fallen forward because his forehead and chest were not only bloody but also smeared with grit, but somehow or other he had rolled himself partly over on his right side and turned his head almost face up. There was a deep gash that ran all the way from his ear to the corner of his mouth. His right arm was doubled up under him, but his left hand was still clutching his private parts, because the lower part of his stomach had been ripped open, and his very insides were hanging out.

He must have been stabbed and cut in almost a dozen different places on his arms and the upper part of his body alone. His silk undershirt was just a mess of blood and sand and rips, and there was I don't know how much blood puddled under him, especially under his waist. There was so much there that it was as dark and sticky thick-looking as fresh liver, and there was something grayish white oozing from his bowels and there was water still dripping from his bladder too.

We stood waiting for the sheriff and the coroner to get there, and Miss Clementee Mayberry was telling it over and over and saying: Lord, I didn't know what to do. I just didn't know what to do, saying Lord this and Lord Jesus that as almost all grown people in Gasoline Point almost always did on such occasions. It was only afterwards that you thought about which ones were the church members and which were not.

Then that part was over. The coroner had released the body to Windham and Borders Funeral Home. Bam Buchanan was on his way back to Mobile County Jail carrying Bea Ella Thornhill whose only statement had been: Yes, I did. Miss Clementee Mayberry had been taken back into the boarding house. The place had been raked to bury the blood, and as the crowd broke up, what was being said was all about Beau Beau Weaver and none of it was essentially different from anything which everybody had been saying all along, except that now that an ugly fate had been witnessed as an accomplished fact, the tone of scandal and outrage which had marked the months of anticipation had become softened to one of shame and pity.

But when Little Buddy and I got back to the barbershop Vanderbilt Coleman was saying that Bea Ella Thornhill was the one people should be thinking about, not Beau Beau Weaver. Because all you were talking about when that had happened to him was the Law of Averages, and nothing anybody said about that was going to make any difference anymore anyway. She was the one who was going to have to suffer the consequences of murder, the least of which was the prison term.

That was when Papa Gumbo Willie McWorthy called it red murder, and that was how Bea Ella Thornhill became Red Ella from then on, which seemed to make most people remember seeing her streaked with blood sitting alone on the boarding house steps waiting to confess. But Little Buddy and I knew that Papa Gumbo Willie McWorthy had said red because what he was really talking about was the blues. Because he was responding to what Vanderbilt Coleman had said was Bea Ella Thornhill's biggest mistake of all: Not knowing that bad luck and disappointment meant not the end of the world but only that being human you had to suffer like everybody else from time to time.

So what he was actually describing was a woman seeing red but feeling nothing. And when she came back from County Farm not only acting like a middle-aged church widow but also looking and even walking like one it was as if she had been sentenced to serve a year and a day in prison and had been paroled to spend the rest of her life either bent over a sewing machine or floating along in a trance. Anyway, from then on she was Miss Red Ella and she always smiled at you as if she were seeing you through a red crepe veil; and no matter who said what—or what you were telling or asking her about, she always made the same reply, which to her was obviously the last word on everything: God doesn't love ugly and doesn't care too much about pretty either.

SOMETIMES Stagolee Dupas used to spend the whole afternoon alone at the piano in the empty dancing room of
Sodawater's honky tonk playing for nobody but himself. That
was when he used to sit patting his left foot and running blues
progressions by the hour, touching the keys as gently as if he
could actually feel the grain of each note with his finger tips,
sustaining each chord and listening with his right ear cocked
(and his right shoulder sloped) as if to give it time to soak all
the way into the core of his very being. When all you could
hear was the piano he was probably thinking up new blues
ballad verses, because when you heard his voice when he was
alone like that he was not singing lyrics but humming all the
instrumental fills, riffs and solo take-off to himself as if he were
a one man band.

Then sometimes he used to spend the next two or three
hours playing sheet music, including such new and recent tunes
as "Ain't She Sweet," "Three Little Words," "Lilac Time," and
"My Blue Heaven," which I used to whistle to myself almost
as much as I used to whistle "Sundown," "Little White Lies,"
"Precious Little Thing Called Love," and "Dream a Little
Dream of Me" (which I still find myself whistling to myself
this many years later anytime anything really takes me back to
those days when I was the schoolboy I used to be and used to
feel the way I used to feel about some of the honey brown girls
I used to know).

There were also times when what he used to follow the blues
with would be ragtime tunes (some of which he used to play
note for note as you heard them on the piano rolls when you
were sent to get barbecue sandwiches from the carline cafe
across from the crawfish pond and some of which were his
own) that always used to make me think about the good time
places in such patent leather avenue towns as St. Louis, Missouri and Reno, Nevada and San Francisco, California, where
he had played when he was on the road.

Then when you heard him vamping into his own very special
stop-time version of "I'll See You in My Dreams" you knew he

was about to ride out in up-tempo, riffing chorus after chorus while modulating from key to key so smoothly that you hardly noticed until you tried to whistle it like that.

When you were lucky enough to be there when he was playing for himself that was sometimes also your chance to find out from him about some of the ABC's of piano music just as you were now and then able to find out from Gator Gus about pitching, when you were lucky enough to be around when he and Big Earl were off to themselves working out. Which is why so much of what I was to learn about music comes more directly from Stagolee Dupas than from Luzana Cholly (who was there first but whom I never saw or heard practicing and never heard even mention either a note or a key signature by name). Because he (Stagolee) was the one who was if anything even more concerned with instrumentation than with lyrics (which as often as not he only scatted anyway—even when the words were his own).

But just as the best of all the very good times to see Gator Gus throwing at top form was when he was in a regulation game, so was the Saturday night jook joint function the very best of all legendary times, places and circumstances to listen to Stagolee Dupas strutting his stuff.

That was what Little Buddy Marshall and I were not so much thinking about or even remembering as breathing in anticipation of at the counter in Miss Pauline's Cookshop, where we sat eating fried mullet with hot sauce and bakery bread and drinking Nehi Orange Crush. I was going to share a piece of leadbelly cake with him and he was going to share his Cincinnati cake with me, and then we were going up to Stranahan's Store and go fifty on next week's package of One Elevens (which we liked better than either Camels or Lucky Strikes in those days) and then we were going to make the rounds.

Miss Pauline stood behind the counter looking at us with her arms folded. Everybody gave her credit for running what was absolutely the very cleanest and most respectable cookshop in Gasoline Point, and when people (especially churchfolks) wanted to eat good cookshop cooking in peace and quiet that was where they used to go. Not that even the most circumspect of Amen Corner church members were ever likely to claim that Miss Pauline, as good a cook as she was, turned out meals in the class with those you got when you ate at Miss Armanda Scott Randolph's next to Stranahan's, or at Papa Gumbo Willie's Hole-in-the-Wall, next to the barbershop. But you never knew what you might get caught in the middle of when you went into Miss Armanda Scott Randolph's anytime after the pay whistles blew on Saturday, and The Hole-in-the-Wall was always off limits to minors even though the barbershop was not.

Y'all going to Sabbath School in the morning, Miss Pauline said as Little Buddy Marshall and I knew she would sooner or later.

Yessum, I said, as much as I had come to dread going to church by that time.

If it don't be raining, Little Buddy said.

Lord, sure do look like it just might, y'all, Miss Pauline said.

You think it will, Miss Paul? Little Buddy said wishfully.

Lord's will be done, Lil Son, she said.

I'm Lil Buddy, Miss Paul, Little Buddy said.

Lil Buddy, Miss Pauline said. That's right. Big Buddy's boy.

I sure do hope it don't, Little Buddy said and Miss Pauline thought he was talking about what she was thinking about, but I knew he was all set to go to see Gator Gus pitch against Bayou la Batre.

But y'all musn't let a little rain stop you from your duty to the Lord now.

Nome, I said.

A fair-weather Christian ain't no Christian atall.

Yessum, I said.

Smell like something burning, Miss Paul, Little Buddy said, and she scooted back into the kitchen, and Little Buddy looked at me and hunched up his shoulders and started fingering the counter as if it were a keyboard.

You know yeah, I said, thinking about our regular listening place in the fence corner outside Sodawater's, from which you could hear all of the music and the dancing too, but all you could see were the silhouettes by the windows and whatever chanced to happen in the yard.

Miss Pauline came back in and stood looking at us again.

How Miss Melba and them, Scooter?

Just fine, Miss Paul, I said and that was when I told her that Mama and Papa had gone up the Southern to visit Granpa Gipson and wouldn't be coming back until around midnight, and that was all I said because that was all I needed to say. Because I knew exactly what Miss Pauline was going to say as soon as she saw Mama the next time: The little man was around to see me Saddy night, him and Lil Brother Marshall. And that would be that, because Miss Pauline would be so carried away about me coming to visit her because I just liked to come by to see her every now and then (which was true) that Mama wouldn't have the heart to tell her that I was there because that was where I was supposed to stay until bedtime. So naturally she wouldn't ever get around to checking up to find out if I had.

Us know good and well where Big Buddy Marshall at, don't we Lil Son, Miss Pauline said, referring to the fact that Mister Big Buddy Marshall had spent every Saturday night of the last ten months trying to woo Little Buddy's mama back home. Where Lil Sue?

Over to Aun Law.

And big Bro and Missy with they ma?

Yamn, Lil Buddy said.

That was when Miss Pauline came from behind the counter and went to the front door and stood fanning the apron up toward her face with both hands. Outside the twilight sky was somewhat overcast, but not yet threatening. Little Buddy and I went on eating, hoping the weather would hold up at least until midnight. It could rain all it wanted to after that and continue on into the morning to boot so long as it then cleared up and dried off in time for the game with Bayou La Batre.

Listen, I remember hearing Miss Pauline saying suddenly, and we turned and saw her with one foot outside and her head lifted and turned to one side trying to catch something with her ear. Y'all come here and listen.

What in the name of the Lord in Heaven is that now? she said, and we jumped down and ran to where she was.

Lord, what is it? she said again and then we heard it.

Lord have mercy on this land, she said. Because it sounded like an automatic pistol somewhere up in the direction of Tin Top Alley and there was also the sound of people yelling back and forth at each other and then there were four quick automatic sounding bursts again.

Jesus, I just wonder what in the name of the Lord these crazy sinful drunken niggers already done started this Saddy night and it ain't even good dark yet, Miss Pauline began saying.

You couldn't make out where it was or what it was, but the very first thing that popped into my mind was Earl Joe Timberlake, the new Deputy Sheriff for the last six months following the death of Bam Buchanan, his notorious predecessor, whose car had spun out of control while he was chasing a bootlegger (probably either Shorty Red or Cholly Chastang) out on the Citronelle Road. Because the very first thing he was reported to have announced as soon as they pinned the star on him was that he was going to ride herd on Gasoline Point niggers until times got tolerable on Saturday nights.

Sound like it might be somewhere up around Tin Top, Little Buddy said sucking his teeth.

I was still thinking about Earl Joe Timberlake.

Hey, Little Buddy said, you don't reckon that's old Earl Joe out here already do you?

Lord I pray, Miss Pauline said. Crackers and niggers. Lord I pray. Crackers and niggers on Saddy night.

Aw shoot, Little Buddy said before I could get the words out myself. Man you know what that is. Man, we supposed to known what that is from the very first off.

Well for God's sakes what in the name of the Lord is it, Lil Bubber?

It's just somebody in a car, Miss Paul, I said then.

Lord, boy what kind of car is that, now?

It's a Hudson Super-Six, Little Buddy told her. But not Mister Long George.

They got it fixed so they can make it backfire like that, I put in.

What on earth for, Lil Man, she said to me.

They just out having them some fun.

Fun? Lord have mercy on some of these old niggers always doing some old crazy foolishness like that now and talking about they having fun. Boy, what kind of fun is that? Lord, I get so sick and tired of these niggers they won't serve God and ain't going to make nothing out they life on earth neither.

Little Buddy and I were listening outside again then and there was no question but that it was an automobile because you could also hear the cut-out roaring closer and closer. And then there were three more pops, and the roar faded on away along US 90 and across Cochrane Bridge and into the canebrakes of Baldwin County.

Man, I don't know who that is, Little Buddy said.

Lord deliver us from niggers like that, don't care who it is, Miss Pauline said. Lil Man, you and Lil Son better not never let me catch neither one of y'all out somewhere cutting up and carrying on like that. Just do what you going to do and go about your business. You don't have to be going around trying to wake up creation just to let somebody know you coming somewhere.

Still grumbling under her breath, she started fanning herself with the apron again. Then as she turned to go back into the kitchen we put the money on the counter.

Be seeing you soon, Miss Paul, I said.

Me too, Little Buddy said. Real soon, Miss Paul.

God bless you honeypie, and y'all stay out of devilment.

And that was also when she said what she said about trouble being the one thing you were always sure to find anytime you went looking for it. (By devilment she meant the kind of mischief she assumed boys like me and Little Buddy were forever initiating.)

Outside we came on through Gins Alley by Miss Blue Eula Bacote's flower yard. It was still twilight but now you could see the headlights coming and going along Buckshaw, and then that was where we were, and you could see all the way up to the light on the sign in front of Stranahan's.

Then we were in and out of there with the cigarettes without arousing anybody's suspicions, and at last it was completely dark. But this time instead of heading for the church supper where the girls were we went on along past the Tin Top Alley corner and on up the red clay hill by African Hill Baptist Church to the Southern Overpass just having a good time walking and smoking and talking with the best part of Saturday night still to come.

But we were where we were and saw as much as we saw of what happened between Stagolee Dupas and Earl Joe Timberlake that Saturday night because when, after all that waiting, it was finally time to head for Sodawater's, Little Buddy said what he said about circling by Joe Lockett's-in-the-Bottom to listen to Claiborne Williams for a little while, since we were already that close to that part of town.

Which just goes to show how things sometimes turn out. Because not only was Joe Lockett's-in-the-Bottom where everybody, including Stagolee himself was that night, but even if what happened had happened at Sodawater's all we would have been able to see would have been people running and scattering in the darkness. Because we would not have been spying from any tree at all, not to mention one as close and branches as thick as that. It was even better than a seat in the grandstand.

Because from up where we were looking and listening that night you could see right down through the wide open double windows to the piano and part of the dance floor. I think Joe Lockett was still using gasoline compression lamps in those days (when electricity was still something very special) but the light near the piano was bright enough for you to see them dancing and see Claiborne Williams at the keyboard with his hat cocked to left and his wide silk four-in-hand tie flipped back over his right shoulder, spanking and tickling his kind of blues. I can still remember the kind of hand tailored high-waist sharkskin pants he always used to wear and how his suspenders and arm garters always used to match because they also were made to order; and something else he always wore when he was dressed up was shirts with French cuffs because he was the one who didn't wear rings but used to like to flash the fanciest cuff links you ever saw.

Then we looked and saw that Stagolee himself was also there. He was on the other side of the dance floor (standing with his left leg dropped back and his right foot forward and turned in and his left shoulder lower than his right) laughing and talking with a circle of women around him. Tonight he was wearing a sporty gray checked pinchback suit, a black silk shirt open at the collar, and a black and gray hound's tooth cap, with the visor unsnapped. All he ever drank during the daylight hours was black coffee, but now he was holding the fruit jar of whiskey that he called his percolating juice, and every now and then one woman would take it and help herself to a sip and then hand it back and give him a kiss on the cheek.

We could hardly believe our luck. The whole house was rocking solid already, and you knew the music was going to keep on getting better and better, not only because Claiborne Williams had not even really warmed up yet, but mainly because, as anybody could see, he was playing as much for Stagolee and himself as for the dancers. Not that he was trying to show off in front of him. Not Claiborne Williams. Because he was too much of an expert in his own right to have to try to impress anybody. Or to have to try to challenge anybody either. Not him. All he was doing was acknowledging that the Stagolee Kid, who was somebody to be recognized, was there and was welcome. Because not only did the two of them like each other too much to challenge each other in front of anybody else, they also enjoyed listening to each other too much ever to do anything except play leapfrog with each other: It was almost as if Claiborne Williams was the pastor making a visiting preacher feel at home by making sure that the congregation was worked up to the right pitch of receptivity before turning over the pulpit to him.

All of which, so far as Little Buddy Marshall and I were concerned, made for the very best of all possible situations. Because a knock-down-drag-out contest between them would have been something to witness all right. No doubt about that. But I for one still don't believe that any music they might have made while frankly trying to outdo each other would have been as good as what you always heard when they used to play as if they were members of the same band. And besides, although by that time we had come to think almost as much of Stagolee as we did of Luzana Cholly (who absolutely could do no wrong) we also liked Claiborne Williams too much to want to take sides against him.

You could see and feel by the way the two of them kept nodding and winking back and forth at each other how much fun they were already having. Then when Claiborne Williams was satisfied that the time was right he played one more low down bumpy grind and began doodling the introduction to one of his shakehouse shouts and that was when Stagolee moved over to where the piano was and put his fruit jar on top of it and stood clapping his hands and snapping his fingers with the women around him doing the shimmieshewobble and the messaround.

That was when Claiborne Williams started talking down to his fingers and the keyboard saying Hey to his right hand, Well all right to his left, and Yeah mama yeah big mama yeah pretty mama to the piano. Saying: Get away skinny papa to his right hand skipping city. Then saying: Strut to me big mama to his left as it walked the dog. Just bring your big old fine big butt self right on here to me big mama. Now listen to skinny papa. Now what you say big mama. You tell em big mama. I hear you big mama.

Bring it to me. Bring it to me. Bring it to me big mama, he said, and then he let his right hand do the talking and his left hand do the walking until the break which Little Buddy Marshall and I could tell was the last break before the outchorus, and that was when he finally shouted: Watch out here I'm coming. Here I'm coming. Here I'm coming. GodDAMN here I'm coming. As we also knew he would.

That was all for him for the time being then, and he stood up bowing and mopping his face, shifting the handkerchief from one hand to the other as he held out his right and then his left arm for the two women helping him to get his coat back on. Then he straightened his tie and turned up his lapels to protect his chest against cooling off too fast, and then he took a sip from the flask one of the women handed him.

You couldn't hear what he and Stagolee were saying, because the whole place was still in such an uproar. But you didn't need to, because all you had to do was look at them and you could see that they were saying what they always said at a time like that: Man you got it. Man you got it and gone. Man not me. Man you the one. Man me I'm just scuffling trying to make me a little meat and bread to stay alive. Man you was mean up there just now. You was cruel man. You didn't show me no mercy at all man. Man I might as well turn around and go back where I come from. Y'all hear this lying dog. Stagolee Dupas you ought to be shame of yourself. Nigger cut out this shit and get your near-yaller ass on down on that piano stool before these niggers realize how much time I done taken up from you already. Just don't scandalize me too bad man. Just remember I still got to live with these niggers when you back over yonder. Then Claiborne Williams moved on into the next room probably to get something to eat.

That was when Stagolee took off his coat and laid it across the top of the piano and sat down and flipped his visor up. He took his own good time opening a fresh pack of One Elevens, took out two, lit one and put the other one behind his ear like a pencil. Then he crossed his legs and, only half facing the keyboard, began fiddling and diddling with his right hand with his left hand still in his lap, deliberately cooling the house down at the same time that he was warming himself up.

Watching him you could tell that he really felt like playing by the way he let his hand dance all the way up to the highest notes and then snatched it back and snapped his fingers and then sent them flittering up the scale again; and for all the differences between being there listening to honky-tonk and zonky-donk music and being on the sidelines looking at a baseball game, what you felt was almost exactly the same sense of all but unbearable anticipation you got waiting for Gus the Gator to dig in.

But the warm-up was all we got to hear that night. Because just as I was about to whisper Here we go to Little Buddy, he hissed to me. And I looked and there was an automobile with a spotlight turning into the front yard, and before you could catch your breath the brakes had grabbed, and the driver had sprung out yelling All right in here you niggers, this is the LAW! All right in here you niggers, let's GO, and people were already stampeding and breaking out through all the windows and hightailing it off in every direction.

Then there was nobody there but Earl Joe Timberlake and Stagolee, plus the two of us who were still outside in the tree because it had all happened so fast that we hadn't had time to get down. Stagolee had stood up and was putting his coat back on not only as if nothing had interrupted him, but also as if Earl Joe Timberlake, standing wide legged in his khaki twill surveyor's breeches and lace-up boots with his star pinned onto his notorious, crisply ironed white broadcloth Van Heusen shirt and his thumbs hooked into his pistol belt, was nobody he had ever even heard of. No wonder you suddenly realized how empty and quiet everything was. And no wonder it was also as if stopping the music had somehow stopped time itself.

I remember the two of them there saying nothing and the two of us outside waiting for time to move again because that would be our chance to get gone. And I will never forget what happened next, because that was the very last thing that either Little Buddy or I could or would have sworn before a Grand Jury that either of us had actually seen or heard: Earl Joe Timberlake with his thumbs still hooked into his pistol belt and his long-blocked, side-rolled sheriff's hat pushed back, walking over and raising his foot to start kicking the keys off the piano, and Stagolee saying I wouldn't do that if I was you, whitefolks, and Earl Joe Timberlake whirling and grabbing for his .38 Special.

All I can remember after that is us running and how I felt when I finally made it inside the chinaberry yard once more. I still can't even say whether we slid back down or jumped down. I can very vaguely remember Little Buddy splitting off and breaking for his house, but mainly because the time between there and the gate was when all there was was the wind in my ears getting louder and louder.

So I didn't hear any shots and neither did Little Buddy Marshall. But late that Sunday morning Earl Joe Timberlake's body was found slumped forward over the steering wheel of his Straight Eight on the other side of town about seventeen miles out on the Chunchula Road with one bullet in his hip and one through his head. And Monday there was a picture of him on the front page of the *Mobile Register* and the news story beneath reported that the circumstances surrounding the murder or perhaps more precisely the assassination of Deputy Sheriff Earl Joseph Brantley Timberlake could only be described as mysterious to say the least what with so much conflicting detail, but that all-told the strongest evidence seemed to indicate that the crime had been perpetrated by one ring of bootleggers who had gone to some lengths to leave investigating authorities the impression that the deed was the work of a rival ring.

And later on there was also some very frank speculation about whether Deputy Timberlake himself had not had ties with one or even several bootleg rings, not all of them local and at least one with a direct pipeline to Cuba. And there are also those who still believe that it all had some connection with the death of Bam Buchanan, which very few ever really believed had been due to an automobile accident anyway.

But as little as we actually saw before we hit the wind, Little Buddy Marshall and I could have solved the so-called mystery with one word: *Suicide*. Because that was exactly what we had seen Earl Joe Timberlake about to commit. Because as bad as he not only went for but in fact was, he still was not that bad, for all the good times he had broken up already that year, and for all that kicking the keys off honky-tonk pianos was already known to be one of his special trademarks.

Man you know what I say, Little Buddy said that next Monday afternoon. Man I say shame on him. Man I say he met his mammy-hunching granny-dodging daddy drunk and no better for him. And then he said: Hey I wouldn't do that if I was you Mister Goddamn Peckerwood Motherfucker. And that was when I said: When you come in here kicking on that piano, Mister Sommiching Whitefolks you kicking on me.

Then Little Buddy said: Hey you know the very last thing that supposed to be so mean-ass peckerwood saw in this life. Them piano keys giving him a great big old pearly grin from ear to ear. And I said: Man you know what I keep thinking about? That wasn't even old Stagolee's own piano. Man, I bet you anything old Stagolee ain't never owned his own piano in his life.

ELJEAN MCCRAY, who was as cinnamon-bark brown as was the cinnamon-brown bark she was forever chewing and smelling like, and who is always the girl I remember when I remember dog fennels and dog fennel meadows, was that much older and that much taller than I was at that time, and she was also two grades ahead of me in school then. So when she finally said what I had been waiting and wishing all day for her to say about me that Wednesday while Miss Tee was downtown shopping, I crossed my fingers.

Then I said what I said. I said Cute is what some folks say about monkeys and puppies, and I held my breath and waited for her to say That's all right about some old monkeys and puppies, ain't nobody talking about no monkeys and puppies I'm talking about you, and she did and poked out her mouth, and she was also trying to roll her eyes. But she couldn't look scornful because she couldn't keep her eyes from twinkling at the same time. Then she started grinning to herself but as if for both of us.

So I said What's so funny girl, but only to be saying something. Because I knew we were thinking about the same thing, which was that Miss Tee, who was the only one who knew we were there by ourselves, was not due back until half-past three. Mama knew where I was (as she usually did, or so she thought) and she knew who else was there because everybody knew where Deljean McCray, who was Miss Tee's husband's niece, was staying that year. But nobody knew that Miss Tee herself was not only not there but was all the way downtown at Askins Marine. Except us. To whom, by the way, her only word had been: If anybody come tell them I say I'll be back directly.

You, Deljean McCray said still pretending to pout, that's what. And I held my fingers crossed but I could hardly keep myself from grinning for another reason.

Because I was thinking about Little Buddy and old Gander Gallagher who were shrimping and crabbing together somewhere near or under One Mile Bridge that day and who thought I was not supposed to go anywhere beyond the china-berry yard because I was being punished—and who could not possibly know that I was only now on the verge of getting my very first chance to do what they had never let me deny I had been doing all along.

We were in that part of the house because that was where we had brought the clothesbasket, and she was standing at the long table because that was where she was separating what she was supposed to press from all the starched shirts and dresses that had to be sprinkled to be ironed by Miss Tee herself. I was sitting straddling the turned-around cane-bottom chair by the window, and outside there was the castor bean plant. Then there was the chicken yard, and beyond that was the empty clothesline; and you could also see across the garden fence and pass the live oak tree to the meadow and the tank yard.

I kept my fingers crossed because that was the way I already was about almost everything even then. Because by that time I knew better than to take anything for granted even when it was something you had not only been promised but had also been reassured about. The best way was to wait and see, as you had long since learned to do at santaclaustime and for birthday presents. Anyway I was not about to make any country breaks that day. Not with Deljean McCray.

She said she bet me that was what I did like, and I said I bet I didn't either, and she said I bet you do too. I bet you that's exactly what you do like, a puppy dog a littleold hassle mouth frisky tail daddy fyce puppy dog. And she kept on grinning her cinnamon bark grin to herself looking at me sideways. So I frowned and looked out through the window and across the dog fennel meadow to the pine ridge sky above Chickasabogue Creek and Hog Bayou Swamp, but I was almost grinning to myself in spite of myself then because she was the one who had said it first. So all I said was How come you say that, and she said Because, and I said Because what, girl, and she said don't be calling her no girl.

Little old mister boy, she said.

Well, *miss* girl then, I said. Because what miss girl?

Because you don't even know what I'm talking about, that's what, she said, and I said That's what you say.

Because I did know. Because I already knew about all of that even before that time playing house with Charlene Wingate when I was not only caught and not only spanked and chastised but also threatened with the booger man who would catch you and cut off your thing with his butcher knife.

That's what you say, I said, but that don't make it so, and that was when she said Well I bet you, and I said Bet me what, and she said You guess what since you know so much about it, and I said okay, and I almost uncrossed my fingers. But I didn't. Because I could hardly wait, but I knew I had to. So all I did was get up from the chair with my fingers crossed in my left pocket.

I was standing that close to her and the Vaseline sheen of her cinnamon scented braids then, and she said: You know something you a mannish little old boy, Scooter. You just as mannish as you can be. Boy, who you call yourself getting mannish with? Boy, what you think you trying to do? Boy you better let your pants alone. Boy, who told you to come trying to start something like that? Ohh Scooter.

She moved back to the wall then and said Ohh Scooter look at you. Look at yours. Look at you already swelling up like that. Did a wasp sting you or something. Oh Scooter you mannish rascal you. But see there you ain't got no hairs like me yet. Just like I thought. See there. Look at me.

Look at my titties like a big girl, she said, smelling almost as much like sardines as cinnamon. Look at my hairs like a wasp nest. And she bent her knees with her back against the wall and put her hands inside her thighs around her dog fennel meadow and her sardine slit. See there. I'm already a big girl little old mannish boy. I'm already big enough to get knocked up. Because a girl grown enough to have a baby just as soon as she old enough to start ministrating. If I was to do it with a sure enough man and he was to shoot off and big me he got to marry me unless he want to go to jail.

That was also when she said what she also said about boys being different. Boys can get stunted: Little old mannish tail boys start messing around with too many big girls and grown women before you man enough and you know what? You subject to hurt yourself and come up stunted for the rest of your life. That's what they say happened to Billy Goat. They say somebody got a hold to him and turned him every way but loose and now he's too big for the rest of his body, and that's how come he have them falling out spells gagging and foaming at the mouth. Some old hard woman bring your nature down too soon and that's when it go to your head and you start craving and playing with yourself and skeeting all the time and goodbye, sonny boy.

That's all right about Goat Bascomb, I said thinking also of Knot Newberry the hunchback who went around whispering and giggling to himself. That's Goat. That ain't got nothing to do with me.

Because if I was going to be stunted I would have already been stunted a long time ago, I said and she said: Who you think you trying to fool, Scooter? Who you think this is you talking to? Who you trying to say you been doing something like that with little old mannish pisstail boy?

Girl you know good and well ain't nobody supposed to tell you who nobody was, I said.

And I bet you I know why too, she said. Because it ain't nobody that's why. Because I sure know one thing. It wasn't nobody big as me. And little old pisstail gals don't count. Because I bet you I already know who it was anyhow. Because it ain't nobody but little old Charlene Wingate with her little old half stuck-up frizzly-headed self, and she sure don't count because she ain't got no more than some little old pimples on her little flat bosom and I bet you anything she ain't got no hairs yet.

That's all right about who it was, I said and I was also about to say that's all right about big girls and grown women and all that too, but that was when I realized that she was standing there grinning at me sideways because she was probably waiting for me to be the one to make the next move. So I said something else.

You said you bet me Deljean, I said. You the one said you bet me.

Well come on then little old mannish boy, she said. Since you think you already such a mister big man. What you standing there sticking out like that for?

That was that first time with Deljean McCray (on the floor under the tent top of the table with my fingers crossed all the while) and she kept saying What you doing boy? Boy what you think you doing you little fresh tail rascal. Boy, Scooter I declare. Boy, Scooter here you doing something like this. Oh see there what you doing? Now sure enough now Scooter now boy now you know good and well we not supposed to be doing nothing like this.

Then she said Now that's enough now Scooter so you stop now and I mean it too now Scooter. Get up off of me boy. You get your fresh-ass self down off me. Then we were standing up again and she said Oh Scooter what you been doing? Boy what you think you been doing? Now you going somewhere talking about you been doing that with a big girl now ain't you? Now tell the truth. Because that's all right with me. Because you better not tell nobody who it was just like you wouldn't tell me on little old skinny butt Charlene Wingate.

Boy Scooter, she said not only pointing but aiming her finger at me with one eye closed, Boy if you tell somebody on me boy you sure going to wish you hadn't when I get through with you. Boy you go somewhere and tell somebody something like this on me and I will natural born fix you sonny boy and I mean it Scooter and if you don't believe it just go on somewhere and say something and see. Because you know what I'm going to do I'm going to say you didn't do nothing but come up there acting just like some little old daddy fyce puppy dog and all I did was start to laughing and laughed you right on out of here. I declare I will. I declare before God I will Scooter.

But then she was also grinning as if for both of us again, and she pushed me and said: I just said that. You know I just said that don't you Scooter? You know I just said that just to see because you already know you all right with me don't you Scooter?

The next time was that day coming through Skin Game Jungle on the way back from taking the twelve o'clock basket to Mr. Paul Miles at Blue Rock mill when she said Hey wait a minute Scooter because I got to squat. Hey ain't you got to do something too? Hey I bet you something. Hey you know what I bet you? I bet you you still ain't got nothing down there but your thing. I bet you you ain't even starting in to sprout your first fuzz yet. Now tell the truth now Scooter. That's how come you shamed to pee now ain't it?

She said That's all right about your thing. Ain't nobody talking about that. I'm talking about some hairs. I'm talking about what I'm doing doing something like that with some little old boy ain't even old enough to do nothing but some dog water. Because when you first start to have to shave with a sure enough razor and lather that's how you know when a boy already getting to be a man enough to make a baby. That's what I'm talking about. I'm talking about some sure enough doing it like some sure enough grown folks with your hair mingling together and all that and then the man shoot off. That's what I'm talking about.

But that was also the time when she said: What you standing there holding yourself looking at me like that for. Come on boy because that's all right about that just this one more time.

———

The time after that, which was that day while Mama and Miss Tee were up in Chickasaw with Miss Liza Jefferson, was my first time in a real bed with no clothes on, and she said I'm going to show you something this time, and she did. She said I bet you you don't even know what that is. That's just the old Georgia grind, and this the gritty grind. I bet you you ain't never done the sporty grind before. She said This the bobo and this the sporty bobo and this the whip and this the bullwhip and this the snatch. She said When the man put his legs like that with his arms like that he straddling the mountain and the woman can do the greasy pole and when the woman put up her self like this that mean the man can come to the buck and when me and you go like this that's what you call bumping the stump.

She said When you see me doing this that's when I'm doing my belly roll to sell my jelly roll. Like Miss Sweetmeat Thompson. Like Miss Big Money Watkins. Then she said What you going do when I sic my puppies on you like Miss Slick McGinnis all the way out in San Fransisco? and I said Sic them back that's all right who like. Because I couldn't make up my mind whether I wanted to be like Stagolee or Luzana Cholly or Elmore Sanders. And that's when she said Well let me see you sic them then and started snapping her fingers and sucking her breath through her teeth.

I don't remember when I uncrossed my fingers that time. All I have ever been able to recollect about what happened next is hearing her whisper Oh shit oh hell oh goddamn and then saying Oh shit now oh hell now oh goddamn now Scooter. And suddenly I was not sure that I was not about to begin to spurt blood from somewhere in the very center of my being and I didn't even care. Because in that same instant it was as if you were coming through the soft stream-warm velvet gates to the most secret place in the world, and I had to keep on doing what I was doing no matter what happened.

And I did. By reaching and by holding and by floating and by pushing and by slipping and sliding and slittering and by hithering and by thithering through cinnamon scented sardine oil and dog fennel thickets and dog fennel meadows.

Then afterwards she said What did I tell you? Didn't I tell you? Oh Scooter see there? Oh Scooter you little rascal you just now losing your cherry. Scooter boy you done lost your cherry just like I told you. What did I tell you? I told you about messing around with big girls now didn't I? Oh Scooter you done lost your cherry and I bet you I know who the one took it.

———————

The one who wrote: *Dear SP guess who (smile) you are my SP because you so cute and also sweet from X guess who (smile) XXX is for hug and kisses for smiles (smile),* was Elva Lois Showers, who was also the one who started saying Please don't now stop that now as soon as I touched her arm. Please don't please don't. Not now Scooter. Now boy you better stop. You better stop that now Scooter.

Please don't what, I said.

You know what, she said You know good and well what. Just behave yourself. Just don't be doing nothing trying to do that. How come you cain't just be nice, Scooter?

That was when we were in the eighth grade and her seat was three rows over and she answered the roll call after *Ross, J. T.* and before *Singleton, Fred Douglass.* So I knew whose handwriting it was as soon as I unfolded the note, because that was also when everybody used to have to go to the blackboard to write sentences almost as often as you used to have to go work problems in arithmetic. I didn't look over that way for the rest of that afternoon, and I could hardly wait for the last bell so I could be all to myself and read it again.

I felt good thinking and whistling about it all the way home, and I went to sleep thinking about it and I woke thinking and whistling about it. But all I did when I got back to school was act as if nothing had happened. So I worried all the way home that next day and spent that night wondering what you were supposed to do, but then the day after that every time I had to stand up to recite I felt that good, warm, feathery-light way you feel when you realize (without having to look) that somebody is looking at you because she has been thinking about you.

Which is why on the way out for twelve o'clock recess I got to the door at the same time as she did and said what I said. I said Hello. (Not only like a big boy but also like a big schoolboy. All I had ever said to her or to any other girl before was Hey. Hey Elva Lois what you know. Hey Elva Lois what you doing. Hey Elva Lois girl where you been. Where you going.) I said Hello and she turned up her nose and ran on out to the girls' play area behind Willie Mae Crawford before I could even say Elva Lois. But that next morning there was another note: S is for secret and P is for passion (smile) F is for how come you try to be so fresh (smile).

So that was the day I carried her books as far as the Hillside Store fork the first time, and all I did was say Bye and came back whistling and the next day there was the next note: *Thinking of somebody very very sweet guess who (smile) XXX kisses (smile).* But as soon as I did what I did that next time she said what she said and pulled away and ran half way down Martin's Lane before she turned and blew lilac time kisses at me from both hands before going through the gate.

The next time and the time after that and the time after that and so forth she also said and said and said: How come you always got to come getting so fresh with somebody, Scooter? Boy, I'm telling you. That's all you think about. How come you can't just be my SP and be nice? How come every time we get somewhere like this you always got to start acting like that? I'm talking about every time, Scooter. I'm talking about every time. Everytime we somewhere out of sight. Everytime we happen to come by some old empty house or something. Everytime we somewhere and it start to get dark. And don't let it start to raining.

There was also the time when she said: How come you can't just be nice like in class? That's when you so smart and neat and everybody always talking about you so cute, and come to find you just as big a devil as you can be, Scooter. Boy, I'm telling you; you sure got Miss Lexine Metcalf fooled. You and David Lovett. That's all he think about too. Just like you. That's what Clarice say and I sure can believe it now. Scooter y'all think y'all something just because Miss Lexine Metcalf think y'all so smart, don't you? Y'all think somebody supposed to let you do that just because she always talking about you and him the two main boys know your homework so good all the time. Well let me tell you something. Don't nobody care nothing about what no Miss Lexine Metcalf say, Scooter. Because she just makes me so sick carrying on like that about some little old fresh boys like you and little old David Lovett anyhow. Because she ain't doing nothing but giving y'all the big head nohow. Because that's exactly how come y'all think y'all so cute somebody supposed let y'all do something like that any time you want to. Especially you, Scooter. Just because some old Miss Lexine Metcalf talking about you going to amount to something so important some of these days.

If that's the way you feel, I said. If that's how you want to be, Elva Lois.

Now that ain't what I said, Scooter, she said. Ain't nobody said nothing about that. You don't even know what I'm talking about. You might know how to get your lesson but that don't mean you know something about what girls talking about. You don't know nothing about no girls, boy.

Then she promised. And I almost believed her. Because that was when she said: Sure enough now Scooter. But not right now Scooter. Not this time Scooter. I got to go now Scooter. I got to be back home now. Didn't I say I would? I already told you, Scooter. This not fair for you to come trying to do that when I already told you. See that's what I'm talking about. And I already said I would.

But she never did. Because what she said that next time was I promised you and now you supposed to promise me something too. And when I said That's not what you said, she said I don't care what I said that's what I meant, because that's what I always meant. When the girl say yes, you supposed to do what she say first, Scooter.

So that was all that ever became of me and Elva Lois Showers that spring which I also remember because the song that was featured during the baseball games was "Precious Little Thing Called Love." Because I was not about to cut my finger and swear by my blood. Not me. I said I don't care Elva Lois. I said That's all right with me because I don't care.

Shoot goddamn right, Little Buddy said when I told him about it that same night. Shoot man what she think this is. Shoot Elva Lois Showers. Shooot she all right but she ain't all that pretty. Shooot tell her she crazy, man. Shoot tell her that's what the goddamn hell SP suppose to mean, some you know what. Secret just meant on the QT. Shoot tell her if she won't, somegoddamnbody else sure will. Elva Lois Showers. Shoot. Man I just can't get over that heifer. Elva Lois Showers. Goddamn. Shoot.

One somebody else who always would on the QT was Beulah Chaney (who should have been at least two grades ahead of me at that time but whose seat was by the window in the first row behind Walter Lee Cauldwell). She was the one who said I got something for you, Scooter, that day at the blackboard while everybody else was outside for Maypole practice.

I ain't going tell you what because if you don't already know that's just too bad. If somebody got to tell you that, all I can say you not old enough yet. So if you want me to give it to you you got to come where I say when I say.

She lived at the edge of Chickasabogue Bottom. To get there you had to go along the AT & N toward Chickasaw until you

came to Blue Poplar Crossing. Then you cut through that part
of Parker's Mill Quarters to the elderberry corner and came all
the way down the three-quarter mile winding slope, and you
could see the barn and the woodshed under the moss draped
trees beyond the open wagon gate.

Well I declare Scooter, she said that first time, Here you all the
way over here sure enough. Boy what if I just said that just to
see? What if I just said that just to see if I could fool you to
come way over here?

But she had not. She was surprised but anybody could see
how pleased she also was, and before I could stop grinning
long enough to put on my frown and say Oh Beulah Chaney,
she said Come on Scooter. I'm just teasing. You know I'm just
teasing you, don't you Scooter? That mean I must like you
Scooter. Because when you like somebody, look like you just
have to be teasing them and all of that just because you might
be kinda glad to see them or something.

But later on in the plum thickets beyond the collard patch
(with everybody away because it was Saturday afternoon) she
was only half teasing: Oh Scooter I'm surprised at you. I'm
talking about you just as sneaky as you can be. How you know
this what I was talking about? I coulda been talking about a
lost ball I found or something like a mitt or something like
that. I coulda been talking about some books and things I
found in the bottom of the trunk or something and here you
come with this the first thing on your mind just like everybody
else just because I said that. You ought to be shamed of yourself Scooter. Now tell the truth ain't you shamed of yourself all
the way over here doing something like this?

As if you didn't already know what would start if anybody
even so much as suspected that you had ever been there: Hey
Scooter where Beulah Chaney? Hey Scooter Beulah Chaney
looking for you, man. Hey Scooter Beulah Chaney say come
there, man. Hey Scooter Beulah Chaney say she sure do miss
you since that last time you come down in the bottom. She
say hurry up back. Hey Scooter guess who they say your girl
now? Old Beulah Chaney. Hey Scooter here come your new
girl. Old big bottom beulah chaney old pillow busom beulah
chaney loping like a milk cow. Hey Scooter you know what she

say? She say she got something for you. She say she got some more for you man.

Not that you didn't know there was another side to it all. Because even as they said what they had said to try to scandalize me in front of everybody in the schoolyard during ten o'clock recess that time you could tell that something else was bothering them. And sooner or later somebody was going to bring it up in one way or another (especially somebody two or three grades ahead of you): Hey what some little old scooter butt booty butt squirt like you doing hanging around some old big ass tough ass heifer like Beulah Chaney for? Boy you know what they tell me? They say you over there trying to mind that old funky pussy. They say you ain't nothing but some little old granny-dodging cock knocker, Scooter. So whyn't you just look out the goddamn way, junior? Look out the way and let somebody over in there know how to handle that stuff. Hey you want somebody to show you how to handle some big old heifer like that? Well don't be looking at me because somebody might find out.

Me myself I don't care, she said. Because you think I don't know what they always trying to say about somebody? You think I don't know they always behind somebody's back trying to make some kind of old fun of somebody and calling somebody all them old names. You think don't nobody know what they doing every time they come running up in my face saying something just to see what I'm going say so they can go back somewhere and laugh some more? They think somebody so dumb. They the one dumb.

You the one got everybody fooled. You the one always going around like you so nice you don't never think about nothing like this because you ain't never got no time for nothing but studying something in some of them old books for Miss Lexine Metcalf and here you over here just as soon as I told you something like that.

Calling somebody riney, she said another time, I ain't no riney and they know it. I might be this color, but that don't make nobody no riney. Because look at my hair and look at somebody like old nappy headed Jessie Mae Blount. Ain't nothing on me that red and nappy, and she even got all them freckles and splotches, and ain't nobody never been going around calling her nothing like that. So that's all right with me if they got to say something. Because I don't care. But anytime they come trying to make out like they cain't stand to be getting next to me without turning up their nose and that kind of stuff, that ain't fair. Because some of them might got a few pretty clothes but that don't mean cain't nobody else be just as neat and clean.

She was more yaller than riney and her hair was more of a curly brown than a kinky red and her eyes were blue-green. So what with her living that close to Chickasabogue Swamp and what with her gray-eyed father being a raft man and a boom man who also had a whiskey still somewhere up in Hog Bayou and what with her tallow faced mother (on those rare times you glimpsed her) almost always wearing a bonnet and an apron like somebody from Citronelle or Chastang, Little Buddy and I always took it for granted that she was probably more Cajun than anything else.

What she mostly smelled like was green moss. But that first time it was willow branches then fig branches then plum leaves. Sometimes it was sweetgum leaves plus sweetgum sap. And sometimes it was green pine needles plus pine trunk bark plus turpentine-box rosin. But mainly it was live oak twigs which she chewed plus Spanish moss which she used to make a ground pallet.

She said: Anybody say I ain't just as clean as the next one just plain telling a big old something-ain't-so. Anybody come talking like I might got something somebody subject to be catching from me they just trying to start something about somebody. Like cain't nobody get them back if I want to. You just let them keep on and see. Somebody always trying to think they so much better than somebody. They ain't no better than nobody else. If they think somebody think they better than somebody they must be crazy. Because don't think don't nobody know nothing on every last one of them.

On the other hand there was also Johnnie Mae Lewis with her johnnie mae lewis long legs and her johnnie mae neat waist and her johnnie mae knee stockings and her johnnie mae prompt princess tapered A-plus recitation fingers and her johnnie mae perfect pensmanship who not only said Not me not you Scooter in front of everybody standing by the punch bowl table that afterschool partytime and not only refused my hand before I could get it up but then danced off with Sonny Kemble of all the knuckleheads that I had always thought she wouldn't even speak to and to "Little White Lies" of all the rain sad honeysuckle melodies that I was forever whistling when I was alone with my boy-blue expections and my steel-blue determination that spring the year before Beulah Chaney.

Nor have I forgotten Maecile Cheatham and her chocolate brown dimples and her glossy creek indian black pocahontas braids, who tricked me into saying what I said so she could go back and tell Claribel Owens who said You think you so slick don't you Scooter you go to be so smart and don't even know better than to try to do something like that with somebody's best friend and I'm talking about the very one that already said that's all you trying to see if you can do. I'm talking about the very one already told me about you and Ardelle Foster and you and Julia Glover and you and Evelyn Childs too Mister think you so much and ain't shit Scooter so good bye.

Then that time which is also the baseball spring and summer I remember whenever no matter wherever I hear downhome trombones tailgating "At Sundown" there was also Olivet Dixon with her big bold olivet dixon eyes and her big bold olivet dixon legs and hips and her underslung olivet rubber doll dixon walk that made her seem two or even three years older than I was instead of one year younger. She was the one who said: The one I like is Melvin Porter because he don't have to always be trying to be some little teacher's pet. Melvin Porter is a real sport. Melvin Porter dress like a real sheik. Melvin Porter is the one all the girls like because he got experience.

melvin porter

melvin porter

melvin porter

melvin porter

He got it and gone all over you any day Scooter. He got experience over you Scooter.

So I said Well good for melvin porter okay for melvin porter hooray for melvin porter melvin porter melvin porter who was the mean sixteen I was still that far away from. Who got her in the family way and hopped a sundown freight train for Los Angeles, California and left her to John Wesley Griffin who was seventeen and who quit school and married her and went to work at Shypes Planer Mill and then lost her to Wendell Robinson who was twenty and was a bellboy downtown at the Battle House and took her to dances on Davis Avenue and got her that way again and went to Chicago and did not send back for her.

———

The one I remember when I remember crape myrtle yard blossoms is Charlene Wingate, to whom I said what I said when she said You suppose to say roses red and violets blue and you suppose to tell me Charlene I love you and you suppose to ask me Charlene be my valentine and you suppose to call me baby and you suppose to say I'm your sugar and when you say you my sweet one and only you suppose to cross your heart Scooter because when you tell somebody something like that that's when you suppose to promise.

I do Charlene, I said.

And she said I'm talking about sure enough now Scooter because I'm talking about when somebody want somebody to be sweethearts.

And I said Me too Charlene.

And she said Well then.

And I looked at her and her Creole frizzy hair and her honey brown face and her crape myrtle blossom smile and waited.

And she said All you said was you do Scooter do what Scooter you suppose to say it Scooter that's the way you suppose to do.

And that was the very first time I ever said that in my life and that was when she said Well you know what the boy suppose to do when the girl say here I stand on two little chips. And I said Come and kiss your two sweet lips. And that is what I did without even thinking about it. And that was when she said You suppose to whisper darling and you suppose to whisper honey because now we suppose to be sweethearts Scooter.

Which was also when she said When you sweethearts that's when you have sweet heartaches every time you just think about somebody and every time you just hear somebody say that name you have to hold yourself to keep somebody from seeing you looking and when you know you going to be somewhere at the same time you cain't hardly wait and when you see somebody coming and it look like the one you want it to be you have to catch your breath because that's your weakness.

Then when she said How you miss me Scooter how much you think about me, I said A whole lot Charlene. But I never did what Little Buddy Marshall used to do when he was thinking about Estelle Saunders. Because not only did he used to say Yes sir that's my baby you know don't mean maybe, but sometimes he also used to limp-walk straddling his right hand while swinging his left arm scat singing Has she got da, de da yes she has got dadeda that certain that certain body do she like do de do yes she like my dodedo that certain body of mine.

What I said that first time in the crape myrtle playhouse was If we suppose to be playing house we suppose to you know Charlene, and she said First you suppose to go to work Scooter and then I'm suppose to bring you your dinner basket and then you suppose to come home and eat supper and then we suppose to sit in the parlor and then you suppose to stand up and stretch because you ready to go to bed. And then Scooter. That's when Scooter.

The Gins Alley victrola music I remember when I remember Deljean McCray all dressed up and on her way somewhere walking like Creola Calloway and like Miss Slick McGinnis as Little Buddy Marshall and I myself used to walk like Luzana Cholly and also like Stagolee Dupas is Jelly Roll Morton and the Red Hot Peppers playing "Kansas City Stomp" as if in the pre-game grandstand with the pre-game pennants flying and the vendors hawking pre-game peanuts, popcorn, ice cream, candy, hot dogs and barbecue sandwiches, and the circus elephant tuba carrying all the way out to the dog fennels beyond the outfield.

But the song I remember when I remember her snapping her fingers and rolling her stomach and snatching her hips and pouting her lips and winking and rolling her eyes at the same time is "How Come You Do Me Like You Do." And she

also used to like to sing "Ja-Da" and You got to hmmm sweet
mama every night or you won't see mama at all. As if she never
even heard of the Deljean McCray who was as concerned as
it turned out she always was about Miss Tee. About whom
she was also the one who said Boy Scooter if she ever find out
about me being the one been doing something like this with
you every time her back turn boy I just know she subject to
just about kill me Scooter. Boy I rather for Miss Melba to be
the one any day. And I'm talking about Miss Tee so nice I don't
believe she even want to kill a flea. But boy Scooter I just know
that woman subject to beat my ass till my nose bleed if she ever
find out about me spoiling you like this. Because evrybody
know how much she like children especially little old frisky tail
boys think they so smart. Because you know what folks say?
They say she had her heart set on being a schoolteacher like
Miss Lexine Metcalf and Miss Kell and Miss Norris and them.
That's how come she got all them books and pretty things
and all them flowers and keep her house painted and her fence
whitewashed like that. Because all that come from way back
when she used to be off in training before she come down here
on a visit and ended up getting married to my uncle Paul Boykin. So that's how that happened. Because Uncle Paul said that
was that about all of that. So that's when she had to give up on
it. And then come to find out they don't look like they going
to even get no children of her own for her to bring up with all
the schooling she still got.

That's how come she so crazy about children, she also said.
And that's how come children so crazy about her. Because she
just like a good teacher because that's the way she talk and she
can tell you all about different things and show them all them
different games and you don't have to be sitting up in no classroom scared somebody just up there waiting for you to make a
mistake or something. Like that Miss booty butt Kell with her
booty butt self.

But boy Scooter you the favorite one she like over all of us
around here and I'm suppose to be in the family. And I bet
you I know how come. You know how come? You want me to
tell you how come you the one her natural born pet and don't
care who knows it. Them books. Because you the one take to
them books like that's your birthmark or something Scooter.

And that's what she like better than anything in this world and here you come just as smart as you devilish. And you know it too son. And don't tell me you don't know you her heart. Ain't nothing she got too good for you and you know it. And you know something else I bet you if Miss Melba and Unka Whit let her she would flat out adopt you boy. Everybody know that. Boy Scooter she give anything to get her hands on you for her own. That's how come I just know she'll cold kill me if she ever was to find out about something like this. Because you know she bound to put it all on me just like you didn't have nothing in the world to do with it.

———————

When I came back for Christmas that time and saw her work-ing behind the counter when I went into Smallwoods Cleaning and Pressing Club she said Mister College Boy. Well all right Mister College Boy. Well go on Mister College Boy. Well ex-cuse me Mister College Boy and I said Come on Deljean. I said How you been Deljean. I said I been thinking about you Deljean. I been wondering what you doing. And she said You the one Scooter. She said You the one better go on out of here. Boy you know good and well you not up there with all them high class college girls thinking about somebody like me. Boy, Scooter, used to be little old Scooter, tell the truth now, you forgot all about me up there now didn't you? Boy you ain't thought about me until just you walked in here and seen me just now. And I said That's what you say Deljean. That's what you say.

I said How could somebody ever forget you Deljean. I said you know something? I don't even have to think about you Deljean to remember you. Just like I don't have to think of Lit-tle Buddy and Luzana Cholly and Stagolee and Gator Gus and all that. Because that's the way you really remember somebody. I said You the one got my cherry Deljean. I said You remem-ber that time. I said You the one taught me what it's made for Deljean. I said You the one used to keep me out of a whole lot of trouble Deljean.

I said Ain't no telling what kind of mess I mighta got all tangled up in if it hadn't been for you Deljean. And she said

Boy Scooter boy you a lying dog. That ain't the way I heard it. Boy who you think you coming in here trying to fool. Because I know exactly who that was from the tenth grade on. You think don't nobody know about you and her. And right under Miss Tee's nose and she so glad you making all them good marks and winning all them scholarship prizes and stuff up there in high school she ain't even suspected it to this day. But see me myself I know you Scooter. I mighta been married and having that baby for that old no good nigger but I bet you I can tell you just about everything you call yourself doing in them days. I bet you. I even know about you and old big butt Beulah Chaney, Scooter, and I know you didn't know nobody know about that. Because you know what? As soon as I seen you coming out from down over in there one time and I said to myself old Scooter think he so slick but he cain't fool me. Because I know you Scooter, at least I used to know you. Because I don't know nothing about no college boys.

But she also said: Boy Scooter if you ain't still a mess. Here we doing this again. And she said Boy I'm surprised at you Scooter. You suppose to be a college boy. I thought college boys suppose to be so proper. I thought college boys suppose to be so dictified. I thought college boys suppose to be such a gentleman all the time.

That was that next evening. And she also said Well all right Mister College Boy. Well go on then. I see you. You think you something don't you. I didn't teach you that. Did she teach you that. You know who I'm talking about. Didn't no high class college girls teach you that. And that was when she said Boy Scooter Miss Tee sure subject to come over here and kill me if she find out her precious Mister College Boy over here putting in time with this old used to be married woman that didn't go no further than the ninth grade. Specially after all she done for me.

She said: Boy Scooter Miss Tee so proud you up there getting all that good education she don't know what to do. That's all she talk about every chance she get. She still just as nice to me as she can be just like she always was. Just like ain't nothing happened. Except keeping Twenty for me so I can work since I made that old no good nigger get his old lazy ass out of here and he finally went on up north somewhere. But you still the

one her heart Scooter. And that's the way she want Twenty to
be too. Just like you. You seen Twenty over there. That's what
they call him. For Quinty. Because his name Quinten Roosevelt. Quinten Roosevelt Hopson. He five and Boy if he turn
out to like his books he got him a home with Miss Tee don't
care what happen to me. Boy she cain't hardly wait to send him
to school so he can get on up there and come by Miss Metcalf
like you. With your used to be little old go-to-be-so-slick self.
But you was born marked for it Scooter.

———————

The last time with Deljean McCray was that night after the
Mardi Gras parade when I came back during that war for that
special occasion. It was that many years after college then,
and she said Look at me with these three children now and
getting almost big as a house. And look at you Scooter used
to be that little old think-you-so-smart-and-cute schoolboy I
used to could make him blush anytime I want to. And I said
You still can Deljean. I said What you think I'm doing right
now. And she said You something else Scooter. She said You
always been something else Scooter and that's how come
you always been all right with me almost as bad as Miss Tee.
And that was when she said That's the only part that make
me feel sorry about all this happening today. Because she not
here to see you come back this time. Because I can just see
her looking at her mister so proud she can hardly stand it. But
that's how come you still all right with me too Scooter. Because that's something everybody got to give you your credit
for. Because the one thing she didn't never have to worry
about right on up to her dying day was you trying your best
to make somebody out of yourself.

Which is also when she also said: You know something
Scooter. Boy you never could fool me. I'm the one fooled you
Scooter. You remember that time when I was the one that got
your cherry. Well you suppose to be the one so smart and I bet
you a fat man you didn't know that's when you got mine too
until I just now told you.

*I*S SHE *your mama's sister? Your papa's sister? Is she your mama's brother's wife? Your papa's brother's wife? Your mama's
own auntee? Your papa's own? Maybe she's your mama's cousin.
Your papa's cousin. Maybe she your big half sister by your mama
or your papa and somebody else, they used to say. And I always
said She's my own auntee. That's why I call her Miss Tee. Because
she is the one who always has been my main auntee over everybody
else in the whole world.*

*Maybe she your you know goodfairy godmother, man, Little
Buddy Marshall said. You know, he said. Because that's what
auntees suppose to be anyhow. That's what mine is and that's how
come I call her my Big Auntee, he said. Because that's just exactly
what they for. And that's where you can always go when you want
to ask for something you already know good and damn well ain't
nobody at home to buy for you. And that's how come you can always depend on them for something else for Christmas and Easter
and your birthday and something special when you stop by there
on the first day of school.*

*That's how come when you don't have them you have to have
a godmother, Little Buddy said. And that really mean she your
guard-mother, because she the one suppose to help your sure-enough
mama watch out over you. And your Big Uncle is the same thing.
Because you know who bought me my big league mitt and mask,
and you don't even have to guess who going to be the one to get me
my first pair of spikes when the time come. Just like you know good
and well you going to be getting yours from the same one your
A. G. Spalding glove come from.*

*Man, look at Aunt Callie Callahan, Little Buddy Marshall
also said. Man she everybody's Big Auntee, he said. Because that's
what she always acting like, he said.*

*And I said Callie the Cat. And he put his hands on his hips,
held his tongue tucked inside his bottom lip like a dip of Garrett's
Snuff and said Chomere and jeer Aunt Chat shome sugar and
spice and shome of all that nice prettiness you little ugly grand
rascal you.*

And I did it too, standing as if I were wearing a pair of unlaced man-sized brogan work shoes. I said: You better bwing your little old rubber butt self on here to Aunt Cat before I bop the flying do-do out of you. Little nasty stinking goodlooking good for nothing honey bung dumpling. Little old billygoat-smelling sugar-coated puppy dog tail. Jeer Aunt Chat shome more of that honey. Trying to be stingy with it already. Don't you be trying to tease me like no jelly bean. And you better not be calling me no Aunt Cat neither. You little mannish pisstail musrat. You ain't old enough to be talking that kind of talk yet. Let me catch you grinning and calling me the Cat and I'm going to wash you mouth out with lye soap. Be plenty of time for you to find out all about that. And you will too, you little devilish-eyed scoundrels. Ain't neither one of y'all fooling me. I seen you pointing them toes and dropping them hips and sloping them shoulders. Don't be thinking you fooling me, I said, still trying to talk holding my tongue like that. No telling what Miss Melba going to do when she find out you rotten to the core under all that sparkle-eyed sweet talk, I said.

Now as for that Lil Buster Marshall, Little Buddy Marshall said, ain't nothing nobody in the world can do about that rap-scallion but get the kidnappers and bootleggers to lose him somewhere up in Hog Bayou Swamp somewhere.

Man, what she talking about? I said. Man, that's where we come from. And he said Yeah in a goddamn skiff boat. And I said Yeah and with no overcoat, remembering Stagolee Dupas singing the dirty verses to "Squeeze Me."

Anytime anybody think I cain't take care of myself in the swamp all they got to do is just try me, he said. Then standing wide legged with his hand down there, he said But man one of these goddamn times she going to be hugging and kissing me like that and godddddamn!

Don't make no difference which side of the family they belong to, Little Buddy Marshall also said one time. Because they don't have to be your flesh and blood kinfolks nohow. Because anybody can be your auntee if they want to. Just like anybody can be your cousin if they want to act like it. And the one you like the best like you like Miss Edie Bell Boykin is your Big Auntee. Just like Aun Law my Big Auntee.

Anybody can be anything you want them to be, he said. And I said the same thing. Then I heard what I heard and had to believe that night at Mister Ike Meadows' wake.

AT FIRST, they were sitting on the porch in the dark talking about death again, and this time it was like an invisible sheet that shrouded down over you. But sometimes it was also something with a cold, icy grip and a stone embrace and sometimes, ghost that it was, it came tripping quietly and sometimes, being as it was God's business, it struck like lightning just to remind sinners that God was almighty. It could come at any time and place and in any shape and form and fashion and it took young and old, good and bad on that long lonesome journey across the River Jordan whether they were ready or not which was why Jesus was the only one who could make up your dying bed.

Then they were talking again about that great getting up morning which was Judgment Day; and that was when, as always, somebody started telling about how he found the truth in the light, got converted and was reborn to be saved in Jesus Christ. And from then on until somebody started another song it was like being in church at confession and determination—telling time, with first one and then another recalling how he was stumbling in darkness until he found the way to the Altar of the Lamb, which was the way to everlasting life.

Somebody kept repeating that, one saying it that way and another saying life everlasting and somebody else saying life eternal; and I thought I knew what the next song was going to be. But when it came it was not "Everlasting Arms," but "Get Right With God"; and when I finally fell on off to sleep with my head on Mama's lap they were singing "The Blood Done Sign My Name," which always made me think how Good Hope Baptist Church people looked coming up out of the baptising pen in the Chickasabogue with the sound of the singing and the shouting echoing all the way across the creek to the canebrakes.

But before that they had been talking about Mr. Ike Meadows himself; and Bro Abe Gardner and Old Tyler McIntosh had started reminiscing and had gone all the way back to the time when the three of them were growing up together back in the farming country; and that was when Bro Abe Gardner told about seeing the first automobile in Brewton; and that was when Old Tyler McIntosh told the one he said Mr. Ike used to laugh himself to tears about, the one about how Calvin Hargroves had made a complete and everlasting, clodhopping fool out of himself the day the first airplane flew over that part of Alabama:

He had left his mule and plow right where they were in the middle of the field when he heard it. And then he looked up and saw it—and struck out across the fence to tell everybody to get ready because the old Ship of Zion was coming. That, of course, was outrageous enough to ruin him for life, but the thing he was never able to live down, the thing that finally drove him north to Cincinnati, Ohio, was the fact that he went running to the whitefolks first.

He spent most of that next year trying to explain that he had only done so because he wanted to find out whether the white-folks had been reading anything about anything like that in the newspapers, since the only things any of the folks he knew ever read were the Bible, the old Blueback Webster and the *Farmer's Almanac*. But that didn't change anybody's suspicions in the least. Because Calvin Hargroves had started running and yelling about the old Ship of Zion, which was what he really believed it was, which meant he also believed it was Judgment Day so the first thing he should have done was go and get his own family ready to get on board, not the whitefolks.

He could never answer that to anybody's satisfaction and it finally got so that all he would do was hang his head. And then when all of it was finally beginning to die down the whitefolks found out that the Negroes had a big joke about it. And they grabbed it and changed the whole point and started it all over again and it was as if it had just happened.

So finally he had had to give up and move on out of that part of the country and on out of the South. Because when that part got started, every time he went into town at least two or three of them would come up to him or call him over to them and tell him that what he had done proved what a good nigger he was, and he couldn't refuse to take the fifty-cent pieces the rich ones handed him and then the rednecks found out about it and got into it and he also had to pick up the nickels and dimes they threw at him and before long even the little hay-haired, rat-piss-smelling, barefooted, splotchy-faced, hungry-looking redneck children were throwing pennies at him.

Then he had to come back among homefolks with every-body knowing about all that and not saying another word about it anymore because the joke was over and all that was left of it was the kind of mess the whitefolks always loved so much. That was when folks woke up one morning and found out that he had packed up that night and left without saying anything to anybody. Some years later they found out that he was living in Cincinnati, and the last thing anybody had heard was that one of his boys was working on the lake boats out of Buffalo and another was a musician in a New York speakeasy.

Then they were talking about the whitefolks and the days of slavery again and the old folks who were there that night were Aunt Classie Belsaw and Uncle Jim Bob Ewing, and when they started recollecting life on the old plantations, the Civil War (calling it The Silver War) and Surrender, everybody sat lis-tening as everybody always did when somebody like that was remembering olden times.

Aunt Classie, who was always dressed in gingham and an apron and always wore plain-toed, old lady comforter shoes and either a bonnet or a head-rag, was sitting in the highbacked cane rocking chair; and everybody knew that every now and then she was going to say And then . . . Ole Marster . . . and pause and rock puffing at her clay pipe; and then say And then Ole Marster say, hum, yes and then the nigger, huh, huh, huh, yesn Lord. Then she would rock back and forth puff-ing and getting the next part together for herself and then say Yes, Lord, again and begin not at the beginning but with the climax and signification: And then so here come Ole Marster just a-coming in there, and then all them other whitefolks they running everywhere like a chicken with his neck wrung and that's when the nigger done figured out something else and biding his time studying about the next chance. That was her way and you knew that she was not ready for anybody else to say anything or ask anything until she finally said So there, by God.

Then Uncle Jim Bob, who was born in slavery, but was freed before he was big enough to realize what it meant to be under the yoke, was talking about being a child during the Silver War and growing up during Reconstruction. He was sitting on the rattan yard chair and he talked with his chin moving up and down against the back of his hand which cushioned it against the top of his Scotch-Irish-Ashanti walking stick. After every three or four words he smacked his lips with great-grandfatherly self-satisfaction as if he were chewing on the cud of wisdom itself while giving you time to let each step of a process become clear before moving on the next. Then to make sure you got the point he would go back over it and condense it: Well, now sir, here's what it all boil down to in a nutshell. The whitefolks they always trying to make out like were none of that nothing but just one great big old free nigger mananial mess. Of course they does, but I'm right here to vouch for them and there were so many cunning ones right there in amongst them. Talking about right here in Alabama in Montgomery and all the way up the line to Washington City, D.C., and didn't none of them old Confederate whitefolks know how that many niggers done found out all that about government business and couldn't none of them figure out nothing to do with them but wait until they got them to call the Yankees on back up North and that's when they started whipping them and killing them up right and left while the Yankees off somewhere studying about something else. But that just slowed them down, but it couldn't stop them long as the answer was in the ballot box. So they still had to cheat them away from there and that's how come today we got Poll Tax which ain't nothing but nigger tax spreading like trying to keep up with mooter grass on down to this day and time and that's what I'm talking about when you hear me talking about the young generation coming up now because they the ones got to know what to do because ain't many of us old heads left because who would even nine thought that I would still be here to see Ike Meadows on his cooling board. Who would thought that because he weren't no child and I was along there with his pappy.

Lord, Miss Et, Jesus, Miss Minnie Ridley Stovall said, because they were all thinking about the wake again then, and Miss Liza Jefferson said When the Lord gets ready for you, Jesus, because God knows Et done what she could.

And I knew they were coming to that part again and I was going to have to hear them go all over all of it again detail by detail from the first day the pain struck. Then they were going to repeat what they had seen and heard and said beginning with the time he took to bed and come all the way up to his very last words; and there was nothing you could do but see the room and the bed and him lying there with the window shades drawn, and then you could hear how his breath began to sink and the dry death rattle settling in and see the glassy look come into his eyes and then there was only the feeble movement of his lips saying nothing and his hands trembling and the last gasp and he was gone for ever and ever and ever.

Like I say, Miss Liza Jefferson said, . . .

Thy will be done Jesus, Miss Ina Hopkins said, That's what the good book say, and thy kingdom come.

Well, the Lord blessed him with Et for his wife, Mister Jeff Jefferson put in then, and he blessed him twice with two fine chillun.

Old Skeeter on his way from Detroit, Michigan, too, Mister Horace Upshaw said. That boy love his daddy and he made a fine man. Up there working for old Henry Ford and got three of his own, two boys and a girl.

An Euralee already here all the way from out in Los Angeles, California.

That's what somebody said, Miss Ina Hopkins said.

That's right, honey, Miss Liza Jefferson said then. She here all right. Et sent for her first and she got in here on the Crescent from New Orleans last night. They got her over at Lula Crayton's so she can get some rest for the funeral. That's how come Lula ain't over here tonight.

Well, I can tell you this much, Mister Jeff Jefferson said Et ain't got a thing to worry about with two fine chillun like that.

Old Euralee sure seeing herself some of the world, Mister Horace Upshaw said, Out there working for one of them picture show women and been all across the water with her.

Guess who else Euralee say out there in California working for some of them big moving picture people? Miss Liza Jefferson said. Luvenia Lewis. Euralee say she out there cooking. Say she so fat and fine you wouldn't even know her.

Out there cooking what? Miss Ina Hopkins said. I know when that child was born, and I ain't never heard nobody say she can even string a chicken.

Lord, whitefolks'll eat anything, Jesus, Miss Minnie Ridley Stovall said.

But that's just what I am talking about these children surprising you, Mister Horace Upshaw said. Little devils subject to be hiding a lot more get-up than me and you give them credit for.

Young'uns, Uncle Jim Bob said, chewing and smacking his great-grandfather cud again, ain't never been nobody's fool.

Lord, Uncle Jim Bob, but some of them, Jesus, Miss Minnie Ridley Stovall said. Lord I pray, but some of these we got around here.

———

I was the only young one still there then. But during the earlier part of the night almost everybody in that part of Gasoline Point had stopped by to sit for awhile and during that time I was out in Stranahan's Lane, and so was Little Buddy and old Cateye Gander Gallagher and so was Estelle Saunders, who was Little Buddy's girl then; and old Gander had his cat eyes on Felisha Coleman; and since Charlene Wingate had gone to spend that summer with her cousins in New York and Deljean McCray had to stay home that night, the one I had was Ella Crenshaw.

It was June and it was warm enough for anybody to be barefooted who wanted to and most of us were and some of the rest of us others took off our sneakers and strung them on the garden gate. There were fireflies blinking in and out of the sunflower clusters along the fence that night and you could hear the guineas roosting in the trees behind Miss Amanda Scott Randolph's cookshop. There was also the smell of dog fennels whenever a breeze had stirred and when you ran down the soft talcum-dry lane the sand dust hung behind you in the moonlight like exhaust pipe fumes.

Some of the others there during that part of the night were Eddie Lee Wilcox, Buddy Baby, and Sister Baby, the Sawyer twins, Martha Ann Pool, Ginny Taylor, Marvin Walker and about ten others plus Nango, Jet, Nerva and Early G. who were there to sing as a junior quartet. At first we were all at the pump shed, which was halfway between the yard where the wake was and the back of Stranahan's store which was where Stranahan's Lane curved and sloped down into Buckshaw Mill Road. That meant that we were far enough away and that our noise would not disturb the wake; and for a while all we did was sit around swapping riddles and playing ring games. But as far as Little Buddy and I were concerned we were just waiting until Big-toed Cateye could finally get Felisha to say yes.

Then we got everybody to play hide-and-seek because we already knew a good place in the thickets along the ridge of the old Confederate breastworks above the crawfish pond. We had it all figured out and came back in to touch base twice, and then that's where we were until they called everybody into the yard to be served refreshments.

Reverend Wilson Mack Palmer was there then and that was when the quartets sang. It started with Nango, Jet, Nerva and Early G. who represented The Intermediate Banner of Good Hope Baptist Sunday School. Then each one of the others gave two selections, and Gaither Williams, whose brother was Claiborne Williams, the juke joint piano player, came on with the Harmonizers and took his famous bass solo on "Remember Me On Mound Caveree." Then after The Pine Star Four from Pine Hill Chapel finished, everybody who was not going to sit until morning said goodnight and left, and I had to stay because it was Mama's committee's time and Papa and Uncle Jerome were on the waterfront unloading a banana boat that night.

That's why I was still there, and when I woke up and realized where I was I guessed that it must have been three o'clock, so I didn't move. I kept my eyes closed and listened but not because I was eavesdropping, I was really trying to hear the locusts and go back to sleep. When Miss Minnie Ridley Stovall started talking to Mama, I was only listening then because lying with your head in somebody's lap like that, every time the answer came you could feel all of the vibrations even before you heard the sound of her voice.

What I really wanted to do was hear the three o'clock locusts and forget about being at the wake and go back to sleep and be ready to go rambling with Little Buddy in Bay Poplar Woods while everybody else was at the funeral the next afternoon. I wasn't even interested when Miss Liza Jefferson started talking about me; because all she was doing was saying The little man all played out and sleeping like a log, dead to the world from ripping and running with all that friskiness from God knows where, but he sure ain't puny no more. My, they sure do grow. Be done stretched on up here getting all mannish before you know it, Miss Melba. And all Mama did was chuckle and run her hand over my head again and say: He's mama's Little Man out there among them. That's what he is, mama's Little Scoot-about Man. I knew all about that kind of talk and I was really trying not to hear it. I was really listening through it and the summertime sound of the swing to the yard crickets and bush locusts, and I was already dozing off again.

So I missed the first part of what Miss Minnie Ridley Stovall said about me this time. What woke me up was Mama responding, and I could tell by the vibrations that she didn't want to have to talk about whatever it was. Then Miss Minnie Ridley Stovall sucked her gold tooth twice as she always did when she was gossiping about something and I knew she was going to say something more, and she did.

Of course me, myself, it ain't none of my business, Jesus. Lord knows I know that, Miss Melba. So that's why like I say I ain't never asked you a thing about any of it before, and I don't even know who the one started it. All I know is what everybody keep saying. So I just say to myself, I'm going to ask Miss Melba. That's the only way to set em straight, if you don't mind, Miss Melba.

Folks always running their mouth about something, Mister Horace Upshaw said. If it ain't one thing it's another and if it ain't another it's something else.

It sure God is, Jesus, Miss Minnie Ridley Stovall said.

And don't none of them know the first thing about it, Miss Liza Jefferson said, Not a one.

That's exactly why I said I was going to ask Miss Melba, Miss Minnie Ridley Stovall said. If you don't mind, Miss Melba.

Ask me what? Mama said.

About Edie Bell Boykin, Miss Minnie Ridley Stovall said.

Ask me what about Edie Bell Boykin? Mama said, and the way she said it made me suddenly numb all over.

Some of them saying he really belongs to her, Miss Minnie Ridley Stovall said.

He belong to me, Mama said.

See there, Mister Horace Upshaw said.

But before anybody else could say anything else Mama's stomach was vibrating again and I felt the sound start and heard it go and then it came out through her mouth as words:

She brought him into the world but he just as much mine as my own flesh and blood. I promised her and I promised God.

The Bible speaks of such things, Miss Ina Hopkins said from the swing. And it speaks of rewards, Miss Melba.

I have my reward, Sis Ina, Mama's stomach and voice said against and above my spinning head and ringing ears.

Poor little thing, Miss Minnie Ridley Stovall said. Poor little lamb.

Poor little thing nothing, Miss Liza Jefferson said. He here, ain't he, don't care how he got here.

I'm just talking about not knowing your own flesh and blood, Miss Minnie Ridley Stovall said.

I promised her and I promised God, Mama said. *And she promised me and Whit before God.*

I was just wondering about his own daddy that spermed and begot him, Miss Minnie Ridley Stovall said. If it ain't asking too much Miss Melba, and like I already said, God knows it ain't none of my business at all.

That's her secret, Mama said. She didn't tell me nothing about that and I ain't never asked her nothing about it and never intend to and I just wish everybody else would just keep their mouths out of it.

Amen, Miss Liza Jefferson said. Amen.

That's exactly what I tell em Miss Melba, Miss Minnie Ridley Stovall said. That's exactly what I always did say and at least anybody can see the other party wasn't no white man, whoever it was.

That next morning my head had stopped spinning and my ears were not ringing anymore and I was no longer numb, but I didn't want to have to talk to anybody or even be near anybody. Not even Little Buddy Marshall. So I kept to myself all day that day and went to bed early and when I woke up the morning after that I had decided to act as if nothing had happened.

It was not until months later that I finally decided to mention anything about that night to Little Buddy Marshall. But all I said was Man you know something? One time I caught Old Lady Booty Butt Minnie Ridley-butt Stovall trying to gossip some old hearsay stuff about me and Miss Tee. But she don't know I heard her—and Mama and Papa neither.

Which is when Little Buddy Marshall said: Man my mama made me promise her on the Bible I wouldn't never say anything about nothing like that until after you brought it up first. But shoot man you want to know the truth? Shoot man the reason I didn't even need her to make me swear? Because man that's good as giving you the inside claim on old Luzana and old Stagolee and old Gator Gus and them and all that. Because man you welcome to Old Lady Metcalf and all that old school stuff. But shoot man. Goddamn. Not that.

I was never able to bring myself to ask Miss Tee anything at all about what I heard that night at the wake. So I have no way of knowing when and how she learned that I had found out who she really was. But she already knew by the time I finished the Ninth Grade and she also must have assumed that I knew that she knew. Because as pleased as she was to see me come hop-skipping up the steps with my certificate and the top prize, what she said without realizing that she was winking as if for me to remember some secret agreement was But My Mister don't you think we better let Miss Melba always be the one to see things first and then ask her if it's all right to come let Miss Tee be next? And I said I forgot. And when I looked back from the gate she was waving and smiling and there were tears in her eyes.

THE SPYGLASS TREE

For Mozelle and Michele

CONTENTS

ONE

Bench Marks

THAT MANY years later, the clock tower chimes you woke up hearing every morning were that many miles north by east from the sawmill whistles along Mobile River and Chickasabogue Creek, and the main thing each day was the also and also of the campus as it was when I arrived with my scholarship voucher and no return ticket that first September.

As you took your place in line with all the other freshmen waiting in the hallway outside the registrar's office that first Friday morning, there was a moment when you suddenly realized that you were actually on your own and you felt so totally all alone that it was almost as if everything that had happened before you came through the main gate (less than twenty-four hours earlier) and saw that many brick-red buildings with magnolia-white eaves and antebellum columns beyond the late summer green shrubbery with the rust-red dome of the dining hall against the bright blue preautumn sky was now already a very long time ago and in a place very far away.

But even so there was also the also and also of L & N express train whistles and creosote trestles, and the marco polo blue skyline mist that is always there when you remember the spyglass view from the chinaberry tree in the front yard of our three-room shingle-top shotgun house on Old Dodge Mill Road. Not to mention the tell-me-tale times around the fireplace and on the swing porch of the house itself. To say nothing of the long since hallowed lie-swapping and all of the ongoing good-natured woofing and signifying you had been permitted to witness outright or had otherwise contrived to overhear in places like Papa Gumbo Willie McWorthy's barbershop and on the veranda of Stranahan's General Merchandise store for that many years.

Another part of all of which was old Stagolee Dupas (*fils*), the flashy-fingered jook joint piano player from New Orleans and elsewhere, with his custom-tailored jazz-back suits and hand-finished silk shirts and handkerchiefs and his deliberately pigeon-toed patent leather avenue walk and his poker-sly watchful eyes, in whose name and for whose sake Little Buddy Marshall and I had in time also come to do things that had nothing to do with playing music, just as I for my part had also already been cocking my all-purpose navy blue derring-do baseball cap and tightening my rawhide wristband like Gator Gus even when the situation I was in at the time had nothing at all to do with being the legendary money-ball pitcher he used to make you also want to be, along with everything else.

Yes, even as the copper-green sound of the vine-dampened reverberations—clinging and clanging over the huddled roof-tops of the surrounding neighborhood—echoed across the rolling central Alabama farmlands and all the way out to the bright clay hills and the gray-green pine ridges of the outlying regions, took you back to storybook illustrations of medieval castles and cathedral towns, there was the also and also of Lu-zana Cholly and his twelve-string guitar and his 32-20 on a 44 frame and his sporty limp walk. Not only because old Luzana Cholly was the one who had once said what he said sitting under the L & N Railroad bridge at Three Mile Creek that time after he had caught me and Little Buddy Marshall trying to follow him and skip city on a northbound freight train and had brought us back as if by the nape of the neck and (for me at any rate) as if specifically to the door of Miss Lexine Metcalf's classroom—but also because of all the things Little Buddy Marshall and I had been daring and doing in his noto-rious name all along.

As for Miss Lexine Metcalf herself and her bulletin-board peoples of many lands, once she had singled you out, you were indelibly earmarked for Mister B. Franklin Fisher and his an-cestral imperatives for the "talented tenth," to whom he said much had been given in raw potential, acknowledged or not, and from whom therefore much in commitment, develop-ment, refinement, and ultimate achievement would always be not only expected but required.

Nor were any of the essential implications of any of that di-minished in any way at all by anything that I had found out by that time, about how everything had finally turned out for the self-same but perhaps not identical Little Buddy Marshall who always used to be there for daring and doing, before he decided to go where he went and tried to do what he always wanted to do.

Incidentally, I can't remember when Mama was not calling me Scooter because I can actually remember all the way back

to the times when what she used to say was not really Scooter
but Gooter. Which was probably all the way back during the
time when I was still trying to crawl because what I remember
her actually saying for Mama's little man was *Mama's yil man
mamam yil gootabout man* and the way she always used to like
to say bless his bones was *betchem bone betchem tweet bone.*

And when I was big enough to go outside the house and
then the yard by myself, not only to play but also to run errands, she also used to say *Mama's little old scootabout man,
lil old scootabout scatabout man out there amongst them. That's
what he is. Out there scooting about all over the place. That's just
exactly what he is. It what him im betchemtweet bone. With his
little old sparkle-eyed buster-brown self and them nimble knees
and twinkle toes just like little old Jack the Rabbit. Just like little old Jack the Rabbit in the briar patch, and Mama wouldn't
trade him for a rich man's share in the Nettie Queen riverboat
with that fifty-thousand dollar calliope.*

*Once I came home from the first grade and Uncle Jerome the
preacher, who was always christening or ordaining something,
said what he said, and it was as if he was conducting one of his
services. He stood up from the rocking chair, looking at me with
his pulpit-solemn eyes and cleared his throat until his voice was
ceremonial and placed his baptismal-firm hands on my shoulder
as soon as Mama said, Mama's little scootabout man, he back
home from all the way over yonder amongst them, he said, Now
there's a name, notion, and designation to conjure with. Gentlemen, sir, as I am a witness.*

*Uncle Jerome may also have been the first one I ever heard
talking about how secret messages from the abolitionists about
the Underground Railroad used to be sent from plantation to
plantation or by the grapevine. Because he was almost always
there in the fireside crescent during midwinter yarn-spinning
nights and he had his own rocking chair on the swing porch in
the summer. In my case, you can bet that he was the one who
wanted you to feel that Scooter was as much the code name for
the fugitive slave zigzagging north by the Big Dipper as it was
for Jack the Rabbit.*

Whenever it was that I first heard about the Underground
Railroad, by the time I had met Little Buddy Marshall at the
pump shed the day after he and his family moved into the

shotgun house diagonally across the street from Aunt Callie the Cat, it was as if I had been calling myself Scooter all of my life. In fact, I still can't remember ever calling myself anything else and I also said, That's what I'm supposed to be able to do, and he said, Hey you too, hey me too, man, you want to let's be good old buddies? And I said, Hey that's all right with me, man. So he said, I live right over there. So you want to come over to my house and I'll get my goddamn mitt and I also got a mask and a breast protector because I got to be a badass catcher, man, and I bat right-handed or left-handed, don't make no difference to me. And I told him I was supposed to be a big-league pitcher one of these days and that I got a regulation-size Spalding glove that last Christmas.

He said, Hey call me Lebo, and before very long I also began calling him Skebo and then we began calling each other Skebootie because that was our way of saying that we were each other's buddies and that we were both bred and born in the briar patch. Which was also our stamping ground. Hey, shit, I reckon, man, he said. Hey, shit, I goddamn reckon.

II

You couldn't see the clock tower from your window but you knew it was on the women's dormitory across the mall on the other side of the dining hall and you also knew that the mall, which was also known as the lawn, was where the band pavilion was, and when you walked up the wide brick steps and across the main avenue to the white columns of the music school and stood looking back that way there were two other women's dormitories beyond the trees at the opposite end, and the main entrance to the dining hall was out to your right facing the clock tower, which was now out to your left.

The only part of the mall you could see from your window was the dome of the dining hall above the cluster of evergreens at the other end of the long four-story academic building that also completely blocked your view of the administration center and that part of the main campus concourse so that you couldn't even see the flagpole in front of the post office, which you knew was only one block away.

What you saw directly across the quadrangle was the corner of the near end of the academic building where the delivery trucks turned off for the service entrance to the dining hall, the campus laundry, and the power plant. You couldn't see any part of the laundry but you knew that the power plant was down the steep hill to your right because you could see the smokestack above the pine tops on the other side of the sophomore dormitory.

The water tank that is probably still the first campus landmark on the horizon after you turn off U.S. Highway 80 at the city marker on your way in from Montgomery and points north or south was all the way back to the left of your window and out of sight between the new science building where most of the academic class sessions were held at that time and the new gymnasium, which was also where dances were held and where concerts and plays were presented and movies were shown.

Back in those days the third floor of that dormitory was known as the Attic because the top half of the outside wall of every room slanted inward with the pitch of the rafters and also that was where the special freshmen students assigned to the upper end of the campus were quartered. But I liked everything about it as soon as I opened the door and saw that next to the window there was a door with a fire-escape landing outside.

As soon as my roommate came in, not more than fifteen minutes later, I liked him too. He was about two inches taller than I was and about ten pounds or so heavier. We had almost the same shade of brown skin, but his hair was coarse grain, almost straight, and almost glossy mat, and mine was soft, with a texture somewhat like moss and a sheen somewhat like steel wool.

He was wearing a tan corduroy sports jacket with khaki slacks and saddle oxfords and argyle socks, and he had opened the collar of his buttoned-down tattersall shirt, but he still had on his navy blue knitted tie. He also had a cloak-and-dagger trenchcoat slung over his shoulders and a tennis racquet tucked under his left arm.

I said, Hi, and he put down his overnight bag and Hartman two-suiter, checking out the room in one ever-so-casual glance, and as we slapped palms Satchmo Armstrong style, he said his last name out of the corner of his mouth like a movie gangster. Then looking at me sidewise but with a conspiratorial twinkle he tucked in his chin like a musical comedy cadet and made a break as if to click his heels and added his first name and middle initial.

Then he said, Geronimo, which I guessed was a nickname meaning now you see me now you don't because whether you played cowboys and Indians or went to the Saturday shoot'em-ups, Geronimo was the chief who was forever escaping again (never mind that he finally ended up on the reservation—in his heyday he was one more badass Indian). Then it crossed my mind that the texture of his hair might mean that his family was part Indian, but I didn't say anything about that.

I said my last name, first name, and middle initial and we touched palms again but instead of my nickname I said Mobile, *seeing Bienville Square once more as you used to see the wrought-iron park benches and the splashing fountain and the tame squirrels when you stood waiting for the streetcar at the corner of Dauphin and St. Joseph with the Van Antwerp building against the sky and the waterfront only two blocks away.*

I also said Mobile County Training School, *seeing Blue Poplar Ridge again with the sky stretching away northward beyond the Chickasabogue and the flagpole above the flower circle and playground where the school bell scaffold used to be when I was in the primary grades,* and suddenly I felt a pang of nostalgia in spite of myself because I wouldn't be going home for the Christmas holidays. I couldn't afford the bus fare. Nor did I expect to be able to afford it for a visit next summer.

He said Chicago and named his high school and then he said that he had come to take courses in architecture and the building trades and that he intended to sneak in as many courses in history and literature as he could choose as electives or would get permission to audit. I said that I was there on a liberal arts scholarship grant but that I hadn't decided on my major and minor subjects yet because I still didn't know what I wanted to do with myself.

He pulled off his jacket and tie and on the way back downstairs to get his steamer trunk I told him that I was there by way of the Early Bird program, and that was when he began telling me about his great uncle (his mother's father's brother) called Old Sarge by some but who sometimes referred to himself in the third person as the Old Trooper and so now was widely known as Old Troop and sometimes addressed as Troop and as Trooper.

The Old Trooper was now in the business of backing entertainers and promoting prizefights but he would always also be one of the legendary Buffalo Soldiers from the old Tenth Cavalry Regiment with an endless repertory of tall tales and historical anecdotes and footnotes about the wild west in the days of Cochise and Geronimo and the Chiricahua Apaches. He had mustered out after the Spanish-American War, and at one time he had managed a cabaret for Jack Johnson and for a while he had also been part owner of a showcase theater on the T.O.B.A. (Theater Owners' Book Association, a.k.a. Tough On Black Asses) circuit and he had also underwritten baseball teams from time to time. One of the prizefighters he and two associates, one in Chicago and the other in Detroit, were backing at the moment was a very promising young heavyweight that I knew the *Pittsburgh Courier* and the *Chicago Defender* were already predicting would become a Jack Johnson and a Joe Gans all rolled into one.

On the way back from the dining hall that first Thursday night I found out that my roommate's family, including the Old Trooper, was really from Fort Deposit in Lowndes County, which was only about seventy-five miles away. As it turned out, it was the Old Trooper who had financed my roommate's family's move north, where he finally settled in Chicago when my roommate was four years old.

Back inside the room again he stood looking around, and then he sat at his desk humming and whistling "Sleepy Time Down South" and "(Up a) Lazy River" and opened his lettering and sketch kits. Then he turned and said, How about this for a start and held up a card that was to be our personalized door plaque which he called our reversible escutcheon, giving me that sidewise glance with the movie gangster, conspiratorial twinkle again.

He had printed "Atelier 359" on both sides. But on one he had lettered CAUTION in red ink and in all capitals and then "work-in-progress" in lowercase, and beneath that there was a black-ink drawing of a hooded monk near the column of a cloister above a quill and a T square crossed over a Leyden jar.

On the other side the word in all capitals was WELCOME and the lowercase phrase was "mischief afoot" and the drawing was of a satyr wearing a top hat playing a trumpet instead of Pan's pipes while cavorting on a keyboard that had a stem glass on his left and a cocktail shaker on his right.

I said, Hey, solid, Gates, and he looked around the room again and said, Not a bad pad, not great but okay for what we came to do, once we fix it up; and he started fixing it up as soon as he finished registration that next afternoon.

In those days there was an eleven o'clock curfew, and lights were supposed to be out at twelve, but that first night we went on talking in the dark until the wee hours, and that was when I found out that it was the Old Trooper who had decided to send him south for his first two years of college to get his bearings. Then he could transfer to any Ivy League or Big Ten university that he was eligible for. Or he could stay on in Alabama and get his bachelor's degree and then still go to the northern university of his choice for graduate studies.

That was also when he told me about how the Old Trooper had taken him around in the limousine to shop for his freshman wardrobe in the college department of the top men's stores in Chicago and when I told him that my Gladstone bag was my graduation gift from Miss Slick McGinnis in New York and that my cowhide looseleaf all-purpose notebook was from Miss Lexine Metcalf and my Elgin wristwatch was from Mister B. Franklin Fisher himself, I couldn't see him in the dark but I knew he was giving me that sidewise look again because what he said was, Heh, heh, haay, heh, heh, haay, and then I also guessed that he had turned his conspiratorial twinkle into a mock penny-dreadful chuckle because then he added, You too, roommate, you too, you too.

III

MISS LEXINE METCALF never did actually say what you were supposed to become or were on your way to becoming or even had already become another one of the very special bright-eyed little boys she was always on the lookout for but had found so precious few of over the years.

She herself didn't have to tell you anything because when the time came there were always plenty of others who had been doing so for her all along. All she had to do was show any special curiosity about you, and you were on the spot, and as soon as they felt that they had seen enough to tell that you were going to be the next one at long last, they began pointing and signifying as if it were all a classroom version of the old playground game in which you had been tagged as the one who was to be It.

Everybody knew that she always made it her very special personal business to know what the new crop of first-termers looked like on the very day school reopened each September. Then, some weeks before Maypole Day during your second-grade year, the speculation would begin about how well who would do next year when you finally made it to Miss Lexine Metcalf and her shawl of many colors and her magic black-board pointers.

But before your classroom was the one with the globe stand and map rack and bulletin-board peoples of many lands and your front-row seat on the aisle next to the planting-box windows, there was first Miss Rowena Dobbs Singleton and second Miss Thelma Caldwell.

When Miss Tee took me through the double gate with the brick pillars and into the school yard that first Monday morning and we came on by the flagpole and the main building to the beginner's area, Miss Rowena Dobbs Singleton was the one who was there, because that was the room where everybody started, and she collected the slip that Miss Tee and Mama had filled out about me, and she said my last name and then my first name, and then my last name again.

Then you had to stand in line along the wall with all the other boys until she called your name again and showed you the table where your seat was and said, Boys and girls, this is the primer grade. This is the beginners classroom and I am the primer teacher and my name is Miss Singleton, Miss Single-ton, repeat after me, Miss Singleton, again, Miss Singleton. Very good, very good, and now quiet, boys and girls, and she picked up her ruler and hand bell and said, Children, children, children, pay attention. Boys and girls who talk in class after the bell sounds will have to hold out their hand for lashes as punishment. Then she said, Answer present to your name, eyes forward, back straight like this. That is good posture. When you slump and slouch like a grumpy grouch, that is bad posture.

Miss Rowena Dobbs Singleton was also the first one to say, *Repeat after me, this is the way we wash our hands, wash our hands, wash our hands, this is the way we wash our hands so early every morning. This is the way we brush our teeth, brush our teeth, brush our teeth, this is the way we brush our teeth so early every morning. This is the way we brush our hair. This is the way we shine our shoes. This is the way we drink our milk. This is the way we raise our hands to recite and ask, repeat after me. May I not can I, may I, repeat, may I please be excused, Miss Singleton. And this is the way we stand and place our right hand over our heart when we say, repeat, I pledge allegiance to the flag and to the republic for which it stands one nation, indivisible, with liberty and justice for all.*

This is A-B-C time. This is one-two-three time. These are letters. These are numbers, also numerals. This is the way letters from ABC through XYZ make words which is spelling. This is the way numbers go from one to ten which is counting, which is the way we find out which is more and which is less. This is the way we spell our name as written. This is the way we write our name as spelled. This is two ways we form letters to make words that form what we say which is writing and also, pay attention, printing. This is the way we say what we write which is reading, which is what storybooks are for. This is the storybook about Baby Ray (who lived in a somewhat but not altogether different place but not in a different time, not once upon a time but everyday, Baby Ray every day).

This is plus which is addition which is the way we do our sums to find more. This is minus which is subtraction. This is the way we take away and find the remainder. This is the way numbers tell us how much and how little and also how long and how short, how far and how near and how heavy and how light and on and on and on.

You were always supposed to sit in the same seat at the same table with the same tablemates, but sometimes everybody had to push all of the tables back and bring all of the chairs into a cozy family circle in the front of the room for story hour, and at other times, especially when the weather turned bad, everything was pushed against the walls to clear the floor for exercises and indoor games.

When you went to the blackboard, you were supposed to have your own eraser just as you were supposed to bring your own tablet, pencil, and wax crayons every day. But what you used at the blackboard was a piece of chalk from the box by the flower vase on the teacher's desk which is also where Miss Rowena Dobbs Singleton used to keep the little bell that she tapped for order. She kept the hand bell in the bottom drawer until she had to ring it for ten o'clock recess. Then she let it stay on the desk by the roll book until she rang it again at the end of playtime after lunch.

At each recess period, tablemates who put everything away and became tidy and quiet in the quickest time got to be the first in the boys' line on one side and the girls' line on the other to march out, and the best all-round tablemates for the whole day were the ones to line up first to go home at dismissal time.

In those days there were so many playthings and bright colors in Miss Rowena Dobbs Singleton's room that it was almost like a toy fair. But when you were promoted to Miss Thelma Caldwell for more spelling and the beginning of Elson readers and more addition and subtraction plus multiplication tables and short division and the beginning of long division and also of such simple fractions as the equal and unequal parts of whole pies and apples and sand tables, when you came into her room that next year that was where you sat in your first regular school desk with an aisle on each side and one seat mate (boys with boys and girls with girls) and two individual pen and pencil trays and inkwells plus an out-of-sight shelf for two book satchels and lunch boxes and also with hinged seats that you were always supposed to leave turned up like a theater seat when you went out for recess and at the end of the day.

Miss Thelma Caldwell also used to say, Boys and girls, and also, Dear children, and also, My dear darling pupils, and for a while you could still recite in chorus with the rest of the class as you had done when you had to repeat after Miss Rowena Dobbs Singleton, but before very long everybody was called on pupil by pupil and row by row, and when it was your turn and you heard the teacher-enunciated pronunciation of your officially registered name once more you were supposed to stand in the aisle with your shoulders square and your head erect and your eyes forward as if the sunny blue sky outside the windows and the everyday working hours sounds and echoes from the nearby neighborhood and street vendors and the call of the wild territory beyond the tree line on the other side of the rooftops of Chickasaw Terrace were not there anymore.

Sometimes during those first two years you could hardly keep from feeling sorry for yourself, not only during recitation and blackboard example time, but even during recess periods. Then when you were finally on your way home at last after the final bell, you were free again for a while. But only until it was school-bell time again the next morning until Friday afternoon and then next Monday there would be week after week until Christmas holidays and then beginning New Year's Day there would be month after month until next May was over.

It was not that I didn't really want to become the buster-brown schoolboy that Mama and Miss Tee had always said that I was the one to be, nor was it that I was any less curious about all that was going on around me in the classroom and out in the school yard than I had ever been about so many other things up to that time. That was the way Little Buddy Marshall was, not me. But even so, school bells always sounded as sad as church bells tolling, until I finally reached Miss Lexine Metcalf that following year and she said what she said about all of the things that reading, including map reading, was always all about.

She said opening books was like opening window shutters. Which was also the beginning of what she always used to say about books, including the newspaper and magazine clippings about peoples of many lands on her bulletin board. It was also in her classroom that you had to go up front to do map and globe exercises as well as blackboard exercises. That was also why everybody could tell that you had advanced to Miss Lexine Metcalf just by looking at you on your way to school, because that was the year when you could stop using your old oilcloth book satchel and strap your regular-size books crossways on your first-year geography book.

When you did something the way it was supposed to be done, Miss Lexine Metcalf always used to nod and smile and say, Very good, and call your name, and say, Very good, again; and when she was very pleased because you had done something that was very special because you had put more into it than was expected or required, she said, Excellent, superb, and put her fingertips together and touched them to her mouth and closed her eyes and then spread them and looked at you again and said, Yes, superlative.

Outstanding girls were wonderful young ladies and marvelous young ladies for whose sake princes also had to be charming no matter what else their ancestral mission required them to achieve. Outstanding boys were splendid young men, and when she called you one of her splendid young men it was precisely as if she were making you one of the Knights of her Round Table, which was no less real for being invisible.

Not that you didn't miss being outside anymore, especially when you looked out of the windows, because from my seat every time you stood up you could see northeast across the vocational workshop area to the poplar tree-line and the sky stretching away above that part of Chickasabogue Swamp and the L & N Railroad canebrake territory, nor was I quite ready to give up rambling and meandering with Little Buddy Marshall. But once Miss Lexine Metcalf was there for you Monday through Friday, I began to make up more and more excuses not to play hooky to do so.

The first time she said who if not you was before class one Wednesday morning. I was there that early because I wanted to have the globe and map rack all to myself while everybody else was either still on the way or waiting and playing around outside until the first bell for the flag formation. When she looked up from her desk and saw me coming in as I had asked permission to do, she said, How conscientious you are, a young man with initiative, and why not, because who if not you.

Who indeed? she said the next time, which was the day I stayed after school because I wanted to read the new bulletin board display all by myself and the time after that was the day I stayed in during the first part of the noon recess to work on my cutouts for the new sand-table project, and when I came out to the playground Simon Ray Hargroves saw me and came up and whispered, Hey, Scooter, boy you better watch out, man, you mess around and let old lady Metcalf get her claws on you and she ain't gone never let you alone. He was whispering not only because he was being confidential but also because you're not supposed to use nicknames on campus. You could get demerits for that, just as you could for keeping your hands in your pockets and wearing your cap crooked or backward.

Not as long as you were at Mobile County Training School, he said, and I said, Not me, man, and he said, Well, you sure better watch out then, because everybody knows she always been dead set on finding somebody so she can help old man B. Franklin Fisher hook him and turn him into a mad genius. Man, before long she going to be giving you a whole stack of extra work and stuff just to see how much more you can do and the more you do, the more she going to keep piling on and piling on.

Which by that time she had already begun doing and was to continue to do right on up through each succeeding home-room teacher until it was time to turn me over to Mister B. Franklin Fisher himself for the Early Bird program, reminding me all the while that some are called and some are not.

And some are also called, she also used to say, and heed not. She said, Some are called to the church, some to the bedside, some as advocates to the bar of justice. While I myself am called to the classroom. Who can tell just what you might be called to do, my bright-eyed young man. For all we know, you may have to travel far and wide just to find out what it is you are called for.

When I came out onto the play area late during another noon recess period, the first one to spot me was Jaycee Robinson from Chickasaw Terrace and he said, Boy, I'm telling you, pretty soon you ain't hardly going to be able to make it out here at all no more. Boy, look to me like she just about got you right where she want you already, and I said, That's what you say, man. That's what you say.

Because by that time I was absolutely satisfied that she was always going to make sure that I got outside in plenty of time to join in whatever games they were playing that day, because sometimes I used to sneak glances back up at the window and find her peeping down to see how well I was making out.

I said, That's all right about some old lady Metcalf, man. I said, Come on, let's go, Jaycee, man. I got your old lady goddamn Metcalf swinging, man. I didn't say what you mean *old* lady Metcalf, because everybody knew that she was hardly even thirty yet, but I also knew that as far as most grade-school pupils during my time at Mobile County Training School were concerned, it was as if she didn't have any business being that young and good-looking and wearing such stylish clothes to

boot if she was also going to be that book smart and that serious about everything anyway, although she was just as nice as
she was strict. When a lot of them had to say something about
her, they always made it sound as if they were talking about a
middle-aged nun from the Saint Francis Charity Hospital.

I said, Man, don't worry about no Miss Lexine Metcalf. I
said, She promised my big auntie to keep a special eye on me,
so you know what that mean. But I wasn't about to tell him
anything at all about how I always felt when she used to say,
You will go where you will go and you will see what you will
see, so you must learn what you must learn because who, if not
you, will do what you must do, my splendid young man.

IV

THE MONUMENT that marked the site of the original campus—
the original log cabins of the old slave compound—had been
in place for some twenty-odd years. It had a triangular base
that supported three bronze men, the one on the right holding a seed in one hand and a hoe in the other, the one on the
left with a hammer and an anvil, and the one in the center
seated with an open book on his knee, and not only had it
been the most famous landmark on the campus ever since it
was dedicated, it had also become one of the national emblems of Afro-American aspirations and achievement through
education.

In the classroom that first Monday morning with my chair
facing in from the wall of shoulder-high windows toward the
lectern and the blackboard because that way you could see the
back row without having to turn and look behind you, and
with everybody hushed and waiting to hear and see whose
name came next, and with the hailing and chattering back-on-
the-scene voices coming and going down along the walks and
hedges outside and with the back-to-work sky music of delivery
truck horns and motors grinding and rumbling and honking
in the distance beyond the nearby tempo of the neighborhood
traffic humming and buzzing and beeping back and forth
along the campus thoroughfare, I said what I said. I said, Here,
meaning not only here as in present in the flesh on the spot as

of now as against absent and thus not here but elsewhere. I said, Here, meaning not only as prescribed and thus required by attendance codes and regulations but also as promised on my own in all sincerity and thus here above all as in partial fulfillment of that which has long since been intended.

Because even as I said it I was thinking, Me and my own expectations me and also the indelibility of the ancestral imperative to do something and become something and be somebody. Then when the instructor finished checking the roster and opened the textbook and held up the blackboard pointer for attention it was precisely as if he were about to say and one and two and three and four and so forth and so on and onward.

The campus was inside the corporate limits of the township that it was named for, but it was also almost like another complete town in itself, with its own surrounding communities and satellite neighborhoods. The main grounds added up to about 145 acres at that time, and the tree-lined avenue that ran from the dormitories near the academic quadrangle and curved and sloped all the way past the trades school workshops and ended on the low hill known as the ag side just about one mile long. Then there were some three thousand more acres of cultivated fields, orchards, and fenced-in livestock ranges.

It had all begun back at the end of the post–Civil War period known as the Reconstruction when it was a makeshift elementary school for freedmen and their families. The first classrooms had been in a cluster of stick-and-dirt cabins in one of the old slave compounds on the old Strickland plantation, some of which was still owned by contemporary Stricklands who were still among the most powerful people not only in the county but in the central part of the state.

The founding fathers, three former fugitive slaves also known as the Triumvirate—a fieldhand, a blacksmith, and a handyman —who had escaped to the North to join the Union army eighteen months before Lincoln issued the Emancipation Proclamation and had in exchange for various personal chores during free time in camp between battles been given elementary-lessons in reading, writing, and arithmetic by Yankee soldiers, some officers, some enlisted men, some abolitionists, some just plain Billy Yanks willing to make a swap.

After Appomattox, which ex-slaves almost always referred to as Surrender, the three of them worked their way back from Virginia to Alabama with the express and unwavering purpose (however vaguely defined at the outset) of initiating their own local Reconstruction program even as other ambitious freedmen here and elsewhere sought to achieve, exercise, and safeguard the rights to full citizenship provided for in the Thirteenth, Fourteenth, and Fifteenth Amendments, by going directly into politics as such, some as local, state, and even national office-seekers, and some as agitators and organizers.

They had begun as sharecroppers, with their own mule, plow, two-wheeled ox carts, jerry-built wheelbarrows, credit for seeds, fertilizer, rations, hand tools, and farming implements at the Strickland commissary plus an option to buy their first forty acres on an installment plan, and before very long they had the beginnings of a school that was to become an attraction for students not only from all over the state and region but also from across the nation at large, so much so that as the names on so many of its buildings indicated, it also attracted a considerable amount of financial assistance from such movers and shakers as Collis P. Huntington, John D. Rockefeller, Andrew Carnegie, and numerous others who regarded it as a pioneering effort in post–Civil War education.

In the early days all students were required to work for room, board, and tuition. There were no entrance fees or incidental charges. Those who could afford to pay were directed to the contributions office where they were given forms requesting their parents to become subscribers to the ongoing campaign for funds. But no student could pay in lieu of work and every student was also required to learn a trade in addition to whatever courses you chose as your primary vocation.

The first two generations of students were summoned to and from field, shop, and classroom alike by the same old bell that had once regulated life on the plantation before the war, and they planted and processed the food they ate. They produced and marketed such farm products as chickens, eggs, dairy products, and also livestock. They also cut the timber for lumber and they made the bricks and constructed the buildings that were to house them, and in the process they also learned to build and furnish their own houses, provide for their families, and develop or improve their communities wherever they settled.

Nor was there any end to the tasks early members of the faculty, whose dedication is a story in itself, had to perform. They had to be artisans, husbandmen, and tradesmen as well as classroom instructors. They had to be church workers as well as health and hygiene missionaries. They had to be fund-raisers combing the country for benefactors and able to convince many of the toughest captains of commerce and industry that by making generous donations to the school they were doing far more than underwriting the education of the children and grandchildren of slaves. They were investing in the future of the reunited United States as a great twentieth-century nation among the other great nations of the world, not in such direct words to be sure, but that was the point they put across.

Anecdotes and details about all of that were very much a part of the indoctrination that your orientation sessions during that first week were all about. And you were also to hear it again as the "gospel of Afro-American uplift," not only during the annual commemoration ceremonies that next spring, but also in allusions and quotations by almost every speaker who addressed the general student assembly on any official occasion.

V

I CAN STILL see myself at the long corner table by the rubber plant in the southeast wing of the main reading room on the second floor of the library, from which you could see part of the gymnasium through the poplar branches outside the windows that also overlooked the traffic circle and the lot where the visiting athletic teams parked their buses.

When you stood up you could also see the ticket shack and the admission gate to the athletic field which was out of sight down the hill. Beyond the high fence a few feet off the right of the vehicle entrance you could also look down onto the tennis courts at the other end of which you could also see the red-brick two-story residence of the dean of men at that time, and in the distance beyond the fence line and scrub-oak thicket there was the open sky above the sweet-gum slopes and the pine ridge somewhere south of Montgomery Fork.

As often as not when there was an assignment with a set of factual details to be looked up, I also used to work for a while at another long table near the open reference shelves at the other end of the main reading room and from there you could see across the thoroughfare to the back entrance to the administration building and the front columns of the old academic hall, and there was also the traffic along all of the walks in the academic area also known as the upper end.

Every time I looked down from that end of the library and saw all of the other students coming and going between class bells during those first weeks of that first fall term, I felt that old pang of isolation you often get when it hits you that you're in a place that you're not yet used to. But I didn't feel lost because I also felt how lucky I was to be there and because I was so excited about all of the things I woke up every morning hoping that I was getting that much closer to. It was enough to make you cross your fingers, and every time I remember how often I used to do just that, I still feel very lucky all over again.

But my usual place in the reading room from the very outset was the table in the corner where the rubber plant was, and this many years later I can still see the chalk white lines against the red clay tennis court and the green-stained bleachers as they were in the late summer sunshine and sometimes also in an early mid-September shower while I was reading about the role of the bards, scops, and gleemen in the evolution of language and literature in England, and also about the origin of civilization in Mesopotamia and about the culture of Egypt and about the Nile Valley and the ancient dynasties.

Along with what I was reading later on about the decline and fall of Rome into the Dark Ages and about the coming of medieval times, and along with English literature from Chaucer through Sir Thomas Malory and also along with selected freshman classics for the Introduction to Ideas and Literary Forms, there was the central Alabama Indian summer outside with the leaves turning from late September green to October yellow mixed with scarlet before becoming mostly shades of the tans and browns and brownish grays of harvest fields and game-bird feathers.

Nothing has ever surpassed the coziness of that corner of the reading room as it was when the first frost came that year. And then in a few weeks it was November and most of the trees were beginning to be bare and the thermometer outside had begun to drop below fifty degrees and then below forty, and inside it was as if you could smell the warmth from the radiators along the walls, but it was really the furniture polish and the liquid floor wax and there was also that trace of stamp-pad ink and binding glue and cataloging-room shellac that almost always used to be there when you used library books.

But before all of that and also before the gauze-thin tree whispering showers beyond the soft steady rattle of the drain pipes, there were those bright days during the first weeks of that September when all of the windows were open and along with the maps and illustrations spread out on the table in front of me there was a spicy smell of recently cut hedges and lawn grass and you could also hear the tennis balls being plipped and plopped and the voices of the referees and sometimes also a smattering of applause.

Then one afternoon I realized that for some time what I had been hearing was only a very casual plipping and plopping, plipping and plopping of fewer and fewer balls back and forth with no referee calls and no applause, because that many weeks of fall-term class sessions had come and gone along with that many social events including the first two home football games and also that much time hanging out on the Strip and in the radio lounge off the main stem, and I also realized that I already knew why I felt the way I felt about being where I was.

In the classroom you were a student among other students and you did what you did among them and along with them and sometimes together with them, not only as in roundtable discussions, seminars, and laboratory and workshop exercises, but even when you were responding to a direct question from the instructor, you were participating in a group session and as such you were also always reacting to and interacting with other members of the class.

But as soon as you came into the library it was almost always as if you were all alone and on your own again, not that you were ever really unaware that you were still actually surrounded by that many other students, faculty, and staff, and also visitors and sightseers. But even so it was very much as if everybody else was there to be an incidental part of what a college campus and a college library were really supposed to be.

Not only that, but what with the biggest globe (revolving on a tilted axis) I had ever seen, and what with all of the maps and atlases and mileage charts along with all of the books and documents and pictures and relics and artifacts only that many short steps away, it was also almost as if you had a sand table of the whole world always all to yourself.

My roommate went to the library mainly to browse through the current newspapers and magazines every Monday, Wednesday, and Friday, mostly during free time in the midafternoon; and sometimes he would also go back again for a while on Saturday morning.

In those days the periodicals room was on your left as you came into the main lobby and you could usually find him by himself at the same table in the corner near the shelves where the technical journals were, but he always began with the big city newspapers. Then he would go through the *Saturday Review of Literature* and then the weekly news magazines and then the monthly and quarterly reviews.

When you saw him up in the main reading room, which was not often and never for very long, sometimes he would be in the open reference section making notebook entries at one of the wall tables where the high chairs were. But usually he went straight to the card catalog section at the main circulation counter, and when he found what he wanted he checked it out and did all of his reading back in 359, sometimes sitting with his leg folded under him in the sea captain's chair that he had picked up from somebody in the furniture repair shop in the industrial arts area, and with the book tilted in front of him on the adjustable drafting board, sometimes with the chair turned so that he could rest both legs across the bed.

But most often he liked to read sitting propped up in bed with the book on his thighs, sometimes smoking one of his fancy pipes which he never took outside the room and sometimes not. But always with a pencil behind his ear and his notebook within easy reach.

The sketches, blueprints, and watercolors on the wall behind the head of his cot and near the drafting table were his own work. Some were class assignments but most were field sketches ripped from his 8½″ × 11″ grid pad and thumbtacked up as mementos that sometimes became entries in his ever-present notebook, which he kept like a sea captain's log and sometimes called his daybook and clay book and clue book, his testament and also his doomsday book of portable property which he used to refer to as the goods not only in the sense of canned, packaged, and dry goods and other provisions for a survival kit, but also in the sense of getting and thus having specific inside information or evidence about something.

Incidentally, in no time at all you could almost always tell when he was about to reach behind his ear for his pencil for another entry, because he would either move directly back from what he was reading, or stand back from whatever he was inspecting and give it his sidelong stare and close his eyes for a moment, or he would rub his hands as if licking his chops and go into his heh-heh-heh imitation of the mustache-twirling, lip-smacking villain of the penny-dreadful pulp story, but then instead of actually saying ah-ah and all of that, he used to say, Yeah, verily.

As soon as I saw and heard him do that the first time, I could tell that it was something he probably always did because it reminded me of what Little Buddy Marshall always used to do. Whenever he was about to have to take a chance on something, old Little Buddy Marshall always used to tilt his head to one side and close his right eye and squint like a poker player, studying his cards through the haze of smoke curling up from the cigarette dangling from the corner of his mouth. Then he would suck his teeth two times and say, Hey, mighty right, hey, goddamn right. Hey, shit I reckon.

When something was good or even outstanding to Little Buddy Marshall, it was either some great shit or some bad shit. So when he judged something to be no good he used to say, Man, that shit ain't going to stack. Man, ain't nobody going to tell me you can make some old thin-ass shit like this stack. Man, I bet you my bottom goddamn dollar. Man, I'm telling you. This shit come from running off at the goddamn bowels. I don't care what nobody say. Because I know good and goddamn well what the goddamn fuck I'm talking about. I'm talking about you looking at some shit that ain't shit and then I'm talking about something you can put your money on.

Anytime Little Buddy Marshall used to say, Hey, shit, I reckon, it meant that he was ready to take a chance on something, sometimes even regardless of the consequences. But it was not very long before I realized that when my new roommate said, Yeah, verily, you never knew when he was also going to say, But, on the other hand. Not that he was less willing to take chances. He was even more of a gambler and a rambler than Little Buddy Marshall ever even dreamed of being. But the chances he took were more a matter of calculated risk. Whereas I always knew that Little Buddy Marshall took many more things for granted than I myself ever did.

VI

AFTER LIGHTS out most nights I used to talk to him about Gasoline Point and Mobile; he asked about the Gulf Coast and about the bayous and sandbars and canebrakes; he also wanted to hear what I knew about Creoles and Cajuns, and I said I knew much more about Creoles than about Cajuns, but that I did know some and I had been to Chastang and Citronelle, which Gasoline Point people always used to think of as Cajun settlements.

He wanted to know which Indians, if any, I had grown up hearing the most about, and I said, The Chickasaws, the Choctaws, the Seminoles, and the Creeks, and I said, Especially the Creeks because from as long ago as I could remember, any time you saw somebody in Gasoline Point with very dark skin and coal-black straight or somewhat wiry hair, it was almost always said that whoever it was belonged to a family with blood mixed with the Creek Indians.

That was something you knew about just as you had always known about how Uncle Jo Jo the African and the people who had originally settled on African Baptist Hill and also founded African Baptist church had come through middle passage in the old *Clotilde* in August of 1859.

I said, Naturally you were always used to seeing Creoles and Cajuns, Choctaws, Chickasaws, Creeks, and Seminoles along with Cubans, Puerto Ricans, Mexicans, a few gee-chee-talking West Indians and a whole lot of others during Mardi Gras every year, not only in the parades but also on the sidewalk all along the route of the procession.

As close as Gasoline Point was to the waterfront of a seaport town like Mobile, you also grew up used to seeing ships from the seven seas flying flags of many lands. And just as you were used to knowing which downtown stores sailors and merchant seamen gathered around and also what points on which downtown side-streets were mainly Cajun or Creole or Cuban, you also knew that when you came toward the foot of Government Street and approached the area of Commerce Street and Water Street, you were always going to hear sailors and shopkeepers speaking more foreign languages than you could identify.

When I told him about Luzana Cholly, he filled me in some more about the Old Trooper. He had mustered out in 1900 and settled in California for a while, had first met Jack Johnson when Old Jack was out there building up the reputation that was to lead to the heavyweight championship of the world in the next five years.

The night club deal was a few years later in Chicago, he said, and I said, Hey, so the Old Trooper was still in during the Spanish-American War. So was his outfit in there with Teddy Roosevelt's Rough Riders? And he said, Well, not exactly. Old Troop was in the Tenth and they were right there with the Rough Riders in that action on San Juan Hill all right. But you know something? They went up that son-of-a-bitch *on foot*, because their horses were still in the Port of Embarkation back in Florida.

That was one of the Old Trooper's one thousand plus one tall tales for later, he said. But actually it came up again sooner than later because within a week or so, we found out that there were some of the Old Trooper's saddle buddies from the Tenth and also from the Spanish-American War along with veterans from the Ninth and quite a few not so old doughboys from the AEF right there on the campus, not only on the dean of men's staff and in the trades school, but also in the academic department, and also the music department.

The first time he ever mentioned anything at all about his father was when he said what he said the night that I told him that Mama and Papa had moved from the old plantation country up in Escambia County where I was born down to the shotgun house on Dodge Mill Road during the wartime shipbuilding boom. He said, when they moved from Lowndes County to Chicago, it was part of the postwar boom, and that was when he also said that his father didn't make it back from overseas, and that was why the Old Trooper had come down and taken the family back to live with him.

I didn't get to know my natural father, he said, because I was not quite two years old when he went to camp. And then he said, so the father whose name I bear is really only a man in a photograph. Three photographs all posed in a studio, one as a young sport, one with his bride, and one in uniform. You know, wraparound leggings, tight coat with stand-up collar, and overseas cap.

That was why I decided to tell him about Miss Tee, something I had never brought up on my own with anybody before. Not even Little Buddy Marshall. I had said what I said to him because after Miss Minnie Ridley Stovall did what she did at Mister Ike Meadow's wake that night while everybody thought I was asleep, I knew people were going to be whispering and I didn't want him to think that I didn't know what was going on.

I didn't say anything about that part of it, but I did tell him that I had never been able to bring myself to ask Miss Tee anything whatsoever about how it all had happened. I had to pick up as much as I could without letting anybody know that I was even curious, and in due time I found out that she had had to leave boarding school and she couldn't face her family and neighbors back in her hometown, so that was why I happened to be born in Escambia County. She had an older cousin who had finished the same boarding school several years earlier and was teaching down there. It was this cousin who was the one who took her in and also arranged for Mama and Papa to adopt me.

But I never did find out anything at all about who my father was, I said, because she was the only one in Gasoline Point who knew. And man, I just have never been able to say anything to her about any of it. And that's when he said, Man, fathers. Just wait until you hear some of the riffs and hot licks I've been grooving and running on fathers all these years. And uncles, too, he said. Not to mention mothers, aunts, godmothers, and some others.

VII

WHEN I STOPPED off in the lounge on my way back alone from the dining hall one night about three weeks into that first September, there were three freshmen and four upperclassmen with their chairs pulled up in a semicircle around the radio console. But they were not really listening to the program of recorded music that filled in the thirty minutes before the news and sports broadcasts. They were listening to each other, with the music which I call downtown department store pop songs—"Smoke Rings," "Isn't It a Lovely Day?" "The Little Things You Used to Do," or "I Only Have Eyes for You"—and instrumentals, in the background like the wall furnishings.

It was a session about what your roommate was really like, and they were mostly just joking, and I found a spot for my chair; and when my turn came, I said what I said and that was how I became the one who was actually responsible for the nickname my roommate was to be known by, although I didn't have that name or notion or any other nickname in mind at all.

Later on I would have said he was by way of becoming a polymath, but I don't think that word was current then. But I had just read the captions to the illustrations of Christopher Marlowe's play *The Tragical History of Dr. Faustus* in my anthology of English literature, so I said, Doctor Faustus, and when somebody said Doctor Whostus, I said, You know about that guy that made the big deal to swap his immortal soul with the Devil, and one of the upperclassmen said, Oh yeah, him. Oh yeah, goddamn, hey yeah, that's a good one. And before anybody else could open his mouth, I realized that they were all thinking about the magicians we had all seen come on stage wearing a top hat and a frock coat and also a black cape with a red lining and carrying a cane and begin by announcing themselves as diabolical craftsmen and technicians who had sacrificed their souls to the devil in exchange for knowledge of forbidden secrets of the universe.

Which made him a witch doctor in a top hat. So somebody said, Snake doctor. Which in a day or so had been reduced to snake as in snake-oil salesman to be sure, but also, and indeed precisely, as in snake in the grass. Because in a week or so even those who were in on the session in the lounge that Thursday night and so had to know that my main point about Doctor Faustus was that my roommate wanted to study and master the entire curriculum seemed nevertheless to have come to take it for granted that a sneaky snakiness was what his sidelong smile and chuckle and his ever-so-casual and offhand manner were really about.

Nor according to some could anything be a sneakier game of one-upmanship than his classroom deportment. He always sat in the back row with his chair tilted against the wall as if he were totally preoccupied with something other than the discussion under way, and when he was called on to recite he always looked up from whatever he was reading, writing, or sketching as if surprised, but he always answered as if he had heard what everybody else had said from the outset. Not only that, but with his quietly conversational responses he not only upstaged everybody else, but also began a brief dialogue with the instructor. Then he would tilt his chair back again as if nothing had happened.

Faust, Faustus, or Snake Doctor, it was all the same to him, he said when I told him about how it all had gotten started in the lounge that Thursday night. But you could tell that he was very pleased at the way it had turned out, so I asked him what he thought a name like that would do for his reputation among the coeds, and he rubbed his palms and knuckles and went into his mock penny-dreadful heh-heh-heh.

They may be academic chuckleheads who are here only to acquire a means for more bread and circuses, he said, but this matter of sobriquets does have pragmatic implications which in this case shall be assayed anon.

And assay he did before the end of the next week and he found out that the Snake had already achieved such notoriety in the girls' dormitories and that getting dates was not going to be a problem. Not that either one of us was ready to take on a regular girlfriend yet. I had decided that all of that would have to come later, and I couldn't afford it anyway. After all, I was not even sure that I was going to be able to come up with the minimum amount of cash you needed for academic incidentals. So money for date favors and treats definitely was out of the question for me.

He could spare the spending change but for the time being he was even less willing to put in the hours you had to spend shucking and stuffing and jiving in the dining hall and on the promenade mall than I was. As a matter of fact, we both decided that we didn't even want to be *invited* to escort anybody to a dance or any other social function, not even entertainment series movies, concerts, and plays, to which admission was by Student Privilege card.

You couldn't be too careful about things like that. Or so they used to say in those days. And he had also been warned by his mother and the Old Trooper among others in Chicago as I had been told time and again by Mister B. Franklin Fisher and Miss Lexine Metcalf among other well-wishers down Mobile way, including the one and only Miss Slick McGinnis, that some coeds came to college to earn a degree but that the certificate that some others were out to get just might be one with *your* name on it.

So Snake was just the name for the game we both had in mind for the time being, and he made the most of it, and so did I. Because it faked quite a few of the more adventurous coeds into taking him on as a city slicker from the big up-north city of Chicago, and as his roommate I was automatically credited with, or accused of, being his buddy from the down-home city of Mobile.

I heard about you, a sophomore whom I will not name but who was from Birmingham and was taking Elementary French Review No. I, said as we were coming out of class one day. I heard all about you, you and that roommate of yours, the Snake. And I said, You can't go by what you hear, and before she could say anything, I also said, The best way is to find out things for yourself, and she said, Aw—you go on now, boy. But when she gave me a playful shove, I caught her hand and she said, What you think you doing, freshman? And I said, Being very fresh and very, very mannish, and she said, See there, what I heard was true. I was still holding her hand and I said, I hope so the way you signifying.

There was also the one who was a junior, no less, from Pittsburgh. She worked in the library and sometimes she was the one at the main circulation desk and after several weeks I could tell she was curious about me and I thought it was because of all the time I was spending at the table in the corner by the rubber plant. So as good-looking as she was, I pretended that I didn't really see her even when she was the one stamping the checkouts. But then one day she said what she said and that was the beginning of that.

You sure had me fooled, she said, and I said, Who me? How? and she said, Here I was thinking that you were kinda cute to be such a bookworm and come to find out you're rooming with the Snake of all people, and I said, What's wrong with that, and she said, He's so stuck on himself he goes around acting like he's God's gift to women, and I said, I'll settle for being God's gift to you, and she said, Well if you aren't the freshest freshman yet. So when her regular boyfriend went on trips with the football team and then the basketball team, she was the one.

That was the kind of on-campus action my roommate and I had going for us that first year, and I still don't know how I got away with it all without ever being called Little Snake or Snake Two or Snake Number Two or the Lizard or the Eel or something like that. Somebody was forever saying that we were two of a kind, but I was known as but not addressed as the Other One.

So much for Doctor Faustus as far as just about everybody else was concerned. But as pre-sophomoric as it probably sounded to an upperclassman coming as it did from a newly arrived freshman, I still think it was a pretty good analogy because what I really meant was the fact that my roommate was the first student I ever met who really believed that everything you studied in a classroom should become just as much a part of what you did everyday as everything else. To him, nothing was just academic stuff, so as far as he was concerned, there was no reason whatsoever why you shouldn't know just as much about the fundamentals of any course in the curriculum as any student who had checked it as the major for a degree. After all, as he had already said as he unpacked his books, the very best undergraduate courses were only a very brief introduction to some aspect of the plain old everyday facts of life that were just as important to you as to anybody else.

Which is why you never knew what his side of the room was going to look like when you came back at the end of the day. Or, for that matter, sometimes when you woke up in the morning. As often as not, the drafting board would be flattened out into a work table and rigged up with whatever equipment he'd have come by for whatever exercise he had underway. One day it might be a makeshift chemistry laboratory. The next day it might be set up for a problem in physics or biology, and when he was reviewing some historical period, he sketched his own maps, and he always got a special kick out of making his own war room mock-ups and outlining the strategies and retracing the maneuvers of the crucial battles of the great army and naval commanders.

During the second week of classes he had picked up the foot-locker now under his bed from a senior in the building trades and that is where he stashed his special equipment, including not only his drafting kit and surveying and mapping instruments, but also his 16-mm camera, binoculars, and the parts he was already accumulating by mail order for the amateur radio set and the model airplane he was to build and operate from time to time that next spring.

Meanwhile, by the middle of October he had begun a window greenhouse project that he always found time to keep going full swing no matter whatever else came up. It started with two baskets of ferns he brought in from the greenhouse out on the ag side and hung above the books on the ledge that he also used as an extension of his work corner. Then a few days later he filled in the rest of the space with two shelves of terra-cotta pots, and before the end of November a fine growth of English ivy, tiger aloe, gold dusk, and silver dollar jade was underway, and by the time that first winter settled in, there were red geraniums and yellow nasturtiums, and deep purple African violets in blossom.

Each plant specimen was tagged with its Latin label, but when he got around to adding orchids he called them his Nero Wolfe project. So the day I came in and he looked around from what he was probing wearing a pawnbroker's eye piece, I started laughing and I said, Hey man, goddamn. Don't tell me you're a jewel thief, too, and he said, Touché, old pardner, and laughed along with me. Then he said, But what about Sherlock and his magnifying glass and what about Benvenuto Cellini the goldsmith and his loupe? Not that the cat burglar doesn't have his challenges for the likes of the old Snake. Hey hey haay, roommate. It's a thought. Good thinking, roommate. Good thinking.

VIII

THERE WAS a time when everybody in Gasoline Point had expected Creola Calloway to go out on the circuit and become a
world famous entertainer. Even before she was thirteen years
old, people were already talking about how every vaudeville
company that came to play in Mobile in those days always tried
to hire her, always promising to make her a headliner in no
time at all.

Nobody doubted it. Her endowments were all too obvious. She was so good-looking that she made you catch your
breath, and when it came to doing the shimmie-she-wobble,
the Charleston, the mess-around, or any other dance step, including ones made up on the spot, she always took the cake
without even seeming to try, and also without making anything special of it afterward.

By her fifteenth birthday most people seemed to have decided that her fame and fortune were only a matter of time and
choice, which they took for granted would be any day now.
Not that anybody ever tried to rush things. After all, along
with all of the fun they had enjoyed speculating about her possibilities, there was also the fact that Gasoline Point would not
be the same without her.

As for myself, once I became old enough to begin to realize
what they were talking about, I couldn't ever think about her
leaving without also thinking of her coming back, and what
I always saw was her rearriving with her own road company
and own chauffeur-driven touring-style limousine wearing a
hot-mama boa and carrying a lap dog. There would be placards about her in Papa Gumbo Willie McWorthy's barbershop,
on the porch of Stranahan's store, and on telegraph poles all
around town. Then her name would be up in a crown of bright
twinkling lights above the main entrance to the Saenger Theatre which was the premier showcase in downtown Mobile in
those days.

Actually by that time the way most people in Gasoline Point
had begun to act whenever she came around you would have
thought that she had already been away and had come back famous. Even when people were standing right next to her on the
sidewalk or in a yard somewhere, it was as if they were looking

at her satin smooth caramel brown skin and croquignole-frizzy hair and her diamond ring and twenty-four-carat ankle chain on stage with their eyes still glazed by the footlights.

Sometimes even when people were talking directly to her they sounded as if she were no longer a living and breathing person in the flesh anymore. It was as if to men and women alike she was a dazzlingly beautiful woman-child beyond everything else, and as such not only mysterious but also unsettling if not downright disturbing. No wonder pretty girls so often seem to be smiling, either as if in response to applause or as if in self-defense.

But Creola Calloway was never to go anywhere with any road show. It turned out that in spite of all the speculation and predictions that everybody else had been making over the years, by the time she was almost nineteen she had decided that she didn't want to leave Gasoline Point. All she wanted to do was go on having a good time, making the rounds from one jook joint and honky-tonk to the next as she had begun doing not long after she dropped out of school (truant officers or no truant officers) even before she finished the ninth grade.

Some people said that she just stayed on in Gasoline Point because she hadn't ever been able to figure out what she was supposed to do about being so good-looking except to act as if it didn't really matter. But most others realized that talk like that had more to do with bewilderment if not exasperation than with insight, because all that anybody could actually quote her as saying was that she did not want to go on the road because she did not want to leave Gasoline Point.

And that was that. She didn't even insist that what she chose to do with her own life was her own private business, because she had already made that point once and for all by dropping out of school when she did. But even so, most of the people who had always concerned themselves about her future all along went right on reacting as if her beautiful face and body were really sacred community commonwealth property and that she therefore had an inviolable obligation to turn into some sort of national credit not only to Gasoline Point and Mobile but also to the greater glory of our folks everywhere.

Nobody ever either accused her of or excused her for not having enough nerve, gall, guts, and get-up to take a chance out on the circuit and up North. Self-confidence was not the problem. Not for Creola Calloway. The problem was her lack of any interest in what, in the slogan of Mobile County Training School (and most church auxiliaries as well), was, A commitment to betterment. Given her God-given assets, that was not just disappointing and exasperating, it made her somebody even more reprehensible than a backslider. It was a betrayal of a divine trust.

That is why by the time she was twenty so many people had given her up as a lost ball in the high weeds and no longer called her old Creola Calloway (with a passive smile) but that old Creola Calloway (with their eyes rolling). Nor did the outrage have anything to do with the fact that she spent so much time hanging out in jook joints and honky-tonks. There were many church folks who condemned that outright to be sure, but the chances are that if she had gone north and become a famous entertainer like, say, Bessie Smith or Ethel Waters, she would have had their blessing along with everybody else's.

But she stayed right on in the old Calloway house on Front Street by the trolley line even after Miss Cute (also known as Q for Queenie and as Q. T.), who had always been more like a very good-looking older sister than a mother anyway, had gone up North and decided to get married again and settle down in Pittsburgh.

She did pay Miss Cute a visit from time to time and she also used to take the L & N up to Cincinnati and continue on up to Detroit to spend time with her brother every once in a while. His name was Alvin Calloway, Jr., but everybody always called him Brother Calloway, not as in church brother but as if you were saying Buddy Calloway or Bubber Calloway or even Big Brother or Little Brother Calloway. He must have been about three or four years older than his sister and there wasn't a better automobile mechanic in Gasoline Point before he left to go and get a job in an automobile factory.

One time he came down for Easter in a brand-new Cadillac and she drove back with him and was gone for ten days, and another time she was away for a month because she also spent some time visiting cousins in Cleveland and Chicago. Everybody knew about those trips and also about the time she went out to California to spend six weeks with her father, whose name was Alvin Calloway (Senior) but who was called Cal Calloway and who had gone out to Los Angeles not long after he came back from France with the AEF. He had a job as a carpenter in a moving picture studio.

I remember knowing that she took the southbound L & N Pan American Express from Mobile to New Orleans and changed to the Sunset Limited, which I can still see pulling out of the Canal Street Station as if with the departure bell dingdonging a piano vamp against the crash cymbal sound of the piston exhaust steam and as if with the whistle shouting California here I come like a solo above the up-tempo two-beat of the drivers driving westbound toward Texas and across the cactus country and the mountains en route to the Pacific Coast which was two whole time zones and three days and nights away.

You couldn't say that she stayed on in Gasoline Point because she hadn't even been anywhere and seen anything else. She went everywhere she wanted to go whenever she wanted to go, especially after Miss Cute left town. But she never went anywhere without a return ticket, and she always came back not only as if on a strict schedule but also almost always before most people who didn't happen to know when she left had a chance to miss her.

That was why even those who knew better used to talk as if she were always in and around town. But then she, which is to say her stunning good looks, always had been and always would be a source of confusion and anxiety. So much so sometimes that people used to accuse her of causing outbreaks of trouble that she had absolutely nothing to do with, as if she caused trouble just by being in town. As if Gasoline Point which had also come to be known and shunned as the L & N Bottoms long before Creola Calloway's parents were born had not been a hideout hammock for bayou-jettisoned African captives and runaway slaves before that and a buccaneer's hole even before that.

When she got married to Scott Henderson, whose family owned the Henderson Tailor Shop and Pressing Club, nobody expected her to settle down, and she didn't. She was going on twenty-two that summer and the whole thing was over in less than a year. Scott Henderson had left town to start his own dry cleaning business down in Miami, Florida. So when Eddie Ray

Meadows, who worked in a drugstore downtown and was one
of the best tap dancers around and also a pretty good shortstop
and base runner, took her to the justice of the peace, people
didn't give him but six months and he barely made it. Then
there was Felton Edmonds from the Edmonds family of the
Edmonds and McKinny Funeral Home downtown. He and
his silk suits and two-tone shoes and fancy panama hats and
Willys-Knight sports roadster made it through one high rolling
summer.

I don't know which ones were annulled and which were di-
vorced, but by the time she was thirty she had gotten rid of
four husbands, because Willie York, better known as Memphis
Willie the gambler and bootlegger who was sent to the penitentiary sometime later, was also with her for about a year.

People didn't know what to make of all of that, but they had
to wag their heads and say something so the word was that she
just really didn't care any more about having married than she
cared about anything else, and they also decided that she didn't
make things happen. She just let things happen. Not anything
and everything, to be sure, just the things she became involved
with. In other words, she didn't get married any of those times
because she had picked out a husband for herself on her own.
She just let one man like her for a while and then there would
be somebody else.

One thing was always clear. She didn't have to marry or become a common-law wife to get somebody to earn a living for
her. Everybody knew that as an heiress to the old Calloway
place she not only had a home for herself and her own family if
any for the rest of her life, but she also had Miss Sister Mattie
May Billings there to run the part she rented out to long-term
roomers. Everybody knew that and most people also knew that
her share of the boarding house once known as River Queen
Inn, which her grandfather had built on Buckshaw Mill Road
back during the days of William McKinley and which was being managed for her and Miss Cute by Brother Buford Larkin,
came to more than enough for her to live well on, even without the old homeplace.

People used to forget about all of that when they got started
on Creola Calloway, or so it seemed to me. But even so, what
all the botheration always came down to was not whether she

could or would earn and pay her own way as expected or would even let somebody else look out for her. No matter what folks said, everybody knew better than that. The problem was that people felt let down because she didn't do enough with herself and the extra special God-given blessing she was born with.

Not that anybody ever really expected to reap any personal profit in dollars and cents from her success. All most expected was that she would come back through town every now and then. It was not that folks had put their hopes on her coming back and changing anything around town. Others were expected to do that. All they wanted her to do was go out and become Gasoline Point's contribution to the world of show business.

Such was people's downright exasperation once they finally came to realize that they might as well give up so far as she and all of that were concerned, that the very way they called her name (behind her back to be sure) sounded as if they had already decided what to put on her headstone: CREOLA CALLOWAY—SHE COULD HAVE BEEN FAMOUS.

And yet nobody ever really hated or even disliked her. How could you not like somebody who was just as friendly as she was good-looking? She was not a nice girl because nice girls didn't ever go into the low-down joints and honky-tonks she spent so much of her time in. Still, she was such a nice person.

Yet even so, by the time I was old enough for Mama to start worrying and warning me about fooling around and getting myself all tangled up with no good full-grown women out for nothing but a good time day in and day out, it was as if Creola Calloway had become the very incarnation of all the low-down enticements that had always led so many promising schoolboys so completely astray.

That was why Little Buddy Marshall turned out to be the one who finally got to do what I too had hoped to grow up to do, if only one time, one day. When he came back from one of his L & N hobo trips and asked me if I had made any move on her yet and I told him what Mama and some others, especially Miss Minnie Ridley Stovall had been preaching for my benefit, he said, Man she may be getting on up there with a few wrinkles after all these goddamn years of fast living and all that, but man I don't care what anybody say I got to see if I can get me some of that old pretty-ass stuff.

He said, Man, I been wanting me some of old Creola ever since I found out what this goddamn thing was made for. Man, remember what we used to say when she used to say what she used to say. Man couldn't nobody else in Gasoline Point, Mobile County, Alabama, say hello sweetheart to a little mannish boy like she could, and I ain't just talking about the sound of her voice. I'm talking about couldn't nobody make it sound that good because couldn't nobody else look at you with a smile like that.

I said, Oh man. I said, You know it too. Remembering also that she was the only grown woman you didn't have to call Miss and say ma'am to. You said Creola because that is what everybody else always said and also because it was what she herself said when she wanted you to do something for her. That was when she always used to say: Hello, sweetheart. Come here sporty. Listen darling, would you like to do Creola a great big favor and run up to Stranahan's store if I say pretty please and promise you something very nice. (Oh Lord!)

What she almost always wanted was a package of Chesterfield ready-rolls and two or three bottles of Coca-Cola and when you came back you knew she was always going to say, Now there's my sweetheart, and you also knew that she was always going to say, Keep the change, sporty. Then she was going to give you a hug and a kiss, and you would be that close, and she would be wearing cologne that always made her smell as good as she looked, even when she was smoking a cigarette. Some lagniappe!

But the more Little Buddy Marshall went on talking and I went on remembering, the more I wanted to change the subject because I didn't want to say anything about being on the spot, since you couldn't bring up anything about school with him anymore. You couldn't, but he could, and he did, because he already knew and he was rubbing it in without ever mentioning it.

As if I didn't know, and I also knew that he honestly felt that he, not I, was the one with the experience and nerve you needed to make a move on Creola Calloway because he, not I,

was the one who had skipped city and made it back from beyond far horizons (although not yet all seven of the seas) and
on his own. But I just let that go. I just said, Old Lebo, I said,
Hey man, goddamn. I said, Yeah man.

To which he said, Hey man, let me tell you something for a
fact. Man, I ain't never stopped having them goddamn dreams
about me and old Creola. Man when I think about all the
times I been thinking about that frizzly-headed quail when I
was climbing up on some tough-ass northern whore, man you
know I got to find out if I can handle that heifer. Man I got
to see if I can make somebody that pretty whisper my name in
my ear.

When I saw him again, it was about three weeks later and
when he saw me he started sporty limping and whistling "Up
a Lazy River," and as we slapped palms he winked and then he
said, Hey man guess what? and stood straddling his left hand
and snapping fingers with his right saying, Hey shit, I reckon
hey shit I fucking fucking reckon.

IX

So WELL now, hello there, Mister College Boy, the one I had
given the nod said as we came on into the upstairs room she
was using that night. She was the same shade of cinnamon-bark
brown as Deljean McCray, but her hair was slightly straighter
and glossier and I guessed that she was about three or four
years older than Deljean McCray, but her legs were not as long
because she was not quite as tall as I was.

I said, Hello Miss Pretty Lady, and she smiled and said, So
where you hail from handsome, and when I said, Mobile, she
said, You don't tell me, and looked me up and down again,
stretching her eyes as if in pleasant surprise and then she
primped her mouth and said, Well go on then, Mister City
Boy, you can't help it. And watched me blush.

Then she said, You know what I heard. They tell me you
young sports from down around the Gulf Coast and all them
cypress bayous and all that mattress moss and stuff supposed to
be real hot-natured from all that salt air and fresh seafood and
fresh fruit and all them Creole spices and mixtures and fixtures

and gumbo and all them raw oysters. And I said, I don't know about all that.

I said, I don't know anything about what other people think about us yet because this is really my first time away from down there, and she said, Well that's what they been telling me for don't know how long, probably ever since I found out what it's made for. And that's when I said what I said. Because I had been warned that if you came across as a smart aleck you were going to find yourself pussy-whipped and back out on the sidewalk in one short verse and about one-half chorus if not a verse and a couple of bars.

I said, Is that supposed to be good or bad, and she said, That's what I want to know, so come on let's find out. If I like it that means it must be good and if I don't, it's bad. And I saw my chance and said, Or maybe there's really nothing to it in the first place and got myself a quick smile and the nicest squeeze I'd had since saying goodbye to Miss Slick McGinnis.

The room surprised me. I already knew that the houses in the district were supposed to be safer and nicer than those in Bearmash Bottom, Gin Mill Crossing, or out on Ellis Hill Road, and that this was the best house in the district because it catered strictly to the campus trade. Not that I had expected any joints of any kind anywhere in that section of Alabama to be as rowdy as just plain old everyday back alley jook houses around Gasoline Point or side-street joints off the waterfront in downtown Mobile. I wasn't concerned about anything like that at all. I just hadn't expected the room to be what it was.

I had thought that there would be just a bed and maybe two chairs and a nightstand with a washbasin and soap and towels and a clothes rack. But it was as if we were in one of the cozily furnished guest rooms of a big two-story house of a prosperous small-town businessman. Not only were there double windows with frilly curtains, a vase of fresh flowers on the chest of drawers, and watercolor prints and sketches of Paris, Rome, and Greece, but also a private bathroom with hot and cold running water, which was something very special everywhere except in deluxe hotels when I was a freshman.

So come on over here, sweetie pie, she said, pulling my arms around her waist and when I moved one hand up and the other down and waited, she said, Nice, very nice, you got nice manners Mobile, and when I moved my hands and waited again she said, Well all right then, sweetie pie, but just a minute, just a minute, and she stepped back and slipped off her boa-trimmed kimono and sat on the bed and kicked off her slippers and when I pulled off my shoes and stripped down, she said, Well hello sweet popper shopper. Let's have some *fun*. Let's do some *stuff*. She said, Let's have us a *ball*. She said, Me and you, baby boy, me and you, me and *you*!

You couldn't hear any voices in any of the other rooms down the hall. There was the static-blurred music and chatter on the radio downstairs for a while, but then there was only what was happening in the room where I was as she whispered sometimes with her lips and tongue touching my ear and sometimes as if to herself. But even so I was still conscious of the dark, damp mid-October night outside and the campus that far away back across town.

I had the feeling that she went on whispering not only because that was something she did sometimes but also because she really wanted me to enjoy myself. So I said, Talk to me, big mama, talk to me hot mama, talk to me pretty mama, and she said, Me and you snookie pie, me and you sweet daddy me and you sweet papa stopper, and it was a very nice ride because that was the way she wanted it to be. Because as smart about things like that as I had already become before I came to college that year, I was also sharp enough to realize that I wouldn't have been any match at all for a pro like her if she had wanted to turn me into an easy trick.

Afterward in the bathroom she said, Here, let me do this, and I raised both arms as if she'd said hands up and she winked and said, I hope you realize you getting some very special brown-skin service over here schoolboy, and I said, You bet I do, Miss Stuff, and she said, I heard that Mobile, that's pretty good Mobile if it mean what some people mean by it, and I said, How about something you knew how to strut second to none how about something you got to watch because it's so mellow, and she said, And what about something you trying to hand because you already so full of it and ain't even dry behind the ears yet.

But you still all right with me, Mobile, she said and then she also said, You a nice boy, Mobile, I mean sure enough nice like you been brought up to be. Don't take much to tell when it come to something like that. When you and your buddy first walked in down there, the very minute I laid eyes on you I said to myself, un-hunh, un-hunh, un-hunh, and then here you come picking me.

And I said, What did you think of that? and she said, I had to wonder if you thought you so smart you had my number but since there was something about you I said to myself, I'm just going to give him the benefit of the doubt and find out what he think he putting down. And I said, I sure am glad you did and I sure do thank you for such a special treat, and she said, Well, that's what you get for being such a nice boy.

While I was pulling my clothes back on, she sat on the edge hunched forward with her legs crossed and her left elbow on her knee smoking and asking me about Mobile and the Gulf Coast and when she stood up I had the feeling that she really wanted us to go on talking. So when she said, You better come back to see me now and I really mean it, I got the feeling that she was just as interested in talking again as she was in doing business.

I said, I sure will, but I didn't say when because I didn't have any idea when there would be enough cash for something like that again. There was no point in putting up a front; and you couldn't put on the poor mouth, so I just smiled and touched her as if I were really looking forward to it, and she said, You sure better.

Then she said, Come on now, I got to get you out of here so you can be back across town before that curfew sound. Ain't no use to you missing that since you already got what you come over here for, and I said, And more, much more, and she said, Tell me anything, Mobile, but you take care of yourself and hit them books and don't be no stranger over here.

Downstairs, she left me in the little sitting room to wait for my old pardner and he came in from down the hall before I even sat down, and back outside in the damp central Alabama autumn night once more with our sports jackets draped over our shoulders cape-style, we slapped palms, and I said, Hey, man, goddamn, hey, man, how can I ever thank you enough for getting Old Troop to include me on this, and he went into his penny-dreadful heh-heh-heh again and said, You can't, old pardner. It's not allowed. Absolutely not. Strictly forbidden.

Rigoureusement interdit! which he articulated better than any student I ever met and which, what with our make-believe capes, also turned us into two elegant *flâneurs* winding our way back across fin-de-siècle Paris from Montmartre to the Left Bank.

But once we were back in Atelier 359 with the lights out but still too high to fall right off to sleep, he said, One more thing, old pardner. Tell me. When you hit the homestretch, did she start snapping her fingers, and I cut in and said, Saying sic 'em, and he said, Yes, and I said, Or maybe sic 'em baby or sic 'em daddy, and he said, So yours too, and I said, Not this one but I know what you mean and he said, It caught me by surprise but it was really something, and I said a little something idiomatic. I said, A little down-home stuff for the city boy from up north. Man, she had your number as soon as she saw us.

On our second visit which was during the study break just before the fall term finals and which was also a surprise treat from Old Troop, it was as if my new friend in the district had in the meantime become my old friend, if not an old long lost friend. When we checked in and turned around, she was looking down from the staircase with one hand on the railing and one on her hip.

Well, look who finally made it back, she said, talking to me but looking over my head as if at nothing in particular. Then she said, Get yourself on up here, Mobile. Where you been, boy? I thought I told you not to come making yourself no stranger over here. You make people feel like maybe you done decided not to have nothing more to do with them or something. And I said, No days like that. I said, Never no days like that for me and you.

I said, You know how it is when you're a first-term freshman, especially when you're on a full scholarship. You got to keep your grade point average up in the outstanding bracket, and you also have to convince the people on the academic merits committee that you are here because you really mean business, you see for me to make just a fair or even a good passing grade is exactly the same thing as flat flunking out.

Hey so you up here on one of them special scholarship things, she said, standing back to look me over again nodding her head up and down in what looked for all the world to me at that time with very thinly disguised fairy godmotherly pride and approval. Now that's nice. Now that really is very nice.

Then she stood back with her hands akimbo, smiling while shaking her head in mock disbelief and said, Now see there. Class. I knew it. Because I can tell. As soon as I set eyes on you, I said to myself, um-hunh, um-hunh, um-hunh, and I also said, I bet he think he cute too, but you didn't smile that kind of smile and that's how come I liked you right off. You know what you smile like with them bright eyes squinting like that? A very nice boy full of mischievousness.

But talking about some more smart eyes, don't think I didn't pick up on how that cute buddy you come over here with was casing this joint right along with all them friendly smiles and respectful manners. Sarajean was telling me about him and she said he is definitely the nicest northern city boy she ever come across and she been in this life for a whole lot of more years than I been. Some we get in here think they so much because they from up there, and don't know doodly squat. But she say your buddy got real class and she swear he also just thumbs down the smartest fellow she ever met anywhere.

She sure did get that right, I said, and she said, I told her ain't no flies on my down-home Mobile boy either. Then reaching for my belt buckle she said, But later for all that. Now come on, show me how much you been missing me because it's been so long.

It was the same room as before. There was the same blurred-static sound of radio music and chatter somewhere downstairs again, but as she helped me out of my shorts and I sat down to pull off my socks this time there was also the dry smokeless warmth from the flame-yellow grill of the gas space heater because the temperature outside was dropping toward the freezing point.

Then as she began whispering and brushing her warm gingerbread-spongy lips against my neck and ears again as before, but also with a few new words added, there was also the shushing and shivery winter night breeze buffeting the shuttered and shuddering window frames and whining and shrilling away through the December bareness of the yard trees. But after a very little while all of that was only another part of what

I would remember as the background for me and her doing me and you and you and me the second time.

So if I ask you who she was you going to tell me? she said, pulling on her kimono and following me into the bathroom again, and when I said, Who *who* was, she said, Now come on boy. Don't be trying to crosstalk me.

She said, Now, you know good and well what I'm talking about and don't come telling me I don't know what I'm talking about. The one you learned all of your nice little bedroom manners from; that's who. You might be one of them scholarship geniuses that can learn anything in a split second. But you can't fool me about nothing like this, boy. You didn't just pick up on something on no one go-round. Some woman know exactly what she doing had a hold of you and don't tell me she didn't.

She sure did, I said, *thinking about Miss Slick McGinnis and her velvet smooth tea-cake tan skin and her Josephine Baker rubber-doll body, and how when she used to come click clacking along Buckshaw sidewalk past Papa Gumbo Willie McWorthy's barbershop and up the steps and into Stranahan's store all the men and boys on the block used to fall silent and then just look at each other and shake their heads and also about how the windup gramophone record that went with the way she walked was the one with the words that said, I want to go where you go and do what you do then I'll be happy.*

But I didn't name any names because that was not what was expected. All you had to do was admit that there was somebody. So I just said that there was somebody who decided that was the way she was going to help keep me out of trouble and finish high school and win my chance to go to college as so many people by that time had come to expect me to do.

Well, good for her, she said, and as we came back into the bedroom you could also hear the wind rising and whirring through the bare branches outside the shutters again. She all right with me whoever she is and wherever she may be these days, she said, waiting for me to put everything back on. I hope you know how lucky you been and I am pretty sure you do and that's another reason you all right with me with your little old cute, sly fox, narrow-eye smile.

Then as she hooked her arm into mine and we came on along the hall to the head of the stairs, she also said, I know you know good and, well, I ain't just talking about controlling your nature because I'm satisfied I don't have to tell you ain't nobody going to be complaining about no wham-bam-thank-you-ma'am in no house like this. Now if I was to be talking about some tough-ass old hens want you spend all night with them, that's another thing.

She said, When it come to all of that what I mean is, you might know how to do what you supposed to do with that nice sweet thing all night, but the first thing you better know is when you supposed to keep it in your pants. So the one that schooled you about that deserve a lot of credit, she said.

And then she said, What I'm trying to tell you right now, that you all right with me because whoever she was she didn't spoil you so rotten that you go around acting like somebody supposed to feel like you doing them a big favor just because you having something to do with them. I'm just trying to tell you how much a woman can appreciate you for being so nice on top of all that other stuff. So now just get on out of here and I hope I see you again before long.

I didn't realize that all of that had anything to do with her in any sense that was directly personal and private until she told me what she told me about herself that next time, which was also the Old Trooper's last treat and so also the end of the orientation leeway he had allowed his two trail recruits to get themselves zeroed in on campus and in certain outlying regions as well.

So what I remember thinking about as we whistled our way through town and then came on across the highway and into the district that night was about how in the letter with my roommate's February allowance (and the treat), the Old Trooper had used the word triangulation, not orientation. Both were about map making and map reading and also about personal adjustment, but triangulation was also a military term that was very much about target practice.

That was what was on my mind when I rearrived in the district on my third visit that Thursday night. It was not as if I didn't also remember everything that had been said the time before. After all, I had repeated it verbatim to my roommate the following morning. But one reason that I hadn't stopped to think much less to consider about any of it was that by that time I had become so used to having people talk to me about such things that most of it usually sounded like reiteration rather than information.

Not that I ever really closed my ears to any of it. Not me. Not Miss Melba's Scooter. Not Miss Tee's Mister. Because for all the clichés, platitudes, and sometimes downright mushy sentimentality about making folks proud (mostly without any mention whatsoever of envy, resentment, backbiting, spite, or slander) and for all the same old stuff about taking advantage of opportunities other people either never had or had and didn't take, there was still the fact that whatever they said was something they sincerely believed they were obliged to say so perhaps the main point of it all was to remind you of precisely that which everybody knew you were supposed to be mindful of already.

Anyway, it was not until she said what she said while I was getting dressed that third time that I realized that she was really concerned about something that had much more to do with her own personal situation in particular than with me on general principle.

She had asked me to tell her some more about growing up on the outskirts of Mobile, and when I came to the part about school and told her about how a lot of students used to come all the way out to Mobile County Training School not only from within the city limits of downtown Mobile itself and from Prichard and Cedar Grove and Chickasaw Whistler and Maysville, but also from as far away across the bay as Daphne, Fairhope, and Magnolia Springs, she said, Now see there, you never learn unless you ask. Boy, that sounds just like the kind of school I'm sure going to be trying my best to get my Roger in one of these days when he old enough.

Roger was a three-year-old son that she had left with her mother, who was now living in Fort Deposit. She didn't even mention anything at all about who Roger's father was, and I didn't ask anything. From what she said about how she ran away from home to go to Birmingham, I was pretty sure that she had not been married and that when she became pregnant she had had to look out for herself, but she mentioned that only in passing because what she was mainly if not only really interested in telling me about was the kind of man she wanted Roger to be.

Not *what* she wanted him to be, such as a doctor, lawyer, businessman, teacher, or a political leader. That was going to be up to him to choose once he had come along far enough in school to make his own choice. The main thing she wanted him to become was somebody worthwhile and also somebody you could always count on.

I just want him to have his chance to make something out of hisself. I sure God don't want him to end up on a chain gang in no penitentiary. I don't want him out there trying to lie and steal and cheat and double-cross his way. Just look at you, she said. That's what I'm talking about. Done made it all the way up here in college because you can make it on your own scholarship. That's what I'm talking about. I'm talking about, I want my Roger to turn out like you turning out so far. Boy, your folks got to be mighty proud of you and I'm sure you know it too, you rascal you.

X

As FOR mothers, I said one night not long afterward, I have three at the same time. Because along with Mama herself there had always been Miss Tee, and then when I had come that far as a pupil over at Mobile County Training School there was also Miss Lexine Metcalf who not only said but also acted as if I also belonged to her.

The only thing I remember that Mama actually told me about my kinship to her was about how all babies came from the soft dark insides of a very special stump hole deep in the brambles and moss-fringed thickets where the baby man hid you like a seed to be found like an Easter egg on your birthday by the woman he picked to be your mother, who was the one who swaddled you to her bosom and gave you nourishment and kept you safe from the bad old booger man. Which was why your mother was the one you already owed your obedience long before you came to realize that you also had a father.

That was all she had ever told me before I overheard what she said that night at Mister Ike Meadow's wake, and that is the way she let it stay even when she told me what she told me about not letting that thing in my pants get me in trouble because she had decided that the time had come when she had to start warning me about getting girls in the family way. As for the contradiction between this version of the miracle of birth and the other, I am pretty sure that she just took it for granted that by that time I had found out enough about men and women to understand exactly what she was concerned about and the main point of it was to keep me from having to drop out of school to get married. In any case, she never revised her original version of the arrival of babies, just as she never revised her original version of Santa Claus.

All I had ever heard about me and Miss Tee was that she was my auntie, and at first that was what I used to call her. Actually, what I used to say was Ann Tee. Then I changed it to Miss Tee. But what she called me was not her nephew but her Mister as in Mister Man, and I always knew that she was a very special kind of auntie, because everybody knew that she was not Mama's flesh and blood sister, like Aunt Sue from Atmore and Aunt Sis from Greenville. In fact, she almost always acted as if Mama and Papa were really *her* aunt and uncle.

For the most part, people in Gasoline Point in those days didn't spend very much time puzzling over such relationships unless there was some special reason to do so. After all, just about everybody in town had aunts and uncles, not to mention cousins close and distant who included perhaps as many if not more self-elected kinfolks as blood relatives. But there were also always at least a few aunts- and uncles-at-large around. Like Aunt Classie Belsaw, for instance, and Uncle Jim Bob Ewing, to name only two, who for their part called everybody not Nephew or Niece but either Son or Daughter or Brother or Sister, meaning little brother and little sister.

I don't remember ever hearing anybody wondering about what all of that was about and certainly not about how it all came about. It was just the way things were and one day you realized that you already knew about it. In due time, you also came to realize that there were also aunts- and uncles-at-large who were called Mama and Papa and Daddy or even

Papadaddy, as in Big Mama and Big Daddy and once again it was as if nobody had ever had to stop and define them because somehow you had already found out that old folks were who they were by virtue of being survivors-in-residence, who were there to tell the tale, who could give eyewitness testimony about bygone but ever-to-be-remembered times in which definitive events came to pass.

Nor did anyone have to question the fact that such mamas (and hot mamas) as Ma Rainey the blues singer and vaudeville prima donna and such papas and daddies as even Papa Gumbo Willie McWorthy were neither older nor wiser than such venerable aunts- and uncles-at-large as Aunt Classie Belsaw and Uncle Jim Bob Ewing who after all were the very embodiment of endurance and wisdom. Hot mamas and papadaddies were who they were because they were not only experts in their line of work but also pros and past masters who were qualified by the unique richness of personal experience to exemplify for peers and juniors alike how things should be done. Thus, when a young man called himself Papa or Daddy, he was bragging that he was so much better than his competitors that he could turn any contest into a demonstration lesson in fundamentals.

What made such youthful presumption acceptable to people in Gasoline Point in those days was the fact that it showed that you were not afraid to put yourself on the spot. If it turned out that you were only running off at the mouth and couldn't perform on the level you had set up for yourself, you only brought public disgrace on yourself. Once you proved yourself, you could admit that you were the champion who must defend his title. That was okay. But any further expression of gratuitous self-esteem was soundly condemned as the height of unforgivable arrogance.

Miss Tee was the expert auntie who told me about fairy-tale beanstalks, and she also used to say Jack be nimble, Jack be quick, Jack jump over the candlestick, ooping me up and out and dedoodling me over and back down and enfolding me to the bosom of herself again. She also riddled me riddles and nourished me on nursery rhymes and caught me with catches and girded me for existential guessing games.

She had a good-fairy smile and fairy-godmother ring fingers, and I can still remember her story-time voice saying once upon a time over my shoulder and that close to my ear as she rocked me rock-a-bye in Mama's rocking chair. It was as if all of that had always been there along with everything else, and even before I was old enough to know what a storybook as such actually was, I could help her turn the page so that I could look at the pictures on the next page while her voice went on spinning out the yarn of the story for that day.

As far back as I can recollect, seeing her coming back again I can also remember that it was as if she had only just rearrived from the far blue ever-and-ever land of storybook castles and boy blue derring-do once more and that I was going to find out something else about how heroes set forth to seek their fortune and about how they prepare themselves to brave the elements and to slay dragons and giants and other dangerous creatures because such, being their destiny, was also their duty.

I was still very young when she got married to Mister Paul Miles Boykin, a stacking-yard straw boss at Buckshaw Mill, but from then on I knew what neighborhood she lived in, because you could see her house from Miss Betty Dubose's corner when on your way up Dodge Mill Road toward the crawfish pond and the streetcar loop; and you could also see it from the end of Gins Alley as soon as you passed Miss Blue Eula's gate on your way to the L & N post office and looked to your left along the street that ran from the tank yard and across Dodge Mill Road to the A T & N and the pecan orchard.

Whichever route you took, her house was only about two and a half blocks away and so was still a part of Gasoline Point although it was also another neighborhood, just as Gins Alley was still another neighborhood. It was called Main Street, but it really should have been called Second Street because the main thoroughfare where all of the business concerns were located and along which most of the traffic came and went was Buckshaw Road, which later on (at the time when the Cochrane Bridge was built across that part of Mobile River) became a part of U.S. 90 and the old Spanish Trail.

When you opened the gate there was a cowbell sound, and there were flower beds on both sides of the brick walk as you came on toward the trellis screening the swing porch. Then when you came up the steps by the potted plants and into the parlor there were heavy draperies that matched the chair cushions and a big bouquet of fresh flowers in a blue vase on the lace-covered center table in front of the settee and bright blue-and-yellow flower patterns on the store-bought wallpaper.

I also remember the high beds with the fancy fringed counterpanes and frilly window curtains I saw as we went through the back rooms on our way to the kitchen that first time, and after we ate a sandwich Miss Tee and Mama went on talking and drinking coffee. She said I could go out into the backyard if I wanted to, and as soon as I opened the door onto the screened-in porch, I saw the toy store playthings.

Then that house turned out to be the first place I was allowed to go when I became old enough to be that far from the chinaberry yard on my own, and in the beginning you had to go by way of Gins Alley because of all the heavy traffic along Dodge Mill Road, and when you arrived she was always waiting either at the gate or on the front steps, and there was always something that she said she had been saving as a little surprise, and when time was up she always went with you to the gate and handed you a package to take back to Mama.

The best times were when Mister Paul Miles Boykin was not there. Because whenever he was, even if he just happened to make a quick circle by the house during the twelve o'clock whistle break, he would be watching and cutting his eyes at you even when he didn't say the same old thing about not being able to waste all of his time playing when he was a child.

One time he showed up at our house as if from the clear blue sky (but probably directly from a spluttering argument with Miss Tee) and asked Mama if he could hire me to run errands and do chores for him on a weekly basis so I could realize that I had to earn my keep and pay my way because nothing comes free in this world. And Mama said, Be time enough for him to realize that, and she said, He got to be a child before he can be a man, and she also said, He sure better mind his manners and show due respect for grown folks because God knows I don't mind them chastising him and I better not hear tell of him opening his mouth back at them neither, let alone sassing them. But me and Whit the ones raising him and I don't want nobody bossing him around and abusing him for no little old

few cents a week, don't care who it is, and don't care what color
neither. To which he said, I'm Edie's husband now and I'm
thinking of his welfare, and Mama said, I want him to grow up
a step at a time, and he sure will be coming to all of that soon
enough. Too soon if you ask me.

Then one day Deljean McCray was there standing on the front
steps below Miss Tee waiting for me as I came through the
cowbell gate. She was that much older and that many more
inches taller than I was and she stood with her arms akimbo,
smiling down at me like a newfound cousin. Then she took
my hand and we went around the house to the backyard, and
the first thing we ever played on was the seesaw, and I still get
a sweet, warm feeling every time I remember how she looked
bouncing and kicking her heels and opening her long rubbery
cinnamon-brown legs with her skirt billowing and shutting
like a parasol as she sang, Seesaw, cut the butter, seesaw. Then
we also had a good time with the toy store playthings on the
screened-in kitchen porch, and when I came back outside to
the live oak and got on the swing, she stood up behind me
and pumped so high that you could see out over the back
fence and all the way across the dog-fennel meadow between
there and the telegraph poles above the mill-quarter's houses
along that part of Buckshaw Road.

  She said, So you the little old cute Scooter boy Miss Edie
Belle always carrying on so much about be coming over here,
and she held my hand again, looking at me with her head tilted
and her eyes twinkling with catlike curiosity and puppylike mischief. Then she said, Boy, Miss Edie Belle sure real crazy about
you, always calling you her little Mister. Just wait till you see
my little Mister. He'll be coming over for a visit. So this is you,
she said, and then she said, and I guess you all right with me,
too. So you want to be friends and play-like cousins.

  I said okay because I was already very glad that she was going to be there. I said, You all right with me, too, Deljean.
Because I liked her cinnamon-brown skin and the cinnamon-
brown tree bark she chewed and smelled like even when she
also smelled somewhat like sardine oil, and I also liked the
Vaseline sheen on her braids although I never did like girls
with braided hair as much as I liked frizzly-headed girls like

Charlene Wingate. In those days I liked it better when girls with hair like that wore it either bobbed and poroed like Miss Slick McGinnis or hot-combed and styled like the most popular blues singers and vaudeville entertainers, and so did she as I found out as soon as she was old enough for it to be dressed for special occasions.

When I went back over there that next time, I could tell that she was glad to see me even before she said what she said, and I said I was very glad to see her too, and she said, Now come on now tell the truth now you're not just playing with me because you come over here to see Miss Edie Belle. I'm talking about sure enough now, Scooter, saying my name exactly as somebody does who has been thinking about you since you were there the last time, and I said, Me too, Deljean. I said, I'm talking about sure enough too. And she said, Well, I reckon we must still be good friends then so come on, let's go play.

The time after that was when she said, Maybe if you ask your mama maybe Miss Edie Belle will let me come over to your house sometime and play too, and I said I would and I did and that was when I realized that she hadn't met anybody else her size to play with yet because Mister Paul Miles Boykin did not want her to get herself led astray by a pack of good-for-nothing mill-quarters niggers. Not that I was really surprised one bit. So I certainly was not surprised when she told me that as soon as he found out that she and I were becoming playmates, he said what he said about her not having any time to be working loafing around playing with the likes of little old mister precious me instead of earning her bed and board.

It was not long afterward that she ran away the first time. She was gone for a week and I missed her as if I had known her all my life. I missed her every day not because I had ever seen her every day but because I didn't know where she was or if I would ever see her again, and when Mama told me she was back, I could hardly wait to see her again and when I got there she saw me coming through the gate and said, Here come Scooter, and she was still trying to smile down at me even with her face bruised and swollen like it was because Mister Paul Miles Boykin had finally traced and found her up in Chickasaw Bend. He had slapped and cuffed her all the way back along the A T & N railroad in the dark.

That's all right. Don't you worry about me, Scooter, she said when I touched her and asked her if it still hurt bad, and she didn't cry when she told about what had happened.

In fact, I don't remember ever seeing her cry about anything. Sometimes she used to get so mad about something that her eyes would water but that was not the same thing as crying because when you cry about something happening to you that means you feel sorry for yourself. But when you get so angry about something that tears almost come that just shows how much determination you have.

She says, Boy you don't know, Scooter. Boy, you don't know nothing at all about my uncle Paul Miles Boykin. She said, Boy you ain't never seen nobody like that in your whole life. She said, I'm talking about every time he think he got to chastise somebody about something, here he come, slapping you up side the head before he even tell you what he mad about, and when you try to move out of the way and ask him what's wrong, he subject to pick up anything he can get his hands on and chuck it at you. And then come talking about he love me because I'm his flesh and blood kin and he don't want me to end up in the gutter and some old stuff like that, I declare, Scooter.

But that's all right with me, Scooter. She also said, That's all right with me because I don't care no more because I know good and well he crazy. I declare before God that man just as angry as he can be. And you know something? If it wasn't for Miss Edie Belle I never would be coming back here no more. Don't care if he tried to kill me to make me come back. He the one always talking about looking after me because I'm his dead sister's child, but Miss Edie Belle she the one know how to be somebody's auntie and treat you like you supposed to do what you do around the house because you at *home* and you got your tasks just like everybody else. But him, I'm telling you Scooter. Boy, you pretty lucky. I know what I'm talking about. You got Miss Melba and Uncle Whit and you got Miss Edie Belle on top of that, and they all treat you like you somebody special, she said, and you know why, and I said, Why? and she said, Because they want you to be somebody special and you know something, me too.

I don't remember how old I was when Miss Tee first said you are my mister because it is as if that is what she had always called me, and I cannot remember when I didn't already remember her voice and her eyes with her face that close and then her cheeks against mine and her godmotherly arms around my shoulders smelling like rainbows look.

But however young I may still have been at the time in question, I was also already old enough to have heard enough of her storybook stories to realize that when she put the tips of her fingers on your shoulders and held you an arm's length away smiling her fairy godmother smile at you, it was her secret way of saying arise Sir Knight and sally forth doing good deeds time after time after time in place after place after place.

So first there was Mama herself, whose little scootabout manchild I already was even before I was yet old enough to stay up late enough to hear the tales told on midwinter nights in the semicircle around the fireplace and during midsummer evenings on the swing porch with mosquito smoke rising and spreading in the chinaberry yard. Then there was also Miss Tee who began calling me her Mister in her storybook voice rocking me back and forth in Mama's cane-bottom rock-a-bye riverboat rocking chair.

By the time Little Buddy Marshall came along, I had outgrown most of the playthings in Miss Tee's backyard and what he and I used to spend most of our times together doing was rambling here and there and elsewhere like explorers and pioneers who were bred and born in the briar patch and we also hunted with a slingshot and the main game we lived to play was baseball. Sometimes I also thought of myself as a boxer with eyes and hands as quick as Joe Gans and a six-inch uppercut like the one and only Jack Johnson.

When he stopped in with me to meet her the first time that day when we were on our way to the shortcut through the kite pasture to get to the foot of Buckshaw Mill Road and the construction camp at the site where the Cochrane Bridge was going to be built, I knew he would like her and the first chance he got he nudged me and whispered, Hey shit I reckon old buddy boy, hey shit I reckon. Then when the time finally came to open her surprise package of sandwiches and tea cake cookies that we had promised to save until the twelve o'clock whistles started, he also said, Man, you sure got yourself some big auntie.

And that is when he also said, Now that's what I call a sure enough fairy story godmother, buddy boy, which was really something coming from him, because as much as he always liked all of the things you found out about from the chimney corner and the steps of the swing porch and especially from the barbershop, he really didn't have very much interest in storybooks as such. As far as he was concerned, there was no difference between storybooks and schoolbooks, and he never did come to like anything at all about going to school, not even the playground activities. He didn't even like football and basketball and volleyball, which were all school-term games in those days. Later on when cowboy movies began to become popular, he liked the adventures of William S. Hart and Tom Mix and Buck Jones and Ken Maynard and hated crooks like Bull Montana as much as I did, but he never did become interested in reading anything about the wild West either, not even the Indians.

But whether Little Buddy Marshall knew it or not, Miss Tee was not only what fairy godmothers were really about, she had also always been a part of what school bell time was all about and when I became school age, she had been the one who gave me my first book satchel and blackboard eraser and collapsible aluminum drinking cup, and Mama had let her be the one to take me to be registered in the primer class at Mobile County Training School that first Monday morning.

XI

YOU COULDN'T see any part of the downtown business district from anywhere on the campus, and except during the wee hours and on weekends you couldn't even hear the courthouse clock striking until you rounded the curve and passed by the wrought-iron gate to the old plantation mansion known as the Old Strickland Place. But you could walk all the way from the academic area to Old Confederate Square in less than twenty minutes.

Then you were at the hub of a cotton market town that was also the county seat, and across North Main Street from the sheriff's office and the jail and the municipal complex was the

Farmer's Enterprise Bank and from that corner you could see along the sidewalk past the movie theater and the next street to the brick and lumber yard of the Carmichael Construction Supply Company and you could also see all of the stores on the other three sides of the elm-shaded square.

In those days there was also a Merchants Bank, and there were also two drugstores, a Woolworth's, a Bradley's Furniture, and I don't know exactly how many clothing stores, specialty shops, cafes, and lunch counters, but I do remember how Goldwyn's Dry Goods store and Ransom's Bargain Emporium used to look, and everybody remembers Tate and Davidson's two-story department store.

My old roommate has a pretty good reason to remember the young women's Intercollegiate Toggery shop that was next door to Tate and Davidson's in those days, but most people have probably long since forgotten Dudley Philpot and his General Merchandise Store. Sometimes I forget all about him, too. I wonder if Will Spradley has ever forgotten, but I'm pretty certain that you would have to prod Giles Cunningham for a while and then he could probably say, Yeah, I think I can picture the old son-of-a-bitch. What the hell happened and what the hell was it all about?

The heavy interstate traffic westbound toward Montgomery and points south to Florida and the Gulf Coast and eastbound toward Phoenix City and the Georgia state line, Atlanta, and points north, came through on the south side of the square, so from the corner where the telephone central was you could see gas stations and automobile dealers' pennants in both directions and the bus stop beyond the light and power building.

The downtown post office was one block due south of the square on the tree-lined street which was called South Main and also South End and which was also where the white supremacist white high school, several white Protestant churches, and the neatly kept but not very old homes of a number of the most prosperous local white businessmen lived in those days.

Most of the downtown white families who could trace their bloodlines back to the earliest settlers lived on North Main, also known as North End which was an avenue of mostly pre–Civil War homes and with a center strip of shrubbery and flower beds and which began on the north side of the square and ended two blocks beyond the corner where it turned into a thoroughfare leading out to the campus.

As I had already found out in the library during the week before I graduated from Mobile County Training School, what the earliest settlers had originally established back during the days even before Alabama became a colony was a French trading post on an old Creek Indian trail. Then the post had become an English crossroads settlement and after that a federal garrison during the time of the Andrew Jackson anti-Indian campaign that ended with the Battle of Horseshoe Bend. It had become a cotton market town and the county seat during the flush times before the Civil War, none of which ever gave it any claim to fame even in Alabama. But since the turn of the century, it had been known all over the country as a college town.

What you saw as the bus pulled in were the mud-caked, dust-powdered jalopies and trucks and also a few horse-drawn buckboard wagons parked diagonally into the curb around the square, and there were the late summer shade trees and the concrete park benches along the gravel walks, and the gray stone Civil War monument to honor the brave.

It was the statue of a Confederate army infantryman facing North Main, and around the pedestal there was a spiked wrought-iron fence enclosing a flower bed in which, as I found out later on, there were always flowers in bloom, even in the dead of winter when they had to be grown in terra-cotta pots in a greenhouse and transferred pot by pot and embedded in straw and pine needles.

So I knew that I would also find out that you-know-which townspeople would have, if not one thousand plus one or more tall tales, riddles, rhymes, catches, and jokes to retell about Old Man Johnny Reb, as they called the rifleman, they would have at least two or three dozen. All you had to do was listen. You didn't even have to be alert. All you had to do was be in the right place at the right time.

And to be sure, there was one that you could always count on hearing repeated or, indeed, replayed every year when the first really hard cold snap hit town. All you had to do was be someplace, say like the old Greyhound bus station when the lie swapping used to get started in the semicircle of hand and rump warmers huddled around the radiator in the waiting room, as if it were an old potbelly stove.

Man, talking about a cold day. Man, Old man Johnny Reb up yonder on the courthouse square feel this weather this morning. Man, I bet you anything old stuff got his boney butt ass down off that goddamn thing last night.

Man, I don't blame him a bit.

Got rid of that old musket and brought his frostbitten peckerwood ass on down off from up there in a hurry, pardner.

Man, when old hawk hit that sapsucker, he said time to unass this area, colonel sir.

Man, so that's who that was I seen all snuggled up over yonder on the sidewalk by the drugstore last night.

Man, doing what?

Man, what you reckon? Asking somebody where he can get him a long pull on a fifth of sour mash, white lightning, rotgut, or anything with some kick to it.

Now, man, you know Old Man Johnny Reb know better than that. So what did you tell him?

Man, I told him that even a short snort been against the law in this county ever since they passed that Eighteenth Amendment back in nineteen-nineteen.

Man, you told him right. Been right up there with the county jail less than a block off to his right elbow all this time now.

But shoot, y'all. Maybe that's exactly how come he know good and well you can get all the bootleg liquor you can pay for right here in the city limits, Prohibition or no Prohibition. All you got to do is make the right contact, and you look just like a drinking man to me.

Yeah, man, but Old Man Johnny Reb suppose to be up there watching out for the Yankees.

Yeah, but, man, maybe the Yankees Old Man Johnny really on the lookout for is them revenue agents. Man, I wouldn't put it pass Cat Rogers. Man, peckerwoods hate them folks.

Man, I don't care what Old Man Johnny Reb supposed to be doing up there, his gray ass liked to froze blue and dropped off last night.

There were also mud-caked and dust-powdered jalopies and trucks and more buckboards all along the side streets where the markets, the grocery stores, and the hardware and repair shops were in those days. But most of the larger trucks and flatbed trailers were always pulled up on the back streets and in the alleys off the back streets where the loading ramps of the seed, feed, and fertilizer warehouses were.

I used to stay away from these blocks, especially on Saturdays, because I didn't want to have to see all of the crap games so many of the farmhands always used to seem to make the weekly trip into town to get into with the local hustlers. Not that I was against gambling as such on any principle. Certainly not on any principle based on the conventional morality underlying the disapproval of the church folks of Gasoline Point.

Not me. Not the self-elected godson of the likes of old Luzana Cholly and Stagolee Dupas (*fils*) plus Gus the Gator all rolled in one. Not the longtime scoot buddy of Little Buddy Marshall. Not the one to whom the sight of sailors and longshoremen rolling dice in the cargo sheds along the piers off Commerce Street and elsewhere on the waterfront was as much a part of the storybook world of the seven seas as the dry-dock elevators and the foghorns and the acres of naval stores out at Taylor Lowenstein's maritime supply yards.

But I felt the way I felt about the back street crapshooters because it was as if they were still stuck in the same rut as the slaves of a hundred years ago, who used to be brought into town by the plantation master or overseer to reload the cotton wagons with supplies and provisions, and then used to spend their free time gambling away whatever slaves had to bet and fight each other about while the master or overseer finished his transactions and no doubt also found amusement elsewhere.

Not all slaves spent their precious free time in town on Saturday, shooting craps and indulging in frivolity, to be sure. According to many of the most often repeated storybook as well as fireside yarns, there were also those would-be and soon-to-be north-bound fugitives who deliberately gave off an air of frivolity not to spend such precious free time to pay court to in-town house servants if not sweethearts brought in on wagons from other plantations, but to make contact with whoever (sometimes male, sometimes female) could pass on the latest news and practical operational grapevine information concerning the signs, signals, passwords, and timetables of the local trunk line of the Underground Railroad.

Surely some instances of runaway slaves using the dice game as a cover have been recorded as historical fact. But in the stories I grew up hearing, the very notion of an invisible network of black and white people working together to help slaves steal away to freedom was no less farfetched to the overwhelming majority of back alley bone-rollers as all of the preaching and praying and singing about chariots taking you to heaven somewhere in the sky, and they almost always poked fun at it one way or another. Some said and may actually have convinced themselves that the so-called Underground Railroad was either a trick that Old Master and the overseer played to find out who they could trust, or it was a trap set up by rogue peckerwoods who stole slaves from one plantation and sold them to another in another place.

Anyway I was scandalized, outraged, and all but exasperated as soon as I turned the corner and saw them and realized what they were doing that bright blue second Saturday afternoon of that first October. There they were and I was already that close and there was nothing you could do about it except try to get on along past it as if I didn't even see them. But one of them had already spotted me the minute I came in sight.

Well, goddamn, if here ain't another one of them.

What they doing coming all around back up in here? Ain't nobody sent for none of them as I knows of.

Me neither. Maybe he lost or something.

I wouldn't be a bit surprised once you get their head out of all them books.

Hey, you lost Mister Collegeboy? Hey, you, yeah, you. I'm talking to you. Yeah you. I axed you a question. You want something around here, Mister Collegeboy? What you looking for around here? What you looking at? Ain't you never seen nobody rolling no bones before? Ain't you never seen nobody drinking no whiskey before? Well, now you can tell them you seen some low-down niggers galloping the shit out of them old affikan dominoes all over the place back in here and looka here, you can also tell them you seen me drinking myself some good old corn whiskey and then tell them I say win, lose, or draw

I'm still going to have enough left to buy me some good old cookshop grub and then I going to buy me some good old city girl pussy. You goddamn right, I'm going buy me some county seat whorehouse pussy.

Aw, man, a not so loudmouthed one said, them college boys don't even know what you talking about. Them college boys studying about bookkeeping and joggerfy and all them kind of things. Them college boys ain't got no time to be fooling around with what you talking about.

Now wait a minute, another one said. That ain't the way I heard it. Now the way I heard it, them books ain't the only thing them college boys like to stick their nose up in, if you get my latter clause.

Hey, wait a minute there, the loud one said again, coming toward me for the first time as I moved on along the block. I had slowed down just because I knew they had expected me to speed up. Hey, hold on there boy when I'm talking to you.

That's when I stopped and turned and said what I said, which had exactly the effect I had wanted and expected it to have.

I said, Sounds to me like somebody is just about to let his big loud snaggle mouth get his bony ass kicked raw, and he stopped where he was and then he said, Who you think you talking to and I said, Ain't nothing to think about, old pardner. I'm talking to anybody too square to know that when the son-of-a-bitch he woofing at get through stomping his ass, he won't even want to *hear* about no pussy for a month of Saturdays. I said, If you looking for somebody to cut you a new asshole, I'm just the son-of-a-bitch to oblige you.

That was when he seemed to decide that moral outrage was the better part of valor. Hey, y'all hear this, y'all heard him, supposed to be some kind of high-class college boy and listen what kind of language he using—you ain't no better than nobody else. But he had turned and was talking to them, not me.

That was when he suddenly had to realize that he had no way of knowing anything at all about me, and my guess is that he didn't really know anything about any other college boys either. So that's when he said, See there, and then said, So that's a Mister Collegeboy for you. Suppose to be up there getting all that high-class education and just listen at him. Y'all heard him. You can't even make a little joke without here he coming talking all that old gutter language and still think somebody supposed to *respect* them.

But he was talking *about* me. Not *to* me. To *them.* To everybody present *except* me. He didn't even *look* in my direction again. Obviously he was somehow totally oblivious to the likes of Daddy Shakehouse Anderson, also known as the Nighthawk or Big Shit Pendleton from Galveston, Texas, or Speckle Red, also known as Florida Red, the Juice Head, or Sneaky Pete Davis, the First Lord of the Outlying Regions and a few other certified campus thugs that I had already met even then. Not to mention my own roommate.

XII

WHAT FINALLY happened to Little Buddy Marshall when I was in the eleventh grade was the end of something that had already been underway for some time even before he began to talk about it the way he kept on doing throughout the whole summer of the year before. Sooner or later he would bring everything we talked about back around to that, and when I said what I said about school I knew exactly what he was going to say again.

He said, Man, like I been telling you all this time, man you welcome to Old Lady Metcalf and all that old hickory butt roll-call and blackboard do-do, and them dripping goddamn ink pens and them goddamn checker-back composition tablets. Man, every time I think about all them old stop and go examination periods, and man don't mention them report cards, and you got to take them home and get them signed!

He said, Man you all right with me, Scooter. You know that, but man, hey shit, I reckon I got to be hauling ass to hell on out of this old Mobile, Aladambama, and all this little old two-by-four stuff around these parts. Man, I got to go somewhere else. Man, I got to hit the goddamn road. Man, that's all I can think about.

He said, Man, you know good and well you always been all right with me, starting right off from the get-go at the pump shed. I know you know that, Scooter. Everybody around here know that. But, man, when it comes to them old henhouse teachers over there on the hill ringing them goddamn bells and flopping them shit-ass foot rulers and watching everybody like a goddamn hawk, I am sorry, man. You can put up with all that kind of stuff because you like books, Scooter, and all them other old games and stuff and that's you. But me, man, I don't give a goddamn shit about any of that old shit and that's me. So that's you and that's me, and I'm just saying I got to get myself on out of here and see me some of the real sure enough world for my own damn self.

Then he said, Any day now Scooter you just wait and see, and I knew better than to try to talk him out of anything once he had said what he had said the way he had said it, because what he had decided was that he was going to take a big risk on something come what may, and practical advice didn't mean anything to him anymore. So I just said, Boy, which way you heading, man? And he said, Shoot, I'm just going, man (because he knew that I knew that his departure heading was going to be due north and then maybe northeast), and when I find me a place I like I might stay there for a while and then move on until I come to somewhere else.

I said, Sheeoot man. I said, Goddamn. I said, I already miss you too much as it is, Lebo. Because ever since I had become an Early Bird I was also almost always busy doing special extracurricular projects not only for Miss Lexine Metcalf but also Miss Edna Teale Wilcox, who is the one I always remember whenever I hear "High Society" because that was one of the piano numbers she used to play as march-in music after the flag-raising ceremony, and who was also Mister B. Franklin Fisher's assembly program coordinator and was also going to be my advanced French teacher and also my college preparatory counselor when I reached the twelfth grade.

There was also the fact that as soon as you achieved the status of a top-perching Early Bird, your name was added to the principal's senior high school campus duty roster, which rotated weekly assignments to such daily details as raising and lowering the flag, checking playground equipment out and back in, and supervising elementary and junior high school playground activities, policing the grounds and overseeing litter removal, providing campus information and escort service to visitors, and so on and on to cover everything the faculty had decided would provide promising pupils an opportunity to develop a sense of responsibility, dependability, imagination, initiative—by all means initiative—and leadership potential.

None of that had ever been any part of anything that Little Buddy Marshall had ever looked forward to. After all, he didn't even like football, basketball, track and field, and tennis, precisely because to him they, unlike baseball and boxing and fishing and hunting and horse-racing and even golf, were schoolboy games and he didn't even want to hear about them.

So naturally you couldn't say anything at all about how you were finding out that the more you knew about geography and history, the better you could read maps and mileage charts and timetables. Not that I was not also the one who had once told him the story I had read about the three princes of Serendip who had set out for no place in particular and had learned to take things as they came. But you couldn't remind him of anything like that either because he may not have actually said, Man, you and them books, Scooter, boy you and them books, but that is what he would have been thinking. So I just let all of that pass but schoolboy (perhaps not beyond but certainly preparatory to anything else) that I had long since become, by that time I couldn't help thinking how much better able to cope with the adventures he was heading for if he already knew as much about the country at large as I did. I could draw a map of the continental boundaries and fill in all the states and capitals and all of the major lakes, rivers, mountains, plains, and deserts, and I could also name and visualize the largest cities and list the principal products and industries.

I said, Goddamn man, and as if he could read my concern, he said, Hey man, remember the good old days you and me used to have. Man, we sure used to have us some times, didn't we, Scooter? And I said, Man, you know it too, and he said, Man, I sure do wish the hell you'd come on and go with me, and I said, Man, you know how bad I want to but, I got to stay here and try to finish up all this stuff first. Because I promised. I promised Mama, man, and I promised Miss Tee and I also promised Old Luze.

I said, You remember that time. But he said, Man, I know what you talking about but that was then. I'm talking about this is now. I'm talking about I don't care what nobody said back then. I talking about I'm *going* this time, don't care what no goddamnbody says.

I didn't say anything else because I knew that you were not going to get anywhere arguing with him. But I didn't really want to try to keep him from saying what he wanted to say, so I just wagged my head with my brows knitted and waited for him to go on, and that's when he said, Man, I didn't really promise Old Luze nothing because I didn't really swear to all that old stuff he was talking about. I just promised him that I wouldn't try to follow *him* no more like that, and I ain't. I just said that because he caught us and he had our ass in a sling and what else could we do? I would've said anything under that bridge that time.

I let that go by also. All I said next was, Aw, man, can't nobody squat back there and call me in there like you, especially with a man on base. And he said, Sheet man, I bet you anything by this next year you going to be ready to get in there and smoke that pill on in there to Old Big Earl himself. Shoot man, you could be on your way to breaking that color line in the goddamn big leagues if it wasn't for them taking up so much of your time with all them old other things over on that old hill.

We were sitting with our legs dangling out of the tailgate of the truck en route to Whistler and as you went on talking, there were also the voices of the other members of the team joking and laughing at the same time, and I can also remember the corridor of overhanging trees and also the power lines along that part of Telegraph Road and how the exhaust fumes used to smell in those days that always become so vivid again no matter where I am when I hear a band playing the channel to "Precious Little Thing Called Love" again. Any time I hear that I also remember how the loose macadamized gravel used to look bouncing along in the red-clay dust the tires kicked back as you rolled on away toward the billboards in the open fields on the outskirts of Chickasaw.

But before we got there we turned off and came on across Kraft Highway which was the only concrete-paved strip to stretch that far beyond the city limits in those days. Then somebody said we were on the Citronelle road and the next turn I remember was the one that brought us into the sandy rut that I always remember when something reminds me of the scrub oaks along the way to the

*playing field and picnic grounds up to the cypress slope from the
Eight Mile Creek swimming place.*

*That was that June, and we had already played home games
against the Box Factory, and the Kelly Hill Nine, and Pine
Chapel and had made one trip to Cedar Grove and had also
played Chickasaw Terrace in Chickasaw Terrace and also back
home. Then on the Fourth of July we played the matinee game
in Plateau and as the summer rolled on we also traveled up to
Saraland, Chastang, and Mount Vernon and out to Maysville
and Oak Grove and also down the coast to Bayou La Batre and
Pascagoula.*

*I don't remember how many games we won and lost that sum-
mer, but then there was no pennant to be won anyway because
there was no organized league. Your team was tough or maybe
about average or a pushover, and that was about it. You sent
out letters of challenge which were either accepted or rejected for
one reason or another, and most of the games took place on open
playing fields to which admission was free and which were kept in
regulation playing condition by the players themselves under the
supervision of the manager and team captain and usually with
the help of a number of faithful fans and sometimes also a few
local commercial sponsors.*

*The main thing about the trip down to Pascagoula was not
that we won the seven-inning matinee preliminary and that the
adult team lost the big game, but the big dance band from New
Orleans playing on a low platform under a wide moss-draped oak
near the refreshment stand. They were there for the home team
and the number they kept striking up every time their side scored
again was "Cake Walking Babies from Home," which I already
knew from Miss Blue Eula's record of old Clarence Williams's
Blue Five with Louis Armstrong, Sidney Bechet, Charlie Irvis,
Buddy Christian, and Eva Taylor.*

*We spent so much of the rest of the afternoon just hanging
around the bandstand that we didn't really try to keep up with
what was happening out on the diamond. From where we stood
looking and listening, you could read the titles on the music stands
and that was the first time I ever saw the score sheets for "Sugar
Foot Stomp" and "Royal Garden Blues" which Papa Gladstone's
Syncopators had been playing in the Boom Men's Union Hall
Ballroom for years.*

We didn't get to hear the band from New Orleans play for the big dance that night because as soon as the third man was put out in the top of the ninth inning we had to pile back into the trucks and head back for Mobile and Gasoline Point. But I could hear "Cake Walking Babies" all the way home and it stuck with me all that next week.

But the band tune that Little Buddy Marshall and I always used to hum and whistle because it went with baseball and Gator Gus and also with the Old Luzana Cholly's sporty limp-walk was "Kansas City Stomp" by old sharp dressing, loud woofing Jelly Roll Morton and the Red Hot Peppers. You would also do Old Luzana's sporty limp to Duke Ellington's "Birmingham Breakdown" and years later I was to make his "Cotton Tail" my very own best of all soundtracks for the briar patch. But at that time "Kansas City Stomp" was our theme song. So much so that even to this day, every time I put it on the phonograph I feel the way I used to feel when he was the one and only Little Buddy Marshall he used to be back before he decided that we had come to the parting of the ways.

One day in the middle of that July he said, Man, you don't really believe me when I'm trying to tell you these my last goddamn weeks around these parts, do you Scooter? But you just wait and see if I don't skip on out of here. And I guess I really didn't believe it, or maybe I was just hoping he wouldn't. But I didn't want to talk about it because I didn't even want to think about it anymore.

The last game he and I played together was the one against Oak Grove in Oak Grove. So that was the last time I ever saw him do that old walk-away limp we used to practice to do when you had to slide into home plate. When you got the jump and beat the throw going into second or third, the thing was to hit the dirt and be standing on the bag dusting your hips and hitching up your pants with your forearms while the infielder was still shifting the ball from the glove to his throwing hand. But when you slid into home plate, you always took your time getting up and then you limped a few steps and then you trotted on into the dugout brushing your pants as if it were all just another little detail in a day's work. I had all of that down as well as he did, but he got to do it more often in a real game because he was so much better as a hitter than I ever was to be.

Then sometime during the week before the Labor Day picnic game against Chickasaw Terrace up on the bluffs, he left town one night without saying goodbye, and that was really the end of me and Little Buddy Marshall as running buddies, because when he came back to town that next year just before the end of the school term, he had already been home for almost a week before I found out he was there, and I didn't actually see him until I just happened to meet him coming along the sidewalk from Miss Algenia Nettleton's cookshop.

We stood where we were and talked for about twenty minutes and all he said when I said, Where you been, man, where you been, and what you been up to, was just, Knocking about here and there doing the best I can, man. But I didn't press him because as soon as I saw him I could tell that he was embarrassed and also that he had not yet fully recovered from some illness, which we never came to discuss or even mention.

But when I heard some ten or twelve days later that he had hit the road again, I was not really surprised at all, and the next time I saw him he could hardly wait to tell me about some of the things he had seen and done in such major league baseball cities as Cincinnati and Chicago and St. Louis and Cleveland and Detroit and Pittsburgh, and I said Hey man, eight down and eight to go, because in those days there were eight teams in the National League and eight in the American League. So there were only four more cities to go because St. Louis and Chicago had one in each league and so did Boston and Philadelphia, and New York had the Yankees in the American League and the Giants and the Brooklyn Dodgers in the National League, and Washington had the Senators in the National League. Which, of course, also meant that once you got to any two-league city, say like Chicago with the White Sox and the Cubs, you were where every team in both leagues came to play.

It was almost like old times for a few days during the first part of that summer, and then he said what he said about what had been on his mind about Creola Calloway for all those years and I didn't see him or even hear anything about him for a while and I took it for granted that he had cut out once more. But then a few weeks later there he was again, coming along through Tin Top Alley from Shelby Hill and as soon as he saw me he made his old you-mighty-goddamn-right-I-did gesture and then broke into a few steps of our old sporty-limp strut.

Then not long afterward I found out that he had skipped the city again without saying goodbye, and I guessed that he had headed north by east to Philadelphia and New York and maybe also Boston, and my guess turned out to be true. It also turned out that the day we stopped to talk for a few minutes in Tin Top Alley was the last time I was to see him alive.

TWO

The Briarpatch

XIII

AT FIRST I couldn't believe that what was happening to Will Spradley was happening to me, too. After all, when I woke up that morning, I had never heard anything at all about Will Spradley and would not have recognized him as anybody I had ever seen anywhere before. But by sunrise the next day, he had told me about his trouble with Dudley Philpot so many times over and in such personal detail that forever thereafter I was to feel that I had not only been an eyewitness but had also been a party to it step by step, breath by breath:

he (Will Spradley) came plunging headlong and lickety-split through the narrow alley leading from the back of the store, his ears ringing, the pain in his side almost bending him double. *Ain't none of it nothing and here I is, all messed up in the middle of it. All tangled and mangled up in it like this and it ain't nothing and ain't about nothing.*

he was aching all over, and he was breathing blood bubbles and spitting blood, too, but he was running now, and he had to keep on running. *All of this now. All of this and it ain't nothing, plain flat-out nothing.* He was wet and sticky with blood and sweat, and his legs were stiff, and he could hardly bear to swing his arms. *I ain't done nothing. I ain't said nothing and ain't done nothing. I ain't done nothing to nobody. I ain't never bothered nobody in my life. Everybody know that. You know me, you got to know that.*

he needed to do something about the bleeding and he needed something to hold his side, too, but he couldn't stop for that. Not yet. He couldn't even think about stopping. He had to keep on running and he had to keep on being out of sight, too. Because at least he was this lucky and this far away from that part of it for at least this long. He had to keep on trying. He had to get to Giles Cunningham now. He had to keep on trying and pulling and get there and be there and be gone.

but he had to get there first and let Giles know. *I got to get there so I can tell Gile. I got to let him know. I got to get there and be the one to tell him and clear myself with him because I ain't said nothing about him. I just said what I said because it was true and that's all I meant. I wasn't trying to get him in trouble with nobody. That's what I got to do now. I got to tell him and tell him I didn't want them to get him, too. Because he the one now. He the main one. Because all this ain't nothing to what they going to try to do to him. Because I ain't the one, because I ain't done nothing. He ain't done nothing neither, but he the one. He musta said something. He musta said something terrible.*

he was sucking and spitting blood and the lump around the gash on his cheek had almost closed his eye already. The raw place behind his ear burned all the way to the base of his neck. But he was pulling and pumping with all his might. Not even looking back. Not even daring to look back yet. There wasn't any time to spare to do that yet. Not now. Not yet. Not even with it this dark. He wasn't far enough for that yet. Not even almost.

not even listening back. Not daring to do that either. Because if you looked back, they would be there, and if you listened back, they would be coming, and he had to be getting away from there now, and that was doing this, which was running, which was going, which was leaving, because your second chance was out in front of you now.

because although he couldn't really know what was going to happen next, he knew what he knew about what had already happened, because that part had happened to him, and he knew that even if it had been worse than it had been, which was bad enough, it was still just the beginning. No telling what was going to happen next. Anything could happen now.

he had to get to Giles Cunningham before they got there. *I got to make time. I got to get in and out of there before any of them get there. I got to be somewhere else when they come there. I got to hold out and do this and then I got to find somewheres else to be.*

he had come out of the alley and across that street and cut through the vacant lot where the automobile hulls were. *I got to tell Gile then I got to be getting further. All of this now. I swear to God, Lord, you never know.* He was coming to the next street then. And then he was across that one, too, and he was crawling through the fence and into the pecan orchard and coming on through there.

it had been raining off and on all day, and the ground was wet and the air was damp, and there was a thin mist among the trees and the night shapes again. It was going to be chilly again but the dampness was still warm now. It was hot to him. His breath was hot, his collar was hot, and his clothes were almost steaming.

he made it to the next fence and got through the railing and was crawling on through there, too, his arms and legs numb now, his head splitting with pain. The whole left side of his face was swollen out of shape, and he could hardly see out of his left eye. He could hardly hear out of his left ear, and every time he stretched too far the pain in his side almost took his breath away.

he was crawling along the garden furrow to get to the next fence, and then he would be at that road. Then he would be coming along there. If they didn't cut him off and hem him in and catch him anywhere along there, he would have a chance to make it to that corner, which was where that part of town began. He was headed for the edge of town and the railroad, but he had to get through here first, and then Higgins Quarters and the lumberyard.

he was running again then, and he had to keep on running until he was there. *If I slow down, I'll be tired. If I slow down, I won't be able to run no more, and I can't make it, and I got to, because I got to get there and tell Gile because I'm the cause of it, but it ain't my fault. It ain't my fault because it ain't nothing no how, and God knows I ain't done a thing.*

he came staving on along the footpath beside the wide, curving road, running in the open, exposed in all directions now, his whole being straining with alertness. He had to be ready to jump in a split second. *I got to hear good now and hear them before I see them because if I don't, they got me.*

the main thing was automobiles, especially coming from behind. If you didn't hear the motor before the headlights came, the beams would hit you in the back and it would be like a charge of buckshot between the shoulder blades. If that happened, it would be too late. If that happened, they would have him again, and it wouldn't be just one but all of them this time. He would have to be there and they would be there all around him, and anything could happen.

that would be here; it would be happening right here. *And ain't none of them got nothing to do with it because it ain't nothing no how. Ain't got nothing to do with it and don't even know nothing about what it's all about, don't know the first thing about none of it. All this time now, and now all of this. But they ain't thinking about that. They don't want to know about that, don't need to know. They ain't going to be asking no questions because they ain't going to be needing no answers. Because I'm the only answer they want now, me and Gile, and it's more Gile than me, because he's really the one, but if they get me it's me, too, and here I is ain't done nothing to nobody.*

everything depended on how lucky he was now. That was all he had to go on now, because all he could do was try to keep on doing what he was doing right now, which was this, which was running, which was all numbness now and pulling, which was pumping, his chest tight, his breath raw, the dull cramp in his side getting sharper and sharper all the time. *I got to outrun this now. This ketch in my side. If I keep on it'll go away. I got to get rid of this and get my second wind. When I get my second wind, I'll feel better and I can make better time. I got to make better time than this. A whole lot better.*

he came lunging on, and then he was there in that part of town which was the last part, and he had to slow down because he had to be ready to break from shadow to shadow now. *This far now. And now I got to get through here.* He was running narrow then. *I got to make it on through here, and get to the lumberyard and get on through there and make it all the way. I can't let them get me now. All of them now, and just me out here all by myself. All over something like that, and it ain't even nothing.* He came darting on, running not on strength but on necessity now, because although it had all started about something which was really nothing in the first place, it was about everything and everybody now. And all he knew about what was going to happen next was that anything could happen, and once it got started there was no telling where it was going to stop.

he came grinding on and the main thing was the numbness. It wasn't the pain anymore. It was the dull bumping numbness and the way his stomach was. *If I can just make it on past there and make it on to that sweet gum I can make it. I got to make*

*it that far now. I got to make it that far and I'll have me a good
head start then, and I can make it on through there.*

*I shoulda knowed better and I did. Ain't no use in them saying
that, because I did, and I was doing everything in my power to do
and I sure God did everything he said and he know it, and then
he started all of that about something like that and I couldn't do
nothing after that.*

because it was happening too fast from then on. Everything
had been going along all that time and then all of a sudden it
had changed to that and there he was right in the middle of it,
all hemmed up in the very middle of it. He couldn't do anything right because he couldn't even believe it that quick. He
saw it happening and he knew it was happening but he couldn't
believe it because he was too stunned to believe it. Because he
was dumbfounded, flabbergasted. Because there he was and
there it was happening before he could even get started on
what he was going to say, before he could even get set to start
thinking about all of the things he knew he had to try to say,
and then it was too late.

he had known good and well that it could happen, but somehow he just couldn't believe that it was going to happen that
fast, and all of a sudden it was like a steel trap springing shut on
you. That was enough to shock anybody. That was enough to
paralyze you. Because there you were and it was like a bear trap
or something and you knew it and you knew you had to unbait
it, and you were trying and there you were being as careful as
anybody could be and all of a sudden it had sprung before you
could even touch it.

but what had really stunned him was the fact that he had
forgotten what it was like, because he was shocked but he was
not really surprised. It hadn't really surprised him. Because surprises come out of the clear blue sky, and this was not like that
at all, because he had been living knowing it could happen
almost all of his life, and knowing that long was waiting that
long, too. But he had forgotten it, too, because he had been
so busy trying to keep it from happening that he had forgotten
all about what it really was, and all of a sudden there it was
and it was him and this: *him facing Dudley Philpot, and Dudley
Philpot holding the pistol.*

2.

I told him and that didn't do no good at all. I told him and he just kept right on. He knew it wasn't my fault and he come lighting into me like that. Just like I was the one and he know good and well it wasn't none of me. I told him I couldn't help it, and he know Gile Cunningham as good as I do. I come right straight on there and told him just as soon as it happened and if he was going to do something he ought to done it then, but all he done was just say that then and I thought I was out of it. I thought he was just going to say that and let me go on and he did and I thought that was it. He wouldn't let me give it to him and he said for me to tell Gile and I did and I figured it was him and Gile then, and it was, and then he come sending for me again and I thought it was all over and done with. I just thought he was ready to take it and let me go on then and here he come with all of this. Just like I ain't had it at all and I had it right there for him to take in the first place. All of this about something like that and I had it right there and he wouldn't let me give it to him, like what difference did that make. All this now and I still ain't give it to him and I had it all the confound time.

he made it on past Neely's Crossing and came on until he saw the sweet gum tree, and then he left the railroad and came on down across the right-of-way to where he knew the trail began. He had to slow down and catch his breath then, but he couldn't stop. He was trotting and then he was walking, and then he was trotting again.

I tried to tell that crazy fool, trouble-making Gile, he said to himself without realizing it. I tried to tell him and that didn't do no good at all. I told him. I said, look, Gile, I got to do that first, and he didn't pay that no attention at all. He made me do it. He made me. He had me and I told him and he made me do it anyhow. He had me then and what else could I do and there I was then and all I could do was go on and I did and I was going along that street and I came on past the sweet shrubs and the warehouse, and then I slowed back down again because I was almost there and I had to think about what I was going to tell him because it wasn't nothing, but I knew good and well he wasn't going to like it and he sure God didn't.

Then I was there and I went on through the store to the office, and he was busy talking to old man Cliff from the secondhand store up the street. Standing there leaning back against the front edge of the desk smoking, looking down at their feet, and then he saw me and looked at me and I waited, and I was still trying to think up something but all I was doing was waiting, and then old man Secondhand Cliff was gone and I was standing there with my hat, like that, and he was sitting in the swivel chair behind the desk again.

"Well, Will?"

"How you, Mister Dub?" I said.

"Pretty good, Will. How you?"

"Not so good, Mister Dub," I said.

"Well, let's see now." He said that like he always did and I heard it and heard that kind of breathing that goes with that kind of talk, and I was thinking, that's the way white folks talk, they have noses like that and they breathe like that when they talk.

"Mister Dub," I said.

"Just a minute, Will," and he took the key from his pocket and opened the drawer and took out that little old checker-back school tablet. Then he took out the metal box.

"Mister Dub," I said.

"All right, Will."

Then I took the money from my watch pocket and unfolded it.

"Take it out of this, Mister Dub," I said.

"Where's that check, Will?"

"I ain't got it, Mister Dub," I said.

"You ain't got it?"

"No, sir," I said, "not this time."

"Well, where the hell is it then, Will?"

"Sir?"

"Where'd you get all that cash money from, Will?"

"Well, you see, Mister Dub, I had another little transaction. I had to take care of that," I said.

"But what are you doing with all that cash money, Will?"

"He cashed it, Mister Dub," I told him.

"Who cashed it, Will?"

"Gile Cunningham, Mister Dub," I said.

"Giles Cunningham?"

"Yes, sir," I said.

"What the hell is that nigger doing cashing your checks, Will?"

"Well, sir, you see I owed him a little something, too, and I was on my way here but I kinda bumped into him first."

"You know I'm the one that cashes your checks, Will."

That's how it started. About nothing, and all I could think about then was all this about a percent. So he can deduct that measly percent and a quarter for surcharge. Gile didn't charge me nothing for cashing it. I did not look at him then, because I know good and well what was coming. I didn't say nothing.

"You know that, Will," he said, not looking at me. I wasn't looking at him either, but I saw him.

"But I got your money, Mister Dub," I said. "I was on my way here."

"Didn't you tell him I cash your checks for you?" he asked.

"Yes, sir. I told him," I said.

"Well, what the hell did he cash it for then?"

"I don't know, sir, Mister Dub. I told him."

"You sure you told him?"

"Yes, sir. I'm dead sure, Mister Dub. But you know Gile Cunningham, Mister Dub."

"You get out of here and get it back."

"But he on his way out of town, Mister Dub. That's how come he done it, anyhow."

"Well, you get out there and catch him and tell him I say send that damn check in here."

"But he already gone, Mister Dub."

"You get out of here and don't come back till you get it."

"Yes, sir, but he gone for four or five days."

"Where'd he go?"

"I don't know, sir, Mister Dub. He didn't tell me that."

"Well, you get ahold of him as soon as he gets back and bring that check in here."

"But I can't make him give it to me, Mister Dub. You know Gile Cunningham, Mister Dub. You know how he is."

"Well, goddamn it, you tell that black son-of-a-bitching bastard I say bring it in here hisself or you tell him I say his black ass'll wish he had."

"He didn't mean you no harm or nothing like that, Mister Dub," I said.

"You tell him what I said."

All I said then was, "Yessir," and I didn't spend a single penny of my own money all that time. My own money now. Mamie and them gone back out to Indian Stand again and all that. All because of that and all of it is just about as near nothing as anything I ever heard tell of in my life. Me waiting around all that time now.

And then as soon as I come back in there and seen his face like that I could tell what had happened and I already knowed, anyhow. Because I know Gile Cunningham and I know Gile Cunningham don't care, trouble or no trouble, and he ain't never been one to bite his tongue for nobody and everybody know it. White folks know that just like everybody else and that's why don't none of them do nothing but look at him and leave him alone. Gile Cunningham don't care nothing about no two-bit peckerwood like no Dub Philpot.

As soon as I come in and seen his face like that, I knowed I was in for it, and I knowed just about what had happened. I had been hoping all day that it was going to be all over, but I knowed that it was just beginning then.

3.

He had been standing there looking toward Dud Philpot then. Knowing that he himself was being looked up and down, but he didn't look him back in the eye. Because he knew white folks and he knew they didn't like for you to do that. They thought you might be figuring on doing something if you did that, and that made them uneasy and there was no telling what they were liable to do to you then. But he was watching him and he could also feel him and he could sense every move he might make as soon as it started. He was waiting then, and then he realized that he was supposed to start talking first.

"I come as soon as I got your word, Mister Dub, and I brung the money too. I was right over yonder at the cab stand waiting all the time I been over there all day."

"What did I tell you to do?"

"When, Mister Dub?"

Will Spradley had moved his feet then. He mad now. He good and mad now. He getting ready to raise hell now. He bound to *raise holy hell now. All about a measly little percent. All because Gile done that and then he couldn't make him do what he said. He got to raise hell now.*

"I done what you told me, Mister Dub," he had said. "I told him what you told me to."

"I told you to bring that goddamn check in here in the first place."

"Yes, sir," he had said.

"Didn't I tell you?"

"Yes, sir. You sure did, Mister Dub."

Dud Philpot had been sitting, holding the desk, looking at him then, gripping it harder and harder every time he spoke, his face getting redder, his knuckles whiter; and Will Spradley wanted to say something to calm him down but he couldn't think of it fast enough then, and the next thing he knew Philpot was standing up.

"Yes, sir, Mister Dub, you sure did."

"Goddamnit, I'm beginning to believe you think you're getting smart, Will Spradley. Trying me. You and that Giles."

"No, sir, Mister Dub, nothing like that, Mister Dub. No sir, Mister Dub, not me."

His eyes were narrow then and he was breathing, coming close, and his neck and ears were getting redder and redder, and he was glaring, and then all of a sudden he started to shake all over as if it had just come to him what he was angry about.

Will Spradley had moved about again then, watching him without really looking at him. *He going to start something now. He bound to start something now. Just as sure as I'm standing here. Just as sure as rain and I'm here. White folks.* He had moved again then, but he didn't really move, he just didn't stand still.

"It was just a mistake, Mister Dub. Gile Cunningham, he—"

"Goddamn your black nigger soul to hell." Dud Philpot struck at him then, reaching, swinging across the desk, but Will Spradley moved, almost without moving, and Philpot missed him and almost lost his balance.

"Aw, Mister Dub, ain't no use of that."

Philpot was halfway around the desk then and he swung again, but Will Spradley twisted to one side and took that blow with his elbow up in front of his face, and began backing away, and then he turned to make a break for the door. But before he could make

*it there, Philpot had leapt back to the desk and snatched the pistol
from the already open top drawer and leveled it at him.*

*"Make one more move, you black-livered bastard, and I'll blow
your nigger brains out. You hear me nigger? Do you hear me, you
sneaky black son-of-a-bitch?"*

*"Mister Dub, I ain't done nothing. I ain't done a thing! What
did I do, Mister Dub? You know me, Mister Dub."*

*Will Spradley was coming slowly on back toward him then. He
got me now. He got me. Goddamn that goddamn trouble-making
Gile Cunningham. And ain't nothing I can do because then
where would I be? All the people in this town and it's got to be me,
and he know good and well it ain't me.*

"You know me, Mister Dub."

*Dud Philpot changed the pistol to his left hand then and swung
his right but missed him and lost his balance again, and Will
Spradley jumped forward to keep him from going down and
jumped back, realizing that he had touched him.*

"Aw, Mister Dub."

Dud Philpot slapped him again then, forehand and backhand.

"I'll teach you."

*"I ain't done nothing, Mister Dub. You been knowing me all
this time, Mister Dub. You know that, Mister Dub."*

"Shut up!"

"But Mister Dub—"

That was when Dud Philpot began hitting him with the pistol.

*"What you going to do, Mister Dub? I ain't done nothing, I
ain't done a thing. What you going to do, Mister Dub?"*

*Dud Philpot struck him a gashing swipe on the side of his head
with the barrel then, and Will Spradley staggered, watching him
through the blood and fell and started crawling toward the door.*

*"Please, Mister Dub, please, sir," he said, but he knew that Dud
Philpot was getting too tired to raise the pistol again.*

"I told you not to move."

*That was when he kicked him. It was not strong enough to hurt,
but Will Spradley pitched himself forward into a sprawl.*

"Get up!" Dud Philpot's voice was almost a whisper.

*But Will Spradley didn't get up any further than his knees,
and he kept his legs together and held one arm around his stomach
and the other hand before his blood-streaked face. I said, Please,
sir, and he still doing it. I told him please sir, because he got me*

and he know it. I could get him, too, but I can't because then it would be all that. I could do it right now if I wanted to. I could ram him right now and grab him and turn him every way but aloose. He ain't thought about that. He so worked up, he forgot about that. I could grab him right now. All I got to do is ram right on into him. Lord, don't let him think about that now. He surely kill me if he think about that. If he think about that, I'm gone and ain't nobody going to do nothing either. White folks.

"Please don't, Mister Dub," he said in a falsetto that was no less deliberate than habitual. "Please have mercy, Mister Dub. Oh Lord, Jesus, have mercy, Mister Dub."

Dud Philpot had started kicking him again then, but he had to stop and catch his breath every time, and at first all Will Spradley had done was keep himself covered as he was and wait.

I said please and he was still doing it, but I was pretty sure he wasn't going to shoot me and he was too tired to aim straight anyhow, and I was thinking it was almost over because he was too tired and weak to be mad, because he was so tired he was going to have to start thinking about it and remember it wasn't me because he knew—good and well knew—it was Gile. So he had doubled over, hoping that would hurry it because he had to get somewhere and get the bleeding stopped.

But the next kick had not come and that was when he had suddenly realized how much danger he was really in. That's the part that really scared me and I was hauling out of there and out here before I knew it, gun or no gun, because I could hear him just standing there huffing and puffing like that, and I knew if he fainted it was going to be me if he come to saying I did it and if he didn't come to, I didn't have no chance at all. White folks. White folks. White folks. But now I got to get there and tell Gile.

And black ones, too. Yeah, them too. Goddamn right, them too. Because ain't no use of them saying that because that don't make me that, just because I didn't do that. They can call me anything they want to, but anybody say I'm that don't know what they talking about. That's all right with me because goddamn the luck I know they going to say it anyhow, because all I want to do now is get there and tell Gile. They can say anything they goddamn want to.

he came on and on and on pulling against the pain and pumping against the stiffness and the swelling and then he had his second wind and his second chance. But he still couldn't really believe it was happening to him.

XIV

NOT THAT I didn't already know people like Will Spradley. I have always known and heard about people like him. But I must say that it has also been my good fortune to have also always known quite a few who could easily have been very much like him but were not. There was Ed Riggins, for instance, better known as Evil Ed Riggins and perhaps even better as Old Man Evil Ed. By which people of all persuasions in and around Gasoline Point meant that he was not only somewhat foul-mouthed as if on principle but also downright badassed when crossed.

He was one I was to find myself remembering again as soon as I realized what turn the story Will Spradley was telling me was about to take. Any time his name used to be mentioned around the fireside or on the swing porch, somebody always had to say something about how he never was one to take any stuff from anybody, especially white people, whom he almost always called white folks. Even when he was addressing them individually, he would say, What say white folks or, Howdo white folks or say, Lookahere white folks and so on, and he was the one who referred to important looking white women not as Miss Ann or Miss Lady but as Miss I Am, as in "Look at Miss I Am up there, call herself clerking on that typing machine. White folks, white folks, white folks. I declare to God!"

Everybody knew the one about how he used to signify at his own boss man back in the old days up in the farming country before moving down into Mobile County during the wartime shipbuilding boom in Chickasaw. All you had to do was be somewhere sometime as I was in the barbershop that time when somebody reminded him of Old Man Jake Turner Cuthbert.

Whoever it was went on to say, I remember one time when damn near half the farm folks in that district was still standing around that little old two-by-four crossroads town after dark, waiting for old man Jake to get back from the county seat with the payroll. You remember that, Ed? And Old Ed Riggins said, Goddamn right I remember it and all them old hunch-shouldered, boney-butt peckerwoods standing around every-where waiting for him, too, just like us, and I'm the one got to tell him. I said, Where the hell is that goddamn old white man with my money I done sweated all the week for? I said, This is Sadday night. I said, I done give him the time he hire me for and now this here is my goddamn time he messing with. He ain't paying me for this and look at all these stores still open so people can settle up a few things and pick up a little something and get on home. Goddamn.

And I told him, too. I said, Man, where you been, white man, just coming in here this time of night? I said, Man, you know this is Sadday. And he come talking about nigger, and I said, Man, nigger nothing. I said, Business is business. I said, Nigger ain't got nothing to do with this. I said, What about all these old hungry white folks around here? Just like everybody else. And he said, Yeah, but nigger. And I said, Man, how you going to nigger your way out of something like this? I said, You know good and well I am eating out of a paper sack. I said, You the one eating out of the cupboard, not me and these people. I said, I'm eating out of a paper sack one can at a time.

I also knew what people in Gasoline Point meant when they said Old Evil Ed Riggins *didn't even lower his voice in the bank* because I was there one day when he came in. It was not that he was loud. He wasn't. But when he spoke in his normal tone of voice, you suddenly realized that the tone everybody else was using was hardly above a whisper and also that they were moving about as if they were not only in church but at a funeral.

As a matter of fact, he didn't even raise his voice when you saw him standing somewhere signifying at everybody in ear-shot as I came upon him doing at the entrance to Hammel's Department Store one day. When he said, Well, let me get on in here and see if I can figure out what these old Mobile, Ala-bama, white folks coming up with this time, he was not really trying to get attention. He was only thinking aloud in public and signifying and scandalizing anybody who happened to be listening.

He also used to like to say, You damn sure better be on your goddamn p's and q's because you can bet your bottom dollar these old goddamn white folks going to be trying to come up with something else, and damn if I believe they know what the hell it is they own selves most of the goddamn time, if you want to know the goddamn truth. Hell, it ain't my goddamn fault. I didn't make them. I'm just trying to find out how to deal with these we got around here.

People used to say he walked with one shoulder hunched just slightly higher than the other because he was so used to wearing an underarm holster for his .38 Special and that when the weather was too warm for a coat or his stiffly starched blue denim overall jumper-jacket, you could tell by a little added drag in his sporty walk that he was carrying his back-up Derringer in a leg holster.

He had started out up in the country as a turpentine worker. Then he had become a woodsman and hunting guide. That was how he got his reputation as the dead-eye pump gun and Winchester expert, bar none. He still hunted bear and deer as well as rabbits, possum, squirrels, and coons, ducks, and quail and now he also had a rowboat that he used not only for channel fishing but also for bagging ducks, marsh hens, and wild guineas up in Hog Bayou (which was also wild boar and alligator territory) and over in the canebrakes of Pole Cat Bay.

The only explanation I ever heard anybody give for the way he always woofed and signified wherever he was around white people was that it was what he did to keep *everybody* reminded that no matter who you were, he was not the kind of man you could mess with and expect to get away with it. Nobody I ever asked or overheard around the fireside, on the swing porch, or in the barbershop or anywhere else ever claimed to know about any specific occurrence that it all could be traced back to. Nor could anybody name anybody anywhere who ever called his hand.

I did know who Dudley Philpot was when I woke up that morning but only by name because of the sign on the front of his store, which I had never set foot inside of but which I knew was about a half of a block off Courthouse Square going toward Carmichael Construction Supply Company. I did not know him by sight and I had never wondered what he was like because he didn't have any kind of reputation that I had ever heard anything about.

Giles Cunningham, on the other hand, was somebody I already knew by sight as well as reputation. I had never actually met him, but I became used to seeing him in the barbershop and on the block during the past three years, and so I had also picked up enough information about him (most of it casual and incidental) to know that he owned the Dolomite Ballroom out near Montgomery Fork, the hillside eating place called the Pit (as in barbecue pit), a short distance out of town on U.S. 80 going toward the Georgia state line, and that the Plum (as in plum thickets and also as in plumb out of town and nearly out of the country), the after-hours spot off Route 33 going south by east to the Florida panhandle, belonged to him.

By the time that I had become the upperclassman and prospective honor graduate that I was when I woke up that morning, I had also learned enough about him to know that he also owned two subdivisions, one near the campus and another out in the hill section where he lived, that he owned a chicken farm and fourteen hundred acres of farmland out in the country, and that he also had part ownership in several other concerns, including a dry-cleaning business which a cousin was operating in Chattanooga and a bay-front resort and fishing camp which his half-brother was getting started down below Mobile and Dog River.

I also knew that his houseman at the ballroom was Wiley Peyton, an old trench buddy from the AEF and that one Speck (as in Speckle Red) Jenkins, an old L & N dining car chef out of Montgomery, took care of the day-to-day details at the Pit and that the man in charge out at the Plum was one Flea (for Fleetwood) Mosley, an old pre-Prohibition bartender and off-time pool shark from Birmingham.

Along with the ballroom into which headline road bands were booked once or twice a week, the Dolomite also had a big bar off the main lobby that was open every night and had its own combo and a floor show. The Pit was strictly an eating place that was open for breakfast and closed after dinner, which was served from 5:30 to 8:30 P.M. on weekdays and 5:30 to midnight on Saturdays. The Plum was an old-time down-home jook joint with a honky-tonk piano player named Gits Coleman.

The Pit was also his headquarters. So that was where he spent most of his time during daylight hours and that was where you called to get him on the phone. He also spent a certain amount of time at the other places, too, but anybody trying to get in touch with him always called the Pit first. Some people also knew that in case of an emergency, you could also get a message to him by calling Hortense Hightower.

He made a daily check of the Dolomite and the Plum either in the morning or early afternoon while things were being set up and then again at night when everything was supposed to be rolling. Sometimes he ran out to the poultry farm once a week and sometimes twice. Otherwise, he left everything up there to Ed Mitchell, a graduate from the School of Agriculture, who sent eggs and dressed chickens into the Pit and also to the clubs. The only time he made regular trips to his other farms further out in the country was during the planting and harvest seasons. Otherwise, he seldom went more than once every two or three weeks.

You could also find him in town for a while every morning because he usually went to the bank before noon, and when Wiley Peyton wasn't with him during that part of the day, it was usually Flea Mosley, and unless there was some reason to check by the courthouse, the next stop was always his office at the Pit because that was where he usually took care of bills and orders. He always put in the big orders himself, and he also booked all the name bands and personally produced and promoted all of the special dances and coordinated the annual galas sponsored by the local social clubs.

As a matter of fact, Giles Cunningham and the Pit and the Dolomite and the Plum (and thus also Wiley Peyton and Flea Mosley and Speck Jenkins) were all very much a part of what was on my mind when I woke up that morning, because as soon as I realized that I was no longer asleep and remembered what day it was, I began thinking about Hortense Hightower and the way she had said what she said.

After all, I had already found out most of what I knew about him and his concerns long before I had finally come to realize that she herself even existed. Nor had I just been hearing about him. I had actually been seeing him at fairly close range although not with any one-on-one personal familiarity ever since the first term of my freshman year because he always came on the block at least once a week. He was always there every Friday afternoon, the big black Cadillac parked head on into the curb in front of the barbershop.

That was when Skeeter always got him ready for the weekend. That included a hair trim, shampoo, shave, and facial, and there was also a manicurist on Friday and Saturday. Sometimes when all of that was over, he would also hang around for a while swapping lies and signifying with Deke Whatley, the owner, or he would come back out and stand in front of Red's Varsity Threads next door, talking sports with Red Gilmore.

You couldn't miss him, standing with one leg dropped back like that, the toes of his highly glossed, elegantly narrow, and thin-soled shoes pointing inward, shoulders erect but with the left ever so slightly lower than the right and with his hat, which always looked brand new, and which he wore tilted toward his left brow, blocked long with the brim turned up all around in what I used to call the Birmingham/Kansas City poolroom homburg style.

Whatever he was wearing always went well with his barbershop-smooth ginger-brown skin and the way he handled himself. He was just about six feet even, solidly built but with a little bulge in the midsection that along with his smartly hand-tailored hand-finished suits and custom-made shirts and accessories made him look more like a road musician or gambler who might go hunting and fishing from time to time than like an athlete.

But as I found out early on, he had started out to be a prize fighter, another Jack Johnson, and heavyweight champion of the world. A lot of boys were going to be another Jack Johnson or another Joe Gans back in those days, and he made a pretty good start and he had kept it up when he was conscripted and sent to camp. But when they shipped him overseas, he got a chance to see another part of the world and all of that had given him a lot of other possibilities to consider.

He had not really been old enough to be called up, but he looked more adult than he was at the time, and he had been putting his age up so that he could hang around the saloons and pool halls so he was drafted and he fought in the Vosges mountains and also in the Argonne forest, and he had had himself some fun over there, too. He had lied to go AWOL to get into Paris, but he and Wiley Peyton had made it there three times. He and Wiley Peyton had been in the same company from the very outset and by the time they reached the embarkation point of Newport News, Virginia, they were buddies, so they had gone on to do a lot of French towns together just as they had done their share of going over the top and through the barbwire together.

When he came back stateside, he had started running on the L & N as a Pullman porter and had also become a dining car headwaiter, and that was when he really began to pick up on how you made good money by providing first-class service. And then he went to Harlem during the boom in the 1920s and got a job in a big midtown hotel, and that's when he decided what he wanted to do and started putting money aside and laying his plans.

Then when the big Depression struck at the end of the decade, he took what he had saved, along with all of the tricks of the trade that he had picked up from the railroad and New York by that time, and came on back down home and went into business for himself, starting with the Pit, which was just another old run-down roadside chicken shack when he made his downpayment on it.

XV

SHE SAID, Hi there, Schoolboy, and I could have said not for very much longer. Because it was already the middle of that third January and I was less than five months away from being a senior, and then there would be the summer and I would be on my way to what comes after commencement. But I didn't say that. I said, I don't deny my name. I said, I don't deny my name because going to school is still my game. And she had to smile and then she winked and said, I don't deny my name either, Schoolboy, and sat on the next stool with her back to the bar.

That was how I met Hortense Hightower. I already knew who she was. Everybody present knew who she was because she was the main attraction in that wing of the Dolomite complex. She was the singer the five-piece combo was there to play behind, and she was also the dancer featured in the Friday and Saturday night floor shows, which also included a chorus line of six dancers who doubled as backup singers, a comedian named Gutbucket, and also a guest spot for a singer or instrumentalist.

All I actually knew about her at that time was how she sounded and the way she came across on stage and what a good-looking, svelte, nutmeg-brown woman she was. I had not yet found out anything at all about where she had grown up and where she had worked before. I knew that she had been in town for five or six years, but I hadn't ever seen her in person until that last Christmas break when I finally went along with Marcus Bailey and Clifton Jackson, two fellow upperclassmen from Birmingham who made the rounds of all the outlying joints several times a month.

On all of my other trips out to the club before then, I had always been in such a big rush to get inside the main hall to get as close as possible to the musicians in the big-name bands that came through on tour that I never had paid any attention at all to the ongoing local entertainment in the after-hours room on your left as you came into the main lobby. After all, the name bands such as Duke Ellington, Jimmie Lunceford, Count Basie, and others that you heard on the radio and on records (and also some of the territory bands like, say, the Sunset Royals) were something you scrimped and saved up for.

She sang some new and some standard pop songs. She sang the blues in all tempos, and she would also do a torch song on request. But you could tell that she got a special kick out of swinging love songs like "My Blue Heaven," "I Can't Believe That You're in Love with Me," and "Exactly Like You" off-time to a medium tempo, and as soon as you heard her shout one twelve-bar chorus with the combo signifying back at her over an ever-steady, omni-flexible, four/four, you knew exactly why they called her Boss Lady.

Not that she was ever actually bossy, not in the least. She didn't have to be. Her authority was as casual as it was complete. All she had to do was come tripping on stage with the combo riffing "At Sundown," and it was as if the storybook queen herself had just entered the throne room, and when she bowed and smiled and waited for everything to settle down, it was (for me at any rate and perhaps on some level of feeling if not quite of consciousness for others, too) almost as if it were about to be Mother Goose tale time around the fireside once more. *Schoolboy that I was and to some extent still am, that was what came to mind at the very outset of the first show I saw her open and just as I was about to whisper to Marcus and Clayton that there were few things anywhere in the world better with some down-home bootleg ale than a good-looking brown-skinned woman with another blue-steel fairy tale, there were the drum rolls, the piano vamping, and her opening proclamation: Let's drink some mash and talk some trash this evening.*

On stage she came across as a seasoned professional at ease and in charge, but sitting next to her at the bar you could see that she was probably not yet in her midthirties, if she was yet thirty, and you also realized that she had seemed taller on stage because she had long-looking, rubbery-nimble legs and she also moved like the dancer she also was. From that alone I guessed that she was size fourteen (36"-24"-38"), which in those days used to mean that along with everything else she was built for speed and maneuverability and also stacked for heavy duty and endurance. It was not until later on that I began saying that she was bass clef, although I had already picked that up from my brand-new roommate during the very first term of my freshman year.

You could also see how little stage makeup she needed for a room that size, and you could tell that the high sheen of her long black wavy hair, which she wore pulled back and clamped into a ponytail, did not come from a hot-comb treatment. All it took was a very small amount of a very light oil and a few routine strokes with a regular dressing-table comb-and-brush set.

I saw you listening, she said, and when she smiled at that range you got a quick flash of one gold filling that looked more like a cosmetic touch than a necessary correction because the rest of her teeth were without any visible flaws at all. And so were her hands and fingers, which, like those of so many brown-skin women I remember over the years, were every bit as small and elegantly tapered as I have always imagined that those of storybook princesses, being of regal birth, were expected to be.

This is not your first time in here, she said, and I said, My third time, my second time on my own, but before she could say anything else somebody cut in to say something nice and give her a show-biz hug and a fake kiss and then there was a couple who did the same thing, and when they left she said, A lot of college boys come in here all the time, but you're the first one I spotted sitting back here all by himself listening with your ear cocked like that, so I said, Who is that one and where did he come from?

So where do you come from, Schoolboy, she said, and when I told her, she said, I've been down through there more than once. So you grew up hearing Old Papa Gladstone and y'all must have more jook joints on the outskirts of Mobile than any other town in this state.

She herself was from Anniston by way of Bessemer, she said, and within the next week or so she also told me about how she had started out in the church choir in Anniston and had become a soloist by the time she was a teenager. She had finished high school in Bessemer and won a scholarship to 'Bama State, but she had dropped out after a year to join a road band barnstorming through the Alabama, Florida, Georgia, Mississippi territory. That was when she became a dancer because the bandleader wanted her to be an all-round entertainer as well as a singer. And for a while she had also played around with the idea of becoming a headliner with her own road show.

When it was time for her to get ready to go back on stage, she stood up and put her hand out and as I took it she said, A lot of college boys come in here all the time, but you're the first one I spotted listening like that, so I just decided to come over here and say something to you and find out what you're putting down. And I said, I sure am glad you did, but what did you find out? and she said, A whole lot. I can usually tell a lot about people from what I see from up there, and it usually don't take me but so many more bars to check them out close up.

Then as she stepped back to head for her dressing room, she gave me a playful one-finger push on the shoulder and said, You just checked out just fine, Schoolboy. I do believe that you just might do. Then, before I could get myself together to say something cute, she winked and waved and was gone and I couldn't believe my luck.

XVI

SO WHEN I finally let myself take time out to think about her again that next morning, I said, Hello, Miss Hortense Hightower, whichever you are. Because I was also thinking about the one and only Miss Slick McGinnis, also known as Slick to some and as Old Slick to others, so-called not because she was so notoriously devious but from the time when she used to wear her hair bobbed and plastered flapper style. The fact that she always looked at you as if she knew more than she would ever tell and as if she always meant more than she ever actually said was really a coincidence after the fact.

She had been right there all along, although not all the time because she also traveled a lot. So much so that whenever you saw her it was as if she had either just recently come back down home from New York City and sometimes elsewhere as well. Or she was only a few days away from going back off again. Or so it seemed. But even so, everybody always used to think of her as being as much of an ongoing part of whatever took place in Gasoline Point in those days as anybody else. And so did I and so did she.

Most of the time she used to be going back and forth between Gasoline Point and New York, but sometimes you also used to hear people talking about something she had brought back from Paris, France, or London, England, or Rome, Italy, or Madrid, Spain, where she, like Jack Johnson, had not only seen but had also met some of the world's greatest bullfighters and had also heard a lot of great gypsy guitar players and had also seen a lot of flamenco dancing which I had also seen on the Spanish floats in the Mardi Gras parade which is why I already knew the difference between the sounds of castanets and the syncopated riffing of the old plantation-style bone-knockers and thigh-slappers you used to hear on street corners in those days.

At first I used to remember her as the pretty lady with the spangle-dangle ear pendants, diamond ring, and string of pearls, who sometimes also sported a cigarette holder that was said to be platinum and ivory. Then later the sound of whatever shoes she happened to be wearing as she came clip-clopping along the sidewalk always used to make me think of bunny-pink bedroom mules and boa-trimmed kimonos.

I always knew that she had been married for a while a few years ago, but didn't have any children, and all anybody seemed to know about her ex-husband was that he was somebody who ran some kind of business up in New York, who refused to come down South even on a week's vacation. So nobody in Gasoline Point, not even his in-laws, had ever seen him in the flesh, which probably was why nobody ever thought of him as an actual person anymore. He was only a shadowy part of a half-forgotten event that in itself was not very real to anybody in the first place. Anyway, by the time I was old enough to become just casually curious about who he was and what his line of work was, nobody could tell you or could remember what his name was (it was not McGinnis, to be sure). Or could say if anybody else in Gasoline Point other than Miss Slick McGinnis and her family ever knew what it was.

I also don't remember having already known anything about what she herself had been doing for a living all of those years before she decided to tell me what she told me after I had answered the questions she asked me about school the day I helped her carry her parcels home from the post office. Before then I didn't have any notion whatsoever that she had a very special job with a very rich high society woman who lived in New York and traveled all over the world. All I knew was that from time to time she traveled a lot.

Then during the next several weeks I was to find out that the high society New York woman she had been working for and who was responsible for her being up north when she went was somebody who was once her blond blue-eyed playmate back when the McGinnis family was living in the truck-gardening area across Mobile Bay near the resort town of Daphne.

That was another story in itself, one about how the blond blue-eyed playmate, whose family was in the drydock business, grew up to be one of the most popular debutantes in the whole Gulf Coast region and about how she married into a family in the shipbuilding industry in New York, and then it was also a story about a mansion on Fifth Avenue and an estate on Long Island with stables and kennels and about a family yacht for sailing the Atlantic and cruising the Mediterranean and the Aegean, and also about how Miss Slick McGinnis had always been able to spend so much time back down in Gasoline Point.

But that was not what we really talked about that first afternoon. All she told me then was that the packages were from some people she lived with up in New York, and then from what she said from time to time later on I found out that her pay was more like an allowance for a member of the family than the wages of a household servant, and that not only could she come and go any time she chose, but that all of her travel was a household expense. The very first thing she mentioned on the way from the post office and the main thing that everything we ever said or did always came back around to was school.

She said, I've been hearing a lot of very nice things about how fine you're still coming along over at the school, which was what most people who knew Mama and Papa and especially Miss Tee also used to say in one way or another. Sometimes all some of them used to do was call your name and nod and smile and give you the highball sign. I was used to that, and I also knew that you never could tell when somebody was also going to use it to try to hem you in with the same restrictions required of boys in training to become Catholic priests.

But as soon as she said what she said the way she said it, I crossed my fingers because I couldn't help wishing what I wished any more than anybody I ever saw in the barbershop or the bench on Stranahan's gallery could help shaking his head and sighing before straightening up and putting on his best manners whenever she came in sight.

So tell me about it, she said as we came on across that part of Buckshaw Mill Road and into the kite pasture, and I started with Miss Lexine Metcalf and by the time we opened her front gate I was talking about Mister B. Franklin Fisher, and we put the parcels down and sat on the front porch, me in the swing and her in one of the two cane-bottom rocking chairs, and that was when I told her about how when you were chosen to attend the Early Bird sessions that automatically put you in competition for a scholarship to college, and she said, Now that's something, now that's really something, and then she said, And aren't you something.

She said, I can't tell you how pleased I am about the way you're turning out. She said, I bet you didn't know that I was keeping tabs on you, and I said, I sure didn't, and she said, See there, you never can tell, and then she said, So from now on I am also going to be expecting to get some of my report directly from you in person. And with my fingers crossed again I said, If you say so.

Then she stood up and said, When do I get to hear something about your plans for yourself and I said, Anytime you say, and she said, Come on, let's go say hello to Mama, and I followed her around to the backyard and saw Miss Orita Bolden McGinnis who was also known as Miss Orita Bolden and Miss Reeta Mac. She was sitting on a wrought-iron bench under the scuppernong arbor, talking to Miss Sister Lucinda Wiggens and when she heard my name she looked up and held out her hand and said, Miss Melba's little old scootabout man, come on over here boy, just look at him growing on up to be a fine-mannered young gentlemen, and they tell me you got yourself a good head on your shoulders too. They tell me that that Miss what's-her-name Metcalf spotted his birthmark for learning the minute she set eyes on him. So you going give me a hug and some of that good old sugar like you used to, and I said, Oh yes, m'am.

Then Miss Sister Lucinda Wiggens opened her arms and folded me into her bosom and I had to give her some sugar on both cheeks and the lips too, and she said, Lord boy you precious, just precious. And she said, So many of our people don't care about nothing these days. Nothing but a lot of the same old foolishness. But some of us does care just like that Professor Fisher we got over yonder and you have our prayers to go right along with his strictness and all that book learning, and we all tells him to lay it on that precious few that got to make up for the many.

Back at the front gate I said, Next Tuesday would be just fine with me too. Then I could hardly wait to get somewhere and be all by myself. So when I came to the end of Gins Alley I didn't turn right and go directly home by way of the live oak shade cluster and the houses from which old Willie and Miss Meg Marlow moved to join Mister One Arm Will Marlow up in Detroit the year before Little Buddy Marshall came to town. I turned left into the old pushcart and wheelbarrow

lane between the tank-yard fence and the skin-game thicket
and came on down across the tank-car sidings and along the
L & N tracks and then back up through cypress bottom to the
chinaberry yard by way of Dodge Mill Road.

When you came through the front door, the parlor was on your
right and the dining room was beyond the arch on your left and
you saw yourself in the big gilt-framed mirror above the long, low
marble-top chest of drawers against the back wall of the vestibule,
and I also remember that there was a telephone beside the mirror
because it was the first one I ever saw in a private home.

In the parlor there was a player piano with stacks of piano rolls
lined up across the top, and there was also a big console-model Vic-
tor victrola just like the best one on display in the window of Jesse
French Music Store on Dauphin Street off the southwest corner of
Bienville Square. As I remember it, Jesse French was the biggest
store in downtown Mobile for sheet music and band instruments
in those days, but what I always used to think about whenever I
heard that name was the black-spotted white dog figure sitting on
the pedestal out front with his ear cocked to hear his master's voice
out of the megaphone of a windup Victor victrola.

She left me on the settee which I guessed had been turned all
the way around from the fireplace because it was summertime,
and you had a view out through the double window and across
the swing porch fern pots and the rose bushes, and in the distance
beyond the open plot between the house across the street you could
also see the sky above where you knew the Tensaw River canebrakes
bordered the route to Flomaton and Bay Minette and also down
into Pensacola and the Florida panhandle.

You could hear her moving about in the kitchen and also the
sound of spoons and ice clinking against glass, and then she was
back with a pitcher of lemonade and two glasses on a silver tray.
She put it on the center table and poured me a glassful and put
a Chesterfield in her jeweled cigarette holder, lit it with a kitchen
match, and sat cross-legged in what I took to be Miss Reeta Mac's
rocking chair, dangling one of the pink-bunny bedroom mules on
the tip of the toes of her left foot.

So tell me some more about yourself, she said then, and what I
said at first was still mostly about school because it was about all

of the campus sports activities I went out for such as football, basketball, and track and field events and baseball to be sure which
I also played off campus because I had decided that I wanted
to be a four-letter athlete as well as be an all-round scholarship
student, even though Mobile County Training School didn't actually award MCTS sweaters because in those days the budget for
interscholastic extracurricular and recreational activities was
barely enough to cover the cost of basic regulation equipment and
uniforms, even when it was supplemented with the fund from the
benefit drives and programs that Mister B. Franklin Fisher was
forever putting on to make up the difference.

I said I could also play tennis, which was also mainly a campus
game in those days (as was volleyball which was only a recess time
pastime at Mobile County Training School when I was there).
But you didn't have time for tennis if you were as tied up with
baseball as I had always been. You didn't have to say anything
about hunting and fishing because both were just a natural part
of living that close to the woods and swamps and rivers and creeks.
But I did mention swimming because I was the first one in Gasoline Point to do the American crawl. Everybody else was still doing the dog paddle, the sidestroke, the back paddle, and the fancy
overhand until I began showing some of them how much more
speed you got when you kicked and breathed like I had learned
to do from a white boy named Dudy Tolliver and also by watching the hundred-meter swimmers in the newsreels of the Olympic
games in Los Angeles.

We went on talking and that was when I found out that Miss
Reeta Mac was already across the bay visiting family people in
Daphne and that she herself was going over to join her the next day
and also go down to Point Clear and Magnolia Springs over the
coming weekend, before heading back to New York the following
Wednesday night on the northbound L & N Crescent Limited.

That was when she began telling me the first part of what she
was to tell me about herself over the next two years between then
and the end of the summer after I got my diploma and my college
scholarship and she gave me my going away present.

The very first thing she wanted me to know something about
was what she did when she was away in New York and elsewhere,
and she also explained just enough about her childhood across the
bay for me to understand why she went to New York in the first

*place and then she told me about some of the things she guessed I
wanted to know about what she liked about living in New York.*

*Then I heard the whistle of the three o'clock switch engine on
the way from the L & N roundhouse across Three Mile Bridge to
the tank-car sidings and realized how long I had been there. But
before I could decide what to say next, she said what she said, and
I had to cross my fingers again.*

*Because as soon as she said, So now tell me something else, I
was just about certain that I knew what was coming and sure
enough, the very next thing she said was, What I want to find out
about now is, how in the world did you manage to make it this far
without getting trapped up in some of all this trouble down here
in these bottoms. After all, she said, this is Gasoline Point. After
all, this is jook joint junction.*

*She said, Unless I miss my guess, you know exactly what I am
talking about and I said I did know and I did because I knew
what had happened to Eddie Lee Sawyer and also to Tyner Beasley, not to mention Clarence Crawford, better known as Crawfish
Crawford, all of whom were once Early Birds while I was still
down in grade school. Eddie Lee Sawyer, who had dropped out of
school in the tenth grade because he had to marry Mary Frances
Henderson, was now the father of two girls and was driving a
delivery truck for Hammels Department Store in downtown Mobile. Tyner Beasley had made it to the eleventh before he took up
with Zelma Gibson and forgot all about becoming an architect
and went to work as a handyman to keep enough money coming in to pay the rent with a little something left over for the
honky-tonks.*

*As for Crawfish Crawford, who had been so brilliant in all of
his mathematics and science classes, he had become so jealous of
Miss Big Baby Doll Jackson who did you-know-what for a living
that he had slit her throat from ear to ear and then had hidden
out in the Hog Bayou for three months until they finally caught
him on a tip from a moonshine runner and brought him to trial,
and state solicitor Bart B. Chatterton had sent him to the penitentiary for ninety-nine years and a day.*

*She said, I sure do hope I'm right about you, because don't think
I don't know what you been up to with all of them nice-boy manners and smiles and them sly twinkles in your eyes, and all I could
say was that I hoped so too, and she said, I damn sure better be*

because after all, you're still just a minor in the eyes of the law, and then she also said, But God knows the truth of the matter is I just hope I didn't hold off until it's too late.

That was how we finally got to that part, and all at once it was as if you had to keep touching the brake pedal because when she said, So well then, she was already standing up and as I followed her down the hall it was suddenly as if what had happened back when Miss Evelyn Kirkwood said what she said that time was about something else altogether, because I was still only a boy then, and now I was almost a man.

But nobody could have made anything any easier than she was to do that first afternoon. She said, Now tell me one more thing. She said, You didn't give me any sugar the other day. You gave Mama some and you gave Miss Sister Lucinda Wiggens some. So how come you skipped me? And I said, Because they asked me and because you're different, and she said, Well can I have mine right here, right now? And as soon as I was that close she said, Well I declare well I just do declare, so I guess I must be different all right. It's a good thing this didn't happen out there in front of Mama. Then as I remember it, the next thing I heard was her saying, You can uncross your fingers now. You're doing fine, just fine.

When we said good-bye before she went back to New York at the end of that last summer before I was to leave for college, the graduation present she had saved to give me at that time was a Gladstone bag, and inside was the one-way ticket I needed to get me to the campus with my scholarship voucher. She said, So good luck, Miss Melba's Scooter, and when I said, Miss Slick McGinnis's Scooter, too, she said, That's just a little secret between you and me, and so is this little going-away present. Then she winked at me and I will always remember how her diamond ring finger felt as she squeezed my hands exactly like all of the other good fairy godmothers I ever dreamed about.

XVII

IT IS just about impossible to keep your thinking from becoming outright wishful when you are with somebody like Hortense Hightower, but I was not about to let myself jump to any hasty conclusions about what she was up to. I told myself that it was probably some sort of little game, that upper-level college man that I had finally become, I was supposed to be up to playing along with it until I found out whatever it was. In any case, the main thing was to keep from being faked into making a country break. Not that I was actually suspicious. There was no reason to feel that I was being set up. It really only was a matter of not taking for granted that somebody liked you on your own terms.

When I went back the week after that, she spotted me as soon as she came on, and at the end of the first set she came over and said, Say, there's my new schoolboy friend. What say, Schoolboy? Take care of my brand-new schoolboy friend, bartender. I was wondering when you'd come back to see me again. I was thinking about how much I enjoyed talking to you.

So there she was, sitting on the next bar stool smiling at me again, and it was not a matter of believing your luck or even of what to say, because after she asked me about the campus routine, she said, You know, when I was thinking about you I was also thinking about how some people come in here all the time because they just like to have some music going on around them when they're sipping a little taste of something and jiving or maybe conniving and carrying on.

Then she said, Now don't get me wrong. They all right with me because that's all a part of what a place like this is here for, too. Always has been. Some people just like to hear it without really listening to it. But you can get to them because they feel it. Just like they dance to it. That's how come when it stops, they stop whatever they're doing and start looking up and around like a fish in a pond you just dried up.

But somebody like you, now, she said, now you're not just hearing and feeling it. You also pay attention like you also got something personal and private going on. Like me, she said, and I don't mean like no musician either. Because I know a whole lot of musicians can't hear doodly-squat. I know some can read anything you put in front of them and then can't play anything you want to hear, and I know some others that'll look at you like you crazy if you want them to go back and read something they just played the stew out of by ear. But later for all that, she said, because I can tell you a few things about musicians. I know some that just come in to watch you working so they can argue about what you did do or didn't do, and you never know when they just looking for something to steal and sometimes when they can't find nothing they want to steal they subject to say you ain't doing nothing. So later for them. I don't call that listening to music because me, I'm just up there trying to help people have a good time.

Which is exactly what she did when she came back on the floor show in which there was also a guest instrumentalist from Montgomery on alto sax whose solo feature was a takeoff of "Sweet Georgia Brown" which was very much like the one that Paul Bascombe was to record on tenor sax with Erskine Hawkins's band of mostly former 'Bama State collegians a year or so later.

I went back again that next Wednesday night and at one point in what was becoming our ongoing conversation, about listening and hearing, she said what she said about some hotshots from the campus who usually seemed to be mainly interested in showing how hip they were by making requests just to find out if she was up with the latest tunes they had been picking up on the radio and from the phonograph and that is how I found out that she herself still had every recording she had ever bought or had been given over the years.

So I said, What about Ma Rainey and Bessie and Clara and Mamie and Trixie? What about Jelly Roll and Papa Joe and Sidney Bechet and Freddie Keppard and young Satch and she just nodded, smiling, and said, Well, no wonder I noticed the way you listen. Because you listen like somebody already on some kind of real time. Because I can tell, and let me tell you something else. When you're already on some solid time you don't have to go around worrying about being up-to-date.

Then she said what she said about a college boy being the one who was supposed to know where stuff came from because that was also how you found out how and when it came to be the way it was as of now. That's what school is supposed to be all about, she said, and a hip cat ain't nothing but somebody trying to be a city slicker, and if you really think you can slick your way through life, shame on you.

Now that's what I say, she said, and that was also when she told me that I was welcome to come by her house and play some of her records if I wanted to, and I said, I most certainly do want to, and when it was time to get ready for the next show, she described how to get to her neighborhood from the campus, and said what the best time was and left it at that.

So it was as if it was all up to me. Bur when she answered the doorbell that Sunday afternoon three days later and saw me standing there and said, So there you are, I could tell that she had actually been expecting me, and before I could apologize for intruding on her precious free time, she said, I'm sure glad you could make it. Come on in and let's get started.

So there I was indeed (with my wishes firmly in clutch and my senior year pretty much within reach and my long-range objectives a matter of no less urgency for being not yet specific), and there was the long living room with a nine-and-a-half-foot ceiling and there was the console-model Magnavox phonograph at the end where the floor-length draperies of the tall French windows were.

Some of the records, most of which were ten-inch and all of which were 78 rpm in those days, were in the built-in storage compartment, some were on the glass-top Hollywood coffee table between the overstuffed lounge chair and a hand-me-down rocking chair facing the console as if it were a fireplace, and there were others along with the stacks of sheet music on top of the white lacquer-finished grand piano near the arch where the Persian rug ended and the dining area which could be closed off with folding glass partition doors began.

I had never seen that many records of that kind anywhere before, and while I was looking through them and trying to make up my mind where to begin, she started the one that was already on the turntable, and as soon as I heard the first six notes of the piano intro I said, Hey, Earl Hines, hey Jimmy Mundy, hey "Cavernism," hey you, too, and she said, That's my favorite dance hall stomp-off and getaway number. Right after the theme, to break the ice and get 'em out there on the floor.

That's the one, she said when it was over, but now here's another one of it that they made about a year before that one and

I like it too. I like those little differences in the call part of that opening phrase, she said, and I said, Me too, and I said, That guitar up front like that is all right with me too. Years later, Earl Hines was to tell me that he and Jimmy Mundy named that piece for a Washington, D.C., nightclub called the Cavern, but it was strictly Chicago music even so, because when you heard it going on the radio in those days, it was as if you were being taken to the South Side, just as Ellington's "Echoes of Harlem" took you to uptown Manhattan and Count Basie's "Moten Swing" took you out to Eighteenth and Vine in Kansas City.

The first side I handed her was old Jelly Roll Morton and the Red Hot Peppers playing "Kansas City Stomp" as if to charge the atmosphere of Gasoline Point with train whistles and sawmill whistles and riverboat and waterfront whistles. So that Little Buddy Marshall and I would have to do Old Luzana Cholly's sporty-limp strut going past dog-fennel meadows and crepe-myrtle yard blossoms en route once more to infield clay and outfield horizons by day and honky-tonk pianos by night.

I remember everything we played and hummed and whistled along with that first Sunday afternoon. After "Kansas City Stomp" I handed her Duke Ellington's "Birmingham Breakdown" which Little Buddy Marshall used to like to whistle and walk to as much as I did, especially when we were making the rounds beginning around twilight time on Saturday nights when the atmosphere of Gasoline Point was also charged with barbershop bay rum and talcum powder and the aroma of cigars, bootleg whiskey, and cookshop food.

And then one that Little Buddy and I also used to think of as our briar-patch music was Fletcher Henderson's orchestra playing "The Stampede." Then I said, Talking about something to make them so eager to get out there and cutting that they can hardly wait in the hat-check line, how about this? and I handed her "Big John's Special."

Then we went on to the one labeled "Wrapping It Up," but which coast-to-coast radio announcers call "The Lindy Glide" (as in lindy hop, another name for jitterbugging, as up-tempo dancing to jazz music was called in those days), and that led to "Back in Your Own Back Yard," "King Porter Stomp," "Stealing Apples," "Blue Lou," and "Sing You Sinners," which, like Bessie Smith's recording of "Moan You Mourners," was a mock church sermon pop song whose words I can still hear Nathaniel Tally, also known as Little Miss Nannie Goat of Tin Top Alley, shouting like stomping the blues with the Shelby Hill street-corner quartet backing him up, especially at a Saturday night fish- or chicken-plate benefit social.

Old Smack, she said, and started it again. Old Smack Henderson from right over there across the state line from Eufaula in Cuthbert, Georgia.

So we listened to it again right then, and we still had to hear it one more time as much as we both also liked "Wrapping It Up." When I realized to our surprise how quickly the time had passed and that I had to head back to the campus, and when I said what I said about the arrangement being strictly instrumental in spite of the fact that the lyrics for it were about singing, she said, That's Smack Henderson and when you got tenor players like Coleman Hawkins or Chu Berry or Ben Webster who is the one on this one, and you got trumpet players like Joe Smith, Red Allen, Rex Stewart, Roy Eldridge, and Emmett Berry who is the one on this and you got Buster Bailey and people like that, you ain't got much for a vocalist to do.

I don't mean he don't like them, she said. He knows what to do with them all right. Ethel Waters, Alberta Hunter, Bessie and Clara Smith, Fletcher Henderson put some righteous stuff behind them and a whole lot of others. Then she said, But what about this? Here I am supposed to be a singer and this whole afternoon was strictly instrumental. But that's just the kind of singer I am, if you know what I mean. Ain't nothing like having all that good stuff behind you. I started out in the Mount Olive Choir and then went on to those bands. As far as I'm concerned, that's the getting place for my kind of singer. All them old pros sitting back there in them sections, and you got to go out every set and make them like having you up there. Now, that's the real conservatory for this stuff.

At the door she said, Wouldn't nobody believe that we didn't get around to but one thing by Duke Ellington, and not one bar of old Louis, and I said, I know I wouldn't and I was right here. Then when I said, I sure do thank you for letting me stop by like this, she said, Well now, you know your way over here and you got this many months left before graduation time.

XVIII

THE MAIN newspaper topic in the barbershop as I took my seat in front of Skeeter's chair that morning was baseball. There were only a few more weeks before opening day in the major leagues, and the preseason exhibition games were in full swing and just about all of the talk was about last year's World Series and this year's most likely pennant winners and how the stars in both leagues were shaping up and also about what outstanding rookie prospects were already beginning to show up.

Skeeter was touching up Red Gilmore who ran Red's Varsity Threads Shop next door and always came in on Tuesday, Thursday, and Saturday mornings to keep from looking as if he ever needed to go to the barbershop. Skeeter's chair was number two. In chair number one, Deke Whatley, the manager whose real name was Fred Douglass Whatley, was working on a sophomore basketball player known as Kokomo because that was the town in Indiana that he came from. The third chair was not in operation because Thursday was Sack McBride's day off, and in the fourth chair Pop Collins was giving a facial to somebody I didn't know.

I did know who Pete Carmichael was. He was taxi number one and he was sitting on the high chair that Deke Whatley, who liked to keep his eyes on the shop and the sidewalk at the same time, used to rest his legs every now and then, but at the moment Pete Carmichael was sitting with his back to the window because he had the floor.

They went on talking about the spring training games of the big league baseball teams, and I heard them, but I was not really listening and following what points were being made because I was rereading the chapters on the commedia dell'arte, or comedy of improvisation of sixteenth-century Italy in a book entitled, *The Theatre: Three Thousand Years of Drama, Acting, and Stagecraft*, by Sheldon Cheney, and remembering how my roommate already knew so much about the masks, costumes, and characteristic gestures and stage business of such stock figures as Harlequin, Pantalone, Pierrot, Columbine, the pedantic Doctor, the swaggering but cowardly Il Capitano, when I mentioned the commedia dell'arte while we were talking about what we had been reading over the summer when he came back that second September. Later on we had also talked about how all of that was related to minstrels, medicine shows, and vaudeville skits, but now he was no longer around so that I could talk to him about what I was thinking about how it was also related to the way jazz musicians play and also to the way they work out their arrangements and compositions.

I was thinking about how whenever you talked to him about anything like that, you were in touch with somebody who was always ready to find out something else about customs, manners, and methods because as a student of architecture he was always involved with matters of design, construction, and engineers, and playing around with stage sets and puppet shows was as much a hobby with him as building and flying model airplanes and assembling and operating ham radios.

Then Skeeter had put the finishing touches on Red Gilmore, and it was my turn and I was sitting in the chair and being swung around toward the wall where all of the pictures, placards, and notices were and along with the chatter and laughter of the ongoing conversation, there was the also and also of clippers buzzing, scissors snipping, and also of shampoo and skin lotion and talcum powder and tobacco smoke, and outside there was the damp, overcast almost-spring weather, and you could also hear the droning and beeping traffic in that part of the morning on that part of the campus thoroughfare.

I looked at all of the long since familiar pictures of Jack Johnson and Peter Jackson and Joe Gans and Sam Langford and of Satchel Paige and Josh Gibson and Buck Leonard and Cool Papa Bell and of such entertainers as Bojangles Robinson and Charlie Chaplin and Bert Williams. Just when I came to the band leaders, I stopped and tried to shut everything out because I did not not want to start thinking about Hortense Hightower that early on in the day that I was going back to see her again, and when I opened my eyes and ears again, the talk was about politics and Deke Whatley had the floor.

He had a freshman in his chair then, and as usual he was working and talking with a short stump of a dead cigar in his mouth, his gold crowns showing as he clamped it in a way that reminded me of how some people hold a coffee cup or a drinking glass with that little finger extended, which is exactly what he did when he took the cigar out of his mouth from time to time.

Red Gilmore was sitting on the shoe-shine stand by the door that led to the back hallway and the toilet. He had the morning paper open and folded to a pad, working on a crossword puzzle as he waited for the bootblack to come in. The others sat listening to Deke Whatley, who kept the clippers in his right hand all during the time that he was doing more talking than hair trimming.

Politics. Politics. Politics, he said. You want to know something about politics? I can tell you something about some goddamn politics. In the first place, it really don't take all that much. It really don't. It don't take a thing but some plain old horse sense mixed in with a little grade A bullshit, and of course you got to have some nerve, too, because how you going to bullshit if you ain't got no nerve. A good politician got the nerve of a brass-ass monkey.

I can tell you something about some politics because I been watching that business for a long time. I been studying that business and watching what some somitches doing, so I'm talking about something I know from experience and mother wit. If you want to get somewhere in this man's world, you got to know how to play yourself some politics. That's a fact. Don't give a damn what nobody say. I'm telling you like it sure butt is as sure as you born. They supposed to be teaching them up yonder on the quadrangle, democracy and all of that no taxation without representation jive. You know what democracy is? I am going to tell you exactly what democracy is: playing politics. That's all it is. That's all it ever was and ever was intended to be and ever will be. Everybody playing politics. Everybody in there trying to get his little taste. You can say anything you want to, but you ain't never seen no somitch yet and you ain't never going to see one that wasn't out there for what he can get. Hell, ain't nobody going to admit it. Goddamn! old pardner, that's just what I'm telling about: horse sense.

He was into another one of his sermons then, as almost always happened when somebody said something academic about freedom and justice for all. He couldn't stand to hear anybody talk about the Constitution as if it were the Holy Bible. To him it was a document that was used for making deals and that was about all it was intended to be.

Ain't nobody but a fool or some old aristocrat going to be going around saying I'm all for me and to hell with you. You don't have to have no sense at all to know better than that. Hell, that other somitch is out there for hisself, too. And ain't no goddamn body going to think more of you than he do his own fucking self. Goddamn, gentlemen, and that's how come I know I don't really understand most of these old white folks to save my life. You see what I mean? You see what I'm driving at? Goddamn redneck somitch think they going to make you want to treat them better than you do your own precious goddamn self. Man, don't nobody come before me, not in my own heart and soul. You follow this stuff. That's something your goddamn dingdong is always telling you. That's all that somitch down there between your goddam legs ever know: me, me, me.

But now let me tell you something about them old aristocrats. When you come right down to it, that ain't nothing but the special few playing politics up there in the high society circles around the king. And don't care how bad-ass the king hisself is, he also got to be working some smooth jive to stay where he is and then if he really got his shit jumping, he can make hisself the goddamn emperor.

You see what I mean? And that's another thing we got to realize, too. I'm talking about us now. Ain't no mufkin white somitch going to give you nothing he don't have to. I'm talking about life now, cousin. This ain't no Sunday school out here. You got to get your ass out there and politic with them. Politic the hell out of them. You just find a way to get in there and dangle enough votes in front of one of them and he'll bring you your little taste, too. See if he don't. That's all it is. Everybody getting their little taste and that other fellow getting his little taste, too. That's what the king and them aristocrats forgot and that's how come so many of them wound up losing their hat, ass, and gas mask. You don't have to have no Ph.D. to dig that. Me, all I ever had was a little old country RFD myself, and I damn sure know it.

All right, now, you take Cat Rogers for instance. Take Cat Rogers right here in this county. You know why he can kick all them black asses and get away with it? Not so much because he so goddamn badass, although he is as badass as almost any somitch I know. You got to admit that. Cat Rogers is one more badass peckerwood, gentlemen. I ain't joking. That's one out-and-out badass somitch on his own, starbadge or no starbadge. Don't let nobody fool you. That redneck somitch will pull off that goddamn badge and pistol in a minute just on general principles. You want to make it something personal? That's all right with him. But that ain't how come he can get away with it, because I know some bad-ass boot somitches just as bad as he is, when you come right down to that. But he can get away with it and they can't because them that puts him in charge of the county jail lets him have his leeway, because it keeps things in line so they can keep their little taste coming like it always has. All this stuff is logic, gentlemen. You got to dig the logic of this stuff. Now get this. When these goddamn crybabies gang around talking about Cat Rogers this and Cat Rogers that, I tell them when you get yourself enough votes to get rid of Cat Rogers, you won't even have to get rid of him because he going to be seeing to it that you getting your little taste just like everybody else. Now that's politics, pardner, and that's what democracy is all about. Don't care what they got in them books up there.

Then he said, Say boy, goddamn! Is your head shaped like this or is I'm cutting it like this? And everybody laughed and he stood back looking at the freshman's head as if he couldn't believe it was real.

Boy, you got the goddamndest head I ever seen in all my born days.

Everybody kept on laughing and the freshman was laughing, too. There was nothing wrong with his head and he knew it. Deke Whatley swung the chair around so that he could look out to the sidewalk and then he turned it so that the freshman could see himself in the mirror and then he went on talking in another tone of voice.

What's your name, son?

The freshman told him.

Where you from?

Birmingham.

You from the Ham?

Yes, sir.

What part of the Ham you from?

The freshman told him.

Goddamn, boy, you ought to *know* something if you come from the Ham. You know old Joe Ramey up in the 'ham?

Yes, sir.

Old Joe the Pro.

Yes, sir.

Boy, you know something. You supposed to know something. That goddamn Joe Ramey is the greatest cat in the
world, boy. What'd you say your name was?

The freshman told him again.

Well, boy, if you know Joe Ramey, you know one hell of a
cat. Hey, this boy is all right. Mark my words, gentlemen.

Hey, what the hell does this Joe Ramey do, Deke? Govan
Edwards asked. He was not waiting his turn. He was there
because the barbershop was one of the places he liked to drop
in on several times a week. I knew him as a sports fan but I was
never quite sure what he did for a living.

Do? Man, that goddamn Joe Ramey can do just about anything he want to. You know him, don't you, Red?

Who, Joe Ramey? Do I know Joe Ramey!

The door opened and Showboat Parker, cab number nine,
the only Cadillac taxi in town, stuck his head in and said, Hey,
in here, and came on in pushing the door shut behind him and
leaning back against it as he checked to see who all was present.

I said, Hey in here, he said, and somebody said, Shoby, and
somebody else said, What say Shoby, and somebody else said,
What's happening Shoby, and he said, Man, ain't nothing happening, and this is the weather for it. What's the matter with
these people? and somebody said, The day is still young, give
them time, Shoby. But you must have picked up some kind of
news out there.

Man, ain't no news, he said. White folks still out in front
that's all I can tell you. And when Pete Carmichael said, Well
that sure God ain't no news, he said, You goddamn right it
ain't. Us white folks so far ahead of you cotton-picking granny
dodgers, it ain't even funny no more. And when Pop Collins
said, Hell, it ain't never been funny, he said, Hell, it better not
be funny. What the fuck, you'd think this is. This ain't no goddamn vaudeville. This is life in the nitty goddamn gritty. You
goddamn people always laughing too much anyhow.

Hey, wait a minute now, Deke Whatley said, holding up his
clippers, Hey now hold on there because that ain't the way I
heard it. The way my grandpappy told me, all that grinning

and laughing is a part of our African mother wit, because the first thing our African forefathers found out after they realized that all them hungry-looking peckerwoods was not going to eat them was that if you didn't grin at them, white folks would be scared shitless of us all the goddamn time and ain't no telling what they might do. My old grandpa told me, if you ain't got nothing but a stick and a brick, you don't go around making somebody nervous that's got cannon and a Gatling gun.

Then he said, But now tell me this. If white folks so far out in front, how come they spend so much time worrying about what we doing? They supposed to have everything already nailed up and they always coming up with another one of these books to prove that we too dumb to figure out how to get it unnailed.

You got me the answer for that? he said, and Showboat Parker said, Now come on, Deacon, you know good and well that us white folks don't have to account to the likes of y'all for nothing we do. It ain't for y'all to understand how come us white folks doing anything. We just want y'all to learn how to read well enough to know your place, and we got a million-dollar school right here to teach you.

They were all laughing again then, and he said, What say there, Red Boy? What say, Skeets and the rest of y'all?

Skeeter swirled the chair, and you could see them in the mirror. Showboat sat in Sack McBride's empty chair and leaned back, crossing his legs and folding his hands over his taxi driver's paunch, his cap tipped down over his eyes.

Where were you last night, Red Boy?

Trying to get somewhere and do myself some good, man, Red Gilmore told him.

The boys missed you.

Man, I couldn't make it. Not from where I was last night.

The stuff was there.

How'd you make out?

Man, me, I ain't held a decent hand yet.

What about Old Saul?

Aw, man, they cleaned Old Saul Baker out way before midnight. Man, Old Saul was probably home in bed by midnight last night.

How about Giles?

Man, don't say nothing to me about no Giles Cunningham. Old Giles, hunh?

That goddamn Giles Cunningham is one of the gamblingess somitches in the world today.

Old Giles checked them to the locks, hunh?

I believe that somitch would have broke the Federal Reserve last night, man.

Old Giles.

Talking about hot, goddamn but that somitch was hot last night.

Yancey got them tonight?

Yeah.

That's what I thought. I guess I might peep me a few of them myself this evening.

You welcome to it, Red. But me, man, the hell with some old poker tonight. Man, I know something else I can do with my little change beside giving it to that goddamn Giles Cunningham.

When I left, they were still talking about Giles Cunningham, but on the way back to the dormitory I was thinking about Old Dewitt Dawkins once more because he was the one that listening to Deke Whatley always made me remember again. Old Dewitt Dawkins who had the best reputation of any baseball umpire and prizefight referee anywhere in the Mobile and Gulf Coast area.

Old Dewitt Dawkins, also known as Judge Dawk the Hawk because when he used to come into Shade's Tonsorial Parlor across from Boom Men's Union Hall on Green's Avenue (always with the latest editions of the Reach and Spalding baseball guides and his up-to-date world's almanac), it was very much as if the circuit judge had come to town to hold court and deliver verdicts, which he did with lip-smacking precision in a diction that was deliberately stilted.

The first thing that probably came to most people's minds when you mentioned Dewitt Dawkins was the way he used to call baseball games back in those days before the radio sportscasters became the voice you associated with the ongoing action. There was a time when all of the baseball youngsters in Gasoline Point used to say *In the window!* for a called strike because that was the way Dawk the Hawk (as in hawkeye) called them.

But what the political gospel according to Deke Whatley had brought back to my mind was something that I had heard from Old Dewitt Dawkins in his high seat on the shoe-shine stand in Shade's barbershop one rainy afternoon in August of the summer before my junior year at Mobile County Training School when he was explaining why we already had too many people signifying and not nearly enough qualifying.

Not that he wasn't still calling balls and strikes. No matter what he was talking about, he spread his hands to give the safe-on-base sign when he agreed with or approved of something. When somebody made a point or he himself was giving the word, he gave the strike sign to indicate it was on target, which was to say *In the window!* So to show his disagreement or disapproval, he jerked his thumb giving the *out* sign to which he would sometimes add with his most stiltedly precise enunciation:

> Tough
> shit (pause)
> you done torn
> your
> na-
> tu-
> ral-
> ass!

Out of my face, out of my face. Out of my face, you disgrace to the human race.

What the hell do we need with some more loudmouth hustlers out there carrying on like they got to get those people told because nobody ever did before, he said that afternoon.

That many of us were all in Shade's because the game with Maysville had been called for weather in the second inning. Hell, as far as that goes, we already had a silver-tongue orator none other than the one and only Honorable Fred Douglass himself doing that all the way back during bondage and on into the war for Emancipation and right on through the whole Reconstruction mess and into the times of old Grover Cleveland, and I don't know anybody that ever did it better since.

He said, We don't need any more horror stories trying to put the shame on those people as if they don't know what the hell they themselves been doing to us all these years. Just look at what they did to *Uncle Tom's Cabin*. Those same people put on black faces and turned the whole goddamn thing into a big road-show minstrel, traveling all over the country.

So much for getting them told, he said, and then he said, Now I'm going to tell you something once and for all about the shame and the blame. If you got the problem and don't buckle down and come up with a solution, hang your own goddamn head in shame, and if you go all the way through college and don't come back with some answers, shame on us all.

XIX

WHAT HAPPENED between Giles Cunningham and Dudley Philpot out at the Pit while I was browsing in the periodicals room later on that afternoon had really begun almost a week earlier when Giles Cunningham and Wiley Peyton had stopped Will Spradley as he came along the railroad spur that used to run from the loading ramp and coal chute at the campus power plant and on through town and out to the siding at the station where trains eastbound from Montgomery and westbound from Atlanta used to stop without being flagged in those days.

It was payday for most people who didn't work on the campus, and before leaving on a three-day business trip up to Chattanooga, Giles Cunningham was making the rounds to collect a few overdue personal loans he had made during the past several months. When he and Wiley Peyton saw Will Spradley, they were on their way to see who just happened to be hanging out in Jack's Chicken Shack just outside the campus entrance near the band cottage.

Will Spradley had been just rounding the bend near the old Strickland mansion and had been coming on walking that loping walk toward where the first downtown subdivision began, when Wiley Peyton who was driving saw him and said, Well, here's your Will what's-his-name over there, and Giles Cunningham had said, Pull over, and Wiley Peyton had brought the big Cadillac onto the soft shoulder and shut off the motor,

and Giles Cunningham had said, Spradley, Will; and Will Spradley had jumped and said, Gile, what say, Gile? and came down
the grade and across the grassy ditch and up to the car and said,
Gile, again. What say, Gile?

Will Spradley had stood looking into the car but at the dashboard, not at Giles Cunningham who was not looking at him
either but at the misty early spring tree-line beyond the fence
on the other side of the spur tracks and who said, Don't you
have a little something to see me about? and Will Spradley had
said, Yeah, Gile, sure Gile, I ain't forgot it, Gile.

I was just going on down into town and I was coming right
on by to see you just as soon as I took care of some other little
business first, Will Spradley had said then, talking and then
listening, but still not looking at anything but the dashboard,
and when there was no reply he had gone on and said, That's
exactly what I was on my way to do, Gile.

Then Giles Cunningham had said, So here I am just tickled
to death to save you that long walk. He still didn't look at him
but he was listening very carefully because he knew that with
Will Spradley you almost always had to read between the lines.

I'm going to have to see you a little later, Gile.

Today's payday, ain't it?

I mean later on today, Gile. I'm talking about today, a little
later on today, Gile.

You been paid, ain't you?

I'm going to see you later on, Gile. I'm going to have your
money then, every penny I been owing you, Gile.

You mean, you ain't got it on you? I thought you just said
you already been paid.

I mean, I just want you to let me see you a little later on,
Gile. That's all I mean. I just mean I can't pay you right now,
he said, and Giles Cunningham said, Now what kind of shit is
this, man? You got your paycheck, didn't you, or is that it?

Wiley Peyton sat at the steering wheel looking along the
corridor of the March green branches of the wooded bend
on the left side of which you could see the turnoff that led to
the stone pillars and wrought-iron gates to the old Strickland
manor house. The strip of off-campus shops, including Jack's
Chicken Shack, was out of sight about a quarter of a mile farther along, and then there was the campus.

He heard what was being said and not being said, and it was all old stuff to him, and besides it was not really anything that concerned him. What he spent most of his time dealing with was the operation of the Pit. But even so he heard Will Spradley say that he had the check with him, and he knew what was coming next.

Aw, hell, man, I thought you were talking about some kind of a problem.

So I'm going to see you later on, Gile.

You already got your check, so see me now.

But it ain't cashed yet, Gile. That's how come I got to be getting on downtown just now.

Man, what the hell you talking about? The goddamn bank been closed for nearly two hours.

But that's not what I'm talking about, Gile. I got some other little business I got to see to first. Then I going to be right on out there to see you.

Where you going to see me?

At your place.

Which place?

Which one you going to be at?

I'm on my way out of town.

Well, when you get back then.

The hell you will. Here, I'll cash your check. He stretched his legs, pushing his shoulders against the back of the seat and pulled a roll of bills out and took a fountain pen and a flat check-holder from his inside coat pocket.

Hey, you can't do that, Gile.

Can't do what, man?

You can't cash it.

Man, you wasting my time. Sign that goddamn check and hand it here.

Will Spradley didn't move. He was looking at both of them then, but Wiley Peyton was still looking straight ahead, and Giles Cunningham just sat waiting and listening as if not looking at anything in particular, but he saw Will Spradley take a step back from the car as he heard him say, I can't do it, Gile. I done told you I'm going to pay you what I owe you and I will, but I owe somebody else and he supposed to cash my check.

Man, what's the difference who cashes it? Now you going to sign that fucking check and hand it here, or do I have to get out of this car and kick your ass? Man, I don't feel like kicking nobody's ass today. I just want my little change so I can be on my way. Look, I'm even going to forget about the goddamn interest. Here, just sign the son-of-a-bitch and get the hell out of my face.

Aw right, Gile, Will Spradley said then. But I'm telling you, man. I'm talking about Dud Philpot.

So when Giles Cunningham looked out from where he was sitting at the desk in the office he shared with Wiley Peyton at the Pit and saw the dull gray Plymouth come crunching onto the gravel driveway and saw Dudley Philpot hop out, not even pausing to slam the door, and come fuming into the dining room, he was not surprised because Will Spradley had already been there with a message from him.

Through the door to the dining area you could see several people sitting on stools eating at the counter and there were several more at a table near the jukebox. Wiley Peyton sat at the cash register because it was that part of the late afternoon when business was always very light and someone had to relieve the regular cashier so that she could always have three hours off before the dinner rush began.

Without really looking up from what he was doing, Giles Cunningham could see Dud Philpot go over to Wiley Peyton, and Wiley Peyton pointing him toward the office and then there he was, just standing with his hands on his hips, trying to look his white boss-man look but also trying to get his breath back without seeming to, and at first Giles Cunningham went on doing what he was doing and then he looked up as if he had just seen him. But he didn't say anything.

Wasn't Will Spradley in here?

I was under the impression that he left out of here some time ago, but I don't know which way he went.

Well, didn't he tell you what I said?

He didn't say nothing that made any sense at all to me, and I didn't have time to be bothered with him today anyway.

You didn't have time to be bothered with Will Spradley? It was me that sent Will Spradley in here. Me.

Well, what he said didn't make no sense.

He was standing up then, and he picked up some papers and moved over to the filing cabinet by the window, dropped them into the wire basket on top and stood for a moment, not as if he were listening and waiting, but as if trying to decide what office routine detail had to be taken care of next.

So what the hell you think I came all the way out here for?

I figured you were trying to catch up with Will Spradley and I told you he ain't out here. He was in here all right, but that was a while ago.

I came out here to see you, Giles Cunningham, and you damn well know it, and you damn well know why, so cut out the horseshit.

Man, I sure must have missed something somewhere along the line, because I sure in hell can't remember ever having any dealings with you in my life. So I don't know what you talking about.

I'm talking about that check.

Well, there sure ain't nothing I can do about that because I already deposited it. I told Will Spradley that and I thought for sure that he had told you by now.

Now listen here, Giles Cunningham, Will tells me he begged you not to cash that check in the first place. Is that right?

It sure is. He didn't tell you no lie about that.

And that's what you got to answer to me for.

Man, you can't be saying that Will Spradley told you something to make you believe I took more out of that check than I had coming to me. I don't know what he did with the rest of his cash after he left me, but he sure in the hell can't blame it on me. Hell, I didn't even take out all I had coming.

But he knew very well that nobody was accusing him of any such thing. He was cross-talking Dudley Philpot and they both knew it because they both also knew what very old and very grim down-home game Dudley Philpot was turning the matter of Will Spradley's paycheck into, although Dudley Philpot would never have called it a game, because to him games were something you played for fun and what he had on his hands was the very urgent obligation to keep things in proper order.

But to Giles Cunningham it was no less a game for being as serious and dangerous as it was. The very way that Dudley

Philpot was standing there just inside the door with his hands on his hips was an unmistakable part of the game, and so was the way he himself was pretending not to notice how much more upset Dudley Philpot was becoming.

Outside the window there was the highway of black rubbery-looking asphalt in the afternoon mist, with the cars and trucks splitting by, buzzing and rumbling as if in a passing parade in a newsreel world apart, and he remembered the trip back from Chattanooga in the rain and wondered when he was going to find time to have that Tennessee and northern Alabama red-clay hillbilly mud washed off his white sidewalls.

Then he realized that Dudley Philpot was swearing at him and he was not surprised because that was a part of the game, too, but at first it was as if all Dudley Philpot was saying was nigger nigger nigger nigger nigger nigger, and that didn't surprise him either, and then what he heard was answer me nigger answer me answer me and he said, I don't answer to no name like that.

You could tell that Dudley Philpot didn't really know what to do next, because then he just stood there clenching his fists and fuming and saying nigger nigger nigger, you nigger you nigger nigger nigger, you nigger, you nigger. Nigger! Then all at once it was as if he realized that he was acting and sounding like a daddy fyce puppy dog in a small-town neighborhood running along inside the fence line yap-yap-yapping at a passerby who was annoyed and alert but was also trying to keep himself from busting out laughing. So that's when he said what he said next.

Nigger, I'm beginning to get the notion that you think you smart or something, but meddling in my business is getting too smart. And when all Giles Cunningham did was just shrug his shoulders at that, he said, Nigger I got a good mind to kick your black ass till your nose bleeds shit right here and now.

But he didn't move from where he was, so Giles Cunningham didn't have to say I know you know better than that. Even so, he couldn't keep himself from giving him his old AEF fixed bayonets eyeball to eyeball you-got-to-bring-ass-to-kick-ass look, and that was more than enough.

All right, you uppity black son-of-a-bitch, you're lucky. You don't know how lucky you are. I'm going to give you one night to get your black ass out of this county, and I don't want to ever set eyes on you again. You got that?

*He said that screaming at the top of his voice so that everybody
out in the cafe and also back in the kitchen could hear him, and
then those in the cafe saw him stomping out, glaring at nothing
in particular, and saw him hop back into the Plymouth and slam
the door. Then they heard the motor stall and start and stall and
then start and hold and saw him throw it into reverse and cut
the front end around as if he were riding a saddle horse and head
back toward town.*

XX

WHEN I CAME out of the library on my way to the dining hall
through the late March twilight of that damp, green Thursday
evening, I was thinking about my freshman and sophomore
year roommate again who would have gone into his old mock
penny-dreadful palm-rubbing and mustache-twirling heh-heh-
hey routine as soon as he looked up and saw how many books
on the commedia dell'arte I had just checked out.

Then he would have reached for his pad of 8½″ × 11″ grid
paper and sketched several examples of the makeshift all-
purpose stage platforms that the old traveling troupes of actors, musicians, and jugglers used to set up on the streets and
in the squares of town after town back in sixteenth-century
Italy and France, and you had to make the connection with
minstrels, medicine shows, and vaudeville acts, after which he
would come up with some fact about the famous drawings and
sketches of Jacques Callot that you had either missed or hadn't
yet come across.

And then for the next several days you could count on him
taking time out from his own current works-in-progress to play
around, dashing off sketches and watercolor illustrations and
maybe even a few woodcuts of masks, costumes for most of
the stock characters and standard scenarios, beginning with
Harlequin (wearing diamond patterns based on Picasso's blue
and rose period Harlequin), Brighella (who was as foxy as Rey-
naud), and including old Pantalone, Il Dottore, Il Capitano,
Pulcinella, Scaramouche, and so on to Columbine and Pierrot
(which he would make sure that you knew was the French version of the Italian Pedrolino or Pierotto).

Nor would he be able to stop here. The next step would be a desktop stage model or a puppet show for which we would have to improvise our own skits for a week or so just as an exercise for the two of us, and only the two of us, because if you as much as even mentioned it to anybody else you would be accused of trying to impress them. As if you didn't know better than that. Anyway, the only part of it that anybody else would see would probably be two or three leftover sketches or watercolors that he would have tacked up on his side of the room where they would be mistaken for examples of class exercises in design.

That was the way he always was about things like that, and that is the way I knew it would have been if he had still been there, and it was also why he was not somebody you tried to compete with. He was somebody to try to keep up with to be sure, but not because you didn't want to be left behind, out-stripped, but because it was as if he were there to keep you re-minded of what Miss Lexine Metcalf's windows on the world bulletin board was really all about.

But he was no longer there on that early spring evening, be-cause he had decided to take the Old Trooper up on his option and had transferred to an Ivy League college for his junior and senior years. That was the very first thing he told me as soon as he came back from Chicago that second September. But it was not until that following spring that he finally got around to saying what he said about the farewell caper he owed it to himself to pull off a few times before cutting out for good.

The main thing he wanted to talk about as he sat unpacking as a sophomore was what had happened during the summer, especially the trip he had made with the Old Trooper that July. The two of them had driven from Chicago to New York, stop-ping long enough in Cleveland, Pittsburgh, and Philadelphia to visit the art museums as well as the architectural and engi-neering landmarks he had wanted to find. In New York he had been given free time on his own to spend in the Metropolitan Museum, the Museum of Modern Art, and the Museum of Natural History and had also made the rounds with the Old Trooper to see the Yankees in Yankee Stadium, the Giants at the Polo Grounds, and the Brooklyn Dodgers at Ebbets Field, and naturally went along to watch the boxers working out in Stillman's Gym and to Madison Square Garden which was on Eighth Avenue between Forty-ninth and Fiftieth Streets in those days.

What he was mainly curious to know about my summer on the campus as a working student was how much reading I had gotten in, and when I told him that along with everything else I had checked off my list I had made it all the way through both volumes of Charles and Mary Beard's *The Rise of American Civilization*, he wanted to know if I had also looked into Beard's *Economic Interpretation of the Constitution*, and he also asked about Thorstein Veblen's *Theory of the Leisure Class* and *Theory of Business Enterprise*, and Frederick Jackson Turner's *The Frontier in American History*, and that was what led to all of the reading and talking about social contracts and political structures and procedures (including socialism and fascism) during the months that followed.

When he saw that I had also checked out the new editions of Louis Untermeyer's *Modern American Poetry* and *Modern British Poetry* on extended loans, he said I also had to get *Axel's Castle* by Edmund Wilson and *Exile's Return* by Malcolm Cowley, which I did as soon as the library opened the next day, and that was what got me going on James Joyce and Marcel Proust (but not Hemingway whom I had already discovered in *Scribner's* magazine and the first issues of *Esquire* magazine back at Mobile County Training School), and not Faulkner who was already there along with and head and shoulders above such other Southern writers as T. S. Stribling, Erskine Caldwell, and Margaret Mitchell whose *Gone With the Wind* had been a best-seller for about a year.

As for his own summer reading, he had knocked off about his usual quota of detective stories featuring Hercule Poirot, Bulldog Drummond, Ellery Queen, Sam Spade, and Nero Wolfe, and he had also read John Steinbeck's *Tortilla Flat*, and Kenneth Roberts's *Northwest Passage*. But the two books he had stuck with all summer and had taken along on the trip east were Sheldon Cheney's *Primer of Modern Art* and Roger Fry's *Vision and Design*, and what he had read on the train coming

down this time was *Man's Fate* by André Malraux, so his first
two checkouts from the library were going to be *The Conquerors* and *The Royal Way.*

*He didn't mention anything at all about any kind of special fare-
well caper until it was wisteria time again that next spring and
he was ready to get started on it, and at first I missed the point
and said what I said about Floorboard McKenzie, who was the
local limousine with the best connections across the line in those
days, and that was when he spelled it out, saying that he wasn't
dismissing anybody for using Floorboard because that way was no
less a matter of life and death in his neck of the woods.*

*But what he had in mind for his own personal derring-do re-
sponse to that particular down-home taboo was something else,
and he said, Don't let anybody tell you that the one in question
whoever she may be is not worth risking your life for, because the
woman is not what really counts. It's the taboo. Because once they
put that life and death price on the taboo that makes them all
worth it, because they have to feel as violated and outraged when
it is a cathouse slut as when it is Miss All-City Belle.*

*So there is no way around it for us either, he said. If you're one
of us, you have to commit a deliberate violation of that particular
taboo before you can really call yourself a man. No matter what
else you ever do, that's something you have to answer to yourself
for, and you're either game or you're not, he said; and then he also
said, Hey, but maybe all of this is all knee-high-to-a-duck stuff
to you, and I said, Not really because I had never thought about
it as being a matter of the kind of taboo and derring-do he was
talking about.*

*What Mama had always been saying about keeping out of
trouble with girls and about not letting friendly white ones grin
your neck into a noose was as much a part of my conception of the
everyday facts of life in Gasoline Point as everything else I was always being warned about. But the way Trudie Tolliver said what
she finally said that day when I met her coming along Dodge Mill
Road from the landing where the skiffs and putt-putts tied up in
Three Mill Bottom made the actual here-and-nowness of it sound
like something you had to be very, very careful about, to be sure,
but not at all like anything that you always had to avoid by all
means. After all, doing something like that was always supposed*

to be a matter of privacy if not secrecy whoever the female partner was.

So the main thing I remember about how I felt about that first time with Trudie Tolliver with her storybook blue eyes and corn-silk golden lashes, lip fuzz, and dog-fennel meadow and her piney woods voice and sweet gum twig breath and tomboy toes is how lucky I was being let in on one more secret, and with Miss Evelyn Kirkwood I remember feeling even luckier because I was still only an early-teen boy then and she was thirty something, maybe going on forty.

At first I had just thought that Trudie Tolliver was a girl who wanted to go everywhere her brother went, so she was always around whenever she could be only because Dudie Tolliver (as in Dude) was the one who used to take me duck hunting and boat fishing and trout-line setting and also swimming and bridge diving, beginning shortly after his family moved into the back of the Last Chance store his father was managing at the end of Old Buckshaw Mill Road and U.S. 90 near the new drawbridge, and he kept it up until his father got a job managing another store and moved on into Mobile.

It was from Duane Dundee, better known as Dude and Old Dudie, Tolliver that I learned to do the American crawl that the Tarzan movies and the newsreels of the Olympics were to make so much more popular than the fancy overhand stroke and scissors kick a few years later, and he also taught me a lot of other things that I was to continue to find out more about by reading Field and Stream magazine later on. So until that afternoon, as friendly as she always was, she was only somebody you had to put up with unless her brother could convince her that it was not one of the times she could come along.

But that afternoon in the bottom, it was as if she and I had been very close friends all along and I knew that she was going to start teasing me even before she said what she said. She said, I bet you wish you knew the secret I know, and when I said, Why, she said, Because it's about you, and I said, How you going to know if it's true if you don't tell me so I can tell if it's so, and she said, Because I saw it all for myself, and I said, That's what you say but it doesn't count if I don't know what it is because anybody can just come up and say something like that. So she said, Well maybe I will if you promise not to tell Dudie, and I knew I didn't have to, because all you had to do was look at how her eyes were mocking you and there was no doubt that she couldn't wait to tell you anyway. But I did promise, and she said, I saw your trigger, and I said, My what? as if I didn't know and she said, I spied on you and Dudie swimming naked down there around the bend from One Mile Bridge. And I tried to get my hand in my pocket, and she said, I see you, Scooterboy, so now you want to root me right this minute and you know it and I know it. And I couldn't deny it because I couldn't even take my hand back out of my pocket.

She said, Keep on going until you get all the way around the curve then turn on around and come on back halfway up the hill and turn off to the trail to the right, and this is my signal, and she whistled one of the bird songs that old Dudie had probably already taught her before they came to Gasoline Point and he started teaching me.

There was a different bird-song signal for every time between that summer afternoon in the L & N thickets and twilight of the last autumn night before her family moved on into the city limits of Mobile. As for the risk I was running for that many months, it was as if once it all got started all of Mama's terrifying warnings about a gang of rednecks tying you up and shucking your life seeds like two raw oysters no longer applied to you if you were always careful enough. You didn't even have to mention anything at all about that part of it, and the closest we ever came to doing so was the time she said what she said about having something on old Dudie because she knew that he gave something from the store to a certain notorious dark brown-skin Gasoline Point party to get her to go into the bushes with him, and then she said, He ain't got nothing on me and he not going to get nothing. Unless you tell him, she said.

With Miss Evelyn Kirkwood it was almost as if you were not really taking very much of a chance at all, because all you had to do was what she said because she was a grown-up and I was only in my early teens, and every time I was in her presence during the four or five weeks that we were doing what we did I was supposed to be running routine errands and then helping her to get packed to join her husband up in Muscle Shoals near the Tennessee state line where he had moved on to a new civil engineering project when he finished his contract on the Alabama State docks along Mobile River. But I was not really working for her because as hard as Papa always had to hustle to make ends meet, he and Mama were dead set against ever hiring me out to white folks. So as far as they were concerned, I was over there as a return favor for something Mister Garrett Kirkwood had done for Papa.

She said, You smell like you just washed yourself with Pine Tar soap. That's nice. That's Aunt Melba and Uncle Whit and all that sweeping and brushing and scrubbing and washing for you. So come on in and come on over here and let me look at you. Nice. Very nice. Don't be afraid. You're not afraid of me, are you? I always thought that you thought that I was a very pretty lady, she said, and I said, I do. Because she was, with what I now remember as her Gainsborough eyes and complexion and her anatomy-sketchbook calves and insteps. I'm not going to bite you, she said. That's a good boy, she said. Nice, very nice. You knew I wasn't going to bite you, didn't you, she said. Because it sure doesn't look to me like you're scared one bit. So I guess I must know something about picking and choosing brown sugar lumps, she said. And she did not say anything at all about not telling anybody because she knew she didn't have to; but she did emphatically say, And don't be calling me no Miss Eve like in evil. Call me Miss Ev. Everybody else called her Miss Evelyn or Miss Evelyn Hughes (as in the old Hughes family and place up the Tombigbee) or Miss Evelyn Hughes Kirkwood, and so did I when something about her came up in public, but in private she sometimes gave me other names to call her along with some of the things she told me to do.

You know something, man, I told my roommate, man, that's just not something you let yourself go around thinking about. I said, Man, once you get away with some stuff like that you're glad it happened, and that's it.

As for the caper that he had decided that he owed it to his conception of himself to try to bring off before ending his sojourn in the Deep South, he had already spotted somebody who met all of his requirements. She was a certified Southern belle from a bona fide antebellum mansion who just happened to be a co-manager of a department store on Courthouse Square a few doors down from Tate and Davidson's, not because she had been trained for a career in the retail business but because she had inherited half-ownership from a childless uncle on her mother's side of the family.

Do you know the one I'm talking about, he said, and I said, No but I'll take your word for it, and he said, Not this time, old *pardner, because sophomores that we still are alas I want to make sure that you don't jump to any sophomoric conclusions about wishful thinking, compensation, or some other Viennese bullshit. He said, I want you to go down there and see for yourself, old pardner, I insist, old pardner. So I did go down as if looking around for a gift for a girlfriend, and when I saw her come out of the office I caught my breath and crossed my fingers, and when I finally came back to the room from the gym that night I said, Man I sure am still a sophomore all right because I do believe you wished it all up and sent me down there knowing that I would see only what you wanted me to see, and he said, No Pygmalion I and no Galatea she. So I said, That leaves us with Herr Doktor Faustus and his snake-oil princess, and he said, Some snake some oil some princess.*

She may have been a year or two older than we were, but she had been away to finishing school and on cruises to Europe and the Near East, and perhaps that along with her several years of very active experience as a businesswoman made her seem older than she was and certainly older than she looked, which was less than twenty-five at most.

Whatever her exact age, she was the kind of very good-looking and casually style-conscious young Southern woman that images of certain New York fashion models have been based on for generations. Also, not only was she herself one of the most prominent young women in town and not only was her store as popular as it was classy, but it also had the most up-to-date college shop in town, which attracted a lot of students from the campus in spite of all of their very strong reservations about shopping in a store facing a courthouse square with a Confederate army memorial as its centerpiece.

So the first step turned out to be easy. He went into the manager's office and introduced himself as a student of architecture and design who wanted to ask her some questions about current trends in fashion, art, and interior decoration for a term project he was working on, and before he came back out he had also made her aware of his easy and thorough familiarity with every type of article in the current and recent issues of Vogue, Harper's Bazaar, Vanity Fair, *and* House and Garden *stacked on her desk.*

Within the next ten days, he was being paged to take phone calls in the booth off the lounge, at first just about every other night, and then every night, and within the month she had begun picking him up either in her sedan or her coupé, sometimes in the traffic circle between the gym and the tennis courts, sometimes near the water tower near the science hall and sometimes in the parking lot behind the library, and they would drive out to one of the campus groves or orchards that were a part of the horizon you saw when you looked out across the fields and pastures from the administration center of the school of agriculture.

Then suddenly after the third rendezvous the whole thing became a very private matter that he hardly ever mentioned except in passing until the final week of his last spring term when he started packing his luggage to pull out for good in the next day or so. I knew he was going to bring it up then, and he did. He said, About my caper I know you would understand what was happening. At first it was something I had to do for the hell of it but as soon as it actually became something person to person, it was no longer my caper but also her caper and so our caper, so from then on the taboo was as much a catalytic agent as it was anything else. If you know what I mean, he said, and I said, I think I do, I really do. But when I said what I said about answers to the old folks' prayers, there was an unmistakable touch of tolerant surprise and exasperation in his old playful sidewise glance and conspiratorial wink and smile as he said, That rather depends on which old folks one's been listening to, doesn't it old pardner? What about the ones who say you can never really call yourself a man among men until you have taken it on yourself to pull the caper I tried and get away with it. Come on man, I thought we agreed that we do indeed choose some of our ancestors.

But don't get me wrong about this caper thing, roommate, and don't play yourself cheap because I'm not. I wouldn't lie to you, old pardner. And he said, You know something? As pleased as I can't help but be about how all of this turned out I still find myself wishing that she had been the one who picked me out. So don't think I don't know that down-home boys who've been through what you've been through don't feel that they have to go through what I took on. I know as well as you do that it can't possibly add up to the same results.

So what now? I said as he went on packing his steamer trunk. And he said, The moving finger having writ moves on. It turns out that she does get up to Chicago on business trips from time to time, and she might give me a call as she volunteered to do. Or she might not. Meanwhile it was what it was and I'm better off for it.

Then three days later, his sojourn in the central Alabama strip of the briar patch at an end, he had cut back out to Chicago once more from where he was to move on to the also and also of other temporary destinations, beyond which there would always be still other horizons evoking newly pertinent ancestral aspirations and expectations and therefore obligations accepted or not, fulfilled or not.

Nor did any of that seem to faze him very much, if at all. Not him who was forever reminding me as well as himself that for all your carefully laid plans and expert training and guidance, a picaresque story line was the perpetual frame of reference for all personal chronicles.

Not T. Jerome Jefferson, T for Thomas, J for Jerome as in Geronimo, Apache or not, and also as in the Hieronymus. Who was never to be called Thomas Jefferson or Jerry Jefferson and certainly not Tee Jay as in Tee Jay period, but who was often called the Snake as in Snake Doctor and sometimes by extension Doctor Snakeshit, to wit, Shakespeare, the author of as many quotations as Anonymous himself! If you were known as snakeshit on the campus in those days, you were obviously somebody for whom doing things as required by the book was a snap, and who could talk as if sounding like a book was the most natural thing in the world.

But even as he used to say yea verily and reach for his notebook to record the goods on something, the T. Jerome Jefferson that I had recognized from the very outset as the best of all possible roommates ever and who was now almost a full year's long since long gone to other encounters elsewhere, always sounded to me as if as far as he was concerned, anything that was to be found in books, especially schoolbooks, even the most advanced schoolbooks, was not unlike the data on timetables, maps, and mileage charts. *Elementary, my dear Watson. Elementary.*

XXI

ALL THE way out from the campus that Thursday evening the main thing on my mind was the stack of Louis Armstrong and Duke Ellington recordings that Hortense Hightower and I had pulled out and started playing the week before. Beginning with "When It's Sleepy Time Down South," we had spent all of the first hour listening to such Armstrong instrumentals as "Potato Head Blues," "Weary Blues," "West End Blues," "Weather Bird," "Beau Koo Jack," and "Struttin' With Some Barbecue" among others, each of which had become an instant standard as soon as shipments of it arrived at music stores and the record counters of department stores all over the country.

Then we had moved on to "Stardust," the national brownskin dance-hall anthem since my junior high school days, "Lazy River," "I'm Confessin'," "When You're Smiling," and "Swing That Music" on which his epoch, yes epoch-making vocals were either matched or exceeded by his solo trumpet choruses. So then there were all of those recent show tunes like "Thanks a Million," "It's Wonderful," "I Double Dare You," "I'm in the Mood for Love," and so on, which made all pop singers want to sing like him from then on.

That took us up to the last fifteen minutes and we closed out with Armstrong taking the vocal and trumpet choruses on his band's version of Ellington's "Solitude," followed by Ellington's playing his own instrumental arrangement of his "Sophisticated Lady," which to this very day still takes me back to the way things used to be between me and the girls at Mobile County Training School between the ninth grade and the year I graduated and left town.

There was only enough time for one more then and since we had finally made it to the Ellington stack, we wrapped things up with a preaudition of the next week by playing "It Don't Mean a Thing if It Ain't Got That Swing," which I then whistled along with "Swing that Music" and Armstrong and the Red Onions' "Cake Walkin' Babies from Home" all the way back to the dormitory.

I already knew what my first selection was going to be and I had started whistling it as I came through the red-brick columns of the Emancipation Memorial Archway with the crown of three rings. It was "Echoes of Harlem," which was also called "Cootie's Concerto" because it featured Cootie Williams (*who was from Mobile!*) but which I liked just as much for the striding piano and bass fiddle figure that also made me think of it as a nocturne that was a perfect movie soundtrack for uptown hep cats on the prowl from after-hours ginmills to the wee hours key clubs along patent leather avenues.

Of course, there was also Ellington's music about the atmosphere of Harlem by day or night such as "Harlem Speaks," "Uptown Downbeat" and "I'm Slappin' Seventh Avenue with the Sole of My Shoe"; and there were other concertos such as "Barney's Concerto" also known as "Clarinet Lament," and for Rex Stewart's cornet there was "Boy Meets Horn," and for the alto of Johnny Hodges there was "Sentimental Lady" among many others.

As I came on toward the point where the paved sidewalk used to end in those days, I was whistling and humming my way through passages that I already knew from "Hip Chic," "Buffet Flat," "Jazz Potpourri," "Battle of Swing," and "Slap Happy," but from time to time in spite of myself I couldn't keep myself from wondering what she had in mind when she said she was playing around with the idea of making me a proposal that she was almost certain was going to surprise me. So I had to remember to pace myself and not get there ahead of time.

But as soon as she let me into the darkened hallway, I could tell that somebody else was already there and that something else was already happening.

Well, here's that schoolboy right on the dot, she said. And I said, As scheduled. I said, Never is to be no CPT for me, Miss Boss Ladee, and she said, Come on back this way, and I followed her to the end of the hall and down the steps to what turned out to be the toilet for the basement party area, and that is when I saw Will Spradley for the first time.

Naked to the waist and with a towel around his shoulders like a shawl, he was sitting crossways on the closed toilet seat holding his bloody and swollen face over the washbasin, grunting and sighing and waiting for her, and she said, This is Will Spradley. He got himself all tangled up in a mess that looks like it might get bigger before it's over. So come on over here and help me with this, she said, and handed me a bottle of witch hazel, a vial of Mercurochrome, a package of gauze bandages, and a roll of tape from the cabinet behind the mirror above the basin and went on doing what she was doing to his face and head with the washcloth and towel, and that's when the phone rang upstairs.

So I took over while she went back up the stairs to the entrance hallway to answer it, and I saw the gashes and knots and puffs on his head and face and the bruises on his arms and torso, and every time he had to make any movement he grunted, and when he was not gasping from sudden stabs of sharp pain he was sighing and mumbling to himself, saying mostly the same thing over and over, answering his own questions as if the right words would undo what had happened. Unh unh unh, just look at all this now. Just look at it. You ever seen anything like this in your life? I know good and well I ain't never seen nothing like this in all of my born days. I swear to God. All of this and what did I do? I ain't done nothing. I ain't done nothing to nobody.

When she came back, she led him out to the couch near the small crescent-shaped bar in the party room where, along with an upright piano, a regular professional rockola, and a console radio, there was also a stack of folded bridge tables and chairs, a big round poker table, and a pool table.

That was him, she said. He's on his way but there's something else he's got to attend to first, and Will Spradley said, I got to see him because I got to tell him, because God knows I wasn't trying to get him in no trouble like this, and she said, Take it easy, Will, we know that; and Will Spradley said, All I was doing was what I was supposed to do and I just happened to run into Gile and that's what I told Dud Philpot and that's all I told him because I wasn't trying to get nobody in no trouble. That's how come I come on out here. Because I didn't want nobody to see me going back out to the Pit, and she said, He knows that, Will. She said, I called him as soon as you made it out here.

All I was trying to do was what I was supposed to be doing and now look at all this, Will Spradley said. I declare before God, he moaned, touching his back and sides with his swollen left hand and pressing the cold damp folded face towels to his mouth and nose as I passed them to him while she went on trying to patch up his gashes and bruises using the Mercurochrome for some, Band-Aids for others, and gauze bandages for the larger ones.

Man, just look at you, she said, so just tell me one thing. How in the hell did you go and get yourself all tied up with some old poor white trash bloodsucker like Dud Philpot in the first goddamn place? You got to know better than that, Will Spradley, and he said, I don't know, Boss Lady. I just don't know, and she said, You hear this stuff, Schoolboy. As for myself, I still haven't been able to figure out how some of our people live to get to be as old as they do. It's a goddamn mystery to me how they don't poison themselves to death through just plain old dumbness.

Wait a minute, just a minute, just a minute, she said then and went over to a closet and came back and said, Here, help him into this, and handed me a faded blue-and-gray plaid sport shirt and put an old worn golf jacket on the chair by the couch. The shirt was size forty-two. Will Spradley was about size forty, but he was just about six feet even, and he must have weighed about a hundred and eighty-five lean hard pounds. I didn't know what Dud Philpot looked like then, but later I found out that he was in his early fifties and was about five-eleven and weighed about a hundred and forty-some bony-butt stooped-shouldered perpetually restless pounds.

I want you to know how much obliged I am to you for this you doing for me, Miss Boss Lady, Will Spradley said. I really do, he said, and I never will forget it as long as I live, he said, and she said, Which thanks to all this mess you now got us all in may not be all that long. And he said, Consarn the luck. I know it, Miss Boss Lady, and that's what bothers me more than anything else and that's exactly why I come all the way over here trying to warn Gile.

And Don't think I don't appreciate that either, she said, and then she said, Look, I hate to be fussing at you like you ain't already got troubles enough, Will Spradley, but goddamn man, there are white folks and there are white folks and you been around long enough to know what kind of white folks Dud Philpot is. Dud Philpot come from some of them old backwoods rosin-chewing-razorback peckerwoods. Any fool ought to be able to see that, Will Spradley, she said, and then she said what she also said about knowing that class of white people once person-to-person. Because, if your folks and their folks have been knowing each other for a while, that made all the difference in the world and you turned each other favors and country folks to country folks regardless of being on different sides of the color line when you came into town.

But if you were just another one of us trying to transact business with one of them that you don't know, they can excuse themselves for anything they do against you. From cheating to lynching. Because all they have to remember is that in spite of the fact that their white skin is supposed to put them above you, even the slaves back on the old plantations were better off than their so-called free but often raggedy-assed and half-starved and mostly despised foreparents.

You're right, Miss Boss Lady, Will Spradley said. Cain't nobody dispute that because here he comes jumping me like that after all them weeks and months I been meeting them time payments. You sure right because I feel like a fool for being surprised and now just look at all this trouble I might be causing all of us. That's how come I'm trying to find Gile. Because it's all my fault and I know it now and maybe it's too late.

I was listening and trying to put the situation together as well as I could and as fast as I could, and at first the problem was that I thought that Will Spradley was somebody who worked at the club or maybe at the Pit and then I had thought maybe Will Spradley was in such a hurry to see Giles Cunningham because he needed to borrow money to pay off an overdue debt to Dud Philpot, whoever Dud Philpot was, and then I realized that I had already become that much a part of something about which I didn't yet really know anything at all.

I sure do hope Gile hurry up and get here because I got to see him and tell him, Will Spradley said, because I don't want him thinking I'm like that because I know what people always subject to say and it ain't fair because it ain't true because I might be poor and sometimes I might have to take low and pick up what I can but I ain't no white man's nigger. I don't care what nobody say. I ain't never done nothing against my own.

He know Gile, Will Spradley went on talking as much to himself as to me and the Boss Lady. He got to know Gile. Everybody know Gile Cunningham, and everybody know Gile Cunningham ain't never about to be giving in to no Dud Philpot, so then here he come buck-jumping at somebody like I'm

the one when all I'm doing is standing around out there waiting for him so I can straighten up with him and get on about
my business.

Then the three of us were just sitting there, waiting as if for
the next weather report as you did when you were down on
the Gulf Coast during hurricane season, and that was when
Hortense Hightower asked him if he felt well enough to fill
me in on what the situation had added up from. She said I was
her young friend from the campus, and he said, Sure because
I'm the onliest one that can tell it to you just exactly the way I
got myself all tangled up in all this mess like this. Sure, because
maybe you the kind of college boy that can see my point, like
I'm counting on Gile doing. Because he the one I'm counting
on. Sure, because most of these other folks ain't no better than
white folks.

But he didn't begin at the beginning. He began at the point
where he was coming along the railroad spur and was stopped
by Giles Cunningham in a car being driven by Wiley Peyton,
and as he went on talking and dabbing his nose and mouth
with the face towel that he kept dipping into the basin of water
on the stool in front of him, he recounted everything, not only
word for word but sometimes also thought for thought and
almost breath for breath. So much so that it was not only as if
you were an eye and ear witness but also the actual participant
himself.

Maybe it was because I just couldn't stop thinking about the
music I had come to play on the phonograph that evening.
Maybe so, maybe no. But as closely as I was following every
detail of the story Will Spradley was retelling, not only for my
benefit but also for his own, as soon as he started telling about
it in his own way and at his own pace, it was also as if you
were listening to an almost exact verbal parallel to one of the
Ellington records that was near the very top of my list for that
night. It was called "In a Jam," but not because it was a song
with lyrics about being in trouble. So far as I know, there never
were any lyrics. The chances are that it was so named because
it was an instrumental composition derived from the interplay
of voices in a jam session.

And yet, of its very nature as a piece of music, "In a Jam"
was also about being in a tight spot. A jam session, after all, is

a musical battle royal, and as such it is always a matter of performing not only with hair-trigger inventiveness and ingenuity but also with free-flowing gracefulness which is to say elegance, not only under the pressure of the demands of the music itself but also in the presence of and in competition with your peers and betters.

All of which also added up to making the jam session a matter of antagonistic cooperation that enriched the overall rendition even as it required each instrumentalist to perform at the very highest level of his ability. Such, as every jazz initiate knows, is also precisely how the jam session also serves to expose the fact that there are times when the personal best of some musicians is none too good. Not that such is the basic function of the jam session by any means. Originally it was simply a matter of participating in a jamboree in celebration of something. Nor did anybody understand all of that more than did Duke Ellington even back then the plaintive emphasis of whose score makes it all too obvious that in this instance he was more interested in the structure of the jam session as such than with what he was later to call the velocity of celebration.

In any case, it was as if Will Spradley's plaintive voice, which already sounded so much like Tricky Sam Nanton's plunger-muted trombone to begin with, was also by turns all of the hoarse ensemble shouts plus the sometimes tearful piano comps and fills of Duke Ellington himself as well as each solo instrument including the alto of Johnny Hodges, the clarinet of Barney Bigard, and so on through the call and response dialogue to the somewhat bugle/trumpet tattoo sound of Rex Stewart's cornet out-chorus solo that you heard every time he made any mention of Giles Cunningham.

When he came to the point where he made his getaway through the back door of Dudley Philpot's store, he stopped and just sat sighing and grunting and shaking his head and dabbing the cold towels to his nose and mouth again, and Hortense Hightower said, Man, goddamn. Man, look like you coulda done *something* to keep that bony butt son-of-a-bitch from kicking your ass like this. I swear to God, Will Spradley, I swear to God.

But all he would say then was, I just want Gile to hurry up and come on over here so I can tell him and explain my part to him because he the one all this is about and I don't care what these old other folks think because they going to say what they going to say about me anyhow. They don't want to know the truth. They just want to talk about somebody. But Gile is a businessman and he knows business is business and that's the way he is and that's what I like about him.

Well, just take it easy, she said. He'll be here in a little while. Just as soon as he can, she said. But goddamn, she said to me then, can you believe all this stuff you just been hearing, Schoolboy? Myself, I know damn well it sure the hell is happening, but I'm still having a hard time *believing* it.

XXII

YOU COULD tell that Will Spradley didn't really believe that it was really happening either. Even as he sat sighing and moaning and nursing his lacerations and closed eye, you could see that he was still expecting to wake up and find that all of the pain and breathless urgency was only a part of a very bad dream brought on by his worries about his money problems which, given just half a chance, he could explain his way out of for the time being.

But when Giles Cunningham finally made it there and filled us in on his part, you knew that he was not having any problem at all in believing in the consequences of what he had become caught up in several hours ago when Dud Philpot had come charging into the office out at the Pit, because all during the time he was talking to the three of us, he didn't miss a step or even pause in the preparations that he was making for his next move.

That was when I found out what he had been doing while I was helping Hortense Hightower give first aid to Will Spradley. She had called him as soon as Will Spradley had showed up, saying what he was saying, and he had clued in Speck Jenkins at the Pit, Wiley Peyton at the Dolomite, and Flea Mosley out at the Plum, and then he had headed over to Gin Mill Crossing to the poker game in Yancey William's club room, because that was where he could find most of the help he was counting on, and when he pulled into the yard and saw the other cars he knew that most of the friends he was looking for were there already.

Big Bald Eagle Bob Webster opened the door and reached out to slap-snatch palms and stood grinning his ever-so-playful but ever-so-steady, bald-eagle-eyed, scar-cheeked grin at him with the others acknowledging his arrival without really looking up from the tobacco-cozy, corn whiskey-cozy, pomade-plus-aftershave-cozy hum-and-buzz at the green-felt-cushioned poker-round table.

Hell yeah, it's him all right, Bald Eagle Bob Webster, whom some called Eag and others called Bar-E, said. Grady MacPherson, who was holding the deck, said, Yeah, come on in here, man, goddamn; and Eugene Glover said, Hey, goddamn right, come on in here. Hey, where you *been*, man? And Felton Carmichael said, Hey that's all right about where the hell he been. Just bring your old late self on into this old chicken-butt house now, cousin.

He had stepped inside but he still stood where he was and waited with his hand up. The others, some sitting around the table as players, others hovering around, some only as onlookers and others waiting a turn—or the right moment—were Solomon Gatewood, Logan Scott, Eddie Rhodes, Curtis Howard, and Wendell Franklin, who said, Man, pull off your coat and money belt, and Logan Scott said, Hey, we been waiting for you, man.

So come on in here with all that money, man, Curtis Howard said, and Grady MacPherson said, All that *long* money, man, and Solomon Gatewood said, Come on in here with all of *my* money, man, and somebody else said, Man, come on in here with all of *all of our* money, and nobody noticed that he was standing with his hand up because they were all so busy signifying at him and laughing among themselves without interrupting the deal going down at the same time that nobody had turned to look at him as yet.

Old money himself in person, Logan Scott said back over his shoulder, still watching the table, Come on money, and Wendell Franklin said, No, man, you talking about *Mister* Money. Come on *Mister* Money. And Curtis Howard said, Hey, wait y'all. What's this cat doing coming over *here* at *all*? With all the money he already got, this ain't nothing but some little old nickel-and-dime stuff to him. And Eddie Rhodes said, Man, that just goes to show you about money people. Now me and you just trying to pick up a little extra change because it will come in handy, but Old Giles Cunningham just like to be *around* money, even if it ain't nothing but a little *chickenshit chicken feed* like this. And somebody else said, No, man, Old Giles Cunningham like to have money *around him*, and Eddie Rhodes said, Hey, yeah man, that's a good one—*right around his waist*.

They were all laughing, and you couldn't help laughing at yourself with them, and you knew that they knew as well as you did that all of you always came together whenever you could, mainly because you always had such a good time just being together. Not that at least a little playful wagering was not almost always a part of it. Indeed, even when they were all emotionally aligned on the same side of some contest. They were likely to make side bets on specific aspects of the performance, such as point spread, extra points, home runs, extra base hits, strikeouts, or knockouts, round-by-round point tallies and so on. But obviously such petty wagering was always far more a matter of ceremonial risk-taking and sportsmanship than of making a killing. Clearly the main reason that they used to make such a big deal of getting together to listen to the radio broadcasts of the important prizefights and the World Series and the Rose Bowl Game back in those pretelevision times was that it was the next best thing to sitting together at ringside or in the grandstand.

So what say, Giles, Logan Scott said, come on in the house, and Wendell Franklin said, Man, ain't you got that money belt off yet, and that was when they all finally turned to look at him and saw his hand up even as he laughed along with them, and that was when he said, Hey wait a minute, y'all. I trying to say something. Bald Eagle Bob Webster said, Hey Ho(ld) y'all. Hold on, hold on, hold on. He stood fanning his hands across each other in front of him and then he cocked his ear and said, Hey, what is it Giles? What's the matter, man?

Hey, I'm sorry I'm late, y'all, he said, but looks like somebody got another kind of little game that just might be shaping up out there tonight. It might be just a threat, he said, but you never know, and that was when he told them about what had happened between him and Dudley Philpot out at the Pit that afternoon and about what Hortense Hightower had told him on the telephone about Will Spradley.

So now I guess it's supposed to be my turn if I'm still here after he told me to unass the area, he said, and Eugene Glover said, Giles, you mean to tell me that Dud Philpot told you that? Not Dud Philpot, Giles. Man, you can't mean some weasly clodhopper like Dud Philpot think he can come up with some old tired-ass peckerwood shit like that. Man, come on. And Bald Eagle Bob Webster said, Just tell us what the fuck you need, Giles, and you got it, man, you know that.

They were all waiting then and he said, Well, Eag, I could use some of y'all over at the Pit with Speck and some others over at the Dolomite with Wiley, and I got a couple of other things I got to see to by myself, and Yancey Williams said, Well, you just go on, Giles. You just leave that to me and Eag. We'll divide them up. You get to Speck, Eag, and I'll get to Wiley. And look, Giles, if a gang of them happen to jump you out there somewhere, all you got to do is make it on back over here. Hell, you know goddamn well ain't none of them going to try to follow you over in here.

Man, Bob Webster said, you couldn't *pay* none of some somitches to come over in here even before they got taught that lesson. I'm quite sure they'll never forget when they let some fool talk them into going up on the campus that time.

Everybody there remembered what had happened (and had not happened!) back some fifteen years earlier when the Ku Klux Klan was on the rise again for a while, following the World War in France. Some could tell you about it from firsthand experience and others had heard about it from somebody who had been either personally involved in one way or another or were around at the time. But the account of it that I have always been most familiar with is the one that Deke Whatley used to recount in the barbershop when he used to get going again on one of his first-chair sermons on the folly of political action without organization.

Anybody think I'm just talking about some kind of old church membership politics already missed my point, he always used to say. I ain't talking about nothing where you got to go to meeting and they collect dues for some sanctimonious hustler in a Cadillac to rake in. *Hey, remember that time when a bunch of them Old Ku Kluxers put on all of them sheets and shit and come talking about they going to bring a motorcade through the campus to show niggers that white folk mean for them to stay in their place? Well, gentlemen, the whole goddamn crew of them goddamn drunk-ass rednecks were all the way onto the grounds before it finally hit their dumb-ass asses that they hadn't seen a soul, not because everybody was either up there hiding under the bed or peeping out from behind the curtains, but because there were all of them combat-seasoned AEF veterans in the student body at that time and they and the ROTC cadets were all deployed in them hedges and behind them knolls and on top of them buildings, all them goddamn sharp-shooters and bayonet fighters and ain't no telling what else, gentlemen. Sheeet, them goddamn crackers got on the hell on through here in a hurry, then, and went on out somewhere and found themselves a hill and burned a chickenshit cross and went on back home and went to bed. Now that's what I'm talking about when I'm talking about organization. Them white folks said, Oh shit, these niggers up here organized! Let's get the hell out of here. And now that brings me to another point. Did you ever notice whenever some white folks go somewhere to pull some old shit like that and you let them get away with it, you going to see it all over the papers, and here comes all them old reporters from up north, can't wait to feel sorry for us and ain't going to do a damn thing to help out. But when some of us turn the goddamn tables on them somitches, all them newspapers act like ain't nothing at all happened in the first goddamn place. That's some more stuff I been studying for years and you know what I found out? I think them somitches know what they doing. Gentlemen, if they had put anything in the papers about how these folks had them people scared shitless because they were organized and just watching and waiting like that, it's subject to drive white folks crazier than the Brownsville raid, and ain't nobody fired one single round of nothing.*

I also remember him saying what he always used to say about Gin Mill Crossing when he used to get going about how the main thing in that connection was to let *them* know that you ain't going to take no shit lying down! *And y'all know good and damn well I ain't talking about getting up somewhere woofing at somebody. You know me better than that. I'm talking about just letting them get the goddamn message that it's going to cost them something because you willing to put your ass on the goddamn line. Otherwise, here they come with some old foolishness like it's their birthright to make niggers jump. But now you take them people over in Gin Mill Crossing. Old bad-assed Cat Rogers himself don't go messing around over in there without first off giving somebody some advance notice, and he's the high sheriff and a tough somitch by any standard. Even if Cat want to get somebody that everybody already knows broke the law and got to go to jail, Cat always going to call Yank Williams or Big Eag, and they'll either say come on in or we'll send him out or he ain't here, and that's good enough for Cat Rogers. That's what I'm talking about when I'm talking about Gin Mill Crossing, gentlemen.*

So you just go on and take care of whatever you got to see to, Yancey Williams said outside on the porch with Bob Webster standing by as the others filed past, some still putting on their coats. Ain't going to take nobody here more than fifteen or twenty minutes to go by home and pick up what they need. What you think, Eag? and Big Bald Eagle Bob Webster said, probably no more than a quarter of an hour at most, and then goddamn it, we'll find out. But frankly, Giles, I can't see very many of them people following Dud Philpot nowhere. Maybe a few of them old razorbacks that been used to ganging up on somebody ten to one and saying shoo.

XXIII

THIS IS my young friend from the campus I was telling you about, Hortense Hightower said when Giles Cunningham finally got there, and he said, What say there, my man? and I said, Nice to meet you, and we shook hands and he gave me a pat on the shoulder and turned to Will Spradley and said, Man, goddamn, just look at you, goddamn! Man, you let a nothing-ass somitch like Dud Philpot do something like this to you? Goddamn man. And Will Spradley said, That's all right about me, Gile. I just been trying to make it to you so I can tell you he done all this to me because you the one he really working

himself up about. And Giles Cunningham said, Well I appreciate that, Will Spradley, I really do.

Then, looking at me again, he said, and I also want you to
know how much I appreciate you giving the Boss Lady a hand
with all of this. But hold up for a minute and I'll be right with
you and we can talk while I do what I got to do and get on
back out of here.

He moved on over to the wall behind the bar and unlocked
the door to the walk-in closet and when he clicked on the light
the first thing you saw was a rack of shotguns and rifles, and
it took only a glance for me to see that there were 20-gauge
pumps as well as single- and double-barrel breechloaders and
that the rifles included a lever-action Winchester, a bolt-action
Enfield, a magazine-fed Springfield, a .30-caliber carbine, and
also a stack-barrel combination 410-gauge shotgun and .30-
caliber rifle called an over-and-under gun.

I could spot any of those in a matter of seconds anywhere,
even in a dim light, because Little Buddy Marshall and I had
learned how to fire and also how to fieldstrip most of them by
the time I was thirteen years old. After all, hunting, like fishing,
was so much a part of everyday life in Gasoline Point back then
that you didn't think much more about using guns and rifles
(but not pistols!) than about any of the other workaday tools
that you were always being warned to be careful about. Pistols,
to be sure, were another matter altogether. Whether revolv-
ers or automatics, they were always special, always redolent of
nimble daring and expert doing and escaping and retaliating.
But then, pistols had just about nothing to do with hunting in
the first place.

Anyway, I already had the gun rack checked out even before
I realized that I was doing it, but it was not until after he had
signaled for Will Spradley to be taken to another room for the
time being that he said, Hey, Poppa, I can use a little help with
this. Then when he opened the footlockers, I saw that there
were also three Thompson submachine guns, also known as
Tommy guns. And I said, Chicago Typewriters because that
was what we used to call the ones you saw (and heard!) in the
gangster movies in those days, and I said, These are the very
first *real* ones I've ever actually seen, and he said, One for each
place, but just in case.

Just in case, he said, and only just in case. I mean, this stuff is strictly for the last resort, he said, and then he said, What I really think they're most likely to have in mind is to come out and scare somebody. So if that's it and they get to any one of my joints and find Eag and the boys or Yank and the boys waiting for them, I think that just might take care of that, because they didn't leave home to go to no battle. They just out to have themselves a little cheap fun, showing off. But since you never can tell when some of them are subject to get all carried away and start trying to burn some property and all that, I got to have this stuff on hand just in case. *But now here's my point. Don't nobody in these parts know I have my hands on no stuff like this but the Boss Lady, Wiley, Speck, Flea, Eag, and Yancey and now you and that's the way I got to keep it. You get the point? And I said, I sure do, and I did. All you had to do was imagine the type of newspaper headlines that would be featured from border to border and coast to coast:* ALABAMIANS MOWED DOWN IN WILD TOMMY GUN MASSACRE BY CRAZED, RAMPAGING BLACK RENEGADES.

I sure do, I said, and he handed me one of the submachine guns and picked up the other two and I followed him out through the back door and up the steps to where the cars were parked and I guessed that the two he was carrying which he put into the trunk of his Cadillac were for the Pit and the Dolomite and that the one he took from me and put into the trunk of the Oldsmobile was for Flea Mosley, out at the Plum. Then on the way back inside, he said, the Boss Lady thinks a hell of a lot of you, my man, and I always trust her judgment about people. So look, he said as we came back down the steps, I'm sending her out to Flea and I really would appreciate it if I could get you to go along riding shotgun for her.

We were all back in the game room again then, and he said, Hey now look now if you have some concern about getting yourself in trouble with the school authorities, I can understand that. And I said, I'll take my chances. And we both knew that it was not just a manner of speaking what with the general campus discipline and specific dormitory rules being what they were in those days, and he said, See there, she knew she could count on you. Boy, this woman's got judgment about people like old James P's striding left hand. *She don't hardly ever miss.*

She herself was still working on Will Spradley's face and all she did was look up and give me a wink that was not a part of her nightclub Boss-Lady-at-the-microphone come-ons, and that was when Giles Cunningham put the clip in the .38 automatic and handed it to me along with the carbine and the musette bag containing a supply of .30- and .38-caliber cartridges. Then he also gave me a wink and feinted a left jab and went on getting ready to go.

I could already see myself in the right front seat beside her with the blue-steel automatic in my hand and the carbine on my lap and the musette bag on the floor between my feet, but before I had a chance to start trying to figure out all of the what-ifs and what-if-nots you had to be ready for, Will Spradley started talking again.

I had to make it to you, Gile, he said, because you the one he really got it in for, Gile, he said, because he came lighting into me like this, and took it out on me just because I was there when he got back from out there and didn't get nowhere with you by himself and he working himself up to get a bunch of them to come at you. Now that's what happen, Gile, and that's how come I'm here. Because if I was one to try to turn it on you just to get it off of me, I wouldn't be here, Gile. I'd be out there trying to get long gone somewhere from this whole place and never come back.

Hey like I said, Giles Cunningham said, I appreciate your concern, Poppa, but don't worry about it. That somitch is mad with me because of what happened when he came out to the Pit. But Will Spradley said, Yeah, Gile, but I'm the one told him about you cashing my check and that's how come he made it his business to come out there like that, and if they find that out they going to say that makes me a white man's nigger. Because I know these folks, Gile, and Giles Cunningham said, Hey, take it easy man. What the hell else could you tell him? You just told him the goddamn truth. Cain't nobody blame you for that. I sure the hell don't.

But you know these folks, Gile, Will Spradley said then. I mean, some of these folks. They get a hold of something like this and there they go, putting the bad mouth on somebody and making somebody a white man's nigger and don't know nothing about it, not a thing in the world. They going to say

I'm that because I ought not to told him nothing. But that don't make me that, Gile. Because I may be poor and got to take low sometimes, but that don't make me no white man's nigger. Because I ain't never tattled nothing on none of us to none of them folks. Never in all of my born days.

I know what you mean, man, Giles Cunningham said, pulling on a single-breasted olive drab three-quarter-length raglan twill topcoat and gathering up the rifles and handguns he had come for. But come on now, man. I got to get on out of here and find out what these goddamn peckerwoods going to be trying to do. You go with the Boss Lady and the schoolboy.

Outside I took the shotgun seat and Will Spradley got into the back, and as we pulled out of the yard ahead of the Cadillac and headed for the secondary road that would take us to the route to the Plum Thickets, Will Spradley said, I never will forget you, Boss Lady, and I want to thank you again for giving me a chance to tell Gile. And then he said, Because the thing about the whole thing is that it ain't about nothing. Some little old percent that ain't nothing but some pennies and nickels and dimes. All of this about something like that and it ain't nothing.

She didn't cut in while he was talking but as soon as he paused she said, Later for that, Will Spradley. What we got to do now is stay quiet and keep our eyes and ears open.

XXIV

AUGUSTUS STRICKLAND, *né* Edward Augustus Strickland II, was somebody I had been hearing about if only incidentally from the very outset of my freshman year. Indeed, unless you came onto the campus by automobile from Montgomery Fork as most students in those days did *not*, Strickland was a name you probably heard on the very same day you arrived, because the old antebellum mansion with its fluted columns and red-trimmed octagonal tower, concrete-patched trees, and wrought-iron fence called the Old Strickland Place and sometimes also referred to as Strickland Acres was the first thing you saw as soon as you came into the elm-lined curve less than a

quarter of a mile beyond which was the entrance to the administration and academic end of the campus.

The first time I ever saw him in person, however, was one
bright and breezy afternoon during the early part of that first
November while I was standing on the corner by the Farmer's
Exchange Bank. I heard somebody say, *Gus Strickland. There
he is. Gus Strickland ain't but the one*, and I looked back across
the street to the square and saw him getting out of the Cadillac
convertible that I had just seen pulling up to one of the diagonal parking spaces facing the Confederate monument, and
as he headed toward the courthouse wearing a tan-and-green
houndstooth-check sport jacket, olive green open-collar knitted shirt, tan whipcord slacks, highly polished jodhpurs and a
tan porkpie hat with the brim turned down all around. I remember thinking that he looked as much like a retired British
army officer as like the rich Southern sportsman that he was—
to whom business matters were mostly handled as if they had
long since become more occasional and incidental than a part
of his daily routine.

As a matter of fact, he had been a colonel in the AEF and
probably still was a colonel if not a brigadier general in the
Army Reserve Corps. But nobody ever addressed him or referred to him as Colonel Strickland, the Colonel, or certainly
not the Old Colonel (which many people, by the way, used to
seem to think meant not one who commands a regiment but
one who owns an antebellum mansion and what was left of an
antebellum plantation).

He was addressed by local white people as Mister Strickland,
and by local Negroes as Mister Gus, but they thought of him
and referred to him as Ole *Gus*, which was not to say *Old* Gus
or *Old Man* Gus, but rather the legendary Gus that you've
been long hearing tell of, which was entirely consistent with
the fact that as often as not, any time you heard anybody say
Gus Strickland, it was just about always as if what was being
referred to was not unlike some elemental sociopolitical force
that could probably be expressed in relative degrees to the nth
power.

By the time I saw him on his way to the courthouse that
afternoon, I already knew that he was the sole owner and pro-
prietor of the Old Strickland Place and also that he didn't live

there anymore. When he came back from the AEF, he had married a woman from Savannah and moved into another mansion, which I was not to see until sometime during the following summer and then only from a distance, but which was out beyond the south side of town and was said to have two tennis courts, a swimming pool, a man-made lake for fish and waterfowl, a stable for riding horses, and kennels for hunting dogs.

I was also to find out that he traveled a lot, not just from border to border and coast to coast, but also overseas. It was easy enough to imagine him in New Orleans for Mardi Gras, in Louisville for the Kentucky Derby, in Virginia for the fox-hunting season, and down in the canebrakes on the Gulf Coast for duck season, and also out in the Gulf Stream for deep-sea fishing. But he and his wife and two youngest daughters were also said to spend several months every other year or so traveling in Europe or the Middle East, and he was also known to have been across the Pacific to Hawaii and the Far East more than once.

Not that I ever had any special and certainly not any specifically personal reason to concern myself with what was going on in the life of Augustus Strickland. Nor had I done so. But on the other hand, he was not somebody that you would not know about or not have any more than a casual or incidental interest in either, anymore than you were likely to have only a passing curiosity about the Old Strickland Place itself. *Even those ever so much better off than thou and ever so deliberately incurious students from up north whose admitted fear of being down south was such that the very sound of a white Southerner's drawl seemed to make them feel as if being on the campus was, if anything, even worse than being foreign legionnaires in a remote desert outpost surrounded by murderous tribesmen wearing hooded sheets instead of burnooses, even they usually turned out to know exactly who he was, by reputation if not by sight. Whenever you heard another one of them saying, so that's Gus Strickland, there was always the same ring of familiarity but not the same overtone of outrage as when they said, So that's Cat Rogers, as if saying, So that's a rattlesnake.*

When you saw him on the campus, it was usually because he had a standing invitation to head a local reception committee of his own selection to greet visitors of state, national, and international distinction. He was not and had never been a member of the board of trustees, because when the original Augustus Strickland had made the land available for the school's first campus, he had decided in accordance with his own personal policy for the reconstruction of freedmen as productive citizens, that in order for slaves to prove to themselves that they could manage their own affairs, no member of the Strickland family would ever serve in any official capacity on a board or any other committee established to formulate policy and supervise operations. And yet the attitude of the family over the years had always remained such that officials fully expected the school either to inherit the Old Strickland Place one day or be permitted to acquire it at a giveaway bargain.

Giles Cunningham knew what he knew about Augustus Strickland, not only as a local matter of course but also as information that had been of direct concern to him as a local businessman for almost ten years. It was, after all, from Augustus Strickland that he had begun buying up the adjacent lots as soon as the Pit had begun to catch on as a not-too-far way off campus roadside rib joint, and five years ago he had bought the property where the Club now was because Augustus Strickland, who knew that he was looking for a site to build a dance hall to book headline road bands into, gave him an inside tip on plans to turn that area beyond Montgomery Fork into several residential subdivisions and had made him a special bargain deal because the kind of classy college-oriented dance hall and night spot he was known to be planning would be a very attractive selling point that developers could use to entice home buyers to settle that far away from the campus.

There was, to be sure, the usual local down-home gossip, speculation, and insinuation about which mulatto and light-brown-skin families may or may not have been blood relatives of this or that branch of the Strickland family of whichever generation. But nobody ever would have said that Giles Cunningham's special person-to-person business transactions with Augustus Strickland were connected in any way whatsoever with anything like that.

As far as Giles Cunningham himself was concerned, information about family bloodlines was not the sort of historical detail that mattered very much unless it had some direct bearing on obtaining clear title to a piece of real estate that he was negotiating to pick up. The relative purity or the degree of interracial mixture of family bloodlines as such was not something he bothered himself about at all. He just took it for granted that with the amount of passing for white he had come to know about over the years, most Americans, like it or not, admitted or not, come from an ancestry of mixed bloodlines.

It was usually as one businessman to another that he got in touch with Augustus Strickland, and once everything was in place that was also the way he felt about what he was doing when he called him and told him about Dudley Philpot that night, and when Augustus Strickland asked him if he had already called Cat Rogers, he said he had not and didn't intend to since he was not going to try to swear out any warrant against Dud Philpot.

I just wanted to touch base with you so that if this turns into some real trouble, you know my position, he said, and Augustus Strickland said, Hell, Giles, let me see if I can find out what the hell got into that damn Philpot and what he thinks he's up to and I'm going to have a word with Cat Rogers, too, Giles. After all, he's the high sheriff and somebody got to see it that he gets a reasonable chance to discharge his responsibilities.

I'm not about to be the one to try to dispute that, Giles Cunningham said then. I just don't want him to get that all mixed up with doing me some kind of personal favor and expecting me to be grateful for it.

I'll get right back to you as soon as I find out something, Giles, Gus Strickland said, and Giles Cunningham said, I appreciate that and I'll be right here at the Pit unless he turns up over at the Dolomite.

XXV

WHEN WE came through town, the streets around Courthouse Square were as empty as they usually were at that time of night. I didn't say anything, but I couldn't help wondering if that meant that trouble had already started out at the Pit or at the Dolomite or maybe even at both places. We circled around to the other side of the square and came on out along South Main Street to the city limits marker and through the outskirts and then we were on our way through the open country with the speedometer moving up to 50 mph and then 55 and beyond.

The bright head beams pushed on through the darkness as the windshield wipers clicked and clacked, swishing and swashing and squigging against the thin, steady, central Alabama early spring drizzle; and with Will Spradley still doubled up on the back seat and with Hortense Hightower handling the Oldsmobile exactly like the expert driver that I was to find out that she had already become all the way back during the earliest days of her apprenticeship in a two-car territory band out on the old southeast vaudeville circuit, the only thing to do was keep on the lookout.

I was pretty sure that nobody was following us, but I also knew that any lights coming up from the rear could turn out to be a carload of drunken, self-indulgent white hell-raisers on their way back out of town after a showdown at the Pit, and there was also a chance that any traffic you met was on its way in to join the mob.

At that time, I was only somewhat familiar with the route we were following, so it was only from road maps of that part of Alabama that I could remember that the next town of any size was Junction Springs, which was all the way across the county line. I knew that we didn't have to go that far and, from the map, I also knew that if you did you could go on south by east to Eufaula and from there you could take the bridge across the Chattahoochee and be in Georgia. Or you could head due south again for the Florida panhandle by way of Dothan, from which you could also go to Jacksonville, by way of Valdosta, Georgia.

We came zooming on along the damp but unslippery blacktop U.S. federal route and when you are traveling in mostly level farming country like that and there are no sharp curves and no other traffic, a steady sixty-five soon begins to feel like only forty-five, and if you start checking and rechecking your watch, you're almost certain to get the impression that time itself has slowed down.

Then there was the weatherworn country crossroads shack that I remember whenever I remember that part of that night, not because it represented any special landmark as such but because when I saw the milepost across from it and realized how far out beyond the town limits we had actually come, that was where and when I suddenly found myself missing the wee hour coziness of my dormitory room and becoming concerned about getting back into the also and also of the campus again.

Up to that point, I had been so completely caught up in the step-by-step urgency of the situation I had walked into and then also with being on hair-trigger alert for what I knew could happen next that it was as if I had somehow forgotten that I was really only a college boy with assignments in preparation and class sessions to attend the next day, beginning at nine o'clock with a lecture period to be followed by a break and lunch and then a session at two in the afternoon.

It was also as if I had forgotten that the also and also of the campus had come to include the also and also of the unfinished matter of one Miss Nona Townsend, a sophomore from Tuscumbia County by way of a freshman year at Alabama Normal, whom I had met back during the first week of that third October and to whom I had said what I said because she looked and moved and also sounded so much like the crepe myrtle–cape jasmine beautiful tea-cake perfect tan brown-skin storybook princess that I had always been looking forward to meeting and making myself worthy of some time later on along the way from the spyglass tree to the also and also of whatever wherever.

You could tell that she was used to having people say ingratiating things to her and as nice-mannered and appropriately modest as her responses always seemed to be, it was also easy enough to see that she was not somebody who really had very much patience with people who were preoccupied with good looks as such or with any of the other superficial values that their flattery suggested. So I didn't say what I said until I was reasonably sure that I could get away with it, and I did get away with it because by then I had smiled and said hello that many times without making a pass, because I wanted her to become curious enough to find out about me and not think that I was some fast-talking hotshot upperclassman on the prowl for innocent newcomers.

But I had not followed through. I had not really backed away either. But I had not followed up. Not because I had changed my mind. Not about her. There was nothing disappointing about her. The problem was that I still could not afford to have a steady girlfriend, because I just simply did not have the extra spending change that you had to have for the numerous essentials in the way of treats and favors you were expected to be able to provide when you went steady with somebody on campus in those days, and I had absolutely no intention of giving up any of my free reading time in the library and taking a part-time job in order to finance my social life. That would violate every promise I had ever made to get to college in the first place beginning back with Miss Lexine Metcalf before Mister B. Franklin Fisher and the Early Birds (knights of the ancestral imperative that they expected to be) and not excluding Miss Slick McGinnis.

And yet there she was as if custom-made, and the next moves were up to me. So I decided to take my chances, and hope that I would be lucky enough to get by with inviting her to go to only those on-campus entertainment events that were covered by the Student Privilege card. The idea was to make it through the rest of the term. Then I would have that last summer to pick up some extra cash for the social obligations of my senior year, and so far I had been able to get by because as a second-year transfer student concerned with making the smoothest possible academic transition from one campus to another, she had already restricted her availability for dates anyway.

You couldn't have asked for a better deal. It was indeed almost as if she herself had suggested that she would be busy doing whatever fairy-tale princesses always do in the castle while the as-yet untried and unproven apprentice knight-errant scoots hithering and thithering about, trying to forge his magic wandlike sword and get himself together to fulfill the mission that he had inherited because he is who he is and that will qualify him for an invitation to the castle.

But now as the Oldsmobile came zooming on further and further beyond the milepost at the crossroads shack, it was as if the main purpose of getting through the night and back onto the campus was to see her the next morning after my first class, when she would be coming down the stairway from room 201 where English Literature Survey Course 203 Section I was held. I wanted to be waiting at the drinking fountain just to say hello and be that close again and walk across the quadrangle with her to the library again.

Meanwhile, Hortense Hightower drove on, cruising between 55 and 60, and without taking her eyes from the road she winked and smiled every now and then to let you know that she was satisfied with the way things were going, but she had not said anything since she pulled out of her neighborhood, and she still didn't say anything until she began slowing down because we were coming to the turnoff. Then all she said was, Here we go, Will Spradley. You all right back there, Will Spradley? and Will Spradley said, I'll just say I'm still here, Boss Lady. I'll just say I'm still here.

She turned off and we came on into the woods and along a narrow winding downhill road to a clearing that was the parking area for the Club, and the first thing we saw was Flea Mosley waiting for us outside under the canopy to the main entrance, and when we pulled up, he said, You sure did get yourself on out here Boss Lady, but don't get out, don't even cut the motor. Giles wants y'all just to turn right on around and come right straight on back into town, and he say ain't nothing happening so don't worry about a thing. Ain't going to be no showdown because the peckerwoods ain't going to show up. Giles say just zip right on back in and drop the college boy on the campus and take Will Spradley on over to the school hospital and he also said find out what time the college boy can be down at the barbershop so Wiley or somebody can pick him up and bring him out to the Pit for lunch tomorrow and he will fill him in then. That's what the man said, Boss Lady, so don't let me hold y'all up no longer.

XXVI

So I DIDN'T find out what had happened to make it all turn out the way it did until I heard about it directly from Giles Cunningham himself during lunchtime out at the Pit that next day.

And that was also when he went on to say what he said about
me and about a part-time summer job beginning the week after school was out at the end of May and lasting through the
Labor Day weekend.

Dud Philpot had not carried out his threat, because within
probably less than twenty minutes after Will Spradley had
moved out of his reach and escaped through the back door and
delivery alleyway, he himself had been taken to the emergency
ward of the county hospital, where he was still in the intensive
care unit under an oxygen tent (that I was to find out later,
incidentally, could always count on emergency backup equipment and supplies from the infirmary on the campus).

To tell you the goddamn truth, Giles Cunningham said as
he and Hortense Hightower and Wiley Peyton and I ate our
soup and sandwiches, I never could see that many of the kind
of white people we have around here letting themselves be
rounded up and led anywhere by some baggy-britches redneck
like Dud Philpot. But you never can tell. So when the Boss
Lady called me and told me about Will Spradley turning up
over there all beat up like that and worrying about me because
I was the one Old Dud was really mad at, I figured I best not
take no chances because even if he came back out here with
just a couple of them old dirt-poor razorbacks from somewhere
out there in that neck of the woods he come out of, ain't no
telling what it could lead to before these people around here
find out what it all started about. Because now let me tell you
something. Don't ever forget how little it takes to set thousands
of normal-seeming white people back not just to all of the old
nightmares their foreparents on the plantation used to have
about the slaves killing everybody in their sleep but on past that
and all the way back to all of the panic the goddamn Indians
used to cause among the early settlers. Man, you don't ever
want to do anything that's going to make somebody realize
how scared they are of you, especially when they happened to
be the ones with most of the goddamn guns and know how to
use them and don't mind using them. Look, you don't have
to let nobody mess over you. But the minute you start going
around trying to prove just on some kind of general principle
that you ain't scared of them, you can get a lot of folks maimed
and killed just because you got it all backward.

So anyway, that's why I also got in touch with Gus Strickland, he said, and I also knew that he would be the best one to find Cat Rogers and get him on the ball; and he called me inside of about ten minutes and told me what happened. Cat Rogers had just had the ambulance come to pick Dud Philpot up from the sidewalk where he had crumpled on the way from his store to the curb where his car was parked, and that's just about the story of how come the trouble didn't go any further than what he did to Will Spradley.

By the way, what about Will Spradley, Boss Lady? I said, and she said, I just circled back over by the campus hospital on my way over here and he's doing all right. They had to put in a few stitches but the way he's carrying on, when the time comes to take them out he intends to be somewhere up north with one of his cousins.

Hey, look my man, Giles Cunningham said reaching over and touching my arm, I really want you to know how much I appreciate what you did last night and when I said, But I didn't really do anything, he said, Don't play yourself cheap. You did plenty. Just falling in with us like that said a lot and the Boss Lady was telling me about how much confidence it gave her to have somebody out there with her acting like he knew what he might have to do. Man, she made you sound like somebody with the makings of just the kind of real pro that I'm always on the lookout for and she already been telling me about how much you like music.

Then he said if I needed a part-time summer job so that I could buy a couple of new outfits and also have some extra spending money for my senior year, all I had to do was let him know by the middle of May and by June we could work out something that I could take care of along with my own campus obligations to the Scholarship Award Program; and I said, I certainly would, and I also said, Absolutely, no doubt about it.

They were all smiling at me then, and when I said, I can't even begin to tell you how much this means, especially at this particular time, he said, You don't have to, and when I tried to thank him he said, Hey, I'm the one doing the thanking my man, and the thing about it is that it is really my privilege because I know damn well that what I'm offering you is just a little two-bit bonus that I know you can get along without, and I said, Yes but that's also what makes it so special.

As we went on talking, he wanted to hear about Mobile, and it turned out that I knew something about some of the downtown people he asked about and that he had also had business dealings with some that I had only heard about. Then while we were finishing our coffee, he lit a cigar and said, So here's my hand. The Boss Lady will get you back on the campus for your next class.

But when she and I came outside, I found that I had another surprise coming. Because when I saw the Oldsmobile there was the head of a bass fiddle case sticking out from the back seat, and she said that I was looking at what the proposition that we hadn't had time to get to last night was all about. She said, I changed my mind about something.

She said, This thing has been downstairs in the closet since I don't know when. Then one day not long ago when I got to thinking about how much more you always seem to hear on all those records we been spinning than most professional musicians I know, I said to myself, I bet you I already know exactly what would happen if he had this thing to play around with. Just for fun. So I said, I'm going to see, and so I had it fixed up for you. So you take it and you got the rest of this term and the whole summer and all of next term.

So that's my proposition, she said, and she said, All you got to do is get somebody in the string section of the Chapel Orchestra to give you a little start with a few rudiments and you'll be fingering and reading and figuring all kinds of stuff out for yourself in no time at all. Because you see, I already know how you whistle and hum along and how you don't just *keep* the time but also have to play around with it.

Which, she said, is exactly what made me change my mind. Because at first I was glad that you were not tied down to one instrument because you always listened to the whole band and not just for the place where your instrument comes in. But in this way I'm going to be able to hear you listening to everything all the time just like the drummer and like when the piano player is the one in charge like Duke and Count.

So what about it? she said as we came on by the old Strickland place and up the slope to that end of the budding green campus, and I said that I had never thought about it like that, and then I said, Never is to be one to not try, Boss Lady, never no days like that.

We were there then, and she let me out on the empty ramp to the front entrance to the dormitory, and I stood with my arms around the neck and shoulders of the bass fiddle and waved and watched as she pulled on off along the campus mainline and went on out of sight around the knoll across from the promenade lawn and then to the turn-off that passed the dormitory where the clock tower was.

Then before going to my afternoon seminar, I had to take the bass fiddle upstairs to 359, which since the beginning of June almost nine months ago I had been lucky enough to have all to myself as my own turret-tall spyglass tree above but never apart from the also and also of either the briar patch itself or any of the blue steel and rawhide routes hithering and thithering toward the possibility, however remote, of patent leather avenues in beanstalk castle town destinations yet to come.

THE SEVEN LEAGUE BOOTS

For Mozelle and Michele

CONTENTS

The castle hill was hidden, veiled in mist and darkness, nor was there even a glimmer of light to show that a castle was there.

—Franz Kafka

ONE

The Apprentice

I

WHEN ROAD band buses used to go west by way of Memphis and Little Rock in those days you picked up Route 66 on the other side of Oklahoma City. Then six hours later you were through Amarillo and the Texas Panhandle country and on your way toward Tucumcari and across New Mexico with a short service stop in Albuquerque and a layover in Gallup, which was thirty-two miles beyond the Continental Divide and not more than thirty minutes from the Arizona state line.

Then early the next morning there would be Holbrook and the Petrified Forest and the Painted Desert stretching away in the distance and as you pulled on through Flagstaff and headed for Kingman and Yucca, it was California here I come. *And I said I come from Alabama and so did Joe States, who by that time had been crisscrossing the country from border to border and coast to coast by rail and by bus as a full time professional band musician for almost twelve years.*

I said I come from Alabama, and he said me and you schoolboy me and you. Which he had been winking and repeating ever since the day I came to Cincinnati as a temporary replacement for the bass player a year and that many months ago. What he had also said then was So you from down in the Beel, well I'm old Joe States from up in the Ham. Then he had gone on to say now let me tell you something, young fellow. Anybody come asking you some old stuff about where your banjo, you tell them what I tell them. You tell them I got your goddamn banjo swinging down you know where.

When I came on board the bus the first time that Monday morning and found that my assigned seat was directly across the aisle from his he said, Like I said Schoolboy me and you my man me and you and the one right back there behind you will be Otis Sheppard, Ole Cool Papa Spodee Odee the box picker. That's the rhythm section minus the bossman because he'll be up in seat number two right behind old Milo the Navigator. Everybody gets a double seat in this organization.

They were en route to New York. But from Cincinnati, they were swinging down into Kentucky for dance dates in Lexington and Louisville, and then turning back north to Indianapolis for two nights before heading across Ohio by way of Dayton and Columbus to Wheeling, West Virginia, and so on through Pittsburgh and Philadelphia.

Now there's somebody that actually did go down into Louisiana with a sure enough country-ass banjo. But he don't come from no Aladambama. He come from outside of Memphis, Tennessee, in other words Missippi. So anyway once he got down to New Orleans, he heard something that made him trade it in for a guitar. He went down there seeking his fortune and that was it, and didn't nobody have to tell him.

Right 'Sippi? he said, and Otis Sheppard, who was as used to being called 'Sippi as Cool Papa, grunted without opening his eyes, and that was when Joe States said, Now me I am the one that can tell you something about coming from Alabama playing music, and I am talking about playing music for a living.

I'm talking about I'm the one that hit the trail out of Birmingham with my trap set in a goddamn cotton sack, and I'm talking about laboring on the L and goddamn N Railroad. And whenever I decided to stop off somewhere for a few days I'd hide my sack in the thickets down by the railroad until I found myself a little gig to pick up enough change to move on.

So you tell them I got their banjo, Schoolboy, he said. And before I could say what I was going to say about how old Luzana Cholly used to snag freight trains out of Gasoline Point with his twelve string guitar slung over his shoulder like a rifle, he said, What I had was a pedal contraption for my bass drum and ride cymbal, a folding stand for my snare, a couple of sets of sticks, a set of brushes and mallets and that was my trap set as we used to call them in those days. And then when I got with the bossman and we started this thing he got now I had to keep adding all this other stuff to keep up because he was always coming up with something he wanted to try out. So when we went over to Paris that first time, and all these French cats kept coming up to me talking about vuzet the battery I said goddamn right I'm the goddamn cotton picking dynamo of this outfit.

I didn't get around to mentioning Luzana Cholly until several days later when we were on our way across eastern Ohio. Somebody started talking about the cities on and near our route that people from places down home went north to settle in back

*during the boom days of the nineteen twenties and I could have
named families who had kinfolks who had moved to Ohio during
the same time when Willie Marlowe, who was the first scootabout
playmate I ever had, left Mobile for Detroit, Michigan. Which
was also when Roger and Eddie Parker left elementary school because they were moving to Pittsburgh. But I said the one I always
thought about when I thought about Youngstown was Luzana
Cholly, who had also been just about everywhere but had never
settled anywhere.*

*I said he had hoboed on just about every railroad line in every
section of the country and he always took his guitar with him and
Joe States said, Now see there, me and you again Schoolboy. Leadbelly, Blind Lemon Jefferson, Big Bill, Robert Johnson, and the
one and only Mr. Luzana Goddamn Cholly. That's right he did
used to spend a lot of time around the outskirts of the Beel. Now I
first met him out on the road. Not on the circuit. Just on the road
hittin' the tonks. I used to have to hit a few of them myself but me
I was always headed for the circuits.*

*So you come up knowing old Luzana Cholly. Goddamn,
Schoolboy, he said. And then he said, But talking about Mobile I
played the Pike Theater out on Davis Avenue when I was on the
southeastern territory circuit, and I also remember playing some
dances in the Gomez Auditorium right down the street from the
Pike.*

*So you know I know Papa Gladstone, he said. Old Papa Stone
was always my meal ticket when I got stranded down there a few
times. Old Papa Glad. He's been running dance bands in that
town longer than anybody and also putting the marchingest band
in the Mardi Gras parade every year. Man, I went down to Mobile looking for a gig one Mardi Gras and old Papa Glad had
three outfits working dances somewhere after the parade every
night; and afterward I cut out on the GM&N and beat my way
on up through Missippi to Memphis and points up the Big Muddy.*

Me and you Schoolboy, he said once more that afternoon as
the bus zoomed across Arizona toward Needles and the Mojave that many months later on what was, at long last, my first
trip all the way out to the Pacific coast. And I gave him the
highball sign, thinking about how I used to dream of going to
Los Angeles as I sat in my secret spyglass place in the chinaberry tree.

Every time somebody else left Gasoline Point for that part of the country the talk, around the fireplace if it was a winter night or on the swing porch in the summertime, was always about how you took the southbound Pan American Express on the L & N down to New Orleans and changed to the Sunset Limited westbound on the Southern Pacific for the Texas plains and the desert and cactus horizons of New Mexico and Arizona.

Then when you finally reached the end of the line and came out of the Union station in Los Angeles that many days later, everywhere you looked there would be palm trees and blooming canna lilies and bougainvillea plants and also buildings with Spanish arches and terra cotta roofing. And when you came to the station exit you'd be at the foot of Sunset Boulevard. And somewhere not far away in the pineapple golden distance beyond the blue Pacific coast horizon was a paradise island of Santa Catalina and the town of Avalon.

That was the way it always used to be when you heard what you used to hear back even before Cousin Bird, whose given name was Roberta, left on the Pan American for a month's visit that time and came back and went back six months later to stay. It was always Los Angeles and not yet Hollywood and Beverly Hills until I began reading movie magazines, especially *Screen Land* and *Photoplay*, when I was in junior high school.

When I reached senior high school, moving pictures and movie stars had become a part of what you read about and thought about as never before, but by that time the main thing for me had become college. So even as I still kept up with not only all of the current movies but also with the fan magazine features about life in Hollywood and Beverly Hills, the place above all others that I wanted to visit was Paris by way of New York and London; and then there would be Rome and all of Europe, the Mediterranean and the Aegean.

But I said what I said because as conscious as I was of what it meant for me of all people to be on my way with the band I was with to play at the Palladium followed by a week in a nightclub on the Strip and three days in a recording studio, the closer we came to arriving, the more I felt as if I had come directly from Mobile on the old Sunset Limited after all.

When the bus rolled on through Topock and came on down to the bridge across that part of the Colorado River, you were at the state line; and you were also leaving the Mountain Time zone for Pacific Time, and in a matter of not as much as thirty more minutes you would be pulling on up the steep grade from the old Indian and Mexican trading town of Needles, beyond which there would be the gray and purple sagebrush and dry lakes of the Mojave, with one cluster of mountains after another in the distance on both sides of the mostly flat desert route all the way to Barstow.

I said California. I said Hey California. And Joe States said, One more time Schoolboy. One more go round for the old Alabama jackrabbit.

Then when we came to San Bernardino and the freeway and there were only sixty more miles to go, he looked over at me again and said, I can clue you in on a few things about these people in this man's town, statemate; and I'm talking about things that will be useful to you whether you decide to stay in this music business or not.

II

THEY WERE already on the bandstand warming up when I got there that morning. You could hear them as soon as the taxi pulled up to the curb, and I also saw the bus in the alley leading to the backstage loading ramp. Then there was the sound echoing in the empty auditorium as you hear it on your way past the publicity pictures and placards in the entrance lobby.

I came on into the auditorium and stood looking at them. The stands with the bossman's name on them were all set up in place, and the five members of the reed section were already seated in the front row, but each one was studying his own score and blowing as if whispering to himself. The three trombone players were standing in a triangle off to stage left working on ensemble riff passages exactly as I had always imagined the hocknet figures had been worked out in Ellington's "Bragging in Brass."

Upstage off to the left each of the four trumpet players was walking in his own private circle doing his own lip and finger exercises. Some dance band trumpet players walked with a stylishly deliberate slouch, but these four held their shoulders as erect as you were required to do in school marching bands.

The guitar player and the bass man were strumming and thumping softly in time with each other, but drummer was still unpacking and assembling his setup. He took his time and examined each piece of equipment as he took it out of the big charcoal gray traveling case with the bossman's name stenciled on it. As he put each piece into place he kept testing it and his stool until he was satisfied.

There was nobody at the piano yet. I didn't see the bossman himself and I wondered if he were backstage in the dressing room that he was going to be using for the next three nights. But I also knew that sometimes he was the first one to arrive, and that sometimes he came along on the bus with everybody else, and other times he would not come in until later on and then would stay on working by himself after everyone was gone except the caretakers.

The club had a long rectangular dance area with tables bordering each side and booths along each wall, and there was a roped off reserved section down front next to the footlights. The floor had already been cleaned and freshly sprinkled with wax flakes, and most of the chairs were stacked upside down on the tables.

I wondered if the purple and gold stage drapery stood for anything in particular. The walls were gray with a shoulder high purple and gold border design. The gabled ceiling was white. But the exposed rafters and beams were black; and there was also a hanging globe of mirror glass mosaics like the one that always used to revolve above the junior/senior prom decorations at Mobile County Training School every spring no matter what the theme for the occasion was.

The cleaning crew had opened all of the shuttered windows, and there was a fresh midmorning breeze from the moist late springtime Ohio weather outside, but there was the not unpleasant nightclub aroma about the place even so. I went inside the roped off area and took a chair down and sat at a table about ten feet from the solo microphone.

I had my fingers crossed, but I felt fine. I had spent the whole night in a day coach from Montgomery, but once I checked in at the hotel and took a shower and shaved and changed, I was ready to do whatever I had to do. So when the desk clerk told me about rehearsal and said nobody would be coming back until mid or late afternoon, I took the cab to the club to report in and get that part over with.

Each section went on working on its own for a while longer. Then the clarinet player, who also doubled on alto and soprano and who was known as The Pro and the Old Pro as in old resident professional or expert because as number one assistant arranger and straw boss (or concertmaster) he was the one who was next to the Bossman Himself, stood up and went over to the piano and waited for everyone else to move into place.

He sat at the keyboard with a pencil in one hand looking at the long master sheet spread out on the rack in front of him and waited until the drummer tapped the shaft of the high hat cymbal. Then he called out the first piece, not by name but by number, and put the pencil behind his ear and played the comp chords all the way through and came back and began a vamp. And on the fourth bar he nodded to the drummer.

I knew what to expect because I had been present at one of their rehearsals before. That had happened back down in central Alabama eight months earlier. I had been in the group of students waiting on the sidewalk in front of the campus guesthouse when the band bus arrived that morning, and when I found out that they were going out to the club right after lunch to get set up and also to run through some new material, I cut all of my afternoon classes to be there.

The Bossman Himself was there from the very beginning that time. The club owner, whose name was Giles Cunningham, had pulled up to the front entrance and let him out of the black Cadillac while the bus was still being unloaded at the stage door, and he headed straight for the piano and before anybody else could unpack and start tuning up, he was already making changes on the score sheets that he brought with him.

What they had begun with that time was something he was still working on, and first wanted to hear how the trumpets, trombones, and reeds sounded separately and then together, but without the piano part and with the rest of the rhythm section also laying out for the time being. Then as he went on pulling out other scores and calling for passage after passage in no particular order that I could figure out but that they skipped to without any confusion whatsoever, I realized that they were not there because they were trying to put the finishing touches on something special for that night. What they were doing was a part of their weekly routine.

Everything they did that afternoon in Giles Cunningham's ballroom was just fine with me because after all of the years I had spent listening to them on records and the radio, there they were in person and there I was that close to them, and to the Bossman Himself making it all happen almost as if as much for my benefit as for his own.

I didn't leave until it was all over, and after the dance that night I went backstage to his crowded dressing room and touched his elbow and said how great it all was, but I didn't actually meet him person to person or even novice to maestro until two days later when Hortense Hightower did what she did and said what she said. And that was when he said what he said and I couldn't believe my ears. And she said, What did I tell you. She said, I know what I hear when I hear something. And he said, That ain't no news to me. But I still didn't know what to think, and then that many months later the telegram came and she said, See there. And Giles Cunningham said, Like I told you before when it comes to stuff like this she's just like old Art Tatum's left hand playing stride. She don't never miss, my man. She don't never miss. Not on something like that.

As they went on working through the first two numbers that first morning in Cincinnati, I kept waiting for the Bossman Himself to walk in any minute. And either slide onto the piano seat beside the clarinet player, or take a chair off to one side, or out in the auditorium. When they stopped for a break forty-five minutes later there was still no sign of him.

When the signal came, the four trumpet players went back through the center exit laughing and talking among themselves. The clarinet player stayed at the keyboard making changes on the master sheets, and the bass and guitar players moved over and stood looking over his shoulder. Two of the trombone players and one of the tenor men moved off into the wings on the left. But the third trombone player stood up and stretched and sat back down, and so did the other tenor man.

The alto player lit a pipe and opened up a magazine, and at first the drummer sat talking to the other reed men about something on a sports page of the *Cincinnati Inquirer* that he had handed them. Then when they passed the paper on along to the third trombone player and started running exercises on their horns again, the drummer made several more adjustments on his equipment, stood up, lit a cigarette, and came to the apron of the bandstand and stood with his legs apart and one hand in his back pocket, looking out into the auditorium.

He was wearing sunglasses, a white nylon baseball cap, a blue short sleeve polo shirt with hard-finished tailor shop perfect gray slacks, and his shoes were gray suede wing tips with very thin leather soles and low heels. I already knew that his clothes were always as natty as his drumming was fly. And I also knew that he was from Birmingham and that his band name was not his real name, which was Jonathan Wesley Gayles, not Joe States. But he was everybody's statemate, because he knew how to make himself at home everywhere, and he could also have called himself the band's elder statesman.

Say now hey there, States, he said, waving and stepping down onto the dance floor and heading toward me. So what say there, my man. And I said, Nothing to me man. And he said, Me neither, my man. I'm just up there trying to keep enough flesh and blood mustered up to drive the man's twenty mule team the way he wants it to go; and, man, sometimes these fifteen mule headed road band scobes can make your job a whole lot harder than a sure enough twenty mule team and a half.

Then he said, Hey I'm old chicken butt Joe States. And I said, Hey man you couldn't deny it if you wanted to. I had you tabbed, man. And, man, you're some mule skinner for my money. And he said, Who me? Man I'm just up there faking. And I said, Some faking, man. You and Sonny Greer, you and Jo Jones. And I also thought about old funny-eyed Dike Spivens, who cut out from Papa Gladstone and Mobile for New Orleans and then worked his way to New York by way of the Southwest Territory circuit.

So what's been happening since we came through here the last time? he said. And I said, Hey man, I'm green on this one, man. And he said, Yeah? Damn man, I was counting on you to put me next to something new. And I said, Not me, man. I just pulled in for the first time this morning. And he said, No stuff. And I handed him the telegram from Milo the Navigator, and he said, Hey Goddamn, man. You're old Shag's replacement. And I said, Temporary replacement, but he let that pass and said, Hey Shag, here he is. And the bass player, whose name was Shelton Philips, turned from the piano and looked out toward us and said, Is that him? And Joe States said, Yeah man, here this schoolboy the bossman been telling us about.

Everybody was looking at me then, and the clarinet player said, Well bring him on up here, Joe. And Shag Philips met us at the footlights and we shook hands, and then the trumpet players came back and we were all gathered around the piano; I already knew all of them by their proper names as well as their nicknames because I had been keeping track of all the changes in the lineup over the years.

The trumpet players were Ike Ellis, Osceola Menefee, Scully Pittman, and Elmore Wilkins. The trombones were Wayman Ridgeway, Malachi Moberly, and Fred Gilchrist, who was no less important for being the single section man who seldom took solos. The two tenors were Old Pro (as needed) and Herman Kemble, who was also known in the band as Big Bloop. The alto was Alan Meadows and the baritone was Ted Chandler. Then there were Joe States, Shag Philips, and Otis Sheppard with the Bossman Himself. I said my name, but they had already picked up the cue from Joe States and were calling me Schoolboy as they were to do from then on; and I didn't mind at all. Not then or at any other time later on, because they always said it just right, even when some of them shortened it to Schoolie and some others said School or Schoo which after all was also short for Scooter.

If somebody had started some of that old what-say-professor or what-say-young-'fess stuff, I just might have turned right around and walked out of there. Not that I myself ever had anything at all against teachers. Not me with my brand new college degree. I just didn't have any intention of tolerating any wisecracks that implied that there was anything either ridiculous or unrealistic about education.

But there was none of that. The way they said it made you feel the way you used to feel when people around the fire circle and on the swing porch used to look at you the way they always looked at you when somebody said what they used to say about taking to school and your books so that you could bring more credit to your people someday whatever line of work you chose to follow.

So by the time I was through shaking hands snatching palms and slapping shoulders with everybody, I was already looking forward to the time when, as much for my ongoing development as for their own technical benefit, some of them were going to begin saying things like, Let's see what the schoolboy has to say about this. Hey, maybe the schoolboy been reading up on this. Hey, maybe the schoolboy dug something about this stuff in some footnotes somewhere. Hey, let's get the schoolboy to put his slide rule on this.

While everybody was getting settled back in place to go on with what they were working on the clarinet player took me aside and told me that Bossman Himself was in New York negotiating a recording contract and was not due in town until the next afternoon. In the meantime, he said, you just relax and start checking these cats out at close range. And don't worry about nothing. And I mean ever. Don't never ever, he said, smiling his Old Pro smile as he gave me a pat on the shoulder that made me feel as only old pros can make you feel about your possibilities. Then he also said, And by the way, you might as well call me Old Pro like the rest of them, Schoolboy.

III

BACK AT the hotel later on that first Wednesday afternoon, Joe States and Shag Philips invited me to come along with them; and after hamburgers at a lunch counter down the block, we checked by the poolroom where they left messages for a couple of local friends. Then we went on to the early evening showing of the current Clark Gable movie, and afterward they took me to one of the eating places where the local musicians, entertainers, and athletes used to hang out in those days.

We made our way along the counter slapping shoulders and exchanging jive greetings and gestures and took a booth from which you could see out onto the street; and that was where

Joe States began telling me what he was to tell me about who was who and what was what in the band and about how much I was going to enjoy getting to be a part of it.

But first Shag Philips said what he had been waiting to say. As soon as the waitress had taken our orders, he held up his hand and said, I just want you to hear this directly from me, Schoolboy. Man I sure do hate to have to be cutting out all these old jiveass thugs in this old homemade road band, and only reason I'm doing it is the situation back home.

Which he said was such that he was the one who had to be right there on the spot to take care of and there was no telling how long he was going to have to run things himself before he would be able to leave somebody else in charge and hit the road again.

Look Joe, he said, I'm just trying to make this young man realize how lucky he is to be coming in with a bunch of fellows like this. He already know that there ain't no better band out there anywhere. So I just want him to know that there ain't no better cats to work with and there ain't no better bossman to work for. If you can call it work. Like the bossman always says, when it comes to music you practice and then when you get on the job you *play*.

He reached across the table and patted my hand, and then he just sat looking down at his place mat because he couldn't say anything more. And Joe States said, Ain't nothing else in the world like this outfit you coming into, Schoolboy, because ain't nobody else in the world like the bossman. Because the thing about it when it comes to him is that it ain't never just about cutting them dots. With him it's always as much a personal thing as it is a technical musical thing.

That's exactly what I'm talking about, Shag Philips said, not minding the sound of his voice or the moisture in his eyes. Man that's what gets you and that's how come I already know it don't matter where I am and what I might be doing, I'm always going to feel like I'm a member of this band, just like I feel like a member of my flesh and blood family.

And when I said what I said about alma mater he said, Hey dig it, man.

The waitress came back with our orders then, and as we ate, Joe States said, You going to like it, Schoolboy. I can tell. You just wait until Friday night. You just wait until you start getting to know these cats up close on a day to day basis from town to town. And speaking of the devil, he said, there's two of them just walked in. And I looked and saw Ike Ellis and Herman Kemble.

Shag Philips stood up and waved for them to come on over, and when they got there, he gave them his side of the booth and excused himself to go back to the hotel because he was expecting a long distance call.

So you all starting right in trying to teach this college boy bad habits already I see, Ike Ellis said winking at me. And Herman Kemble said, You better watch 'em, Schoolboy. And Joe States said, Who me man? Come on man. Ain't much these college boys ain't already been into these days. Both of y'all know that.

But sure enough now Joe, Ike Ellis said. What you cats up to for later on? And before Joe States could get halfway through saying Ain't nothing happening, Herman Kemble said, Man don't come trying to hand me none of that old hype. You rhythm section thugs been the chick chasingest cunt hounds in this band since in the beginning was the word and the word was you know what.

So come on, man, Ike Ellis said, What you timekeepers got on the line? And Herman Kemble said, It may be a big grizzly bear but she's always out there somewhere, everywhere we stop. One horse town, tank town, any old crossroad, Schoolboy.

I know good and well that you all got something in Cincinnati for this schoolboy to get next to, he said. And Joe States said, Come on, Bloop, does this schoolboy look like he needs somebody to fix him up with anything? Man, what this cat's going to need is somebody to help him fight them off.

I already knew that Herman Kemble's nickname was Bloop and that sometimes he was also called Big Bloop and I was also to find out that when the bossman wanted a certain kind of tenor sax solo he called him the Bishop. He got everybody all revved up and rocking and shouting and when they came to the solo chorus he would say, And now, the Bishop. Or say, You tell them, Bishop. Or say, Go tell them, Bishop.

Plenty of time for the trillies, Bloop, Joe States said. First things first, man. We were just about to give him a quick inside rundown on the bossman. And Ike Ellis shook his head in mock sadness watching me out of the corner of his eye and

said, You'll need it, Schoolboy. And Herman Kemble said,
Lord, will he evermore need it.

But I knew they were just signifying because they couldn't
really disguise the mischief in their eyes or in their voices. So I
pretended to be alarmed, but I couldn't hide the twinkle in my
eyes either. So we all ended up laughing at ourselves. And then
Joe States looked at me and started.

Now the first thing, he said, is that the goddamn man is a
goddamn musician. And I'm talking about first, last, and always. And I'm not talking about somebody that folks call a
musician just because he can play some kind of instrument because he learned it from a book and can run down something
you hand him on a sheet of paper. That's not what I'm talking
about and I'm not talking about calling somebody a musician
because he can get a job playing music. Ain't never no time
when it's really a job to that man, Schoolboy.

And Ike Ellis said, He sure telling you right about that,
Schoolboy. Ain't never been no time like that for that man.

That's because it's the man's life, Schoolboy, Herman Kemble
said. When something is your life, man, that makes all the difference in the world; and that's why that somitch ain't never shucking and jiving. Don't care what kind of place we been booked
into and how few of any kind of people turn out to hear us.

Tell him, Joe, he said. And that's when Joe States said, The
thing about that is it don't make no difference who else you
booked in there to play for, you always playing for him. It's
like he's the goddamn microphone and then he sends it all out
through the amplifiers and speakers and he don't never want to
have to be sitting there hearing some old half-ass bullshit. And
just remember most of the time the stuff you playing is his, and
the rest of the time it's something he picked out because he
wants you to do it his way.

Which brings me to another thing, Ike Ellis said. You know,
a lot of times when something is somebody's whole life like
that, the somich is subject to become a goddamn fanatic or
maniac or something. You know what I mean? And Joe States
said, Like that somitch I saw in a goddamn movie a long goddamn time ago. You remember that old movie that old John
Barrymore did? I think it was called *The Sea Beast* or something like that. And old John Barrymore was this peglegged

schooner captain and his whole thing in life was hunting down this goddamn tigertoothed whale all over the seven seas.

Hey yeah I remember seeing that, Ike Ellis said. Now that was one more tormented cat. Man, seem to me like I can still see old John Barrymore glaring like he's out to tangle with the devil himself, and I swear I can still hear that pegleg bumping back and forth on the captain's deck—and man, unless I'm mistaken that goddamn movie came out way back before there was even Vitaphone.

But you see now that's just the thing about our bossman, Schoolboy, Joe States said. You ain't never going to catch him up there, in there or out there anywhere acting like everybody else got to put up with some crazy ass shit from him because he's the one that's the mad genius.

Not him, Herman Kemble said. You never met a more regular cat than that stud, Schoolboy. I'm telling you. Ain't nobody in this band can put him the shade when it comes to partying. And Joe States said, Look you're talking about the champ because he can be out there balling till the swallows came back to Capistrano, and then be the first one up the next morning just like ain't nothing happened but counting sheep.

Inking in some more dots, man, Ike Ellis said. Ain't nothing ever going to get in the way of that. And Joe States said, Inking them dots. Inking them dots. The first thing he heads for every morning (sometimes even before he goes to the bathroom) is the nearest piano and there are all them little scribbles on all them little scraps of paper in his pockets he's got to deal with.

That was when I asked about Old Pro and about how soon he was usually called in when something new was in the work, and Joe States said sometimes right at the beginning but mainly because Old Pro just happened to be there at the time. But most of the time the first to be called in was always somebody or whichever section he had in mind for some particular passage he was working out.

Sometimes he would pass out fragments of the manuscript and make changes as he listened to the run-through. And other times he was just as likely to compose directly on the horns by dictating the notes to each instrumentalist, by humming them, by name or by sounding the tones on the piano. Then he would make his first draft of the score from the playback.

As a matter of fact, Joe States said, Old Pro might not get to see how the whole thing is laid out until it is ready for the first run-through by everybody together. All he knows up to then is his part in the reed section.

Now me, I'm just about always the last one to see what's actually written down, he said. And Ike Ellis said, Yeah but let me tell you something about that, Schoolboy. He don't even need to see it then and probably ain't never going to look at it no more. Tell him, Bloop, he said. And Herman Kemble said, It's the goddamnedest thing you ever saw, Schoolboy. After all the years they been playing together Old Joe's so tight on the bossman's case that when the bossman's nose itches, he can always count on Old Joe to be ready to sneeze even before he himself realizes that he wants to.

You hear this stuff, Schoolboy, Joe States said. Now that's these horn blowers for you. All I'm doing is just doing my goddamn job and here they come signifying some hocus pocus bullshit.

Yeah but you just wait till you see the stuff, Schoolboy, Ike Ellis said. And Herman Kemble said, Man, it's uncanny. And Joe States said, You hear this stuff. Man, all you all talking about is plain old experience. When you got enough experience, you might not know exactly where somebody is going, but it don't take much time to figure out which way he's headed.

They went on drinking what they were drinking, signifying at each other for my benefit; and then on the way back to the hotel Joe States locked arms with me and said, Me and you, Schoolboy. Me and you. Ain't nothing for you to worry about, because the bossman handpicked you himself and that means that he knows that you can already do exactly what he wants you to do. So anything else you need, get to me fast.

IV

WHEN I FINALLY made it back to my room that first night in Cincinnati, I lay awake in the dark going over what I had been hearing about the bossman. Then even as I began to think about what I was going to have to say to him the next day, I was already remembering what had happened when he came into the club to catch Hortense Hightower's one o'clock show that Saturday morning that many months ago.

I didn't find out that Hortense Hightower had set it all up, until she called me that next afternoon to tell me what he had told her. *All she had said that night was, Well look who just came in. And what I saw was him being led to a table right down front, and I knew that the one who came along with him was Milo the Navigator, his road manager; and all I thought was that they were there mainly for a late night snack and also because Hortense Hightower and Giles Cunningham were among the many longtime friends he had made in towns all across the country over the years.*

But it was really her doing, and I didn't have any idea of what was really going on. Even when she left us playing instrumentals for the rest of the set and went down joined them and sipped her usual ginger ale, while he and Milo the Navigator had their fried chicken, potato salad, and beer. I just thought that, being the official hostess as well as an old personal friend, she was out there to help lay on the good old special down home brownskin service.

So when he got up and followed her when she came back on stage for the last set, I just thought he had talked her into letting him back her for a couple of numbers so that he could listen to her from his usual position at the keyboard. Then when he stayed on up there jamming with us until closing time, I just thought he was probably doing something he liked to do from time to time to unwind before turning in; and when he said what he said afterward, it occurred to me that sitting in like that was also one of his most direct and practical ways of keeping in touch with (and ahead of) whatever was happening among local musicians in all sections of the country the band traveled through on its swing around the coast to coast circuit every year.

That was very nice, very nice, very nice, he said, looking back from the front seat as Giles Cunningham headed for the campus to drop him at the guesthouse and me at the dormitory. Milo the Navigator had already left after Hortense Hightower's last number. They were pulling out that next morning en route to New Orleans for a theater date at the beginning of the next week.

How did you come by stuff like that? he said. And I told him I guessed that I had just picked up here and there, more from listening to the whole group than from practicing the bass fiddle because I'm still in my first year of trying to do that. And he said, That may be so but you've been a musician all of your life, my man.

I can tell one when I hear one, he said. It's my job, he said. I don't know what the hell else you do, and I bet you're damn good at whatever it is, but you've also been a musician all of your born days, if you know what I mean. Some people think you're a musician if you can play anything they put in front of you but to me a musician is somebody who makes his instrument say something even if he can play in only one key and can't name that.

Then he asked me where I was from, and when I told him he said, I wondered about that. I thought that was what I heard in there. That's old Gladstone's town. So you're one of old Gladstone's boys. And when I said in a way I guess but not really because I never ever even touched an instrument in Papa Gladstone's presence, he said, That's all right about that, if you grew up down there that's who you grew up hearing.

And I said, Beginning with Mardi Gras and at baseball games and picnics way before I was old enough to know what dance halls and dance bands were really all about. And even as I spoke it occurred to me that I couldn't remember when I didn't already know what honkytonks and juke joints like Joe Locket's in the Bottom were all about.

Old Papa Gladness, he said. And I said, Then later on when I was in junior high school I used to go all the way into town to listen to Papa Gladstone rehearsing a band just as I also used to go by the assembly room to hear the Mobile County Training School Musical Demons add new numbers to its dance book, which I already memorized cover to cover, note for note by ear.

So it looks like I had you tabbed right away, he said. And I said, You sure did. And he said, That's old Papa Gladness for you. He's got as many children forever turning up somewhere as old Uncle Bud in that old bone knocking rhyme, Giles; and not just children he might have forgotten after all these years, but a whole slew of others like this young fella here that he didn't even know was one of his in the first place.

Then he said, If you're from down there, you must also know something about an old barrelhouse piano player named Doodlebug McMeans. And when I said, By name, reputation, and riff quotations only (because he always played in a place way down on the other side of town), he said, Now let's see now, I guess old Riverboat Shorty was before your time because hell he was getting on up there when I first met him; but he was the one that used to tangle with old Jelly Roll Morton when old Jelly used to come up to Mobile from New Orleans.

He was still around when I left, I said; but he wasn't playing very much anymore. I used to see him out at baseball games getting on up there but still sharp in his peg top pants and silk shirts and either a straw katie or a Panama with the brim turned down all around and you couldn't miss those rings, that cigar holder and that watch chain and fob which is why he always wore one of his fancy vests even when he wasn't wearing a coat.

That's Riverboat all right, he said. This boy knows something, Giles, he said. And then he said, What about the one they call Red Bird and another one known as King Velvet? And what about singers? What about Velma Mackie, Cleo Quitman, and the one and only Miss Big Money Watkins, who used to be out there on the trail making some of the same rounds as Ma Rainey and Bessie and all the rest of them red hot Smith mamas.

And I said, Now you're talking about some of the places I was beginning to be able to get into by the time I was at the end of my first year of high school. (By which time I had also begun memorizing all of the records I liked—and some I didn't—without even thinking about it. Somebody would just walk up and say, Hey Scooter what about when old so and so said, and either hum or whistle the solo passage and also the background including grunts for the rhythm; and if you had heard it you always joined in to prove that you had picked up on it too.)

We went on talking about Mobile all the way to the campus, and when Giles Cunningham pulled up behind where the band bus was parked in front of the guesthouse, I said I would walk from there and got out and took the bass from the trunk and waited until the two of them decided what time the bus would circle by the Pit to pick up the box lunches on its way out of town the next morning.

They shook hands and after Giles Cunningham headed back toward the main gate, the two of us stood there on the sidewalk under the elms talking a little while longer with him asking if I knew Pensacola Slim, who was the one who had begun by taking him to places in the Grove and out on Chinchula Road back when he first brought his band to the Pike Theater years ago; and I remembered Pensacola Slim as a man about town whom I knew only by sight, by automobile and reputation.

Which was also the case with the Yates brothers and their well to do family who were the TOBA circuit people in Mobile as well as the owners of the Davis Avenue ball park and the sponsors of the Mobile Black Bears baseball team. For me they were no less legendary when you saw them in person than they were in the stories you heard about them and about Cleve Huddleson The Contractor, not only around the fireside and in Papa Gumbo Willie's barbershop but also in some of Mr. B. Franklin Fisher's morning assembly talks.

But to him they were people he had done business with and also had fun with during brief stopovers in Mobile, and he mentioned going with them down to their summer house and fishing camp at Coden, a place everybody knew about because Booker T. Washington once spent a vacation there with them. I didn't mention it but I also knew Coden by sight, because it was only about two miles from Bayou la Batre and about eight from the picnic beach at Mon Louis Island.

Pushing the fiddle case along the tree lined avenue to the upper end of the campus and the dormitory, I could still see the Mobile people and places he had mentioned, and then I also began to think about what it was like to be a full time big league road musician. Your headquarters would be in New York but your home would be nowhere in particular and everywhere in general which is to say anywhere at all.

Anywhere you parked your bus. Anywhere you unpacked your bags. I said anywhere I hang my hat. Anywhere I park my feet, remembering myself all the way back to the me I used to be when my best of all possible running buddies was Little Buddy Marshall who said, Hey shit I reckon and set out for the seven seas and the seven wonders, ready or not, compass, spyglass, maps, and mileage charts or no compass, maps, or even mileage charts.

My good old best of all possible roommates, who reckoned always in terms of calculable probabilities, contingencies, and comprehensive implications would have said, Yea verily. But only after having carefully estimated, however casually, the risks and having given due consideration to the alternatives.

On the subject of road musicians he would also have reminded me of all our conversations about the Chansons de Geste of the troubadours in medieval France and the improvisations of the commedia dell'arte during the early years of the Italian Renaissance; and he would have pointed out the connection of what he used to call the ineluctable mordality of the picaresque (because all yarns like all tunes actually begin and end with and, as in: And it came to pass and so it went) and the ultimate rootlessness that is the perpetual condition humaine.

As for what had been said about how I played that night, I couldn't help thinking about it again once I stood the instrument in its rack in the corner and sat on the bed taking off my clothes but I also knew that the best way to take it was as very nice words of very generous encouragement from a famous professional to an eager to please beginner. In any case, since I didn't think of myself as being a musician, not even a part time one, or even a potential one, what it really meant was that I hadn't messed up. And I could always say I got through the whole session with the Bossman Himself without being told to lay out. It never once crossed my mind that anything else would ever come of it, certainly not within the next twelve months.

Not that I had actually forgotten what I had heard over the years about how the great personal sound of his band was based on the fact that he was so good at turning beginners into the expert sidemen and soloists that his always very special arrangements and compositions required. Somebody was always talking about that, and I never questioned it. I just didn't think it would ever have anything to do with me.

V

HE FINALLY came into Cincinnati from New York that Friday morning, but he was not at rehearsal that afternoon; so I didn't see him until Joe States took me to him when we got to the club that night.

In that band in those days you were always due on the scene an hour before opening time, and he was already there when we came backstage. The door to his dressing room was open, and he was talking to Old Pro. He saw us and held up his hand and said, Hey there you are. Come on in. And Old Pro said, See you later. I got to go get pretty; and as he passed me he said, You know how it is, Schoolboy. Even when I don't take solos I'm sitting right up there on that front line where people can even see my goddamn socks. And Joe States said, Me and you, Pro. Me and you. I just popped by to bring you our schoolboy, bossman. Me and you later, Schoolboy. Anything you need, get to me fast. Well, look like you done it again, bossman. All I got to say is when it comes to that you got a knack second to none.

So then there was only the two of us for the first time since that last night on the campus that many months ago. And he said, How was your trip? And I said, Fine just fine thanks. And he said, I sure am glad you're taking me up on this. I've been thinking about you, and I believe I might just be on to a little something for you before long. We'll see. Meanwhile, Pro tells me that he and Shag and Joe and Otis have already started getting you clued in on the book; and they all say you're a very quick study. And I said, Well so far it's been more like fun than work. And he said, No wonder you've made such a good impression on everybody just like I knew you would.

He also said, Just pace yourself and keep your eyes and ears open and let things soak in and you don't have to worry about anything, because that's really how you become a part of us. If you know what I mean. And I said I thought I did. But the best part was what everybody had already said about him never asking you to do anything that he didn't already know you could do whether you yourself knew it yet or not.

Through the open door I saw Osceola Menefee and Scully Pittman coming toward us, and he said, Stick around. They're just checking in. First they let Milo know they're here because he's the timekeeper. Then they see Pro because he's in charge of the book, and they just kind of look in on me in case I might have worked up some little something different that I might want to drop in there somewhere during the evening.

So I was also there when everybody else came by that first night, and they all gave me a pat on the shoulder, and sometimes also an avuncular wink like the hometown baseball team going onto the field from the dugout and as if to say what somebody in log carriage crew at the Buckshaw sawmill always used to chant when the one o'clock back to work whistle blew.

When all of them had come and said what they had to say and left, he said, So here you are on board as we weigh anchor and head seaward. Which to me whose first scoot buddy was Little Buddy Marshall meant seven-seaward. And I said, Aye aye Sir and snapped to, not with my first year roommate's sidelong glance of conspiracy but with the grin you couldn't ever really repress when Miss Lexine Metcalf or Mr. B. Franklin Fisher designated you with their blackboard pointers.

It was curtain time then, and everybody was standing in the wings and he said, Okay, now for the time being, there's a chair for you right next to the piano. I want you to just sit there and get used to hearing how everybody sounds when you're that close to me and Joe and Otis.

That caught me by surprise, because until then I had been picturing myself spending the first few nights in a chair in the wings off the rhythm section side of the bandstand. But there was nothing to do but to nod okay, okay, okay, if you say so, it's all right with me. Then when we heard Milo the Navigator give the all on, all on call, he gave me a pat on the shoulder and said, So there you go. See you in a minute. And I left him rolling his shoulders and dangling his fingers.

There was a very important difference in the way the band sounded when you were listening from where I was sitting. Everything was there and it was all together exactly as it had been rehearsed to be. But as Joe States was to point out when I said what I said later on: Everybody on the baseball team is in on all the action and they all respond to every pitch and every swing and crack of the bat and they all call the play by the same name, but no two of them ever see it from the same point of view, if you know what I mean. Just like the reed section is down there from us like the infield and there's a trombone section and the trumpet section, and you also got the rhythm section like the battery.

When you sat listening from where my chair was, you also felt you were already a part of the team effort. So much so that I found myself actually trying to help the other sections push the notes out into the auditorium. But when everybody stood up to take a bow at the end of the first set, I stayed put in my chair and applauded along with the audience before following Joe States backstage.

That was the way the Bossman Himself wanted me to spend the band's opening night in Cincinnati, and every now and then he would look at me and wink; and sometimes he would name the progression he was playing, and at other times he would name the changes and variations that Shag Philips was running. The second night started out the same way. But when we came back from the first intermission, he said, well how about it?

He was already noodling and doodling at the piano before the rest of us started filing back on stage, and at first I thought it was just a little something to go with the glass-clinking, table-hopping intermission atmosphere. But then I realized that he was really playing for himself and that what he was fooling around with was either something new or a new treatment for something already in the book. You couldn't really tell because he kept going back over it again and again, as if he were only vamping until everybody was back on stage and in place and ready.

I listened expecting him to weave in a figure that would be the signal for the band to find the score sheets for the next number, but before he did that he looked at me and winked again and said what he said. And when I said, If you say so, he went on vamping and I scooted into the wings and was back in place with my bass before he finished another chorus and he said, yeah and went into one note per measure and Joe States came riding in on the high hat cymbal going chickachee chickachee chickachee chickachee, like whispering locomotive steam over a steady driving four/four on what he called his boom boom pedal.

Then when Otis Sheppard strummed the first two bars of the changes I took the second two as a fill and also as if in a quick response to his call and when he repeated as soon as I also repeated, Joe States brought the whole ensemble in shouting like batting hell for leather. So I did what I did because nobody had to tell you that we were going to be highballing it until the bell and flag sign came from the bossman's piano.

Meanwhile Osceola Menefee, Big Bloop and Old Pro would have done their jive time lying, signifying and tall tale telling and retelling in the number of choruses the bossman wanted from the trumpet, tenor and clarinet before sending old Malachi Moberly out with his dirty toned trombone to take it up to the bridge before the outchorus.

That was how I got to make my first bow into the applause along with the rest of the band, and just before they sat back down, Alan Meadows said, Shame on all of you old thugs. This is this young fellow's first time up here with us, and you all got him out there chomping all through this stuff like he got on boomman's hip boots or something. And Joe States said, Well he showed you didn't he? And Ted Chandler said, Yeah he did. And Wayman Ridgeway said, You bet he did. And Osceola Menefee said, Ain't nobody said he didn't. And that was when Scully Pittman said, Hey Boots, Yeah Boots what about Seven League Boots? That's a pretty good one, bossman.

The Bossman Himself was also smiling and he looked at me and winked again and as the audience settled back down he began the next vamp and he kept me going for the rest of the set. But when he brought in the arrangement of what we had played, he called it "Outbound Express" because it was a turn-around on "Alabamy Bound" and he also kept in the "Banjo on My Knee" licks that Joe States and I had sneaked in.

VI

SHAG PHILIPS left at the end of my second week, because by that time Old Pro and Joe States had taken me through almost all of the arrangements in the folders the band was using on that tour; and they said I was ready to take over full time. And Otis Sheppard, who always sat in with us whenever Old Pro wanted him there, also said what he said about the only other thing I needed was the experience of holding the job down on my own.

So the Bossman Himself said okay and that Shag Philips didn't have to worry about leaving him in a bind. And that very next morning he himself began talking to me and Old Pro about some of the notions he already had in mind for me to

start getting ready for two of the numbers we were going to record when we made it into New York at the end of the month.

You ain't got a thing in the world to worry about, Schoolboy, Joe States kept saying on the way back from seeing Shag
Philips off on the train to Florida that second Sunday night.
Like I say, you were hand-picked by the Bossman Himself in
the first place, and I mean right off the bat; and he don't ever
do that unless you got something he been looking for. You
might not ever find out exactly what it is, but if he sent for you,
that means you got it, poppa. And you got me and on top of
that you got Old Pro.

Old Pro, he said. Old Pro—and if you didn't know it already
you been around here long enough to find out for yourself
that we call him that because that's exactly what he is in this
mammy-made outfit. And when I said what I said about what I
had already heard about Old Pro's reputation as one of the best
straw bosses in the business, he said, Not one of the best, the
best. Barring none, Schoolboy, barring none that ever did it.

Old Pro, he said again. When the bossman want to set the
quails up to flip and put the house in an uproar all he got
to do is sic the gold dust twins on them, referring to the in-
house nickname that had finally been settled on for Ike Ellis
and Scully Pittman because of the way their trumpets alter-
nated and then came together on the verse to the band's special
arrangement of "Stardust."

We also got that big one-two tenor solo punch of Old Pro's
setup coming after Wayman Ridgeway's alto getaway and followed by Big Bloop in the cleanup position or vice versa; and
when he want to make sure everybody still going to be out in
the alley for the next go-round, here he come with old Malachi
Moberly taking a couple of nasty-talking trombone choruses.

Talking out of school, I cut in to say, and under nice folks'
clothes. And he said, They're the ones you're going to be hearing people talking about and calling for just about everywhere
we go. But it takes more than a string of knockout solos to add
up to the kind of music this band plays, and that's where Old
Pro comes in again. Because he is the bossman's A-number-one
musician's musician.

In the first place, he said, the somitch can play any instrument in the band. This band or any other band or any other
kind of band not leaving out a string band. And I don't mean

just to show off enough to prove some chickenshit point. I'm talking about cutting some dots to get a sheepskin from a conservatory. Because that's what he did, and he also used to be a school bandmaster. And you know what that means, don't you, Schoolboy, he said. And I said, It means you have to know how to show everybody how to hold his mouth and/or fingers and how to start out being letter perfect.

That's exactly my point, he said. And it also means he can read anything you put in front of him, and he can write anything he can hear. Then in the third place, he is also a pro when it comes to dealing with all the different kinds of people you got to deal with in this trade, not just musicians but this whole entertainment business thing out here. Man, Old Pro can step in for Milo the Navigator bright and early tomorrow morning without missing a beat. Old Pro is a pistol, my man. He don't go around looking like a high priced dentist for nothing.

Joe States was also the one who said, Get Old Pro to tell you about him and the bossman back in the old days when they used to knock around Harlem together. Ask him about all them old stride time piano sharks like Willie the Lion Smith and Luckey Roberts and James P. Johnson, and just wait until he gets going on some of those old master musicians like Will Marion Cook and Harry T. Burleigh; and you'll find out about a lot of heavy historical stuff that's behind this band that people don't realize is there.

Everybody's always carrying on about how hip and out front this band has always been; but, man, this stuff we play is also *historical.* Everything this band plays is connected with some kind of story about something that is flesh and blood and history, he said. And then he said, Old Pro is going to see to it that everybody is cutting them dots, but that's just a convenience like a map. It's always that little story that counts with him and the bossman.

And I said, I can see that. I can hear that. Because I will always remember what my roommate during my first year in college used to say about the best way to get to the meaning of a poem was to see it as a part of an ongoing conversation.

Get to Old Pro, Schoolboy, he said. All you got to do is just catch him when he got a little spare time. Because I know him just like I know the bossman, and I'm telling you it'll mean a lot to him. Because you're a college boy. Because to him and the bossman all the flesh and blood and history in this music they got this band playing makes it just as classical as them preludes and études and sonatas, cantatas, and fugues and all the rest of that symphony hall jive. Because if you can give people them deep itching goose pimples you're doing your job as a musician.

He said, Just watch your chance and get to Old Pro. And I said I would and one day during the week I was in New York that first time I did. *When I came out of the movie that afternoon it was raining and I stopped in at the Peacock and the first one I saw was him sitting by himself at a table for two by the window smoking a cigar and sipping what I knew by that time was bourbon on the rocks in an oversized Old Fashioned glass as he turned through* The New York Times *folded the long way.*

There were also several other daily newspapers and current magazines at his elbow next to the window; and along with the tall glass of water chaser in front of him there was also a dish of ice cubes. He waved me over to him and it was a good time to get him started and I did, and he said, I thought I already knew something about music. I was from Atlanta and my folks had always sent me to the best teachers and I went for smart. I had won every contest and scholarship I ever tried for, and I was making straight A's at the conservatory.

Several of us were down from Boston between semesters, and this particular night I had come uptown with some friends I was staying with down in Greenwich Village, and we were making the rounds with some guys I had known since they were in Atlanta at Morehouse, and that's when it happened. I'm sitting up there listening to stuff I had been hearing and liking and taking for granted all of my life, and all of a sudden it was as if it was all brand new and something had happened to me. And when I looked around there was this one special very fly and together-looking cat smiling at me at the next table as if he had been watching me all along and could actually see what was going on inside me. That was really the beginning of me and bossman. Because he said, Hey fella you look like somebody who has just heard the word and seen the light. And I said, Amen. Man, this stuff is something and I mean really something. And somehow he knew that as good as the performance was, what I was talking about was the music as such because he said, Ain't nothing better. Not to my ears.

We kept nodding and shaking our heads at each other through the next three numbers, and at the end of the set he introduced himself, and I told him where I was in town from, and he invited me and my friends to come along with him to a couple of other spots. And who was in the first? Nobody but old Willie the Lion all by himself except for that cigar and derby hat but what he was doing on that piano made you think about things you could do with a whole band.

Then at the next and last stop for that night there was old James P. wearing no hat but lolling his cigar about with his teeth, tongue, and lips as if getting your fingers to do what you wanted depended on knowing how to hold your mouth exactly right. That was some night, Schoolboy. Man, every time I hear him taking off on old Edgar Sampson's "If Dreams Come True" it all comes back to me like yesterday. Man, you bull fiddlers got to love cats that stride like The Lion and James P.

Anyway that was the night I met the bossman and from then on, it was me and him every time I could make it down from Boston. I don't want to go into all of that now. I'll just say he was already looking forward to the day when he could make a full band out of the pickup group he was just beginning to gig around town and the nearby sticks with on a catch-as-catch-can basis, whereas for my part I had never thought of playing that kind of music for a living. Not that I hadn't always liked it. But when you went to the conservatory in those days, that meant that you were preparing yourself to follow in the footsteps of Harry T. Burleigh, Clarence Cameron White, and R. Nathaniel Dett and such like. So what I was looking forward to was a job as bandmaster and maybe head of the music department at a big city central high school or college one day so that I would have time to compose and train enough student musicians to organize my own concert orchestra.

So I went on and got my degree all right. But in the meantime there was this thing the bossman and I had going, and through him I had come under the influence of Will Marion Cook and Royal Highness. Remind me to tell you about me and the bossman and Dad Cook sometime. I'm pretty sure the Bossman Himself is going to take you by to meet Papa Royal before we leave town.

Well as I was about to say I went on out there and started doing what I did in Kentucky for three terms, and it was not really a bad job at all. But my whole outlook was different by then and when the bossman got in touch and said he was ready to go for a full contingent, I came on board as first mate, and I'm still here because we've got something going and it's getting better every day.

It was still raining, and we went on talking until it was time to meet Milo the Navigator and Joe States in the Braddock Bar at the corner of Eighth Avenue and 126th Street, one of the main spots musicians and entertainers working in the current shows at the Apollo Theatre used to pop in and out of in those days. And when we got there Old Pro said, You were right Joe somebody has been schooling this schoolboy from way back and we do have a lot to talk about. And Joe States looked at me and said, Temporary replacement. Some stuff. And Old Pro said, We'll have to see about that, won't we Joe?

VII

BY THE time I got around to catching Old Pro with enough free time to spend telling me what he told me about himself and the bossman as we sat looking out at the traffic splashing along 125th Street in uptown Manhattan that rainy afternoon, Joe States had already told me something about the personal background of everybody else including Milo the Navigator, whose real name was Miles Standish Barlow. Milo was from Columbus, Georgia, the pleasure town of Fort Benning, where he was given his start in the business end of show business by Pa and Ma Rainey, who took him on the road as an errand boy while he was still in knee pants. When he struck out on his own he worked his way up to an advance man on the Toby circuit and began dreaming of the day when he would own his own theater or maybe even a string of theaters and maybe also a baseball park and his own team that would challenge the Kansas City Monarchs, the Pittsburgh Homestead Grays, and so on. But when he met the Bossman Himself, it was as if being the honcho for the greatest band in the world was the very thing he had been preparing for all of his life.

Me and you, Schoolboy, Joe States said patting the spare seat beside him as the bus hummed on out to the open countryside en route from Cincinnati to a string of one night stands that would take me through Pittsburgh and to New York for the first time. Then after that there would be New England, from which we would head south along the Atlantic Seaboard.

Like I said, Schoolboy, he said. And I said, If you say so, Unka Joe. And he smiled because he knew all the uncles I meant. And he said, I do say so, Schoolboy, I do say so, which means get to me fast. He patted his seat, pointed his finger at me, and jerked his thumb.

So I sat with him for the rest of that morning and that is also what I was to do for a few hours every day during the week that it took us to work our way on out of the Midwest and into Pennsylvania. And while he was talking about Otis Sheppard we saw one of the trumpet players reach up and put something in the overhead rack and that was why the next one he told me about was Osceola Menefee, who had straight black maybe part Creek or maybe part Seminole hair and sometimes was also called the Kid from the Okefenokee, because the region of Florida where he was born was as close to the Georgia state line where that particular swamp was as to the national park that commemorates the same chief he was named for. (It was also only a few miles from the Sewanee River, but the only thing that had been made of that so far was a riff pattern that the bossman had woven in behind the trumpet solo in his variation on Louis Armstrong's "Lazy River.") He had gone to elementary school in Jacksonville and high school in Charleston, South Carolina, which was where he became so good on his instrument that he dropped out of school to go with his first road band.

Now you see old Scully Pittman up there calling them hogs already, he also went on to say that first morning on the road. Well, he ain't got no Indian in his blood, but he's the one that grew up around what was left of all them tribes and nations that got resettled in the old Oklahoma Territory, because his family moved out there from somewhere in East Tennessee somewhere near Chattanooga when he was still in his diapers. Now he can tell you something about Indians from firsthand and fireside and everyday neighborhood facts of life. Just like somebody like you from down in your part of Alabama when somebody asks you about Creoles and Cajuns. He don't go around trying to claim no family connections or anything like that, but anytime we come across any Indians in any part of the country and you want to know something about them, get to Scully Pittman. He can run it down for you, cousin. Beginning back before Pocahontas and not skipping from the last of the Mohicans to the last of the Apaches.

But now when it comes to that trumpet, you can tell he grew up listening to the old Blue Devils band that used to range from Oklahoma City all through the southwest territory. And there is some U.S. Cavalry mixed in there, too, and I'm not just talking about "Bugle Call Stomp" and stuff like that. I'm talking about for a while back when he was growing up, he used to dream about running away and going up to Fort Riley, Kansas, and enlisting as a bugle boy.

That's what he told me, Joe States said. And then he said, Hey did you all know about the 9th and 10th Cavalry down Mobile way? And I said, We did but not as much as about the 24th Infantry over at Fort Benning, Georgia. And then I said that I had always thought of trumpet players as having the most military bandstand posture. And he said, And trombone players. From all them John Philip Sousa marches and them school bands. I think I know how come the reeds get farther away from holding their shoulders like that than the brass. But later for that.

But it ain't never later for him when it comes to the ponies, he said looking out at the network of neat white rail fences and mostly flat Kentucky bluegrass pastureland, and I knew that as we rolled on toward the next settlement I would soon be seeing the manor houses and private stables and training tracks such as I had seen only in movies until now.

Him and Mojo Wilkins. And there's our man Otis. Not that they're the only ones. They're just the regular ones. Because when we are spending a few days in certain towns where they're running, you're going to find quite a few of the rest of us out there trying to pick them too.

And that includes me too, Schoolboy, he said. And sometimes you might even see Old Pro and the Bossman Himself out there studying them forms, placing them bets, and hanging on the rails, especially and the big ones like Belmont Park when we have enough time in New York. And out on the Coast it's Hollywood Park and Santa Anita and down in Miami it's Hialeah.

But don't get me wrong, he said. Quite a few of us like to go for the old two-dollar window from time to time, but this is really a baseball band. Man, some of these clowns are almost ready to come to blows about their favorite big league baseball teams, especially between Labor Day and the World Series.

Baseball and big time boxing, he said. Hey man, this goddamn band hauls our softball gear around everywhere we go just like all the rest of our stuff. Which brings us to old Malachi Moberly, he said, because he's the one that almost went on the road as a shortstop. And he could have made it on up to the Kansas City Monarchs or the Homestead Grays and such like. But we came through Bogalusa and the bossman heard him playing trombone one night and told him he could be a big league musician and play twelve months a year for the rest of his life.

You take me myself now, he said. I used to go for a jackleg tailor back in The Ham; and I guess I can still get by at it if push comes to shove. But music is my natural hustle, Schoolboy, and I wouldn't change what I do for the bossman with somebody managing money for J. P. Morgan.

Of course, it's always a good thing to be able to do something else along with being a musician, he said. And then he said, Now when it comes to any kind of gadget the one to get to is Old Plug. And I knew he was talking about Alan Meadows and I said, Didn't I hear somebody call him Juice the other night? And he said, Ted Chandler. That's what Ted Chandler calls him because he's always tinkering around with something plugged into electricity.

And when I said there was a cat back on the campus that we all used to call Juice because of all of the cans of grapefruit juice he used to spike with chem lab alcohol, he said, you want to watch that stuff, man. That stuff will drive you crazy and make you blind to boot. And I said, Not me. I said, This guy was in organic chemistry. And Joe States said, Me I want to see them when they break the seal.

Then he said, When it comes to drinking, old Wayman Ridgeway got everybody in this band beat cold and I don't mean just drinking. That clown can drink it and then carry it. Hell, if you don't smell it on him—and you can't even do that most of the time—you don't even know he's been anywhere near any. Be sitting up there steady sipping on that nickel-plated flask and playing as much music as anybody that ever picked up a trombone. Ask Malachi. Ask the Pard. Somitch play that slide horn like it's got keys on it. Battle a trumpet in a minute. But after all, he came up on old Louis too. And believe it or not, so did the Pard, he said, referring to Fred Gilchrist, also known as the silent partner.

I looked back at Wayman Ridgeway across the aisle from Osceola Menefee, sleeping with his head on a pillow against the window, his patent leather sheen hairdo held in place with a tight fitting baseball cap. And when I asked about his hometown and Joe States said Chillicothe I said, I thought maybe you all called him Big Sip because he was from Mississippi like Otis Sheppard. And Joe States said, Chillicothe, Ohio, out of Roanoke, Virginia; and that leather gut somitch ain't never missed sipping nothing.

And another leather gut in this band is old Ike Ellis up there wearing that stocking cap. Ike ain't no steady drinker, but if he's somewhere among a bunch of lushes putting it away, he can put as much of it down the hatch as the next one and wipe his mouth and walk on out of there like it was lemonade or coffee or something. You probably already know that he's from Little Rock, Arkansas. But did you know that the bossman just about kidnapped him out of a machine shop down there? Old Ike's daddy wanted him to be a master mechanic or engineer or something like that. But his uncle came along and gave him a start in music. You see that cornet he doubles on sometime? His uncle used to blow that same horn with the old Sunset Royals down in Florida.

When I said What about Herman Kemble? as we went on with my orientation session that morning en route from Louisville to Indianapolis before heading east to Dayton and Columbus, he said, Who the Bishop? That's the Bishop, Schoolboy. I don't know. I think maybe if they had let that big butt bastard stay in school, maybe he might have turned out to be a lawyer or something. Maybe he really would have turned out to be a bishop. But they kicked him out of the eleventh grade for knocking up a girl and wouldn't marry her, and all he been doing ever since is just blowing that old blooping foghorn, which is what he had started doing with a little hotshot local semipro crew as soon as he was big enough to start sneaking into the joints.

Houston, he said. And then he said, Beaumont, Dallas, Oak City. We got him from Ross Evans in Wichita. We happened through there on our way out to Denver, and they were trying to hustle their way back to Houston; and the bossman hired him and let Ross hold enough cash to haul the rest of them home. Old Bloop had just one change of threads to his name and just about the raggediest ass tenor you ever saw in your goddamn life. But boy was he ready. He was evermore ready, Schoolboy. Challenge any of them. Battle to a fare-thee-well, and then blow ashes to ashes over them. That's where that bishop stuff comes from. We mostly call him Bloop, but one night at a jam session somewhere somebody called him the Presiding Elder and after a while it got changed to the Bishop. So we call him Bloop but sometimes when we are talking about him he's the Bishop.

Don't let him fake you out now, Schoolboy, he said as I turned to look down the aisle to where Herman Kemble lay stretched out across the backseat. He might get a little juiced every now and then, but don't be surprised when he start asking you a lot of deep questions about stuff. Because in a way he's still a schoolboy too. And I'm not just talking about somebody getting his lessons and winning prizes. I'm talking about genuine curiosity right on across the board. Man, the first thing he could have been was a mathematician, but his grade school math teacher was also his first music teacher and the school bandmaster.

The morning I asked him about Elmore Wilkins and Ted Chandler, he said, Frederick Douglass Chandler from Richmond, Virginia, and Elmore Lincoln Wilkins from outside of Nashville by way of Detroit, Michigan. But just let me get back to old Sporty Otis for a minute. When he slung that old country sounding banjo over his shoulder and snagged a freight for the Crescent City, the one that turned him into a guitar player and made a road musician out of him was old Choctaw Cheney. Old Choctaw must have come through Mobile with them twelve strings and that diamond stickpin and them railroad and work camp blues and swamp hollers.

It was old Choctaw Cheney that hooked him up with one of the greatest piano players that ever tore up a jam session. Old Blind Baltimore Livingston. That was in St. Louis, and old Baltimore with a drummer named Plug Willis and a bass player calling himself Bull Montana, was swinging down through that territory to Galveston and back around the Gulf states to Florida; and when the bossman, Shag Philips, and I went to check old Baltimore out one night in Chicago, they had come up the Atlantic Seaboard and barnstormed the mining towns; and we all agreed that Otis on guitar was just what we wanted.

Get old Otis to tell you about what a hell of a musician old Baltimore is, he said. Then he went on to say that Ted Chandler was the son of a Richmond doctor and that his mother, who was a graduate of the Oberlin Conservatory of Music and a former concert pianist, was a music teacher. There was an older brother who was a surgeon and one sister who was the older sister was a nurse and another who was a school supervisor.

Everybody in the family and the neighborhood had expected the youngest Chandler to be a dentist. But at the end of his second year in Washington as a premed student he decided that the musicians you heard at the old Howard Theater in those days were much more important to him than what he was supposed to be doing on the Howard University campus. So he told his mother that he had decided to go up to New York and become a professional musician.

He left it up to her to make everything right with the old man, Joe States said closing one eye and touching his temple with two fingers, which she did even though she knew he wasn't going to any conservatory because he knew she had all the confidence in the world in what he would do with all of that practicing in all of them hard keys she brought him up doing every day. And when the bossman and I ran across him he could blow the hell out of anything with a reed in it. And the bossman promised him if he took the baritone chair he'd see to it that he would have plenty of chances to double on anything else he wanted to.

Now old Jomo with the mojos, he said finally nodding toward Elmore Wilkins. I don't have to tell you about nobody got nothing on him when it comes to that plunger and any of them mutes and any kind of derby fanning. Our other name for him is Mucho Moola, Big Money because he can be rich anytime he want to. His family is well off up there in Detroit. His old man came up to work for General Motors and saved his money and set himself up in business and hit the pay dirt. And that's what he was trying to bring old Jomo up to take over but the trumpet changed all that. As a well off kid he was started out on the best piano and violin lessons money could buy in Detroit, because his family could afford it. And they could also afford the best instruments, and before long the violin was getting him more attention at summer camp than his athletic ability. Until one year when some little fat kid named Fatgut Gus Something Something turned up from somewhere down home with a trumpet and started stomping and scatting and shouting some up tempo blues and took the spotlight.

But just for that one year. Because when they came back that next summer, old Jomo had gone straight home and got himself a trumpet and he was ready for old Fatgut Gus. Not just because he could play all them notes on the trumpet he was used to hearing on the violin but even more because of all that signifying he could already do with his plunger and about five different mutes, plus a plastic, an aluminum, and a felt derby, which he called his mojo tools.

That's how he first got to be known as the Jomo man, and then Jomo with the mojos; and when we came to Detroit a few years later and heard him, and he heard what the bossman was doing with old Malachi and Bloop, he agreed that he belonged in here with us, and that's where he's been ever since.

So much for the family business, Joe States said pulling his cap over his eyes and letting his seat back. But what the hell, you might as well do what you really want to do with your life. And Jomo Wilkins can afford it, Schoolboy. You see him up there curled up in them two bus seats like he's lucky to be in out of the weather? Man, with what he going to have coming in automatically from his old man's side, he can live on easy street, and I mean in high style without ever hitting a lick at a snake again. Look at him. Shout you some blues, too, when you need him to. As you well know. Low down dirty or otherwise. Clown you some novelty with capers. Croon you some jive-sweet when the Bossman don't want to sic old Osceola Menefee on the trillies. Or when you want him to either join or follow some of old Ocie's mellow come-on stuff.

VIII

WE HAD pulled into New York on Sunday night, but we were not due in the recording studio until Wednesday morning. So Monday was a free day, and we spent all of Tuesday in a rehearsal hall uptown on 131st Street off Seventh Avenue around the corner from the old Lafayette Theatre; and on the lunch break we all went around to Big John's, and the treat was on Milo the Navigator.

There was all of the new material the bossman had been working up during the tour, and as usual he had also made changes in several of the old arrangements that he wanted to record again. Not as a matter of updating in terms of the going fashion of the moment but rather because to him some compositions were like the canvases some painters keep putting back on the easel not because there's anything wrong with them but because they like them so much that they have to go on playing around with new touches here and there.

It was also already pretty clear to me that when you rehearsed with that band you were never really working to get the score as such letter perfect. Usually that was only the beginning, because most of the tricky passages and special problems of execution were almost always worked out and double-checked by Old Pro beforehand. So the main thing was not whether you could execute what was on the music stand but how close you could come to the feeling being signaled from the piano. What mattered was what the bossman wanted to hear, sometimes for the time being and sometimes maybe from then on.

When we finished the last run-through, it was six o'clock. And Joe States said, What did I tell you? Didn't I tell you? You see what I'm talking about? Been in here rolling like a bunch of cotton wharf dockhands since this morning and still blowing like they trying to make the lineup and get a letter sweater or something. And the man ain't cracking no whip. He just punching some chickenbutt piano keys.

But what can I tell you, Schoolboy, he said as he started breaking down and packing his setup. This man has got himself one hell of a crew of musicians, and they ready to tear this stuff up down there tomorrow. Hell, I'm kind of ready my goddamn self. Hell, we'll blow the goddamn *Encyclopaedia*

Britannica for him, all it takes is a quick little segue not even a vamp.

You already know what happened when he starts laying down them extended vamps, he said. And I said, I sure do, remembering how he brought me on that night in Cincinnati. And Joe States said, I been in this band since forever, and the somitch can still raise big fat goose pimples on my hidebound behind anytime he really wants to; and that's when I'm subject to drive the rest of these thugs right on into the jaws like them six hundred troopers in that poem.

Milo the Navigator told everybody to be downtown at the studio before nine o'clock. He printed the address, the studio number, and the bus and subway numbers on a portable blackboard for those who would not be taking the band bus down Seventh Avenue from the Woodside at 7:45 with a stop at Hotel Theresa at the corner of 125th Street.

There were several questions about the new uniforms that we were supposed to be measured for before leaving town, and then Old Pro began collecting the folders section by section and when he came to me he said the bossman was in the office on the phone at the moment but wanted me to stick around. So I told Joe States not to wait for me.

Old Pro sat at the piano and started checking through each folder. I waited on a high stool by the window from which in those days you could look out across the rooftops of that part of Harlem to the ridge that stretched south to Morningside Heights and Columbia and north to CCNY and Hamilton Terrace.

When the bossman came back in, I stayed where I was until he finished looking over the sheets Old Pro showed him, and then he held up his hand to let me know he was ready to leave; and when I joined him on the way out I found that I was in for a double surprise.

I was wondering if you'd like to run with me for a while tonight, he said; and all I could get myself together to say was, You're the bossman. You're on. Because I could hardly believe my ears and he said, I mean beginning as of right now. No change necessary. And I said, I'm with you, bossman. I'm with you.

We came on downstairs and out onto the sidewalk, and he said, Well good but now are you sure that this is not cutting in on something you already had up for the evening? And I said, Absolutely. I said, Nothing special and nothing definite. I was just going to look around up here a little more and turn in early for tomorrow. And he said, This won't keep you out late at all.

He flagged a cab heading up Seventh Avenue, and when he got in he gave the driver the street number and settled back and said, I'm going up to see Daddy Royal, and I thought you might like to come along and meet him.

And I said, Not Royal Highness.

And he said, Ain't but the one, Schoolboy, ain't but the one.

And I said, Grant Simpson.

And he said, Ulysses Grant Simpson.

At that time Royal Highness, the contemporary peer and sometime nemesis of such legendary show stopping dancers, vaudeville entertainers, and musical comedy headliners as Ernest Hogan, Williams and Walker, Miller and Lyles, Slow Kid Thompson, King Rastus Brown, and Bojangles, was living in a penthouse up at 555 Edgecombe, across 155th Street and north of the main part of Sugar Hill and also overlooking Coogan's Bluff and the Polo Grounds, which was the home park of the New York Giants National League baseball team in those days.

In the lobby there was a woman's voice on the intercom responding to the buzzer, but when we came off the elevator upstairs, Royal Highness himself was waiting for us in the open door. He was around five feet nine and he looked as if he were just about the age his father must have been in the publicity pictures of him that I remembered from the *Pittsburgh Courier*, the *Chicago Defender*, and the *Baltimore Afro-American* back in Mobile County Training School. And his smooth medium brown skin was exactly the shade I had always thought it was, although all of the photographs of him that I had ever seen had been black and white.

Here's my bandleader, he said. Back in town from another go round. What say there, maestro. You all come on in here. And the bossman bowed, making a flourish with his hat, and said, Daddy Royal. Ain't but the one. And we stepped inside and they stood holding each other at arm's length and the bossman said, You looking fine, Daddy Royal. You're looking great. And then he said, This is the new bass player I was telling you about.

So I did my little bow, and he patted me on the shoulder with a warm down-home grandfatherly twinkle in his eyes and said, You're already welcome in the band, so you're automatically welcome up here young soldier. I make it a practice not to shake hands with finger musicians. Hell, their goddamn hands are too valuable for any and everybody to be coming up and grabbing and wringing and twisting them all the time. Hell, people ought to remember that's your goddamn bread and butter and also the keys to your soul bank they putting all of that extra wear and tear on.

Then the first thing he said after we helped ourselves to drinks from the sideboard and sat down was, Boy you thought I was dead didn't you? A lot of them think old Royal is dead. Boy, I ain't near 'bout dead yet. I might not be getting around much anymore like I used to, but I'm here and I'll be here after a lot of them check out. Right up here watching to see what you young splibs got going to deal with them jaspers.

But now don't get me wrong, young soldier. Let me get this straight right now. Don't you ever let nobody tell you that you were put here on God's earth to spend your life worrying and bellyaching about some old jaspers. Excuse my language, but fuck that shit, young soldier.

I'm starting right in on you like this, he said. But I ain't never bellyached to no jaspers in my life. Because the notion I was brought up on down home was that you just go out there and show the somitches. Do whatever the hell you do and let them get to that. Some of them are always going to be looking for ways to deny you your talent. Hell, that's the game of life, young soldier. You ever played any game in which there wasn't somebody trying to deny you something? Boy, now this is exactly what gets me. Don't nobody love tangling in baseball, football, basketball more than splibs—and don't mention boxing. So how can any honest to goodness splib turn around and start bellyaching because some jaspers are out there doing the same thing? Like I say that's life and it's also life that there's always some others out there that will invest in any promise that you might show—and it don't take but one when it's the right one. Look at Irving Mills. Look at Joe Glaser. Now what

I want you to remember always is that everything else I say
about splibs and jaspers comes down to this. So now just make
yourself at home.

The first thing he wanted to hear about from the bossman was
how the band was getting along financially; and the bossman
said fine better than ever in that the new recording contract
looked very good. They started talking about agents and details of the entertainment business then and I was not really
listening anymore. So I picked up my drink and started looking
at the multiple rows of photographs that lined the walls and
shelves and also the top of the ivory white grand piano.

There were glossy blowups of familiar sports page portraits
and prize ring action shots of Jack Johnson, Joe Gans, Sam
Langford, Harry Wills, and the young still up and coming Joe
Louis, all personally inscribed to Royal Highness—as were
those of Rube Foster in his warmup sweater, Satchel Paige following through on the mound, and Josh Gibson in his catcher's gear with the grandstand in the background.

As I moved on to the panel of entertainers and musicians,
there were copies of some of the same promotion portraits
that I had first seen as a little boy waiting my turn in Papa
Gumbo Willie McWorthy's barbershop next door to Stranahan's General Merchandise Store. There were also some that
reminded me of myself as I was when as a teenager I first
started stopping by Shade's Bon Ton Barbershop and Shoe
Shine Parlor across from Boommen's Union Hall Ball Room
on Green's Avenue.

Then there was a special gallery of autographed originals of
entertainment page sketches and caricatures of Royal Highness
himself, usually sporting a coronet at a jaunty angle (something he had never actually done). In some of the snapshots
he was wearing a top hat and tails, and in others a homburg
with gamble striped pants, or a derby along with patent leather
shoes and spats. In still others he wore no hat at all so as to
show off his widely imitated footlight glossy hairdo.

To keep out of range of the conversation I skipped the end
of the room where the mantelpiece, the piano, and the big
console record player were and crossed directly over to the opposite wall where contemporary paintings, mostly from Paris,

were hung along with various tribal masks, shields, and spears from the Benin, Senufo, and Yoruba areas of West Africa.

When you came to the next wall, you were at the door to the terrace, from which there was a view of the after dark Manhattan skyline that brought back the way I used to feel about New York not only when I saw such scenes in cops and robbers movies in the Saenger Theater in downtown Mobile, but also whenever I used to hear Cab Calloway either on record or radio singing about Creole girls in a revue tune called "Underneath the Harlem Moon," back when I was still in junior high school and had not yet read Alain Locke's book *The New Negro* and found out about the so-called Harlem Renaissance.

After that many years I could still whistle the melody to "Creole babies walkin' 'long with rhythm in their thighs . . ." note for note as I used to do. But even as I began to do so, what I found myself thinking about again after that many years, was how at first like just about everybody else around Gasoline Point I didn't pay very much attention to what the lyrics were really about, and when I did I hated them because they were about highbrows going slumming whereas what I had always pictured to myself as I whistled was a panorama of frizzly headed copper colored girls all dressed up and strutting their stuff along Lenox Avenue at twilight with the midtown skyscrapers twinkling in the distance.

What remembering all that also brought to mind was an old James P. Johnson ragtime piano roll titled "If You've Never Been Vamped by a Brownskin, You've Never Been Vamped at All"; and at the very instant that I realized that such was the sort of tune that both Royal Highness and the bossman would be pleased to reminisce about there was the bossman's voice at the door telling me that something was about to be served.

So I came back inside and the three of us went into the dining room, and that is where I met Stewart Anderson, who was much better known as Stewmeat Anderson (as in Pigmeat Markham), because he was once half of an old vaudeville comedy team billed as Stewmeat and Small Change (Small Change Flint, formerly Skin Flint because his real name was Glenn Aldridge Flint).

Over the years the stage name Stewmeat had been shortened to Stew (for stew chef as in sous-chef), because when bookings became scarce during the Depression the act broke up and he started a hole-in-the-wall eating place on 132nd Street between Seventh and Lenox avenues with himself as chief short order cook and bottle washer; and with two-thirds backing from Royal Highness, an old hometown boy from Norfolk, Virginia, he expanded into a neighborhood hangout on 134th Street between Lenox and Fifth avenues where the most popular special was not a stew of beef and root vegetables but down-home pork neckbones and rice.

It was his wife's voice that we had heard on the intercom in the lobby. The two of them were sharing the large apartment and keeping house for Royal Highness, who had been married three times but had no children and no close relatives and so not long after his last divorce had invited them to move into the north wing to keep him company. By that time all three of them were in retirement, but they were also still business associates because they had held on to part ownership of the restaurant, which now under new management was paying off better than ever.

In the publicity pictures of Stewmeat and Small Change in costume Stewmeat always wore a very gaudy vest padded to look like a bay window. In the amusement page snapshots of him in street clothes he looked as much like a stylishly tailored athlete as like an entertainer, and at dinner the night I met him, you could have mistaken him for a retired prizefighter who treated himself to regular massages, facials, and manicures and still dropped by his favorite Lenox Avenue barbershop to check through the sports pages of the daily papers while having his shoes shined.

His wife whose name was Cherry Lee from Cherie Bontemps a cafe au lait Creole former dancer from New Orleans had worked in the chorus line at the Cotton Club, at the Apollo, and at Small's Paradise before marrying him and helping him run the original hole-in-the-wall restaurant.

After saying the blessing Royal Highness, who had pointed me to the first place on his left, went on with the tête-à-tête conversation he had going with the bossman, who was sitting on his right directly across from me. Then as he turned in my direction he said, So this young fella is all set for his first recording session in the morning. And the bossman nodded and winked at me, and I said, I hope so. And Royal Highness said, You just go on down there and play that bull fiddle. Them jaspers down there in that studio ain't got no stuff for you.

Boy, any time you can play music to suit the bossman and Old Pro, you can forget about them jaspers down there twisting them knobs and watching them dials. Hell, a lot of them jaspers don't know anywhere near as much about them highfalutin studio gimcracks as you might think. Let alone splib music. They're doing what they're doing and you're doing what you're doing. Hell, I know a lot of people that can talk your head off about Mozart and Bozart and don't know the first thing about the kind of Mose art that band can put goose pimples on anybody's behind with. He told you about them goose pimples, didn't he?

He turned back toward the bossman again then, and they went on talking as before but on the way back into the parlor he left the bossman with Stewmeat Anderson and guided me into his huge dressing room and showed me a double row of handmade shoes that he had been ordering since the mid-1920s from a London cobbler recommended by the Prince of Wales and he said, You know what I want to do? When them records you all going to start making tomorrow come out, I want to put on one of my favorite pairs of old hoofing boots and just sit in my old rocking chair in there just listening and snapping my fingers and wiggling a toe every now and then.

Don't worry about it, he said again. But watch yourself. And watch out for them bright lights.

And I said, I'm trying to. And he said, I'm talking about not losing sight on the world like some I've seen. I'm talking about when you see what you see and hear what you hear you really going to find out that a lot of this stuff up here ain't nothing but some of the same old jive all wrapped up in a big city package. I'm thinking about how some folks come up here all wide eyed, and when them bright lights from them tall buildings hit them, they think the first thing they better do is get rid of the good old tried and true down-home stuff that got them all the way up here in the first place.

Boy, don't you ever let nothing make you forget that what's always out there waiting to rip your drawers is that same old bear you been tussling with all your life, and man that somitch is just as grizzly in the city as he is in the swamps. Boy, it's just exactly like what the old folks always used to tell me it was; the bear comes in any and every shape, form, and fashion, and sometimes in no shape, form, and fashion that you can really describe. Just like you can't describe the goddamn blues, even when they got the mug on you like ugly.

When we came out into the hallway the bossman and Stew-meat Anderson were standing by the sideboard where the drinks were. Royal Highness told me to serve myself, and I chose seltzer and he made himself a bourbon on the rocks. Then we all followed him on back to the living room where he sat in the high back Scandinavian rocking chair and lit a cigar and took a long puff followed by a sip of bourbon and said, So now tell me, Emp, is this young fella going to take You Know Which What in that cool booted seven league stride you been telling me about? Or should I say Miss You Know Which's What. And the bossman said, Joe thinks so. And Royal Highness took another puff from his cigar and winked at me and held up his glass and said, A good word from Joe States goes a long way with me, young fella.

What I'm talking about now, son, he said, is when them dazzling bright lights twinkling at you happen to be the blue eyes of some of them mane tossing ponies prancing around with all that ofay enthusiasm for flesh and blood and nitty gritty. Boy, the stuff you got to deal with in the circles you moving into now is totally different from tipping on the Q.T. with Miss Ann down yonder.

Boy, sometimes I wonder, he said. As I took a quick look at the bossman and realized that what Royal Highness was saying was as much a part of what the visit was about as anything else. Boy, sometimes I wonder. Boy, I'm not sure. But sometimes I do wonder if the admiration of some of them people don't screw up more splibs' heads than just plain old segregation as such ever did. If you know what I mean.

I mean all that bad taste some of the classiest jaspers I ever met sometimes go for. I mean how some of the very jaspers that supposed to know so much about everything, can turn around and excuse splibs of some old half assed shit that ain't no other splib would ever let you get away with. So I'm also talking about how you always got to be on the watch out for the kind of ponies that will make you feel that you're already God's gift to women and don't need to change a thing.

As he went on talking, you got the impression that you were being warned against an occupational hazard that was every bit as dangerous as alcohol and narcotics. But what he was to say when he brought it up again during my third visit was: Don't worry about it. All you got to do is just remember that they're supposed to be able to put you next to something else besides what's between her legs, and even in her pocketbook.

You see all of this fine stuff all around this apartment? I didn't hustle it, son. I'm not talking about playing them. I'm talking about handling yourself out there in that same classy world you went to college to qualify for.

So now look here, young soldier, he said, when the bossman and I stood up to take our leave that first time, I know you got all your spare time booked solid with things you want to find out about New York all by yourself. But when you come back in another time, you know where to find me. Hell, we didn't get around to talking about old Gladstone yet. Hell, I know Papa Gladness down there on the Bay, just like I know Fess Whatley in Birmingham and Willis James down at Bama State.

Then the bossman and I shook hands and held shoulders with him at the door, and at the elevator we turned and waved again. And he said, Where the hell is that goddamn Joe Ass States? Tell him I say he better get his skinny butt self on up here with all them new lies he always saving up to add to my private stock. Tell him I say don't lighten up on that high hat, but get to me fast.

IX

IN THE cab rolling south along St. Nicholas Avenue toward 125th Street, the bossman told me that it was Royal Highness who had insisted that he begin building his full band when he did, and that Royal Highness had also helped him get its first bookings and had helped to underwrite its first tour. But it was Royal Highness himself who was to fill me in on how their very special relationship got started.

Me and your bossman go back a little ways, Schoolboy, he said at one point when I went back up to see him the next time the band had several free days in New York, I'm the one told him he was on the way to become The Emperor of Syncopation. I said, With the stuff you putting in the game, if you just keep on charting enough of the territory you heading into you can stake your claim to a whole empire, and that means you'll be the Emperor. If he told you I was one of the ones back there that helped fan a blaze under his young behind, all I can say is the spark was already there and there was plenty fuel everywhere.

But now don't get me wrong, he also said. I'm not really talking about just plain old everyday egotistical competition. What I'm talking about is what can result from just trying to do the best you can, whatever it is you do, no matter who else is also trying to do it. Because when it comes to musical competition, even when you turn out to be better than every living and swinging somitch in sight, what about all them others who may be out of sight but not out of earshot, like Bach, Mozart, and Beethoven? They still right there in the music store while a whole lot of others have come and gone.

That's what I told him right at the outset. I said, You get to be the kind of Emperor I'm talking about not because you're out to wipe out everybody else. I'm talking about doing what you're doing in a way that commands everybody else's respect. I told him, I'm not going to knock the money and popularity that hype can bring you. But it's the genuine respect you command that makes you the goddamn boss.

The first time he came backstage to see me, I asked him if he wanted to be another jackleg dancer, and he said he was a musician. He was already on his way as an after hours piano player and he was also doing pretty good gigging around catch as catch can with his own sextet. There was something about him that really impressed me right away. He was good looking enough not to have any kind of trouble getting with the quails. His threads were fly, and he carried himself with cool class. But the main thing for me was the expression in his eyes when he got going about music and about music and life experience.

When he said what he said about music and dance, I said, goddamn, boy. You know something don't many people know. I said, Don't many people realize the meaning of what you're talking about. Because, he said, Some people say dance is about music so dancers need musicians. But to me music is about dance because the way I hear it dance actually came before music, and that's why we measure music in dance time. So musicians should be trying to dance whatever instrument they play.

I was working down on Broadway in one of the headline live variety acts being featured with a big first run movie. We were doing five shows a day between the film feature, and when you were not on, you could just stay around backstage and have visitors or you could go and hang out somewhere in Tin Pan Alley. Or visit backstage with friends who happened to be playing at other Broadway theaters at the same time.

He caught the act that first time, and I told him to come back to see me and I told him to just come on back to the stage entrance and ask for me next time.

That's how it began and he would drop by from time to time. And then one day he brought me a piece of music he said he had written, and when I asked him what it was about he said it was about me and for me. So I took him over to the piano back there and made him sit right down and play it over, and I couldn't believe my ears. That young fool had me coming out of that piano, comping for me with one hand and doing me with the other. He was mostly just hinting and half kidding, but he had me, young fella. I knew exactly where he was going with it, and I also knew he was a born musician. And you can bet a fat man that old Daddy Royal knows one when he hears one. He told me it wasn't really filled in yet but he just wanted me to hear it at this stage. And I said, You got it going all right. But, boy, what you need for your kind of music is a full band. I said, Boy, your true instrument is them eighty-eight keys in a fourteen to sixteen or eighteen piece orchestra.

I took him around and put him in touch with some master musician friends of mine, and when they heard him they all said the same thing, which was the same thing I had told him. I'm talking about solid professional writers and arrangers like Will Vodery and Ford Dabney and I'm pretty sure that a college boy like yourself knows about old Will Marion Cook and Harry T. Burleigh.

And I said I sure do and told him that Cook's "Swingalong" and Burleigh's "Deep River" were school glee club songs just as J. Rosamond and James Weldon Johnson's "Lift Every Voice" was the general assembly period anthem along with "My Country 'Tis of Thee" and "The Star-Spangled Banner." Then as he went on talking, the other tunes that came to mind were "Sweet and Low," "East of the Sun and West of the Moon," "California, Here I Come," "Avalon," "The World Is Waiting for the Sunrise," and the mock church testification song that went: "Oh Yes, Oh Yes and When You Die . . ." because the sound of that kind of music was also a part of the atmosphere that Mr. B. Franklin Fisher brought to Mobile County Training School along with Miss Lexine Metcalf.

People forget what kind of musicians these men were, he said. Everybody knows that some of them wrote hit tunes and could play some fingerbusting stride piano. But I'm talking about something that goes all the way back before the old Clef Club down in Hotel Marshall at Seventh Avenue at 54th Street. When you're talking about people like the ones I'm talking about you're talking about masters of all kinds of harmonics for ensembles of just about any kind of instrumental combination or voice mixture you can come up with.

I'm talking about people with solid experience of being not just arrangers and composers but musical directors to boot. So anyway, they all heard what I heard and told the young fella he was not just a born musician but a born composer just exactly like I said. And they all still got their ears cocked and he knows it. Jimmy Johnson, Willie the Lion, Will Vodery, Old Will Marion. We all dropped it on him. We were the ones that told him to forget about all of the hotshot all-stars and pick his own sidemen one by one because they fit in with what he was trying to do as a composer. Because what I realized as soon as he played that little sketch for me was that he needed a full band that he could play just like he played the piano.

He came backstage to see me because I was supposed to be The Great Royal Me and I as much as told him that's all right about me. I said now it's your turn to do what you can do about being the Almighty Imperial you.

Now, he was to say at one point when I went back up to see him again the day after the band came back to town the time after that, Let me tell you a little something about how old

Daddy Royal started out in this racket. Maybe you've heard about it or read something about it, but I want you to get it directly from me. Boy, I got my goddamn start as a blackface minstrel comedian in one of them fly by night circus tent medicine shows—or maybe I should say one after another of them. And then one day I said to myself I said, Hell, I ain't cut out to be no two-bit tent show clown. I'm a goddamn dancer with enough stuff to be a class act. And I got on out of there and I worked my way on up into vaudeville.

Back then when a road show hit town and there was somebody in it doing something, and you figure you could beat him doing it, you could challenge him and battle him right then and there. Of course now if you were not ready, shame on you. But if you really had something, you also had yourself a job, sometimes maybe even his job.

This was in Savannah, and I started woofing and stuck my fish and he decided to teach me a lesson. So he dared me to come up on the stage, and *boy*! I was *up* there before he could get the words out of his mouth. Because I knew I was ready, and I low more scandalized him. Man, I didn't just put him in the dozens, I put his butt in the wind.

They started calling me Kid Stomp the Royal High Stepper and stuff like that, and I battled my way on down through Atlanta, Mobile, and New Orleans to Beaumont and Houston and all the way out to Los Angeles and San Francisco and then all the way back across to Kansas City, St. Louis, and I worked out of Chicago for a while. And when I say battle I mean you never could tell when the next local tiger was going to try to ambush you.

So when I hit New York that first time I figured I was ready. I was already being billed as Kid Royal the King of the Stompers, and when I made the scene to pay my respects to the joints along Lenox and Seventh, I would be wearing one of my homburgs or derbies and my chesterfield or my alpaca with the maestro fur collar. I was dressing the part as if to say Who says I ain't? It didn't take but just a few days for the word to get out that there was this young hotshot in town, and when I made it to the Hoofers Club later on that week they were expecting me as I knew they would be. Well, they didn't run me out of there, Schoolboy, because I wasn't jiving. I was laying some stuff down and everybody knew it. But I did find out that I had to go and come again. Which I did, and when I got to be one of the top dogs around there, I promoted myself to Royal Highness.

At one point during another visit later on that year he was to remind me of how much territory his stomping grounds had covered. It not only stretched beyond Harlem and Broadway to most of the four star showcase theaters from Boston all the way across to San Francisco and Los Angeles but also took in a string of the choice music halls in western Europe.

In my heyday I was billed and booked as Royal Highness all over that part of the world too, Schoolboy, he said when he came back into the living room from the study where Stewmeat Anderson had called him to the phone and saw me standing in front of the panel of framed foreign language placards and marquee displays. Boy, you should have seen me over there moving among them hereditary royal dogs. Man, me and them and them and me.

Them trying to get with old Mose and old Mose trying to get with all that gold plated castle and palace routine. All that confetti, spaghetti, and filigree stuff. And of course you know I had to get next to some of that royal intrigue poontang, me being an old triggerman ever since I found out what it was made for. So talk about tipping on the Q.T., me and them pedigreed stone foxes, some of them grandmamas, and them and me. Boy, ain't nothing like hearing your name whispered close up in one of them European accents early in the morning just about the break of day, sometimes in a wing of one of them old rambling castles or while you're all bogged up in silk and downy pillows in one of them forty acre flats with garden terraces overlooking some world famous boulevard or other.

Hey, what you talkin' 'bout, young fella! he said and took a long pull on his cigar, his eyes twinkling not only because he was remembering how it was but also as if he knew that the way he said talking 'bout would evoke all of the old yarn spinning and lie swapping places in my down-home boyhood.

Another thing me and old Jack Johnson used to talk about, he said taking another sip of cognac and another pull on his cigar. Boy, one of the main things about the people I'm talking about is the sporting life, and that was just like putting old

Br'er Rabbit in the briar patch. Anytime you start carrying on about handling horses and hunting dogs and wing shooting and deer and bear tracking, and stuff like that you just bring out the down-home stuff I was bred and born to. Boy, I fished all the way from the crawfish pond to the Gulf Stream, and I used to hunt cheechees with a slingshot, possums with a forked stick, and rabbits and squirrels with lightwood knots. *Whatyoutalkinbout!*

Every now and then old Jack Johnson used to come up and whisper something about the whereabouts of my royal skids, because once when I had a show in Zurich, Switzerland, I went up in the mountains with a bunch of them and decided to get on a pair of skis, something I'd never done before in my life. But, hell, I was a dancer, and I had also skipped along the top of quite a few boxcars in my young hoboing days. So I got with that too, for one afternoon. Then the people backing the tour moved in and called a halt to that egotistical bullshit as if to say "It may be your ass but it's our goddamn money."

Every time old Jack Johnson used to bring that up, I would always say, Hey, just look who's talking. Ain't you the same Jack Li'l Arthur Johnson that woofed himself into the Plaza de Torros to go bare knuckles against the horns of a goddamn Miura bull?

Boy, you tell them young splibs I say Old Daddy Royal is still here, he was to say when it was time for me to head back down to Seventh Avenue again. You tell them old Daddy Royal say old rocking chair ain't quite got me yet. Tell them I say if they don't know what to make of what I'm all about, shame on them. Because I'm a goddamn fact, and when you deny me you denying history. And that's just like trying to deny the law of gravity. You tell them I say even when I'm dead and gone I'm still subject to be a fact for some time to come.

X

SOMETIMES WHEN *we left town late at night, everybody would already be curled up and asleep even before the bus made it out beyond the outskirts and settled into that cozy soporific open country hum again, and unless there was an early morning relief stop*

*at a service station or at some wayside inn or crossroads general
merchandise store, you wouldn't hear another word from anybody
until we pulled up in front of the next hotel or boarding house.*

*But there were also times when you could wake up and tell
where you were even before you opened your eyes because all you
had to do was listen, and somebody would start calling off and
repeating either the place name, like an old time railroad conductor, or start signifying about some street name, building, or
other identifying landmark as Ike Ellis did for my benefit on the
next morning of my first trip south from New York by way of the
Atlantic Seaboard states.*

*Well, there's old man Johnny Jim Crow, Schoolboy, he said just
loud enough not to disturb anybody else. And I knew that we had
recrossed the line and were back in the section of the country that
had been a part of the old Confederacy and that we had stopped
for a traffic light in a courthouse square that had a gray monument of either a CSA officer on horseback, or a pack bearing
rifleman, facing north.*

*Still up there, Ike Ellis said; and Alan Meadows said, Still up
there trying to make out like them people didn't get the living
dooky kicked out of them. And Ike Ellis said, Man, did they ever
mo. Man once them Yankees got all of their stuff together and got
them gunboats rolling down the Mississippi and then cut across
Tennessee to Georgia and the sea, kicking every living and swinging ass until times got tolerable, I'm telling you, mister.*

*Grant and Sherman, Joe States said. Old Grant and old
Sherman, and I'm not forgetting Mr. Sheridan and old Chickamauga Thomas either. These people had old Stonewall Jackson,
but the Union had the rock of Chickamauga. Him and Sheridan
are my boys too, and old Admiral Farragut down in your neck
of the woods, Schoolboy. And Otis Sheppard said, Hell, I know
something about that one. Damn the torpedoes, full speed ahead.*

*Hey, but wait a minute, Joe States said. Here's what I'm
talking about now. I'm talking about once old Abe got rid of that
simple ass McClellan and turned things over to old Grant, and
Grant teamed up with old Sherman, and they got that one-two
punch going, it was all over for these people. Fare-thee-well, land
of cotton, jump for joy.*

*McClellan, Malachi Moberly said. Man, goddamn. Where the
hell did they get that McClellan from? They say he was a badass*

somitch on the drill field and on maneuvers. But all he ever did on the battlefield was make Robert E. Lee look good in the newspapers. Man, that clown made Lee look good even when Lee was having to retreat because he had gotten his ass in a bind. But now when they put Grant on old Lee's case it was like stink on doodoo all the way to Richmond.

Man, Joe States said, Old Sherman told them at the very outset. Old Sherman was from up north but he was working in a military school down in Louisiana when they first started talking all that old loudmouth secession jive. He told them. He said, Personally I like you all, I really do. He said, Some of the best friends I made up at West Point come from down here. But when you all start talking some old stuff about messing with the Union, I'm sorry, you all don't know what you all are letting yourself in for. That's what he told them, and when that didn't do any good he showed them.

Oh but did he show them, Ted Chandler said. So much for the Seesesh. Don't care how mad these old peckerwoods anywhere down here get about anything, the one thing you don't ever hear any of them ever talking about no more is secession. They wave their flag and give that old rebel yell but that's as far as it goes, buddy.

These people, Wayman Ridgeway said. These people and all this old hype, and they keep on passing it on from generation to generation. That's one of the main things I can't understand about this whole situation. Look, Schoolboy, what about this shit. Now they put the badmouth on old Benedict Arnold for whatever it was he did, and then they turn right around and let these people get away with all this old stuff. And I'm not talking about the denying us our birthrights, I'm talking about glorifying old Jeff Davis and Lee and Stonewall and them, even old Nathan Bedford Forrest.

Man, that's right, Ike Ellis said. Man, they ruined Benedict Arnold's reputation forever, and here these people down here still putting up all these old monuments and hanging out all these old Dixie banners all over the place on holidays, national holidays.

Then he also said, Look, you all I'm talking about the Constitution. Wasn't no Constitution when Benedict Arnold came along. Man, old raw-boned, frozen face Jeff Davis flat out told them. He said, Look, these are my niggers just like these are my livestock, and if you all don't let me have my way about how I run my business I'm going to tear up this piece of paper because that's all it is to me.

What about all this old stuff, Schoolboy, Osceola Menefee said, What did them college profs say about all this old historical hype? And I said, As far as my profs were concerned the greatest Civil War monument is not some piece of stone or bronze sculpture up on a pedestal anywhere, not even the Lincoln Memorial on the Washington Mall, Grant's Tomb above Riverside Drive, or Sherman facing south in the Grand Army Plaza. The way they see it the Civil War memorial that really counts for us and for the whole country, north and south, east and west is that little statement that Lincoln read from a page of a scratch pad up at Gettysburg, Pennsylvania, on the nineteenth of November almost a year and a half before the war was over.

I could have gone on to say that all colleges like the one I went to were Civil War memorials, but I didn't because I just wanted to go on listening to them; and also because Ted Chandler was already saying, Hey well all right, Schoolboy. And then he said, Hey you all hear this deep stuff our schoolboy is laying down for us? And Ike Ellis said, Them college profs sure did school him right on that one. And Alan Meadows said, Because they want him to be dedicated to the proposition. And that was also what he was to go on talking about that afternoon when he came into the Snack Shack across the street from the auditorium and sat at the counter with Joe States and me.

Say now look here, Schoolboy, he said. That was some heavy stuff we were getting into this morning. Man, by the time you hit the ninth grade, everybody in our school already knew that address by heart. You had to commit it to memory word for word and get up before an audience and recite it with the same feeling that was always there when you heard "Lift Every Voice."

Heavy, Joe States said. Man, you talking about something heavy as church. And Alan Meadows said, In church it was the Lord's Prayer and the Lord Is My Shepherd, and in school it was I Pledge Allegiance and Four Score and Seven. And Joe States said, You know something? Until I hit the road and started to get to know some of our folks up north, I didn't realize that they didn't do all that up there like down the way.

Man, what we really talking about now is the old folks and the old landmarks, Alan Meadows said. And Joe States said, God bless them both. And then he said, Let me say this again because I can't say it too often. When it comes to education, the old folks have always been on the case.

I'm talking about like way back before Emancipation. If you found a way to learn to read and write and figure it was like outfitting yourself with a pair of them seven league boots, that somebody—who was it?—mentioned the other day, for the Underground Railroad. Then after Surrender, every time somebody put up a new school they saw it as another Amen to Appomattox.

And said as much, I said. And he said, You know it too? And I said, To them it is still as if every good mark you make on your grade school report card is like another bullet to help bring about old Stonewall Jackson's final Waterloo.

But schoolboy that I still was (and still am) I also knew that you should never forget that there were also those who did not listen to the old folks because sometimes they acted as if what they scoffed at as "book learning" was a bigger threat to their well being than segregation. So much so that some of them not only pulled for poor students against good students, but were also very likely to insist that good students' achievements were the result not of conscientious application and integrity but of luck, hype, trickery, or favoritism. Not that they really thought of schoolboys as being more dishonest than anybody else but that book learning and everyday common sense and the practicality that added up to success didn't go together. So to them schoolboy was a term of contempt.

On the way out to the West Coast that first time it was Elmore Wilkins who started signifying about landmarks of another kind; and as soon as the others began joining in, you could tell that they were saying what they were saying not only because there was a schoolboy along this time, but also because it was something they had been doing among themselves from time to time over the years.

One more time, Elmore Wilkins said looking out across the plains at the mountains against the sky in the distance. One more once, Schoolboy, he said. Now, you know what I always have to think about every time we head out this way? Them folks making this trip back in the old days of the covered wagons. And Joe States said, Man, I know what you mean, but what about them cats that were all out through here way back before that? What about all of them Spanish studs tramping and camping all out through here looking for gold? Man, do you realize that they came all the way across the Atlantic Ocean from the old country and left them ships anchored back somewhere on the coast, and didn't even have any maps to go by?

Maps? Osceola Menefee said. Man, them cats were making themselves a map as they went along. Man, what can I tell you? Man, don't forget you're talking about the same somitches that navigated their way all the way across the wide open seas. And Joe States said, Them cats were making history. Man, them cats had history in their blood.

And passed it on to the ones that became the early settlers and the forefathers that turned all of this part of the hemisphere into one nation under one flag, Ike Ellis said. And Malachi Moberly stood up and stretched and put his magazine in the overhead rack and said, Man, what about that goddamn trip your forefathers made in the bottom of that cattle boat? And Ike Ellis said, Aw man, don't nobody feel like playing no dozens today. And Malachi Moberly came and sat beside him and said, Man, ain't nobody trying to put nobody in some old dozens.

Damn, man, he said putting his seat in a reclining position and stretching his legs, They're my forefathers too. Come on, man, you're talking about making history and making the flag. Man, there's a whole lot of doodoo all mixed up with all that other stuff they come up with to stick them stars and stripes together with. Man, all that old coonskin and log cabin jive is all right with me but man, history is all in the way you look at it.

Now me, he said to the bus at large, What I can't help thinking about every time we head out this way is Indian history. Man, them folks messed around and lost everything to these people. And when Ted Chandler said, Yeah Jack, but them goddamn Indians went down swinging, Jack, he said, but Jack, them goddamn Indians ain't swinging no goddamn more, Jack. Man, that's exactly what Indian history comes down to, and that's what I'm talking about. Man, me, I don't intend for us to go down at all. Man, look out the goddamn window and see what they left these folks with. Man, how you going to ever swing anymore when you ain't got doodly squat to swing with? Man, ain't nobody in history ever got themselves faked further out of position than these folks. Which just goes to show you that it takes a whole lot more than being brave or even making people scared of you. Ask Scully.

Well thank goodness Old Mose has played it smarter than these folks, Joe States said. And Ike Ellis said, So far, man, so far. Which is a goddamn miracle when you stop to think about how loud and wrong some of our people can sometimes be. Scully knows this.

We rolled on westward and I was following the route on the road map and mileage chart, and nobody said anything else above the ongoing sound of the bus. So I nodded off thinking about the Continental Divide, and the next voice I heard was Osceola Menefee saying, Now you know what this kind of country put me in the mind of, Schoolboy? Science, man. Science.

And I opened my eyes and saw that we were less than a mile away from the foothills of the Rocky Mountains. I was wide awake and I opened the map and mileage chart again.

Man, Osceola went on saying, What Joe and you all were talking back there a while ago was history. But man, this kind of stuff we pulling deeper and deeper into now was out here even before history. Man, you start thinking about what you looking at in this kind of country the next thing you know you also thinking about not just mineral deposits and wildlife and livestock on the open range, and all that but also glaciers and volcanoes and earthquakes and planets. Man, you're going to see more telescopes and stuff like that out this way than in any other place I ever been in the whole United States of America.

As soon as he had mentioned science, it was as if you were back at Mobile County Training School where you had studied animate and inanimate specimens in the room with the long laboratory table and on the wall above Mr. Troupe C. Hodges's desk there was the Periodic Table of Elements that you would be using when you came to study physics and chemistry the following year and the year after that.

I would have used the word primordial instead of before history or prehistoric, but since I didn't want to sound academic all I said was that he and I were thinking along the same lines. And Wayman Ridgeway said, Hey Scully, you hear who up there going all whatchmacalogical on the schoolboy? And Scully Pittman said, Man, I'm listening to this stuff. And Wayman Ridgeway said, Hey Bloop, you been knowing this cat for a long time. Where's he getting all this new jive from? And Herman Kemble said, Man, don't be looking at me. Man, I wouldn't know. Maybe that's some of what he's been getting from some of all of them little Miss Goldilocks he been bagging and heading for the shed with *all by his goddamn self* these past few years. And Alan Meadows said, Well, if that's where he's getting it he sure got a funny way of getting it. And everybody was laughing then, not because what Alan Meadows said was hilarious but because they were pretending that they had heard something questionable about Osceola Menefee's manhood.

Hey what's happening back there? Milo the Navigator said from the front seat, pretending that he hadn't been listening all along. And Osceola Menefee said, Man, nothing but the same old sixty-six. Here's somebody trying to use some intelligence about man and the environment, and here they come in the goddamn gutter. And Scully Pittman said, Man, All I said was you sure have a funny way getting what you getting from them college girls.

Okay, man, Osceola Menefee said shaking his head and laughing along with everybody else. Okay, he said, and then he said, You see there, Schoolboy. These are your folks, man. How you ever going to get their head out of the goddamn gutter long enough to make some kind of progress? Them other people trying every way they can to qualify, and all you can really count on your folks to do is come up with another way to signify about some ofay poontang.

Yeah, Herman Kemble said not long after everybody had settled back down into the ongoing sound of the California bound bus again. Yeah, but don't let any of this fake you out of anything along that line of action, Schoolboy. Because, man, as far as I'm concerned all of that bright-eyed and bushy-tailed curiosity is as much a part of my birthright as anything else out here.

Especially seeing as how you can just about always count on so many of them being stacked so fine, Otis Sheppard said.

And Ike Ellis said, With them bass clef calves and treble tipping toes and insteps. And Herman Kemble said, And all I ever seen any of them looking for is some meaningful experience as they call it, to help them get themselves together for life. And ain't never stingy about nothing that really matters to me.

You tell him, Joe, he said. Am I fakking or just yakking? And Joe States with his seat still reclined as far back as it would go and with his baseball cap still pulled down over his eyes said, You ain't yakking, Bloop. You fakking and cadillakking. But you ain't telling our college boy nothing he ain't already hip to.

Then he said, Of course now, me myself, now speaking of birthrights, every time another one of them latch on to me and start hitting me with all them questions about the beat and syncopation and blue notes and, oh boy, improvisation, improvisation, improvisation that gives me a very solid notion that they feel that I am as much a part of their birthright as old Unka Remus used to be. Yeah, Unka Remus, he said. Because if you believe that Unka Remus was some old harness mender all bent over with rheumatism sitting around spinning yarns for some little old shaggy-headed boy from the Big House, you talking about them people's Unka Remus. Not my Unka Remus.

XI

IN THOSE days you left Route 66 at the junction with the San Bernardino Freeway, which came all the way into the downtown Los Angeles interchange at Civic Center, and that was where you picked up the Hollywood Freeway. Then you came on past Western Avenue and turned off and circled back on to the overpass and you were on Sunset Boulevard.

Well, here's this old two-by-four factory workers' town, Schoolboy, Joe States said as we came on by the local broadcast studios on both sides of that part of the street. And Otis Sheppard said, Don't pay no attention to that kind of old talk, Schoolboy. He's just as glad to be coming back out here for the umpteenth time as you're glad you're finally making it for the first time.

And Joe States said, Yeah glad. Who said I wasn't? Not me. This is one of my most favorite side hustle towns in the U.S.A. You damn right I'm glad. The way I rake in these people's ready money for a little hot jive piecework here and there in this town is a sin and a shame. That's exactly what I'm talking about. Everybody knows about the big fat world famous studios, because that's all a part of the Hollywood glamor mill hype. But, man, it's that network of subcontracts that most of these pretty houses and this good living come from.

We rode on past a long Paramount Pictures building and a Columbia Pictures headquarters was in the next block. Then there was CBS followed by Music City; and we came onto Highland Avenue and La Brea, and I saw the Screen Actors' Guild and the Screen Directors' Guild and after we passed Fairfax Avenue and stopped at a traffic light near Schwab's Drug Store, we came on past Villa Frascati and I saw the huge plastic statue of a blond drum majorette wearing a white cowboy hat and tasseled white boots, revolving on a pole advertising Las Vegas as the place for Beverly Hills people to go for fun and games.

The bossman and Old Pro got out at the Château Neuf, which was in the same neighborhood as the Garden of Allah; and we headed back along Sunset and took La Brea across to Hollywood Boulevard and came on along past Grauman's Chinese Theatre, Max Factor's makeup headquarters, and the Pickwick Bookstore to Vine Street and pulled up the hill to the Vineyard Motel.

Last stop. Last stop. All out and everything off but my tools and the music stands, Joe States said standing up. And then he said, Get to me fast, Schoolboy.

So when I found my room I just left everything there and came back out to the courtyard, and he and Otis Sheppard and I walked back down the hill past the Capitol Records tower to Hody's and I had my first Hollywood hamburger and malted milk.

We went for a short walk beyond the Pantages Theater then and came back up the hill again, and when I finished my shower and got into bed, it was almost two o'clock, and as I was falling off to sleep I heard Herman Kemble opening his door across the hall and saying, Don't nobody be bothering me about nothing in the morning, and I mean nothing under a hundred dollars coming this way. Don't nobody call my name before twelve o'clock. Anybody see me up and about before 2:00 P.M., you can bet a fat man I'm walking in my goddamn sleep.

I found my way around Hollywood on my own that next morning, and in the afternoon I went out to Beverly Hills and walked all the way across Rodeo Drive to Wilshire Boulevard. Then that night Ross Peterkin the disc jockey, local man about town and longtime cutbuddy of Joe States, came by in his Roadmaster convertible, and Joe States and Herman Kemble and I rode across town to West Los Angeles with him. That is where I met Gaynelle Whitlow.

We were standing at the bar in The Home Plate, and she came in and sat in the stall next to the jukebox while Ross Peterkin was ordering our drinks, and when I asked him who she was, he said, Hey, that's somebody I want you to meet. Hey, Joe, this schoolboy got good eyes to go with his good ears. And Joe States, who was talking trash to the cashier said, Who you telling? That's my states from down in The Beel.

Ross Peterkin waved, and she smiled back and he took me over and introduced me; and she said, Well, hello there, Mr. College Boy. And Ross Peterkin said, How about showing this down-home boy some big city fun? And she moved over to make room for me beside her and winked at him and said, I thought you just said he was a big-time college boy. And Ross Peterkin said, So what? Right now he is a brand new road musician on his first trip out here to glamor town. And one thing for sure, this college boy got three legs just like the rest of the thugs in that band.

Joe States and Herman Kemble were there then, and Joe States leaned over and put his arms around her and kissed her on both cheeks, smacking his lips and sighing and rolling his eyes in exaggerated blissfulness saying, All this fine brown, mellow frame and her own eight cylinder rolling stock to haul it all about in.

And she said, I thought maybe you were not speaking tonight. I was wondering if you'd decided to pass or something. And when Herman Kemble said, Pass for what? she said, I don't know. But you know how some of you old big-time musicians can sometimes get, from having all them people running after you. And Joe States said, You looking so good, baby, I had to hold back and get up some nerve. And she said, You hear this stuff, Bloop. And Herman Kemble said, Baby, he's just trying to tell you like it is. And she said, You guys. Especially you guys in that band. Every last one of you, trying to be just as bad as that man himself.

So look here, Ross Peterkin said then as the three of them bowed and backed on back toward the bar, Maybe we'll run across you all later on, maybe at the Five Four or somewhere. And she said, We'll see. And then she said, So you're Shag Philips's replacement. People out here keep tabs on that band just like other places. So tell me why they call you Schoolboy. And I said, Well it's not really just Schoolboy. It's also Scooter-boy and also Scootboy and also Scooboy.

Then when she asked me about college I also went on to tell her something about Mobile County Training School; and that was what we were still talking about when we came outside and drove along West Adams to the Rumpus Room, where she left a note for somebody with one of the bartenders. After that we came on past the University of Southern California, Exposition Park, and the Los Angeles Coliseum; and shortly after we crossed the Harbor Freeway and turned right, she said, I'm sure you've been long hearing tell of Central Avenue. And I said, Ever since I first started hanging round the barbershop. And she said, Well here it is.

She said, They say everybody from down home had at least one cousin over in here somewhere. And I said, And somewhere on the South Side of Chicago and above 110th Street in Manhattan and in the Black Bottom section of Detroit and so on depending on the part of the old country you hail from.

We stopped at the Crossroads Tavern, and she introduced me to Ford Shelby, whose place she said it was; and as soon as she told him that I was with the band he rapped on the bar to get attention and said, Hey folks, I just want you to know that a brand new celebrity just walked in. And everybody wanted to buy me a drink, but he said everything I ordered was on the house. Then he said, How's the bossman? And I said, Still rolling.

And still the best that ever did it, he said. Tell him I'll be out there tomorrow night.

They started reminiscing about the band as they had known it over the years then, rehashing tales that I had already heard on similar occasions in town after town from coast to coast, about what Joe States said to somebody somewhere one night and somewhere else on another night, and about how from the very beginning anytime anybody from the band walked in anywhere the music always picked up. Not because they had come to challenge anybody in a cutting session, which none of them ever did anymore. But because along with everything else hearing blues music was supposed to do for you, the boss-man's band had also always been the one that represented that special class (or easy high style and elegant or swinging manner) that always made you feel that however well you already did whatever you did, you should try to do it better.

When you dance to that music, somebody said, It is not just a matter of going out there and doing something to show that you can get down with the latest do. You feel something deep inside yourself when you hear that music.

That's exactly what I've always said, somebody else said. And sometimes that is also what puts you on the spot. Because if I'm out there dancing I feel like I'm missing something up on the bandstand. And if I'm just standing down front looking and listening I feel like I should be back on the floor doing something to go with the way the music makes you feel.

Then a voice down at the other end of the bar cut in and said, Hey I got a question I want you to answer, young fella. And I said I would if I could. And he said, Is the bossman really the one that thinks up all that stuff can't nobody else play but you all? And somebody at the opposite end of the bar said, Well there's old Govan for you. Always coming up with some old back-fence signifying jive. And the one called Govan said, Man, didn't nobody ask you nothing. I'm talking to this cat here. He the one in the band. You ain't in nothing.

I said, Naturally the bossman is always the main one. That's why he's the bossman. And he said, What about Old Pro? And I said, He's the straw boss, and he writes some few things too. And he said, The way I heard it, the man ain't got nothing on Old Pro. Of course, me myself all I can say is Old Pro is supposed to be the one that went to the goddamn Boston Conservatory of Music.

And Ford Shelby said, Don't make no goddamn difference who went the hell where, when you hear that band playing something, it always sounds exactly like the bossman wants it to sound, don't give a damn if Shakespeare wrote it. Then he turned to me and said, You tell him I said I'll be over there tomorrow night. You tell him Ford Shelby. He knows me. You tell him old Ford is still out here fighting that bear and dodging cold weather.

We made it to the Twilight Lounge just before the second show began, and that's where I met Silas Renfroe. He was leading a five piece combo that night, playing tenor, alto, clarinet, and flute himself, with Eddie Sinclair on piano, Jamison McLemore on bass, Nelson Scott on trumpet, and Fred Stokes, better known as Red Folks, on drums.

Our table was right next to the stage, and at the end of the set all of them came and spent the whole break sitting on the knee high apron of the crescent bandstand talking to us. And when I told Silas Renfroe that I had heard the bossman telling Old Pro something that he liked about one of the combo's recordings, Eddie Sinclair said, What did I tell you. I told you that man don't miss much, and don't forget nothing. And Silas Renfroe said, You sure did, but it's still hard to believe.

Jamison McLemore said, Of course, don't nobody have to tell you that you got the best bull fiddle gig in the world. And I said, talking about hard to believe, man, I keep expecting to wake up and find out that I fell asleep listening to records and have been dreaming that I was doing Blanton and Oscar Pettiford rolled into one.

When it was time to go back on the stand, Silas Renfroe gave me his phone number and said, Anytime you're out here and have some time off give me a buzz, and I'll pick you up and we can have some Mexican food at my house, and maybe some Sunday we can drive down to TJ to the bullfights. And Red Folks said, You tell that Joe Ass States I said he could at least get sick or take some time off and go to Hawaii while the band is out this way, at least once in a while.

When we pulled up to the Five Four there was a crowd out-side, and when we got upstairs there was elbow room only. But we did get to dance two times before the end of the set, and we stayed long enough to hear old Decatur Wilcox play some barrelhouse piano and sing three lowdown way down-home blues numbers. Then we went on to the Safari and sat in an alcove and sipped sour mash, and she told me about leaving Gulfport, Mississippi, and living in Chicago and Detroit before coming to Los Angeles.

Then she said, Now I'm going to take you to get some of the best barbecued spareribs I ever tasted anywhere on this side of the Rocky Mountains. So our next stop was the Wagon Shed, and when she put in our order, she said, I know you're a big boy and all that, but you just got to try some of this lemonade, and when I took a sip I said, I see what you mean. This is the real stuff, right off of the down-home church picnic grounds and hey, ain't no flies on this potato salad either.

From our booth in the dining room you could hear the jukebox in the bar, and somebody kept playing "9:20 Special" all during the time we were eating, and when we left she was humming it and snapping her fingers, and when I joined in she said, Do you guys ever play that? And I said, Sometimes, think-ing about how Count Basie's band, whose tune and recording it was, played it like a transcontinental express train batting hell for leather across the wide open spaces en route to or from the Pacific or the Atlantic coasts. Whereas the bossman had us doing it sometimes somewhat slower and sometimes not but always more like an East Coast limited reverberating along the cuts and fills and against the urban density of Washington, Bal-timore, Philadelphia, New York, and Boston.

I always did like that number, she said. And I said, Me too. And when she said, You know how some pieces make you feel good in a very special way, I said I'd tell the bossman that there was a very heavy request for it tomorrow night. But I didn't tell her that in our current arrangement the bossman and I had a piano and bass spot just before the out chorus.

You took the Imperial Highway across to the Harbor Free-way and there was no inbound traffic and only a very light premorning fog, and she drove on humming "9:20 Special" with me drumming bass time on the dashboard, and we were turning up the slope to the Vineyard Motel in fifteen minutes.

Then before I could decide which magic words to try first she said, What time is it? Which was all the vamp I needed, and I said, Just about that time. And she said, Well we better get on in here and do this thing and get some sleep. You got to work tomorrow you know or is it already today?

When we woke up it was almost two o'clock that next afternoon, and as she headed for the shower I said, Breakfast, brunch, or lunch? And she said, Make mine just plain old ham and eggs and grits and black coffee. So I put the order in to room service and joined her in the tub and by the time we got back into our underwear the trays were delivered.

She said, Call me sometime. And I said, When? And she said, Sometime when you get back around to the likes of me. And when I said, What about tonight? she said, I'll be there and I'll be listening for my number, but don't look for me. She said, I don't care what you say, I know good and well ain't no Alabama cutie pie out here on his first trip really want to hook up with no old down-home broad before looking over this crop of mane tossing ponies this town is so famous for.

Outside on our way through the patio we waved at Ted Chandler and Osceola Menefee, who were sipping beer at a table in the shade of a big California bright beach umbrella. Malachi Moberly was in the telephone booth, and Milo the Navigator nodded at us from where he stood in the office door talking to somebody inside.

So, you just go ahead and help yourself to some of all that eager pink stuff that's out here waiting for you, she said stopping me at the entrance. Then when you get back east you can tell them about how it was with somebody in the movies. Then when you come back out here sometimes and get a little homesick for some down-home cooking, that's when you might really want to give your new brownskin kissing cousin a buzz, and we'll see how you follow up on that nice little lick and a promise.

She gave me a lotsabrownskinmama hug and kiss and patdown-there then, and then she winked and turned and did that fine brown cake walking babies strut all the way to her parking space. Then she turned and waved and winked again.

It was not until we had finished our West Coast tour and were back beyond the Rockies heading for a string of one-nighters leading into Chicago that Joe States told me how Gaynelle Whitlow came to be my first date in Los Angeles. The bossman himself had set it all up and left the rest to Joe States and Ross Peterkin. Everybody else in the band knew about it because that was the way things were on the road with the band in those days. But the Bossman Himself was the only one who never mentioned Gaynelle Whitlow.

XII

AT THE Palladium that next night everybody except the Bossman Himself was backstage even earlier than the usual forty-five minutes before curtain time. At least half of the lineup was already there when Joe States and I came in with Old Pro just ahead of the others and when I got dressed and started tuning my instrument, we still had thirty minutes in which to warm up, primp, and woof at each other.

You knew that the bossman was also somewhere on the premises, but I hadn't yet seen him when Old Pro gave the all on whistle, and he was still nowhere in sight when Old Pro gave the downbeat for the first number. So I figured he was checking us out and also getting a sense of the audience from somewhere out in the middle or back of the auditorium, and when I looked over into the wings as we hit the out chorus of the third tune and saw him looking at us with his eyes stretched in mock astonishment, I was not at all surprised.

He stood with one leg dropped back and his forward foot pointed inward, his body erect but with one shoulder ever so slightly lower than the other, both rotating ever so gently, his arms hanging relaxed and his fingers dangling as if fresh from the manicurist; and when we did a repeat on the tag, he nod-ded to Old Pro and waited for the applause to fade. Then he made his entrance, doing that thin soled imperial patent leather sporty limp, wide legged stride, saying, Thank you thank you thank you and now.

The applause started up again as he reached the microphone and it was for him this time and it was an ovation, into which he bowed smiling and saying, Thank you thank you thank you again, as he backed away and moved over to the piano. He sat waiting for the crowd to settle back down once more, and the next time he said, And now, and now, he began the vamp to our theme song, and when he raised both hands, and Joe States brought us in, it must have sounded as if we had been playing the first three numbers behind a scrim.

We did two repeats on the out chorus then instead of following up with a bright getaway jump tune so that Scully Pittman could call out the dancers with a high register trumpet solo, and Big Bloop could pile on the goose pimples, he made a fast segue into the new twelve bar riff tune in C natural designed for theaters and concerts and called "Showcase," because it had enough space for as many solo spots as he chose to use.

Everybody had a four bar solo spot that night, and we took it out with Ike Ellis and Scully Pittman blowing at each other from opposite sides of the stage as if from coast to coast; and when the applause and the thank you thank you thank you died down, we took our concert stage routine bows, one by one, section by section, beginning with the trumpets, followed by the reeds and the trombones and then Joe States, Otis Sheppard, and finally me. And Otis Sheppard said, I always did like this town. And Joe States said, Now let's lay some stuff on the natives. I ain't showing nobody no mercy at all tonight, Schoolboy. When we walk into that after party I want them trillies waving some trimming at me.

That was the night I met Eric Threadcraft. He was among the first people who came backstage during intermission. Joe States and Otis Sheppard and I were standing by the sprinkler control unit, and I saw him waving at us as he worked his way through the crowd, and I thought he was somebody from the entertainment section of one of the newspapers or magazines and I was pretty certain that he was coming to talk to Joe States not me; and I didn't want to have to listen to any more of the same old questions about what jazz really is and where it came from and where it's going and who is taking it where. So I said I'm going over here a minute. I'll be right back.

But Joe States said, Hey, wait a minute, I want to introduce you to this cat. I want you to meet this cat because I want you to have some business connections in this town. You always need to know somebody like this in a town like this. This is one of the cats I was talking about. I'm already set to do some Q.T. stuff for this cat next week.

Eric Threadcraft was there then and he said, Hi, fella. And I said, What say, man. And Joe States said, I know you already started picking up on what we putting down on the bull fiddle these days. And Eric Threadcraft squinted shaking his head saying, I can't really believe it yet. And Joe States said, Man, ain't nothing you can do but believe this stuff because it makes your bones remember.

He was talking with his arm around my shoulder, and I wondered how much Eric Threadcraft's ofay background prepared him to know about Uncle Bud, Uncle Doc, Uncles Ned and Remus—or really Uncle Bud-Doc-Ned-Remus; and I decided that he had probably heard of Uncle Remus just as most fay boys had heard of Uncle Tom (not of Harriet Beecher Stowe but of the ever so black political rhetoricians) but his Uncle Remus was probably only old Joel Chandler Harris's good old arthritic darky harness mender and spinner of backyard yarns for towheaded down-home boys from the Big House. But my Uncle Remus (or Bud or Doc or Ned) was another avuncular proposition altogether. *But Joe States was his unka Remus even so.*

As Eric Threadcraft and I shook hands, Joe States began telling him about how the bossman had heard me during the fall of my senior year and had decided to try to entice me to come in as a second bass player (after graduation, of course) even before he had to realize that family circumstances were going to cause Shag Philips to give notice.

So, we got ourselves a blue ribbon college boy, he said; and then he said, And I didn't say conservatory. I'm talking about that deep classical and philosophical and diapirical economical psychological scene, man. That's what he got a degree in, man; and that's what we're working on because he still got to realize that he's supposed to be a full time musician. He still thinks he just lucked into a new side hustle that will bring him in enough loot to get him to and maybe through some graduate school or something. Man, we keep telling him ain't no university ready for this stuff yet. This stuff belongs out here in the everyday world that this band is all about. Like where we at right now and will be tomorrow.

What can I say, my man, Eric Threadcraft said. I just heard you out there and I take my man Joe's word on you even if I hadn't.

At that time he thought of himself as an apprentice arranger-conductor, and his main occupation was making records. Most of his jobs were with pop singers, and most of his scores were written for big studio bands that included strings and such symphonic woodwinds as flutes, piccolos, oboes, and bassoons. He also used a certain number of instrumentalists who played our kind of music, and he always used our kind of rhythm section even when he also had the whole percussion section of the regular studio orchestra on hand. That was how he and Joe States had been brought together, and they had been friends for about three years when I came along.

I really get a big kick out of working for this cat, Joe States said, slipping his other arm around Eric Threadcraft's shoulder. All of them sugar coated saw fiddles and wine stained reeds, and me in there in the middle of all them opera tools! Of course I'm just taking his money for doing next to nothing. Man, all I have to do is just sit in there and pat my feet and twiddle my sticks and stir and flap my brushes and be ready to boot all that mess up every now and then when my old good buddy here points that teacher stick at me.

And Eric Threadcraft said, That's doing plenty, fellow, believe me. It's money well spent. And Joe States said, See what I'm talking about? That's what I like about working for this cat.

And that was when Eric Threadcraft turned to me again and said, I'm already all set with a bass player for next week. But you can count on something with me the next time you're out here, if you're interested. And I said, I'm interested all right. And he said, A fellow with all the stuff you got going can always make a good living in this town. Man, there's no telling how much Joe States could make if he stayed out here for a while. Just freelancing. And I don't doubt that you can do the same thing.

It was time for the rhythm section to be getting back in place for the second set then. So we shook hands and he said, Next time. You can count on it. And I said, I'm game. And as he headed away waving he said, That's good enough for me. It's a deal. And as Joe States and I came on into the wings, Otis Sheppard, who was waiting for us, said, Man, some of these gray boys sure got a lot going for them in this town.

And Joe States said, Especially that one. You keep in touch with him, Schoolboy. And I said I would and he said, You two are going to get along just great. Hell, you can even talk some of all of them deep thoughts back at him. He'll like that.

That was also the night I met Felix Lovejoy. During the second intermission I was on my way upstairs to look at the dance floor from the balcony, and as I came on to the landing, somebody tapped me on the shoulder and said, There's that man. How's the new bass champion?

And I said, That's not me, man. You got me mixed up with somebody else. And he said, Hey man, I've been in this business long enough to trust my ears, and I call them as I hear them.

He introduced himself then and told me about his radio program and invited me over to his table to have a drink and say hello to his friends. And that is how I also happened to meet Shirley Comingore the same night. She was talking to another Scandinavian looking blonde who, like her, had long legs with the kind of shapely calves I always spot right off and who also gave me a smiling squint and a nose wrinkle as she said, Hi there.

What are you doing afterward? Felix Lovejoy asked me. And I said there's a party or something up in the hills somewhere. And he said, Well let's talk business right now then. I want you for my record show the day after tomorrow afternoon, and I'm also inviting you to my jam session at The Key Sunday afternoon. I know the band's policy against sitting in, but I just thought you'd like to dig the scene as my guest.

Somebody cut in on us at that point and he excused himself and stood up and stepped aside for a minute, and when he turned back to me he took a business card from his wallet, wrote a figure on it, and handed it to me and said, How's that for the day after tomorrow? And I said it looks pretty good to me, man. And he said, There's more and there's fun. This is a money town and a fun town. And I said, That's okay by me too, man.

As I was leaving, Shirley Comingore invited me to get to The Key in time for her vocal set. And I did and that was when she said what she said about getting in touch with me the next time the band was in town, because she was thinking about some changes and working up some new things that she wanted to run through with me. But as things turned out we didn't see each other again until over a year later.

XIII

WHEN Joe States and Ross Peterkin and I got there the after party was in full swing. You could hear the music and the noisy chatter and laughter as soon as you came along the curving drive to the parking area. We came on up the wide flagstone steps to the main yard, and I saw the big rambling house, and there were people moving about on the long cantilevered balcony where the lanterns were, and others clustered about the tables on the patio around the swimming pool.

The three of us came on past the couples sitting and strolling about in the darkness of the palms, and suddenly the cool moist breeze reminded me of how close I now was to the Pacific Ocean. *And I said, California. I said, Hey California. I said, Here I am from Alabam. Me and my expectations and my obligations and now my speculations.* And I crossed my fingers.

They were dancing in the drawing room. There was a trio (piano, bass, and drums) from Central Avenue playing after hours gin mill blues extensions, and as we circled around the edge of the floor, I saw Osceola Menefee dancing with a sandy maned Texas looking woman. For some reason I guessed (correctly) that she was a successful booking agent who had once been an extra and a starlet. She was dancing in her stocking feet with her eyes closed, and old Osceola Menefee was looking all nonchalant and doing an old down-home barrelhouse bump and roll on the sly.

We passed Ike Ellis talking to two very pretty brunettes who looked like chorus girls and also looked like old fans of his; and I saw Scully Pittman and Wayman Ridgeway going to the sliding doors that opened on to the patio. I didn't see the boss-man, but when we got to the bar there was Old Pro. He was sitting on a high stool talking to a silver gray man and two elegant women who did not look like entertainers, and I could tell that one of them was French by the way her lips moved.

Among those who either said hello or shook hands and said their names or waved or gave us a smiling nod of recognition as we moved on around from one room to the next, there were more good looking women of all ages than I had ever seen at one party before. There were no flies on the guys either, not in Hollywood. But you were not really going to have to compete with them that night. Not only because there were so many more women present, but also because more than enough of them were mainly fans of the band in first place.

When we got to the bar and tasted our drinks I said, Man, the stuff is here just like you said. I said, Man, everywhere you turn. And Joe States sipped his drink and said, Cool it, School. Man, ain't no rush. Man, let's eat first. Man, I know what's going to happen. Man, if we don't grab us something to eat right goddamn now before we start meeting folks we subject to never get another chance at it. I don't know about you, but I'm hungry. I been driving this mule train. Man, I'm the goddamn pick and shovel of this goddamn aggregation, remember?

Then he said, Man, you see all them pink pussycats out there licking their chops? Man, I ain't about to tangle with any of that overeager stuff on no empty stomach after what we laid on them down there this evening. They expect something special after that, and I got my goddamn reputation to keep up. So first, I'm going to get something under my belt, and then I'm going to jive around until my system's settled back down, and then in the cool calm of the wee wee hours I'll be ready to take care of some business.

The food was being served out on the west terrace and we ate looking out over the patio and the garden. The fog had not begun to roll in yet and you could see beyond the nearby hills to the distant network of sparkling lights spreading away across the Los Angeles basin toward where the Pacific shore-line, which I had not actually seen yet, was supposed to be.

Ross Peterkin and I served ourselves from the seafood smor-gasbord and the salad table, but Joe States said, To each his own, Schoolboy, to each his own, and headed straight to the corner where the charcoal grills were; and when he came back to the table we had taken he said, Treble clef for you, bass clef for me. Like I said, Schoolboy, I'm vamping for heavy duty.

When we finished, the two of them went down the steps into the patio. They went along the edge of the pool to the table where Herman Kemble and Malachi Moberly sat with nearly twice as many single women as couples sprawled at their feet. I came back into the drawing room. I wanted to look around before joining in the festivities. It was my first chance to see what the inside of a Beverly Hills mansion was like.

The Bossman Himself was there then and they had him surrounded. I saw him standing as if stashed on one of his favorite mainstem corners once more, ever so relaxed, but missing nothing, kidding about music with the fellows, and talking trash with the ladies at the same time. I didn't stop to listen because by that time I was as familiar with the current chitchat line for local variation as I was with the themes in the current bandbook. *Oh that was mainly some of our leftover last year's stuff. Wait till you hear some of our this year's stuff, which also includes some of our year before last stuff mixed in with a preaudition of some of our next year's stuff. Oh hello, Miss Excitement. The outrageously beautiful people are over here. They stand back there only as long as it takes for us to click on our shields against the radiation. In your case we'd still be taking a chance if you stood back there all night. So you've heard about the misinformation they've been passing out about you. Gross distortion. Scandalous misrepresentation. Because do you know what they said? They said that you were very pretty, but they didn't say that you were going to be this pretty.*

I made my way across the floor and came up the steps to the level where the library was. The door was open, and the lights were on. So I stepped inside and saw that the bookshelves were on one side of the room and that the opposite wall was a gallery of paintings, watercolors, drawings, and sketches, among which, thanks to the influence of the roommate of my first two years in college, I was able to identify those by Monet, Matisse, Picasso, Paul Klee, John Marin, Stuart Davis, and Charles Sheeler.

There was a long conference table in the center of the room, but the main desk was at the other end facing a glass wall of

sliding doors that opened out onto a balcony beyond which
you could see across the valley and Los Angeles to the Pacific
Coast darkness once more. I checked the time on the wrist
watch that was my commencement present from Miss Slick
McGinnis when I graduated from Mobile County Training
School, thinking: *This many miles from Gasoline Point. This
many miles from Dodge Mill Road.*

Then just before I turned to start back down to the drawing room, I realized that someone had stepped in from the
hallway and was about to say something. I could tell that it
was a woman before I looked around, and I hoped she was
somebody from this part of town, and she was. And she had
the diction I wanted to hear and the sailboat tan to go with it,
and she said, Golden Boy, and introduced herself as Morgana.

But not before what she said about some of the paintings.
Do you like the Tamayos? That was what she was already saying
as I looked around. And when I said, Very much, she said, Well
good for you and good for Rufino. The next time I see him I
must tell him that I found a bass player in a library looking at
two of his pieces while a big Beverly Hills party was going on
downstairs.

It so happened that as few examples of Rufino Tamayo's work
that I had seen up to that time (mostly in book, catalog, and
magazine reproductions) I was already much more taken with
his work than with what I had seen by Diego Rivera, Orozco,
and Siqueiros, who were much more famous. Yet even so the
Mexican artist that I was most familiar with in those days was
Miguel Covarrubias, because of his drawings and caricatures in
Vanity Fair, *Vogue*, and *The New Yorker* magazines, and also
because he had published a book of caricatures called *Negro
Drawings*.

I didn't say anything about any of that however because I
didn't think she really wanted to go on talking about art, and
I knew I didn't. So I waited to see what else she would say,
and she said, You were followed, Golden Boy. You were spotted, stalked, tracked, and now stand bearded. That makes you
mine, Golden Boy. So let's play games.

And I said, I never argue with beautiful women after midnight. And she led the way back down through the drawing
room and across the patio, and fifteen minutes later we were
dancing naked in the dark in her house in Bel-Air, where it was

as if the music came floating in on the breeze along with the fragrance of the subtropical flowers outside.

She said, When I saw you up there on that bandstand holding that warm brown female shaped thing against your left thigh and shoulder and making it respond to the deft manipulation of your fingers like that as if you were Gaston Lachaise playing around with auditory putty, I knew you were the one for me so I went to the party and waited, and when the three of you came in I've had a bead on you ever since.

As she spoke she put my hands where she wanted them and we danced down the hall to a door and she backed through it clicking on the lights, and we were in the bedroom, and you could see us everywhere you looked, because there were mirrors on all of the walls and also overhead.

From then on I was so busy doing what we were doing that there was hardly any time to look around and check things out, but you couldn't miss the way the streamlined design of the room itself, along with the functional Scandinavian furniture, set off the period piece chaise longue and dressing table with matching chair and old silver and ivory accessories.

You couldn't miss the Picasso drawings of nudes and satyrs and the Matisse studies for odalisques, but I didn't see the Braque painting of an artist and model until it was time for me to go back into the living room and gather up my clothes the next morning. And that was also when I saw the wall of shelves where books and records were, but there was no time to find out what was there. So I didn't even mention it.

When I said Morgana Who, Morgana Which, Morgana What, Morgana Question Mark, she said, Morgana Period. She said, Morgana Exclamation Point. She said, That's my name for myself after dark, Golden Boy, especially from midnight to daybreak.

It doesn't make anything any less real, Golden Boy, she said propping herself up with three pillows against the headboard of the rumpled silk garden flower patterned ever so subtly perfumed bed. It only makes things less literal. Or somewhat less literal in any case.

She then lit her first cigarette since the one she finished in the car on the way from the party. But she took only several pulls on it before putting it aside to start teasing me again, saying,

Let's see now where were we? Saying, How about right about here? And how about this? Followed by this which brings us to such as this. And when I said, If you say so, she said, I do say so, Golden Boy. I most certainly do.

And so hithering and thithering on we went, doing the also and also required for the also and also she desired. And what came after what she said what she said about that, could only have been a very brief nap because when she said what she said next, it was as if I had just closed my eyes.

She said, And now I've got to get you home and be back in place before seven. She said, I turn back into the daytime me on the final stroke of seven. She said, No more Miss Night Creature until after dark. And only sometimes even then, she said, such as when Golden Boys from fairy tales materialize in an atmosphere as earthy as that at the Palladium last night.

I got dressed in the not yet warm Palmolive green dampness of Bel-Air in the early morning thinking, *A sunkissed missy don't be late. Thinking California, hey, California.* And school-boy that I still was, also thinking: *Your smile, eyes, nose, and your tutti frutti et cetera.*

Then outside we came winding back toward the main residential section of Beverly Hills not in the convertible but in the station wagon that I guessed she used mostly to go to the marina and the stables, and there were willows and olive shrubs and date and banana palms all along the sidewalk just as there were in the lush Estate Gardens and that was also when I found out that the tree you saw most often along all of the streets everywhere in Los Angeles was called the black acacia.

When we turned left on Sunset Boulevard at 5:45 radio news time and I saw that the traffic was already building up I remembered what Joe States had said about Hollywood being a factory town, where headline stars and their supporting casts had to get to work almost as early as the technical crews, including the makeup and wardrobe experts. That was when I realized that I hadn't asked Joe States about how all of those unemployed and mostly broke people hoping to be picked as extras in crowd scenes got to and from studios as far out as Burbank and Culver City.

I looked over at my very intriguing hostess at the steering wheel, and she smiled and nudged me with her elbow without taking her eyes from the traffic, but neither of us said anything. But when the music that came back on following the weather report turned out to be a set of four of the recordings the band had made on my first trip to New York, she looked at me and nodded and began rubbing her palm against my left thigh in time with the figures I was playing on the bass and kept it up all the way to the corner of Vine Street.

Then when we pulled up to the motel entrance she said, We must do this again sometime. We really must. And I said, If you say so. And she said, I do say so. But she didn't give me her telephone number and I didn't ask her for it. I said, Whenever. And as I got out, she said, I'll let you know. And I stood on the curb watching as she made a U-turn and waved and headed back down the slope and across the smoggy dimness of Hollywood Boulevard.

When Ross Peterkin drove by and picked Joe States and me up again that afternoon, the first thing he said as we headed across town was, Hey Joe, how about that fine fay fish I saw our college boy cutting out with last night. And Joe States said, And didn't get in till daylight this morning either. And Ross Peterkin said, Fay Morgan. That's some big league and bass clef stuff there, Schoolboy.

Then when he said, How did that action go, man? And I said, Fine man, great man. But when he said, She's somebody that can really make it worth the time and energy, I missed the point. Which I realized as soon as I said what I said when he asked what he asked next.

Because when he said, So what kind of righteous response did she lay on you, my man and I said, Nothing really weird or anything like that, my man, just solid box with a few nice frills, he looked at me and looked back at the traffic and said, Box? Come on, man, you know I ain't talking about no box. Hell, it's all among friends. What kind of loot did she lay on you for a start? And when I said that I hadn't even thought of any deal like that at all because I was just out to have myself some fun and that I had enjoyed myself and that was that as far as I was concerned, he said, Hey Joe we got to school this schoolboy some more.

He didn't say anything else until we crossed Melrose and came on by the Wilshire Country Club, but I could feel him looking over at me and then back at the street. And then he said, Yeah Joe, we got to clue this young fellow in on a few more facts about life in this neck of the woods.

Look boy, he said, patting me on the knee, in the first place, you don't ever want to be going around talking about how much you enjoyed fucking no rich white barracuda, don't care how good looking she is. Man, I know you ain't hard up for none. So how the hell you going to enjoy wrestling with some tough ass horse riding, tennis playing, sailboat bitch you don't even know?

And that's when he said, Hey Joe, let's circle over by my pad for a minute. I want to show our young friend here something.

He had taken Vine and Rossmore to Wilshire Boulevard, and at the next corner he turned right and came along Crenshaw to West Adams and on across to Baldwin Hills. And when we came into his deluxe bachelor apartment, what surprised me was not all of the custom made furniture and state of the art electronic gadgets. All of that was completely in keeping with the range and quality of his wardrobe and the style of his two automobiles. And I had also expected all of the personally inscribed photographs of sports stars, entertainers, and musicians, many grinning into the camera alongside him, some taken in the room where they now hung. And I would have been disappointed if his record collection hadn't turned out to be one of the most comprehensive (what with all the European issues) that I had ever seen up to that time.

What I had not foreseen was a wall of books that he guided me straight toward so that I could see that along with all of the detective and Western stories and novels of adventure and intrigue and all of the nonfiction about music, science, and current topics; there was also a six-foot shelf of histories of families such as the Astors, Biddles, Mellons, Rockefellers, and Vanderbilts, among others, and about such men as August Belmont, Diamond Jim Brady, Jim Fisk, J. P. Morgan, Leland Stanford, Stanford White, and so on and on including the top people in the movie industry up to then.

Now here's my point, my man, he said. I just want you to realize that when you start messing around with the class of stuff you cut out of that party with last night, you got to check it out just like everything else you learn about in college.

He moved over to the coffee table and picked up the current issue of *Town and Country* from a spread of magazines that included *Vogue*, *Harper's Bazaar*, *Vanity Fair*, and *The Diplomat*, and when he found the page he was looking for he held it up to show me a full page closeup and a facing page of action snapshots and said I just wanted you to know who you spent the night with last night.

Man, he also said, When you rubbing up against somebody like this you ought to know what you're doing. Because on the one hand you could have yourself the next best thing to old Aladdin's magic lantern but on the other hand she could be just another rich white babe out to slum on you like it's her natural due. If you don't know any better than to let her, he said. And I could have said, Hey man, she's doing what she's doing, and I'm doing what I'm doing. But I didn't. All I did was nod my head and say, Hey we can't have that. So that's some more stuff I've got to watch.

All during the time Ross Peterkin and I were talking, Joe States stayed carefully out of earshot and didn't join in at all: But back outside, as we stood waiting for Ross Peterkin to finish answering a telephone call, he put his arm around my shoulder and said, Everything is cool, statemate. You ain't scandalized nobody. That's just his way of cluing you in on the Bel-Air neck of the swamp. He can tell you a whole lot about them people, because he started out as a backyard boy, you might say. Because his folks came out here from somewhere near Bluefield, West Virginia, to work on the household staff of one of them big estates in Santa Barbara back when Hollywood was still just getting started. Remind me to fill you in on old Ross and all them rich kids he used to play with before they went east to school and over to Europe.

When Ross Peterkin rejoined us a few minutes later, he also gave me a playful hug and a mock left jab and said, No sweat, Schoolboy. No sweat, my man. And that was also when he said, It's just that the first kind of box that came to my mind when you said Fay Morgan laid it on you is the fancy gift wrapped kind that comes from Hermes and A. Sulka.

XIV

I SPENT THE next Monday morning riding around with Osceola Menefee, who had the use of somebody's Oldsmobile convertible for several days. The weather was fair, and along with the warm mild breeze there was the aroma of freshly trimmed shrubbery and lawn grass and yard blossoms. There was also some gray blue haze in the near distance but the Los Angeles Basin smog was not as thick and bothersome in those days as it was to become a few years later.

I said, California. I said Hey, California. I said, Me and my postbaccalaureate contingencies. I said, All the way from the spyglass tree and dog fennel meadows and the L & N canebrakes and Hog Bayou. I said, This many miles from Chickasabogue Swamp and Three Mile Creek Bridge.

We turned off Vine onto Bellamy Boulevard, which we took to La Cienega and came all the way through Restaurant Row to Wilshire and cruised along the Miracle Mile shopping district in the busy traffic of the forenoon bargain hunters. But instead of going all the way into Civic Center, we turned and came back to the La Brea Tar Pits and found a parking area and spent the rest of the morning in the Farmers Market.

Osceola Menefee bought California souvenirs to mail to female fans in six cities, while I was deciding on something for one very special person who like me also had what amounted to ancestral expectations and obligations to fulfill before becoming formally engaged to take on the personal responsibilities of marriage and parenthood.

That was also where we ate lunch that day. Then it was time to head back to Hollywood, and we took Fairfax Avenue, and at three o'clock we were in Studio 2B, 7000 Santa Monica Boulevard, and I was all tuned up and ready for my first West Coast recording session to begin.

Milo the Navigator passed out the music in the sequence that it was stacked on the table by the piano, and as Old Pro took each section through its revised passages and then had us all run the whole arrangement down together except for solo parts, the Bossman Himself sat in the glassed-in control booth checking the balance and sometimes dictating further revisions over the speaker system.

Then when he was ready to take over, he whistled into the microphone and held up his hand and said, So now that everybody else seems to know what is supposed to happen, let's see what our first chair keyboard man has to say about it. If he can't take care of his awesome executive responsibilities, this session is in big trouble and believe me he will be docked.

He stood up and came down out of the control booth walking his crotch-airing, knee-loosening, back-straightening, shoulder-adjusting sporty limp walk and took his place in the center of the studio rigged setup facing the reed section on the floor level, with me and Joe States and Otis Sheppard on his left. The brass section was on a split-level platform behind him, the trombones up one step, the trumpets up two.

And now, he said as he began a vamp that he kept going until he was absolutely sure that he had everybody worked up to hit the groove he wanted. Then as he went on repeating the progression as if only for himself, he said, Hey trombones just remember that all your stuff is supposed to be jive time fanfare. Everything. Foreground and background.

And all the trumpet stuff is monkey business, he said. You come leapfrogging in and everything you do is acrobatic like jugglers, tumblers, and trapeze artists. Solos, riffs, every phrase should be like a jive quotation from the signifying monkey. And the reed section growls and roars and it can slither and twitter and also thunder like a herd.

So Joe, that makes you the cage boss this time around, he said. And then he also said, Old Clyde Beatty himself with a stool and a whip and a pistol. And with a set of spurs, too. Because this thing has got to come on with cymbals streaking and flashing and clashing like lightning even before the fanfare blows away the thunderclouds like parting the curtain for the acrobats.

He was looking at me then, and he said, Elephant boy. He said, Bull fiddle, I want you to walk those goddamn elephants right up through the middle of all this stuff like you don't even know it's there. Or better still, just like you wouldn't give a good goddamn if you did know it was there. Like, What the hell is this? Because you are en route to your next camping site out on safari at a steady pace that will get you there before sundown.

He set the tempo again then and dictated the bass line by naming the notes as he played them for me on the piano and when I started thumping and got it right, he said, keep it right there. He went on through the progression again and nodded to Old Pro and held up his hand and stretched his eyes toward the control booth and said, Let's do it up flashy like Ringling Brothers and Barnum & Bailey.

But before bringing his hand down for take one, he said, Maybe something like "Nonstop to the Big Top." Or maybe "Flipping the Flop in the Big Top." Or even maybe something like "Three Rings Three." Or what about something as simple as "Elephant Walk" as in "Camel Walk," and "Cakewalk," with the circus show time atmosphere speaking for itself?

Then he said, Name to come. Just remember this is my Hollywood open air carnival stuff. Don't be confusing this with my Broadway footlight stuff. My Broadway stuff is something else. That's my midtown stuff that I compounded from the uptown stuff that we brought back from the road in the early days. This is my California stuff.

He also said, Don't be getting this stuff mixed up with my other pit band stuff. That's our black tie stuff and our white tie and tails stuff. This is our out here stuff that I got from our tank town and our showboat on the river stuff. But what the hell, just don't forget the hot dogs and hamburgers and the peanuts and popcorn and Cracker Jack and cotton candy. Which made me remember a poem my roommate and I used to read about the Emperor of Ice Cream. *The only emperor is the Emperor of Ice Cream.* What would old Daddy Royal make of that?

We took a break at six o'clock, and when we came back at seven-thirty the studio audience had grown from the cluster of local musicians, entertainment page reporters, and Hollywood hipsters who had been looking on from the corner by the door to the control booth during the afternoon to a double row of chairs that Milo the Navigator had arranged to have set up along the wall between the main entrance and the table where the refreshments were.

When Osceola Menefee's date came in, he told me that her very pretty early thirtyish-looking blue-eyed brunette friend had come along to meet the bass player. So during the next playback I went over with him to where they were and found out that her name was Enid Metzger and that she was a staff designer in the costume department at MGM, and also that her shade of olive skin made freckles invisible until you were close enough to shake hands.

I said, I hope you don't mind having to sit through all this repetition. And she said, Are you kidding? I just hope we're not in the way or anything. And I said, Not at all. I said, The boss-man likes to have a general public audience in the studio when we're recording, because that way we're playing for people not microphones and mixers. And Osceola Menefee said, How you going to be in the way when you so much a part of what's happening? And when his date, whose name was Beryl Boyd, said what she said about divided attention he said, Let me tell you something about these musicians in this band, baby. The bossman couldn't be happier than to see you all in here like this because he know good and well these thugs ain't never going to mess up his music in front of this many pretty women.

This is really something, Enid Metzger said when we went back over during the next playback. And Osceola Menefee said, I guess I know what you mean. But to tell the truth, baby, me I'm just up there trying to make myself a living. Another day, another dollar. And she said exactly what he expected her to say. She said, That's not the way it sounds at all. It sounds won-derful. It sounds simply marvelous. And he said, Well, that's because you and my inspiration are here.

On the next break I said, You never know. We might be here for quite a while longer. And she said, Mox nix. I'm only sorry we couldn't get here earlier. So when the bossman finally called it a day, I said, You're invited to the private party. And she said, How private? And I said, Very. I said, I will be the party of the first part and you will be the party of the second part. Or vice versa. And she said, That requires some serious deliberation. Yes. And we followed Osceola Menefee and Beryl Boyd on out to the convertible. But when he came to the final stoplight before turning left onto Vine, I told him to let us out and we shopped at the old Ranch Market and took a taxi on up the hill.

There was nobody in the patio of the Vineyard when we came through it with two chicken salad sandwiches and two cartons of hot tea with lemon in the takeout bag I was carrying

and an assortment of California fruit and nuts in the small tourist packet she had; and as we came on along the hallway, she
clutched my free hand and fell in step and said, Is this another
kind of elephant stride? And I said, Not really.

I said, I think of an elephant stride as being a lumbering
gait, just as a lion or a tiger has a stalking gait. And at another
time I probably would have gone on to tell her that the circus
piece should not be confused with program music, because
rather than being intended as a more or less literal imitation
of specific sounds as such, it is a matter of making music by
playing around with sounds that obviously go with the festive
atmosphere of circuses. But that would have broken the spell
of what had gotten under way during the ride from the studio.

So I said, No I guess you could call this a Harlem stride of
sorts. I said, Let's call it the swinging patent leather avenue
gait of the after hours creeper en route from the last gin mill
to some action that brings more satisfaction than can ever be
reduced to a powder or put into a bottle of whatever proof
or vintage. And she said, What about strutting as in strutting
one's stuff and strutting with some barbecue?

But we were there then, and I opened the door and clicked
on the light and said, See, nobody here but the very best people. Like you and me. Then I said, Remember who you came
with now. I said, Or better still, no cutting in. And she said,
Don't turn on the radio. She said, I can still hear the band. She
said, All I have to do is close my eyes for a minute so don't turn
off the light either.

She had to leave early the next morning because her production unit was getting its kits assembled to be shipped to the
shooting location in Europe that she was scheduled to leave
for in three days. But she said she would be the party of the
fourth part that night if invited by the party of the third part.
And I said, Consider yourself not nearly so much invited as
beseeched. And she said, See you here. Then she also said, My
treat this time.

She's fine people, Schoolboy, Osceola Menefee said when I got
to the studio that afternoon. Man, you're going to be thanking me for a long time for putting you next to some people
as special as Enid Metzger. Now that's something with some

follow-up the next time we swing out this way. And the thing about her is that she could have made it out here just on her looks and being stacked so fine. But she never traded on that, because she's just as deep as she is good looking; and what she's really deep into is not some entertainment and jive but all of that historical and geographical costume stuff that I'm sure you all going to have a lot of fun talking about between the rounds. Man, wait till you see that nice place of hers. Man, she's keen on all of the same kind of things you see when some of them hip globe trotting Ivy League profs throw parties for members of the band.

There were three professional photographers at the session on assignment that afternoon and evening, and I also saw a big bushy bearded weatherbeaten man sitting off in a corner by himself working with his huge sketch pad against an easel shaped like a lyre.

One of the photographers was so preoccupied with the Bossman Himself that it was almost as if everything else were incidental. The other two moved from section to section framing individuals and groups in various clusters and from various angles, one of them using three Nikons, the other alternating between a Contax and a Hasselblad, the one zeroing in on the bossman with two Leicas on neck straps and with another Leica and a Rolliflex on tripods set up in the curve of the piano.

The three photographers worked so smoothly that you could hardly tell them from the studio sound crew. They did all of their shooting while we were rehearsing. Then during the actual takes they moved back to the wall and stood looking on and listening along with the reporters and other visitors.

The big man with the sketch pad sat patting his feet as he worked away at his easel, and as I kept checking him out from time to time I got the very strong impression that whatever he was painting was more involved with what he was hearing than with what he was seeing. Because the only thing he was really looking at was what was on the easel. Every time he raised his head from that he closed his eyes.

He was wearing thick-soled rawhide sandals and a pair of baggy khaki safari shorts, with his faded blue denim shirt open like a bush jacket, exposing his shaggy chest and stomach; and when Otis Sheppard saw how I was keeping an eye on all of the squirming and frowning and leg pumping and smiles and sighs of release and relief he said, Man, what can you do about a cat like that, Schoolboy? All this stuff we're here laying down all these years and that somitch over there still missing the goddamn beat. And man, forget about the groove.

He would have gone on but Joe States cut in then and said, Hey Spode, you didn't tell him who that is. That's Django the artiste, Schoolboy, and if he ever heard anybody in this band saying what Spode was just saying it would wreck his whole frigging life. Man, old Django's whole thing is that his kind of painting is exactly the same as our kind of music. You see that design of that easel, don't you? Man, sometimes you see him over there using his brushes just like me. I mean using two goddamn paintbrushes just like me with my wires. And don't get him started on us and Africa for God's sake. Man, when he gets going on about being the paleface missionary from Shango, he can make it sound like you just got off the boat straight from the paradise lost land of gumbo and barbecue.

You know what old Joe told him one time, Schoolboy, Otis Sheppard said. Old Joe said, Hey Django, man, my family is from a long line of highly distinguished zebra jockeys just like all them Kentucky Derby winners beginning back with Oliver Lewis and coming on through Willie Walker, Isaac Murphy, who was the greatest that ever did it, Soup Perkins, Willie Simms, and Jimmy Winkfield.

But Joe States said, That's all right about what I told him, Schoolboy. Every time you see old Django rip off another one of them sheets that's another umpteen thousand dollars.

XV

WHEN I MADE the trip all the way out to the West Coast with the band the first time, my status had already been changed from stopgap temporary to extended indefinite, because I had already said what I said to the bossman about staying on for a while longer when I talked with him that morning that many months earlier down in Bay City, Florida, on our way around the Gulf Coast.

I had talked to Joe States the night before, and when he wanted to know what the bossman had said I said I hadn't been to see him about it yet but that I would do so the first thing in the morning. And I did. I found him working alone at the piano in the empty ballroom with a chrome coffeepot, a breakfast tray, and a package of cigarettes on a tête-à-tête-size ringside table in reach just beyond the bass clef end of the keyboard.

We were booked into the Bayshore Casino entertainment complex for the Labor Day weekend, and from where I was standing as we talked, you could see the pier leading out to the pavilion where we were to play open air matinees on Friday, Saturday, and Monday; and there was also the landing for the excursion boat. Off to the left there was the amusement park, and back to your right was a public beach and then the sand dunes curving away and the rolling whitecaps breaking out of the rising morning mist.

He was wearing slate gray slacks and a stone blue polo shirt and he still had on his silk stocking cap under his hat, a neutral brown porkpie with a navy blue band and with the brim turned up all around. And he was also still wearing his lounging slippers. He looked at his wrist watch, put his pencil behind his ear, lit a cigarette, and squinted through the smoke at the music rack in front of him. And said, I thought everybody else was sleeping late this morning. And I told him that Herman Kemble and Wayman Ridgeway had gotten up at five-thirty to go deep sea fishing with some local friends.

I'm the only other one up and about, I said. Except you, I said. And he said, We know about me, so what's your story morning glory? And when I told him and he said, So you changed your mind. I said, Somewhat. Only somewhat. Because what I had said when I agreed to meet him in Cincinnati the week after graduation, I did so not because it was the greatest break in the world for somebody who wanted to become a certified professional musician (something I had never thought about being). I had agreed because briarpatch scooterboy that I had always fancied myself as being and also felt you would always need to be, it was such a fabulously appropriate way to pick up additional ready cash you always needed to supplement the basic expenses covered by the fellowship I had won to do graduate work in the liberal arts. So I had said Labor Day and maybe also the fall semester. And he had said, So let me know around Labor Day. Don't worry about advance notice. Milo always has somebody on standby for emergencies. Anytime during Labor Day weekend will be fine.

Somewhat suits me just fine, he said looking at the empty Gulf Coast beach that would soon be teeming with people making the most of the last hot dry weekend of summer. Then, no doubt because he was no less aware than I was of the faint but unmistakable touch of early autumn in the late August weather along with the back-to-school shop windows and sports page items about football as well as the coming World Series, he said, But what about the university deal? And I told him it was still on.

Because I had found out that the award would still be valid that following year. So I had decided to go on working a while longer to build up a big enough cash reserve so that I could complete all of the requirements for both the M.A. and the Ph.D. in three consecutive years of residence and not have to take a year or more off to earn enough from the salary of an M.A. teaching somewhere.

I told him that I had not really changed anything fundamental. I said all I was doing was changing my schedule. But even as we went on talking I also began to realize that my ultimate career plans probably did not sound nearly so firm as my determination to earn graduate degrees may have suggested. Still it was not until later on that I could acknowledge to myself that for all the indoctrination in the ancestral imperatives as promulgated by Mr. B. Franklin Fisher at Mobile County Training School, I was really planning to go on into advanced training not because I knew what I wanted to become but because I still needed to find out more about the world at large before I could decide what I wanted to do in it.

Not that I still thought that there were any clear-cut answers. That was something my roommate and I had worked over in our after hours gab sessions during my first two years in college, and for him at that time it always used to come back to what Jake Barnes in Ernest Hemingway's *The Sun Also Rises* had to say one restless night in Paris: *All I wanted to know was how to live in it. Maybe if you found out how to live in it you learned from that what it was all about.* To which he used to say, Yea verily, much the same as Little Buddy Marshall back in Gasoline Point would have said, Hey, shit I reckon. But my roommate already knew that he wanted to be an architect, just as the bossman knew that being the kind of musician he had become was what he was really all about. And the same was true of Joe States and everybody else in the band.

Which brought me back to the proposition of being an answer to the old folks' prayers that I had already absorbed from talk around the fireside and on the swing porch even before Luzana Cholly all but took me by the nape of the neck to Miss Lexine Metcalf who in turn delivered me (which is not to say relinquished) to Mr. B. Franklin Fisher and the Early Birds of the Talented Tenth, which intentionally or not, brought me and Little Buddy Marshall (who acknowledged no obligation to anyone not even Luzana Cholly) to the parting of the ways. Because even as he was making up his mind to drop out of school because setting out for the seven seas was a matter of serendipity I was beginning to think of school bell time as Miss Lexine Metcalf's map rack and globe and compass time along with her bulletin board windows on the world. So, by the time Little Buddy Marshall actually skipped city on his own, I was not only on Mr. B. Franklin Fisher's pre-first bell Early Bird schedule, but was also looking forward to college (with its chime times and spyglass tree castles) to be followed by the graduate school time required to earn what would be equivalent to the seven league stride of the heroes in rocking chair story times.

So thank you again, I said looking out beyond him and the Bayshore Casino ballroom piano to where the early shift caretakers and stall-keepers were beginning to come to work along the beach. And he said, No, let me thank you for bringing me some good news to go with all this fine Spanish Main weather. And by the way, as things are shaping up it looks like you'll still be with us when we go out to California and the West Coast again before long.

Then when I apologized for the interruption he said, No sweat. He had been sitting back from the piano with his legs crossed as he sipped another cup of coffee and smoked another cigarette; and the way he tilted his head with one eye closed against the upcurling smoke, suddenly brought back to me once more how much he still reminded me of Stagolee Dupas, *fils*, sometimes. Who sometimes used to like to get up and go and play all by himself in the early morning emptiness of the Gasoline Point jook joint known as Sodawater's. Old Soda-water McMeans.

No sweat, he said. I'm just kind of fooling around with this little thing I picked up somewhere. He bent forward and played the changes ever so lightly in think-through tempo with only an offhand hint of the rhythm. Then he uncrossed his legs and pulled his seat all the way up to the keyboard again and put his cigarette on the ashtray and played sixteen bars in the intended tempo, naming the instrumentation and humming the part section by section and also saying, Ike, Bloop, Wayman, and so on.

All you got to do is drop it on us, I said. And he said, We'll see, we'll see. I just might spring it on Old Pro in a couple of days. Nothing special you understand. No big deal.

XVI

When we pulled out of Cleveland on the last leg of the trip back from the West Coast to New York for what was to be my first Broadway showcase theater date, Earlene Copeland, a local singer that the bossman and Old Pro had been trying for at least four or five years to add to the lineup, finally decided to put in with us for a while.

She's somebody very special, Schoolboy, Joe States said when he passed the word on to me as we came outside after breakfast and headed for the bus and the Pennsylvania state line that Monday morning. She finally made up her mind, he said. And I told him I was not really surprised at his news because I had guessed that something extra special was in the works as soon as I saw her at rehearsal that first day.

Even before I asked you who she was, I said. In fact, that's why I asked.

Not that I had guessed what he had just told me about. His news didn't surprise me because what I had guessed was how good she turned out to be, how smoothly she was going to fit in as our special feature soloist for that week in Cleveland. Which I was able to do because by that time I had covered enough territory to know that you could almost always count on hometown entertainers on our circuit living up to or maybe even exceeding their recommendations, no matter how down-right legendary all of the frankly partisan pride and praise set them up to be. You could count on them coming through be-cause such was the respect that people everywhere had for that band in those days that nobody would even mention any local hopefuls that might not pass Old Pro's preliminary standards and then bring some special stimulus to the bossman's imagi-nation. You could always rely on that and in the case of Earlene Copeland there was also the example of Hortense Hightower, who had done what she had done for me, but whose own re-sponse for hitting the road again was, Not now, I'll tell you when.

We were all set up in the empty club on Euclid Avenue working on the new material that had to be ready for New York, and I was running down my parts with my eyes closed, because that way I could see the lead sheets that the bossman and Old Pro directed from, because I had memorized them verbatim exactly as I used to learn everybody else's lines and cues in the Dramatic Arts Club productions back in Mobile County Training School, a practice that was even more useful when you were playing in an orchestra than when you were acting in a play, especially if you were in the rhythm section with the Bossman Himself.

Sometimes I also kept my eyes closed and went on fingering my parts while the next selection was being chosen. That was why I missed seeing anybody come in. When I closed them no-body was out in the audience area, not even the cleaning crew. But when I opened them again, the first thing I saw was that a very stylish but casually dressed young woman with teacake tan skin, Afro-Asian slanted hazel eyes, and black naturally wavy very lightly oiled but firmly brushed hair, had come in and was sitting by herself at a table on the right side of the center aisle just three rows back.

You could tell that she was somebody who was not only expected but was also used to dropping by on a pop call on her own whenever the band was in town. My impression was that she was just about old enough to have finished college the year I became a freshman and I wondered how far she had actually gone in school. But before I could ask Joe States who she was, I saw the bossman acknowledging her presence by blowing kisses in her direction at the end of one of his short segues and I closed my eyes again.

But even as I went on thumping my part and memorizing everybody else's as before, I could still see her ivory ear loops barely dangle as she tilted her head ever so gently to the left on the afterbeat of the time we were playing in—and that she was keeping with first one foot and then the other—snapping her fingers so softly that there would have been no sound even if she had been standing at the solo microphone.

As the gray green mist outside turned into an intermittent drizzle I found myself remembering once more how it used to be when the weather would suddenly become too wet for my track and field workout and I would come into the assembly auditorium and sit listening as Carl Mike Thompson led the Musical Demons through his arrangements adapted from the Louis Armstrong recordings of "Sleepy Time Down South," "Lazy River," "Stardust," "Wrap Your Troubles in Dreams," and "He's a Son of the South." And also from such Ellington recordings as "Sophisticated Lady," "Rocking in Rhythm," "Mood Indigo," and "It Don't Mean a Thing if It Ain't Got That Swing."

There was also something about the cozy atmosphere of the bandstand that overcast morning in Cleveland that made me feel the way I used to feel when I settled all by myself at the table by the rubber plant in the corner of the main reading room of the library where I used to spend most of my forenoon free periods beginning the first week of my freshman year in college.

At such times it was as if you had the whole world at your fingertips. Which is why it was also as if the campus at large, which was only a little more than two hundred miles north by

east of the chinaberry yard up the L & N beyond Chickasabogue Bridge, was the best of all spyglass places so far, exactly
as Miss Lexine Metcalf and Mr. B. Franklin Fisher had obviously intended me to find it to be.

As a member of the band you knew that what you also had
to have at your fingertips at all times as an ongoing everyday
bread and butter matter of course wherever you were, was not
only the bossman's entire repertory as such, but also as much
of the world at large according to him as you could come by.
So as aware of the striking newcomer as I continued to be, I
still kept my eyes closed and my attention focused on the new
material.

There were two more instrumentals to wrap up before moving on to the background charts for a set of pop vocals and up-
tempo blues features. The first instrumental was a jump number
that was a Hollywood exit shout originally labeled "Checkout
Time" and then "Wake Up Call" and finally "Rise and Shine."
The piano vamp, which sounded to me so much like an early
morning clock tower chime, had the instantaneous effect of
arousing and bestirring the whole ensemble to three shouting
choruses. Then Malachi Moberly did the trombone getaway
solo, and Alan Meadows followed suit on alto. And that set up
Ike Ellis for his centerpiece trumpet spot that Old Pro followed
with a clarinet continuation the elegance of which was a signal
for Ike Ellis to come back and take the out chorus up into
the stratosphere. Meanwhile what Otis Sheppard and I had to
do through it all was just go right on stomping the blues as
if tomorrow were as certain as yesterday, while old Joe States
rumbled his thunderbolts and crashed his cymbalic lightning as
if clearing the eastern skyline for sunrise.

The other instrumental was called "Skipping City," but I
thought of it as "The Mohawk Express" because the bossman
had me laying in there like an upstate New York locomotive
chugging the blues on the double from his piano intro to the
tag, except for one eight bar modulation. Ike Ellis had three
high register solo spots on that one, the first following Alan
Meadows's alto setup, the next behind Big Bloop's evangelical
centerpiece, and finally in the out chorus after the bell tinkling
piano sequence.

There was hardly ever any real problems with jump numbers like those two. Putting the sheets for material like that in
front of that band was like handing certain Hollywood studios
a script for a Western or a gangster movie. It was a case of the
rabbit in the briar patch from intro to coda, from breeze to
fadeout and credits.

We went directly from the second instrumental to the first of
the five background arrangements for the vocal set that was
being worked up for New York. There was no coffee break.
Everybody just turned to the next sheet on the stand and listened to the variations the bossman noodled and doodled as
he vamped his way to the downbeat. So I wondered if we were
giving the good looking woman out front an overview because
she was the guest singer, or if we were being taken through a
preliminary for our own benefit while we waited for the guest
singer to arrive.

As he almost always did when we were getting background
charts ready for guest singers, Joe States filled in the vocal
lines, sometimes stage whispering the actual lyrics, sometimes
humming them, and sometimes scatting them while mugging
like who else but Louis Armstrong himself. Mostly he made
it seem as if he were doing so because he was working out his
drum and cymbal accents, but it didn't take many guest singers
long to realize that not even Old Pro could give them a better
demonstration of how the bossman wanted the lyrics voiced
against the band's special background treatments.

Joe States, who was forever making eyes and pretending to
pine and sigh on sweet groove instrumentals, and who was always likely to become a one man amen corner any time we got
a straightaway blues set, vocal or instrumental, going in any
tempo, was also a great one for setting riffs verbally. He would
come up with some significant catchphrase (usually from some
figure the bossman would sneak in on the piano) and start saying it over and over flashing his heads-up signal at the trumpets
or the trombones or the reeds or even the whole band when
what the bossman wanted was a unison shout.

Such verbalized cues or mnemonics might sound somewhat
like anything from an old work chant or an old field or swamp

holler or some old saying, slogan, or motto or some current wisecrack or brand new jive line. There was no big mystery about it. As soon as I saw Joe States looking the way he looked at the section he had in mind when he began an offhand repetition of something like, *Say now hey pretty mama, let's get it on;* or *Well let's go Big Shorty let's go, let's go;* or *All night long,* as he did the very first time I ever went to watch the band rehearse.

But you could also tell that what was now happening was strictly a spur of the moment thing between the bossman and Joe States, and that not even Old Pro knew when it was coming until it was already happening. Which is also why everybody knew that there was no use complaining when Joe States suddenly started cracking the whip as if the band were dragging when it was already in high gear. All anybody was going to get was what Herman Kemble got that time when he forgot himself and shook his head on the way back from the solo mike as if to say, Man, what you trying to do?

The first thing he got when the set ended was an answer, Man, don't be shaking your head at me. Man, don't even be looking at me. Man, I'm just doing my goddamn job. I'm giving the bossman what he wants. Man, I'm just sneezing by the numbers, and if you can't get with it shame on you. But hell, Bloop, you did cut them dots, and look at the big ovation you got.

We ran right through the five background charts for the vocal set plus one encore, and then it was break time, and I let myself check out our good looking visitor again. I saw her stand up as the bossman made his way toward her with his arms already outstretched. They hugged and kissed and stood talking with their arms still around each other, and then he brought her back to the stand and everybody gathered around sighing and signifying.

She knew everybody and she greeted them one by one, signifying right back at the best jive passes they could come up with. I was the only one she didn't know, so when she got to me she said, So we got ourselves a brand new bass man. And the bossman said, This is our very clean, keen, and ultraspecial schoolboy, with a college degree no less. And she shook my hand giving me a very genuine smile and said How about that—and kind of cute to boot!

She also said, I was listening to you just now, and I also have the new records and have been catching some of the broadcasts, and I think I know exactly why they picked you for Shag Philips's replacement in this band.

Then as the bossman steered her on over to the piano and we headed backstage Old Pro said, No stuff, Schoolboy, she's so right for this band it gives me goose pimples to think about it. Wait till you hear what she does with this stuff tonight. Wait till you hear her shout some blues. Wait till you hear that lovely creature sing any goddamn thing.

Private stock, Schoolboy, Joe States said as I handed him a mug of coffee. Man, every band on the road is after that honey tree, but we saw her first; and we've been bringing her up to our own specifications every chance we've had. Hell tell him Pro. Like I say private stock. Tell him about all that stuff you and the bossman sketch up and don't put in the book until we come back through Cleveland because it's for her.

One of these days, Old Pro said, one of these days. One of these days, she's going to give in and do some records with us and that's going to bother a whole lot of people. Mark my words. But now let's get this straight now because I'm not trying to predict that she's going to become an overnight jukebox sensation. What I'm talking about is somebody who's going to put her stamp on everything she touches, and I'm saying that's going to turn a whole lot of people around.

When we came back on the bandstand she was still sitting on the piano bench with the bossman and that was where she stayed during the rest of the rehearsal, and the two of them were still there when the rest of us left for the hotel. So the first time I got to hear her strut her stuff was when she came on in the guest spot that night.

And strut her stuff is exactly what she did. She had it and she knew precisely what to do with it. As soon as she came on, it was as if she had been working with us every night. Her timing was perfect. Her beat was exactly where it was supposed to be, and her intonation was as natural to the band as the bossman's uniquely voiced brass and reed sections were.

I can still see her at the microphone as I did from my position in the rhythm section with the jampacked, spellbound crowd in the dimness beyond the footlights. She was wearing a strapless black sheath dress that did to a T what it was designed to do for the rubbery elegance of her not quite café au lait tan, size ten body. And she had her own way of standing and moving and doing that cold stroking walk off routine all the way into the wings and pausing before coming back doing an upbeat one-sided strut, almost like posting on a right diagonal. As we riffed an old off time vaudeville shout theme above the applause.

You have to be there and see as well as hear the band on a night like that. Everything is right and everybody is ready; and before you know it you're in the middle of something you'll never forget. The Bossman Himself can't really explain what is really happening on a night like that and he doesn't ever try to. He just sits there working with it, making the most of it as only he can.

That was the way things got going that first night, and the next night just picked up where we left off and kept going, and the same thing happened the night after that and night after that and after that.

XVII

SHE'LL BE catching up with us in the Apple, Schoolboy, Joe States said when he saw me looking for her because everybody else was in place, and the bus was getting ready to pull off on schedule. Then he pushed his seat into the reclining position and said, Actually she didn't make up her mind and give the word until after the last show. So she needs a little time to take care of a few things before cutting out.

We were booked for two nights in a ballroom in Pittsburgh, and then we would be en route via Harrisburg, Lancaster, and Philadelphia to New York for one open date and two rehearsal afternoons in Harlem before opening down in the midtown theater district as a headline feature in the stage variety show on the same program with what was billed as a major first run movie production.

That's the deal, Schoolboy, he said. So we finally got ourselves the singer we've been waiting and wishing for. And not because of the Broadway thing either. Not really. I'm not going to say that Broadway didn't have anything at all to do with it. But I will say it didn't have as much to do with it as the recording deal, and if you want to know the truth, I really don't think that had but so much to do with it either. I think the main thing was that she just decided that the time was right. And what did that was the stuff we laid on her this past week. I think that's what swung the record thing. I really do. Because she knew about the Broadway gig before we came, and there was always a guaranteed recording proposition. But, boy, when the time came for us to break camp this go round she realized that she was just not ready to say good-bye like before. Not yet. Not with all the stuff that was still building up. So she said okay if you still want me I'll give it a try and see if I'm up to it.

So what you think about it all, my man? he said as the bus worked its way toward the suburb and the route to Pittsburgh by way of Youngstown. Did you ever get a chance to have a get acquainted chat on your own?

And I said, Hey man. I said, Yeah man. I said, Hey she's all right with me man. And he said, Hey we're not just talking about a hell of a singer that's getting better and better every go round. I'm also talking about the fact that she's such special people. And I said, Hey man I could tell that as soon as I laid eyes on her and that was when I told him about what happened when I was window shopping my way along Euclid Avenue near Terminal Towers that Thursday afternoon.

I'm going your way she said, and I looked and there she was about to step into the driver's door of an Oldsmobile Eighty-eight parked at the curb; and when I said, Now just let somebody try to tell me I haven't been living right, she said, I don't know about that and I wouldn't bet on it since you're a member of that band of old rounders and reprobates but you sure have been playing right.

Then she said, I haven't had a chance to thank you for that fine and mellow bass line you've been laying down back there. The more I hear it the more I realize why I like it so much. It makes me feel that I'm back among family folks. Not just hometown folks, which is fantastic enough, but family bosom folks.

Which made me think about how beginning back during the fall of the year I left Gasoline Point for college, every time I hear Louis Armstrong playing "When It's Sleepy Time Down South" it takes me back to the family bosom coziness of the tell-me-tale-times around the fireplace and on the chinaberry yard swing porch with the fireflies in the distance above dog fennel meadows.

But what I said was, I sure am glad to hear you say that it comes out that way, because I know that you know what it means to be up there trying to keep up with the likes of Joe States and Otis Sheppard, not to mention the Bossman Himself.

And she said, I do know and I also know enough about that band to know that you've got them trying to outdo themselves every time around. Hey I think it's just great and so do Uncle Joe, Uncle Bloop, Uncle Ike, and all the rest of them.

And bossdaddy couldn't be happier, she said. And I said, Who always has something else for you to get to. I said, Talking about different strokes for different folks and not because he's always trying to find something new either. Not at all. Novelty is not what he's after. Absolutely not. Not him. With him it is not a matter of updating as such but of making music that is suitable to the situation. So you always have to be ready for changes in accent and shading here and there, to say nothing of extensions that come from his just about perfect sense of how the local response is shaping up.

You're sure right about that, she said. If there's such a thing as absolute audience pitch, he's got it. And I'm sure you know all about him adjusting the sound of the band to fit the variations in acoustics from one auditorium to another.

Oh yes, I said, so far as he is concerned that is as much a part of the game as tuning up the band in the first place. That was one of the first things Joe States told me.

Incidentally it was also Joe States who had confirmed the old tale I had heard in college about the time when two arrangements had to be adjusted to utilize a studio feedback noise because the recording technicians couldn't get it cleared up before the end of the session, and the band couldn't come back the next day because it was pulling out of town first thing in the morning.

Then when she said, So where are you headed? And I said, Nowhere in particular, just feeling my way around, trying to get the hang of things, she said, Well come on, get in and I'll give you a quick zip around just to get you started with a picture of how all this stuff is laid out.

Trust me, she said as we pulled out into the traffic. I know how much fun it is to find your way around in a new town on your own, and I promise that this won't spoil any of that. It's just that I've got these wheels and you don't have but so much time.

And I said, Spoil? Lady how could you spoil anything? And she said, Well you know how it is with down-home welcome do. Ain't nothing like it. But when it gets in the way it's a real drag. I mean really. Like a millstone.

She said, I was born up here but my folks are all from down there. So that's the way I was brought up, and I've also spent some time with my grandfolks down in Anniston and Gadsden, Alabama, and Rome, Georgia, back when I was just a tot. I haven't been back down that way since but when they used to come up here from time to time, they always expected to see the result of all the old landmark teachings. She pointed out the sights along Euclid Avenue, and as we cruised on toward Eighty-ninth Street she asked me if I had ever heard of the Karamu Playhouse. And I told her how I had found out about it from the director of the campus little theater during the fall of my freshman year. So even before we came to the curve that led to the grounds of Western Reserve University she had already started asking about what campus life was like in a small college town in central Alabama. And as we drove by the main academic buildings and circled past the Museum of Natural History, the Museum of Art, the Garden Center, and the Historical Society I went on to tell her about my first roommate, whose self initiated research projects were as important to me as the course of study that led to my degree.

I could tell that she liked hearing about college life and that being a college graduate made me somewhat special in her eyes, but I didn't go on with any more details because we were coming to other landmarks and also because I wanted her to have something to ask me about when we ran into each other again.

The rest of the quick spin included a turn through Rockefeller Park that brought us to Lakefront and along Memorial Shoreway and then back to the Terminal Tower, from which she pointed out that Cleveland was a city of heights stretching away from Lake Erie. I had heard of Cleveland Heights, University Heights, and Shaker Heights but not Garfield, Maple, or Bedford Heights, and so on. When she dropped me off at the hotel, she said, So that's it for a start for the schoolboy. Meanwhile for the road musician's Cleveland I leave you in the capable hands of a certain drummer and a whole crew of the smoothest thugs that ever hit this town in my day. See you backstage. And hey, thanks again for what you're laying down back there.

She's very special people, Schoolboy, Joe States said sitting up to look out and check landmarks and mileage markers and then settling back down again as we zoomed on toward Youngstown, East Liverpool, and our Pittsburgh stopover.

Very special people, he said again, pulling his cap back down over his eyes once more. So she took time out for a little hometown hospitality. That's her all right. She's got class and she knows class when she sees it. I knew I could count on her to find time to begin to form her own personal opinion of our college boy. Man, I didn't even have to think once let alone twice about it.

She don't miss much, Schoolboy, he said. Especially when it comes to what's happening in this band. She knows good and well that we're a bunch of thugs. But that don't keep her from also knowing that we got ourselves a band with class second to none. And class is what she's about. You don't need to put on no airs when you've got what she's got, Schoolboy.

No two ways about it, statemate, he said turning toward the window and curling himself into his open country sleeping position. The only thing about it is I don't know how long we're going be able to keep her out here.

XVIII

WHEN WE opened on Broadway the following week, it was as if she had been a regular member of the band all along. You had to be there to appreciate how smoothly everything she did fell into place. And the audience liked her as soon as they saw her, and she came right on down front and justified their first impression with the same ease with which she had responded to the completely partisan hometown enthusiasm back out in Cleveland. And was called back for an encore at the end of each set.

The reviewers and show biz chitchat tidbit columnists not only singled her out for special mention, but most of them also made a point of saying that she was a first rate newcomer with a very bright future as a headliner in her own right. Some went on to compare her with Ethel Waters in her glamor days, Adelaide Hall, Valaida Snow, and Nina Mae McKinney. Even the jazz reporters who had come mainly for the band's instrumentals decided that she was not just a pragmatic concession to show biz commercialism but was an excellent in-house vehicle for the bossman's songwriting genius. Which was second to none.

It was the kind of opening you hoped for, and everything got better as the first week moved on along and we really settled in. Meanwhile it also turned out that our new singer could take the daylong schedule in stride, as if doing that many shows between midmorning and 1:00 A.M. were the most natural routine in the world.

All I can say, she said, brushing questions about it aside with an echo if not a riff on an old work holler that I used to hear the sawmill hands down at Blue Rock on the Chickasabogue give when the afternoon back to work whistle used to blow. All I could say, she said, is the work ain't hard and the bossman ain't got a mean bone in his body.

To the entertainment page interviewer who came backstage the second afternoon to find out how she had managed to seem so unfazed by the fact that she was making her debut in one of the biggest theaters on Broadway, she said, Of course you know good and well where you are, but believe it or not, it actually didn't make all that much difference. Because you're really doing what you're doing for the bossman wherever you are. When that piano calls you out there you go, and when you get there it's like having him cradling you in his arms. And with all of my uncles back there supplying everything the bossman even hints at wanting, you don't even think about confidence. You go with the feeling that nobody else in the world can give you like this band.

That was also when she brought up the old one about the bossman and the New York telephone directory, which I had first heard somebody passing on as a bunch of us sat listening to the radio in Shade's Barbershop back when I was still in my first year of senior high school.

No question about it, she said. Not in my mind. If he decides to make jump arrangement on it in any key in any tempo, the band will swing it and the minute it starts to swing it, I will know exactly how I'm supposed to sing it. Sometimes this band comes up with things that sound weird to a lot of other people, but you know something? It always sounds perfectly natural to me.

Because that's the way she was brought up, Joe States said. Talking about somebody being earmarked. We've got it right here in the flesh and blood. And if the bossman wants her to sing the goddamn Milwaukee, Wisconsin, telephone book she'll make all of them w-i-c-z's and c-z-y-k's sound just as red, white, and blue as Jones, Smith, and Ben Franklin on the Fourth of July—and like she said in any key, any rhythm, any tempo.

As for how it was for me, the main thing was that the bossman was so pleased and so was the band. Not that he said so in so many words and neither did the band. Not even Joe States. Everybody just gave me the same nods and winks they usually give you when things are clicking even better than usual on a one night stand out on the road somewhere. Nobody mentioned anything at all about the fact that I was opening on Broadway for the first time.

My guess is that the reason the reviewers who singled me out for special comment made no mention of my debut either, was that they were familiar with the recordings I made with the band by then and so already thought of me as a regular part of the lineup. In any case it all added up to the impression that I was doing better than just good enough.

So from the very outset I was free to make the most of being in midtown Manhattan all day every day, and as soon as I found out exactly how much time you could actually count on having to yourself between all-on calls, the first thing I did was to make my way over to Brentano's on Fifth Avenue between 47th and 48th streets and buy the copy of the guide to New York City that I've kept all these years. And from then on, break time was not only old movie catch-up time and nearby theater playgoing time, but also New York Public Library or Museum of Modern Art or Metropolitan Museum of Art or Madison Avenue and 57th Street gallery time. And that was also when I started browsing and shopping at the Gotham Book Mart on 47th Street in the diamond district.

We were extended for an extra week. Then after one day off we spent the next three afternoons in a midtown studio recording Earlene Copeland. That was all the time we needed for two solid takes on each number on the contract, plus three extra instrumentals that the bossman and Old Pro had worked up just in case there was any session time to spare, which there was.

Following that, as usually happened before you went back out on the road again after a Broadway run in those days, there was a sold-out week up on 125th Street at the Apollo Theatre, where the audience would be made up mainly of Harlem people, among whom there would be many from down home and also of another of other people from elsewhere in and around the city some of whom had already been to see us on Broadway, some more than once.

The two main hangouts for musicians and entertainers between shows at the Apollo at that time were the bar in the Braddock Hotel on Eighth Avenue and 126th Street and the one off the main entrance to the Hotel Theresa on Seventh Avenue at 125th Street, which was not only the favorite shucking and jiving stand for the ever so hip or fly uptown cats and chicks (as they were then known as) but also the most strategic checkpoint for sportswriters, gossip columnists, political reporters and commentators, and various hype artists and feather merchants as well.

Playing at the Apollo Theatre and also at the Savoy Ballroom up the east side of Lenox Avenue between 141st and 142nd streets was a very special New York experience in those days. Because as soon as you came on cracking and popping the audience response made you feel as if you were a member of a very popular baseball team taking the field in your hometown park. So much so that every time somebody else come out to the solo microphone it was like a local boy stepping into the batter's box and having everybody from the grandstand all the way out to the center field bleachers pulling for you to ride one out of sight. They even picked up on section riffs, ensemble obligatos, and solo call and section and ensemble response exchanges as if they were matters not unlike running bases and executing double plays, squeeze plays, and so on.

That was the way it was uptown during those years not only for us but also for any band with the right stuff, which at the time also used to be called the righteous stuff and also the mellow stuff. It was a matter of having the stuff that hit the right groove, which was the one that took them down home to tell-me-tale times around the fireplace and on the swing porch once more, wherever you were from.

Not that such an audience response was unique to Harlem. It also happened elsewhere. Because as my old college roommate would have said, recordings and the radio and the jukebox had made the band no less a part of their mythosphere than of their atmosphere, which made your live performance in a sense the experience of the fable become flesh. Hence their sense of kinship. They were part and parcel of the down-home flesh from which the fables came.

Down in midtown I had been eating most of my meals at a Chock Full o'Nuts counter and in the Automat in Times Square. But the Apollo was only a few blocks away from Stew-meat Anderson's hole in the wall. So I had to go by there a couple of times to keep in touch with Royal Highness. And you also had to stop in at Big John's place up on Seventh not only for the special that one of Fletcher Henderson's brother Horace's jump tunes was set to celebrate, but also to spend some time in the company of the people who used to hang out there in those days.

Incidentally one of the things about eating in Harlem during my first week long gig at the Apollo was that there were Chinese restaurants everywhere you turned, and that most of the meals delivered backstage seemed to be Chinese. Before that time I had no idea that so much chop suey, chow mein, and egg foo yung was eaten in uptown Manhattan. That came as a big surprise and another surprise was the rice. Unlike the best down-home rice, which is cooked so that each grain is as freestanding as it is moist, the rice served in Chinese restaurants was downright *gummy*! So much for something I had wondered about for a long time. Chinese would have one hell of a time trying to eat properly cooked down-home rice with chopsticks.

XIX

ROLLING, ROLLING, ROLLING, I repeated to myself as we zoomed on along from the Blue Ridge Mountains of Virginia in the early morning mist, because what I woke up remembering again was how much my old roommate used to love to chant the opening lines of Rilke's "Cornet": "*Riding, riding, riding, through the day, through the night, through the day. Riding, riding, riding. And courage is grown so weary, and longing so great. There are no hills anymore, hardly a tree. Nothing dares stand up. Alien huts crouch thirstily by mired springs. Nowhere a tower . . .*"

We were circling back down into the southeast again on a string of one-nighters and weekend specials that would take us across the Carolinas and over to Knoxville and Chattanooga before entering Georgia by way of Dalton. Then after Atlanta, Macon, and Savannah there would be the Florida resorts along the oceanfront all the way to Miami, from which we would head for New Orleans by way of the Gulf Coast route north from Sarasota and west through Pensacola, Mobile (in the wee hours), and Gulfport.

There was a very good turnout everywhere we played, just as Milo the Navigator had promised, sometimes even better than he had estimated. And I also liked going back through as much of the territory as I had already covered with the band, because that was the way you became more familiar with key landmarks and also more intimate with new acquaintances, and so acquired another part of the seasoning that made the difference between being an ever so promising apprentice and a fully qualified professional road musician in every sense of the word.

But even so and even with our new vocalist not only on board but also spending as much time as she spent sitting with me as I checked through my maps, mileage charts, and regional guidebooks every time we got ready to pull out for the next scheduled stop on the first half of our itinerary I couldn't keep myself from thinking about how far away Chicago still was, and about what a long and roundabout way I was having to take to get there for the first time.

Commodious vicus of recirculation indeed. Until we left Miami we were always rolling on and on in the opposite direction, even as the scheduled time of arrival became shorter and shorter. Then when we finally hit the trail northbound from New Orleans on the way out of the bayou and delta country, with a sold-out stopover in Memphis, going to Chicago in city-skipping four/four hell for leather time was what everybody had in mind, including old Milo the Navigator himself, who was always supposed to be at least five towns ahead of all the rest of us, including Old Pro and the Bossman Himself.

I was the only member of the band who had never been to Chicago before even on a visit. But that was only one of the reasons that I was so much more eager than probably anybody else to get there and get settled into the routine of work for which we had been booked into the Regal Theater. Going up to Chicago, Illinois, and also up to Detroit, Michigan, not unlike going out to Kansas City and California Here I Come, was already a part of what skipping town for the seven seas was all about. Some years before all of the souvenirs brought back to Mobile County Training School from the Century of Progress Exposition by Mr. B. Franklin Fisher, who had taken the top three prizewinning seniors of the Talented Tenth Early Bird program of that year up to see it when I was in the ninth grade, there were the Windows on the World bulletin board pictures of the Hub City of the North Central states and the railroad center of the nation as a whole. And long before that, there were almost as much fireside and swing porch tale spinning and lie swapping about Chicago as about anywhere else. Along with all of which and everything else over the years there were all of the times that Chicago had been featured in the movies.

Added to all of which was also the fact that Chicago was also the hometown although not the birthplace of my good old very best of all possible roommates. Not that I thought that I would be able to look him up, or that he might turn up backstage one night. There was hardly a chance of that, because the last letter from him was postmarked Mexico City, where he had gone to serve an apprenticeship after graduating from the Yale School of Architecture. And from there he planned to go on down to Brazil where he hoped to be hired as a journeyman with Oscar Niemeyer, whom he had met while at Yale when Niemeyer came to New York to help design a pavilion for the New York World's Fair in Flushing Meadows.

In his letters there were always references to and quotations from books and magazine articles that he hoped I would find time to look into, which I always did and which also made me miss our after lights out exchanges in Atelier 359 more than anything else about college because I had graduated from college, but you never graduate from the likes of him.

As things turned out however I didn't really miss him very much while the band was in Chicago that time. I thought about him a lot all during the time we were there to be sure. But I was much too busy doing what by that time I was used to doing on my own to familiarize myself in a new town, to miss anybody—even him.

But even so sometimes no matter where I am, when something makes me realize how much I still do miss him, it is as if the first weeks of the fall semester of my freshman year were only yesterday: *when the dormitory cot, the chest of drawers, the desk with its own bookrack and straight-back chair were the only items of furniture on my side of the room, and the only thing on the wall was a school year calendar from the bookstore until I added maps from back issues of* National Geographic Magazine. *What with the library I really didn't think I needed much more than that for the time being.*

But what he had in mind for his side was an all-purpose studio, laboratory, and workshop for the artist, craftsman, research technician, and engineer. So in addition to a drafting table and the sea captain's chair he had bought during the first week of class he also got permission to design and attach a seven-foot bookshelf along the wall beside his bed, because he wanted to have five feet of the great literary classics of the world and twenty-four inches of science and technology within easy reach at all times.

Which didn't surprise me at all, because I had already noticed that the first two items that he had taken from his overnight bag that first Thursday were a recent edition of The Odyssey *in a prose translation by T. E. Lawrence (under the name of T. E. Shaw), and* Technics and Civilization *by Lewis Mumford. Then when we picked up the packages that he and his uncle The Old Trooper had shipped ahead by parcel post, in addition to his drafting, surveying, mapping instruments and his camera and binoculars, there were also his own copies of* The Iliad, The Decameron, The Song of Roland, Gargantua and Pantagruel, Don Quixote, Candide, The Tragical History of Doctor Faustus, *and* The Three Musketeers, *which were at the end of the shelf nearest his pillow along with* The Testament *of François Villon*, Cyrano de Bergerac, A Study in Scarlet, The Sign of Four, *and Don Marquis's* archie and mehitabel.

There were also library copies of Sticks and Stones, The Golden Day, Frank Lloyd Wright on Architecture, *and Sheldon Cheney's* Primer of Modern Art, *which he kept with the textbooks lined up on the window ledge beyond the drafting table and which he would continue to renew until somebody else put in a request for them.*

He was very pleased that I intended to use my wall mainly for maps, but above the bookshelf on his side he tacked up a line of glossy magazine tear sheets of color reproductions of modern paintings beginning with Cézanne's "Landscape Near L'Estaque" and continuing with Picasso's "Nude Couple" and his "Jeune Fille à Mandoline"; Fernand Léger's "Paysage Anime: L'Homme au Chien," Lyonel Feininger's "Toc Turm," John Marin's "Lower Manhattan," and Charles Sheeler's "City Interior" and his "Classic Landscape."

There was no federal guide for the city of Chicago as there was for the city of New York, but there was a 115-page section on Chicago in the one for the state of Illinois, which I had bought before leaving New York and studied en route along with Old Pro's copy of *Chicago, a Portrait* by Henry Justin Smith, illustrated by E. H. Suydam, whose sketches for books about New Orleans and Los Angeles I was familiar with also.

So I had my own orientation agenda worked pretty much by the time we arrived, and there were also the rounds that I had to make with Joe States, whose favorite book on Chicago, Herbert Asbury's *Gem of the Prairie*, I had also been reading on the bus. The only other Asbury books I knew about at that time were *The French Quarter* about New Orleans and *The Barbary Coast* about San Francisco.

Joe States took me to meet people who worked or hung out in places like Club DeLisa, the Grand Terrace, the Rum Boogie, and at least a dozen other clubs, bars, and lounges in the South Side area that included Garfield Avenue, State Street, Calumet Avenue, and South Parkway and environs. He also took the personal responsibility of cluing me in on the pimps and prostitutes in that part of town. The point, he said later, was not that he didn't think I could figure things out for myself but that Chicago was so different from New York and Hollywood and he wanted his young statemate to hit the scene copping what was popping from bar one.

On my own I started out at the Art Institute and went on along Michigan Avenue to the river, the Tribune Tower, the Wrigley and Daily News buildings. Then after familiarizing myself with the vastness of Merchandise Mart I went on out a few blocks farther along the shopping strip of Michigan Avenue before coming back to Randolph Street, the library, and the Loop.

The next day I started out at the Field Museum and came back to the library and the Loop and the day after that I spent the late morning looking around the campus of the University of Chicago before going on across 57th Street to the Museum of Science and Industry for most of the afternoon. Then for the rest of our stay I just took things as they came, which as usual included catching up on the new movies and also the reruns that happened to be showing while we were in town.

The band was always a big attraction in Chicago. And this time there were new and recent recordings in the music stores and being played on the radio throughout the day, every day; and there were also all of those longtime local fans who were eager to find out how Shag Philips's replacement on bass and the recently added vocalist came across in person. And who also made a special point of letting you know how keenly aware they were of the shadings that each instrument in the lineup represented.

Not that Chicago didn't have its own absolutely first rate world famous hometown band. Because there was Earl Hines and his by no means provincial Grand Terrace orchestra. And at that time Chicago was also still the functional hometown of Louis Armstrong himself. But even so our fans in Chicago, like so many

others in most towns from border to border and coast to coast,
identified with the bossman's music as if it belonged not one bit
less to them than to the people of New York.

As for press coverage, Chicago was second to none. Along
with a very enthusiastic arts and amusement section, reporters and reviewers of the dailies and their Sunday supplements,
there were such national publications as *Down Beat* magazine and R. S. Abbott's *Chicago Defender*, and there was also
Esquire, the Magazine for Men, whose elegance and prestige
were comparable to that of such women's magazines as *Vogue*,
Harper's Bazaar, and *Vanity Fair*.

Esquire's ongoing special interest in our kind of music was
such that for a number of years it was one of the three top
magazines covering the subject. The other two were *Down
Beat* and *Metronome*, both of which were publications devoted
exclusively to covering music. It also came to sponsor national
popularity polls, annual achievement awards, and all-star concerts for a while.

The bossman, Old Pro, and Milo the Navigator, ever mindful of the connection between enthusiastic reporters and choice
bookings and big advance sales, were always cooperative and
charming in all of their contacts with journalists and disc jockeys. But nobody got a bigger kick out of kidding around with
and manipulating so-called jazz critics than Joe States. He was
forever sneaking some catchword or phrase into his backstage
or ringside table interviews precisely because he knew that ever
so hip reporters picked up on what you said and published
it as their own special insight into the secret dynamics of the
bossman's music.

This time around the subject was Earlene Copeland and the
phrase was "torching in jive time," and they went for it just
as others over the years seem to have gone for "blue note,"
"groove," "stride," "shout," "soul," "flatted fifth," "trumpet
style piano" "walking bass," and so on. We were going along
the alley from the stage door of the Regal and he looked at me
with a poker face that meant that he was winking and rolling
his eyes; and when I saw her the next day I said, Mark my
words. By the time we get out to the Coast, the Hollywood
disc jockeys will have audiences clamoring for at least two jive
time torches and at least one encore in kind in every set.

XX

BACK ON the road again after Chicago, we headed for St. Louis and Kansas City, and from there we went on out to Topeka and down through Wichita and Oklahoma City to Dallas and Fort Worth before dipping farther south to San Antonio to make the long haul out of Texas north to Denver by way of El Paso, and then up through Albuquerque and Santa Fe.

Rolling, rolling, rolling, I began repeating to myself again as we cruised on across the Mississippi River Bridge from Illinois into Missouri that Tuesday before dark. Because I was thinking about my old roommate again. But this time the writer he brought to mind was not Rilke but Walt Whitman, about whom he had said in response to my letter about joining the band for a while: *Boy, what old footloose Whitman wouldn't have given to be able to traffic with the likes of that perpetually roving crew of festive but ultimately unfrivolous merrymakers.*

Song of the open road, yea verily. And also the also and also of it all. Hithering and thithering from here to there and from there to elsewhere after elsewhere. According to my old roommate, old Walt Whitman, barnstorming troubadour par excellence that he was, could only have been completely delighted with the interplay of aesthetic and pragmatic considerations evidenced in the maps and mileage charts and always tentative itineraries of Milo the Navigator of transcontinental as well as transoceanic meandertrails.

It was Ralph Waldo Emerson who spoke of "melodies that ascend and leap and pierce into the deeps of infinite time," my roommate also wrote, which, by the way, would make a very fine blurb for a Louis Armstrong solo such as the one on "Potato Head Blues." But, he went on, it was the old wayfaring bird of passage himself, whose "minstrels latent on the prairies" were counted among the pioneers "soon to be heard coming wobbling, soon to rise and tramp amid us."

Walt Whitman, to be sure, singing his specimen days "singing the great achievements of the present, singing the strong light works of engineers, our modern wonders (the antique . . . Seven outvied). In the Old world the east the Suez Canal / the New by its mighty railroads spanned / the seas inlaid with eloquent gentle wires." Yea verily. Or as little Buddy

Marshall would have sucked his teeth two times and said, Hey shit I reckon, skebootie, hey shit I goddamn reckon.

None of which, my good old roommate was very careful to point out, was to imply that your position as a sideman in the bossman's far ranging road band was also like that of Ishmael on board the *Pequod* in Herman Melville's *Moby-Dick*. Not at all. The bossman, as my old roommate knew as well as I did, was completely ordained and dedicated, to be sure; but not to the point of hell-fired obsession. So, very much unlike Ishmael, who had no options because he had signed on for the duration, you for all your junior apprenticeship status had the prerogative that, although it was completely unsanguinary, was no less authoritative than that of the all powerful Shahryar, the king to whom the tales of the Thousand Nights and a Night were told. Because all you had to do was give notice and pack your fiddle.

But wait, he went on to add as if you could hear his voice on the page and also see his sidelong glance across the dormitory room as he used to sit slouched in his captain's chair with his stocking feet propped against his bed. Leave us not forget the relevance of the three princes of Serendip (now known as Ceylon) to all the riffing and sundry improvisational carryings on, which I need not remind you, is no less personal than musical. Or should be.

Same old roommate, I wrote in reply, only more so. Picaresque by any other name were no less riff-style. The bossman's got your old commedia dell'arte swinging, old partner. And I do mean cracking and grooving as the occasion requires, whatever the occasion. Dance halls, roadside joints, clubs, vaudeville stages, picnics, outdoor jamborees, political rallies and barbecues, oom-pa-pa bandstands in city parks, Milo the Navigator books them and we play them, and I don't mean just knock them off. We play them barring none. No shucking allowed ever.

Stamping grounds and stopping places, I also wrote. Naturally there are some that you can't help becoming more excited about but there were none that you were ever allowed to discount. No lackadaisical nights in this man's outfit. The prestige of certain very special places did count for a lot, to be sure; and there was always a certain amount of special preparation. But the atmosphere and audience response mattered most even so. So much so that sometimes we were even better in some ramshackle roadside joint than on Broadway, in the Loop, or on the Strip and there are radio air checks to prove it.

So, a word more about those one thousand nights plus one, old pardner. Your point about my prerogative to cut out is well taken, but I'm really something of a very special case, because I'm still not sure of what I want to do with myself, whereas in point of fact, it is always the bossman who is Shahryar the headcutter. As everybody tells you when you show up for your first rehearsal, he's the one you have to make want to hear more tomorrow night.

You never knew when his next letter would come. Sometimes there would be one in a month or so but it was most likely to be more than six months between times. Because it was not so much a matter of keeping up to date as of keeping in touch in a random sort of way each on his own terms. And unless there was a question that called for an immediate answer you responded whenever you got around to it—sometimes as if picking up a conversation that had been interrupted by a telephone call three minutes ago, an old campus game we had begun playing with each other the day after reading that it was something that James Joyce did upon reencountering literary friends days, weeks, months, or even years later.

All I wrote about Chicago was that I had finally made it up there and had checked out most of the high points and found everything to be as advertised over the years. But right after my first trip to Boston I sent him an all but verbatim copy of the log I kept of my week of schoolboy explorations, which began with me finding my way along Tremont Avenue to Boston Common and Beacon Hill from the rooming house and eating place where most of the bands used to stay and hang out back during that time.

Then on my free time during the week that followed, I made my way from such downtown Revolutionary War era landmarks as old North Church, the Old State House, the Massacre Site, and Faneuil Hall among others (and also including the Augustus Saint-Gaudens Civil War memorial honoring Colonel Robert Gould Shaw and the Massachusetts 54th) over to Harvard and Radcliffe by the second day. I skipped Massachusetts Institute of Technology for the time being. So when I took off from Harvard Square late the next morning I took the Paul Revere route to Lexington, Bedford, and Concord; and by the time the bus pulled out of Boston and headed westward on the Old Post Road for one night stands in Springfield, Hartford, and New Haven, I had also been to see Walden Pond, the Concord Bridge, the Emerson, Alcott, and Hawthorne houses, and also the Bunker Hill Monument and *Old Ironsides*, which I had already seen and boarded as one of Mr. B. Franklin Fisher's Early Bird Explorers when it called at the port of Mobile and tied up at the foot of Government Street that time.

On the day that I had gotten around to going back over to Cambridge to see the Massachusetts Institute of Technology, I had actually spent most of the time revisiting the Fogg Museum of Art at Harvard. I also went to the Boston Museum of Fine Arts twice and the Isabella Stewart Gardner Museum, both in the Back Bay fens area.

Several months later my old roommate responded to my Boston notes by reminding me of Van Wyck Brooks's *The Flowering of New England*, which we had read during that second year because on his own he had been reading and rereading *Sticks and Stones* and *The Golden Day* by Lewis Mumford as background material for his course in architecture, and which had also led him (and then me) to read *American Humor, a Study of the National Character* by Constance Rourke, which is still one of my basic bibles on the subject of life and art in the United States.

The historic figure whom my references to the monument to Colonel Shaw and the Massachusetts 54th brought to my old roommate's mind was Frederick Douglass. We had read *A Narrative of the Life of Frederick Douglass, an American Slave, Written by Himself*, which he had checked out of the library during February of our freshman year. Since that time he had also read *My Bondage and My Freedom* and *The Life and Times of Frederick Douglass*. I had read *My Bondage and My Freedom* during the summer following my sophomore year but had not yet got around to *The Life and Times*. . . .

Frederick Douglass had been a very influential supporter of and also a highly successful recruiter for the Massachusetts 54th. But the main thing my old roommate had in mind this time was the world of the abolition movement, the fugitive slave, and the Underground Railroad, the point of which was to suggest that the itinerary of a road band probably took you to a lot of places that were once stations on the Underground Railroad. I got the point immediately and the first place that came to mind was Oberlin in Ohio, which I had not yet seen but which was already famous at Mobile County Training School as early on as I could remember, not only for its role in the antislavery movement and as the first coeducational as well as interracial college but also as a conservatory of music.

In fact I had already heard of Oberlin as a music conservatory even before I realized how many different kinds of junctions and layover spurs the Underground Railroad actually had. Come to think of it, Oberlin was probably the very first musical conservatory I ever heard of, because Miss Lucy Ariel Williams the concert pianist and daughter of Doctor Roger Williams of downtown Mobile had studied there, and so had R. Nathaniel Dett, the composer of "Listen to the Lambs"; and Will Marion Cook, who wrote the music for Paul Laurence Dunbar's "Clorindy, the Origin of the Cakewalk," and also created the Southern Syncopated Orchestra, was sent out there from Washington, D.C., as a student of the violin at the age of thirteen and had gone on to the Hochschule in Berlin to study with Joseph Joachim and had also taken lessons with Dvořák during the year Dvořák had spent in the United States circa 1893.

I knew about all of that before I went to college, not only because of what Mr. B. Franklin Fisher told us when he brought Miss Lucy Ariel Williams out to play "The Juba Dance" from R. Nathaniel Dett's "In the Bottoms Suite" during National Negro History Week that year, but also because Dett's "Listen to the Lambs" and Will Marion Cook's "Swing Along" were as much a part of the musical atmosphere of assembly room time as "Lift Every Voice and Sing."

Old Pro was the one to talk to about what for better or worse had been happening at Oberlin over the years. And incidently he was also somebody you could chat with about Will Marion Cook, whom he had come to know through the Bossman Himself, whose well-known apprenticeship to Cook had been arranged for by none other than Royal Highness, the only, who had also seen to it that the bossman got a chance to work under the direct supervision of Will Vodery.

At the time, my impression was that in recent years the reputation of the Oberlin Conservatory had been eclipsed by Juilliard, Berklee, and Eastman. But even so for me it was somewhere I looked forward to visiting, because its unequivocal commitment to the antislavery movement and its pioneering policies as an unsegregated and coeducational institution made it a hallowed and inspiring landmark that symbolized the Civil War and the Emancipation era much the same as Bunker Hill, Concord Bridge, and the Liberty Bell symbolized the period of the War for Independence and the principles articulated in the Declaration of Independence and the Constitution.

XXI

Meanwhile there was the also and also of me and Miss You-Know-Who, from what region of my mind, who was still a student down in central Alabama.

When I told her that I had decided to accept the bossman's invitation to come with the band for the summer, beginning the week after I graduated, we agreed that there should be at least one exchange of letters each week, and that I would make one Sunday morning telephone call every month, and that I would also send postcards whenever the itinerary took me somewhere that was of some personal or academic interest to either one of us. Souvenirs were a discreetly unmentioned option that I was only too happy to use to make such surprise and special occasional gifts as I could afford without violating my financial plan to supplement my graduate school fellowship grant.

The possibility of a short layoff time visit every now and then was not even considered until I changed my mind about staying on with the band beyond that first September. Then there was the all too obvious fact that the band always expected to be booked into some special spot during all holiday weeks and weekends the year round. So for the time being, we decided to wait and see how things turned out. As for the likelihood of the band being brought back to town to play out at the Dolomite again within the next year or so, no such luck.

When I said what I said about the Mobile County Training School Doctrine of the Ancestral Imperative, she said, So that's what they call it down there. And I said, And also the obligation of the Talented Tenth and told her about the Early Birds. And she shook her head smiling and said, *Up my way you were also earmarked by the time you reached the ninth grade, at which point the question was whether you could qualify to be included in the Circle of Young Achievers, who earned distinctive armbands much the same as first team athletes earned letters and sleeve stripes, but which were worn only on the school premises and when you were representing the school as a participant on some formal public ceremonial occasion.*

The first requirement was outstanding classwork. That was basic. But excellent grades as such were not really enough. Along with being in the upper ten percentile, you also had to exemplify that certain something that made not only faculty members schoolwide but also civic leaders and church elders feel that they had ample reason to expect you to become one in that precious number of the divinely chosen and endowed few who in answer to the prayers of old folks long since gone would sally forth and so acquit themselves in the world at large that generations yet unborn would arise and call them blessed.

In other words, I said, *some Early Birds were specifically groomed and charged to hit the open road of endless obstacles and opportunities in quest, if not conquest, of whatever wherever forever, while others were no less carefully counseled to "let down your bucket where you are," which meant that some in that category were expected to go to college and come back into the Mobile and Gulf states area as professionals, and that others would go directly from high school graduation into the local workaday world either as inspired progress oriented apprentice artisans and business men and women, or by way of one of the part time or full time technical courses recommended by the vocational guidance counselor.*

But let me tell you something about that bucket jive, I said. *Most people I know don't know anything at all about the point Booker T. Washington was trying to make when he said what he said in that famous speech. They just take what he said at that point as a very wise old saying about not overlooking something valuable right under your nose so to speak. To them it goes right along with what old Booker T. also had to say about our people prospering in proportion as we learn to dignify and glorify labor and put brains and skill into the common occupations of life.*

That's what it all adds up to for me too, I said, *and I also knew a few other things about that historic speech in Atlanta. And I've also read the inscription directly from the monument at Tuskegee.*

But what Booker T.'s bucket always brings to my mind is a church song that goes as far back in my memory as the Sunday school shout that goes "Jesus wants me for a sunbeam. . . ."

And she said, Oh, I bet you I know that one, and said, Don't tell me, let me guess, and said, Oh, this is very easy. I bet you anything it's "Brighten the corner where you are," isn't it?

All I could do was open my mouth and stretch my eyes and nod my head and as we held each other and pressed cheeks, I thought about the difference between our obligations to our hometowns.

Hers was more specific and also more binding than mine. All I had to do was promise that I would always do my best and if I ever accomplished anything noteworthy it would be something that not only home folks but also others elsewhere could be proud. That was as far as the Early Bird program went. You earned your scholarship to college, and the rest was up to you. But in her case there was an ongoing relationship with her hometown sponsors. Unlike fellow Young Achievers whose training in medicine, dentistry, and law was being underwritten, she had not had to sign a commitment to come back and practice her (as yet unchosen) profession in her hometown for at least a certain term, but she had agreed to a sponsorship plan that included completing all residence requirements for a master's degree in the field of her choice one year after college. When she said, So that's my story and I said, So what about our story? and she said, Well I guess we're going to have to make that one up as we go along, won't we, I said, Touché said the big bad bull fiddle player-to-be, touché. And she squeezed my arm and brushed her lips against my cheeks and said, My Mister. Hello my Mister and got the Buster Brown blush that she knew Miss Tee's old riff and leitmotif was always good for. Then she said, I must say this. As much as I'm going to be missing you it's probably best that we're going to have to be separated for a while. I really think so.

And I said Me too, alas, me too. You didn't have to mention wedding bells as such on that campus during that time of year in those days. Because from wisteria blossom time on through the commencement season, few other rumors were more a part of the daily gossip than those about what graduating senior was getting engaged to marry whomever of whatever class level.

As for the next chapter (or following stanza, fit, canto, chorus, or sequence) of my own story, by the time my roommate and I said so long for now at the end of our sophomore year he (who referred to it as the Scooter Saga or Scooter Cycle to be) had made me aware as I never had been before of the fact that regardless of your career objectives your own story was something that you make up as you go along. Not that I was entirely unaware of it before. After all, as Early Bird conditioned as I was, I still had not settled on my career field.

And almost two years after his exit to the Yale School of Architecture, I still had not made up my mind except to continue my course of study in the Department of Liberal Arts with a major in literature. But my notions about my obligations to hometown expectations had undergone significant modification indeed. They had become more and more a matter of existential implication and less and less obviously a matter of personal social and political progress as such, without becoming any less pragmatic than direct involvement in concrete action as such, precisely because they were concerned with that upon which such action at its best must be predicated.

In any case, the closer I came to the bachelor's degree in liberal arts the easier it was for me to realize that what I really wanted to do next was to go on to a big university for graduate courses in the humanities. Because my personal preoccupations and concerns had far more to do with underlying assumptions, functional definitions, and basic issues than with direct hands-on professional involvement with the day to day operations of any programs and institutions as such, however prestigious.

Ancestral imperatives, yea verily, my brand new roommate had said as soon as I said what I said about Mr. B. Franklin Fisher and the Early Birds in response to what he had just told me about the support and implicitly heroic but deliberately unspecific expectations of the great uncle, a former hard riding member of the 9th Cavalry regiment whom he sometimes referred to as The Old Trooper and sometimes as Old Troop.

Ancestral imperatives, indeed, he said again then (and also time and again later on), yea verily, who would gainsay that which so obviously goes without saying? Forsooth not I, who am absolutely nothing if not ever mindful of antecedents and derivations. But even so, he also said, but even so. But even what most certainly does not go without saying and gainsaying is the question of WHICH ancestors among which.

Which among which indeed, *I thought. It was not until sometime later that year that I suddenly realized how Luzana Cholly had eliminated himself. But when I did, I also realized that the one I had always assumed he retrieved me for was not the ever so pragmatic and no less comprehensive Mr. B. Franklin Fisher himself with his primary emphasis on brown-skin achievements in social and political service, education as such, business, and public affairs, but to Miss Lexine Metcalf, who was to say Who if not you, my splendid young man, my splendid young man, who if not you? And who was also to say, Who knows but that you may have to travel far and wide to find out what it is that you are called to do and be.*

It was when I told my roommate about how I still felt about Miss Lexine Metcalf that he vamped our after hours yak sessions into the first of a string of riffs on what he called the actual, or in any case, the functional and thus the true or real ancestors—opposed to the conventional flesh and blood and thus official or legal ancestors.

Mind over matter, roommate, he said. Mind over matter, if you know what I mean. Materiality is nothing without mythology. Your Mr. B. Franklin Fisher himself was never talking about flesh and blood ancestors, was he? Of course not. And nobody down there at that school of yours ever thought he was. Everybody knew very well that he was talking about picking and choosing, roommate, picking and choosing. As you pick and choose among tools and weapons, roommate.

Then he said, Chacun selon sa faim, *roommate,* et après, peut-être, selon son goût. *Then he also went on to say, I submit that necessity is the mother of fairy godmothers, roommate. And also of earthly godfathers and Remus wise uncles of all shapes and fashions. So of course, Miss Lexine Metcalf, roommate. And but of course, Miss Lexine Metcalf. Who else if not she could carry on better for Miss Tee, my splendid young man, my splendid young man.*

Eunice Townsend, Eunice Townsend, Eunice Townsend, I said as we sauntered arm in arm and cheek to cheek across the spring fresh tree lined campus thoroughfare with only that many more weeks before Commencement. And she said That's the official me of my birth certificate and also the make believe me of my aspirations, which according to you and the Snake also makes it the personal me, doesn't it?

By that time she had long since explained that Nona was a nickname that had nothing at all to do with her hometown identity. It came from the tune that Erskine Hawkins and the former 'Bama State Collegians had recorded and was given to her by members of the 'Bama State Hornets basketball team during an after game dance party at Alabama Normal.

We came on down the wide concrete steps and past the side entrance to the Dining Hall and found a park bench in an alcove of shrubbery of the Promenade Mall near the empty bandstand, and I said, First things first and she agreed and we held each other with our eyes closed for a while. Then when I said, So will you weave and reweave to keep the suitor wolves of Ithaca at bay, night and day? she couldn't resist putting her hands on her hips and mocking me with her eyes and saying, While the cat's away at play? And I said, Well not exactly. I said, More like while the self-styled Alabama jackrabbit is out somewhere trying to get from here to there in the road musicians' briar patch with his pelt if not untattered at least none the worst for fair wear and tear.

All the same, she also said on the day I left the campus to take the train to join the band in Cincinnati. All the same, there are so many occupational hazards out there in the world of music and entertainment I can just see crowds of good time people with all kinds of enticements lying in wait for their favorite bands in town after town all across the country.

But she didn't say if you can't be good be careful. She said, I'm satisfied that your Mobile upbringing will keep you on your p's and q's anytime you come anywhere near any women with a pigfoot and a bottle, mug or tankard of beer.

Then she also said, As for all of those good looking conjure women cleverly disguised as gay divorcées, who might sometimes sound so much like your Miss Lexine Metcalf, I'm sure I don't have to remind you that neither your Miss Metcalf herself nor your Mr. B. Franklin Fisher ever told you anything that would lead you to believe that there will ever be any shortcuts either to the Holy Grail or the Golden Fleece.

That was all she said on that subject, and I said, I know what you mean. I know exactly what you mean. And I couldn't keep from smiling and shaking my head as I blushed, because what she

*never could have gone on to say next was precisely what old Deke
Whatley had already said earlier that same day when I stopped in
to take my leave of the barbershop.*

*Say now look here, son, he said holding his clippers in one hand
and his chomped on cigar in the other as I stepped back to salute
and cut out, Now look here. Now you got your college degree and
you're on your way to join up with the greatest musical aggregation that ever was and music ain't even your chosen profession.
So that shows the kind of stuff you can lay down if you want to.
But just one more detail—and I know good and well you already
know this or you wouldn't have made it this far. But I'm going to
say it again anyhow, son: That thing down there can get you into
far more trouble than it can ever get you out of. It can get you
into a lot of good places too. But how many bad places have you
ever hear anybody say it got them out of.*

*Remember that now, he said and looka here. Send us a postcard
every now and then, and let us know how you're doing up there in
the big league. Hell we all betting on you my man. We're not just
pulling for you, we're betting on you.*

XXII

As THE bus cruised on across North Dakota toward Montana
en route to California by way of Idaho, Washington, and Or-
egon, Earlene Copeland came back to sit with me for a while;
and Milo the Navigator followed her and slid in beside Joe
States, and the two of them briefed us on the upcoming dance
and theater dates in Spokane, Seattle, and Portland.

Then for the rest of the time between Fargo and Bismarck,
she stayed on long enough to add something else to what she
had been saying about what made that particular band so special. In her first interview back when she opened with the band
on Broadway, she had said what she had said about singing and
playing for the bossman even more than for the audience as
such. Not that the audience was only incidental, she had added
in another interview later on out in Chicago. Not at all. But in
this band you always played to the audience through the bossman, even in your own hometown. Even then you didn't go
out to the microphone as if to say, Hey here I am whom you've

known since I was knee high to a duck, being featured by no less than the Bossman Himself. What the hometown folks actually heard you saying was This is the way my little part of our good old hometown stuff sounds to the bossman.

I've been thinking about this stuff, Schoolboy, she said, sounding almost exactly like one of the best looking and most popular senior class women on campus talking to an ever so self-centered but likable sophomore with a high grade point average. I've been giving it some more thought, especially since we came on farther west from places like Duluth and Minneapolis, and what I was trying to say to those reporters still goes, but there is also something else that goes along with it.

What I'm getting at is—well let me first say this: People in places like New York, Chicago, and out in L.A. and Hollywood, especially back in New York, always just take it for granted that they're the ones that get to hear all of the bands at their best, and I'm not going to try to say that they don't have a pretty good case, because the bossman always works up a lot of special stuff to spring on them. And naturally when that curtain opens and they have just come back off the road everybody is raring to tear up some stuff just to let everybody know who's back in town.

New York has got to be special, she said. And so is Chi-town and L.A. But you still can't really say that this band holds stuff back for the big city audiences. Not this band. Here we are way out here and just listen to this stuff we're putting down for these folks every night. Look, what I'm saying is this. If you heard this stuff on the radio you couldn't tell where we were or what kind of spot we're being picked up from. Not from the way this band is popping.

You sure couldn't, I said. Then I said, Hey what you're talking about is exactly why some of us in the dormitory used to spend so much after hours time in the darkened radio lounge fishing the airways. And now here I am out here as a part of this crew, and, like you say, just listen to what we're laying on these people like they're from somewhere down home.

But after all, I also said as we went on talking about the mainly German and Slavic backgrounds of the people you played for in this part of the country, but after all, that's radio and phonograph records for you. That's why Milo can come up with itineraries like this in the first place. These people may be way out here but they know exactly what to expect from us.

And that's exactly what the bossman never forgets and never lets you forget, she said. So come to think of it, that's why people who want to think that he holds back on the best stuff until we hit New York just might have things backward. I never really questioned it before, she said. But now that I'm out here with him I know better, and I'd say the new stuff has to get by these people out here on the road before he'll take it to New York.

That's how much respect he has for the people we play for all across the nation, she said. And that's when Joe States said what he said. He had been nodding ever since Milo the Navigator went back up front. But now he had been awake long enough to get the point we were trying to make. And he said, This is what I told myself about all of that a long time ago, not long after we started touring and I realized that there was never going to be any letup. I said, You know what this cat's really like? A master chef that don't never intend to serve nobody no bad meals anywhere ever. And that's what I still think. If it's your first gourmet meal he wants your first impression of his stuff to convert you to his way of cooking. And if you're already converted he wants to keep you coming back for more.

And another thing about him is that he never forgets about the people out there on a big special splurge that they've been saving up to treat themselves to. He wants them to wake up the next day feeling that what they had to scrimp and save to come and hear us was worth it. That's this man and that's this band, kiddies. Take it from Papa Joe.

When we came back on board after a snack stop in Bismarck, where I picked up a book about the Lewis and Clark Expedition and also one about Frederic Remington in a souvenir shop, Earlene Copeland took her seat up front behind Milo the Navigator and across from the bossman and Old Pro once more. So as we droned on and on along the four hundred mile stretch to Billings, I read about the adventures of buckskin explorers among the Mandan Indians until I dozed off, and when I woke up because we were making a comfort stop I checked the map and we were in Montana.

In the letter along with the souvenir postcards of Home Stake Pass through the northern Rockies that I mailed to Eunice Townsend, I mentioned that I had been reading about Sacajewea (or Sacagawea), the only woman serving as an Indian guide for the Lewis and Clark party. But as we came on from Butte toward Missoula and the narrow strip of northern Idaho I was thinking about my old roommate once again.

Because when I wrote about finding a copy of the Remington book, I also mentioned that on the very first day we met, my roommate had told me about the collection of original Remington paintings and sculpture in the Art Institute of Chicago while he was filling me in on his great uncle and benefactor, an ex–9th Cavalry man whom he referred to as The Old Trooper. And what that brought back to mind again was how she used to like to tease me about him from time to time, and then I was thinking about one time in particular.

When she said, *You and the Snake. You and the Snake. You and that snake doctor roommate you used to have.*

Then she said, It's just like him to have been here and gone by the time I came on the scene. So tell me, are you sure he was who (and what) he said he was? Anyway whoever named him snake doctor just might have been on to something. Because just about everything you've been telling me about him makes me wonder. To tell the truth if I didn't hear so much about him from so many other people I just might think he was somebody you made up. And as it is he still sounds like an updated disguise for old-you-know-who in English 322.

Are you sure that's not where you got him from? she said, looking at me with a mock pout that was as irresistible as it was mischievous. And I said, What I'm absolutely sure of is that he would have been no less impressed with such jolly good liberal arts talk like that as I am. Then I said, Because according to him making things up is the name of the game.

Indeed it was. As he made so unmistakably clear when we got back around to the matter of mothers and aunts and fathers and uncles during one of our after hours sessions near the end of that first September.

He remembered what I had told him about not being able to ask Miss Tee anything about the circumstance of my illegitimate birth, and he said, All she probably could have told you was something that she finally worked out for her own peace of mind when she could no longer deny that she had gotten herself into serious trouble.

That was pretty rough stuff, fellow, he said, and as for your father, she couldn't even tell you his name although she knew it.

Not after she had made that promise to Miss Melba all on her own, he said. And I told him that I realized that at the time, and I could also have said that I had not really been interested in any details that might change the family relationship I was already used to.

But I just let that go for the time being and he said, The name that really counts in this league or any other league from now on is the one you make for yourself and likewise the fathers that count are not necessarily the ones that begat us but the ones we choose for ourselves as we need them in certain situations and predicaments as we need and choose our own personal tools and weapons.

Then he clicked on a small flashlight that he had rigged up on his drafting board and sat up and opened his notebook, and as he wrote he said, Fathers comma, and then he said, Necessity as the Mother of. Which I guess was a new topic heading because he underlined it. Then he reached across the bunk to his bookshelf and took down his personal copy of The Odyssey, *saying, Telemachia, Telemachia, yea verily the Telemachus in us all, perceived or not, acknowledged or not.*

Then he said, Listen old pardner, one's mother is whoever is there and says she is, if she does what mothers do. To most practical interests and purposes, mother is verb as well as noun. Mother is if mother does. Mothers mother you. Like Miss Melba. But fathers are somewhat a trickier matter. Even when one bears the same legal name and is the spitting image of the man of the house. Or so I would have it.

Take Telemachus, he said. What he needs and goes looking for is somebody to help him rid the premises of all those rowdy and self-indulgent suitors camping and swarming all over the grounds and stinking up the goddamn place. He needs someone who is good at just the sort of cunning stratagems the ever clever Odysseus is past master of. As for Odysseus being his flesh and blood father as such, here is what Telemachus says right up front in Book One: "My mother says I am his son; for myself I do not know. Has any son of man yet been sure of his begetting?"

Pretty strong stuff, he said closing the book. *But if you think he is putting himself in the dozens, you miss the point. Because as I see it, his most urgent concern is with the pragmatic function of fatherhood. In other words, old pardner, what this youngster named Telemachus hits the trail to find is an adequate father figure, or in still other words, someone whose manhood is worth emulating.*

I said, I know what you mean, old pardner. Because I got the point about necessity and I also knew why he said what he said about the dozens. Not only because I already knew the story of the patient Penelope even before I found out it was part of The Odyssey *but also because I had always known that those who play the game of insult called the dirty dozens place the main emphasis on the mother not the father. It is her virtue that counts. It is by implication taken to be no less sacred than that of say, the Madonna. And any suggestion to the contrary is the ultimate offense, and is almost certain to lead to a violent showdown.*

Because what is at issue is whether or not one is a son of a bitch, which is to say whether he was conceived as a result of his mother acting like a bitch or was in any case treated like one. A son of a bitch can never be certain of his father because his mother is a slut and if one's mother is a slut then her husband and one's official father is lacking in manhood and is either to be pitied or laughed at. But since he after all is not really one's father, it is still one's mother whose honor has been besmirched and must be defended.

In the game as I grew up knowing it, the dirty words as such were not actually spoken. In a sense, to play the dozens is to make insinuations that provoke one's adversary in a verbal duel to respond as if he has been called a son of a bitch outright. The insult is oblique. The allegations are signified or hinted at in an offhand and even seemingly playful manner. The game is over as soon as one of the players (i.e., verbal duelists) becomes angry, loses his composure, and begins using raw and direct epithets. Because from that point on, either might resort to physical violence.

The difference between playing the dozens and putting somebody in the dozens is in the manner. In both instances you're bad-mouthing somebody's family background by "talking about his mama." But in contrast to playing around (the point in playing the dozens), you can put somebody in the dozens as directly and crudely as you wish, depending on how eager you are to provoke a fight.

I said, But speaking of the plain old everyday facts that Telemachus was trying to find out about when he said what he said to old Nestor and also to Menelaus in the passages you just read. And he said, From Book Three and Book Four. And I said, Sometimes you think about that part of it too. So every now and then I used to wonder where my father actually was and what he did for living and for fun and all of that. But most of the time it didn't even cross my mind. Not even I might have added, during those times when I used to have to think about how lucky I was that Mr. Paul Miles Boykin was not my father. He got married to Miss Tee but as far as I was concerned that didn't even make him my stepfather.

Sounds to me as if to all practical intents and purposes, the identity of your, ahem, consubstantial father, has been mostly only a little matter of occasionally restimulated curiosity about some chickenshit gossip you once overheard and then overheard reminders of, old pardner, he said. And I said, Hey come to think of it. And he said, Whereas the Telemachus in us all is always a very urgent matter of fundamental necessity. Not curiosity, old pardner, not curiosity.

XXIII

IT WAS at the end of the last week of my fourth trip to Hollywood that I decided that the time had come for me to leave the band. I hadn't planned things that way. I just woke up that morning and realized that as much as I still liked everything about being on the road with the Bossman Himself, I also wanted to stay around town as a freelance musician for a while.

Just like that. And also postponing graduate school once more as if the ever so obvious possibility of registering as a part time graduate degree candidate at the University of Southern California (across from the Coliseum) or at the University of California at Los Angeles (off Sunset Boulevard in Bel-Air) did not exist, not only because I had always thought of doing my graduate work on an Ivy League campus, but also because I still had not made up my mind about what I wanted my graduate degree to add up to as a profession.

Which, as I was finally beginning to admit to myself by that time, was also why I had decided not to leave the band at the end of that first summer. I had stayed on then not because I actually needed more money to supplement the fellowship grant for the year required to earn a Master of Arts degree. At the time I said what I said about sticking around for a while longer to accumulate a large enough nest egg to supplement on campus living expenses and incidentals straight on through the Ph.D. program. But the fact was that I had been having such a great time going where we went and becoming a part of things, that it was already past the registration deadline before I ever got around to thinking in any specific terms at all about any given course of study in any of the several catalogs that I had brought along.

And yet even as I woke up that morning thinking about sticking around to try my luck in Hollywood for a while, I was never more mindful of Miss Lexine Metcalf and her bulletin board windows on the world of peoples of many lands and her fairy tale castle towns. Because who else if not she (as if for Miss Tee) would say, Go where you will go and you will do what you will do as splendid young men have always found their own ways of doing, wherever they came to be, however they came to be there.

Miss Lexine Metcalf to be sure. But perhaps not Mr. B. Franklin Fisher, who after all was far more given to the statistical imperatives of social engineering than to such no less patent leather than blue steel avuncularities as were to be come by around the fireside, on the storefront, and in the barbershop.

So no perhaps (or ifs, ands, and buts) about it at all for such uncles as Bud, Doc, Ned, and Remus, for whom it was only a question of whether you were game enough to risk whatever you had to lose. Not that you were ever expected to take any risk that you had not calculated. No better for any fool who went around acting as if life were a dice game. *It may be a gamble young fella but it's a matter of much more than rolling them bones and snapping your fingers.*

As for what my old roommate had to say in response to my news about leaving the band to freelance around Hollywood for a while, I expected him to approve and he did. And then he also went on to bring me up to date on how he had come to feel about what his formally certified professional training as an architect was adding up to so far.

Shelter. By all means, he wrote at one point. Shelter. Yea verily. Still should not all basic architectural decisions be predicated upon fundamental assumptions about lifestyle, which is about nothing if not the whole human proposition as such? For what was ever more human than design as such? Shelter by all means indeed and also with every means and with whatever available material. But oh the ineluctable modality of it all, whether in caves or with sticks and stones or with Bedouin skins and fabrics or adobe and brick and so on to "I" beams and plate glass.

When he wrote like that, not only could you hear his voice and the way it went with his offhand manner and sidelong glance, you could also see him sitting in his sea captain's chair at his flattened out drafting board again, because the statement he was playing around with was as much an entry for his logbook as it was a part of what was already an ongoing dialogue with you.

Ancestral imperatives, to be sure, he was also to go on to write several weeks later. *Ancestral imperatives, yes and again yes. That is not the question. As you know I've said so many times before. The question is which ancestors and what priority of which imperatives. Moreover as I've also maintained from the outset, even as the names that really matter when it comes to the determination of actual identity are the nicknames we choose for ourselves—or the ones we accept as appropriately definitive when suggested (sometimes even as a joke) by others, so it is with ancestors and their imperatives.*

The point of which I already knew from a long string of riff sessions about the Telemachus factor of fatherhood and hence forefathers, beginning back during our very first month as roommates: That vocational choices and indeed the underlying assumptions of all vocational guidance programs as such, not only *could* but absolutely *should* be called into question or in any case reexamined as a matter of course from time to time. In view of inevitable modifications in our perception of the nature of the actuality as well as the implications of things.

Which was entirely consistent with what I somehow realized that Miss Lexine Metcalf wanted me to be prepared to take in stride when she used to say what she always used to say to me about journeys the ultimate destination of some of which could not be determined until you were already en route, and also about destinations that you might not be able to recognize as such until you got there.

And as for what Miss Lexine Metcalf may or may not have known about such ever so advanced seminar, laboratory, and field project subject matter as my old roommate and I were forever playing around with, she knew what fairy godmothers always know about what fables and fairy tales are fabricated to deposit in our consciousness as if on the dynamics of time-release capsules.

Nor come to think of it, was Mr. B. Franklin Fisher himself for all his messianic devotion to social engineering for community uplift as such ever really unmindful of such legends as made the point that the ultimate goal of many pioneers and trailblazers no less than that of explorers and discoverers was to find what there was to find.

XXIV

WHEN I said what I said to Joe States at breakfast that morning, he said, Man, don't come trying to scare nobody with some old jiveass joke like that. Man, I ain't been up long enough to be dealing with no stuff like this you hitting me with. Man, I ain't even finished my first cup of coffee yet.

We were sitting in Hody's and from our booth you could see the traffic stopping and going through the intersection of Hollywood Boulevard and Vine Street. He was nursing his coffee while we waited for his ham and grits and eggs sunny side up and my waffle and sausage patties. I had finished my orange juice and was having a bowl of mixed California fruit.

Come on, man, he said, what kind of old henhouse do-do is this you putting down for me to squish my toes in this morning? And I said, Man, I'm trying to tell you. And he said, I know, man, but I just don't want to hear it. Then he said, Damn, man, you sure got some heavy stuff to lay on the bossman this morning.

And I said, Don't I know it though. I said, Man, do I know it. But man, this is one of those things. I said, Man, this is something I owe it to myself to check into. I owe it to myself to try to find out what this stuff is really like and if I can hack it on my own for a while. I don't know for how long but for a while.

That was when I told him about the recording dates that I had been asked to do with Radio Red for Decameron Records, and also about Felix Lovejoy; and when I said what I said about some of the things Eric Threadcraft wanted me to give him the go ahead to line up, he said, Like I told you that first night backstage, that's somebody on his way somewhere in this town. Hell, my man, that's your room and board right there and with some to spare. You can count on him for that already and he's just getting warmed up.

So at least I don't have to worry about you being stranded out here because you too proud to call the bossman and come back out on the trail, he said. And then he also said, I know how you feel. I really do. I'm telling you, man. I almost stayed out here myself some years ago. But man, me, I always been so much a part of this thing the bossman's got going. And then too, I guess I got too much gypsy in my soul. After all, I first hit the trail riding the rails in what old W. C. Handy calls a sidedoor Pullman car.

When we came back outside and crossed Hollywood Boulevard, we were headed downgrade along Vine and we passed the Huntington Hartford Theater, and on the other side of the street was the Brown Derby Restaurant; and up ahead was the corner of Sunset and Vine. We then crossed Selma Avenue and came on along Sunset past the ABC Studio to Music City.

I followed him upstairs and he bought a new set of mallets, and we walked on over to the NBC KRCA building, and when I stopped at the door, he knew exactly what was on my mind. So he said, Hey I tell you what, I'm going in here and call the bossman myself and tell him and ask him what time you can come to see him yourself.

And I said, Come on man, you don't have to do that. I said, It's really my responsibility. I said, I'm just going to have to face him.

But I got his point, and I waited while he went inside and made the call; and when he came back he said, So, okay you ain't got nothing to worry about. You surprised me but not

him. But hell that's another reason he's the boss. I told him
you'd be coming over during the noon hour. So there you go.
It's all in the family. I just told him you needed some time off
on your own to check out a few things and he said why not,
I'm pretty sure he knows his way around here by now and I
trust his judgment.

Which goes for me too, he said. And all the rest of these
thugs in this two-by-four outfit. So everything is going to be
copasetic with them also. Because as important as all of us
know this goddamn band is, and as pleased and amazed as everyone of us was at the way you just came right out of college
and fell in with us and all this stuff, we all knew that you were
going to have to move on after a while because there's so many
other things you got to get together besides music. None of us
know what it's going to turn out to be, but the way we figure
it music is just a part of it.

It was ten minutes to ten and he had a recording session
with a local pickup combo starting at a quarter after. So I threw
him a jab, which he ducked and tied me up in a clinch. Then
he gave me a shove and waltzed away as if to his corner of the
boxing ring. And I went back across to Music City and found
a booth and listened to six of Radio Red's latest blues releases.
Then I sampled two batches of show tunes arranged and conducted by Eric Threadcraft until eleven-fifteen and then I came
back outside and stood on the corner of Sunset and Vine and
waited for a taxi.

When I got to his suite at the Château Neuf the bossman was
listening to the transcriptions of the material we had done earlier that week. He was lying on the couch wearing one of his
navy blue polo shirts under a stone blue V neck cashmere pull-
over, gray worsted slacks, and with fleece-lined slippers instead
of the black loafer moccasins he wore to the studio. He was
also wearing one of the fancy silk skullcaps that helped to give
his always neatly dressed hair the special footlights sheen that
was one of his sartorial trademarks.

As was also usual when he stretched out like that in his dressing room or somewhere backstage during a performance, he
had his eyes covered with a neatly folded hand towel, which
he did not remove to look at me when he extended his hand

to greet me and point me to a seat by the window, and Milo the Navigator closed the door behind me and went back to the paperwork spread out on the table in the dining area.

Old Pro was operating the playback machine and also checking each bar against the lead sheet spread out on the music rack of the piano that was always a part of the bossman's furniture whenever the band was scheduled to be in any big town for three or more days. I had recognized which takes they were reviewing as soon as Milo the Navigator opened the door. It and the one that followed were two of the three we had made of a new piece called "Central Avenue Inbound," and from where I sat as I listened along with them, you could see down across that part of Sunset Boulevard to the Plush Pup Pet Shop, and on your right and across Havinghurst was the site of old legendary Garden of Allah motor court cottages, now replaced by a savings bank but once the setting for movietown off screen capers that the no less legendary movie magazine gossip columnists used to thrive on embellishing or even fabricating for people who used to be as preoccupied with the private scandals of movie celebrities as with the pictures they played in.

You could also look back up past Villa Frascati and Pandora's Box to the intersection where Schwab's Drug Store was. But Sunset Strip was out of sight around the bend in the other direction, and Beverly Hills was beyond that, and beyond Beverly Hills was Bel-Air, and then there was Westwood. Then if you turned left when you came to Wilshire Boulevard you could go all the way back to downtown Los Angeles by way of the Beverly Wilshire/Rodeo Drive shopping area and the Miracle Mile, then from the Civic Center interchange you could come down off of the Harbor Freeway and pick up Central Avenue outbound.

I didn't expect the bossman to ask me anything about what I had told him about staying in the band beyond that first summer to build up enough of a backlog for graduate school expenses, and he didn't. At the end of the second playback of "Central Avenue Inbound" he gave Old Pro the cutoff sign, but he didn't take the hand towel from his eyes. He hummed a riff phrase to himself so softly that you could hardly hear it and said, Hey let's try this, and hummed it again so that Old Pro could take it down.

Then after dictating three more phrases, what he said when he sat up and turned to me was, So you need to take some time off to follow up a few things on your own for a while. And I said, If we can work it out. And he said, We'll do everything we can as much as we hate to have you absent for any time at all. After all, you've been very nice about this whole thing of being out here with us this long without a break.

Old Pro and Milo the Navigator came over to where we were then, and Old Pro gave me a wink and hooked his arm into mine and said, You'll do just fine. And then he also said, Meanwhile how about that kid you liked in St. Louis? Scratch something or other from somewhere in Kansas. What about him, and who do you like out here that we can get on a short notice? And I said, Scratchy McFatrick in St. Louis and Jamison McLemore out here. And Milo the Navigator said, With that house combo Silas Renfroe has at the Twilight Lounge and the bossman said, Right, now that you mention it.

Then he looked at me and said, So do you like him enough to recommend him as your fill-in? And I said, Definitely. I said, He's not just a good combo man, he also does a lot of studio orchestra work around town.

And when he said, Do you think he would like to play our kind of stuff? I said, I know he would. No question about it. He probably knows most of the book already. Like everybody else in that combo, I said, and he and Old Pro looked at each other.

I don't know how long you can count on him staying out on the road I said because he has a family here. But I do know that he'd like nothing better than a chance to play with this band at least for a while, in fact for as long as he can swing it.

So let me get right on this and see if this kid can go up the Bay Area with us next week, Milo the Navigator said leaving. And the bossman stretched back out on the couch and put the hand towel over his eyes again and said, Okay and get me some samples of his latest things with Silas and also a couple of the studio band things.

Then he was talking to me again and he said, So what do you like and think I might like about this Scratchy McWhat-hisname fellow in St. Louis? And I said, Fatrick, Scratchy Mc-Fatrick. Theodore Roosevelt McFatrick. Scratchy Mac. What I like about him is that sometimes when he really gets going he executes stuff on that full bull fiddle as if it's some little old toy saw fiddle tucked between his chin and shoulder.

As for his nickname I explained that it came from the fact that he had been a child prodigy, who had begun scratching out impossible riff figures on a hillbilly neighbor's saw fiddle in the Missouri Ozarks before his family moved up into Kansas when he was eight years old. Ever so hip jazz people tend to forget how nimble fingered some of those so-called hillbilly musicians sometimes are. Never mind how sad-assed so much of that kind of singing sounds to people who prefer music for stomping and shouting and tipping on the Q.T. as played by down-home and uptown musicians, when it comes to cutting a lot of dots in a hurry there are hillbilly fiddle, guitar, and banjo players who can get up and go with the best that ever did it.

I said, You know how the show biz part of the world of music is about clowns and acrobats. Well so far nobody seems to know what to do about all of that technical dexterity of Scratchy Mack except to use it mostly as a show stopping gimmick to be enjoyed as a trapeze or contortionist act. Which he is already good enough at to become a big time headline feature right now. But working for you in this band all of that virtuosity would always have to add up to music not just novelty.

He sat up again then and said, Hey Pro this sounds like something I can't afford not to look into. If this local boy is available we'll take him up into the Bay Area and also keep him for a while longer if he would like to stick with us. Meanwhile see if Milo can get this St. Louis wonder kid to meet us in Dallas. Hell, let's go for doubles on bulls for a while.

The doorbell rang then and he said, Hey there's lunch and your name is in the pot so stick around. And when the room service staff came in pushing the cart I guessed that the cuisine was Chinese and when the table was spread the main dish he had ordered for me was moo shu pork, which was my main choice in those days, and as always he also got a special kick out of suggesting which other selections you should try and file for future reference.

The only other thing he said that afternoon that had anything to do with the fact that I was staying behind in

Hollywood for the time being was a question about how I had come to know about Scratchy McFatrick, and when I told him that Joe States had taken me to hear him, he said, Naturally, who else but?

That next morning we went back into the studio and after the second take of the revised version of "Central Avenue Inbound" he said, Hey these guys are wide awake already. These guys feel like playing some music this morning.

He started his new nightclub piano vamp, then stopped and gave the control booth the signal that he was ready to roll, then started again and kept noodling and doodling chorus after chorus with me and Joe States and Otis Sheppard until he decided which groove was exactly the one he wanted. Then when he pulled everybody else in he kept us going with one tune followed by another with only a modulation, a cue figure, and a segue in between for five numbers at the end of which he said, That's what I say about some people. They come by one day and tell you they got to split and then the very next day here they are in here playing your music like it's the main thing they were put on this earth to do. Not showboating to rub it in. Too much class for that. Just hipbone connected with the thighbone connected with the footbone stuff. So much the worse.

Then there was only time enough for one more. So he winked at everybody else and gave a signifying nod in my direction and began with a down-home meeting bell vamp as if to sic the whole band on me. Not to make me hustle and strut my stuff but in a medium church rocking bounce so that all I had to do was keep time and listen to the ensembles coming sometimes as if from the Amen corner and sometimes as if from the congregation at large and as if invoking and also responding to a big blooping tenor sax sermon by Herman Kemble, a short deaconlike baritone prayer by Ted Chandler followed by two thirty-two-bar choruses of very elegant riff shouting and carrying on after which the bossman, Joe States, and Wayman Ridgeway, got their little licks in before Scully Pittman took it up into the choir chancel from which Ike Ellis pushed it on out through the stained-glass windows and into orbit.

You guys, I said as we packed our instruments. You guys. And Joe States said, Not you guys. Us guys, every good-bye ain't gone, homeboy. Not for good.

The morning they pulled out for the Bay Area, there must have been at least twenty-five or thirty other people on hand to see them off. We were all in the patio of the Vineyard Motel, and when the bus rolled up at nine-thirty, I helped Joe States take his luggage out to the curb. And while they were loading, Ike Ellis started signifying about why I was staying in Hollywood. And Scully Pittman said, Now come on old buddy, you don't have to jive the Skull. And Moe said, If he want to get in the movies, that's his business. And Ike Ellis said, Maybe so. But only up to a point. After that, it's all our business. I'm talking about don't be letting them have you up there beating out no hot jazz with no shoeshine rag. And don't be letting them pull off all them fly clothes and smearing no jungle Vaseline on your brown velvet skin and don't be hopping no bells in no tap shoes. And don't be flipping no flapjacks like the goddamn stove is Joe States's drum set.

There was a circle of people around us laughing and nudging each other then, and Herman Kemble said, Boy, if I ever see you up there talking about Yassir Mr. Charlie and rolling your eyes and flashing your pearly teeth your natural ass is going to be my personal shit stomping ground. And when Malachi Moberly said, Hey Bloop, man, you talking to a college boy. Man, you don't have to worry about no college boy pulling no burnt cork stuff like that on his people, Wayman Ridgeway said, Hey I don't know about that. Don't be too sure. Look at what they had old Paul Robeson up there doing, and he went to more and bigger colleges than our schoolboy and on top of that he's always somewhere bragging about how radical he is and don't care who know it.

So see there, Herman Kemble said. That's why I'm telling you, Schoolboy. And I said, Ain't never going to be no days like that, Bloop. Forget it man. And Joe States said, College or no college, that's my statemate. Don't worry yourself about him when it comes to some old tired ass hockey like that. You ain't never seen this boy do anything that wasn't a credit and you never will. The bossman and Old Pro whose luggage was already on the bus pulled up in some Hollywood friend's chauffeured limousine and while Old Pro was talking to Jamison McLemore the bossman made the rounds shaking hands and chatting and kissing all of the women good-bye. Then he called me and I followed him to his seat on the bus, and he said, I know how you feel about all of this. And when I said, I don't really feel so good right now, he said, I'm not talking about that, you'll get over that. I'm talking about taking on a town like this all by yourself. I'm talking about being game and having the kind of guts you had to have to come on the road with us straight off the campus in the first place.

Milo the Navigator came in then and took his seat across the aisle and opened his briefcase and winked at me and handed him a check for me and as I stood up to go, he waited until I slapped palms with Old Pro in the seat behind him, and then he said, I know I don't really have to tell you this, but I'll just say it anyway. Out here you get Arabian nights not just every night of the year but also twenty-four hours of every day. So the special thing to remember about this town is that the fun out here is always better when you're also working. Always remember that, especially when you have to tear yourself away from something just before it gets to be as good as you think it can be if you stick around.

Everybody was in place and they were ready to roll then and I stepped back onto the curb, and as the motor idled I came back along the sidewalk to the window where Joe States sat with Jamison McLemore beside him. And when the motor revved up and the door closed, Jamison McLemore said, Man, I just got to say it again. Man, thanks for remembering me. Man, because of you I can die happy.

And as the bus pulled away all old Joe States could do was look at me and wave ever so tentatively and shake his head, not in disapproval or in bewilderment or even with any last minute misgivings as such, but only as if to say, And so it goes young fellow and so it goes in this business. I almost forgot.

When I opened the envelope on my way back through the patio, I found that the whole band had chipped in to add a substantial bonus to the already generous paycheck, and there was also a note stating that I could always draw an advance against my return any time I gave notice that I wanted to do so.

TWO

The Journeyman

XXV

I HAD BEEN on my own in Hollywood for six weeks when I was approached by Jewel Templeton as I stood on the sidewalk outside the Keynote Lounge that Sunday night. I was waiting for a taxi and behind me the fairyland cobweb red and purple neon sign blinked as its yellow border flowed, and you could still hear the music of the ongoing jam session back inside in spite of the sound of the horns and motors and tire treads of the extra heavy weekend traffic both inbound and outbound along that part of Sunset Boulevard at that always busy time of the evening.

You could see who she was as soon as the Rolls-Royce pulled up to the curb and stopped directly under the streetlight. She was driving and she was alone, and I guessed that she was about to say something because she leaned toward me smiling; and since I assumed that she knew who I was because she had probably seen me with the band, I thought she was going to ask me something about the bossman, and maybe also about why I was no longer with the band. But when I stepped forward and she said what she said, I realized that whatever else she wanted to talk to me about she was also there because she had decided that I myself was somebody she wanted to talk to.

So, here you are. Mr. Bass Master himself, she said smiling somewhat more like an infrequent backstage visitor than a movie star. And I said, Not quite. I said, Accidental apprentice at best, who may or may not be ready to become a side hustle journeyman of sorts. And she said, Some journeyman. Radio Red. Eric Threadcraft and also that many recordings with his Imperial Highness himself to begin with. Some apprenticeship. Some journeyman I must say.

The Sunday afternoon jam sessions for which the Keynote Lounge was so well known in those days began at four o'clock, and I had played until seven and picked up my check and promised to come back the next Friday night at nine. Then I had put on my light London Fog trench coat and zelin cloth porkpie hat and stepped out into the not quite chilly Southern California after dark breeze and was on my way back to my room to drop off my instrument and change clothes before heading across town. I hadn't been along Western Avenue to West Adams and then to Crenshaw in two weeks. I hadn't been on Central Avenue in almost a month.

I had seen her inside. She had been there three nights in a row, and she had come by herself each time and had sat in the same alcove sipping what looked like the same tall cold drink that I was pretty certain was only a seltzer and lime, and tapping her fingers ever so tentatively on the napkin. You couldn't see and judge how she kept time with her feet, but every now and then she would tilt her head to one side as we accented here and there.

In those days the Keynote Lounge was the kind of place whose regular patrons were always more interested in music and musicians than in movie stars, and so it attracted a significant number of movie stars, who came because they had a special interest in the music as such and also because it was a place where they could enjoy being out just for the fun of it without being preyed upon by overenthusiastic admirers and autograph seekers. In the Keynote Lounge it was the music fans, especially the record collectors (among whom were a number of movie celebrities), who were the seekers of autographs.

That was why the only reason I was somewhat surprised when I saw Jewel Templeton that Friday night was not because I had expected her to like music. It never occurred to me that she was someone that wouldn't like it. What impressed me and made me curious was that her interest was so obviously that of a serious newcomer, and I wondered whether it was professional or a matter of personal development—or maybe both; and I decided that it was not a matter of casual or frivolous exploration whatever it was.

When she came in that Friday night wearing a blue sheath and a single strand of pearls and carrying a silver fox stole, I speculated that she was dropping by on her way home from a recital or maybe a ballet or modern dance concert, and you could also tell that she had made a reservation and was expected not because she was a regular patron but because she was who she was.

She came back Saturday night for the ten o'clock show, wearing an outfit that suggested she had spent the day, and perhaps had also had dinner at some nearby place out of town, probably some place I had not yet seen but had read about in the movie magazines back in high school—or so I found myself free-associating as she was led to the same alcove as the night before.

On that Sunday she came in at 6:20, just as we were about half way into the six choruses we ended up jamming on "Royal Garden Blues"; and as soon as I saw the slacks and blouse she was wearing with a blue blazer draped over her shoulders I assumed that she had come directly from home this time and probably intended to go directly back there afterward because she was either studying a new script or was in the process of choosing one, probably about a nightclub entertainer or hostess, I found myself speculating again, or maybe a detective story with a pop or torch singer in it.

She was that close to the bandstand again then and you couldn't help being aware that she was there even when you were not looking out beyond the footlights, and suddenly I was sorry that I hadn't decided to stay on for the whole session. Not only because she was who she was but also because I always get a great kick out of playing for people who listen the way she did. I like to think of the sophistication of such people as being so cosmopolitan that they can be frankly curious or even downright square but who regard their inability to connect with something unconventional not as a question of ignorance or barbarism but simply as a matter of specific idiomatic orientation.

When I finished my last set and took my bows I smiled as I turned in that direction without actually looking at her or anybody else, but as I made my exit I did look back that way because I wanted to see her that close once more, just in case she did not show up again that next week. Then hoping that she would, I decided to sign on for every set Friday through the Sunday late show.

She said what she said as she pulled up to the curb where I was, and I answered as I did; and the next thing she said was exactly what you couldn't admit you hoped for until it happened, and I crossed my fingers. She said, If you're not waiting for anyone in particular you always need a lift in this town. And I said,

Now that you mention it, I guess I do at that. And when she said, Well then, I opened the door and braced my instrument on the backseat, and as I got in beside her and gave her my address I made a little weak crack about rolling stock.

I said, Here I am all the way out here on the western frontier without my own pony and packhorse. I'm going to have to fix that very soon. And she said, I'm sure you will, because my guess is that you're going to be a very busy fellow around these parts.

Then she turned the headlights back on and got ready to move out into the traffic, but with her foot still on the brake pedal she said, Meanwhile if you're not really in a terrible hurry because people are waiting for you somewhere, I wondered if you would mind talking with me a bit about this fascinating world of very special and wonderful music that I've been only superficially aware of all these years.

So close and yet so far, she also mumbled to herself as we waited for the light to turn green, and when I said I was not in any particular hurry to get anywhere I either promised or was expected to be, she said, Well then in that case. And when the light changed she pulled into the traffic going in the opposite direction from Vine Street.

You stopped playing early tonight, she said as we rolled on along the Strip toward the Interlude, the Crescendo, and the awnings and tables on the terrace of a place that was called Pupi's in those days.

My time was up, I said. I got started early. And when she said how sorry she was that by the time she got around to calling in to check the Sunday schedule the first session was already under way. And when I told her that she hadn't missed anything that was really special, she said she thought that what she caught of the session the night before was very special.

Especially those two friends of yours, she said then, the ones that kept playing back and forth at each other. They made a lot of difference. Their sheer delight in just playing around with the musical possibilities in each tune like that was instantaneously contagious. Where were they tonight? Are they somebody that even someone who is as uninitiated as I am is expected to know about already?

The trumpet player is Sonny Craig, I said, and the alto man is Jay Wheeler. Tonight they're working their way back east by way of the southeast rhythm and blues route (which Joe States used to call the back alley circuit). They're somebody not many people may have heard very much about if anything at all yet, but the general public just might be very much aware of them before long. Not necessarily as a team. Probably each on his own. But as kindred spirits.

The three of you really had something going up there, she said. And when I said, We did have fun, she said, The way you kept looking at each other with mock frowns and stretching your eyes and smiling each to himself as well as at each other as if you were swapping previously unrecounted anecdotes and episodes of some old yarn the outlines of which you all shared a common recollection to begin with. That was terribly intriguing and it was just fascinating to be that close to such informal but precisely controlled and relentless, yes, relentless indeed, improvisation.

I was completely taken with the fun and games elegance of it all, she said as we settled into the tempo of the traffic and came on beyond The Seven Chefs and around the bend from Hamburg Hamlet. But I also had the feeling that I was missing something because I really didn't know enough about what it was about. I could tell that something was being said very well indeed, but I didn't know what it was.

That's good enough for me, I said. So long as you have been taken with it. And that was when she said, All the same I hope you don't mind talking to me about such idiomatic things as that, because I just love to have you tell me what I should do about it sometime. Sometime when we get to know each other well enough to ask about things without feeling that I'm sounding like a tourist, if you know what I mean, she said looking at me and smiling again and I had to squint and press my lips together to keep from grinning from ear to ear.

I might as well tell you, she said, I've been doing some homework on that special world of music you work in. For personal not professional reasons, she said. Very personal reasons and by that I don't mean personal hobby rather than current production project, although I don't rule out the possibility of finding a role as an eventual consequence. I mean personal in the sense that my books and art pieces are personal. My garden is a hobby, cooking is a hobby, if you know what I mean. Anyway, what I must begin by telling you is that I know who you are because it was while I was doing my homework that I came across an item about His Imperial Highness leaving town with a local musician filling in for his regular bass player who was staying behind to work on several projects around town for the time being.

And when I said, But that was only a teeny weeny squib in a pop music rag, she said, you get used to picking up all kinds of little details like that in this town. There are people out here who make their living getting things like that put into show biz news tidbit columns for clients. And there are others whose livelihood depends on picking up on what is barely mentioned in passing and also spotting names that are merely mentioned for the first time.

Mainly I've been reading things and buying recordings, she said. And I would like to find out what you think about what I have. And I said okay and that records were the main things for getting it all together if you listened to enough of the best. Even if you were already pretty certain about what you preferred, a wide sampling of records was the best way to relate your special interests to the rest of it. Because with records you could have some of the best of all of it right at your fingertips long before you could get around to hearing enough of it live.

So I've been led to assume, she said. And that is why I would like to have your opinion of what I've come by so far. And I said, Anytime you say. And she said, What about tonight? Or do you have an early call in the morning? Maybe you could at least take a quick look-see and give me your general impression for starters. Would you mind doing that for me?

Not at all, I said. And when I also said, Tonight is fine with me, she said, Oh, wonderful. And does that mean that maybe we could listen to a few of them, too? Would you mind terribly? And when I said not at all, she said, Are you really sure it's not a bother, a presumptuous imposition? I said, Absolutely. I said, Absolutely not. I said, I would absolutely love to. And the pleasure would be mine. And she said, No angel, mine, mine, mine.

We were that far beyond the Beverly Hills Hotel then and she turned off Sunset to the right and when she had come on through the tree-lined residential streets and began winding and climbing up toward where the hillside began there was no other traffic either coming or going. So, for the time being there was only the two of us alone together in the softly purring vehicle which she steered with all of the expert ease that I had taken for granted she would.

Neither of us said anything for a while and then you could tell that there was not much farther to go as soon as she looked over at me and said what she said next.

I hope you really don't mind this, she said. I hope this is not going to be too boring for you. I'm very much aware of the indulgence I'm asking for on such a short notice. After all what I'm so newly excited about must be such old stuff to a top flight professional like yourself.

And when I said, Not all that old and not so topflight professional as all that either, if at all, she said, All the same what I'm talking about is kindergarten stuff as you well know, and I can't tell you how pleased I am that you agreed to run the risk of spending the evening having to respond to a lot of dumb questions. And when I said, We'll see about that I was thinking Jewel Templeton, Jewel Templeton, Jewel Templeton. On some level of consciousness or subconsciousness people who have earned that level of international esteem know very well that they can afford to be as square or naive-seeming as they need to be in order to find out what they think they need to know about. In fact sometimes when it suits their purpose they may even go so far as to invite condescension in order to make sure that they are adequately drilled on the fundamentals of whatever it is they're trying to get at.

No, the ones most likely to be a downright drag are almost always those ever so persistently friendly ones dead set on impressing you with how much inside stuff they already know about the music (and "the musical life" as well) as a natural result of their intimate association with other performers young and old, local and nationwide over the years.

I said, I absolutely cannot imagine you being boring about anything whatsoever, and certainly not about music. You never get away from fundamentals in music. And when it comes to the way we play what we play, I said, thinking about Eric Threadcraft, curiosity about idiomatic details comes under the heading of fundamentals.

To which she said, How nice of you to put it like that. But all the same I'd just as soon not turn out to be somebody who comes across as being all but hopelessly unfamiliar with too many things that should have been an intimate part of my life all along.

Then she said, Well, in all events, here we go. And when we leveled off again we were there and I could see the house and the trees and the dark grounds with the other hillside house shapes above the sparkling valley and the lights of that part of Hollywood reflecting against the sky. We came on through the archway and along the upcurving drive to the carport above which were servants' quarters, and I saw that she also had two other automobiles and a station wagon.

I followed her along the breezeway to the shallow steps and into the wide entrance hall, and the split level drawing-dining room opened out into the patio, the pool, and the view across the dim valley to the distant hills. Nearby, you could also see another wing of the house with a second story sundeck and steps leading down to the poolside, which I suddenly remembered having already seen in movie magazine photographs over the years.

The recordings in her collection of the great European composers, musical comedy scores, and popular standards were on the same waist-high to eye-level shelves of the white built-in, wall-length floor-to-ceiling bookcases along with the art books and portfolios of sketches for fashion, costumes, and set designs. There were no shelves from waist-level to the floor, only closed-in cabinets and drawers in which she stored back issues of magazines and some of her less important shooting scripts and a few souvenir props of early films in which she had bit parts.

Most of the recent purchases that she wanted me to spot-check and react to were on a long limed oak bench near the ultra deluxe sound system. But there were also quite a few others stacked on the rectangular glass top coffee table in front of the long tuxedo style linen covered lounge.

Just pick out something you yourself would like to hear, she said heading toward the one step up to the dining area level where the bar stood near the door to the patio and the pool. That's how I would like to begin if it's all right with you, she said. Not something for me, just anything that happens to strike your fancy. Let's start that way and then later on or maybe even some other time we can get around to some of those that I have had in mind to ask somebody about.

So when she came back pushing a highly polished brass serving cart outfitted as a portable bar I had decided to begin with the Kansas City bands, piano players, and singers, because I still enjoyed the ones I picked out as much as I did when I first heard them during my sophomore year in college, and also because having her responding to them along with me at the outset would make it easy for her to appreciate the notions that I was pretty sure I was going to try to get across about the nature and function of the traditional down-home blues in jazz improvisation and composition.

She clicked on the turntable and I handed her the first record and she adjusted the volume and came back to the cart and said, Help yourself or name your poison. And I helped myself to one jigger of bourbon over three ice cubes in a sparkling crystal glass for Old-Fashioneds and added water from the silver pitcher, and she said, Me too, and made her own and held up her glass to be touched and said, Well then so here we are. So nice of you to come. Oh, this is great fun already. Then after one ceremonial sip along with me, she said, I'll be listening upstairs as I slip into something more homelike and I'll be right back down. Meanwhile, do *faites comme chez vous*, as they say. To which I made a stage bow with my glass extended and as she turned and headed on up to the mezzanine landing I took another sip and moved back over to the bookcase again where, as I had expected, there were more novels, short stories, and plays than anything else. But in addition to the tall art books there were also some about the history of the theater, stagecraft, the history of music, and the lives of the great European composers. Biographies also outnumbered volumes dealing with special historical periods and general historical surveys.

That didn't surprise me either because I guess I had always assumed that movie people were more concerned with the daily texture of life in given time periods and places than with political and social issues or even military problems as such. After all, the characters you were cast to play might turn out to be on the side of an issue you personally opposed. Such characters had to be made as believable as the ones on the side of the issue you supported.

When I came to the section of books on travel I was not surprised that it was not very large, because I had already assumed that she kept her collection of tour guides and foreign language manuals along with her maps, atlases, and other basic reference materials in a special inner sanctum workroom somewhere upstairs, which was also where I guessed that she kept most of her books and artifacts related to American history and culture as such.

There were also travel books in the collection of international cookbooks on the shelves lining the short corridor between the dining area and kitchen. That was some few years before Samuel Chamberlain came to write and illustrate *Bouquets de France* and *Italian Bouquet*, which Waverley Root followed with *The Food of France* and *The Food of Italy*, but Jewel Templeton's kitchen library, which is a story in itself, had evolved from the same emphasis on the interrelationship of food and travel.

When she came back downstairs wearing a pale blue silk smock with off white raw silk slacks and patent leather flats, she had also combed her hair so that it was shoulder length, and she looked more like the famous screen and fan magazine personality than the no less glamorous but somehow somewhat less familiar woman who had just brought me home with her.

The woman I had met less than an hour ago outside the Keynote had in effect been a familiar all but improbably friendly stranger with whom I had instantly become involved in a very cordial person to person relationship that was as yet undefined. Now suddenly she was the Jewel Templeton you had come to know so intimately from all of the closer than life closeups, special camera angles, and sound effects that you felt that you could not only read the way her eyes and lips and nostrils reacted in a whole range of intimate situations but also how her breath already sounded before the words came.

She put her empty glass on the serving cart and stood with her left hand behind her neck, her cheek against her forearm, her hair falling around her raised elbow; and when she saw that I was following my shot of bourbon with a tall glass of seltzer she helped herself to the same, and after her second sip she said, Oh say, if you worked from the first set you've not had anything to eat since lunchtime, or midafternoon at the latest. So how about something to eat? And suddenly remembering that all I had eaten since breakfast was a hamburger with a vanilla malted in the midafternoon I said, Well, now that you bring it up.

Which was when she slapped her forehead and said, Oh my God, there is dinner! I had completely forgotten all about it. Now that's really something, I mean really. You have no idea. Not that I have a huge appetite. But mealtime is not something that often skips my mind. Unless I'm deeply absorbed in some special undertaking. So I guess I must be even more excited about all this than I realized.

The help had left at six, she told me as she beckoned for me to follow her up to the dining area, where she set two plates, but except for a few little personal finishing touches that she always insisted on adding, everything was ready and waiting.

Then I also followed along as she went on into the kitchen, and when she saw how curious I was about all of the special equipment and utensils, she said, I have accumulated all these fancy gadgets because I myself am something of a fancy cook. You have no idea what a special thing this food thing is with me, in spite of all the concern about staying thin that the mere mention of Hollywood brings to mind. I actually designed this kitchen along with my first husband, who as you probably know was a set designer and also something of an architect—or in any case a collaborating architect.

As for the size of the kitchen library, she had been given her first guide to French food and a handbook of French wines in preparation for her first trip to Europe when she was eighteen and had begun adding new and old titles before the trip was over, and before long food and wine books had become a very special enthusiasm. Her taste was basically French, but she also was almost as taken with Italian cuisine, and then came German, Polish, Scandinavian, and other European dishes; and her menu might include Spanish, Portuguese, and Latin American specialties any day of the week.

Not unlike many other people along the Pacific Coast she also ate a lot of Polynesian, Chinese, and Japanese food, but with so many outstanding Far Eastern restaurants and caterers so readily available, she had never felt the urge to try out any Far Eastern recipes at home except when among the gift packages that she received from fans from many lands there were Far Eastern food items with recipes included.

Among her special food loving friends there were, to be sure, also a number of winemakers, those in France and Italy predating those in northern California, who had in due course come to outnumber them by a considerable margin. Some of these also belonged to a special circle of "mushroom friends," many of whom also grew their own herbs and spices.

The main dish that night was neither strictly French nor Italian. She called it Escallops in Short Order and explained each step as she zipped along. The pieces of veal were already cut and dusted in flour so all she had to do was sauté them quickly in olive oil and splash in the right amount of dry vermouth and beef stock, let the gravy thicken slightly, and then sprinkle in already prepared fresh rosemary, chopped scallion, and parsley and wafer thin slices of lemon. And *voilà*, in less time than it took to play through three selections of approximately three minutes each.

She made a salad dressing of olive oil, fresh lemon juice, and sea salt in which she tossed Bibb lettuce and sliced plum tomatoes in a wooden bowl rubbed with a half clove of garlic. She said that there was a choice of a red wine, a chilled white wine, or both but that the red would go better with the cheese course. So that's how I came to have my first taste of Barolo and the cheese was gorgonzola and for bread you had a choice of crusty French or Italian rolls or you could either cut or break the French ficelles to suit yourself.

Meanwhile the records I had chosen included "Six Twenty-seven Stomp" (as in Musicians Local 627), with Pete Johnson on piano with a seven piece group of Kansas City all stars; "Piney Brown Blues," with Joe Turner singing along with Pete Johnson and several of the same all stars; "Baby Dear" and "Harmony Blues," with Mary Lou Williams on piano with her Kansas City Seven (from Andy Kirk's band); "The Count" and "Twelfth Street Rag" by Andy Kirk and the Twelve Clouds of Joy, with Mary Lou Williams on piano; "Good Morning Blues" (with Jimmy Rushing on vocal) and "Doggin' Around" by Count Basie; and "Moten Swing" and "I Want a Little Girl" by a group led by Eddie Durham, trombone player, a pioneer electric guitar player and key arranger for the late Bennie Moten and the early Count Basie orchestra.

We skipped dessert and coffee and brought the leftover wine back to the main part of the drawing room, where she curled up in what was obviously her favorite overstuffed chair and I took over the operation of the sound system; and when I said, You can go either way from Kansas City, south to the blues and New Orleans and Louis Armstrong and all of that, or east to stride time in Harlem and Duke Ellington and all of that, she said, Whatever you say, maestro. So I said, Why don't we just stick with what we already have going? And she said, Why don't we indeed?

Then she also said, May I take that to mean that you approve of what you have found so far? And when I said, No question about it and said, I can't get over finding so much of this stuff up here in these elegant hills, that was when she told me that she had been shopping from a list prepared for her by a newfound friend in St. Moritz last winter.

Believe it or not, she said, that was really the first time I ever stopped and listened to the blues as you listen to what is called serious music. I must tell you all about that because that is really what all this goes back to: the Marquis de Chaumienne, my favorite twentieth century human being. He is an extremely handsome sixty-seven-year-old French diplomat, sportsman, and patron of the arts, whose family involvement with America goes all the way back to the time of De Tocqueville, and whose knowledge of the things that make America American is absolutely staggering, especially to somebody with my conventional midwestern upbringing.

Oh I really must tell you about what happened when I finally got to meet and become friends with him over there last winter. I most definitely must and now that I think of it, I can hardly wait. But not tonight. He himself would not have me interrupt this music for that.

So we went on playing the records I had set aside. And in answer to questions that she would signal for a pause to ask from time to time, I said what I said about the infinite flexibility of Kansas City four/four, riffs, and riff chorus compositions, about stomps, jumps, and shouts, about voicings, timbre, mutes, plungers, aluminum, plastic, and felt derbies and also about how the old Kansas City jam sessions were said to be similar to and different from the ones in the Keynote.

Then to call attention to how late it was getting to be I said, And now for an example or so of the after hours groove if the time will allow. And she said, Oh by all means. And when I began with Count Basie on piano with his rhythm section of Walter Page on bass, Jo Jones on drums, and Freddie Green on guitar playing "The Dirty Dozen" from the stack that also included "How Long Blues," "The Fives," "Hey Lordy, Mama," "Boogie-Woogie" and "Oh Red," and she said, Perfect, just simply precious. I can't wait to tell the marquis about this. Oh I don't believe this really.

Your choices are among his favorite examples of what he calls the functional and therefore truly authentic American chamber music, she said. According to the marquis, whose explorations in the United States also included the back alley honky-tonks, jook joints, and barrelhouses, it was in the gin mills, cocktail lounges, and small intimate after hours hole in the wall joints that you found the twentieth century equivalent to the music you heard in the elegant European chambers of the old castles and châteaus of yesteryear.

She stood up and began moving around the room doing dance studio warmup stretches and she dimmed the lights. Then when I put the Eddie Durham octet version of "Moten Swing" on again, she came striding back in my direction with her back ever so statuesque, her shoulders square, her legs and thighs moving like a Busby Berkeley chorus girl and I began snapping my fingers and tilting my head on the diagonal.

We were facing each other like that for the first time then, and as she opened her arms she also stepped out of her flats saying, Do you know what this shoe thing is about? And when I said, What kind of old shoe thing? she said, This barefoot thing some of us have. There's supposed to be some big symbolic something about it. There are these friends of mine who insist that there is something about this kind of music that all but literally undresses them, that makes them respond as if they are or should be naked.

I don't know about that, I said, as we stood vamping in time, in place. But hey, I'm all for it in some situations that I can think of. To which she said, I hear that twinkle in your voice, young man. We stepped off and did a very nice trot and she also took her first spin very well, but when I tried to take her from a soft stomp to a cozier and groovier shuffle, she missed a beat and became somewhat self conscious, but as soon as I began snapping my fingers she picked right up and relaxed and smiled and said, I don't know. Those girls out in those places along Central Avenue seem to have their own special way of handling all this. I don't know. Some marvelous way of stylizing it without destroying the truth of it. Some way of controlling and even enhancing it in the very process of giving themselves to it.

I said, That's all right about them, lady. What you do just being yourself will do just fine. And she said, Well thank you, gracious sir. Thank you for being so consistent with the impression that I've had of you from first sight.

Then she said, I was watching you. Friday night, last night, and tonight. Did you realize you were under surveillance? and I said, Not really. I said, I could tell that you were listening to what I was playing. I was pretty sure of that, and I began to play around with certain little things just because somebody special was out there paying attention.

Well thank you again, sir, she said. I had no way of knowing that, of course, but I did like everything you played, as if with such nonchalant elegance, and I might add incidentally that I kinda like what you're doing at this very moment. And also that I am absolutely certain that I'm going to like what it is all leading up to.

XXVI

THAT NEXT morning I remembered where I was and what day of the week it was as soon as I heard the shower running and realized that I was awake and who was in the bathroom. So when I saw how early it still was, I closed my eyes again and settled back into the pillow, and when I woke up again it was half past nine.

When you rolled over and sat up with your feet on the floor, you were facing a wide picture window through which you could see the houses on the nearby hillsides and the sky fading from bright to silvery gray as it stretched away beyond Hollywood toward downtown Los Angeles. The temperature was seventy-five degrees, and there was a breeze that made the fluffy pink and metallic gray bedroom smell as blossom fresh as it was cozy.

On your left beyond the foot of the wide bed there was a glass paneled door that opened out onto the sun deck, and when I pulled on my shirt and slacks and stepped into the terry cloth slides that had been left along with the hapi jacket for me and came outside and looked down into the patio I saw Jewel Templeton in broad daylight for the first time. And I think that was probably the first time I ever crossed my fingers after the fact.

She was sitting in a deck chair by the swimming pool wearing a black bathing suit, and she had on white rimmed sunglasses and a white gondolier style straw hat with a wide red band, and on the low table at her elbow I saw a wicker basket full of mail. There were also several new books and a stack of new magazines along with two spring binders that I took to be screenplays under consideration.

When she looked up and saw me and waved I said, Movie stars sure do get up early. And she said, Old studio habits. As a rule they also turn in early.

Musicians sleep late, I said. And when she said, So I see, I said, When they can, which is not all that often, but there is always the bus and the ever so soporific open road. And before I could say what I was going to say about how early the Bossman Himself often got up, she said, Soporific is not what I've ever found any dressing room to be, not in the studio, not on a remote back lot, and not on location.

So all I said was that I imagined that directors were somewhat like bandleaders such as the Bossman Himself when it came to the hours they kept. And she said, I would not be at all surprised. After all they have everybody's part in the whole cast or band bouncing around in their consciousness. It's a wonder they ever get any sleep. But then it may well be that the difference between sleeping and waking is not the same for them as for people like myself.

Then she said, Tell Maurice what you want for breakfast and tell him to serve it out here. Meanwhile why don't you come on out and take a dip. There are trunks and clogs. Esther will bring them up.

You could hear the midmorning radio music downstairs and also the cook and the maid moving about. I looked around the airy bedroom again and peeked into the workroom, and then I looked outside again, and beyond the pool there were wide steps leading down to the level where the two tennis courts were, the white chalk lines sharp against the clean red clay, the chain-link fence interlaced with splotched ivy, the gate framed with bougainvillea. I could also see the greenhouse and a low red brick garden wall beyond which there were beds of flowers and a plot of kitchen herbs.

Somewhere nearby somebody was operating a power mower, which you could hear beyond the radio and the voices downstairs. And you could also smell the freshly cut grass and the lawn chemicals in the breeze and see the hillsides in that direction and that part of the sky getting clearer and clearer as the valley mist became thinner and thinner. *California, hey California.*

The water was just right and I swam half of the first lap under the surface and finished with the Australian crawl and paused and came back showing off my three beat American crawl. Then I did a racing turn and a few rolls and a few backstrokes and breaststrokes and climbed out and dried myself and draped the towel around my neck and came along the poolside to where she sat smiling and holding out her hand.

We touched cheeks backstage style, and she stood up and came with me to the table under the umbrella where Maurice, a graying pale tan Creole from Louisiana, served me a glass of orange juice and a bowl of Polynesian fruit to be followed by a two-egg ham-filled omelette and toast. All she had was a cup of tea with lemon, and when I finished we came back to the deck chairs, and that was when she told me about being between pictures.

From the gossip columns I already knew that she had been between husbands for the past five years and that she was also between regular escorts. Her last divorce was number three. Her last publicized romance had ended before she flew to Europe in the late autumn of the past year to spend time on the Côte d'Azur and Provence before going on by way of Paris to Switzerland for the winter season.

She had not decided on a next movie script yet. She was not in a hurry, because in the meanwhile she had become involved with a very special personal project that had grown out of a friendship she had come to have with the Marquis de Chaumienne, who had given her a new insight not only into her profession but also into herself as an American and as a twentieth century person.

I told her about the deal I had with Eric Threadcraft, and we talked about Felix Lovejoy; and she wanted to know about all of the clubs that I had been working in around town. Then she asked about the records I had played on with the band, and that was when I started telling her about how I came to be in the band instead of graduate school and about Joe States and Old Pro; and when I came to the Bossman Himself she said that she had always known that he and Louis Armstrong were in a class above and beyond everybody else but that it was not until recently that she had begun to understand why.

That was all she said about that at that time, and then she began to tell me about some of the things that had happened back during her early days in show business, and as she settled back recalling the names of faces and places it was not long before you realized that she was reminiscing perhaps as much for her own benefit as for the ever so casual orientation of an acquaintance of less than twenty-four hours.

Because what she was not only recalling and relating to me but also in effect if not intent sharing with me was not at all the usual movie magazine personality profile platitudes about how you pick up on the tricks of your trade on the road to fame and fortune. What she had begun remembering herself back into was her innermost sense of the texture of the existential quest for your personal definition, for which public recognition is often mistaken perhaps by most people and certainly by press agents.

As I sat listening to what she went on to tell me about how the stock companies used to make their way across the country, I was also thinking about Milo the Navigator, who when he used to say "fifty roads to town" also as often as not meant fifty roads to fifty towns, all of which were only way stations en route to the castle town that was your ultimate personal destination.

Which is why when she finished what she was telling me and patted me on the thigh before turning back to her mail and magazines, what I closed my eyes and nodded off thinking about was the Bossman Himself, whose castle town destinations were exactly the same matter of the same maps and mileage charts as those of Milo the Navigator, to be sure, but who even so would also have been described by my good old best of all possible freshman and sophomore roommates in terms of the barnstorming troubadours of the yesteryears of storybook times.

When I realized that I was awake again and that I could hear the horns and motors in the distance because the sound of the nearby power mower was gone, I could tell that the sun was now directly overhead even before I opened my eyes. You didn't have to open your eyes to know that you were still in Southern California either, but even so there was something about the hillside breeze and the smell of the freshly cut lawns and freshly trimmed shrubbery that made me feel the way I used to feel every time I walked across the campus during the first term of my freshman year.

I said, California, hey California. But I didn't make any sound or move my lips because I knew that I was being looked at. I kept my eyes closed a little longer and then opened them and saw her smiling at me and wondered if I myself had been smiling without realizing it so I tried to wink but all I could do was squint and grin, and that was when she reached out and meshed her fingers in mine and said, Well then, shall we go back upstairs for a while?

We didn't come down for lunch until the middle of the afternoon. It was a chicken salad lunch with Bibb lettuce, a platter of fruit and a napkin covered wicker serving basket of warm French rolls. The wine was Pouilly-Fuissé, and when she held up the bottle and I pronounced the name to her satisfaction she smiled and touched my arm and said that my musical ear stood my school book French in good stead. And that was also when she promised to have me sample such lighter weight red wines of the Beaujolais region as Fleurie, Moulin-à-Vent, and Juliénas before moving on to the vintage Burgundies and Bordeaux.

After lunch we settled down in the living room area and went on playing the records left over from the night before, and for a while she closed her eyes and kept her own time. But when I looked again she was taking her clues from my foot tapping and finger snapping, so I began naming dance steps that went with the rhythm, tempo, and the beat of each number; and when we came to Jimmie Lunceford's "I Wanna Hear Swing Songs" she stood up for me to show her how to do the Florida Off Time, after which she was also up for the steady four/four velocity of "Time's Awasting" but not for the all out killer diller clip of "Swinging on C."

She led me over to the deep tuxedo couch then and sat in the corner facing me with her finely shaped and carefully tanned calves and ankles tucked under her, and after lighting a cigarette she told me what she decided about us.

I do hope you will take this in the way that it is certainly most sincerely intended, she said, because I was never more serious about anything in my life. So here goes. I've decided that there is something about you that I would not like to treat as a pleasant but brief encounter.

I must have said something in response, and I can think of a lot of things that I could have said; but I don't remember anything at all about what I actually said or what I did. I don't remember that I was really surprised. So I think that I must have felt the way you feel when you're playing a game (or doing anything for that matter) and you become so taken up with doing what you're doing that you forget that there is any prize or reward involved. Anyway, the next thing I remember her saying was what she said about my eyes.

Maybe it's the way they always shine, she said. And curiosity and sincerity are only the beginning of it. There is humor and patience that add up to a precocious wisdom. Then she also said, I'll just bet you something. I'll bet you were always everybody's little bright-eyed boy back in your hometown. Whether they liked you or not, she said. I can just tell about things like that. After all, who was I if not little Miss Sparkle-eyed Goldilocks of Small Ridge, Wisconsin?

That was that Monday afternoon. I moved my things into the studio apartment above the garage that night.

XXVII

THAT TUESDAY morning she went down and came back with the breakfast trays and we ate in bed and sat propped against the pillows talking, and that was when she told me about the Marquis de Chaumienne. She described him as having classic Gallic features, a deep almost leathery ski-slopes-and-shipboard tan, neatly clipped iron gray hair, and a military mustache. He was of medium height, trim, elegant, his bearing casually correct, his presence magnetic; and as soon as you heard him speak you could tell that he retained his charm and authority in many languages. He spoke nine fluently and not only was he at ease (and among acquaintances) in most of the capitals of the world, he also knew his way around the countryside, the back country, and the back alleys.

She had finally met him that fateful night last winter in Saint-Moritz. The American born wife of an Italian film executive had introduced them during a gala in the grand ballroom of the Palace Hotel. He had bowed from the waist and kissed her hand and held it smiling, and she still couldn't get over what followed. He had already known who she was. Not only that but he had taken her in tow immediately and had started telling her all about herself as a screen actress, naming her roles and discussing them in a way that made her want to rush out and see them all over and over again.

When she laughed and told him that she was quite certain that none of her producers and directors had ever been seriously concerned about or even remotely conscious of most of the implications, overtones, and relevancies he was suggesting, he had only smiled and folded her hands in his, kissed her again on both cheeks, and said, Of course of course, producers were in the business of manufacturing for the general public but that it was precisely in the process of turning out clichés, popular romances, and pulp adventure yarns, things of that sort, that they sometimes wrought far better than they ever really intended. But there were, after all, many truly gifted craftsmen in the film industry, and they sometimes went beyond their immediate popular commercial orientation and became literary artists without ever really intending to do anything except the same old thing a little better, or maybe only a little sleeker.

The two of them strolled arm in arm along the edge of the dance floor and left the ballroom and made their way to the bar, where he seated her in a quiet corner and ordered whiskey. Then looking at her again, the mature approval of his knowledgeable eyes suddenly reminding her of the producer who had chosen her for her first starring role, that warmly personal way he had of putting you at ease so that you could function at your best. He talked about the marvelous and marvelously curious American girls in the stories of Henry James; and he told her that she herself was another one of what Henry James had called "the heiress of all the ages," in a sense perhaps even Henry James himself had not visualized. Certainly she projected a dimension of earthiness that he didn't find in James's ever so inquisitive and adventuresome American princesses. Also, whatever her studio press agents really meant by their glib characterization of her as a sex symbol, she was in effect an American-born heiress of all female fundamentalities from Eve to James Joyce's Anna Livia Plurabelle.

She forgot all about what was happening in the grand ballroom, and they spent the rest of the evening in the bar talking about what he called the archetypal plurabilities of the all-American Anna Livia Plurabelle. *Which is why back in her room she had dreamed of playing two-handed then four-handed piano duets with Henry James for James Joyce who suddenly looked like Abraham Lincoln, Henry James playing the right hand keys, herself playing the left.*

The next morning he had taken her skiing, and they had eaten lunch on the sunlit terrace looking out across the town and the scattered settlements along the wooded valley of the upper Engadine. There was a usual elaborate buffet and they helped themselves to soup and shellfish salad and sat sipping champagne until the middle of the afternoon, the conversation ranging from the Alpine terrain before them to his boyhood fascination with the romance of the Rocky Mountains and life in the old American West, which had also led him to his long-standing special interest in American horse breeding. He was especially interested in that all-American circus performer, cow pony, and fourth of a mile racer known as the quarter horse. He still scheduled occasional trips to California to coincide with the quarter horse racing season.

He also talked about the western railroad lines that he had come to know in his youth, and when he told her about his several visits to Indian ceremonials near Gallup, New Mexico, he had promised to take her to see the priceless kachina dolls in the private collection of a literary friend of his the next time he and she were in Paris at the same time. He himself had begun by collecting firearms, traps, and tools of the old fur trappers, traders, and mountain men. Then it was the hardware and equipment of the range and cattle trail.

So when she went to dinner at his chalet two nights later she was not surprised by the number of western objects in evidence, but she was absolutely amazed at how by displaying them on the walls and about the drawing room as he did, he had transformed such homespun workaday nineteenth century American ranch items as branding irons, corkscrew horse-tethering pins, bits, rowels, stirrups, bullwhips, lariats, and various strands of barbed wire into artifacts with a patina that was both prehistorical and *dernier cri*. The collection of branding irons and tethering pins was especially impressive and eye opening. In fact she was already reacting to them as art objects before she suddenly realized what they had actually been designed for.

She was also immediately impressed with the Marquise de Chaumienne, a stunning soft spoken woman in her early fifties, whose tawny hair was streaked with silver and whose clothes made you conscious all over again of the kind of elegant women who produced so many great French and Italian fashion designers.

There were two other dinner guests, a young Italian contessa whose family manufactured musical instruments and parking meters; and a Danish baron who had once competed in Olympic ski events. The marquise had not been at the gala. She and the contessa, who was also her houseguest, had just returned from Amalfi by way of Milan that morning.

When she thought about it on the way back to her hotel afterward she realized that she would not have been surprised if the food had been chuck wagon chili or pigs' feet, black eyed peas, collard greens, and corn bread or red beans and rice. But what the menu really featured was the cook's special dish of game birds and a fine red wine from the marquis's vineyard in Médoc. But after the cheese course the marquis had led them into another room promising her that along with coffee and Armagnac there would be some delightful messages from the United States to the world at large.

The first thing you noticed was the screen, so you looked for the projector but then you also saw the recording and playback system. So when he turned the sound on she had thought that he was tuning in on some special American broadcast over one of the State Department shortwave radio channels that European diplomats and foreign correspondents listened to and she had not known whether to expect a special news roundup or some new high level policy statement. So much for my estimate of the situation, she said.

What came out of those huge high powered speakers was the absolutely startling downbeat of a jazz orchestra, which broke into something that sounded like the blues and a war dance at the same time, the trombones hoarse and rowdy, the saxophones moaning, the trumpets shouting and screaming, the rhythm pounding as much like the beat of a transcontinental American express train as the beat of movie soundtrack tom-toms.

She was flabbergasted. It was as if the whole evening had suddenly become some kind of carefully prepared European joke about American jukebox culture or something or other. She closed her eyes and held on to herself and made up her mind to be amused. But what she saw when she stole a look around the room was the baron patting his feet in all seriousness, the young contessa moving her head from side to side and snapping her fingers soundlessly but confidently. The marquise sat smiling, rubbing her palms along the arms of her chair, her eyes twinkling with excitement. And as for the marquis, himself, he was pacing back and forth tapping his stomach with the flat of his hand. She settled back relieved. But before she could get her attention focused on the music as such again, the first selection was over and they all had turned toward her smiling and applauding.

Since that night she had been spending as much time trying to learn all she could about American music as she spent trying to find a new screenplay. She had passed all the next afternoon at the chalet listening to recordings, air checks, and transcriptions, and asking questions. And on her way back to Hollywood she had stopped off in New York for fifteen days shopping for the selections on the list the marquis had made up for her and also making the rounds on all of the nightspots he had mapped out for her.

I called him last night she said. While you were picking up your things, she said, getting out of bed and standing on her fine tan legs and insteps with only the transparent shorty shorts between me and her and the window. It was eleven o'clock and she wanted to swim and spend some time in the sun and eat lunch on the patio before going down into Hollywood to keep several appointments. I was going to spend the afternoon practicing and then I was going to take a long nap before getting dressed and taking the Ford runabout that she called her auto incognito to meet Eric Threadcraft at Hotel Watkins across town on West Adams. She went into the dressing room and came back wearing a very brief black two piece outfit from the Côte d'Azur. All I had to do was step out of my pajama shorts and into the swim trunks.

He's at his place in Médoc, she said. He's back from some mission in the Far East. We talked about you. He never ceases to amaze me. He knows exactly who you are, and thinks you're awfully good. He has those last things you did with the band. He gets advance promotion copies of everything along with the reviewers and disc jockeys. You didn't tell me you had an original piece coming out.

I haven't heard any evidence of it, I said. I know we made some tapes, but you never know what they're going to use. Anyway it's not really all mine. It's just one of my riffs that the Bossman Himself told me and Old Pro to set up for the band.

He says you have true talent for thinking in terms of the whole band, she said. He says the contours of your musical personality are already becoming distinctive. And I must also tell you that he's especially pleased that my first jazz musician friend is as he puts it bass clef.

Did I tell you what he said about me and the bass clef that first night? she said. He said what he said about me and Daisy Miller and then he said but as great as Henry James was, he was a trifle treble for the likes of me. He also said I had ragtime in my ways, blues in my bones, and spirituals somewhere deep down in my soul.

Then later as he was driving me back to my hotel in the sleigh, there I was all wrapped up in my most elegant mink and wearing my most sparkling Cartier carats and the most expensive coiffure that money can buy in Saint-Moritz and he calls me one of Ma Rainey's children, one of the sparkling daughters from the muddy waters of the upper Mississippi. The blue-eyed first cousin to Bessie, Mamie, and Trixie Smith.

And I said, The Big Muddy. Hey, Wisconsin is on the upper Big Muddy as is Davenport, Iowa. I'll take you over Bix Beiderbecke any day.

XXVIII

DURING MY first months in Hollywood, Eric Threadcraft and I did most of our work in the canyon view hillside apartment that he always referred to as his old air conditioned woodshed with drafting tools. We hardly ever went down to the record-ing studio to rehearse anything either then or later on until he was satisfied that all of the parts of whatever we were working up arrangements on were ready for a full band run-through just before the first official takes.

In the beginning we actually spent most of the time talking about what he liked so much about the Bossman Himself and his band, which he said was always one and the same thing with his music in much the same sense as Picasso and his pal-ette and easel were the same as his painting. When you said Picasso you meant the paintings. When you said the Bossman Himself you meant the music.

It was also during that time that he used to like to come along every now and then when I made the rounds to the spots across town along and off West Adams and along and off Cen-tral Avenue. And nothing pleased him more than being invited to sit in on piano on occasion here and there. To which he always responded not with a solo but by vamping and comping not only to avoid making himself a target in a cutting session but mainly because that way he would go on listening as the arranger-composer and conductor that he was (but admitted only to an apprenticeship to).

Hey fellow, if only I had grown up having to earn my way into sessions like those, he always said afterward. Hey wow! Man, there's no telling. Because so much of this wonderful stuff depends on nuance and scruple. The idiomatic nuances one absorbs growing up and the scruples peculiar to the con-vention from which your definitive aesthetic judgments are derived. Hey fellow, I'm talking about growing up learning how to break the proper rules properly and mispronounce the right words correctly because you are not so much taught as conditioned to know that something goes not like that but like this.

But the main thing during those first weeks and months was what I could tell him about being as close as I had been to the Bossman Himself. Tell me. Tell me. Tell me, my man, he started saying at the very outset, and as much like an ever so enthusiastic amateur as he almost always must have sounded to some people, as soon as you stepped into his picture

perfect streamlined workshop, you could see that his collection of recordings, band equipment, and memorabilia and
his files of articles and photographs were those of a professional whose dedication to his métier was longstanding and
comprehensive.

Naturally I'm already pretty much clued in on the vital statistics, he said. Man, just wait till you see some of the background
stuff I've been picking up from the Washington and Baltimore
of his boyhood days and the years of his apprenticeship. Hey
fellow, it turns out that there were fantastic piano players all
over that Potomac and Chesapeake area in those days. Some
with formal training from the conservatories and others who
could play anything by ear as soon as they heard it and run variations on it for an encore. And then there were those TOBA
showcase theaters featuring all of those headliners from New
York and everywhere else. Man, don't let anybody try to give
you the impression that there was anything provincial about
that Washington and Baltimore scene of those days.

And don't forget how those Washington people felt about
their schools and colleges, he also said. And then he said,
okay, so I know that our man didn't go to college and I also
know that it turns out that there was no college and certainly
no conservatory for him to go to. But I would like to talk to
you sometime about music in those colleges. I know about
the choirs, the so-called jubilee singers and the groups singing
spirituals, but what about our kind of musicians? I really hope
we can get into that sometime.

Anytime, I said, anytime at all. So let me just say this about
it now. There were college dance bands as well as marching bands for parades and ceremonies. But what has always
counted with the dance bands is not the music department
but the road bands: what you heard them doing in person, on
broadcasts, and on records was what you had to contend with
no matter what was happening in formal courses in the music
department.

There you go, fellow, he said. Man, that tells me a lot already
because it's just like what happened in painting and literature.
Contemporary painting didn't come from any of those Paris
academies but from people like Cézanne. And current fiction

didn't come from what was being taught in the universities but from people like Joyce and Proust and so on. Oh say but this is going to be just great. And great fun in the process.

Things got under way before the end of that same week. He agreed to orchestrate a portfolio of twenty musical comedy hit tunes for one of the several recording studio bands he worked with from time to time, a thirty-five-piece all-purpose outfit that included the string section of violins, cellos, and also a harp. He was also going to conduct and I was going to be his main man in the rhythm section.

As special assistant to the arranger-conductor, my job was to go by his apartment and listen to what he had in mind and supply the bass line and also make suggestions about the overall treatment that he came up with for each selection. The main thing he wanted from me this time around was the beat. He was gearing everything to that he said, and not even the band itself would know what was getting to them. And that was also when he said that it was what I could do for his left hand that would make me his right hand man in the studio.

So, here we go, fellow, he said on the phone when I checked in with him that morning. It's not the World Series, but it's not bush league either. And I said, Hey man, I'm a rookie in this stuff. Man, I need all the spring training and exhibition workouts that I can come by in this league.

Look, fellow, this could very well be the beginning of one hell of a team, he said. I hope so, because that way I could also count on having you there to save me from any obvious ofayisms. Among a few other things, he said. And when I said, Come on, man, he said, I know what you're going to say, but I want your ear on this stuff all the same. I'm talking about nuance and scruple, man, remember?

All I said when he said what he said the next time around was what I've been saying for as long as I can remember. He said, The only question is how long you can stand to be involved with this much of this kind of stuff. *And I said, As far as I'm concerned it all goes with the territory, my man. Always did and always will. No less than newsprint, fashion magazines, run of the mill movies with popcorn. I said, also remembering myself window shopping along Dauphin and then Royal Street in downtown Mobile, Alabama, and how the current songs you heard not only from the mechanical megaphone in front of Jesse French Music Company but also in the department stores always went with the gas fumes and the sound of the traffic and the latest styles on display in the haberdasheries and sporting goods show windows and with the blue steel fairy tale glitter and smell of drugstore counters and soda fountains.*

If you know what I mean, I said. And he said, I do. I do, my man, I do. In other words pop stuff is really urban folk stuff. That's precisely what Tin Pan Alley has always been about. City stuff, all the way from the street corner and the hole in the wall and after hour joints to vaudeville, the road shows and the palatial showcases during the days of the annual Follies, Scandals, and Vanities and so on to the Hit Parade charts.

Two weeks later we were ready to start recording, and when I signed in at the studio that Monday morning he was already there, and so were most of the band members. They were laughing and talking as they settled into place and got ready for the sound check, and he was in the control booth reading the *Los Angeles Times* with Felix Lovejoy, the popular local radio host and record producer who was now working his way into the movie business, peering over his shoulder.

When Eric Threadcraft looked up and saw that I had found my place and was all set up, he raised his baton and waved for me to join them, and the three of us slapped palms and went through our new buddy-buddy greeting routine and he said, So let's drop it on them, teammate. And I said, If you say so, maestro. And when Felix Lovejoy, whose nickname was Felix the Cat as in the old funny paper and silent movie cartoons, said what he said, shortening maestro to mice as Ernest Hemingway had done in an article I had read in *Esquire* magazine back during the fall term of my freshman year in college, Eric Threadcraft said, Me with my Cat with the Golden Paw on the one hand and my Cat with the Golden Fiddle on the other.

Then as he and I came on back out to the bandstand, he hooked his arm in mine and we went over and slapped palms with Ted Ripley, who was the drummer on that session and who had only recently come back into town after four weeks in

Las Vegas. Then before heading for the podium he said, Mice yeah mice, hey mice. So let the Cat get to plucking away and just listen to how the mice will play.

Every section was tuned and waiting then and he opened the first score and called out the folio sequence number and raised his baton, and from the very first rundown, everything went along so well that by break time we were ahead of schedule. He stabbed the baton at me playfully and turned and almost ran to the control booth for the playback. Everybody else headed outside to the rest rooms, the telephones, the vending machines and/or snack bar.

Ted Ripley overtook me on the way to the newsstand in the snack bar, and started telling me about the job he had just finished in Las Vegas. And as he talked lowering his voice and cutting his eyes about him, screwing up his face and holding his stomach as if the memory itself were enough to knock him out all over again, I remembered meeting him the night the band opened at the Palladium on my first trip to town.

He had come backstage to talk with Joe States after every set, and I had also spotted him in the second row at every concert we played in Southern California that time around, his lips moving, his head bobbing, his eyes never leaving the stage. He owned every recording that Joe States ever played on, and he knew each arrangement note for note. He had the same drum set as Joe States, some of it once owned by Joe States himself; and when he played he moved his elbows like Joe States, holding his head at the same angle, his ears cocked, his eyes narrow, even when he was smiling his stage smile, even when he was being nonchalant. Sometimes on upbeat numbers he would forget and close his eyes and hum to himself as if gritting his teeth, but even so he kept his tempos as steady as a metronome and he was always right there with something to go with anything you tried.

So how do you like it in there this morning? he said as we moved from the newsstand to the Coca-Cola machine. And when I said, Pretty smooth hustle so far, he said, Man, like why not? With the stuff we're laying down for them. But I also mean what do you really think of this kind of gig? he said making a face suggesting a mild cringe. And when I said, It's all right. It's fun, it's interesting, he said, Hollywood stuff, man, and looked as if he could taste it. Cocktail lounge sonatas, soda fountain concertos, plush after hours joint whiskey sipping *études*. Man, you can shuck your way through all that stuff. Then he said, But what the hell I'm a pro and I do have eyes for the kind of checks that come from this scene.

And that was when I told him that I liked that kind of music for what it was. Because I did and I still do. I don't have anything against cocktail lounge music. On the contrary, I liked the idea of hearing myself on the sound systems not only in swanky cocktail lounges but also department stores, lunch counters, and all of the other places of the workaday world. And then there were also all of those homes of all kinds that kept the pop music radio stations tuned in almost all day, almost every day.

Speaking of being a pro, I said, to me this is just another dimension of the trade. And he said, Hey that's cool with me, man. I can see you know what's happening. And that's what I like about that Eric. Hey that Eric knows what he's doing. That helps, if you know what I mean. He's not kidding himself. That's the difference. He knows exactly where it all goes. That's why in my book he's the greatest thing out here. I mean really. I mean you've got to hand it to him. He's got it all working. I mean like he can hear from blues to bop, and he can chart them from heads to Bach, Beethoven, and Brahms. From twelve bars to twelve tones. Hey and he knows who to get help him swing them.

By six o'clock that evening we had completed all the takes and retakes, and after the others had packed up and gone, Eric Threadcraft, Felix Lovejoy, and I sat together in the control room and listened to the retakes of the first three tunes again and decided that they were as good as we had hoped. Then the three of us came outside into the still early twilight brightness of that time of year in Hollywood, and I stashed my instrument in the auto incognito and as we headed down the north side of the sloping sidewalk, Felix Lovejoy said, It's my news so it's my treat.

He took us to a place across from the Vine Street Brown Derby, and outside the window where we were seated you could also see the Huntington Hartford Theater and beyond

Selma Avenue there was the local American Broadcasting Company station. And farther on up along Sunset Boulevard you would come to the Palladium, where the two of them had first heard me play in person.

The waiter who had seated us came back and took our orders and as he turned and started for the bar, Eric Threadcraft said, And now the news. And I leaned forward and cupped both my hands to my ears and that was when they told me that the contract that they had been negotiating for a full length feature movie score was finally in the bag.

In this bag, my man, Felix Lovejoy said, and opened his briefcase and took out two movie scripts and Eric Threadcraft took one and pushed the other toward me as Felix Lovejoy went on to say that all we had to do was read the story and think about it and then go back through it scene by scene and knock together something that would put the audience in the groove that the director was going for. And Eric Threadcraft said, We're going to give them a different kick to get on, and the thing is to get them on it before they realize what's happening. Of course we could put out a manifesto and dare the smart set not to be up to date, but you don't have to do that with the kind of music we've got.

I said, I know what you mean, man. And I did, but as he and Felix Lovejoy went on talking about the actualities of feature film production all I did was look at the title and studio logo. I didn't even try to skim the first page. I didn't want to start thinking about the actual work until I could settle down by myself. I was not even going to mention anything about it to Jewel Templeton until I had done that.

You could tell that Eric Threadcraft was already familiar with what the project was about (and perhaps also with earlier drafts) by the way he flipped through his copy of the script while Felix Lovejoy made scratch pad notes from several documents in his briefcase. *I took another sip of the tall drink and looked outside at that part of Hollywood again thinking: Me too, this time. This is the way it happens when it is happening to you.*

Oh boy, I heard Eric Threadcraft saying. I can hardly wait to get going on this baby. And I said, When do we have to start? And he said, I wish we could start tonight, but that's just it. Looks like I'm going to have to be tied up for at least the rest of the month doing what I still have to do on all that fantastic stuff we laid in today. And I do mean fantastic, he said. Fabulous. So I'm afraid that's my situation as of now, you guys.

But when I asked how much time we were going to have he said, Plenty of time. No sweat on time as yet. It's just that I really can't afford to let anything intrude on the current stuff in progress. So why don't you just check it out and see what you can come up with for a start. In the meantime, just don't give me any hints until I'm free to turn my undivided attention to them.

Just read the script for the story and make your own musical response to the action, beginning with atmosphere. Just remember it's how you feel about the scene as well as the people in the action that really counts. Don't bother yourself about any of the technical stuff. That's just routine. That's the last thing. Any studio hack can take care of that in his sleep. How many bars here? How many bars there? That's all that is.

So on my way back up into Beverly Hills later on that evening I couldn't keep myself from thinking that my Hollywood gamble was paying off, and that I had reached another landmark. But even so I also realized that I still didn't know what my ultimate destination really was.

XXIX

I READ THE script in the garage apartment that night and did not bring it into the main house, because I liked the story line and I was already beginning to have a strong sense of the overall atmosphere that the music had to generate, but I wanted to go back over everything scene by scene at least two or more times and then read the novel before talking about it with Jewel Templeton or anyone else.

So all I said about it during breakfast at the poolside the next morning was that Eric Threadcraft had asked me to start playing around with some ideas for a new project that he and Felix Lovejoy had lined up for us as soon as he was done mixing and editing the material that we had finished recording the day before. I didn't say anything about a film score; and she didn't ask for any details, because she wanted to tell me her own news.

I, too, have myself a new project, she said. So what do you think of that, Mr. Studio Pro? And I thought she had finally agreed to make another movie, but it turned out to be a trip to New York to see new Broadway plays.

Studio business, she said. They called me this morning to remind me. I hadn't really forgotten about it, but somehow the dates had slipped up on me. I was thinking in terms of next Tuesday and it's really tomorrow.

Through the weekend, she said, and when she said, Esther and Maurice will be on part time, but if you need them for anything don't hesitate to call on them, I said, If it's all right for me to use the kitchen I'll be just fine on my own, and they can just check by at their leisure.

And she said, That's no problem, I'm sure, since they both like you so much. Believe me, I've never known them to be like this about anybody else, star status notwithstanding.

I pretended to duck behind my forearm as if from a brickbat and said what I said to change the emphasis back to her trip. I said, Hey meanwhile maybe there'll be enough spare time for you to get around to some of the music spots. And she said, That would be a wonderful bonus, but I'm not counting on it. They choreograph every move you are to make on missions like this. It's no junket. Or rather it's their junket not mine.

What a shame, I said, but at least you don't have to feel bad about missing the Bossman Himself. He's out on the road and won't be back for months.

Then when instead of making any mention at all of who was actually going to be where around town during the time she was going to be there, I said I hoped it turned out to be a good trip, she said, Oh I'm certain of that. I'm not really counting on the stage, but there are always the gallery and museum circuit. The fact of the matter is that the people who will have me in tow may be ever so deeply involved in the production and distribution end of this business, but when you come right down to their personal preferences they'll take still pictures on canvases over moving pictures on celluloid any day.

She took off for New York early that next morning, and I stayed in and practiced until midday. Then I drove down to the Pickwick Bookstore on Hollywood Boulevard and found a copy of the novel that the script had been ever so freely adapted from. I wanted to find out how much of the atmosphere evoked by the flow of the author's words on the page had been retained, missed, or deliberately left out by the scriptwriters. Because I was pretty certain that whatever the case, if the author was any good at all his narrative voice as written would of its very nature suggest sound track music as the script as such could not, or at any rate had not. I had not talked to Eric Threadcraft about it yet, but my assumption or working notion was that the sound track should help make the audience feel about the people, the situation and action being projected on the screen the way the storyteller's voice on the page made you go along with how he felt about whatever he was telling you about.

I was almost halfway through the three hundred page novel and was taking a nap on the couch in the drawing room when the phone rang that night. The first play was over and she was back at the Sherry Netherland with a few minutes to spare before changing into what she was going to wear at a party at the Plaza.

The first play was only so-so, which was about all she expected it to be. But even so there was as always nothing like being back in a Broadway audience attending a live performance, because along with everything else you shared with regular New York playgoers, there was also the fact that it put you back in touch with your craft and made you feel not only like an apprentice once more but also as if you were always an apprentice/journeyman no matter how many times you've seen your name up on the much bigger and brighter marquees of the Times Square movie showcase theaters of those days.

Anyway the visit was off to a good start, and was bound to get better no matter how the other two plays turned out. It would be nice to see something that you liked well enough to recommend to the studio of course. But she had agreed to come east not because she herself had any special interest in screen adaptations of Broadway plays. She had always preferred adaptations from books, she said. And I said, I think I know exactly what you mean. But I didn't mention the book I was reading, because I still was not ready to tell her what I was getting into; and that was when she said when you come to New York from Hollywood on any kind of visit it was always like coming back to the seat of empire from one of the far-flung outposts. Then she also went on to say what she said about the red carpet treatment in New York being an absolutely indispensable part of what being in demand in Hollywood added up to.

It was time for her to begin the stroll across Fifth Avenue and Central Park South to the Plaza then, and she remembered that I was going to be working at the Keynote that Thursday night and Saturday night. So she said her next call would be during the daytime, no earlier than late morning and no later than midafternoon, and that unless something urgent came up, probably not until she had seen the third play.

But when she called that Sunday around noontime all she said about the third play, which she had seen Friday night, was that it was okay but not for her. The second play, which she had seen on Thursday, was a musical comedy. It was that and the modern dance program that she had seen that Saturday afternoon and the ballet she saw in the evening that she was looking forward to talking with me about when she came back that Monday afternoon.

There you were, she said. As soon as the downbeat came. You and the Marquis de Chaumienne. And I must say. I really must. What with your off-the-cuff demonstrations of his brilliantly cosmopolitan implications, I will never again listen to music or look at dancing as I once did. At all three performances it was as if he were sitting on one side of me, and you were on the other; and that made me so much more acutely aware of all sorts of missed possibilities that never would have occurred to me before. So I liked just about everything somewhat, if not a whole lot, less than at other times. But it was still a wonderful experience. Because I felt so much more mature and knowing about everything. It was just marvelous.

So you were saying, she said that Monday night as we settled down in the drawing room after dinner. She had come in from the airport and had started right in on what she had to say about the Broadway musical even as she headed for the bathtub, and during the meal I had told her about some of the details I had picked up from Old Pro (and from sources he directed me to) about how the old minstrel shows, ragtime, the cakewalk, the fox trot, the blues, and some of the early so-called syncopated orchestras had influenced the evolution not only of American popular song but also the Broadway musical and so also the Hollywood musical comedy.

The names of such turn of the century and first quarter musicians and performers as Will Marion Cook, Bob Cole, Bert Williams and George Walker, Ford Dabney, and Will Vodery were already somewhat familiar to her because the Marquis de Chaumienne had mentioned them from time to time; and when I said, James Reese Europe, she remembered that he had been the musical director for the famous Vernon and Irene Castle dance team, the forerunners of Fred and Adele Astaire.

When she went on to tell me about how interested the Marquis de Chaumienne also was in American ballroom dance steps as such, I started talking about the way many of the old "how-to" pop song lyrics used to promote new dance fads, and that is how we came to spend the rest of her first evening back from New York with me showing her what I remembered from my childhood on the outskirts of Mobile about how to do such steps as the Strut, the Shuffle, the Black Bottom, the Breakdown, Balling the Jack, the Mess Around, the Georgia Grind, and so on through the Charleston and the Suzie Q to jitterbugging and the stomp as done elsewhere, even before the Savoy.

XXX

By that next Friday afternoon, I was ready to start trying to find out how many of the little melodic figures, riff sketches, and themes I had come up with could be worked into a first draft. But I decided to put it all aside and spend the weekend making a few pop calls with the bass, while Jewel Templeton was sailing off Catalina Island with the studio people responsible for her trip to New York. I hadn't been into any of the spots in West Los Angeles and out on Central Avenue in several weeks if not a month.

I felt very good about what I had been able to come up with so far, so much so that I was already beginning to speculate about which of the passages would be accepted as is, with the orchestration as indicated. There were some leitmotif riff figures and a few uptempo and slightly cacophonous blues shout choruses to accompany several of the action sequences that I was just about certain that Eric Threadcraft was not going to be able to resist. And by that time I also felt that I was beginning to know enough about him to guess what direction most of the modifications and elaborations he decided to play around with would take. *Yes, yes, yes, I know exactly what you're getting at. Yes, yes, yes. Then he would say, And perhaps also . . . And maybe also . . . And hell, even something like this—or even this. Say you've given us a million options on this thing, fellow.*

As little as I knew about the piano, there was nothing like the keyboard for working up what I was trying to get together, and the Pleyel in the garage apartment was what I hunted and pecked on every morning until midday. Then I would tune the bass and spend at least an hour working out on it until it was time to take a dip in the pool and have lunch.

Sometimes, Jewel Templeton, who always woke up and got started on her various routines before I did, would spend most of the morning in her workshop and then go down to the pool. On other mornings, she would putter around in the garden or with the house plants; and there were also times when I wouldn't hear or see her until she was turning into the driveway from an early shopping trip, sometimes to downtown Hollywood, sometimes to Civic Center, and sometimes to Farmers Market. But that Wednesday she was already at the poolside when I came down to the patio, and that was when she said what she said about the finger exercises I had been zipping through just to keep in shape.

I was listening, she said, and I must say. I really must say. My God, you sound like somebody who was born doing calculus and trigonometry. And I said what I had to start learning to do right after I was born was the Jackrabbit. Because I was born in the briarpatch, I said. And she said, But aren't we all? And isn't it all a matter of idiom? That's what the marquis would say, and he would also say that idiom is a matter of convention, which is basically a matter of how and maybe why you do what you do where you come from. And by the way, to him, that was what the storyteller's traditional opening lines were really about. *And I said absolutely, thinking: Once upon a time in a place perhaps very far away, what came to pass among some*

*people perhaps quite different from us in many ways, nevertheless
applies to us in a very fundamental sense indeed.*

I do so hope that I'm doing justice to what the marquis had
in mind, she said; because I do so feel that it is precisely the
very foundation of that cosmopolitan point of view that he
represents so much more casually than anybody I ever met.

In any event, she said—or perhaps I should say at all odds—
your briarpatch is somebody else's wilderness or somebody
else's highlands or somebody else's bayou lowlands and canebrake and so on and so on. If you know what I mean, she said.
And I said, I do, I do, I really think I do. And she said, He
would say we were talking about a basic disposition toward adventure and its requirement for improvisation. And believe me,
what I just heard was high velocity improvisation indeed. And
I said, I think I know exactly what you're getting at, I really do.

Then when I said, But I must tell you, what you heard up
there just now was only some offstage stuff, some offstage
warmup stuff not actual performance stuff, she shook her head
smiling and said, There you go again. You and the marquis.
You and the marquis. There's a story, which he corroborated
for me, that his standard answer to those who responded to
some of his jazz recordings by asking if such musicians could
be taught to play the great masters was that he knew many jazz
musicians who played the great masters as warmup exercises.

She thought it was a great story and so did I. And I said, the
marquis knows his stuff all right, but I also have to confess that
I'm not one of those by a long shot. What you heard me doing
up there was something I had memorized from Tricky Lou
Cartwright in Mobile years before I came to promise anybody
that I would try to learn to play that thing myself.

And by the way, I also said, Old Tricks used to call that
kind of accelerated warmup routine his Paganini Orini jive, and
once I got started running finger exercises one of my goals was
to be nimble enough to play note for note all of the figures I
could remember him cutting, and in the process I also began
making up some of my own. Not that I ever had any notions
of ever becoming a pro on that thing, not even a part time pro.
All I was trying to do was to see how quickly I could get to be
good enough to jam with the combo led by the one who had
given it to me.

Paganini Orini? she said. Really? You're kidding. You're pulling my leg. Oh the marquis is going to be completely delighted when I tell him I heard this from you who got it from a Mobile, Alabama, pool shark. Oh when I get you two together. Just you wait, my bright-eyed, nimble-witted, sparkle-fingered friend from the here, there, and elsewhere of road musicians.

El hombre de época, she went on to say and was to repeat from time to time from then on. *Hombre de época*. Do you happen to know what that expression is? she said. And when I nodded remembering my roommate once more who had come upon it in a book by José Ortega y Gasset when he returned for the first term of our sophomore year. That's what the marquis has in mind when he talks about the ideal person that should be the natural product of the American experience, that our schools should be geared to turning out, given the ready accessibility to modern innovations in ever more precise and efficient communication and transportation facilities we enjoy.

Or words to that effect, she said. Then she said, Of course, as far as I'm concerned what it all adds up to is somebody very much like the marquis himself, whose point was precisely that an American would not have to begin with all of the family means and privileges that a European aristocrat such as himself was born to. As a matter of fact, he insists that to be truly representative of the possibilities inherent in the contemporary epoch one must not inherit but achieve one's aristocratic status. Much the same—oh and I do so enjoy telling you this— much the same—although I suspect that fabulous roommate of yours has already realized it—much the same as all of those literally fabulous jazz kings, dukes, counts, earls, and barons have given themselves titles and obligations that they then are expected to live up to.

When I think of the ever expanding implications of some of the very first things he said to me, she was to say and repeat from time to time, sometimes to me but mostly for her own benefit even so. When I suddenly realize how many ramifications some of his most casual remarks have, I can only marvel. And even more marvelous to an American schoolgirl like myself is the fact that he is not like a big time university scholar or deep thinking intellectual type at all.

Which, she went on to say, just goes to show how naive I've been about how things go. After all, what made that circle of people so attractive to me in the first place was that, to me, they were what the world of the international playboy was all about. Then somewhere along the line I became so bedazzled by *haute couture, haute cuisine,* and the glitter of the galas that I lost sight of the obvious. Such people, especially the very richest ones, are seldom less concerned with nuts and bolts than with fun and games.

What I'm only now just beginning to come to terms with, she also said, is something that I really can't say that I didn't already know. Such people don't let their formal education show. Not as such. Not any more than is the case with some of their various other acquisitions.

Some years later I would have said something about education as a matter of collecting ever more highly calibrated tools and devices for your work kit. Because what it all added up to was a phrase I had picked up from Mr. B. Franklin Fisher's Seniors Pregraduation Seminar, in which one of the main discussion topics was "The Aims of Education." What they were about was the knowledge, skills, understanding, awareness, and appreciation to be gained from such subject matter as Language, Mathematics, Science, History, and Religion. But according to Mr. B. Franklin Fisher, of all people, whose doctrine of the ancestral imperatives was not always distinguishable from the Horatio Alger all-American work ethic, what they all added up to was Worthy Use of Leisure Time.

So that's what I told her I had always thought playboys and the international smart set were really about. And she said, Me too, and so they are, in spite of all the emphasis the tabloids put on their self-indulgences and perversities that some are, have been, and probably always will be guilty of. To me whatever else some of them might be, some others are not only the most important patrons of the arts, ranging all the way from the so-called angels who back stage productions to those who establish endowments and those who donate priceless collections that make up the treasures of our great museums.

Everybody knows about their staggeringly expensive jewels and playthings, she said. But who buys more expensive books or more of the better and best books? And where would the most imaginative architects be without them? But so much for my personal theory of the leisure class. You get the point.

That was when she stood up with her finger to her lips and then went up to the dining level and into the kitchen and came back to hand me the bucket with the iced Dom Perignon and went and came back again with a tray on which there were the stemmed glasses and caviar and said what she said about certain things should always be a matter not only of leisure but also of ceremony and celebration.

To which I said, Hey, you know something Miss Lady? This is some pretty deep stuff we're getting into now. But you know something else? It also sounds like an invitation to a dance.

And she said, The dance, Mr. Bright Eyes. Invitation to the dance.

XXXI

EVERY TIME Jewel Templeton said what she always liked to say about why she was so pleased that you had come along when you did, all you could do was shake your head and squint your eyes and tighten your lips and look around at nothing in particular.

Not that you doubted her sincerity when she said what she said about how much she was learning from you about music and what she said about how impressed she was with the bright-eyed enthusiasm with which you went about things in general, or even when she kept coupling your name with that of the Marquis de Chaumienne as if to do so were the most natural juxtaposition in the world.

Nor was there any question whatsoever of flattery on the one hand or of all too obvious and all too ofay-eager naiveté on the other. Her praise was nothing if not generous, to be sure, and her frank curiosity was a matter not of naiveté but of a sophisticated self-confidence that on occasion could become downright aristocratic in the exercise of its freedom not to have known already.

As a matter of fact, what your instantaneous, even if not unplayful, reaction was in response to was precisely the ring of sincerity that made what she said add up to being as much a matter of ongoing high expectation and indelible obligation as was the case when Miss Lexine Metcalf used to say, *Who if not you, my splendid young man, my splendid young man? Who if not you?* And earmarked you for Mr. B. Franklin Fisher and the Talented Tenth Early Birds, which was the name of his special accelerated study program for those students considered to be most likely to fulfill the ancestral imperatives.

Apropos of all of which, and in accordance with your own long established conception of the scheme of things, you are not about to allow anything, no matter how genuinely adulatory, the certified glamorous and internationally famous Miss Jewel Templeton said, fake you into forgetting that you, not she, were the apprentice. Because at the same time that she was whatever she was in her own mind and to other people here there and elsewhere as well, in your mind she was no less another one of those good fairy godmothers that you may or may not be lucky enough to encounter in various guises at some point along the meandertale route from Mama, Miss Tee, and Miss Lexine Metcalf, than was Miss Slick McGinness.

Miss Slick McGinness West, I might well have said. Miss Slick McGinness redux, Miss Slick McGinness as of this juncture. But I didn't. Because there was no need to do so. Because what really mattered was not an articulation of the minute particulars of the relationship but rather the compatibility that was already there by the time the two of us settled down in the drawing room after supper that first evening. She had said what she said about music and had liked my response and that was the beginning and what followed happened as such things do when one step leads as naturally to the next as do the also and also choruses in a riff session.

You were who you were to her and she was who she was to you. And since the fact that the person to person dimension of the relationship, however intimate and however unfrivolous, was only an incidental detail, went without saying, that was all that was necessary.

So whenever she would say what she would say again and again about what she was not only learning but also coming to terms with because you were there, all you had to do was turn your head as if from well meaning but gross exaggeration and then change the subject back to the point at which her enthusiasm had interrupted you.

It worked every time, and that was how and why the conversations never became an ongoing exchange of compliments during which you would have said what you could have said about what she meant to you. Which was probably all the same to her, since the reason you were there in the first place was that she was so preoccupied with the Marquis de Chaumienne, who had convinced her that there was something that she was supposed not only to represent as a performing artist but also to embody and exemplify as an American in the contemporary world at large.

But still and all and still in all and still withal, however else she saw herself and in whatever other personal terms she defined her relationship to you, such was the perhaps ineluctably mythological nature of the also and also of things that she was also your fairy-tale godmother in the most functional sense of the word, the undeniably sensual and even incestuous implications of which were already very much there indeed in Miss Lexine Metcalf's all but disconcerting good looks.

All of which is to say that Jewel Templeton, in spite of the fact that she never once said anything to me that anybody could possibly interpret as the expression of any kind of authority of status or seniority whatsoever, was my fairy-tale godmother on the scene at that time, even as Miss Eunice Townsend continued to be the fairy-tale princess in the storybook world of my as yet far from specific aspirations and expectations, and would, I hoped, continue to be so for sometime to come.

It was a gamble to be sure, but no chance taking no adventure and no adventure no hero and no hero no story and no story no storyteller and no storybooks, and no storytellers and story books, no need for compass, maps, and mileage charts since all purpose and action involves risk; and inertia has no destination. Even as entropy has no shape, form, or fashion.

So far Eunice Townsend was still willing to gamble on her expectation that whatever escapades a young part-time journeyman road musician might become involved in during a sojourn in Hollywood or anywhere else in the world of entertainment, for that matter, were likely to be only a part of the also and also of the rights of passage that should help him achieve the personal experience, conditioning, and cosmopolitan outlook that would qualify him for the obligations and expectations of husband and father. Most references to Prince Charming are made with tongue in cheek but the requirement that he and his experience questionable or not be there for damsels in distress and people in need of deliverance is no less urgently expected even so.

In any case her gamble was not a matter of the expectation of puritanic abstinence. Her gratuitously dismissive statement about that was what she said when she said what she said not about being good but being careful. A statement I have never been able to imagine myself making. But then are women ever really as insecure about such things as most men seem to be? Scandalous gossip aside to be sure. And even if it came to that, Miss You-Know-Who would never insist that the passing embarrassment of the deceived wife was as awful as the eradicable disgrace of the cuckold whose status as a father is forever in doubt.

So, the so-called double standard based on the assumption of the absolute equality of male and female options and pre-rogatives was not an issue for her or even a matter of serious discussion. But for you there was first of all the question of how long you could expect her to extend the amount of time required by the indefinite nature of your postcollegiate appren-ticeship and travels.

At present she was still so deeply involved with her own ob-ligations to the ancestral expectations of her hometown spon-sors and potential clientele that your continued absence was actually a convenience. But for you it was all a gamble never-theless. After all, there was also the undeniable matter of that which my old roommate, in the process of applying his notion of the inescapable necessity of taking calculated risks, used to call *the what if*'s that can never be answered until after the fact because they were precisely the ultimate means of mea-suring the skill, efficiency, and determination underlying good intentions against good fortune. *For yea verily, I say unto you, my dear Vatson, good intention without good fortune availeth naught in this man's league.*

Once upon a time indeed, he also liked to say. *But what about next time? What about this time? What if, my good fellow? What the hell if? That is the question, is it not, stated or not, that is always there, before, during, and after all undertakings. We're talking about the nature of things, to wit, the primordial actuality of things, my worthy fellow. Which brings us by a vicus of recirculation, commodious or not, back to the ultimate notion of entropy itself, does it not? And thereby also to the aboriginal assumption of adventure, without which, needless to say, there can be no story to tell.*

None of which was in direct reference to what you had going on with either Eunice Townsend or Jewel Templeton, neither one of whom he knew. You had mentioned Eunice Townsend in letters from time to time but mostly only casually and in passing. He had never seen her because when she came on campus, he had already transferred to Yale. About Jewel Templeton you had decided at the very outset not to mention her to anybody whomsoever. Not only because of all of the things that were said and signified by Joe States and Ross Peterkin the day after the night in Bel-Air following your first time in the Palladium, but also because to do so might give the impression that you were not yet up to taking such things in stride.

As for what Esther and Maurice made of my relationship to Jewel Templeton I still haven't really figured that out. They simply fell in line with it without ever missing a single beat. I was a young musician on leave of absence from the rhythm section of the world-famous orchestra of the Bossman Himself, and I was there in the studio apartment (also with run of the house) for the time being because I was an essential part of a new project that she had come to be preoccupied with beyond everything else since she came back from her most recent trip to Europe, and that was that. Every now and then she herself would say something about how much they liked and admired me. But for their part I was just simply accepted without any discernible reservation of any kind. No thinly disguised one-upmanship formality on the one hand, and no phony conspiratorial nods and winks on the other. I don't know what she told them about me, but by the end of my first week there, the casualness of our routine interactions was such that all of our verbal exchanges had already taken on a second chorus intimacy. No vamping around the bush. No ever so careful segueing into an unmistakable first chorus. You could begin with the second chorus with or without a vamp or segue and then move on to the out chorus, or skip to the out chorus. Or begin not with the second chorus but with the out chorus.

I never did find out whether they were surprised by the way things turned out with me and Jewel Templeton. If there was any surprise neither one showed any sign of it. Both took my exit almost as casually as they had taken my entrance. Almost but not quite. On my arrival they both shook hands with me and smiled as if to say, We don't know you but we know her, so we also know that you wouldn't be here if you're not somebody special. On my departure they both gave me a tight hug, patted my back, and held my hands as they looked me up and down at arm's length and then turned and left without a word; and I decided that they already knew why I was leaving so suddenly and that it was something they would never discuss with anybody.

XXXII

IT WAS exactly one month after he gave me my copy of the screenplay that Eric Threadcraft left a message for me with the answering service. It was waiting for me when I called in late that Monday afternoon, and I drove over to his house the next morning.

It was nine forty-five when I turned into the yard and he was standing in the door wearing a faded red polo shirt, blue jeans, and rope soled shoes; and he was smoking a dip-bowl meerschaum pipe. He was letting his hair grow long. He pushed it back with one hand, holding the pipe with the other and said, Hi ya, fellow. How are you, really?

And I said, Nothing to me, Mice, as I stepped out of the auto incognito with the manuscript in the briefcase. And he said, It's a hell of a day to be working, as he pushed his hair back again and then shook my hand. I hope you don't mind too much.

The bougainvillea hung down from the overhead trellis. The yard was in full bloom. The sky was almost too bright and blue to look at. I followed him up the stairs to the sundeck and into the studio.

I really hope you don't mind, he said. And I said, Not at all. I was beginning to wonder when you'd call. And he said, This is the first free day I've had.

There was coffee, tea, rolls, and a big bowl of fruit on the sideboard; and he handed me a cup of tea. I skipped the Danish pastry. He poured himself a big ceramic cup of strong black coffee and refilled his pipe. Then he said, Well I certainly hope you've had better luck getting started than I have. I just simply haven't had any time at all. And I said, I don't know, but here it is such as it is. I unzipped the case and when he saw how thick the manuscript was he said, Say, fellow, you've been working. And I said, I started that next morning.

I handed him the lead sheets and he spread them on the piano and stood turning through them, his lips moving, his head nodding, his free hand waving the pipe like a baton. Then as he sat down to the keyboard and went on turning the pages he said, Say you really have been working. And I said, I just thought I'd try to see what I could do. And he said, You've got a whole thing here, fellow. And I said, I had the time. So I just kept on going. And he said, I'll say you did.

He turned back to the first page and sounded my opening chord, sustained it, and then sounded it again. I sat across the room with the shooting script and waited. He played the opening theme three times, studying it carefully, accenting with his head and then tossing his hair away from his forehead. I listened from where I was. And then, when he was ready he moved over and I sat beside him and we started at the beginning again.

He kept nodding to himself and I knew he was pleased and I thought about the Bossman Himself and Old Pro again and wondered what they would think about what I was trying to do. If you didn't have it all working together they would see right through you. They wouldn't knock your hustle, but I didn't want them to have to be nice to me about it. If the Bossman Himself liked it he would say, Hey, that was a pretty little thing you did. And if he liked it Old Pro would probably like it too and would probably say, I heard a couple of nice little tricky things in there, to which I would say, They probably came from you. I just hope I'm not distorting you. But if old Joe States or somebody else started talking about how much money you were making and about all the profitable new contacts you had, they didn't want to talk about the quality of the music at all.

I certainly didn't want anything like that to happen. Anything but that I thought. Not that I was worried about being too commercial for them. None of them would mind that at all as long as you got a few of your special licks in somewhere. Hey you hear my old States up there bootlegging all them old mammy-made riffs in there among all them dollars and cents. Boy, I don't know what's going to happen when them people wise up to the kind of stuff you're trying to put in the game.

Eric Threadcraft stood up, and I slid over to the center of the seat and went on playing, with him reading over my shoulder. Then he began walking back and forth across the room behind me, stopping every now and then to check the score against the shooting script. Then he came and stood in the curve of the piano listening and directing with his eyes closed and I went on plunking until he said, This is good news, fellow. This is great news.

He made another cup of tea for me and poured himself another cup of coffee and refilled his pipe and said, Say listen, man, I feel so good about all this I can't even work on it any more this morning.

I followed him out to the sundeck and saw the terrace and garden again. He pulled at his pipe and squinted against the sky. Then he turned to me and said, Look, fellow, maybe we can get out and take advantage of this fine weather after all. I know that an old smoothie like you always has something lined up, he said winking and pushing his hair back again. And I promised some people I'd come out to Malibu if we finished up here in time.

I had no idea that there would be this much time, he said. I was just hoping that you'd come up with something to get us started, and here we are in business and I haven't written one bar yet. So now let's see what I can come up with. Maybe a day at the beach is just what I need to get me going. Let's see what I can do before we get together again. Say in about a week or so. But meanwhile I think we have something pretty great already, I really do, fellow.

I don't think you realize what you've done, he said walking back and forth again as I got ready to leave. If we had to we could really start rolling tomorrow. All we really have to do is zoom in on the instrumentation a little more tightly.

I went on noodling and doodling around on the keyboard for a while every morning for the rest of that week just for the fun of it. And by the following Wednesday I found myself thinking as if I were back with the band playing for the Bossman Himself and Old Pro again. And that was when I began jotting things down with all of the instrumentation in mind, and that is how I started coming up with full band arrangements all by myself.

The first I did was a getaway stomp for Osceola Menefee, which I called "Seminole" because I wanted an Indian word to go with his first name and also because the Seminole was a legendary railroad line that I remembered tales about along with references to the Piedmont, the Atlantic Coast Line, and the Seaboard from fireside, swing porch, and barbershop tell-me-tale times. So I played around with train whistle riffs for the reed section and Florida palmetto swampland echoes for the trombones; and the solo line for Osceola Menefee's trumpet was based on an old train whistle blues that Luzana Cholly used to strum as he strolled his way up out of the L & N bottom in the twilight on his way to Miss Alzenia Nettleton's cook shop on Buckshaw Mill Road next door to Stranahan's General Merchandise store. I had old Joe States highballing and also taking care of the exhaust piston steam with his cymbals and brushes, and there were also parts for his mallets and the Indian tom-toms that a lot of drummers used in those days when some trap sets also used to include Chinese wood blocks. As for the locomotive arrival and departure bell and the ongoing punctuation, you could leave that open and any good blues oriented piano player would hit it right off, as would also be the case with the way he would share the chomping sound of the drivers with the bass player.

I felt that I had it well enough under control to set it aside by the weekend and when I ran through it again that next Monday morning I still liked it enough to move on to something else, and by noon I settled on one of old Herman Kemble's old gutbucket riffs, which I decided to try to expand into a background gospel shout for the whole band and call "Presiding Elder," because if I could get it right, I'd have old Bloop all set up for one of his surefire church rocking tenor sermons with the trumpets as his choir, the trombones following Fred Gilchrist's soulful call and response lead as his amen corner and the reeds as the organ; and this time the piano would ring church bells, not train bells and also suggest not gothic but down-home stained glass windows.

What I found myself moving on into next was a five-note twelve-bar blues riff that I decided to use as a frame for a string of five solo choruses, each beginning on a two-bar break (followed by a sharp pickup) and lasting twelve bars. The piano would begin things by plunking the riff figure three times over twelve bars of the steady four/four of the rhythm section and moving on to the channel, after which Otis Sheppard would lead off with a getaway train whistle guitar solo to be followed by Scully Pittman with Harmon mute and felt derby, following which would come Big Bloop's street corner woofing tenor, Malachi Moberly's trombone with plunger, and Old Pro on clarinet, which would take it to the ride out.

In a sense it was like routining a jam session, but even so it was also a basic way of composing what was in effect a home-grown equivalent to the European sonata, namely the instrumental, the structure of which is not based on exposition, development, and recapitulation, as is the so-called classical sonata, but rather on a series of choruses of various kinds (most often of either twelve or thirty-two bars each), which function like stanzas or chapters in a narrative.

Now that, as you and that fabulous freshman roommate of yours and my incredible marquis know very well, is what ad-lib theater is so very much about, Jewel Templeton said when I plunked and hummed and described and explained my way through it for her at the piano in the drawing room that night after dinner. I still had not made any mention of Eric Thread-craft's movie assignment because I didn't want her to start thinking about me in that context yet, but the three standard full band arrangements that I had just gotten up represented exactly the sort of workshop examples of the interplay of the arranger's overall control with individual improvisation (and impromptu obbligatos by sections as well) that she found so intriguing about jazz composition.

That was one reason I brought the score sheets along with me when I came down to dinner that night. The main reason I did so that particular night however was that I wanted to have somebody listen as I ran through what I had done. Because I wanted to check out how I felt going through it with some-body listening before I mailed everything off to Old Pro.

When I said what I said about how everybody in the band would already know what the overall voicing was, I also said that the composed parts of each solo were set up in charac-ter. And that was when she said it was not unlike growing up and learning how to drive Daddy's car. And I said, Somewhat like that but perhaps even more like learning to ride Daddy's special mount, given the band's long since all but organically conditioned response to his slightest whim and touch.

In other words when you set something up to be played by Ike Ellis, Ted Chandler, Fred Gilchrist, or anybody else in the lineup it was much the same as playing it on the keyboard of an organ designed by the Bossman Himself. The old joke about Joe States sneezing as soon as the bossman's nose began to itch is only a part of it. The other part is that Joe's sneeze just might become an official part of the orchestration, as was also the case with Herman Kemble's bloop, Ted Chandler's belly bellow, and so on.

I mailed all three sketches off to Old Pro in care of the home office in New York that next afternoon, and on Friday of the following week there was a telegram from Detroit that said: Shaking down nicely minor adjustments only before using on Chicago theater date week after next spot for Fred nice touch everybody says big ears check follows hope more where this came from.

XXXIII

HEY, MAN. Hey, this is great, man, Silas Renfroe said when I called the number he had left with my answering service the night before. Hey, great, just great. Then he said, Say now look here, man, what I was wondering about was if I could get you to help me out on a little out of town gig I got coming up. I was wondering if you could spare from Wednesday through Sunday, coming back by Monday night.

Then going on before I had time to make any response at all he said, Hey, man, I'm talking about Frisco, man. I'm talking about classy stuff, man. I'm talking about a real swanky joint. I'm talking about gourmet spareribs and chitlins à la Waldorf-Astoria, if you know what I mean. I'm talking about The Gray Falcon. Hey, man, I know that something like that is just another one among many in the kind of booking you're used to. But hey, man, I really would appreciate if you can see your way to helping me out.

And I said, Hey, man, I'm weak, man. I'd like to, man. But I have to check with a couple of people and get back to you later on today. Not later than tomorrow morning, I said. And he said, Hey, man. Oh, man. Great, man.

All I had to do was tell Jewel Templeton only as a matter of procedure, because I knew that she herself was all set to go down to La Jolla to visit friends for a few days including the weekend; and also as a matter of procedure I wanted to make sure that Eric Threadcraft and Felix Lovejoy got advance notice just in case they were not counting on my being out of town.

At the end of our opening set at The Gray Falcon up in San Francisco that Thursday night, the management had to limit our encores to seven minutes overall, because by that time the line of the sellout crowd for the second set stretched all the way around the corner; and the early arrivals for the third set were already beginning to form another line on the opposite side of the entrance.

Hey, man, Silas Renfroe began saying as soon as we were far enough into the first set for him to relax enough to look around and realize that there was a full house. Oh, man. Hey, man, is this us? In San Francisco? Hey, man, how am I going to believe some stuff like this? And this is just Thursday. Man, them cats back in L.A. are going to think I've been trying to hand them some kind of old Bay Area fish story, which you didn't really expect them to believe because you didn't really believe it yourself.

But believe it or not, that was the way it was to be right on through the entire weekend, and you also had all day every day all to yourself because the only numbers Silas Renfroe was calling were arrangements of his own that I had already sat in on at the Rumpus Room from time to time and didn't need to rehearse; and on the spot heads on blues changes and such standard surefire pop tunes as "All of Me," "Blue Skies," "Tea for Two," "Sweet Georgia Brown," and the like.

I already knew my way around downtown San Francisco from my first trip there with the band, when I had bought a map and a guidebook and started out at Civic Center and went to Museum of Art and when I came back outside into the hazy sunshine it was midday and I walked along Market Street, and from the sidewalks and the older shops you could tell that you were in an old seaport town even though you were not as near the waterfront as you would have been when you came along Government Street in Mobile or Canal Street in New Orleans.

That time, I had eaten lunch in a snack bar in Union Square and took a cable car up Powell Street to Nob Hill. Then I went to see Chinatown by daylight and came back and spent the rest of the afternoon looking into the shops along Post and Kearney streets and had bought myself a suede jacket in Abercrombie & Fitch and I also stopped in and had I. Magnin ship a silk scarf and a bottle of French cologne to Miss Eunice Townsend back you know where.

When I came back to the hotel nobody in the band was still around, and there were no messages. So I decided to study the map and guidebook and take a nap, and when Joe States woke me up to tell me that we were all going to Fisherman's Wharf for dinner before going to work it was as if he were pulling me away from a San Francisco of earlier banjo plucking ballroom piano times, when the old harbor was a thicket of clipper masts and sails as well as steamer stacks and an endless variety of smaller towing, rowing, and ferrying craft; and everywhere you looked along the gaslit streets teeming with carriages and stagecoaches there were amusement arcades, dance emporiums, music halls, and theaters, which presented everything from minstrels and vaudeville variety acts to Shakespearean and operatic stock company offerings.

The next morning of that first time in the Bay Area I had set out again with the itinerary that I had worked up from the guidebook and map and by the time we pulled out for the trip back east that last week I had gotten around to every site on my checklist. Afterward I had also finished reading Joe States's copy of Herbert Asbury's The Barbary Coast *before we came back to the Great Divide.*

So what I had planned to do during the short stand at The Gray Falcon with Silas Renfroe was to retrace as many of my steps as possible. But after the very first set that Thursday night the club manager brought Elliot Marchand backstage and that was when I was invited to spend the next day at his place.

I remembered his face and voice but not his name until he reminded me that I had been introduced to him by the Bossman

Himself and that what the three of us had talked about was ragtime and Harlem stride piano music. Then he said that he had come by because when he read that I was back in town for a few nights he decided to find out if I would like to spend part of whatever free time I had tomorrow checking out his special collection of ragtime piano rolls on his 1912 vintage Steinway eighty-eight-note player piano.

Sounds great to me already, I said. And I also said anytime between breakfast and one hour before show time. And he said, Why not include breakfast? And I said, Why not? So by ten o'clock that Friday morning he had picked me up in his runabout and we were on our way across the Golden Gate Bridge to his place in Sausalito.

Alongside the player piano there was also a 1910 vintage eighty-eight-note upright regular piano. And at one end of the room there was a concert hall grand and at the other there was an old-fashioned country church organ. The two uprights were collector's items from Sedalia, Missouri. The grand was a local heirloom. The church organ had been brought west by a family from Georgia.

His wall to wall collection of records, transcriptions, and air checks was in an adjoining room, which he called the Amen Corner and which was where he usually spent most of his listening time. But which we were not to settle into until later that afternoon.

We spent the rest of the morning playing rolls by Scott Joplin, James Scott, Luckey Roberts, Jelly Roll Morton, and James P. Johnson; and when we were called for lunch we were joined on the terrace by Elliot Marchand's wife, Kimberly, who had just driven back from a committee meeting at the museum in Civic Center.

My guess was that like her husband she was in her middle to late forties but there was no gray in her sandy shoulder length mane and she had very friendly hazel eyes, and I was not surprised when I found out later on that she was one of the best dressed women in San Francisco.

I was also to find out that she spent thousands of dollars every year to help poets and painters and that the two of them also underwrote art exhibitions as well as dance groups and music and dance performances on campuses and also in public concert halls. It was also sometime later on that I came to realize that the two of them helped to finance the publication of some of the noncommercial journals of the arts that I saw in their library that afternoon.

She shared her husband's enthusiasm for ragtime and stride piano music but the first thing she wanted to talk to me about during lunch that afternoon was what it was like to work that close to the Bossman Himself, which she said she hoped would not be a drag for me to go back over yet again; and I said, Not me, and told her how it had come about. And she said my account was entirely consistent with her conception of his creative genius.

When Elliot Marchand brought the conversation back around to Harlem stride piano music his wife also wanted to know what details about the menus and recipes typical of the old rent party spreads had passed along to me by people of that generation. And that led to questions about eating your way across the country in a road band. That was when the three of us began to realize that we were becoming newly found food friends as well as music friends and that was why they drove me back into town early enough to change clothes and have dinner at one of their favorite restaurants before show time. And when they came backstage after the first set to say good-bye they made me promise to notify them of my next trip to San Francisco in advance so that they could take me for a tour of the vineyards in Napa Valley.

Silas Renfroe pulled back into Hollywood early that next afternoon and I had him let me out at Sunset and Fairfax and took a taxi. When I gave the driver the address he looked at my instrument and suit bag and said You play up that way much? and I said, I guess you could say that. I don't know what he thought was in the overnight bag, probably something to go with my act.

Beverly Hills, he said. They have some wild parties up in here, and you musicians get to see it all up close. Say now that's something, that's really something. You could learn a lot of fancy tricks up in this neck of the woods.

Hey here we go right here, my man, I said. And he said, Well all right. This is going to be a good one I can tell. And I said, Keep the change. And he said, Hey, yeah, well thanks old buddy, and good luck and remember, see no evil, hear no evil, speak no evil, but I don't have to tell you. And I don't have to tell you to keep tabs on the kitty either.

Jewel Templeton was still in La Jolla and Maurice was taking the day off so the only one at home was Esther and she was getting ready to leave on an errand to downtown L.A. when I arrived. I decided to stay in and raid the pantry and read some more about San Francisco as I waited for the call I expected from La Jolla. And I also decided not to get in touch with Eric Threadcraft until that next morning.

XXXIV

WHEN I COULDN'T get Eric Threadcraft on the telephone by that next afternoon, I called Felix Lovejoy, and as soon as you heard his voice you could tell that things were going much better than he had ever let himself even hope they would. Not that he didn't have high horizons of aspiration, but his immediate expectations were always based on practical considerations rather than wishful thinking.

There's that man, he said as he always did when he had good news. How was the trip, old buddy? I've been waiting to hear from you since last night. Eric is in Europe. Things are happening, my man. Fantastic things. Uptempo and splitting. I mean really, I mean quantum leaps. Incredible! Looks like we're just about in there, good buddy. And I do mean there.

And when I said, Hey I'm listening, man, so hey lift the veil, man, he said, Not over the phone. You free tonight? And I said, Nothing yet. And he said, So let me buy you a fancy dinner and clue you in. And I said, That's all right with me. And he said, About eight. And I said, Fine. And he said, Benvenuto's okay with you? And I said, So long as it's your money, man. And he said, Correction. Corporation money, man. See you between eight and eight-thirty.

You could always depend on him to be on time, so when I came through the door at Benvenuto's at exactly eight he was already there leaning on the piano holding a drink and listening to Curtis Howard, who was working as a single at that time and who when he saw Felix Lovejoy and me nodding at each other segued into a few bars of the intermission band call riff of the Bossman Himself and winked at me and then went on to the next chorus of his cocktail lounge variations on "Dream a Little Dream of Me."

On the way through the main dining room, which was already two-thirds full, I saw several people I knew by sight and one couple waved for me to join them at their table and when I indicated that I was already with somebody they smiled, applauded silently, and blew kisses as I followed Felix Lovejoy and the maître d' on out to the terrace.

From our table you could see the lights and the traffic along Sunset Boulevard, and across the busy intersection was Schwab's famous drug store. And I could also see all the way to the curve of Crescent Heights Boulevard, where I had parked the auto incognito. It was his treat and choice of restaurant so I said I would go along with his recommendations from the menu and we began by sharing an order of clams Vasto style (Arselle alla maniera di Vasto), and he suggested that I try the quail en polenta and for himself he selected rabbit gourmet style (lepre alla maniera dell ghiottone), which he was to insist that I sample and there was also a huge green salad for the two of us.

We talked about San Francisco until the clams were served. Then he turned to the business at hand, and that was when he said what he said about the corporation, which he said was primarily a moneymaking proposition, but which would be no less effective as a device for career development, because it would stand for high quality as well as something very much in demand.

Because that's what this town works on, getting to something that is in demand. So why not us? My job will be to make it us.

Okay. So we're already beginning to be a team, right? So now we become a corporation, which stands for professional teamwork. Professionally organized and programmed teamwork that adds up to big time production under one made-up name that we promote into a brand name with its own trademark. If you know what I mean. Whatever name we finally choose, which as you and I know could really just simply be

Eric Threadcraft, as in Eric Threadcraft, Inc., because as of now that's what our first buyers are going to think whatever name we choose stands for anyway. Because he's already perceived as up and coming. But Eric doesn't feel that would be fair to you given how he feels about your creative input and editorial say-so. And I agree. But on the other hand he also had to admit that coupling your name with his at this stage of the game would not add anything to his market value. So we decided to go along with long established Hollywood practice and propose a screen name and what he came up with for a start was Youngblood, Inc. Ernest Youngblood, Inc. Ernest Youngblood of Maestro Music, Inc. Which is not bad when you consider the riff he's playing on that Ernest Hemingway crack about maestro that you're always pulling on him.

Inside, Curtis Howard was playing around with "Three Little Words." Across the street at Schwab's Drug Store clusters of young and hopeful actors, writers, studio technicians stood around talking near some convertibles and motorcycles at the curb, some around the entrance and along the showcases in both directions. As I looked at them, the first thing they reminded me of was the autumn of my sophomore year and how it was when you came along the walk from the clock tower and the music hall at the upper end of the campus to the block where the Varsity Drag was. Then what came back to mind were the drug store blocks as you saw them in the early evening as the band bus made its way from town to town and coast to coast. *Soda fountain U.S.A.*, I thought. Mostly with the same movie magazines along with whatever else in the line of pop fare.

As I said, Felix Lovejoy said, It's only a proposition. So it depends on the agreement of the parties concerned, and naturally that depends on how you really feel about the overall thing at the very outset. Hey, but wait a minute, he said, I said this was supposed to be a money proposition and here I am about to get the cart before the horse. The basic proposition is the split. And what we're proposing is fifty, thirty, twenty for Eric, you, and me in that order.

You don't have to answer now. All I'm supposed to be doing is giving you something to think about. That's what Eric had in mind and as I know you fully understand, the only reason he's not here doing this himself is this European thing, which happened so fast all he had time to do was get on over there.

This is just to alert you to what looks to us like a more professional way of handling the kind of really big time stuff we're beginning to get into. No more freelancing. We'd like to be able to deal in corporate terms. It carries a bigger impact when you talk with a corporate budget in the equation.

I said I would think about it. And he said I wish I could tell you when Eric is going to be able to make it back. But right now he really doesn't know how long this Paris, Rome thing is going to take. He just knows it's worth the time, and he will clue us in as soon as he gets back because that is most likely to be the sort of thing that he wants a corporate setup to handle.

I said okay. I said, But don't forget this music scene is something that I'm just into for the time being. Not that I have a definite cutoff point in mind yet, I said. But I don't see myself as being in for the long haul either. Not as a full time professional, I said. And he said, We'll see about that, good buddy. We'll see about that. We'll cross that bridge when we come to it.

Then as we slapped palms outside on the sidewalk before I headed for the auto incognito, he said, Got any club dates? And I said, There's always the Keynote on weekends. And he said, Whenever you want to line up something else just let me know. Eric and I are always good for local spots in this part of town. Just give a buzz.

And I said, You bet.

XXXV

I CAME CRUISING along West Adams and turned into Crenshaw and the first thing I saw when I pulled into the parking lot behind the Home Plate (as in down-home plate and home cooking) was Gaynelle Whitlow's robin's egg blue convertible. I came through the restaurant and saw her sitting in the bar.

She was alone in a booth near the jukebox, and I recognized the medium tempo instrumental blues that I had made with Radio Red not long after I began freelancing. I had a copy of it along with everything else I had recorded, but that was my first experience of walking in and hearing myself thumping in a place like that. She looked up and saw me and waved. She was wearing dark glasses and her hair was swept up and her earrings were large hoops of brass. I went toward her walking deliberately out of time with myself on the jukebox.

Hey, where you been, home boy, she said. And I said, Across town. I gave her an exaggerated show biz kiss on each cheek and stood back and looked her up and down and she pretended to ignore me. Then she cut her eyes at me with her hands on her hips, and then she smiled and said, Somebody said you were still out here. What you been doing with your cute down-home self around this big old ultrafrantic hick town?

Making records and trying to learn how to scratch out a few charts, I said. And she said, Well good. Well nice. Well fine. Sit down. And I slid into the booth beside her. She was sipping a margarita, which she let me taste, and I ordered one for myself and another one for her.

The jukebox played on, and beyond the music you could hear that hum and buzz of the other conversations and the sound of clinking flatware that all dining rooms seem to have in common. I looked around but I didn't see anybody I knew.

Hey, you seen Ross Peterkin? I asked. And she said, Not lately. I think he must be down around Acapulco or somewhere like that. He's got himself some new thing going. And the last time I saw him he was doing a lot of talking about a boat, so I figured he and whoever she is must be down there somewhere cruising around. You know that Ross.

Somebody played another number by Radio Red, and there I was again dragging the beat so that the atmosphere would be honky tonk cozy enough to suggest a down-home menu. There was a piano, bass, and drum opening and when we hit the second chorus she stopped talking and started snapping her fingers soundlessly, moving her head and shoulders ever so slightly, and humming the background accents. Then there was a break, then the other sections came in and faded away for the vocal.

Ray Red, she said. Old crazy Ray Red. He may be full of stuff but he can sure get down with some good old good time blues when he wants to. And when I said, You see him around anywhere? she said, Not over this way. I think they're still out at that place off Central. And when I said, What about Silas

Renfroe? she said, I saw him the other day. He told me about that great gig you all had up in San Francisco. I don't think they're in the Rumpus Room. You playing over somewhere this way tonight?

I shook my head slowly from side to side looking at her until she spoke again. Which is when she said, So what are you doing over in this neck of the woods? Looking for some of your kinfolks? And I said, Looking for you. And she said, You guys. She said, You guys in that band. And when I said, I'm not in that band anymore, she said, Don't make no difference. She said, You were in there long enough.

I don't know what you're talking about, I said. Then I said, I was just cruising around hoping I would run into you. And here you are the very first one I see. And she said, See there. There you go. You know where I live and I distinctly remember giving you my phone number, because everybody ain't so lucky. To which I said, Yeah baby, but I didn't know whether or not you would remember me. And she said, Look you can't help it can you? Once you've been around with that band and all them thugs you're ruined for life.

I really don't know what you're talking about, I said. And she looked at me laughing. And while I was trying to look puzzled, the waiter came back and I ordered another round of drinks. There was a jump number playing on the jukebox then and she started snapping her fingers again, her head tilted, her big earrings dangling, her leg brushing time against mine under the table. I thought about that night at the Vineyard. But I didn't say anything.

So you got out there and forgot all about me, huh, she said. And I said, You know better than that. And she said, Ways and actions, that's what I go by. Ways and actions. And forgetting myself I said, You know something very special I remember about you? And she said, Tell me anything. Boy, you didn't think about the likes of me until you walked in here just now and saw me.

Your hands, I said.

My what?

Your hands, I said. You have hands like a princess. And you know something else? You've got a lot of regal stuff going anyway. Elegant stuff.

And she said, So now you're going to try to pull some of that fay boy stuff on me too, huh? Or is that just some of that college boy stuff? And I said, You know better than that, baby. And that's when she said, Well you know I heard all that. All that African queen stuff, all that Coptic princess jive. Hey you know something else? I'm so regal I'm supposed to be a regal fritillary.

A regal what-illary? I said. And she held her unlit cigarette out at an angle turning her hand and tapping it on the ashtray with her forefinger. A regal fritillary, she said and she pointed to the pin she was wearing. It was shaped like a butterfly.

I was going with this fay cat from out at Caltech. He was an architect but he also had this freakish thing about butterflies. Sometimes we would be driving somewhere in the country and this big hairy butt clown would stop the car and grab that little goddamn fancy net that was always on the backseat and take off across the field like he had bees at his bottom or something. You know what that butterfly stuff is called, I said. And she said, some crossword puzzle sounding name. And when I said, Lepidopterology, she said, No better for him.

Then she said, He also had a freakish thing going for Billie Holiday and you know flesh and blood singers and dancers, no clothes on. I don't know, maybe his papa snuck up to the Cotton Club one night and came home and got his mama pregnant on the afterbeat. Anyway one night he was taking me to eat at this place out on the Strip and he kept saying, They'll think you're an exotic entertainer. You know you really could be from the Middle East. And I finally said, I don't want them to think that. I want them to think you're a rich businessman and I'm your secretary, like in *Esquire* magazine. He never did get that. I bet you every time he remembers me he thinks I want to be a dumb blonde. Some fay boys. I'm telling you, home boy. Almost as bad as some boot cats I know.

Hey, it sure is good to see you, I said, hooking my arm in hers. And as I looked at her cutting her eyes at me like that again, I knew that she was also pleased to see me. Then she said what she said.

Tell me anything, she said, half pouting half smiling. You know. Down-home girl. Way out here all by herself. Green. You know what I mean. A well-stacked country girl, frantic, and cute enough so we don't have to hide her, but not in the class with them sophisticated Fisk and Spelman girls, them Bennett College cuties, them Howard hincties. You know what I mean. Big time musician, girls all across the country, schoolgirls begging for your autograph. Blondes and brunettes climbing all over each other trying to get to you. Rich bitches swelling your head. Any old line for the likes of me. If you happen to run into me.

I know you know I know better than that, I said. I was still holding her arm. She held her head back from me. But she had to stretch her eyebrows above her dark glasses to keep from smiling. And I could tell she was having fun playing with me.

I'm the one don't know no better, she said. I'm the one, you know, they got me out of the back country a long time ago, but there's always a chance they ain't got all of the back country out of me yet. And as I tried to snuggle up to her again, I said, Hey what you brought out of the country, baby, is exactly what makes the city the city. She looked at me and shook her head again, making that down-home big mama noise of disapproval with her tongue and teeth.

You really can't help it, that's all there is to it. It's that band. It's that man. Turning all of his little half-smooth children loose on the nation. Then she opened her purse and refreshed her lipstick and said, Come on here, smoothie. And I called the waiter and paid for the drinks.

But hey, wait. Are you sure they don't have you over here looking for people to pick cotton in another one of them Gone with Scarlett O'Hara movies, she said. And I said, No, m'am, not me. No days like that. And she said, You know there really was some little half hip fay boy over here a few months ago trying to get on sometime with all that old stuff about recruiting extras. They used to pull that stuff. Boy, how they used to pull that stuff. But that last clown never did find out that anybody could have scored with them lushes he was getting with all that whiskey he was buying. Girl, I said, talking about that band. You can swap lies with anybody in that band any time.

That's when she said, That's all right about that. So you want to run with me tonight, huh? Boy, if they ever find out that you're out here playing around with Gaynelle Whitlow they'll never let you back in college. They won't even let you into barbers' college. And when I said, That's all right about college—I got their college; she said, Well, you know what I was sitting here getting ready to do when you walked in. I was just getting ready to go home and pull off my shoes and put on a stack of dirty low-down blues and get in the kitchen and cook me a good old home folks meal and sit right down and eat it barefooted. Some hogmeat, some black-eyed peas, some thin corn bread, some finger collards and okra. That's exactly what I'm going to do tonight. So, you still want to run with me? And I said, I just hope I got here in time to get my name in the pot. And she said, and also I also have the fixing for a sweet potato pie. All I've got to do is mix it.

We came outside and she saw the auto incognito and stopped in mock surprise and started nodding her head from it to me. I walked on over to it and opened the door and started rolling the windows down. Hey nice, she said. And I said, I'll be right behind you. But still looking the auto incognito up and down, she said, Yeah, very nice, home boy. You're doing all right for yourself out here.

So I said, don't lose me now. And she got into the convertible and backed out and waited and I pulled out into Crenshaw Boulevard and trailed her. We crossed Santa Barbara Avenue and stopped at a supermarket and came on toward Vernon Boulevard. It was almost seven o'clock then and there was the starless twilight sky above the six lane traffic, the neon signs, and the pale street lamps. I drove watching for her turn indicator.

She was living in View Park in those days. I followed her up the hill and along the winding tree-lined street and turned into the driveway behind her. She pulled all the way into the carport and came back toward me, arching her neck and making eyes at the auto incognito again.

So you've got yourself some fancy wheels, she said. And as I got out with the shopping bags, I said, Just something I borrowed. And she said, I thought maybe you were getting ready to start hauling your own little combo around or something. And I said, What kind of old chickenbutt combo? And she said, I don't know. I figured maybe you were getting your own little combo together by now, you being an ambitious college boy and all that. Now if you were still back down the way I might think you just got yourself a little red wagon, a little yellow basket for some of that kind of action. But I know good and well you don't need nothing like that out here.

That was when I told her who the station wagon belonged to and I said I was driving it because she wanted somebody to put some more miles on it and it was just what I needed to get my instrument to and from work. As we came on across the walk to the house I told her about how I met Jewel Templeton at the Keynote. Then I started talking about Eric Threadcraft.

The apartment was on the second floor, and as we came into the living room I saw the black and tan batik draperies and a long low couch and batik pillows. There were also hassocks and three fanback rattan chairs. Two Siamese cats lay curled on a large flokati rug. A snow white Persian padded in from the bedroom and started rubbing itself against her legs, its back arching, its mouth making soft meows.

This is Kitty Boo, she said. And this is Kitty Doo Doo and this is Mr. Skatrosantalango.

The base of the huge lamp on the long, ebony coffee table in front of the couch was a bronze cast of two entwined Hindu dance figures, one male and one female, of course. There were also several busts and torsos of Gaynelle herself on other surfaces around the room. And there were three large oils and a number of expensively framed sketches of her decorating the walls.

Here's this new thing old big butt Gomer put out, she said, holding up the album as she turned on the record player. And I said, I haven't heard old Gomer in months. And she said, And here's old Zonk. And I said, I've met him a couple of times, but I've never played with him. But I did jam with old Gomer one night in Greensboro, North Carolina.

She turned, snapping her fingers to the music, and I followed her through the dining area and into the kitchen. And the first thing she did was make a long cold fruit punch and then she started dinner. And I slid into the padded breakfast nook by the window. She moved about nodding her head to the music. It was dark outside now and beyond the sloping backyard you could see down the hill and out across the lights at the Crenshaw Shopping Center and Linet Park.

So, she said. Jewel Templeton. Is she supposed to be on some kind of music kick or something? And I said, She's got a lot of deep stuff going about the blues. Artistic stuff. Philosophical stuff. And she said, What kind of old philosophical stuff? I thought she was still trying to break into high society. And I said, One of her high society friends is a French marquis who collects all kinds of flesh and blood music.

The phone rang. She answered in the bedroom and while she was talking I had a chance to move around the living room and look at the pictures. In one large oil painting she was a Coptic princess, in another she was an odalisque, and in a third she was a dancer with her breasts bare and her hair done up in a topknot and she was wearing a banana skirt à la Josephine Baker at the Folies Bergère. On most of the drawings and sketches she was either a dancer or a torch singer. There was also a long collage made of light and shadow photographs of her posing nude.

She came back in and saw me looking at the watercolor near the record player. It was titled "Miss Georgia Brown" and it showed her walking along a Harlem sidewalk and in the background there was some abstract design representing the Savoy Ballroom, the Apollo Theatre, and Lenox Avenue north from 135th Street.

How about that stuff! she said smiling and shaking her head. She had changed into a blue gingham dress and as I followed her back into the kitchen I said, So you model some too. And she said, Well in a way, I guess. Somebody's always coming up with some weird idea about what I really look like. A guy named Django did the one you were just looking at. He did some of those little things too. He's always after me to let him sketch me. It's a wonder you haven't run across him by now. He is a real freak about flesh and blood music, she said. And I said, I know about him. I saw him in a studio one night. 7000 Santa Monica. And shaking her head she said, I don't know. Then she started to say something else and stopped and said, I don't know.

I sat looking at her moving about the kitchen in her flat house shoes, her apron nipping her waist like that and suddenly it was almost like seeing old frizzly headed Creola Calloway again, who used to break everyone's heart in Gasoline Point doing that same brown-legged, sweeteyed, sweetmeat, gold-smiling walk, going to the store in her pink bedroom mules, a thin five dollar gold piece on a chain around her left ankle.

She put the pork on, washed and picked greens, made the corn bread, and started mixing the potato pie. She sat on a high chair with the big old fashioned crockery mixing bowl in her lap, her head tilted, her earrings dangling, her cigarette drooping to one side, her eyes squinting against the curling smoke. So that's what you're doing these days, she said. Putting some more miles on it for Jewel Templeton. She kept a straight face and went on creaming the potatoes. And when I said, Hey, is it all right to leave it in the driveway like that? She nodded and smiled and said, They don't call you Schoolboy for nothing, do they? And I said, Joe States started that stuff the day I joined the band. And she said, See there, he knew you were an all-American genius. And I said, He knew I was just coming out into the world and that I had a lot to learn. And she said, A chick like Jewel Templeton can do a lot for you. I know you know that. That's why I know you're smart. Ain't no telling what I could be by now if I had your education. And that Ross Peterkin, he could be an ambassador or something.

She made the piecrust and I watched her put the design around the edge with the fork, remembering Gasoline Point again. Whenever I start thinking about how good old fashioned sweet potato pies can really be, I always found myself remembering how they used to taste on Saturday afternoons at Miss Alzenia Nettleton's cookshop next to Stranahan's store if you got there before they were all gone. And there was also Miss Pauline's cookshop in Gins Alley, where you could also get the best blackberry pie in season. You could go on and on about Gasoline Point and sweet potato pies. There was Miss Nicey Tompkins, who used to pass our house on her way to Buckshaw Corner balancing one basketful on her head and carrying one basketful in each hand. Then there was Octavia Wilcox, who used to have to make her mix in a big dishpan because Old Buttheaded Tom Wilcox used to lean crosslegged in the kitchen door and eat as many as three before he would move, folding them like apple turnovers as fast as they were cool enough to come out of the pans. And of course there was also Mama. She didn't have to back away from anybody making sweet potato pies either. But she made them only for special occasions like Thanksgiving, Christmas, and church suppers. What she was always making were the best syrup bucket tea-cakes and ginger bread muffins in the world.

But sweet potato pies, sweet potato pies, sweet potato pies. And then there were sweet potato pones, which were even rarer than fruitcakes used to be. Everybody including Miss Nicey backed away from Miss Alzenia Nettleton when it came to making sweet potato pones. Not only everybody in Gasoline Point. Everybody in that part of Alabama. After all, not only had she cooked for the governor, but governor's wives still sent for her to come all the way to Montgomery just to make sweet potato pones for one of their fancy banquets.

Hey, you really do kind of go for bad in the kitchen, I said to Gaynelle Whitlow. And she said, Yeah, bad. Ain't no use me trying to deny it. And I said, Spices aside I could tell by the way you move. And she said, I could tell by the way you move too, cutie pie. But you know, like I say. Tell me anything. But what I'm thinking is what I'm thinking about what's happening. Boy, you ain't driving that station wagon around just because Jewel Templeton just found out about flesh and blood music.

That was when she went on telling me what she had started telling me about herself and Hollywood. She was twenty-six years old and had not been married and didn't intend to be. Not any time soon, at any rate. She had been living in California since she was twenty-one. She had left Mississippi on her nineteenth birthday and had spent a year with an aunt in Chicago and sometime with another aunt in Cleveland. Then she had gone to New York and worked in a beauty salon for a year and saved enough money to pay her way out to the West Coast.

She had started out working in a beauty shop on Central Avenue and also taken a clerical course and worked at the Golden State Mutual Insurance Company about six months, after which she had helped to manage a little dress shop. Then, because she also knew how to sew (both of her aunts were seamstresses), she worked in the fitting department of a specialty shop on Wilshire Boulevard, from which she had gone into a fashion designer's establishment in Beverly Hills.

When I asked her if she had ever tried to get into the movies, she said, Believe it or not, and maybe you won't, but I could be in movies. By one means or another. I'll tell you about that sometime. Boy I can tell you some things and with your college education we could write a book.

When everything was ready to come off the stove we served our plates and I slid back into the padded nook facing her. She bowed her head and whispered a blessing. Then she picked up her knife and fork and winked at me as her bare feet touched my leg under the table. Then she went on talking.

The first white man I ever got tied up with in my life was a big and I mean big *rich* Hollywood producer, she said. He came in to talk to my boss about some designs we were working on for one of his movies and he saw me and flipped right there in front of everybody. You know how some fay guys start carrying on with all of that two-finger old ooh and aah artistic stuff and get all toted away when they see something they like. He came running up to me with his neck and ears getting all red talking about setting me up for a screen test. And I just looked at him. I had already been out here too long to fall for that kind of bull hype. But he was really gone on me and he kept on calling me and started sending me all kinds of expensive stuff. And I finally started seeing him and I had to quit that job so he set me up in one of those fine apartments that looked like it came right out of his Technicolor movies about the smart set and stuff.

There wasn't a cheap bone in him, and he was really straight about wanting to put me on the screen too, she said. He was always outlining some story and telling me about the part he wanted me to do, and sometimes he used to bring all kinds of fancy costumes by from the studio wardrobe and have me model them while he described scenes that I could wear them in. He had ideas for all kinds of stuff. Nightclubs, harems, slave ships, pirates' coves, Creole balls, South Sea islands. And he was sure enough toted out about that old African queen jungle princess stuff. Wait till I show you some of the wild jewelry he used to bring me. You saw those big paintings in there. He's the one that had them done.

What happened about the movies? I said. And she said, I told him I didn't want to be no actress. I told him if I was going to be in show business I could have been on the stage a long time ago. I got all kinds of show people right in my family. Folks in my family been in some of everything from the medicine shows and the riverboats to the Cotton Club and Paris, France. And I can sing and dance myself and know it. I just ain't going to be no stage entertainer. That's all. You know something? I've been hearing about California and dreaming about coming out here to Los Angeles all my life, but I didn't realize that Hollywood and Los Angeles were in the same place until I got out here. I just didn't. I just didn't care that much about it. I really don't care all that much about the movies. I never did. I used to go and I used to read the magazines just like most of the girls. But I was always more interested in the clothes and the places and the houses and all of that.

So why should I want to try to be an actress? she said as we went to get second servings of everything. There I was in the money and living like that jus because I was who I was. Just because I was a fine woman. Just because I was me. You know something I always used to do? I used to walk through all the swankiest stores in town and just look at the chicks who were buying all the best stuff. I used to do that back home. I used to do it in Chicago. I used to do it in Cleveland and I did it in New York. I used to just look at them and wonder who they were. And it was always the same old story. They were just women. Every now and then you might see one that was famous but just every now and then. Most of them that you saw in those places every day were just women with the right kind of man. And it's the same thing out here. And it's the same thing when you look at all them fine houses and apartments. Even in Beverly Hills, most of the people living in all them fine places out there ain't no more famous than me and you.

So what finally happened? I said, not considering the point she had just made until later on. And she said, He had to break it off for his health. After all, he was in his middle fifties and had not had that much of that kind of action before. Naturally he had been playing around with some of his young actresses a little, every now and then. But he was really just a middle-aged family man with a couple of grown-up children. He had everything under control when we started out. He'd come around two or three times a week and sometimes he'd spend the weekend. He'd come by and relax, play his kind of music, and tell me about all kinds of interesting things.

Then something happened and all of a sudden he was getting all frantic on me and starting to act like he just found out what it was made for, and he oversported his constitution. I still don't know whether it was really me or something to do with his work or his home life. But he started spending as much time as he could around me and then he started coming down with all kinds of ailments. I hate to sound country but I really do think rich folks get all kinds of diseases other folks never heard tell of.

We finished the main course of the meal and while the coffee perked, I helped her wash and put away the dishes. Then she took a tray with the pie and dessert plates and coffee cups into the living room and I brought the coffeepot. She was about to go on with the story but when I tasted the slice of potato pie she handed me, I held up my finger and said, Hey, this pie is as good as it looks. You really are some cook. You really are some girl, lady. And she said, I do like to hear that kind of stuff. I guess all women do. But you know something? I really am a bitch in the kitchen. I just flat am. I was just brought up that way. I used to fix one of my good old dinners for old stuff every now and then and knock him dead. And he knows about good cooking from all around the world. I'll just fix some old down-home something every now and then. Not often enough to give him any ideas about having himself a cutie pie who'd double as Aunt Jemima. Anyway the first time he just happened to come in on me fixing it for myself and I didn't make it no better or worse and he kept talking about how good it was smelling. And so that's how that started. And he really was a very sweet guy.

I didn't intend to cut in on you, I said. So what happened? And she said, He had to retire. He was in the hospital for a while and then he decided to move to Italy. She sat silent for a moment picking at what was left of her wedge of pie with her fork. Then she went on. When the time came to go you know what he did? He called me and offered to set me up in my own business. I had mentioned something about having my own little beauty shop or maybe my own style shop one time. And he remembered that. I told him I wasn't ready to start on anything like that yet and he said he was having his lawyer set up a nest egg for it anyway. And I have the papers right over there in that drawer.

We finished the coffee and she took the tray back in the kitchen and came back holding up a plain old fashioned flat pint hip flask of what was obviously a kind of down-home bootleg corn whiskey.

Hey, what's this? I said stretching my eyes. And she said, Boy, I'm on this kick tonight. And she put another stack of records on the turntable and came back and sat on the couch beside me and poured me a single and herself a double and we settled back with the Hammond organ, guitar, bass, and drum quartet playing a walking blues in the background. She sipped her drink and I tasted mine and waited for her to go on.

He was a sweet one, she said. Of course everybody I ever had anything to do with like that was really nice to me. But this guy was just kindhearted. He sure didn't owe me anything after all the other stuff he had given me. You know what I mean? But boy, the next guy. Like I say, they were all nice to me, but I can tell you some pretty funny stuff too. I met this next guy at a party for the guys in the Count Basie band one night. He couldn't dance a little bit. But he was one more fine looking thing. He was in his middle thirties and he had black hair with specks of fresh gray in the temples. In a way he kind of reminds you of a Spanish bullfighter, except that he was a bigger kind of guy and he wasn't built that neat. He was also collegiate looking. He wore those heavy black rimmed college boy eyeglasses and he dressed kind of like you.

He really was one low more no dancing cat, but he kept trying and he kept saying he was having himself the time of his life and it was all because of me and well, you know. So we get out to his place about six o'clock that next morning. And I looked up and there was this great big old delta plantation house sitting up there facing down toward Coldwater Canyon. Big old white columns, honeysuckle vines, magnolia trees, and all. I guess they were honeysuckle and magnolias. I'm sure they were the nearest thing you could find to the real thing. I bet you that.

Then when we got inside there were all kinds of old Civil War stuff everywhere. All kinds of slavery time stuff framed up like art. A large full length picture of Robert E. Lee with the Confederate flag on one side and the Virginia flag on the other was the first thing you saw when you came into the ballroom size living room. And when you stepped into the dining room there was old Stonewall Jackson. I didn't say anything. I just kept checking all that stuff. And when you looked out into the backyard there was all kinds of old corny Stephen Foster stuff all scattered around. You know, all that old wrought iron stuff and all them old trees under the care of tree surgeons. The swimming pool had so many weeping willows drooping around it that it looked like the Swanee River.

You know what he turned out to be? A rich *and again, I mean very rich* city boy. And he was on that kick because he really believed he had missed a big part of the fun of being an American white man because he hadn't grown up on a planta- tion down in the good old Deep South with a lot of us folks surrounding him.

Oh yeah, I know all that old stuff, I said. And then I said, You know I can still remember how folks used to talk about stuff like that saying, The first thing some white people do as soon as they get enough money to pay the rent and start eating regular is go out and hire a bunch of the *folks* to be around them. And she said, Yeah I know about that too. But this cat is all tangled up in a way I personally had never seen before. He had his whole life all tangled up in it. He's supposed to be one of the biggest consulting experts out here for any kind of production about the South. That's what he got his degrees in. He's got a whole library full of southern stuff. And right in the middle of it stretching away from his work desk is a long sand table where he can lay out any battle needed for a Civil War movie.

What does he look like? I said. Don't tell me he goes around looking and acting like a Mississippi riverboat gambler on his way to New Orleans. And she said, No. He isn't that kind of guy at all. Like I said, he's a college looking guy. You know, he's been to Harvard, Yale, and Princeton. And the University of Virginia. And you know something? He'll believe just about anything if he can find enough about it in some books. And he wouldn't believe something he's looking right at, touching, smelling, tasting, or even fucking until he found out what the big book authorities had to say about it. Look. Sometimes he'd start out on some long line of that old unreconstructed moon-light and molasses stuff about what the South was really all about or something like that, and every time I tried to set him straight he would look at me with that little grin like I couldn't possibly know anything about it at all and start talking about what's your authority, what's your source, what's your second-ary source, and what's your primary source? And I would say, Man, I'm my own authority. Man, I was born knowing better than all that old stuff you talking about. I said, You talking about where I was bred and born and raised. That's my pri-mary source and common sense is my ultimate authority.

Too bad he didn't grow up around some of us folks, I said. It really might have been good for him. And besides, I looked at her and winked and said, If you're going to mess around with this stuff, best you get started early.

But the main thing about him, she said, ignoring my wink, is that he is really a nice guy. I mean really nice. He doesn't be-lieve in any of that old Jim Crow stuff at all and never has. Let me tell you something. He used to take me almost everywhere. We used to eat all up and down the Strip and across La Cienega and we walked into the first class clubs and have tables as good as any movie stars, and if anybody ever even looked like they wanted to question it he'd turn the place out and pay for it. But wait a minute, what I didn't tell you was that all that old consulting stuff is really just a hobby. He definitely don't need the money. I'm talking about the kind of rich boy that could buy the whole joint just to fire the waiter.

Well, as I was saying, he didn't take any foolishness at all about anything like that. But then when we would get back home, he would always want to try to get one of his old weird games go-ing again. And when I said, What kind of old weird games? She said, Bedroom games. Historical bedroom games.

Well. The first one he pulled he just wanted me to take all my clothes off and stand on a hassock and he would just walk around looking at me stroking his chin and feeling me. An-other one he used to like was to come up behind me as soon as I stepped out of all my clothes and tie a maid's apron on me with a hundred dollar bill in each pocket. All kinds of stuff like getting in bed wearing a big wide West Indian straw hat and smoking a long black cigar with a bottle of rum on the floor. Or sometimes it might be a little thing like me letting him tear my panties off. Or me putting on a pair of old fashioned mammy made drawers he got from the studio wardrobe department.

And one night I woke up about three o'clock and there he was trying to handcuff me to the bed, she said. And I said, Hey come on, Gaynelle, not really. Come on. And she said, Why would I lie about something like that? Then she said, He wasn't really trying to start anything rough or anything like that. He was just trying out something he read about or probably had come across in a script he was working on. It wasn't rough. It was really funny to me. I mean funny as hell because the cat was wearing a goddamn patch over one eye. And one silk scarf tied around his head and one around his goddamn waist.

Well what did you finally do about him? I said. And she said, I had to put him down. And I said, What happened? And she said, I don't know. All kinds of weird stuff. In the first place he started getting more and more jealous of my musician friends. Now remember now, after all this cat met me at a band party. I've been knowing band guys ever since Chicago and Cleveland. Some I've been knowing since home before they got with a band. Well you know how you old thugs carry on with all that hugging and kissing and signifying. Man, I suddenly realized that all that old jive time carrying on was scaring the stuffing out of this cat. He'd been reading about some of the old piano players plunking all night and partying all day and he got it all tangled up with all that old historical southern stuff about slavey time stud horse niggers. And Reconstruction time jellybean gamblers and pimps. And it started backfiring on him and almost drove him crazy. I really thought that he was going to flip his lid. And like I said he was really a nice type of guy.

What happened? One night he came in and started raving about he didn't want no Scarlet Creeper spending the money he was giving me. And when I said, What the hell is a Scarlet Creeper? it turned out to be somebody he had read about in a book about Harlem. And another time he came in asking me about what us folks mean when they say black snake. And when I told him, Hell man, we mean what everybody else mean, he started talking about all them old songs about black snake hanging round my door, black snake creeping in my room, black snake coming in my bed. All that old stuff.

I interrupted and said, Hey I used to know a guy. He used to play all the old black snake songs on the guitar. And boy, I used to like the way he hopped a freight train as much as I liked the way he picked that box. But go on.

Then he really got weird. You know what the last straw was? You won't believe it. You can't believe it. I'm a hip chick. I know it. And I never heard anything like it in all my born days. You know what he did? He offered to give me a twenty-five-thousand-dollar down payment to let him get a baby on me. How about that? He had it all figured out. Not in cash. He was going to give me five thousand cash when he got the results back from the rabbit test and set up twenty thousand in escrow to be paid when I came out of the hospital after the birth. And he was also going to buy me a new convertible and set me up in a house somewhere like on Buckingham Road. You ever heard anything like that in your life? And he wasn't kidding. He offered to go out and get some legal papers drawn up. Well now you know good and well I had to unass the area when he kept coming up with that kind of old stuff, she said.

And when I said, Girl, you know some stuff, she said, Me, I just chalk it all up to experience. I don't know. Sometimes I think I is and sometimes I think I ain't. But you know something? Sometimes I think this cat I'm tied up with now is passing. He knows just a little bit too much. Sometimes I think he keeps me set up like this just so he won't have to be homesick for Dixieland. I really do. He's out of town on a business trip now, but I really wouldn't be a bit surprised if he's really down home visiting some of his flesh and blood kinfolks.

You really think he might be pulling some stuff like that? I said. And she said, It keeps crossing my mind. Every now and then a little something will happen. Not that he's raising all that much extra hell and getting all greedy and acting like it's going out of style. But you know, every now and then he really does remind me of one of them high yaller boys, half with it and half running from it.

I said, Like I said, girl. You sure do know some curious stuff. I said, Girl, you could get in there and trade choruses in any key and any tempo with the one and only Miss superhip Shari herself. And she said, The one and only Miss Shari who? And when I said, Zaad, she said, Oh her. Then she said, Did she really jive that horny stud out of it every night for a thousand and one nights in a row and him being a certified sheik with a whole harem full of so many of the best looking and best stacked chicks that he could afford to kill one every night just because he didn't want anybody else to have any of what he had been with?

And I said, Not really. I said, The idea was to keep him coming back every night because she had something more to offer than just her body. And she said, Okay, yeah, I can dig that. So she had some geisha jive going for her. And I said, She sure did. And with her it was a matter of life or death.

Then I said, Because the thing was not to keep him from doing it but to avoid the gorilla reaction to detumescence. I said, You know what they say about the gorilla? They say once that somich blows his stack, shoots his wad, busts his balls, he's through with the female and is subject to kick her ass out as if she (not he!) were an empty carton.

And that was when I also said, As for Scheherazade preserving her cherry, it turns out that at the end of that thousand and one nights she and old King Shahryar had begotten three boy children, one walking, one crawling, and one sucking. And she said, See there. Look at that. Boy you're something. Boy you're deep. Boy they don't call you Schoolboy for nothing.

When we went to bed she started kidding me about Jewel Templeton again, and all I could do was take it and squirm and wait for her mood to change. And when it did she said, Okay, I just wanted to see if you let that big name bitch go to your head. Some guys do, she said. Some guys act like it's the greatest thing in the world to look up there and see all that stuff all spread out against that big screen and be able to say that they been next to it. Like what is that? Plenty of guys and I mean plenty are willing to pay all kinds of alimony and shit for the rest of their lives. Especially the ones that didn't do anything with it when they had it.

Boy these people, she said laughing. Then she said, So you got the big head about that famous bitch? And I said, No, ma'am, not me. And she said, Now you gonna lay up here and try to tell me that Jewel Templeton is just another piece of well stacked meat to you? All right now, all right now, all right now. And I said, I didn't say that. And you know it.

And she said, Well okay. Because I was just about to say that driving her station wagon around must be giving you something even worse than the big head. Because if there's one thing I know it's you flesh and blood cats and that's another thing I have against fay chicks. They always spoiling you. Ain't no flesh and blood woman going to be spoiling you like that. Unless it's some kitchen mechanic and she ain't going to take but so much of you either. And there are plenty brownskin cuties like you walking around wearing all kinds of switchblade and razor tattoos to prove it. I bet you that's exactly how your old bossman got that cute little scar on his cheek. I bet you fifty dollars he made some bat salty and she went upside his pretty head. You can't tell me much that I don't already know about flesh and blood, she said.

Then she said, So tell me about it. And I said, About what? And she said, About all this stuff you got going with the famous Miss Almighty Jewel Templeton. And I said, Well now, you also have to admit that she is also one more fine looking woman fame or no fame. And she said, I'm not talking about that. She said, I wouldn't try to take anything away from her looks. Yeah she's fine. But good looking women come a dime a dozen and you know it. And you also know good and well you're used to seeing even better looking chicks than her hang around the bandstand every night all across the country. Better looking, better built. Both younger and older. And easier. But not famous. Me, I don't care anything about all that myself. I'm just trying to find out whether you got the big head. And I said, Well I'm not going to say her name doesn't have anything to do with it because I know you know better. But I do say it's not really the main thing.

And she said, I know, I know. I'm just teasing you. Ain't no big deal. I don't know. Maybe it's because I'm surprised at how pleased I am to see you again after all this time. So you really took me at my word that next morning at the Vineyard, didn't you. You showed me, didn't you. Jewel Templeton. Not bad, home boy. Not bad. Even for a college boy.

Then she said, But there I go teasing you again. But I really am glad to see you, home boy. But you got to prove you're not lying when you said what you said. So, come on over here and show me how much you missed me all that time up in the hills. And I said, If you say so. *And then there was only the two of us again as in you and me and me and you equals us and we were doing what we were doing which was what we had been doing plus what we were then doing which was what I was doing within that which she was doing and beyond the bed, the room, and that part of Los Angeles Hollywood was far away and there was all that which I was going to be doing plus that which I had already done and I thought this is what I shall have done.*

What woke me up that next morning was her saying, Hey is that daylight out there? Don't tell me that's daylight out there. That can't be daylight this quick, she said. I just closed my eyes three minutes ago. I don't believe this, she said. And when I opened my eyes I saw that the darkness was gone and that the time was six o'clock plus. *California, hey California.*

Now I know good and well the famous Miss Pink Nippled, Pink Toed, Mane-Tossing Jewel Templeton ain't about to be keeping you that busy, she said. She got her famous face to worry about. Them pale tailed chicks come out of a night like that with telltale splotches and stripes all over them.

You could see all around the room. The air was damp. But not as aromatic and chilly as it was in Beverly Hills. You were in California all right but this was not Hollywood and Beverly Hills and Bel-Air. This was Los Angeles, West Los Angeles, and Baldwin Hills and View Park territory. I pulled the spread up and closed my eyes again as she was saying, I know you know better than to be expecting this kind of old carrying on every time you just happen to come over this way Mr. School-boy Wonder. But I'm just telling you up front because I don't want you to be getting no wrong ideas about anything. You know what I mean. Because if I don't know about you flesh and blood cats when it comes to this kind of fooling around I don't know nothing about nothing.

And I also know all about how some of you all act when you're around them fay bitches. I know exactly how some of you all go around putting on all them classy airs and pulling all that old ooh la la hype. And then come around us and act like all they know what to say is, Come on baby. And all they expect to do is not go somewhere looking at fancy pictures and listen to high class music and stuff, but just to do that and eat and sleep. You hear what I'm saying? Like somebody like the likes of us ain't even intelligent enough to want to get the news on TV. And I said, You want to get the news on TV? You want me to turn it on? And she said, I'm not talking about you personally. She said, I'm just talking, boy.

But you know good and well them fay broads ain't going to let you lay up like this all the time even when they are rich enough to be keeping you. And they don't even have their hair to worry about. This sweaty mess is going to cost me money to get untangled, boy, she said. And I said, All chicks worry about their looks. I said, All chicks spend money on their hair these days. All sharp chicks, that is, I said. And she said, okay, smarty.

She got up at seven-fifteen and made coffee and fed the cats. And then she got up again at a quarter of nine and I dozed back off and when I woke up hearing the radio I was also smelling bacon and eggs. It was nine-fifteen and on my way to the bathroom I heard her talking to the cats.

We sat in the breakfast nook, me in my fancy shorts and her wearing a shorty short peignoir. She had done her hair up in pin curls, which she had covered with a silk scarf that she wore like a turban. There were grits, bacon, eggs, and hot biscuits; and as we ate you could see the morning mist lifting outside; and the windows of the houses stretching away down the hill were beginning to glitter although the sky was still streaked with haze that was going to become part of the late morning smog.

And don't be expecting this kind of brownskin service every time either, she said smiling at me. She looked almost as good in the morning with her face freshly washed and without makeup as she did all dressed up and out zipping around town in her convertible.

I know Jewel Templeton can serve you squab on toast every morning, she was saying. But just remember I did all this with my own two hands. Just remember that. Cotton field princess fingers and all, Mr. College Boy.

She poured herself another cup of coffee and lit a cigarette and looked out of the window. On the radio there was a program of show music. I watched the sky clearing beyond Linet Park. And when I looked at her again she was yawning. She saw me looking at her and almost blushed. I never was to see her really blush. And I never was to see her really angry either. She was always signifying about something and I still haven't figured out how much she was signifying at me and how much was really meant for herself.

The music played on and I followed each melody remembering most of the words without humming them. Then the one playing was "Blossoms on Broadway," which was somebody's radio theme during my freshman year in college when my roommate and I always kept up to date with what was happening in show business, not only by going to the periodicals room to read the entertainment section of the *New York Times* and the *New York Herald Tribune*, but also by reading the copies of *Stage* magazine passed on to us by young Associate Professor H. Carlton Poindexter from Hamilton College and Howard University and the University of Chicago. He was the one in whose class we both studied Introduction to Ideas and Forms in Literature, and he was also the one who was to become the faculty equivalent of my best of all possible roommates when my roommate transferred to Yale, even as he was already the college extension of Mr. B. Franklin Fisher.

Boy, I heard Gaynelle Whitlow saying then, I must be out of my head or something, messing around here, playing around with my birthright like this. And I said, Is that what they call it now? And she said, That's what I call it. And in imitation of the jive line that I knew she would spot as coming from the Bossman Himself, I said, I never argue with beautiful people. Not in the morning, I said. Not on a beautiful morning like this. Not in such delightful circumstances as these. And she let me get away with it and said, Naturally. I don't blame you. Look at you. Just look at you. You should be ashamed of yourself, she said. And I said, Aw come on, baby. And realized how it sounded as soon as I said it. But she let me get away with that too and said, Boy, what am I going to do about you? And I said, You'll think of something.

When I got ready to go that afternoon, she decided to trail me as far as Crenshaw and Adams and we stopped at the Home Plate to have a quick one for the road. And she said, Call me sometime. Like the last time, she said. You know. Anytime for me. Sometime when you get around to it. Sometime when you think you might be coming over in this part of town again.

One day when you wake up with them old down-home back alley blues again, she said. And I said, Come on, Gaynelle. It's not like that and you know it. And she said, Yes it is too. And ain't nothing wrong with it. Ain't nothing in the world wrong with knowing where to go to find something good for what ails you. I'm just letting you know you're welcome to give me a buzz sometime when you don't have anything better to do.

And I said, Why are you talking like that? And she said, Like what? And I said, Like that. And she said, Me, as far as I'm concerned, I'm just glad to know you. And I said, Now see there, here you come again. And she smiled and said, One of these days I'll probably be happy just to say I used to know you. And I said, Okay, okay, okay, but me, I'm just as happy as I can be just to say I know you right now.

Then she said, Yeah but I'm talking about you're on your way somewhere to be somebody important. And when I said, Everybody is somebody important, she said, I know all about that. I told *you* about that already. I told you about me and show business. I made up my mind about that a long time ago. Before I left Mississippi. I used to read all them movie magazines just like everybody else. But all the other girls were dreaming about being stars and seeing their names up in lights. And what I was dreaming about was mostly the clothes and the houses and stuff like that. But you know what I really want? I just want to live good and know a few fine people in different walks of life as friends along the way. That's me just like what you out there in the professional world trying to find out what you really want to do is you.

When we came back outside she walked over to the auto incognito with me, and when I started the motor she said, Be sure not to give my regards to Miss Jewel Templeton. But I do wish her well, because I wish you well, honey boy. And that's also why I got to say this. Boy, you be careful over there now. There is a lot of big money invested in that chick and I know you know as well as I do that it don't take much to make some of them people nervous, and I mean very nervous.

XXXVI

ALL Jewel Templeton said on the telephone just before dusk that Monday of what turned out to be the last week I was to spend in Southern California for several years was that she was glad that I was already there and that she was on her way. But the sound of her voice gave you the impression that there was a problem of some sort that she wanted to tell you about as soon as she could get through the rush hour traffic along Sunset Strip.

So when she finally came in almost forty-five minutes later I was surprised, because she seemed every bit as unruffled as she usually was; and she said what she said as if what she had in mind didn't have anything to do with any problem, only a quick shift into uptempo for a few measures before settling into another groove.

That was why when she told me what she told me later on I suddenly realized that I had actually stopped thinking of her as an actress. Not that you ever really forgot that she was a movie star. Maybe because it was as if a movie star was somebody who practiced the art or craft of make-believe only when there were locations, sets, lights, cameras, crews, and a director. Otherwise movie stars spend most of their time trying to be free to be whoever they really and truly were, warts and all! Whereas it seemed to me that it was not at all unusual for actors and actresses of the theater to approach real life situations as if they were scenes in a play. Anyway it was easy enough for me to forget that Jewel Templeton was, after all, first of all, or rather along with everything else, an actress because there was hardly anything theatrical about the person that I had come to think I knew as well as I did.

Not that anything would have turned out any better or worse if I had been aware of the whole story at the time. And besides what the way she said what she said really amounted to was pretty much the same old fake-out that long trusted good friends are forever using to set up a surprise party. When you look back, the subterfuge although not entirely untrue is also transparent but not at the time of the come on.

What she did when she came in that evening in Beverly Hills was make me a proposition that we both knew I could hardly refuse. The first thing she said was what she said about being held up in traffic. Then she said, So this is what's up. But then with just the right touch of feedback twinkle in her voice as well as her eye, she said, Speaking of the ever so definitive matter of improvisation the existential implications of as I have or think I have come to understand it from you and the marquis, how flexible are your various projects and contractual obligations as of now? Or perhaps I should say how portable?

And when I said, As flexible and portable as almost always, which I hope is enough, she said, Does that by chance also mean that you have a current passport? And I said, It just so happens it does. I said, Not that I've ever used it yet. But that's one of those professional personnel details that Milo the Navigator sees to it that you take care of right away, even while you're only a temporary replacement in that band.

And she said, I thought as much, because as little as I knew about that part of the world of music before I met the marquis I always knew that the Bossman Himself like Louis Armstrong was an international American force. Then came the proposition that you knew you were not only expected to accept or decline immediately but also be ready to act upon in a matter of several days at most.

She said, How would you like to join me on an expense free trip to Europe for an unspecified number of weeks or maybe months? And I said, Very much. Then I said, What part of Europe? And she said, the South of France, arriving Nice Saturday you by way of a change in New York and me from business matters in Paris after other aspects of the same in Milan.

I leave tomorrow night, she said, And we meet in Nice Saturday. All I have to do is call the travel agency in the morning and your kit will be delivered here before noon. So what I was hoping was that all you have to do is pack a bag or so and make a few phone calls. There's cash on hand for all incidentals between now and Saturday and some to spare. Oh yes, just in case you're wondering, it's studio money all of it. So as you will see everything is strictly first class.

Oh this is fine, she said then. Just fine. As I hoped it would be, she said, and now I must zip up to Esther and get together what I need for two conference stops before setting down in Nice. The Côte d'Azur is to be sure no problem. Not for people from these parts. But let me go so there will be time for a brief toodle-oo until Saturday.

You couldn't keep yourself from wondering what it all was really about, but once she had presented it as a game of improvisation at the very outset, you couldn't start asking for explanations and the usual routine details without running the very likely risk of creating the devastatingly scandalous impression that you were hesitant about committing yourself to a spur of the moment situation that was after all obviously only a real life equivalent of the jam session.

She had said where and she had said when and if she had wanted you to know any of the specifics of wherefore at this time she would have told you that too. So to ask why could easily imply that you actually had doubts about her intentions. *Which was not the case at all. Quite the contrary. You had no reason whatsoever not to go along with anything she was so eager to share with you precisely as fairy tale aunts in whatever disguise have always done. Who have become guardian angels when necessary but never wicked witches. Not so far at any rate. And whoever else ever took such sheer delight in springing surprises. Who themselves were nothing if not surprises in the first place.*

So what I settled for was the immediately credible possibility that what she had taken advantage of some studio project to set up was a trip that would include meeting the Marquis de Chaumienne perhaps as much as a surprise for him as for me. Not that I didn't cross my fingers, but further questions were *out* of the question because there was also the totally unnecessary risk of being a spoilsport.

Which is why it was not until we had been in the South of France for a week and a half that I finally found out that the slight edge of agitation that I had thought I heard as soon as her voice came over the telephone that afternoon was actually only a bit of not quite controlled excitement involved in the elaborate game of one-upmanship she had worked out and was on her way home to spring on me.

Not that it had taken me that long to ask about it, because I never would have done that. Not me. Not about anything that had to do with studio transactions and policies. If she brought it up, fine. Otherwise no mention. Maybe if she had been in production during my time there, things would have been different. But that was not to be.

What brought the sound of her voice on the telephone back to mind that many days later was her response to what I said about not going back to Hollywood when she went, because the time had come for me to move on into the also and also of whatever else I had to find out about myself and about what I was going to do about which of the inescapable ancestral imperatives.

That was what I had been getting myself ready to tell her for several weeks, and then we were already where we were, and I had already gone through what you go through whenever you have to pack up to move on, but as soon as I drew my breath to say it I suddenly realized that she not only already knew what I had in mind but had also already known it long enough to plan the open-ended junket we were on. Something she had long since planned to do for and with me before I myself either went to rejoin the band or decided not to put off going east to graduate school any longer—or before she herself came across a script she liked and became caught up in the all-consuming details of her next production.

I went ahead and said what I said, which was only enough to make the point I wanted to make about the never stated but never ending obligations that come with the endlessly bountiful hospitality of storybook guardian aunts. And that was when she said what she said about fairy tale aunts existing only in the self-made world of storybook princes.

Apropos of all of which, she was also to say, as we made our way down to the surf after lunch and siesta that afternoon: Tinsel Town, Tinsel Town, Tinsel Town. That's Hollywood, to be sure. But if you believe that there is less make-believe in the South of France or anywhere else than is concocted in those studio sound and special effects stages and all of those far-flung "location" picnics you are most assuredly and totally mistaken.

Of course there's make-believe and there's also make-believe, she said, as we spread the towels on the stony sand, and the difference is a matter of taste, which is, as the marquis points out, much the same with life and the arts as with cuisine, that is to say, *a sense of the optimum quality, proportion and processing of the ingredients in the recipe.*

So put that into your big brown oracular goddess of a bass fiddle and pluck away my bright eyed nimble fingered road musician, she said as I sprinted ahead to the damp sand and water's edge thinking, *This many miles beyond Chickasabogue Bridge and the canebreaks and the bayou, this many more miles along the way.*

THREE

The Craftsman

XXXVII

A FEW YEARS later on there would be the Great Circle Route from Los Angeles International nonstop over the pole. But at the time that I left California to meet Jewel Templeton in Nice, you didn't really feel that you were actually on your way to Europe from anyplace in the United States until you finally took off from Idlewild International in New York and headed out across the Atlantic on a trajectory that was pretty much the same as the one that took Lindbergh and *The Spirit of St. Louis* to Le Bourget back when I was in the seventh grade.

So my first transatlantic passage by air began by also being my first cross-country flight all the way from the Pacific Coast to the eastern shores of the early colonials, traversing the legendary deserts and the Bad Lands, the Great Divide, the Great Plains, the Mississippi Delta, and the foothills of the Pennsylvania Appalachians at speeds beyond any super express train and at altitudes that made falcons and eagles seem earthbound.

Also in those days as was likewise the case back during the high times of the transoceanic liners, when the ports of embarkation had to be reached by road or rail, the stopover in New York gave you what was not only a two-part journey but in effect was also two distinctly separate journeys altogether, each with its own significantly specific objectives. Because as incidental as the first part was to the second it was no less a destination as such than a junction, even so.

New York, New York, I said as the flight pulled on away from El Segundo and beyond the Sierras. *Back to the Apple yet again*, I said, realizing even as I did that I would be there in a matter of only hours and minutes this time. By super streamlined train it was a matter of days. By road band bus it was a matter of at least several weeks of one night stands and theater dates at best.

From Mobile back when New York was as much the Phila-mayork of fireside and swing porch yarn spinners as an actual point of arrival on a timetable, you took the L & N north-bound to Montgomery and changed to the eastbound West Point route to Atlanta, from which the southern took you on out of Georgia and through South and North Carolina and

Virginia and into Washington, the border town of Dixieland and the transfer point for the Pennsylvania Railroad and the last six hours it took to get through Maryland, Delaware, the state of Pennsylvania, and New Jersey and into Penn Station at 33rd Street and Seventh Avenue.

The trip from Mobile by train was also a matter of perhaps three days at most (with fair connections). And the thing about it in those days was that most of it took you through what had become of the old Confederacy, most of which (largely because of the notorious Hayes-Tilden Compromise of 1877) was not only far from being reconstructed in accordance with the Thirteenth, Fourteenth, and Fifteenth amendments, but still in violently reactionary defiance thereto.

Mobile, to be sure, was also a part of the old Confederate South, but even so you never thought of Mobile as being a Civil War town as Montgomery, Atlanta, and Richmond were. Montgomery was where old Jeff Davis was sworn in to lead the seesesh against Lincoln and the Union to defend to the death their freedom to own slaves. Atlanta was Sherman, Sherman, Sherman, and the wages of rebel yells. And of course Richmond was the actual wartime capital of the ever so arrogant but ill-fated C.S.A. from which Jeff Davis had to flee once Grant did what he did to Lee. But Mobile as I grew up knowing it was always somehow different. On the one hand it was nothing if not loyal to the southern cause, and the Battle of Mobile Bay was a very important Civil War event, indeed, coming as it did after the fall of New Orleans. So there was no shortage of C.S.A. monuments and Confederate flags.

But on the other hand along with forever advertising itself as a City of Five Flags (Spanish, English, French, Confederate, and American), it was not only an international seaport into which ships and seamen came from all over the world, it was consequently also a place with downtown streets and side streets along which it was perfectly natural to find yourself among people representing so many of the languages and customs and even costumes of so many of the lands that Miss Lexine Metcalf's Windows on the World bulletin board made you realize what classrooms were also about.

Eastbound by air from Los Angeles International it was at times somewhat as if you were cruising above a sand table mock-up of a physical (not political) map of the Zone of the Interior U.S.A. Not that you could actually see very much except when the altitude and visibility were such that the pilot would announce over the speaker system that you were approaching this or that landmark on the right or left. But even so your ongoing reaction to the flight was that of a map reader superimposing overlays of political boundary lines and historic sights over natural earth shapes and features.

Along with all of which there were the recurring times when you nodded off and woke up again feeling the way you felt because as soon as you realized that you were still airborne, there was the also and also and elsewhere and elsewhere of moving on once more, and each time you checked your watch and closed your eyes again thinking, *Yes, very much the same as if alone on horseback with saddle pack, even so. Very much the same, indeed, for you and who if not you will go where you will go. Riding, riding, riding through the night through the day, riding, riding.*

I said, I come from Alabama. I said, This many miles from the spyglass tree and the also and also of the train whistle guitars of Gasoline Point and the saw mill bottoms on the outskirts of Mobile north of the bay and the coast of the Gulf of Mexico. This time by way of California, hey California. This many months after the elsewhere and elsewhere of road band bus routes. I said, This time after the first time since the campus of being in one town long enough to become used to not being used to being there. Which was pretty much the same as I realized that I had come to feel about the campus that spring as commencement time approached. Then on the road with the band you became used to not being used to being in the same place for more than a week or so at most. Which is why that is also what I said when old Ike Ellis said what he said about me being a quick study on the bandstand and also a quick study of life on the road. I said, Hey man, I'm just getting used to not being used to this stuff out here just as I'm getting used to not being on the campus anymore or back down in Mobile anymore. And he said, Hey man, that's deep, college boy. They don't call you Schoolboy for nothing. That's psychological. That's very psychological.

In New York I checked into Hotel Theresa and headed straight down to midtown to the Libraire de France off Fifth

Avenue on the promenade to Rockefeller Plaza and bought the latest editions of the Michelin and Blue guidebooks to the Côte d'Azur, Provence, Burgundy, and Paris. I had taken French at Mobile County Training School as well as in college, but that was also when I picked up a copy of the beginner's exercise book that I was later to use at Alliance Française.

Then I walked up Fifth Avenue to 53rd Street and went to the Museum of Modern Art mainly to revisit the permanent collection, especially what there was of Cézanne, Matisse, Braque, Picasso (*Ma Jolie*, *Woman in the Mirror*, and *Guernica*), Léger, Klee, Miró, Mondrian, Modigliani, and so on, in those days, the first two catalogs of which I still have.

There was also time to go to a special current exhibition of architectural design. Then afterward, I took the bus down to Greenwich Village to see a few of the writers and artists that I had kept in touch with since my times in New York with the band, and the first one I called invited three others to meet us at a cozy place off Sheridan Square where they treated me to a light early dinner and we talked until I had to leave to get uptown in time to pop in on musician friends working in spots along Seventh and Lenox avenues on my way to catch the first set at the Savoy Ballroom.

My New York stopover agenda for the next day included an early start for revisits to at least three of the landmarks that I had preselected from my ever handy old Federal Writers' Project guide to the city and environs (which I still have and which is mostly long since not up to date but which continues to become more and more important as a historical document of the period during which it was published).

From Jewel Templeton's collection of Phaidon volumes on the great masters I had also preselected what I wanted to see during a midday page-flipping-tempo visit to the Metropolitan Museum, from which I went on uptown and arrived at Sugar Hill on time for my pre-Idlewild visit with Royal Highness who pointedly reminded me of what he had already been telling me about his travels across the water; and also said, Now this is what I have to say: Boy, ain't no telling what I would have come back from over there in them parts with if I had been the kind of schoolboy you had sense and guts enough to become, young soldier. And don't miss my point about coming back. Because that's the main point of going over there in the first place. Don't ever forget that. All some splibs talk about when they tell about being over there is how free they felt from these old color line problems over here. And that's important. That's very important. But frankly, between me and you, young soldier, I can't name one refugee splib that's putting out anything even in the class with this homegrown stuff we turn out a dime a dozen. Let alone being out of sight of us because of all the advantages that they're supposed to enjoy by being over there. Not a single one. And you know why? Because it takes more than just being somewhere away from all this old cracker mess we got over here. So you can't put all the blame on them jaspers.

Of course now, if you want to become a brownskin Frenchman or refugee or some other kind of foreigner over there, that's your personal business because after all it's your life. But now, as for me, I just want to be the goddamnedest world-beatingest American I can get to be, because that's my birthright. Hell, young soldier, I know Josephine Baker, Sam Wooding, and Spencer Williams and most of the rest of them, and some of them might even have their French papers, but they're still foreigners to them Frenchmen as crazy about them as them Frenchmen supposed to be. And what they do is still something foreign from over here. Don't care how much them Europeans like it.

But hell, I'm satisfied that you're already on to what that's all about. So the main thing I'm hoping about you is that you will go on over there and see and learn about as much as you can. Because my point is you don't know enough about the world until you learn some more about it the way they've been dealing with it from over there down through the ages. Look at them Japs. Look at them Chinamen. They got some stuff that goes all the way back to ancient times too. And they know good and well that it all counts for more when you're tied in with all that stuff you're headed for.

But like I say. I'm satisfied that you know what my point is. So go on over there and find out as much as you can firsthand about all that stuff you already been reading about and studying up on in school. Then come on back over here and see what you can do with it.

Which reminds me of one more thing I'm counting on you for, young soldier. Whenever it come down to the point of being a splib dealing with them jaspers, don't ever forget that the main thing about this country we got over here is that so much of it is still a matter of unfinished business. Don't ever forget that. And don't forget who told it to you. Me, an old broken down entertainer. Maybe you're one of the ones that realized this rock bottom point from school. But don't nobody practice it better than splibs in show business. Take old Louis Armstrong. When old Louis puts his mark on a tune them jaspers find out that's what this country's music is supposed to be like. Don't care what they say in them conservatories. But hell, I don't have to tell you. The bossman and Old Pro and them got you branded from now on regardless of what you brought out of school.

That was the only mention of me and the band and the Bossman Himself during the whole visit. And that was the way I let things stand.

XXXVIII

WHEN THE flight to France finally taxied out to its takeoff runway and climbed to the assigned elevation and leveled off into its cruising speed I adjusted my seat to the coziest position for reading and pulled out the map, guide, and language workbook; but what I found myself thinking about was all of the first fireside and swing porch talk about the AEF troop transport crossings from Newport News, Virginia, to Brest on the Normandy coast back when Uncle Sam joined John Bull on the Western Front in the world war against Germany and the Kaiser (a.k.a. Old Kaiser Bill, he of the piked helmet, satanic mustache, and shriveled hand), *which was that many years before I found out where over there was because I can also remember hearing war songs and also talk about submarines and submarine chasers before I was yet school age and you didn't have to know about maps and geography until you reached the third grade.*

By which time it was as if I had known Soldier Boy Crawford from as far back as I can remember either the fireside or the swing porch. But the fact of the matter was that the way he used to tell about it that many years afterward made it all seem as if you had been over there in the trenches and at the outdoor cafés, in the country wine cellars, over there tramping in hobnail boots, eating hardtack and drinking cognac, over there talking parlez-vous, voulez-vous *zig zig.*

Old Soldier Boy Crawford, who talked French as much with his eyes, shoulders, and fingers as with his voice and lips, saying sand meal killing my trees easy to Paris, with his fingers articulating the syllables as if on a guitar (which come to think of it he couldn't even play). Old Soldier Boy Crawford, whose Parisian experiences as related in Papa Gumbo Willie McWorthy's barbershop were even better than any of the stories I had overheard about Storyville and Algiers down in New Orleans or about the Barbary Coast of San Francisco; and whose notorious and long since dog-eared deck of French postcards of positions for doing it (including sixty-nine a.k.a. reverse ninety-six) Little Buddy Marshall was finally to find a way to borrow for our ever so casual but hardly calm perusal from time to time. In much the same manner as he used to borrow Mr. Big Buddy Marshall's .38 Smith & Wesson six-shooter every now and then for one another of our derring-do capers.

Old Soldier Boy Crawford. There was his France and his Paris, and then after Miss Lexine Metcalf and the earlier times of Charlemagne and Roland, which were followed by the even earlier times of Julius Caesar when it was not yet France but the Gaul of the first of two years of Latin conjugations and declensions that made first year French easier than it would have been without them. Meanwhile along with the movies and no less than the Wild West pulp magazines there were the Three Musketeers and D'Artagnan that many school years before the Paris of the Champs Élysées, the Arc de Triomphe, the Eiffel Tower, and then Montmartre and Montparnasse.

Sometimes it was as if the France of Mr. B. Franklin Fisher began with Louis XIV and then brought forth Jean-Jacques Rousseau whose writings including The Social Contract *helped to bring about the American war of independence and constitutional democracy thirteen years ahead of the French Revolution and the Declaration of the Rights of Man. And other times it was as if it had all happened so that a schoolboy genius like Napoleon*

Bonaparte could rise from the obscurity of Corsica to establish France as a supreme international military power and Paris as the most cosmopolitan of all cities.

What my good old best of all possible roommates had in mind when he sketched the design for the reversible escutcheon that tagged our digs as Atelier 395 was life in the garrets not only of Montmartre, the Belle Époque of the Moulin Rouge out of which came Picasso, Braque, and Matisse, but also of Montparnasse during the postwar period of the so-called lost generation of American artists and writers. And that turned out to be only the beginning. Before midterm test time arrived he had read Helen Waddell's novel about Peter Abelard and Héloïse and passed it on to me. For my benefit he had also read aloud his favorite ballad stanzas from François Villon's Legacy *and* The Testament *and was insisting that I be well into Rabelais'* Gargantua and Pantagruel *before the Christmas holiday break.*

Farce, my good fellow, he was to say time and again whenever Rabelais was the topic, the ridiculous, the hyperbolic, the ludicrous, the downright outrageous, without which there is no need for mathematical actuality and hence no engineering. Look to your pathetic repeat pathetic categories, my good man. Tragedy represents an engineering failure; comedy and melodrama represent engineering resolutions whereas farce—now there's entropy, old pardner, no less for metaphorical connotation than for factual denotation.

Which brings us to poetry whether in verse prose or drama, which includes the bawdy, robust, tongue-in-cheek and thumb-in-nose Rabelaisian along with the no less earthy but also more elegant world of our very own Ernest Hemingway. Item: the chilly beads of sweat on the bottle of white wine when Jake and Bill take it out of the clear, pebbly bottomed almost icy stream for lunch during that fishing trip in The Sun Also Rises. *Nothing counterstates the vanity of vanity or futility of futility that the book's epigraph is all about. Indeed much goes to show that whenever it was that his Côte d'Azur play pal Gerald Murphy said living well is the best revenge, our boy Hemingway already knew that the indispensable element in living well is elegance.*

Elegance is the best and perhaps even the only revenge against chaos, my good old trail buddy, he said. And the key to elegance is play. As who knows better than our fun-seeking verbal jeweler the intrinsic importance of the play repeat play of light and shadow and also sheen, sparkle, glitter, and twinkle? If you miss that and the verbal and auditory equivalents to it, such as connotation in words and overtones, chords and so on in music, shame on you, my good man. You might as well be a stone, or a particle or wave. Because we're talking about the quality and potential range of human consciousness, my fellow sojourner.

But back to Rabelais, mon semblable, mon frère. *You're going to be hard put to come up with anyone who better understood the basic function of slapstick and slapdash in this matter of forming meaning. Back to the vulgarity and popularity of the commedia dell'arte. But even so, your* Gargantua and Pantagruel *is no less notorious for its scholarly sophistication than for its irrepressible exuberance and its unflagging zest for fun and games. But then is it not written that Rabelais was "a monk by convenience, a doctor of medicine by instinct and choice, an editor by disinterested zeal and, finally, a writer because the medium of literature alone allowed him to express his infinite exuberance."*

That was the way such sessions almost always went during those two sine qua non, yes, sine qua non years that he was there. And then when he went on to the Yale School of Architecture, no new roommate turned up for my next year but from that midsummer before my junior year on through to graduation there was Mr. (associate professor but not yet doctor) Carlton Poindexter of the English Department who was already the faculty member that my roommate and I had identified most closely with from our very first Monday morning in English 101. Not only because he was already so obviously a big league college professor before he was yet thirty but mainly because of all of the current books and magazines on the shelves and the conference table in his office that looked out across the unclosed quadrangle to the library and the gymnasium with a parking area for the tennis court and the alumni bowl in between.

The current books and magazines along with the photographs and travel posters of textbook places as well as the color reproductions of contemporary art around the walls made him seem accessible to me and my roommate to a degree that was not even thinkable to me in connection with anybody on the faculty or staff back at Mobile County Training School. Nor was I yet as ready for it as I began to be as soon as I realized that I was in college and on my own without any hope of any financial support from any relatives anywhere. Which is also why I was ready to do what I did that summer. Because by that time I had not only taken two of his electives along with the two courses required by the prospectus, my roommate and I had also been asking him all of those historical and literary questions and also borrowing books from his office that were not directly related to any subject matter that he was teaching on any level. Meanwhile for his part he had also begun passing along things for us to read, not as teacher to student but as fellow enthusiasts, albeit somewhat less advanced. Nor could anything have been more flattering than the fact that he seemed to take it for granted that our extracurricular preoccupation would not intrude upon our required assignments in any other classes.

So from that summer on to graduation, he was the one who was there as my official faculty adviser and also as the nearest thing to a replacement for my roommate, whom he knew how much I missed because he missed him very much himself. Not for the same reason to be sure. But, given his sincerity as a teacher, perhaps not much less acutely even so. In any case, even as the two of us reminisced about him during the week before my commencement it was still as if his absence was only temporary. He was still my legendary roommate and still his most legendary of all pupils although his major field was architecture.

As for Carlton Poindexter himself, the difference between his authority and that of Mr. B. Franklin Fisher was especially significant to me at that time. Mr. B. Franklin Fisher's authority was that of a headmaster whereas one of the most striking things about Carlton Poindexter was how tentative he was about what the subject matter he knew so much about added up to in the workaday world at large.

Not that Mr. B. Franklin Fisher was ever dogmatic about literal application but his world of secondary education was the realm of pragmatic fundamentals, the world of carefully monitored drill sessions and the elements of grammar, mathematics, science, and the precise documentation of historical events and geographical relationships.

Which was entirely consistent with the all too obvious fact that at Mobile County Training School it was almost always as if the highest premium was placed on meeting the precise standards of *eligibility required by the occupations and professions that added up to social, economic, and political betterment as such. Nor could anything have been more consistent with community expectations, not only in general and in accordance with conventional ancestral imperatives that book learning was assumed to be about, but also with the specifics of what they had expected from him in the first place.*

I can remember them talking and speculating about him all that summer before he came. It was also the summer before I was to be in the third grade and carry my books strapped onto my wide First Year Geography *instead of a primer grade book satchel, and everywhere you went sooner or later somebody would mention something about the coming school year and the fact that there was going to be a new principal. There were sermons and prayers about it at church and discussions and arguments about it in Papa Gumbo Willie McWorthy's barbershop, and you heard no end of gratuitously avuncular signifying about what he was going to be like as you moved around the neighborhood and during swing porch visiting time at home.*

They tell me that new principal, that Professor B. Franklin Fisher is supposed to be rolling in town the day before Labor Day, and they say he is a natural born pistol. They say he has a way of just cutting his eyes in the direction of any kind of naughtiness that'll make these young rascals and freshtails straighten up as fast as cracking a whip; and they also say he got a tongue that can take the hide off of a Hog Bayou alligator.

"Lift Every Voice" was already a school bell song along with "My Country 'Tis of Thee" and "Oh, Say Can You See," but when he arrived that Monday morning it also became the anthem that specifically evoked the ancestral imperatives of the Talented Tenth. From then on it was also a school bell song that resonated as if surrounded by stained glass windows. That was a very special day indeed.

We were all there waiting, students, a number of parents, welcoming committees from civic groups as well as churches; and at five minutes before the last bell, the Ford bringing them, Mr. Hayes, who was driving, Miss Duval and Miss Lexine Metcalf, turned in and rumbled across the cattle-guard and came flivvering on up the drive with two carloads of faculty of staff people following.

Mr. Hayes got out first. He was wearing surveyor's boots and britches, and he was carrying a tricorn folded flag, and on the chain around his neck there was a whistle, which he blew and began lining everybody up parents and all for the Pledge of Allegiance ceremony. Then he marched us all to the entrance to the Assembly Room, and everybody was thinking that he was the one, until we got inside and found out who was going to speak.

He was standing at the podium wearing a dark blue hand tailored suit, and as soon as people saw him we could tell by the look on their faces that most of them were either mumbling or wondering is that him? That boy? Is that boy the man? Because what he looked like was a boy evangelist. The other teachers except Mr. Hayes who was standing at parade rest in back of the room and Miss Duval who was at the piano, were seated on the stage looking not unlike the evangelical chorus that they in fact turned out to be.

The music Miss Duval had been playing for us to get in step with as we came up to the landing to march into the assembly and find our seats and stand waiting by was a very fancy strutting New Orleans march called "High Society." But I guessed that the first number that we were going to have to sing together was "Lift Every Voice" because it was already the sound that went with school bell times and classroom smells, but that was the first time it also made you feel like being in church, which is exactly what Mr. B. Franklin Fisher wanted, and somehow even before he opened his mouth to say the first words you knew he was about to begin a sermon. And the first thing he said was that he was beginning an old time revival meeting that was going to last for nine months.

I've come here to these notorious sawmill outskirts of the historic and legendary seaport town of Mobile, Alabama, he began in a voice that was nothing if not that of a boy evangelist, to revive the spirit that that song from the turn of the century was composed to generate. It was first performed by schoolchildren such as you as a part of a celebration of Abraham Lincoln's birthday. But for me it is song of songs. For Mobile County Training School it is to be by my decree the clarion call to excellence.

The spirit of the extended revival meeting which I have come to conduct for this student body is the same that motivated and sustained the fugitive slave on the Underground Railroad, Harriet Tubman, Frederick Douglass, the nonpareil nobility of the *magnificent volunteers in young Colonel Shaw's Massachusetts 54th. It was what motivated bondage-born Booker Washington to service and uplift as freeborn white youths were inspired to wealth and status by the books of Horatio Alger.*

Who knows perhaps the grounds of our campus like those of some of our outstanding universities, colleges, and normal and industrial institutes were once a part of a plantation that our forefathers were bound to. Well true or not, it is in effect another kind of plantation with another sort of overseer. And I intend to raise my kind of crops on it. Yes, I come here to raise crops that will supply this town with the civic nourishment it hungers and thirsts for: Instead of catch as catch can common laborers, expert technicians and artisans who will prosper by putting brains and skill into the common occupations of life; crops of dedicated professionals with certification second to none and along with everything else in every walk of life our people need leadership, leadership, leadership, the potential for which may even now be fermenting in the most lawless and backward seeming corners down in Meaher's Hummock.

Apropos of all of which there was also to be that assembly session that I remember from the term in which I was in the ninth grade. He began naming famous leaders and their historical achievements and calling them our appropriate ancestors and he singled out old Elzee Owens and said, Citizen Tom Paine and when old crazy Willy Lee Berry whispered what he whispered to old Elzee about being put in the dozens the assembly which usually lasted from ten to ten-thirty each Wednesday went on until three o'clock with only a twenty minute break at one o'clock.

The dozens, he said. Stand up Willy Lee Berry. So now you're wondering how I heard you. Well, I got twenty-twenty vision as well as absolute pitch, so I didn't have to hear you. All I needed was to see you lean over and I didn't even have to read your lips. The dozens. Boy, I'll tell you something about the dozens. Boy, we were already in the dozens generations before we were born. Boy, they brought the flesh and blood ancestors of our people over here in chains in 1619. Boy, I'm not up here talking about bedsprings and berry thickets. I'm trying to tell you something about history and responsibility. I'm talking about you and your obligations to yourself and your allegiance to the principles on which the United States of America is founded.

If you call that playing the dozens, then I'm going to be playing the dozens with you from now on. All of you. Every last one of you. Boy, Tom Paine is precisely the great-great-great-granddaddy that suits the signifying you seem to think you're already qualified to whisper while your principal is addressing the junior high school student body. Citizen Tom Paine, yes, Citizen Tom Paine. Boy, I forbid you to put your number eleven feet on these grounds that we are in the process of hallowing until you read enough about his life and work to explain why I match you with him. And I'm going to be right here waiting for you at seven-thirty tomorrow morning. We'll all be here at seven-thirty and when we've heard from you we'll hear from your good friend Elzee Owens.

Then before Elzee Owens could figure out whether he also was supposed to stand up, the voice from the podium went on to say, In fact, I don't think we should slight any one of you, if you know what I mean. I mean I'm going to be standing right here pointing my finger and ready to pat my foot if it takes the rest of the week for every last one of you to testify. I mean I am herewith promulgating my grandfather clause. The Mobile County Training School corollary to the grandfather clause, effective as if of tomorrow morning at seven-thirty and appertaining to everybody in the seventh, eighth, and ninth grades. Your homeroom teachers will be right up here on the stage with me tomorrow morning and when they call your name you will answer by giving the ancestor you've chosen for emulation. You may change to someone else later as your aspirations come more and more into focus as you advance to graduation, but the ones you select for this exercise had better be suitable. Duplication of choices will be permitted but your reasons must be yours and yours alone. And please don't let me catch you using anybody's name in vain.

At that time I had my own reason for wanting to say Benjamin Franklin, but I knew very well you could never get away with that. And nobody would ever let you live it down. So I said what I said about Frederick Douglass as fugitive slave and said, For the time being.

That was the instantly legendary Mr. B. Franklin Fisher who had come not only in response to the official call of the school board and community elders but also as answer to the old folks' prayers down through the generations. And yet this was also the selfsame Mr. B. Franklin Fisher who said what he said when I won the award I won in the tenth grade: Note bene, note bene, note bene. *Every time some bright-eyed pupil like this comes out of the sawmill bottoms of Gasoline Point and makes straight A's in Latin 1 and 2, not only because he studies his lesson as required but also because he likes the history and the stories that he's able to translate, we are witnessing yet another personification of hope for the survival of the human proposition as such.*

But then who if not he was the one who said what he was to say when he presented me my diploma and announced the college scholarship award. Everybody stood up and applauded and he said, We expect special things from this one. He said, All we ask of this one is that he try to the best of his God given ability and considerable potential.

And even as I said, I promise that I will always do my best, I was not at all unaware of the ever growing number of previous Mobile County Training School graduates who were already declaring their eternal gratitude to him because the vocational guidance he had literally forced them to follow had been so specific.

I said, I promise. I said I promise that I will always do my best and he nodded smiling his satisfaction as he led the audience in the applause that lasted until I got back to my place among the other members of the graduating class. I said, I promise. Which is also what I had already told Miss Lexine Metcalf when she said what she said that many terms earlier when she said, You will go where you will go and you will do what you will do, my splendid young man. Because, who if not you, my splendid young man? Whatever it is, my splendid young man. And who if not you is to say?

I said what I said because I was also talking to Miss Lexine Metcalf, Miss Tee, and Mama, who were also smiling and applauding, and when I found Mama and Miss Tee on the way out and handed Mama my diploma, which she handed to Miss Tee, they looked at each other and began shaking their heads, and then they put their arms around me and started laughing and crying at the same time.

Then when I went on over to say good-bye to Miss Lexine Metcalf, who was going up to New England for the summer, she put both hands (instead of her magic wand blackboard pointer) on my shoulders and held me at arm's length, moving her fairy-tale face up and down in A-plus approval. And I said what I said

*again and said good-bye and when I looked back to wave one last
time I could tell that she had just dabbed her eyes with the dainty
handkerchief that she switched to the other hand before waving
back.*

*When I promised what I promised Mr. B. Franklin Fisher as he
handed me my Mobile County Training School diploma, it was
good enough for him for all of his primary emphasis on career specific vocational guidance, just as it had been already good enough
for Mama and Miss Tee long before Miss Lexine Metcalf was to
say, There is as yet no telling what a young man of your caliber
and potential can make of yourself once you decide what it is you
want to be.*

*The word (for a while) on Mr. B. Franklin Fisher among career
experts of a decade later on would have been that he had either
discovered or in any case had decided that you were inner-directed
not other-directed. But by that time Mr. Carlton Poindexter had
already said what he said along with his congratulations on your
graduation from college. He would talk about graduate course
content but never about personal vocations. All he said that day
was, Now you will see what you see and you will make of it what
you can.*

The also and also of the ongoing transatlantic flight sound
was always there as if it were what your sense of the stream of
time consciousness itself was. But at the point that you also became aware of the intrusion of the preliminary intercom static
and then the buzz within which the voice of the pilot announcing that the coastline of Europe would be visible in less than
five minutes, you realized that you had fallen asleep thinking
about Mobile County Training School and that you were now
heading into sunrise over the province of Normandy. *And I
said, This many miles from Mobile Bay. I said, This many miles
along the way.*

What I also realized the instant I turned my wrist to check
my watch (because I was thinking of the early risers in the
towns and countrysides that we would soon be flying over),
was that we were now heading into a time zone that was five
hours later than the Eastern Standard Time of New York,
which was three hours later than the Pacific Standard Time of
Los Angeles and Beverly Hills. When you were that close to
Europe you were also that close to the prime meridian, which

was the zone of Greenwich Mean Time, the mean that was the basis for universal time.

The South of France, like Paris, would be one hour later than Greenwich Mean Time, which is also the time zone of London.

XXXIX

THE VILLA was on a hill above Juan-les-Pins and the sea, and beyond the pines, the palms, and the terra cotta rooftops along the slope you could see sails and the long white streaks from the speedboats cutting back and forth on the blue water as the clear Mediterranean sky stretched away to the south toward Corsica, Sardinia, and North Africa; and on the distant horizon from time to time you could see the sails of larger craft and also the deluxe cabin cruisers. Sometimes there was a long white yacht with festive flags and sometimes there were also the ocean liners and freighters that came in that close because they were en route to Nice and Villefranche.

Beyond Alpes-de-Haute-Provence were the Alpes-Maritimes, which came all the way down to the coast at Monte Carlo, on the other side of which was Menton and the beginning of the Italian Riviera. Northeast beyond the Maritimes was the Italian region of the Piedmont. It was only five hundred kilometers from that part of Italy to the Swiss border, and fewer than six hundred kilometers across Switzerland by way of Berne to the Rhine and Germany. North beyond the French Alps and Haute-Savoie was Geneva. *You were that close to all of that then and you could say all the way from the seat by the map stand, eight thousand miles from the U.S.A.*

There was a grand piano in the long high beamed drawing room where soirees and parties were held, but I used the Danish spinet in the studio on the second floor, and through the wide window which opened out onto the balcony overlooking the vegetable garden and what was left of an old sandstone wall, you could see the mountains again. These were the Pré-Alpes de Grasse.

There was also a balcony outside the great bedroom where we slept, and from there you could see the traffic along Avenue

Guy de Maupassant and the flags along Promenade du Soleil; and with the binoculars you could survey the beach and the surf and watch the water skiers. You could also see the casino and the curve of the cape beyond which was Antibes.

From the dining terrace above the tropical gardens you could see west along the dense and teeming shore toward Cap-de la-Croisette and Cannes; that was the route past the Massif de l'Estérel to Saint-Tropez, above which was the Massif des Maures and beyond which was the rugged route to Marseilles, north from which was Provence. Southwest beyond Montpellier, Narbonne, and Perpignan was Spain.

When you looked toward Antibes it was as if you were looking due east, but the actual direction of the coastline at that point was northeast. You couldn't see very far looking that way from where I was because of the trees, but the Hôtel de Ville was only two kilometers away and going there was like going into the old town from the suburbs. But actually you were not aware of crossing any town line at all.

On the way to the Musée Grimaldi on the bicycle I passed Place Charles-de-Gaulle, circled through Rue de la République, and strolled pushing the bike through the market. Then I found my way through the narrow streets to the sea and came pedaling along Promenade du front de Mer. The museum was an old château with a square tower, and close by was an old church and not far away was the old harbor. There were white breakers and the curving shoreline of the Baie des Anges. And then there were the blue-green mountains against the pale sky above Cagnes-sur-Mer.

I locked the bicycle and went inside and bought my ticket. In the lobby I was still aware of the bright, blue high afternoon sky and the mountains, and I can also remember how you could still feel the nearness of the sea. I looked at the floor plan. The main thing about the museum was the special collection of paintings and ceramics by Pablo Picasso, but there was also a permanent exhibition of historical documents, maps, pictures, and regional antiques, which I decided to look at first.

I had been reading about Antibes in the travel guide before breakfast that morning and I had also checked the maps and looked at the pictures in the travel brochures. In a way I guess I've always been a student of geography and history.

I've always been a student of just about everything. Old Joe States, he didn't know how right he was when he nicknamed me Schoolboy. Or did he? You never can tell about old road musicians. Especially if they're from Alabama by way of the T.O.B.A. circuit and have been swapping that many lies in that many wayside inns for that many years.

In any case I knew that Antibes was the old port town of Antipoles, which went all the way back to the time of the ancient Greek sea merchants. Nice was also an old Grecian port. Its original name was Nike, which meant Victory. The original name for Marseilles was Massailia and then it was Massilia. I didn't remember what that meant but it always used to make me think about Marsala, which was a wine, and that made me think about the wine trade but I also knew that Marsala was in Sicily and I guess that it had also been a Grecian settlement. I knew that Marseilles went all the way back to the Phoenician sailors.

I also knew that southern France had been a part of the Roman Empire. I had known about that since junior high school where *Gallia omnes in partes tres* was *divisa*. In ninth grade declensions nominative, genitive, accusative, dative, ablative, and very very vocative under Miss Kellogg the Conjugator. And in the tenth grade there was still more Julius Caesar and Gallic Wars, which had begun with the Helvetians who lived in Switzerland. And there was also Cicero who called upon Catiline, oh Catiline in oratorical accents to be used in assembly programs. And Virgil told about Aeneas and Dido when North Africa was known as Carthage, while algebra moved on toward what Mr. B. Franklin Fisher called the quixotic windmill country of quadratic equations and springtime adventures in quest of cube roots.

I was thinking about all of that then and I don't remember what I saw representing the Middle Ages but something made me remember Roland and Oliver fighting for Charlemagne in Spain in fifth grade. That was adventures in literature. Switzerland was adventures in geography like the dikes and the wooden shoes of Holland. The French Revolution was adventures in world history like the Battle of Waterloo and also the campaigns of Alexander the Great, Hannibal, and Scipio Africanus.

There was a special exhibit on Napoleon. He had landed in Antibes in 1794 and had returned from exile in Elba by way of Golfe Juan in 1815. He came in the eleventh grade along with first year French for some including me and first year Spanish for others. But he was in another classroom which was the homeroom where I was an all around student and a four letter athlete with never a thought of ever becoming a musician of any kind to say nothing of going on the road with the big league band that was the champion of all big league bands, but I did prefer Duke Ellington to the Duke of Wellington even then and not only did I get away with ad-libbing "It Don't Mean a Thing if It Ain't Got That Swing" in my cleanup rebuttal that time in the citywide debate finals against Frederick Douglass High School, I brought the house down dignitaries and all and won the trophy for M.C.T.S. and went around tipping on Sugar Hill patent leather until the track season began.

I came outside and saw the sea from the terrace and walked through the garden looking at the sculpture and there were some of the largest storage urns I had ever seen. There were also fragments of ancient columns and sections of bas-reliefs from some of the local ruins. Some of the urns that had been brought up from the bottom of the old harbor had once been used in the wine and olive oil trade. Some of them were almost five feet high. They were now used for decoration and as planters.

The garden was in full bloom. The bright flowers moved sparkling in the keen salty breeze and the warm sunshine. I sat on the thick wall, which had been a part of the ramparts of the old fortification, and looked at the gulls circling and swooping over the glistening water. Then I looked back across the promenade toward the beaches and the point of the Plateau de la Garoupe, which I guessed had been an invasion point since ancient times.

I went back inside and looked at the paintings and drawings remembering what I had seen in California and what I had been reading about in the guide books and the library at the villa. Picasso was like the Bossman Himself. He could do everything any other painter could do and do it better, and there were all kinds of other things that he could do that nobody else would even try. Joe States used to swear that the Bossman Himself could even make a business report sound better than the next best musician sounds with lyrics. He probably would have said that Picasso could stain a wall with a stream of you know what better than the next best painter. For my money he could.

There was always somebody like that. It was always worth more of my money to see Sugar Ray Robinson working out on the speed bag than I would pay to see a lot of other good fighters win a title by knockout. It was worth the price of a World Series ticket to see Willie Mays warming up in any base-ball park, or even on a sandlot; and I would trade a touchdown in the Rose Bowl by almost anybody else just to see Jim Brown run signals. As for the Bossman Himself, he could sit at a pi-ano better than most musicians could play it. The band always played better with him there even when he didn't do anything but sit there and point and make faces.

At one end of the grand salon there was a large triptych of a satyr, a faun, and a centaur with a trident. All three panels were very simple black and white drawings on a white back-ground and they looked like enlarged sketches from a book on Greek mythology. But as soon as you saw them where they were you realized that all of that was also a part of the life you saw around you every day on the Mediterranean. You didn't have to think about it. All you had to do was be there and look at it after seeing the plage at Juan-les-Pins.

At the other end of the same room there was a painting of Ulysses and the Sirens, and through the door you could see related paintings and sketches on the walls ahead. There were also still-life studies that showed some of the local fruit and regional seafood. The reclining figures were also local. So were the sailors. One sailor was eating sea urchins. One was yawn-ing. Another was dozing. All of that went with the old har-bor. And later on I read about another related painting called *Night Fishing at Antibes*, which I was to see again when I got back to New York. That was that afternoon at the Museum of Modern Art where I was playing in the garden with Eddie Larkin's pickup group and during the intermission I found it on the third floor landing and on the way back down to the garden Eddie Larkin kept saying, *Night Fishing at Antibes*. I like the way that makes you think about Rock Skipping at the

Blue Note. You dig? Makes you think about a beach in France, makes me think about a club in Chicago. Man if you were getting to more of them in France than I was getting to in Chicago, you were getting to a lot of them.

I remember the design stylized from sea urchins in picture after picture. They were used very much as riffs were used in music. I had never seen so many sea urchins before in my life. I grew up in a seaport town and I don't remember ever even being aware of such a thing until I went to college. I don't remember knowing about them in California, not even in San Francisco. I was too busy with yellowtails, flounders, and sand dabs in California. I didn't even get around to alba-core. In Gasoline Point I was too busy crabbing and shrimping for gumbo. And the standard fish were croakers and catfish. Channel cats came from Mobile River and mudcats came from Chickasabogue Creek.

I tasted sea urchins for the first time the day after Jewel Templeton and I arrived. We stopped at a seafood stand near the beach and she ordered them and the vendor could tell that I didn't really know what they were and she showed me what part to eat. And when I tasted it and nodded smiling, she said, Now you're on the Côte d'Azur, *monsieur*. Now you are truly there. That night I had côte de veau de la crème and the next day we drove all the way to Toulon's for my introduction to bouillabaisse.

I liked the paintings, and as I moved from room to room I also liked the way everything blended into the remodeled interior of the fine old castle. So much so that before I was even halfway along I had already decided to come back again as soon as possible. It was too much to take in on one visit any-way. All you could really do was find out what was there and pick out what you wanted to see the next time.

I also liked seeing the other visitors and hearing that many languages spoken everywhere you went, all day, every day. That was something else that was part of being on the Côte d'Azur. I had played in some fine casinos all over the United States and I knew a lot of beautiful beaches, but none of them compared to the South of France. They had their points. They had the sand and the water but people were forever getting fed up with them over one holiday weekend because of other people. But creeps, jerks, bandits, thieves, and other criminals have always swarmed all over the Côte d'Azur and they haven't ruined it yet. Not for me. But maybe I'm just a down-home high school boy after all. I really don't know. But there is such a thing as style and class in places just as there is style and class in say singers and boxers, and Miami Beach doesn't have it. Las Vegas doesn't have it. Monte Carlo does.

A tall distinguished looking middle aged man and two slightly younger looking women came in and stood looking at the painting called *Joie de Vivre*. The man, who was deeply tanned and had a neatly trimmed sun bleached mustache, was wearing a cruising cap, a blue double-breasted blazer with white shorts, and was carrying a camera and a swagger stick. The women were wearing straw hats. One was wearing a sheer red and white polka dot dress. She looked like an Italian. The other, who looked French, was wearing a gray and yellow candy striped blouse with a white finely pleated skirt. Both were carrying straw bags. All three were wearing espadrilles.

They stood talking softly in English and French. The man was explaining the composition in English using the swagger stick as a pointer. The way he moved it made me think about a conductor waving a baton. He had a British accent and he had the kind of vibrato that went with London town houses and country manors. I guessed that he had his own private art collection, his own racing stable (or maybe it was polo ponies), his own yacht, and maybe his own plane. That was an old bandstand game we used to play in all of the swanky nightclubs. Somebody, say old Malachi Moberly, would pick out a ringside party while he was at the solo mike and when he was laying out he would ask somebody in the rhythm section what kind of whiskey was being served and sometimes the answer was big steel whiskey or oil well whiskey or automobile whiskey department store whiskey and so on. Old Otis Sheppard used to look at the way certain girls were dressed and the way they acted when the waiter was there and classified them as rich bitch stuff, expense account stuff, pay raise stuff, big chance stuff, and so on down to wide-eyed stuff and meal ticket stuff.

Regardez, regardez, the French woman was pointing to one of the fauns in the picture, *comme* Picasso *à* something something too fast for my textbook French at that time. *C'est mignon* something something something something in machine gun staccato.

The other woman answered in Italian as I had guessed she would and the French speaking woman caught her breath twice, batting her eyes, and I suddenly realized that she was not gasping but was saying, *ah oui, oui* as in oh yes, yes. *Mais définitivement.*

Tu sais, the man said to her as I moved on away. *Eh bien*, the great painters of the Renaissance. *Habituellement, ils ont* something something. Not only the faces. Most of the background landscapes.

I moved on toward the ceramics and the pottery. That was what Jewel Templeton was excited about during that time. She had been reading everything she could find about it all that week and she had been to see it three times already although she had been coming to the Musée Grimaldi for years. I liked it too. I had my own reasons and I also knew what hers were, and when I got back up to the villa late that afternoon she was waiting to go for a drive before dinner, and the museum was the main thing she wanted to talk about. And the first thing I said was, That Picasso. He's together. He's got it all going.

We were passing through Golfe Juan, and she knew that I knew we were that close to Picasso's villa because she had pointed it out and told me about all that the day after we arrived. She looked at me and smiled behind her new Italian dark glasses. Her hair looked like a shampoo ad. We drove on through Cannes.

When she asked me what I liked most I said, The bullfight dishes and the female jugs and bottles, looking at her looking at the road. At the intersection she decided to take the route through the back country of Estérel to Fréjus and Saint-Raphaël and come back along the sea. Still looking at the road she reached one hand into her bag and took out a purple headband. She put it around her neck like an elastic collar and then lifted the front end over her face and swept it back to keep her hair from blowing in the wind.

And I also see what you mean, I said. And she said, About my food thing. And shook her head and then said, It's incredible. It's absolutely incredible. And I said, I thought it was the most natural thing in the world. And she said, That's just it. All this time and all of a sudden I realize that. What was I thinking about before?

We zipped on through the town of Mandelieu. I looked it up on a carte Michelin. It was twenty plus kilometers from Fréjus and well on our way up into the rugged green Massif. The sun was still high but at that altitude the temperature was already beginning to be cool.

What was I thinking about all that time? she said shaking her head again. And I said, All of the things that all of those wild forms and figures make you think about. That's enough to make you forget all about the fact that what you're looking at is pottery.

And she said, Maybe you're right but you didn't. And I said, Maybe because I was already clued in. Otherwise I might have been thinking about beach toys or something. Mexico or something. Pueblo or something like that. And she said, Maybe you're right. Then she said, You remember the "Ode on a Grecian Urn"? I'm sure you read that poem in college. And I said, In English 104, 5, or 6. Ideas and Forms. One, 2, and 3 were Freshman Composition.

Maybe it was something like that, she said thinking about it. After all it's not really pottery anymore. It's not really decorated utensils. It's art based on decorated utensils.

She thought about it again. She was always thinking something out. It never embarrassed her to let you know when she didn't understand something. She would ask you about anything if she thought she could get the information she wanted. She never minded starting out sounding stupid because once she learned whatever it was that she didn't know before she had it from then on. Maybe it was because she was that good looking and that famous she didn't have to be already hip to everything. That was also the way certain rich people were. They were so rich and powerful that they didn't have to prove that they were also smart. Once upon a time there were aristocrats who didn't even read. They didn't need to. There were plenty of people to read for them. Her good looks made her an aristocrat of sorts. And she was smart too. But she didn't confuse it with being hip.

She drove on looking at the road and then she said, I've always had this thing. I've always had this big thing about buying my kitchen stuff at the hardware store and the restaurant supplier. We were zooming along through the hills then, the motor echoing in the trees and gorges. She took the curves with ease. She enjoyed driving in terrain like that. Sometimes she did it for relaxation and sometimes that was the way she memorized new parts. I had read that in a magazine in college. According to the articles she did it alone then, late at night and early in the morning on 101A north from Santa Monica, on 66 east toward San Bernardino, and on 60 and 111 to Palm Springs. She was not really the same person I read about. I was not really the same person either. In a way I was. In a way you always are. When she was not there she was almost always Jewel Templeton, especially at first. More than later. When she was there she was who and what she and the relationship was about.

I took the map from the glove compartment again and located Mont Vinaigre. We came on through the Col de Roche Noir. And I pinpointed the Tour de Mer and the Pagoda. And then there was the old Roman town of Fréjus. I saw the ruins of the aqueduct and we came on through the gate that was left from the old fortified wall and circled by the ruins of the ancient theater and arena. But we didn't stop that time and we headed back along Route N98.

We were on the Côte de l'Estérel then, where the blue water crashed and foamed white against the rugged red rocks, and some of the backwash looked like it had been stained with fresh blood. I had seen the California coast south from Monterey and Carmel and that was something too, but I had never seen rocks that made reefs and miniature bays and islands and natural swimming pools like these. At some points the pools were so still and clear, and the jagged escarpments were so sharp that you could look down and see all the way to the bottom even that late in the day. On our left was the Massif de l'Estérel against the westward sky.

She drove toward Miramar, Théoule, and La Napoule-Plage. She had seen all of that many times. And every now and then she would pronounce the name of the town we were going through. Anthéor, Pic du Cap Roux, Clanaque de Maubois.

She drove on and the next thing she said was, But this pottery thing. Suddenly it is the most fascinating thing in the whole world. I don't really remember what I said to that if I said anything. Maybe I just nodded or touched her without taking my eyes from the sea.

Present company excepted, of course, she said watching the serpentine road and patting me there at the same time. I put the map away and we came on back toward Cannes, the incoming breakers foaming phosphorescent on the beaches in the twilight and in a few minutes the streetlights twinkling like stars.

I'm going to buy some of it, she said finally. That's what I'm buying this time.

The next morning we drove up to Vallauris. And I saw the workshops and the kilns and we watched the craftsmen. There were also vineyards and olive groves on the outskirts of town and everywhere you went there was also the odor of the flowers that were grown and distilled for the perfume industry, the focal point of which was Grasse. We saw where the special potter's clay came from and I found out that Vallauris had always been mainly a pottery town. Its earthenware utensils had been used all along the Mediterranean for centuries.

See what I mean? Jewel Templeton said. In the old days it was like pots and pans from the hardware store. And I said, That's exactly what I was thinking. I said I was thinking about tinware. I was also thinking about galvanized water buckets and washtubs and cast iron skillets; and I remembered a tinware repairman who used to come onto our street from Gins Alley carrying two charcoal furnaces, which I used to think looked like railroad lanterns, who used to call himself the tinware man, the inware man. Inwamp! Inwamp man!! He also called himself the devil's disciple. And if you called him a tinkerer and said, Inwamp or inowamp he would chase you with a red hot soldering iron. Sometimes when you followed him around too long he would suddenly whirl on you brandishing it like Satan's pitchfork. And if you pointed your finger at him it was as bad as playing the dozens.

The people from Gasoline Point, Alabama, used baked clayware. They also used crockery churns for making buttermilk and sometimes they used them to ferment wine in. Most of the time it was blackberry wine and muscadine wine, but sometimes they also used elderberries and wild cherries. You could get drunk from eating too many of the kind of wild cherries that grew in Gasoline Point. Old Cateye Gander Gallagher once fell out of a tree doing that.

Now they put frames around it, Jewel Templeton was saying. I nodded and she went on and I was looking at the black pine smoke moving skyward from the kilns. It rose above the pink tile roofs and the trees and faded away in the upper air. I looked at the horizon. There was no view back down to the sea. They frame out the connections, she said. But I still don't see how I missed it all this time. I never missed it with porcelain.

We stopped in Place Centrale and looked at the statue of the man carrying a young sheep. And she told me about it. But from the rear he looked like a saxophone player taking a solo as you see him from where I stand by the piano. All he needed was to have his toes pointed in a little more like Herman Kemble. But he could almost rock as he was. Maybe he was taking a sweet solo. Maybe he was cooling it because he had it all in his fingers, all in his head and fingers like so many ofay musicians. Maybe he was trying to riff like Charlie Parker. Maybe he was the man with the yardbird horn. Too bad Picasso didn't get onto the blues as he got onto African sculpture. He would have had a ball just sketching old Louis. He could have done all kinds of harlequin things with Dizzy Gillespie, the crown prince of arabesque. Too bad he never made the Harlem scene not to mention the cross country scene with the Bossman Himself.

The statue was called *L'Homme au Mouton* and from the front he looked like a businessman carrying a sheep. There was something about that which made me think about Old Pro. Not that there was any physical resemblance. Maybe it was the neatness of his hips. There was something about the neatness of Old Pro's trousers that went with the spotless way he copied out his manuscripts. There was something about the statue's neck and shoulders that made me think of trumpet players. There is almost always something military about the way most trumpet players hold their shoulders, especially when they're playing as a section. When they solo you get something else. You get a lot of things you don't even see in the dance groups. I wish Picasso knew all about that. Then he could do musicians as the Greeks once did athletes. He could do them on plates like his bullfight plates. And they could be chitlin plates, I thought. He could have a blues period to go with his blue period and then he could have a Kansas City period and maybe an uptown downbeat period that would really cause a downtown uproar. I wonder if Picasso would go for down-home cooking.

I didn't say anything about any of that and Jewel Templeton must have thought that I was still thinking about the statue and she called it the dignified banker with the billy goat and I said, Left holding the billy goat without horns and she said, Passing out billy goats without horns.

We headed back down the hill toward Golfe Juan and then there was the sea again. She pulled off the road and we sat looking at it beyond the palms. The damp breeze stirred the leaves on the hillside. The rooftops shimmered under the open sky. The sun, like the vegetation, was tropical again, but you could still smell the lavender and jasmin from Vallauris.

As soon as I heard her voice, I knew that she was changing the subject from pottery to something else. She was excited about pottery. She was suddenly solemn about what she was thinking about now. I tried to be as casual about it as possible and waited for her to go on. And she said, I don't know when I've been so happy. Really happy. Not with success, not in triumph, just plain happy.

I was having a good time too. I was having the time of my life. But somehow or other I did not think of myself as being happy, and there was something about the way she said she was that was suddenly almost like an embarrassing confession. It was as if I was not yet old enough. Happiness was something I was still getting ready for as I was still getting ready for life with Miss You Know Who. So what she said made me suddenly aware of the difference between her age and mine. She was not really old but she was that much older than I was. She was as old as most of my teachers had been. She was as old as Mr. B. Franklin Fisher himself. She was older than Carlton Poindexter. But that still didn't make her very old and I didn't really have to remember that because I had never actually forgotten it. It only made me feel very young. It made me feel almost too young to know what I was really doing there. It made me remember how many young men my age were still in school. Well so was I.

And now I'm going to tell you something else, she was saying then. Now I'm going to tell you a big, fat secret.

I looked at the palms and the sea. I was sitting with my legs crossed and my fingers clasped together around my knees. Then she was looking at me again and I wondered if she had changed her mind about what she was going to say. Because she reached out and touched my wrist, her hand covering my watch. I unclasped my fingers and put my arms around her shoulders.

Then what she said was, I never say things like that anymore, absolutely never. Every time I say I'm happy about something, I get frightened. I look back over my shoulder. I cross my fingers. I can't help it. Maybe it's just show biz superstition.

I held her and looked at the Mediterranean and thought about the day I had decided to extend my stay with the band. And then I was thinking about the day I decided to stay in California. I wondered what was going to happen next, but I was really too busy to think about it. Too much was happening now. I was too busy keeping time every day, me and my almost middle twenties years and my bull fiddle from Miss Hortense Hightower and my bright-eyed curiosity.

So much depends on luck, she was saying. So much depends on chance.

XL

ON THE way along Autoroute Estérel–Côte d'Azur from Biot, where we had spent the afternoon making the rounds of all of the pottery works on the list she had made, she began telling me about her maiden trip to the South of France on her delayed honeymoon eighteen months and three productions into her first marriage.

Speaking of fairy-tale dreams come true, she said as we zoomed on in the direction of Nice to the intersection with Route N7, which would take us back toward Antibes and the turnoff to the hills above Juan-les-Pins, my first time in these incredible parts was as the saying goes nothing if not precisely that. And more. Because at the very same time it was also an excursion into all of those historic moments and events that you are only very vaguely aware of before, but that our Baedeker,

Michelin, and Blue guides were forever referring to. And don't forget. The groom himself was an art director. So dressing up and making the scene in Monte Carlo was great young movie celebrity fun, but when we went up to Èze and La Turbie he threatened to try his hand at writing a historical novel, because of a sudden urge to submerge himself in the study of the manners, architecture, and costume of those times. He didn't follow through on the novel, but his enthusiasm was real, and he did get a chance to apply his researches as a designer on a couple of class B costume productions. Nothing on the scale of Cecil B. DeMille, but he had fun.

I must say, she said, you couldn't have picked a better traveling companion. It was a fairy-tale episode all right. But not kid stuff by any means. He was not really Prince Charming. Being slightly older and representing that much highly professional authority, he was somewhat more like a bachelor king who marries one of the slightly younger not entirely naive but not quite yet cosmopolitan ladies of the court, if you know what I mean. Anyway that honeymoon was, as you like to say, storybook stuff for a midwestern schoolgirl type like me.

The trips to Europe she had made with her family during her childhood had been tours of such major cities as Paris, Rome, Milan, Venice, Vienna, Berlin, Copenhagen, Amsterdam, and London, during which she had seen the countryside mostly en route between stops on the itinerary prepared for her father by his travel agent. But the honeymoon was a matter of deluxe and completely casual serendipity, which made his ever expanding scholarly inquisitiveness even more exciting to her undiminished schoolgirl curiosity than it already was when she was attracted to him in the first place.

Up to that time she had said whatever she had said about him ever so casually and almost always as if only incidentally and also as if referring to something I already knew anyway— and I reacted in kind and related it to what I had read about him in the magazines and trade papers. But after dinner that night she went on reminiscing about that part of her life, and that was when she finally got around to telling what she wanted me to know about what he had meant to her.

Speaking of self-made men, she said, he qualifies on all counts. Then she said, When I told the Marquis de Chaumienne the story that I'm about to tell you, he said the matter of personal identity is not at all the same in America as it is in Europe, and his very first example was a story that F. Scott Fitzgerald told in *The Great Gatsby*, which I had read as a Jazz Age novel about status seeking but which he described as a novel about passing. He knew very well that to almost all Americans passing meant mulattoes crossing the color line to be accepted as white people. But *his* point was white people passing as whiter people, if you will pardon the expression. Anyway I reread it, and there was that self-improvement routine right out of Horatio Alger and all.

But Mark Howell, *né* Marcus Aurelius Howell, from that little town down in Arkansas, she said, saying his name to me for the first time, was no Jay Gatsby.

I got the marquis' point all right, she said. But unlike Jay Gatsby, Mark Howell would have seen straight through Daisy Buchanan. Mark agrees with Fitzgerald that the very rich are different and he also liked Ernest Hemingway's quip that it was because they have more money. But Mark himself was about living well being the best revenge.

Mark Howell had hitchhiked his way from Arkansas out to California the summer following his graduation from the local technical school with a diploma in carpentry and woodworking and had found a job with a scenery construction crew; and in six years he had completed enough academic as well as laboratory courses in architectural history and design and in film technology to be well into a career as an all around production technician, as ready with specific details about the geographical and historical background of the story in production as he was handy with on the spot technological adjustments.

When the two of them met at a producer's party, he had been in California eight years and his reputation as a highly regarded art director was such that it attracted a higher level of publicity for their courtship and marriage than her bright very promising new star status. Her publicity was about glamor. His was about taste and class, which gave him an edge in local social circles that she enjoyed rather than resented. After all, some reporters scored his class as a conquest for her glamor.

When I met him, she said, he was just enough older than I was so that it was easy to feel very close to him and defer to him at the same time. Naturally I was very much impressed by his position and his authority with studio bigwigs but he himself was much more concerned with his personal development than with his career per se. He told me his story quite candidly. No games, and without the slightest impulse to impress. He was much too serious about himself to misrepresent his past.

He described his Arkansas background as being redneck, hillbilly, and white trash. And why should he not? After all look at what he was making of himself. You were listening to somebody who had used the accessibility of the movie industry's fantastic collection of international experts in just about everything to perhaps an even greater and certainly no less immediately personal advantage than your ideal Ivy League student uses his venerable professors. Or so I'd like to think at any rate.

In any case, his reputation as a classy guy was no hype. It was something he earned and something I think he understood better than Jay Gatsby, and F. Scott Fitzgerald too, for that matter. He certainly knew more about what to make of Hollywood than Fitzgerald did.

But you know something? As I told the marquis, for my money Fitzgerald, for all his fame and the impression he made in certain New York and academic literary circles, never really outgrew being the wide-eyed overeager young man from the provinces come to seek his fortune in the big city. If you know what I mean, she said. And as I said I did I was thinking about that subsequent generation of immigrant boys out of the Lower East Side and Brooklyn, who went to C.C.N.Y. and to the 42nd Street library, the Metropolitan Museum of Art, the Madison Avenue and 57th Street galleries, somehow came by cheap seats in Carnegie Hall and the Metropolitan Opera, and who hung out in Greenwich Village. But I did not say anything about that because I wanted to hear what else she was going to say about Mark Howell.

And that was when she told me what she told me about how it had begun. Each already knew who the other was when they were introduced at the producer's party, but that was the first time they had actually seen each other in person. He was not as strikingly handsome as Hollywood matinee idol types go, but he was good looking enough in his tastefully cut clothes, and when he smiled, the sincerity of his eyes matched the warmth of his voice, which might have been that of a professor in the liberal arts department of a Big Ten university. So even as they shook hands she realized that she was hoping that they would stroll and chat for a while before the evening was over.

Being of the theater, she said, smiling in anticipation of my mock shock at her all too deliberate stock company of theater, and therefore having a more professional interest in twentieth century theories and experiments in production design than the usual starlet, I decided to ask him if he had any personal contact with Robert Edmond Jones who was at U.C.L.A., and you couldn't have picked a better topic. Except for several brief separations for one or the other to chat with old associates and acquaintances, we spent the rest of the evening talking about such pioneers as Max Reinhardt, Norman Bel Geddes, Jo Mielziner, and Lee Simonson among others, and a week later we began dating.

She didn't go on to talk about their life together, since she had already referred to that ever so matter of factly all along, and I had already seen her photo collection and fan magazine files, which is also where I came across what I know about her other two husbands to each of whom she was married only briefly (six months and eleven months) and neither of whom she ever mentioned to me by name. Somewhat (I couldn't help cracking to myself) as if they had been miscast leading men in two mercifully forgotten class B movies.

Nor did she ever say anything at all about why she and Mark Howell had not had any children during their seven apparently enjoyable and certainly unstormy years together. Nor did I ever mention anything about that either. But since Mark Howell for his part had gone on to become the father of two children by his second and only other wife, I simply assumed that studio control of the private affairs of performers at that time was such that production schedules represented a higher priority than family development; and that the momentum of her approach to stardom had not permitted time out for childbearing.

So, for the time being at any rate, she had chosen career enhancement over motherhood, and if she had any regrets she never mentioned them, or said anything to suggest them. Not that she placed her career above everything else, but only that at that time she did not feel that she was far enough into it to run the risk of not moving beyond the threshold.

As she went on talking about the honeymoon almost as if it were something that had happened only months ago, you got the impression that Mark Howell was not only somebody that she still admired and respected as much as she ever had, but he was also somebody with whom her relationship was still no less cordial for being altogether less intimate. *Which I said was great, because I was thinking it must be a great satisfaction to be able to change a choice without having to regret having made it in the first place. And when she said there was nothing to regret about her choice about Mark Howell because there had never been anything about him that was misleading and that neither could she bring herself to regret her choice of a career over a relationship with him, I said, I see what you mean because I really thought I did, given the schoolboy promises I had made as much to myself as to the expectations of anybody else, beginning back even in the preschool times of Mama and Miss Tee before Miss Lexine Metcalf and Mr. B. Franklin Fisher.*

But even so I crossed my fingers as I always found myself doing whenever something for whatever reason made me so sharply aware once more of the also and also of Miss You Know Who back down you know where as if meanwhile back in Homeric Ithaca that many ages before medieval castles with fairy-tale princesses. Not that you had to be reminded from time to time any more than Odysseus himself had to be, whose fingers were already crossed for the duration of the ten years of the Trojan War before the ten that as every schoolboy should know included Calypso, the Sirens, and Circe.

XLI

I DON'T HAVE to tell you that this is not good-bye, do I, Mr. Brown Eyes, she said when the time came. We know very well that this is only for the time being, however extended it may turn out to be. You know that as well as I do, she said, perhaps even better. Then she said, After all, it's you not me who got us into this fairy-tale-aunt business. So you know very well that fairy-tale aunts never say good-bye, don't you, Mr. Brown Eyes. They will always be there, won't they?

I had decided to go to New York by way of Paris. She was going straight back to Hollywood, stopping in New York for only as long as it took to change planes. I was taking the auto-bus route up through Provence and Burgundy so that I could stop off in Avignon, Lyons, Mâcon, Dijon, and maybe Vézelay.

As for myself, she said, trying to keep her eyes from twinkling, What I had in mind when I came back from Saint-Moritz was finding myself a trail guide for an expedition into a terri-tory that I had been made to feel that unless I could not only come to terms with but could relate to no less than to apple pie that I was neither as American nor as cosmopolitan as I thought I was by way of becoming.

That was what I had in mind when I saw and heard you at The Keynote, she said, and then not minding the twinkle in her eye she also said, Not that I remember having had any objec-tions to finding one that I just might also be tempted to share a bedroll with from time to time. But that by my reckoning is a pretty far piece from being a bedable fairy-tale aunt, young pardner.

But as we say in the trade, it was not a part that I was out there looking for but when it turned up I couldn't imagine my-self turning it down. In strictly professional terms, the wicked witch, as any agent will tell you, is almost always the juicier part for your career. But in the personal world of private fantasy the good fairy is really the one you always wanted to grow up to be, beginning all the way back with the very first cradle rocking bedtime stories you ever heard.

On the other hand, I said, I guess I fell into that trail guide role pretty fast myself, native overtones and all. And she said, Well what I was actually thinking in terms of was the idiomatic rather than the native implications. But I must admit that it does carry all too American overtones of the forest primeval and the westward movement nor can I deny that the marquis is almost literally a white hunter of sorts.

A French Denys Finch-Hatton, no less—if you know what I mean, she said. And I said, I think so. Because after my room-mate and I read Hemingway's *Green Hills of Africa*, "The

Short Happy Life of Francis Macomber," and "The Snows of Kilimanjaro," we had also read Isak Dinesen, *née* Karen, who became Baroness Karen Blixen. Denys Finch-Hatton, no two-finger Swahili expert, he, I said. And no Stephen Foster either, I said.

And she said, All the same, Mr. Brown Eyes. All the same. I'm beginning to miss you already.

We were standing that close together again then, and there was that all too familiar catch in her breath that made you close your eyes because you did not need to look into hers, and before I could think of saying what I was only going to mumble anyway, she put two fingers to my lips and said, Story-book, history book, or clay book, who wouldn't miss such a well brought up young man of parts as you? Just look at you this very minute. Always the completely charming proportion of ever so tentative but undeniable naughtiness and irresistible enthusiasm. No wonder you became such a wonderful bass player in such a short time.

We were already beginning to do what came next as you do it when there are only that many days left before you wave so long for the time being. So I didn't say anything about such up-bringing that I had come by beginning with Deljean McCray, Trudie Tolliver, Miss Evelyn Kirkwood that many boyhood years before Miss Slick McGinnis. As for Hortense Hightower and the bass fiddle, I was absolutely certain that I had neither said nor implied anything that could be mistaken about that, but I did like the notion that the gift suggested that Hortense Hightower had my number on all counts.

It had all turned out as if scheduled. When I came back up to the villa from an informal workout in Juan-les-Pins with a group of French musicians, some local and some down from Paris, the news she was waiting to tell me about was that by noon she had finished reading and rereading a new script that she had found not only suitable but also so actually exciting that she had already agreed to go back to Hollywood within a week or ten days because she wanted to be in on all of the preliminary production conferences. She had already agreed to the studio proposal, which included approval of the director plus input on all story line revisions and final editing.

I won't bore you with the current version, she said but I will say that as of two readings it is very much the sort of thing that I've been looking for ever since coming under the influence of the marquis. In any case I'm eager to find out what I can do about this sparkling daughters and muddy waters of the upper and lower Mississippi business that he has made me so conscious of, and if I bring it off you will deserve much of the credit. And if I don't bring it off, I'm going to insist on as much remedial work as your circumstances will permit. But I must say, I really do think I'm on to something, Mr. Bright Eyes. We shall see. We shall see. We shall see. Won't we, Mr. Bright Eyes?

That was that Monday, and she already knew that I was all set for a place to stay during my stopover in Paris. So all she said about checking out of the villa was soon maybe very soon. But no rush, because there were still a few details in the contract to be cleared up and finalized over there and also a very personal matter that she was still hoping to take care of over here before pulling out this time.

So, as it says in the song, she said, Soon maybe not tomorrow but soon. Or better still, she then went on to whisper as if into a hand-held after hours microphone, *not now, not now, not now. I'll tell you when.* And I said, I'm with you, sweet mama. I'm with you. Then with the back of my hand to my mouth in a mock stage aside I said, No torch singer this one. Not this mane tossing sparkling daughter from the upper waters of the Big Muddy.

To which she said, Oh but aren't you ever the bright-eyed one. Then she said, But seriously. And that was when she said what she said about my having come over to the Côte d'Azur as if on a split second segue and thereby earning the luxury of going back stateside by way of Paris as if on one of the ever so many totally casual seeming modulations she had come to think in terms of after listening to me practicing and playing on records, especially along with the Bossman Himself plus Joe States and Otis Sheppard.

I was all set for Paris because through music loving artists and literary friends in Greenwich Village I was in contact with an American couple who was spending eighteen months in

Europe with the Hôtel de Londres on Rue Bonaparte in Saint-Germain-des-Prés as a base of operation as they had been do-ing from time to time for more than a decade. All I had to do was get in touch with them twenty-four hours in advance of my estimated time of arrival.

Meanwhile it was easy enough to go on doing what you had been doing on the Côte D'Azur where, after all, there was al-ways more of the same along with something even better. But as soon as Jewel Templeton said what she said about the lat-est script, everything suddenly became a matter of vamping in stoptime to the out chorus. No rush, to be sure, but no more lollygagging either.

Then when I pulled in from Cannes that Thursday afternoon the personal call that she had been waiting for had come through, and she had decided when we would be pulling out. But first she wanted to tell me what the call was about, and she said, Of course you know who's arriving Nice just in the nick of time. And I said, Who else but. And she said, It's touch-down and takeoff but we meet for dinner tomorrow night, early dinner followed by need I say what somewhere, maybe some little informal spot where they will insist that you take a turn.

If you don't mind of course, she said. And I said, Okay by me, I said. I know more places between Antibes and Cannes than between Nice and Monte Carlo but whichever, since all it takes is a word from him anywhere in these parts. And she said, This is all so wonderful. She said, I can't tell you how much it all means to me to have things turn out like this, and I do so hope that it's going to be as much fun for you as I'm absolutely sure it's going to be for him. And for me too of course, she said. And when I said, Hey why not, she said, Okay, okay, okay, okay, I know, I know, I know, I know. But it's still something that you might find yourself going along with more as a favor to me than because you really feel like joining in on your own impulse.

And I said, I know what you mean. I said, I know exactly what you mean, but hey, I'm expecting to have a ball. And that is also when I said, After all without him not. Repeat not. I said, without him none of this. No him, no you and me. No us.

And hey, I also said, look at all the fun I'm going to be having up there pretending that I'm not checking on how you're responding to the riffs I'm sneaking in there just because I know you're going to realize that I'm signifying about us.

Which made her smile and shake her head as I knew she would. Then she said, But aren't you the sly one. And I said, Not me. That's my old roommate. I'm supposed to be the nimble one. I'm the one from the briar patch and the candlestick. He, not me, was Reynard the Fox long before I came up with that stuff about Dr. Faustus during our freshman year. Which only led everybody else to turn him back into Reynard the Fox in a disguise of the snake in the grass. Not because he was really snake-sneaky but because he was almost always so offhanded that it was as if he were downright sly and tricky.

The main thing the marquis wanted me to talk to him about during dinner at the outdoor restaurant he took us to in Cannes that Friday night was the time I spent playing with the band and when I told him how it had all come about through Hortense Hightower he said, *Formidable, merveilleux, incroyable!* Directly out of college and into the very center of the pulse of that incomparable orchestration. One had the immediate impression that you were realizing if not a childhood dream of your own, then certainly one derived from dedicated parents.

Which reminded me once more of the fact that nobody had ever set any specific goals for me. Nobody. Not Mama and/or Papa or Uncle Jerome. Not Miss Tee. And neither Miss Lexine Metcalf, nor Mr. B. Franklin Fisher himself, who was known not only as a fisher of men but also as a molder of men and women commensurate with ancestral imperatives not only of Frederick Douglass and Harriet Tubman in America but also of heroes and heroines in the storybook world at large.

But I didn't say anything at all about any of that. I said, Not me. I said, I didn't realize that I could do what I did until the time came. I said, I never thought anything at all about becoming a musician of any kind, certainly not a professional musician. As much as I've always taken for granted that it was an indispensable part of my life, after all cradle songs and oop-de-doodle bounces were already there before songs became fairy tales.

I said, All I can say is that as far as I was concerned the way that band played music was the way I had come to think about music. I said, What I heard when I heard that band was not only the sound that went with the way things looked and felt but also the sound of how I already felt about things. It was the sound equivalent of whispering to yourself. *The sound not only of my blues bedeviled situation, I said, but also of my aspirations, my fears and frustrations, and my celebrations and exhilarations.*

I said, Once you were in the middle of all that it was not a matter of being able to play through anything that was put in front of you. Nobody expected you to be able to do that. The kind of musicianship they wanted in that position at that time did not begin with technical virtuosity as such. It began with what you heard or thought you heard or wanted to hear. As was also the case with painters and writers. They don't begin by being able to zip through exercises of all kinds of examples. They begin by evolving their own conception of writing or painting and then they have to develop the technique to bring it off.

That was the principle Joe States had in mind when he told me that the band was a bunch of homemade all-stars. We don't hire them, Schoolboy, we make them. Of course, now special talent and/or manifest genius is another matter. We know what to do with it, and we can't stand to let it go to waste or be misdirected. Hell, we don't really need it, but if we happen across it we create a need for it. First the Bossman spots the possibilities. Then there's Old Pro with the necessary touch-ups. And then we see if he can get by the old trickmaster himself.

In my case, Marquis, I said, it was not only like the rabbit in the briar patch, it was also almost like the rabbit in the pet shop. And he said, I can't begin to tell you what this means to me, and I do hope that my how do you say it amateur curiosity is not going to interfere with your appetite or be bad for your digestion, because the cuisine here is really quite good. And I said, Not at all. I said, I really don't mind one bit.

Because I really didn't. I hadn't expected his questions to be anything like those of an entertainment page reporter, and they weren't. They were completely consistent with everything I had been told about him. And I could also tell from the very tone of his voice that he had taken at face value what Jewel

Templeton had said about me, beginning with the fact that my nickname in the band was Schoolboy.

I really don't mind at all, I said. I've been looking forward to this ever since I first heard about you. And he said, I must tell you. I made reservations here because I know you grew up in the Gulf Coast seafood area of Alabama, and I'm counting on the superb seafood cuisine here to offset the banality of my hyperenthusiasm about all of this.

And I said, Hey, no days like that. Not from you. And Jewel Templeton said, We're in for a treat, Mr. Bright Eyes. Nothing but nothing can possibly spoil anything the marquis orders anywhere. If we were in Texas I would want him to choose the chili joint. And speaking of seafood, if we were in Spain, you could be sure whose paella choice I'd follow.

They both said that I'd never forget the langouste thermidor and I haven't. We were a party of three for the evening. The marquise was flying in from Italy that next afternoon and along with her would be two couples who were looking forward to meeting Jewel Templeton when we joined the marquis again at the bullfights in the old Roman arena in Nîmes that Sunday afternoon.

During dinner I also agreed to spend several hours between midmorning and midafternoon listening to old radio air checks and transcriptions that the marquis had brought along from his collection hoping that I could not only supply missing and garbled titles and explain puzzling ones but could also identify some of the soloists that he didn't recognize or was uncertain about.

When we stopped in at the Vieux Colombier in Juan-les-Pins later on that night, and I was invited to join the house combo for a set, I suggested that we play whatever the marquis wanted to hear, and everybody agreed and he made three requests, which was all you needed for a generous set in the totally informal atmosphere of a club like that. After all, since the primary emphasis was on the quality of the improvisation you could extend one number for the entire duration of the set if the response made you feel like going on and on. As the marquis knew very well. But he had his own reasons and the musicians were very pleased with each choice.

The first was "Indiana" (Back Home Again in). The second was "Sweet Georgia Brown," and for the third he wanted us to run as many riff ensemble and solo choruses on any twelve-bar blues progression in any key or keys of our choice as would take us to the end of the set.

So I kicked off "Indiana" as a medium uptempo Kansas City jump tune, which got an immediate bravo from him. Because as anticipated, he was to say shaking my hand and clasping me to him when I finally made my way back to the table after two reprises of blues out chorus, what you did changed homespun nostalgia into a cosmopolitan celebration of arrival. And that was when he also said, I must tell you. One day when I'm in America again I must do something that has been on my agenda for years. A small thing perhaps but very personal to me in my fascination with Americana. So many brownskin jazz bands have such marvelously jubilant arrangements on such an obviously, how do you say it, ofay standard, that I would just like to see what I can make of their response as I sit listening in a predominantly ofay audience in an Indiana Hoosier town like Fort Wayne, Muncie, or even some suburb of Indianapolis, for instance. I don't know. Perhaps they take it simply as expertly ingratiating entertainment for white folks not unlike the blackface minstrels of the old times. But given such music I suspect their response is a matter of much more complexity than that. Here are these troubadours who are just dropping by en route to somewhere else and they make the place sound more enticing than any native Hoosier ever has. You can't help wondering what they make of it. The arrangement you played in the band makes it sound like a state anthem. On the recordings of Count Basie's radio broadcasts from the Famous Door it sounds like the perfect place for a holiday romp. And there are the Lester Young combo recordings that make you feel as if you are somewhere being caressed by an elegant lullaby.

Then he said, "Sweet Georgia Brown" was a different matter altogether. With "Indiana" you could have missed, especially with a combo of musicians not native to the idiomatic nuances of jazz, who may alas actually be charmed by the standard version precisely because it strikes them as being as American as a Norman Rockwell cover for The Saturday Evening Post. *But with "Sweet Georgia Brown" you couldn't possibly miss. It can only be a syncopated rhapsody. She is as earthy as she is elegant.*

And when I said what I said about the appropriate tempo of her ineluctable down-home plus uptown modality and he said what he said about Anna Livia Plurabelle, I didn't say what I could have said about Deljean McCray and Charlene Wingate and Creola Calloway and Miss Slick McGinnis, all I did was snap my fingers on the beat and tilt my earlobe on the afterbeat. And he said, Voilà, voilà, voilà. *There you are. Even the pulse of it is idiomatic. That is what is so difficult to come by over here. And without it your authenticity is questionable no matter how competent your musicianship.*

I said, As for your request for a blues based wrap-up. By the time we got to that point, the right groove was no problem at all. And he said, So I noticed and so I had hoped. And incidentally, I can't thank you enough for the totally unexpected pleasure of being granted the privilege of making those requests.

I waved to the musicians, and they all came to the table to say good-bye, and when the three of us were outside again the marquis reminded me of the audio research project scheduled for the next morning and also made sure that the details of our Sunday rendezvous in Nîmes were all clear. Then he began shaking his head again as he had been doing from time to time throughout the session.

I must say, he said holding my hand once more, you inspired them and kept their exhilaration under excellent control at the same time. So they exceeded their technical competence. They, how do you say it, outdid themselves. Then he also said, So you must concede this much to the French. We may appropriate here and there but nothing is also more French than our genuine appreciation and respect for the idiomatic wherever we find it. Yes, we borrow and enrich ourselves thereby, but not only do we remember the source we also return to it time after time for replenishment.

XLII

AT TEN o'clock that Saturday morning I met the marquis in front of the music store at the street number in Cannes that he had given me during dinner, and we spent three hours listening to old air checks and radio broadcast transcriptions that he had brought along from the main part of his comprehensive library of recordings, which he kept in his archives in Paris. Incidentally, most of the impressive collection that Jewel Templeton had seen in Saint-Moritz was only his portable selection of vacation duplicates.

The playback equipment in the back room audio workshop was available to him for as long as he needed it over the weekend, but he had brought only twenty items because his time in the vicinity was even more limited than my own had become. He was flying back to Eastern Europe on Monday. I was heading for Paris by midweek.

We didn't need the services of the resident technician because the marquis himself was fully qualified to operate the system we were to use. So we settled in immediately and by noon we had played through all twenty selections, repeating whatever passages I needed to hear again and again, and I was able to come up with answers for fifteen, which he said was at least twice as many as he had allowed himself to hope for.

But of course, he would say as I supplied title after title and identified soloist after soloist. But of course. And he was especially pleased whenever I could also name a well known popular song that the selection in question was a takeoff on, as was the case with one of the band's unnamed getaway shouts that I told him was another one of our many versions of "Please Don't Talk About Me (When I'm Gone)" that so far as I knew was still in the book each with its own call code in the bossman's piano vamp system.

And so it is, he said shaking his head and nodding agreement as I hummed snatches from three examples. And so it is. *Bien sure, bien sure, bien sure!* And furthermore what we have is not simply three variations on the same melody, what we have for the band's functional intents and purposes are that many entirely different compositions. But then such is the nature not only of this music but also of the act of aesthetic creation in general. That what really counts is the treatment. It is not the raw material as such but the treatment that adds up to the aesthetic statement that we perceive as the work of art.

But yes, he said again then, *bien sure*. That is why it is as it is with this magnificent man. Given his ultraspecial sensibility it is as if it is all the same with him. A melody from a highly chic

Broadway musical is no less a piece of raw material to be repro-
cessed than is a folk ditty. I mean really. Indeed, I find myself
very much in accord with those who suggest that Tin Pan Alley
has been a major source of raw material for jazz musicians ever
since the band backed vocals that Louis Armstrong recorded
several years after the Hot Fives and Hot Sevens.

That is also when he said what he said about Louis Armstrong's singing being no less a revolutionary influence on
contemporary music than his trumpet. Then in the time left,
we listened to four of the most recent Armstrong releases
available at the counter out front, and after each one he said,
Bravo, bravo, bravo. *Voilà, voilà, voilà. Comme il est formidable.* But it is always there, is it not? He is definitive, no question about it.

And on the way along the sidewalk where the cars were
parked he said, Speaking of idiomatic nuance, the problem for
most outsiders, by which I mean those not native to it, is very
complex indeed. First there is the matter of authenticity. Ooh la
la, what could be more difficult? It is precisely the same as with
speaking a foreign language. There is always the problem of
the telltale foreign accent, which the natives almost never miss
and which immediately destroys the illusion for them, because
their instantaneous response is that of detrimental empathy.
If you know what I mean. It is precisely the same as occurs in
the theater whenever something happens to make the audience
identify emotionally with the actor's stage problem rather than
his make-believe situation in the story. A very serious matter
indeed, he said, which reminds me of a chat about singers and
the basic blues that I had with your bossman some years ago in
Paris. He knew very well what I was getting at; and how could
I ever forget what he said: that the timbre, vibrato, and pulse
were no less matters of idiomatic authenticity than slurring and
mispronouncing the words *correctly*!

A very serious matter indeed, he said again as we came to
where the cars were parked. Then he looked at his watch and
held up his hand to indicate that there was still plenty of time
for him to drive to the airport in Nice before the marquise
landed. Then he said, Another problem is that all too often
the outsider's fascination with the idiomatic is likely to be the
same as with the exotic.

If you see the connection, he said. All too often it is a matter of escape, rejection, or even full blown rebellion and revolution, or in any case a matter of being deliberately unconventional. Whereas when you are native to the idiom you're simply being conventional if you see what I mean. Your basic objective is to measure up and then maybe excel and in some cases also exceed.

It is not at all a matter of rebellion or revolution or even counterstatement or anything of that sort, he said. Not really. It is, on the contrary, a very urgent matter of mastering the fundamentals of an established or, yes, traditional local way of doing something. Basically, you play the blues the way you play the blues because that is the way people among whom you grew up conditioned you to hear and play the blues—without, by the way, denying either your individuality or even personal idiosyncrasy. Such, as I see it, is the nature of the source of idiomatic authenticity. The effect on outsiders may well be tantamount to revolutionary innovation. But it is not all a matter of experimental trial and error to insiders.

And yet, he also went on to say as he settled himself into his convertible. And yet. It is through the impact that it makes in the larger, richer, and more complex context of the outside world, is it not, that the vernacular achieves universality. Otherwise it remains provincial as is the case in language in the matter of regional dialect, shop talk, or slang.

As for myself, he said turning on the motor and gunning it but not very loudly and then letting it idle, As for myself, I insist that your wonderful American music is anything but the folk art of a subculture. It is the music that I find to be the very embodiment of the rhythms and disjunctures along with the sonorities and cacophonies of our epoch. And one day we must discuss the profound significance of its being extended into the world at large by those to whom it is indigenous as compared with the efforts of very gifted and well-intentioned appropriators.

Until tomorrow then, my marvelous young friend, he said pulling off. Until tomorrow.

That Sunday afternoon Jewel Templeton and I met the marquis and his party for lunch at the Cheval Blanc, which was directly across the thickly shaded plaza from the partially restored ruins of the ancient Roman arena where the bullfights were held. According to the travel guides this Spanish ritual became a local event back in the middle of the nineteenth century. Before that the Visigoths, who came after the Romans, turned the old stone structure into a fortress with a moat, ramparts, and towers, later removed.

The other guests were two very elegant fiftyish-looking Italian wives, whose husbands were to join them at the Chaumienne château in Médoc when the marquis returned from Eastern Europe two weeks later. I hadn't decided whether I would still be in Paris or somewhere else in Europe by that time or already in New York, but Jewel Templeton would definitely be back at work in Hollywood.

I didn't have any idea of why the marquis was going wherever he was en route to and I didn't ask Jewel Templeton anything about it because she was the one who had made me realize back at the very beginning of our relationship that you never ask such people any direct questions whatever about their personal involvement in business or political matters not to mention international relations. And she said if they themselves volunteered information about such matters it was almost always more likely to be some sort of cover story than anything factual. In such matters it was as if everything involved espionage and intrigue she had said shaking her head knowingly. But that's the way it is, believe me.

The trip to the bullfight was really the fulfillment of a promise to the Italians year before last in Cortina. The marquis had insisted on being the one to introduce them to it because he wanted to make sure that they responded to it not as a barbaric spectacle or gruesome sport such as the Romans had built the arena to stage but as a profound ceremonial Spanish reenactment of the condition of mankind. The Roman arena was a secular place, he began by reminding the Italians, but to the Spanish the bullfight was about very sacred matters indeed.

Jewel Templeton had been invited to come along and bring me not only as a means of adding that much more time to our all too brief encounter, but also because the marquis knew that she was someone who for a number of years had attended bullfights in Spain and in Mexico as well. I had known about that all along because it was something else that dated back to her first husband, through whom as the marquis also knew she had come to have personal acquaintanceships with several well known matadors on both sides of the Atlantic.

As for myself, I hadn't seen my first actual bullfight until Joe States and Ross Peterkin took me down to Tijuana one Sunday during my first trip to California. But before that there were the movies and then in college there was Ernest Hemingway with *The Sun Also Rises*, *Death in the Afternoon*, and "The Undefeated," which my roommate and I had gone through in my sophomore year along with all of the other Hemingway stories and articles you could find in current and back issues of magazines.

When we came to our seats in the arena, the marquise sat between me and Jewel Templeton, and the marquis sat between their two guests and began explaining the structure and sequence of what was about to begin. Jewel Templeton brought the marquise up to date on the current status of the forthcoming production that was taking her back to Hollywood. Then when she also mentioned that I was going to make at least a short stopover in Paris on the way back to New York the marquise said, Yes I know, and opened her purse and handed me an embossed memo card with a list of people to call, places to visit, and things to do and said, As many as time will allow or as many as you fancy. As for the people, Yves is absolutely certain that all will be delighted to be in touch even if you only have time for a call. All being aficionados of your music, speak English, somewhat amusingly to you in some instances, but you would have no problem understanding them.

At the sound of the bugle I looked over at the marquis and nodded and he held up his hand and nodded back smiling. Then he leaned over and picked up his binoculars and settled himself again. His two guests also smiled across at me and then sat forward looking down into the arena, and I got the impression that they were confident that they had been adequately briefed on the minimum essentials of the five acts within which the three classic *tercios* must be accomplished with each of the two bulls that each of the three matadors would have to take on.

So all I expected the marquis to do once the action got under way was to identify specific passes and comment on the quality of their execution from time to time. Otherwise he would hold off on his commentary and evaluation until after each matador had dispatched his second bull. After all it was not a matter of converting the Italians, or even of overcoming any anticipated squeamishness about the bloodshed. They were simply uninitiated, not skeptical. They were curious but not at all naive. To them it was only a matter of close-range on-the-scene orientation.

I myself knew what to expect in each of the five acts because I remembered what I had read about them when Joe States had set up the trip down to Tijuana. I had bought an illustrated book at the Pickwick Book Store on Hollywood Boulevard not far from Grauman's Chinese Theatre, and I still have it along with six others that I picked up over the years.

It was during dinner in Aix-en-Provence that night that the marquis said what he said about bullfighting and playing the blues. As we sipped our apéritifs Jewel Templeton was telling the Italians about how she, like so many other Americans, had grown up thinking of matadors as daredevils who took unnecessary risks just for the thrill it gave the bloodthirsty spectators, who callously accepted the fact that the bull would still be slaughtered even if he won the contest. It was not until her first husband persuaded her to read *Death in the Afternoon* on her first trip to Spain that she came to appreciate how interwoven the ceremony of the man and the bull was with the Spanish approach to things. Before that trip she had not realized that the corrida was more ceremonial than spectacular, much more a matter of existential profundity than of festive amusement. Before that she had also shared much of the American view of Hemingway as a tough guy. In Spain she had come to realize that machismo was not a matter of aggressive arrogance but of a disposition to confront unfavorable odds. The world of the bullfighter was a world of fear. Machismo was not a matter of displaying force. It was a matter of overcoming fear with grace and style as well as with skill.

Speaking of your Ernest Hemingway, the marquis said when Jewel Templeton finished her account of her initiation, I think I understand why it was F. Scott Fitzgerald that your journalists and social historians most often mention when they refer to the American high times of the 1920s as the Jazz Age. But in my view it is Hemingway whose work is actually closest not only to jazz but also the underlying blues that make the best jazz a possibility. Even when the material at hand is really a thirty-two-bar popular song chorus. Fitzgerald may evoke the twenties decade in a reportorial sense much the same as leafing through illustrations in old stacks of magazines of the period.

Which reminded me that the Ernest Hemingway whose stories and articles had become such a very special part of what my old roommate used to call the goods that I had come by during my first year in college, was not a part of the New York speakeasy scene of the decade following the Prohibition amendment in 1919 as Fitzgerald, who had published *This Side of Paradise* in 1919 and followed it with *The Beautiful and Damned* and *The Great Gatsby*, came to be. After the war Hemingway had returned to Paris to cover Europe as a foreign correspondent and to begin his career as a writer of serious fiction. It was during this period of apprenticeship that he came to realize that what he learned from the bullfight as ritual was directly applicable to the art of fiction, both in terms of style and of fundamental content.

We were at a rectangular table, with the marquis at one end and the marquise at the other. I was on his right with Jewel Templeton on my right with the two Italian guests facing us across the center decoration. When we finished our *pastis*, the marquis suggested Tavel because we were in Provence and also because we were having a quick supper not a full French dinner. *Then when the waiter left with our orders and the women began to chat among themselves, he turned to me and said, I find much in the bullfight that is entirely consistent with the existential implication of the blues when fully orchestrated. First there is the bull, which is nothing if not the blues made visible, the blues in the flesh, destruction on the hoof, chaos personified, the symbol of all dragons and monsters, in a word, anarchy! Then there's the matador in his suit of lights with his myrtle wreath of a pigtail. He's nothing if not, as Thomas Mann put it, "life's delicate child" who must survive not by his strength and power, but by his flexibility, his wit, and his style. Is not that very much the same as the musician who must contend with the blues? For all of the power that the percussion and the incredibly high notes that your music is noted for, it is the musician's elegant improvisations, especially on the brink, that I find so basically relevant to the disjunctures of contemporary life.*

XLIII

EARLY THAT next Wednesday morning Jewel Templeton drove me down to Cannes, and I shipped the bass directly to Paris by railway express. Then we came on to the autobus station, and I checked in my luggage for the trip to my stopover in Avignon and came back outside, and we sat in the open Jaguar until boarding time, and that was where we finally said what we said instead of actually saying good-bye.

She had picked up a copy of the Paris edition of the *New York Herald Tribune* for me while I was inside, and after skimming quickly through it she refolded it and handed it to me. Then as we sat saying nothing for a few minutes, it was almost as if I had slipped all the way back to the day Miss Slick McGinnis gave me my high school graduation and going away present. It was Miss Lexine Metcalf who not unlike Miss Tee, had always said You will go where you must go. But when graduation time came you could also tell that the ever so slick Miss Slick McGinnis, who herself was forever coming and going, was also more preoccupied with anticipation than the separation at hand.

As so now was Jewel Templeton sitting thigh to thigh in the Jaguar outside the autobus station in Cannes that many years later and that many miles away from Mobile Bay, Mobile River, Three Mile Creek, and the Chickasabogue who looked at me and then looked ahead through the windshield again and said, So have fun doing Paris on your own and all of my very very special good-fairy best wishes or whatever for whatever you decide when you get back to New York.

And I said, And all the best to you back on the Coast and also in the box offices border to border. And remember: no better for such reviewers as don't even get the most obvious point of the effort but presume to grade the outcome. And she said, You said it, Mr. Bright Eyes. You said it. No better for plus than for minus and by the way the moneychangers have already declared themselves certain of fat profits regardless of reviews. Not that such matters concern me at this stage of the game. I think you know very well what concerns me at this stage of the game.

After all, she also said then, you're the one. Not me. As excited as I am about the possibilities of this new thing, it's still mostly a matter of going back to the same line of work with a keener perception of nuance and a new resolve. Not that I'm not as pleased as I can reasonably expect to be. But when I think of all of the options that you still have coming I literally tingle for you.

So anyway you have fun doing Paris, she said again. And I have no doubt whatsoever that you will. After all, who now comes to town? Not just another one of those small town sports from the provinces such as Balzac sent there as Eugène de Rastignac in *Le Père Goriot* and as Lucien de Rubempré *né* Chardon in *Lost Illusions.* Or such as Flaubert sent as Frédéric Moreau in *L'Éducation sentimentale.* No, this time it is who else if not *le vrai lapin agile,* if you pardon my midwestern high school French, from the Alabama briar patch by way of here there and elsewhere.

We sat saying nothing then, and I remembered what she had said one time when we were talking about the all-American elementary schoolboy and schoolgirl in us all. *She had said, Even now I am still almost as much the schoolgirl as I ever was. Incidentally I do not say that motherhood is not for me but I do keep on saying not yet. And that is when she also said, Alas it may very well be as Edna St. Vincent Millay declares in that poem when she says whether or not we find what we are seeking is idle biologically speaking.*

Maybe so, she said, maybe so. But what counts with the schoolgirl in me and the schoolboy in you is how we feel about things. What counts is that we are seeking whatever we are seeking. And I had said, In other words it may also be as Lord Raglan the Fourth Earl of Fitzhugh suggests in his book about the origins of civilization when he points out that the most natural state of human existence may be a state of low savagery. But even so, if there is always entropy, there is also always the ineluctable modality of the perceivable.

To which I was later to add what I also came to understand about the incessant interaction of imaginative exaltation (or self-delusion) and ever impending banalization as I continued to try to come to terms with the ever more comprehensive implications of the Mobile County Training School doctrine of the ancestral imperatives, which amounted to nothing less than the human proposition itself.

When I turned to kiss her and go because it was time to move to the boarding line, there was her voice vibrating that close again and her saying, I really must thank you once more for being so wonderful with the marquis, who thinks you're just fantastic. Oh, it was as if I had used my magic movie star wand to conjure up a golden brown storybook prince who was by way of becoming the very embodiment of what the music you play is all about.

Oh, I very much doubt that anybody from *Burke's Peerage* or the *Almanach de Gotha* could match your impact on him. As for myself there you were once more as you were the night I accosted you as you stood at the curb outside The Keynote with your arm around the neck and shoulders of that rich toned earth brown earth mother of a bass fiddle looking for all the world as if you had just alighted from a foam flecked steed. Oh, I must say, she said.

And I said, And now it is my time to thank you for arranging me to have such a very special one-on-one personal encounter with a truly contemporary cosmopolitan who is as much to the manner as to the manor born. Who, I could have added, like other sophisticated Europeans almost always apt to strike Americans such as ourselves as being casually insightful rather than academically or even intellectually brilliant.

I could also have pointed out that in any case there was seldom if ever any trace of the schoolboy and schoolgirl left in sophisticated Europeans once they were grown up, as if they had just simply evolved as organically as a plant evolves into what it is cultivated to become but I didn't say anything else because she had clicked on the ignition.

And now you must go, she said, not looking at me again and also as if to say, We shall see what we shall see as you go wherever you must go to do whatever you must do. Then as I turned and headed for the departure gate I heard the Jaguar pull away, but I didn't look back until I was sure it was out of sight.

XLIV

ON THE way out of Provence and into Burgundy by way of the Côtes du Rhône and Saône, I began thinking about the band again, not only because I was on a cross-country bus trip again and suddenly missed being a part of the lineup as I hadn't had time to miss it when I stayed behind in Hollywood, but also because of a train of thought that my exchanges with the Marquis de Chaumienne over the weekend had started. And there was also the matter of my forthcoming functional identity as a musician among musicians in Paris.

After finishing the Paris *Herald Tribune* I spent most of my waking time between Cannes and Avignon tracing the route in the Michelin guide and reading, mostly about the old days of Cézanne but also about Van Gogh and Gauguin in the pocket sized booklet on the beginnings of contemporary art that Jewel Templeton had picked up for me to browse through. I had already been playing around for some time with the notion that Louis Armstrong's influence on the music most representative of our time was comparable to Cézanne's influence on contemporary painting, and as I thought about it again that afternoon with Mont St. Victoire in the distance I suddenly realized that I had missed a chance to mention it to the Marquis de Chaumienne, but I was pretty certain that he would have agreed with the analogy.

The side trips out from Avignon were strictly all-American schoolboy stuff. So at Pont du Gard, as had also been the case with Arles and Nîmes, you were back to the illustrations in your ninth and tenth grade Latin textbook. At such points as Les Baux-de-Provence, Gordes, and Roussillon you were back in your first and second year French language, literature, and culture textbooks once more.

At one turn during the guided tour through the Palais des Papes I became aware again of how impressed I had once been with what Frederick Douglass had been able to make of what he saw there on his journey through that part of Europe in the mid-1880s.

His ruminations about the headquarters of the popes being at once a palace and a prison, with halls of judgment, halls of inquisition, halls of torture, and halls of banquet, like the remarks he also made about the Roman arenas in Nîmes and Arles, had struck me as being very wise observations about the contradictions that are as much a part of the universal condition (or fate) of mankind as everything else.

But even as I considered this as noteworthy evidence of how far this magnificent ex-slave omni-American ancestor of mine had transcended the intellectual restrictions of racial provincialism, I couldn't keep myself from also remembering that alas this same Frederick Douglass, himself a mulatto, now traveling with a white wife, had then gone on to Egypt and in effect claimed a special kinship with the ruins of ancient Egypt, not as a part of his natural inheritance as a human heir of all the ages, but as a darker skinned American some of whose foreparents were captives from West not East Africa.

Nor are matters helped when Douglass goes on to say that his trip to Egypt had "an ethnological purpose in the pursuit of which I hoped to turn my visit to some account in combatting American prejudice against the darker races of mankind, and at the same time to raise colored people somewhat in their own estimation and thus stimulate them to higher endeavors."

Because I had long since come to revere his magnificent ancestral status as much for his wisdom and intellectual sophistication as for his courage, I had come to assume that Frederick Douglass's conception of the human proposition underlying the American promise was more profound than such pathetic defensiveness reveals. Feeling an urgent need to prove to Union, the abolitionists, and the Confederacy alike that downtrodden slaves are able, ready, and eager to fight for their liberation was another matter altogether.

Not that my disappointment amounted to a major disenchantment. As far as I was concerned Frederick Douglass was still the unsurpassed embodiment of *Homo americanus*, warts and all. And with the autobus rolling on beyond Montelimar and Valence toward the next night's stopover in Macon it was almost as if you were seeing the countryside from your old seat in the band bus with Joe States (whose take on the ancient Egyptians I definitely preferred to the implications of Frederick Douglass as I understood them at that time) nodding across the aisle from me once more.

Egyptians? Come on, man. But I will say this much for them. They were some great undertakers. And they left some pretty conspicuous tombs. If you go for such things, which I don't. Man, just look at them frozen butt friezes or whatever you call them and stuff. Man, them people ain't swinging. They ain't stomping cute. And what kind of old stiff-kneed shuffling is that? Man, them goddamn people always look to me like they're on their way to a funeral. And when I think of all them goodies them frigging pharaohs took to them tombs with them instead of parceling that stuff out among all them hungry survivors.

In all events whatever you inherited from ancient Egypt you had to come by like everybody else, not because of any special kind of kinship whatsoever. As for ancestral antecedents, elsewhere on the vast and ever so demographically varied continent of Africa Joe States was pretty much on the case on that too. Not that it was a matter that ever seemed to concern him very much. *Africa? Africa? Africa? Let's be realistic, home boy. This band is a class act. We don't play no music for no rusty-toed clod busters dragging and whirling around for no chief. Man, we don't even want to look out there and see some somitch that need his shoes shined and his pants pressed.*

Africa? Africa? Africa? Hey, that's all right with me about the great-granddaddy of my drums and the grandmammy of the mellow brown in my complexion and all the little cousins of the kinks in my hair. This music ain't got nothing to do with sending no messages to some chief across the river somewhere over yonder. This music we play is about going somewhere and getting on some time in the United States of America.

Man, what I'm laying down for these thugs in this outfit is strictly stateside stuff and mostly down-home stuff to boot. Man, by the time I came along the granddaddies of my drums were them honky-tonk guitar players strumming their driving rods under them fret-fingered train whistle guitar blues in tempos all the way from slow dragging locals and switch engines all the way up through express and highballing express to limited express. Boy, I was already way into all of that I don't know how many years before I put my trap set into a cotton sack and hit the L & N northbound.

As the autobus made its way through Vienne bringing back more recollections of textbook illustrations from Mobile County Training School classrooms and settled into the stretch that would take us on beyond Lyons, I began thinking again about how the marquis was to the manor and manner of the château born, and about how Jewel Templeton and I and most other Americans were born wherever and however we were born to be reborn on campuses. *Certainly the most basic of all things about universal free public education in the United States is that for all its widespread and longstanding entanglement with racial segregation it is predicated on the completely democratic assumption that individual development, self-realization, and self-fulfillment is a matter of inspiring learning contexts not of one's family background and certainly not a matter of one's ancient racial forebears. So assumed Miss Lexine Metcalf and Mr. B. Franklin Fisher, neither of whom ever confused race with culture. Windows on the world indeed. Windows on basic patterns and idiomatic variations in human behavior.*

Joe States Joe States Joe States, I kept thinking as the Paris bound autobus pulled on away from Dijon heading for Avallon and the swing over to Vézelay before continuing on to a turn through Auxerre. *Joe States Joe States Joe States, Uncles Bud, Doc, Ned, and Remus as same height big brother in bespoke tailoring second to none.* Everbody's main man was the Bossman Himself to be sure. And everybody's undisputed master craftsman of musical nuts and bolts second only to the unfathomable genius of the main man himself was who else but Old Pro. But even so, who else but Joe States was the band's self elected and unanimously approved elder statesman? *Who said, me and you, Schoolboy. Get to me fast. You may be just what this band needs at this stage of the game.*

Listen, Schoolboy, he kept repeating during my first month or so in the band, this stuff we play for this band is not just music. This stuff is life, Schoolboy. Life! LIFE. Man, I mean I'm not just talking about cutting some dots. Man, I'm talking about making them dots mean something.

Being a member of this outfit is not just a matter of being an expert in cutting some weird dots, Schoolboy. When you come right down to it what I'm talking about is having your little story to add to the bossman's big story. And don't ever forget that this is a dance band, whatever else it might be. It's the bossman's stories with all of our little chapters in there that make people want to move something.

You know what we're always up there trying to do when we're out there on them concert and stage variety tours? Trying our best to make everybody down there in them orchestra rows and over them boxes and up in them balcony tiers wish they could get up and get out on the floor and dance.

One of the first things you found out as soon as you came on to the stand to play your debut dance set with the band was that Joe States was the one who always made sure that you were keeping close tab on how the couples out on the floor were responding. Your job was not just a matter of being good enough to fit in with the rhythm section he said, it was also really a matter of helping the bossman please them people out there trying to get on some time.

The bass player is not just some kind of picture frame or pedestal, Schoolboy, he said. The bass is always there to lay that indispensable foundation for the ongoing stories. Them pistons and drivers got to have a track under them. And that was when he also insisted that what you did in every bar could also be just as personal as what the featured horn men did in their solos and fills.

Hey man, my motto for this band is let's get them dancers first, he always used to say. Even when they're lying in bed listening to the radio. Even if they're all entwined together somewhere out there in lovers' lane. You keep them dancers happy and you ain't got nothing to worry about because they'll be coming back. Like I told the bossman back when we were just starting out. I said, We got to make people want to dance that think they can't dance. And know what he said? He said, You can dance with a lot of things other than your feet.

So naturally, Joe States was the one who said what he said that night in that ever so classy country club in the suburb of that midwestern town that I won't name because the band always has been and still is so popular there. Hey like I said, Schoolboy, this stuff we put out is supposed to make people want to do things, but man, sometimes I also wonder. Man, sometimes some people go into action before they get the message. Now here I am making damn sure this band puts this hall in a groove that's hip deep, and just look at what some of them people out there doing. Man, goddamn. Man, I declare. Man, but what can I tell you except there it is again.

But what the hell, he also said two numbers later. We got them up and out there trying and having themselves a hell of a good time in the process. So there you go, Schoolboy. We do what we can. And if they didn't like what we're about we wouldn't be here.

Then as we file offstage after the first set there was somebody behind me saying Just keep thumping, Schoolboy. Just keep thumping. And I didn't recognize who it was at first because I hadn't been in the band very long yet, and when I looked back I was surprised because it was Fred Gilchrist, the first trombone man, who was called the Silent Partner not only because he took so few spotlight solos but also and perhaps mainly because he did not talk very much to anybody about anything whatsoever.

Just keep thumping that bull fiddle, Schoolboy, he said again backstage. Man, I used to think I'd never get used to some of the stuff people do out there. Man, sometimes I used to have a hard time just trying to keep a straight face instead of laughing or frowning. But then I realized something. Man, we got them people doing their best to try to get with it.

That was only a few weeks after Joe States had introduced me to the band as a newcomer at that rehearsal in Cincinnati that first morning. His smile and handshake had made me feel as welcome as everybody else's had and he had also stopped by the booth to shake hands again when Joe States had taken me out to see some of Cincinnati that first evening. But that night between sets was the first time he ever said anything to me person to person. And he never actually brought up the topic again, but every now and then when we were playing another dance in a similar place somewhere and he saw me looking back at the trombone section he would nod his head toward the dance floor and wink.

The scenic route to Paris from the South of France by way of Provence and Burgundy was not through Flaubert country, to be sure. Flaubert's native territory was Rouen and environs in the northern province of Normandy. But regional differences notwithstanding, it was Flaubert's famous remark about peasant life that kept coming to mind as the bus made its way through the small towns and smaller settlements and on past the vineyards and farms and rolling pasturelands along the Côtes du Rhône and then the Saône with what I took to be the hunt country in the distance.

As a matter of fact the legendary pronouncement that I hadn't heard since the night Eric Threadcraft kept repeating it as we drove back across town from a jam session out on Central Avenue to take the Hollywood Freeway to the Sunset Boulevard exit, popped into my head the very first time the bus made a rest stop that was long enough for a short visit to an open air market.

Ils sont dans le vrai, ils sont dans le vrai, ils sont dans le vrai, Eric Threadcraft had kept repeating as much to himself as to me. And I told him that was the first time I had heard anybody actually say it since my old roommate and I used to play around with its implications as early on as the first term of our sophomore year. *Then my roommate and I had become more impressed with what William Empson had pointed out about how sophisticated artists and intellectuals used pastoral (or the glorification of peasant life) as a literary device or rhetorical strategy to depict "an inversion of values" by representing peasant life as being richer in the basic virtues of humanity than aristocratic refinement and elegance!*

So I said, Hey man, he was talking about country folks. I said, he was talking about peasants. I said, Man, you got to watch that "blisses of the commonplace" jive, if you know what I mean. I said, Hey man, don't go sentimental on me.

And he said, Not me fellow, not me. He said, I'm not talking about folk music. I'm talking about Kansas City four/four. I'm talking about not losing touch with the fundamentals. As Count Basie never does. As the Bossman Himself never, but never, never has and never, never will. Hey, fellow, I'm talking about keeping the flame.

So then I said, Maybe that was what old Flaubert was really talking about too. And you know good and well that I'm all for it. But man, don't ever forget that the hometown expectations that made me the schoolboy that I became are about raising the horizons of aspiration of the so-called common man. *What was important to the folks in my hometown was not that*

you could have a good time among the so-called common people
of Gasoline Point on the outskirts of Mobile, Alabama, but that
such a place could produce people of extraordinary potential and
achievement.

After the stopover in Dijon during which there was a side trip
back to the vineyards of Nuits-Saint-Georges, Clos-Vougeot,
and Gevrey-Chambertin that had been passed up after stops
at Poligny-Montrachet, Meursault, and Pommard on the way
to Beaune, I finished the travel books about the dukes of Burgundy and France in the Middle Ages.

Then on the way to Auxerre after Avallon and the side trip to
Vézelay (where references to Bernard of Clairvaux and Richard
the Lion Heart took you back to the Crusades) I wished for
something to read about storybook castles, knights, and troubadours. But when you pulled on through Joigny and headed
for Villeneuve and Sens, it was as if you were already approaching the outskirts of Paris.

So I took out the Michelin and Hallewag city maps of Paris
(both of which showed the key landmarks in three dimensional
drawings that looked like the cutouts on Miss Lexine Metcalf's
third grade sand table) because even as we rolled on past the
turnoffs to Fontainebleau and Corbeil and Senlis, *I was thinking first the banlieues and then the arrondissements and thinking
when you see the Eiffel Tower and the Seine you're there.*

XLV

WHEN YOU came out on to the narrow sidewalk in front of
what was the Hôtel de Londres on Rue Bonaparte in those
days, you were facing a grilled entrance to a courtyard of the
École des Beaux-Arts, which meant that you were in the Latin
Quarter. So when you turned right and went to the corner
tabac to get the newspaper, directly across Quai Malaquais and
the Seine was the Louvre, and the French Institute was in the
block on your right.

On your left along Quai Voltaire was Pont du Carrousel,
which led to the gateway through the courtyard of the Louvre
by way of the Arc de Triomphe du Carrousel, which you could

see was in a straight line with the center walk of the Jardin des Tuileries, the Obélisque in the Place de la Concorde, the Avenue des Champs-Élysées, and the Arc de Triomphe in the Place de l'Étoile.

From the exit on the other side of the courtyard of the Louvre, you crossed the Rue de Rivoli, Rue Saint-Honoré, and you were on Avenue de l'Opéra, at the other end of which only a few blocks away was the Paris Opéra itself, a stroll to which would take you past Brentano's Bookstore, the Grand Hotel, and the Café de la Paix. Then when you crossed Boulevard des Capucines you were not only at Place de l'Opéra but also Rue Aubert and at Hotel Scribe and the legendary Paris office of American Express.

Across Boulevard Haussmann directly behind the Opéra were Les Galeries Lafayette and Au Printemps, the two most famous department stores in Paris. That was as far as I went on my first exploration of the Right Bank. But when I had to go back to use the American Express exchange service a few days later I went on as far as Gare Saint-Lazare and came back by way of Madeleine, the Place de la Concorde, and Quai d'Orsay.

When you turned left from Hôtel de Londres, Rue Bonaparte led to Église Saint-Germain-des-Prés, which was the name not only of the small square but also of that whole quarter of Paris, and its main thoroughfare was Boulevard Saint-Germain. Across the square from the church were the sidewalk tables of Café des Deux Magots, across the street on the other side of which was Café de Flore, across the boulevard was Brasserie Lipp. These were all literary checkpoints, and the main checkpoint for American musicians, not only in Saint-Germain-des-Prés, at that time was the Vieux Colombier, which was a downstairs club in the same building as the Café des Deux Magots.

If you took Boulevard Saint-Germain to Rue de Tournon and turned right you came to Place de l'Odéon, Shakespeare and Company bookstore, and Palais Luxembourg, in which there was a gallery that I knew about from reading Hemingway and there was also the Odéon branch of the Comédie Française; and beyond the Palais was the Jardin du Luxembourg, which took you all the way to the Place de l'Observatoire beyond the intersection of Boulevard Saint-Michel and Boulevard du Montparnasse.

I turned right and headed along Boulevard du Montparnasse for Boulevard Raspail and the Dôme, the Rotonde, the Select, and the Coupole, cafés I had read about in *The Sun Also Rises*. I had a beer in the Select and studied the map and guidebook and decided that I would come back through Luxembourg Gardens again the next morning and turn left along Boulevard Saint-Michel and visit the Panthéon and the Sorbonne on the way to Notre Dame and then browse my way through the book stalls and go on along the quais past Île de la Cité back to the French Institute and Rue Bonaparte once more.

It was also in the Select that I decided that on the day following the trip down Boulevard Saint-Michel and back along the Left Bank from Notre Dame, I would find out how to take the bus to Montmartre and then another bus across to Étoile and walk on over to Palais du Trocadéro, Palais de Chaillot, and the Musée de l'Homme. Then from there you could go on across the Seine to the Eiffel Tower or there was the Musée Nationale d'Art Moderne on the way back along Avenue New York at the crossover to Quai d'Orsay.

When I left the Select I went back to the Hôtel de Londres by strolling along Boulevard Raspail to Rue de Rennes, which took you directly to Saint-Germain-des-Prés. Then after a nap I took a shower and changed clothes and ate at the nearest bistro on Rue Jacob. Then I headed across Pont du Carrousel to my first encounter with the ladies along Boulevard de la Madeleine and Boulevard des Capucines.

Not because I actually expected anything more fancy or exotic than what you had already been initiated into as an apprentice road musician in those days, and certainly not after having spent as much time as I had spent freelancing around Hollywood. But really because it was something that I had fantasized about ever since I had been ever so subtly permitted to contrive to overhear the capers Soldier Boy Crawford and other AEF veterans reminisce about in Papa Gumbo Willie McWorthy's barbershop.

It was not at all a matter of curiosity, exploration, and revelation for me as it had been for old Soldier Boy Crawford and the other doughboys who after all were still as oblivious to the existence of the *Kama Sutra* and the *Perfumed Garden* for instance (as I was not by the time I had finished junior high school) as they were of Miss Lexine Metcalf's bulletin board and sand table peoples of many lands. No, with me it was really a matter of personal verification of the actual texture of the also and also of the fable and the flesh.

And as you turned off Avenue de l'Opéra, there they were, walking that walk and talking that talk that made all the difference in the world. And on my way back to Pont du Carrousel and Hôtel de Londres afterward, I was to tell myself that what made it worthwhile and worth doing again had as much to do with the idiomatic nuances of Parisian French as only they spoke it and with Parisian perfume as only they wore and projected it (not without the faintest pleasant hint of bistro garlic and bistro carafe wine withal) as with any unconventional range and specifics of the choreography as such.

As a matter of fact such was the tone and tempo of the one to one intimacy that was so instantaneously generated during my first and second evenings that as much as I had also picked up over the years about how there were always pimps keeping tabs on the streetwalkers with the same authority as house madams had over their ladies, I forgot all about that part of it much the same as you forget about the proscenium, the footlights, and the director as soon as the curtain opens on the stage set. And not only was such the case the first two times, but even as I spotted the signal as my choice of the evening passed a corner bar on my next exploration, it made no more difference than when you passed the stage manager in the wings on your way into the action on stage.

There were also the ladies of the sidewalks near Gare Saint-Lazare and also of Montmartre and the kikis of Montparnasse and such also was the also and also of the "parlors" on your checklist that even as each madam began her all knowing smile the schoolboy in you stepped into the plushest pleasure domes of the *flâneurs* and grand horizontals not only of the Belle Époque but also of Balzac's Paris of fifty years earlier.

Meanwhile there was also the also and also of all the other reasons you were stopping over in Paris en route to New York. Which in addition to guidebook tours on your own also included mornings or afternoons and sometimes whole days in the Louvre, the Orangerie, Musée Nationale d'Art Moderne, and the Musée de l'Homme. Along with which there was also not only the also and also of the contacts with fellow country-men on the scene, made available by backstage friends in New York, but also those chance encounters that sometimes turn out to be even more memorable than some of the key items on your carefully prepared agenda.

By the end of that first week I had also started checking out what was happening in jazz clubs around town, beginning with the Vieux Colombier in Saint-Germain-des-Prés because it was only a few blocks away from Hôtel de Londres and also be-cause I was already as familiar as I was with the Vieux Colom-bier in Juan-les-Pins.

The one in Juan-les-Pins was on the beach on your right as you pull out heading for Antibes. The one in Saint-Germain-des-Prés turned out to be somewhat smaller than I had imag-ined because of its reputation among musicians. But there was no reason to doubt that it was one of the most important clubs of its kind in all of Paris at that time.

Another not very far away spot on my list was Chez Inez (Cavanaugh) over near the Sorbonne, and after that there were several other now mostly forgotten ones in and around the Latin Quarter. Then when you cross over to the Right Bank and made your way on up to nighttime Montmartre you were entering the part of Paris in which American entertainers and jazz musicians had become *all the rage* back during the heyday of Place Pigalle and all of the other hot spots you grew up hearing and reading about in stories about Josephine Baker, Bricktop, Frisco, Spencer Williams, Sidney Bechet, and the one and only Royal Highness.

The Montmartre that I had visited by day was what was left of one ever so bright-eyed schoolboy's Belle Époque world not of musicians as such but of the entertainment provided in places like the Moulin Rouge by such legendary night crea-tures as Yvette Guilbert, Jane Avril, and La Goulue among oth-ers, and celebrated by Toulouse-Lautrec and Édouard Manet, among others.

Nor was there very much of what you had imagined of the heyday in what you came across in nighttime Montmartre. But it was still very much the capital of Parisian nightlife, and as such was second to no other such district in the Western world. After all, entertainers like Josephine Baker were still around and so were Bricktop and Frisco as were musicians like Sidney Bechet and a number of others including Don Byas and Kenny Clarke. But as far as I was concerned the best sets that I heard while I was in Paris at that time were not in any club including Vieux Colombier but during concerts in auditoriums like Salle Pleyel in the Palais de Chaillot and during the dances I went to in Salle Wagram because some group on tour from the States was booked there.

Not that the state of American music in Paris was really a matter of any urgent concern to me at that time, because as completely involved with music as I had been between the time that I went on the road with the Bossman Himself and the day I left Hollywood, I was not stopping over in Paris as a journey-man bass fiddle player or even as a part time semipro freelancer. I knew very well the chances were that I would be spotted and invited to do guest shots from time to time by somebody who recognized me from the context of the band, and I didn't mind obliging. Not only because it provided an easy way to choose new friends, but sometimes it could also lead to a little extra chicken change, not that I was looking for it.

Incidentally unlike a lot of horn men and guitar and chin fiddle men, who perhaps more often than not used to take their instruments along with them when they made their rounds in those days, I didn't take my fiddle into any club in Paris until after I had been asked to fill a request on the current bass man's instrument and had then been invited back. Actually the only time I ever took my instrument along when I was making the rounds anywhere was when I left the band and was getting started as a freelance newcomer around Los Angeles. And the main reason that I could bring myself to do so then was that having the use of Jewel Templeton's auto incognito made having it at hand seem so casually incidental. After all the last impression you wanted to create anywhere was that you were expecting or hoping to be invited to join in.

Anyway, although I didn't really mind being recognized be-ing flattered and applauded, I had not come to town to en-hance my reputation as a promising young musician. As useful as such an identity was especially in Paris, I was there only for a stopover for essentially the same reasons that I would have spent the summer and only the summer there between college and graduate school if I had been able to afford to do so at the time that I had gone on the road with the Bossman Himself as temporary replacement for Shag Philips.

Not that being in Paris at long last was no more (or any less) of a schoolboy's dream come true than it ever was when I was in college. But by the time I actually arrived, there was also the also and also of my recent personal encounter with the Marquis de Chaumienne, whose catalytic impact on me had already become no less than his undeniably crucial influence on Jewel Templeton through whom indeed his effect on my conception of coming to terms with my functional definition of my personal identity and universal whereabouts had already begun during that first morning when she told me what she told me about meeting him in Saint-Moritz.

So in a sense it was very much as if the actuality of being in Paris was so consistent with all of your longtime anticipations made you somehow almost restless to complete your visit and so have it as an accomplished dimension of the firsthand personal experience that was an indispensable part of the equipment in your existential tool kit (*and thus also a part of the back home practice sessions you so often find yourself all but yearning for as if precisely because things are turning out so well for you elsewhere*).

Not that I ever seriously or even tentatively considered shortening my checklist. But even so, what the also and also of the day to day patina of Paris at firsthand clearly stimulated beyond all else was an irrepressible urge to be back stateside getting on with what was to come next, whatever it was.

Which was a reaction that turns out to be much closer to how Jewel Templeton came to feel about her trips to Europe as soon as she entered the charmed circle of the Marquis de Chaumienne and his cosmopolitan friends than to how any of my idiomatic cousins among the Americans I met in Paris felt about being there.

Ezel Adams, for instance, an after hours piano player from the outskirts of Chattanooga by way of Pittsburgh, uptown Manhattan, and Greenwich Village piano bars, who was rooming in a pension in Saint-Germain-des-Prés when I was there, and who said, Hey, what about this Paris, man, and said, Man, this is the life, and said, Man, every time I wake and realize that this is where I really am I have to pinch myself to prove that I am really here in the flesh and blood and not just dreaming.

I had heard him play two sets at the Vieux Colombier, and I had also seen him come in with friends during my second guest shot in there, and we had nodded and smiled and made the high sign to each other each time. But we didn't actually meet each other until he came over and introduced himself while I was sipping a *citron pressé* at a sidewalk table of Le Petit Mabillon on Boulevard Saint-Germain several blocks away from the Café des Deux Magots in the direction of Café Tournon.

Hey, what say there, my man, he said, sounding down home and uptown at the same time, I just wanted to tell you how much I enjoyed your gig the other night. That was some nice stuff you laid on them, man. Nice, nice. Very nice. And they picked up on it too. And I said, Hey, thanks, man, and nodded for him to join me, and said, Man, I was in there when you laid some stuff on them yourself, remember? I said, Man, there they were with all their ever so Parisian and international chicness and you eased them right on out into the back alley and had them responding as if it was the most natural place in the world to be.

And he said, Hey, man, that's this Paris for you. Ain't nothing like it. Man, this goddamn Paris, France, is the place I been heading for all of my born days. Now I'm not saying I always knew it or anything like that. I heard enough about it to want to see for myself and when I got here that was it for me.

When I told him that I was there only for a stopover, he said, What a pity and a shame. So, when I told him that my limitation was self-imposed all he could do at first was shake his head and say, Hey, come on, man, you expect me to believe that? And I realized that he just might be thinking that I was trying to cover up the fact that I was either short on funds or uncertain about my chances of making a living in Paris as a musician.

Whatever he actually thought, the first thing he said when he introduced me to Calvin Curtis at Café Tournon a few days later was, Man, this cat is incredible. Man, this cat is on his way back stateside on his own timetable when he could gig around over here for no telling how much longer if he wanted to. And Calvin Curtis, who was knocking around Europe as a reporter and features writer from Chicago said, Man, what for? And when I said, Unfinished business, man, he said, Come on, man. Or do you mean that you got yourself a big fat surefire deal waiting that you just don't want to string out any longer? And I said, Hey, man, what can I tell you? I'm just here to touch a few bases before getting on back to the matter of some very important unfinished business. That doesn't mean that I'm not already planning to come back from time to time. It just means I'm not sticking around but for so long this time. And he said, Hey, man, it's your call. It's just that a lot of home boys over here wish they had the option to stick around that you musicians have. And I said, I think I know what you mean man, I really do.

And that's when I also said, Listen, man, what they like is American musicians playing American music. Our kind of American music. Don't forget that. Man, I don't know anything about them wanting American musicians to become French musicians. Or American writers to become French writers. If you're an American musician and you move to France they still expect you to play music in an idiom that is authentically American.

Then I also said, And as for painters, man, ain't nobody in the world more crazy about Paris than American painters and sculptors have mostly been over the years. But I don't know any instances where the French have ever sent for any of them as they send for our kind of American musicians.

And he said, You got a point there, my man. You got a deep point. I can tell that you really have been thinking about all this stuff. I really mean it. In fact, I'm beginning to wish you'd stick around a while longer just because you're so different to talk to, my man.

Danny Dennison, a writer from New York, was also somebody I had exchanged nods and waves with in Vieux Colombier before we said hello and had a drink together at Le Petit Mabillon. I was to get the impression that he had become much more involved with my kind of music and musicians as such since coming to Paris than he had ever been back in New York. He had grown up in the very heart of Harlem, but his was the Harlem of church folks rather than the Harlem of bars, nightclubs, and ballrooms. The clubs and bars he had come to frequent when he grew up were those where certain writers and artists hung out in Greenwich Village. In any case, I remember him as identifying much more intimately with folk and hot mama blues and the earthier forms of down-home church music than with jazzing, swinging, stomping, riffing, grooving, bopping, and so on. Although he was anything but square and could get up to date with it on the dance floor if the occasion called for it.

To each his own is what I always say, he said in response to being told of my self limited stopover status. To each his own. He flourished his Gauloise *bleue* cigarette, his instantly friendly "smart cookie" eyes twinkling playfully. Or as they say over here, *Chacun selon son goût.* Or in my case, *selon sa faim.* Because in my case, it was truly a matter of life and death. No two ways about it, baby. When it really hit me. When I could no longer deny what those awful people over there really had in store for me it was a matter of hauling my black ass out of there, pronto.

Some stay and submit. Some stay and contend. And believe me when I say I honor and celebrate them because I really do. But these nevertheless are such personal matters. Whatever they saw there must have inspired or indeed fired them on. But what I came to see was myself being consumed whole soul and body—*soul before body!* Many bodies survive through street smarts, but the survival of one's soul is another matter altogether. The existence of my soul depends on me being a writer and I could not become a writer in that place. It was as if it were against the law. Against the law for us, I mean.

He always referred to himself as being black, which I took to be a matter of principle or policy, because he was in fact only a slightly darker shade of brown than Ezel Adams whose hair texture before processing was also pretty much the same as his. He was also shorter and slighter than Ezel Adams who was about five feet eleven and weighed about one-eighty and had a slight paunch that is not unusual in piano players even before they are thirty.

Also, unlike Ezel Adams, who dressed like the well-tailored after hours piano player that he was, and who did a version of the patent leather avenue limp walk that gave the impression that he was wearing house shoes even on the bandstand, Danny Dennison's clothes and carriage made him seem as much a part of the world of ballet and modern dancers in New York as the world of writers and artists in Saint-Germain-des-Prés.

Calvin Curtis was a not quite high yaller northern city schoolboy type that some down-home folks regarded as being a bit too concerned with proper speech and bearing. But as far as I was concerned the main thing about him was his pre-occupation with academically certified conventional standards of excellence, whether in personal appearance or professional performance. And I found myself thinking that he would have made a much better military officer or say airline pilot, than a newspaper reporter and features writer he had become at that time. Precisely because he would have derived far more personal satisfaction from proving that he could measure up to the most stringent professional standards than he seemed to be getting from trying to express his personal point of view of things in his published articles.

We didn't talk about vocational choices although my own choice was what was very much on my mind at the time. But whenever something brings him back to mind I can still see the look of personally achieved security on the face of the air force officer or airline pilot as he and glamorous guests are seated at a ringside table in one of the exclusive clubs that I used to play in. (Incidentally it would not be the uniformity of the uniforms that he may or may not wear to the nightspot that attracted him but rather the challenge of sartorial perfection required by the air force and the airlines.)

I met the painter Roland Howard Beasley one afternoon at Montparnasse when I happened to be sitting close enough to his table to overhear him referring to Royal Highness as if to a longtime acquaintance. He and his companion, who turned out to be a college English professor and poet on a traveling fellowship, were talking about old vaudeville performers who were always in and out of the old Lafayette Theatre, the Harlem Opera House, and the Alhambra when he was growing up on 135th Street off Seventh Avenue.

There were not many people in the Coupole during that part of that midweek afternoon. So you could hear what conversations at nearby tables were about without really paying any specific attention. But when I realized that Royal Highness was being mentioned I stopped reading what I was reading, and when I heard Roland Beasley referring to him as Daddy Royal, I decided to introduce myself to him on the way out; and the three of us left together and at Boulevard Raspail, Roland Beasley and I promised to meet at the Closerie des Lilas that next afternoon.

When I got there he was waiting by the statue of Marshal Ney and on the way inside he began telling me that he was going to be on his way back to New York in several weeks when the term of the special courses in contemporary French culture and philosophy he was taking at the Sorbonne would be over. He had hoped to extend his stay in France a few weeks longer but he was also looking forward to getting back to his studio.

Man, what can I say? he said as we waited for our drinks. You can't beat this goddamn Paris, especially if you're a painter, but it ain't home, if you know what I mean. And you being a musician I'm pretty sure you do, because you know there's all the difference in the world between playing music for people over here and doing it for folks back home.

Because, he went on as we tasted our drinks, it is a matter of making up the music for them. Because you're making it up out of something that you and that audience over there share so much of. That's where you start. Then if you go on and get good enough you just might also turn some of what you come up with into something that people all over can relate to. And by that I mean as if it's the most natural thing in the world of here and now and maybe for some time to come.

The fact of the matter is, he was to say later on, that I came over here to find out as much as I can about how these people came up with all this stuff that's so fantastic and so much a natural seeming part of everyday life in the workaday world. And how much of it I need for the express purpose of doing my own thing with my own stuff. So you know what? I guess that makes me one of the truest sons of that bunch that Malcolm Cowley wrote about in *Exile's Return*. Man, as I'm sure you know, that bunch was over here loving every minute of it.

But their best stuff was about being Americans if not about the United States itself.

And remembering reading Cowley's book at my favorite table in the main reading room of the library during the fall of my senior year in college (with tennis balls plopping back and forth outside but with my best of all possible roommates not there to discuss such things with anymore) I said, Hey, man, you know it too. Hey, too much, man. I said, Man, you *know* something. *Because there we were sitting in the very same Closerie des Lilas where Hemingway had come up with some of his back home four/four prose (derived in part from the style sheet of the* Kansas City Star*) that in its own way was as idiomatic, valid, reliable, and comprehensive as the "St. Louis Blues."*

I stuck out my hand because I was absolutely certain that he knew what I was thinking, and as we slapped and snatched palms, he smiled and then laughed with his tongue between his teeth like a schoolboy, and his eyes became moist, as I was to find that they always did when he was especially pleased about the way something connected with something else. It was the same prankish schoolboy chuckle that I was to see when things were going well in his studio when I visited him in New York time after time during the years that followed. And I decided that it was as if a joke was being played on the complexity of actuality. As if the joke was the means by which form was achieved from the actuality of the undefined.

Anyway, my man, and I do mean my man, my brand new cousin, he said, wiping his eyes that afternoon in Paris that many years ago. As much as I really would like to stick around a little while longer and also zip back through some of the places I've taken in, that is why I got to be getting on back across the pond to my little old dinky woodshed and see what I can come up with. Hemingway could do it over here and other places too. But man, as much as I love it none of them cats knocked as many people out overseas as old Louis Armstrong and the Bossman Himself.

My woodshed and my launching pad, man, he said, because what old Louis and the bossman make me realize, when I listen to them over here, is that when you talk about achieving universality in the arts you're talking about something that is really a matter of intercontinental ballistics, my man. When you listen to that stuff over here you keep thinking about where you know old Louis and the bossman are coming from back home.

As for me and Daddy Royal, he finally said several afternoons later when we met at Brasserie Lipp as we had agreed to do, Johnny Hudgins, the comedian, was there first. But Daddy Royal became one of my main uncles. By which I mean along with being the headliner he was for everybody else I got close enough to him for him to become the same kind of uncle as Uncles Bud, Doc, Ned, Remus, and Zack, if you know what I mean and I'm sure you do, home boy.

And I said, Down-home boy. Which makes us idiomatic cousins, I said. And he said, Idiomatic. You said it, man. So let's keep in touch, cousin. And I said, By all means, thinking this is also what the also and also of being in Paris can add up to.

XLVI

Zone of the interior, I began thinking again as the plane settled into its cruising speed en route from Le Bourget to New York. *Zone of the interior from border to border and coast to coast (plus twelve) of the continental limits of the United States, which began with a gradual settlement of the lucky thirteen aboriginal colonies that somehow and anyhow came to predicate a nation that was a new kind of nation on the principles underlying their declaration of independence from the England of King George III.*
  That was the precise phrase become poetic notion that had popped to mind again on the way back to the hotel from dinner with Roland Beasley at the Mediterranée in Place de l'Odéon the night before. We had spent most of the meal talking about what I later came to think of as the vernacular imperative in the creative process. But we had also spent some of the evening questioning the depth and scope of the sense of alienation that so many of the idiomatic relatives we had met in Paris were forever talking about. So when we said so long, and he went along Rue Monsieur-le-Prince and I came on to Boulevard

Saint-Germain and headed for Rue Bonaparte, that was what I was thinking about again and I said, As for me, it's back to the zone of the interior.

Which was part of the terminology I remembered from the junior high school textbook for physical geography and so already knew when I came to political geography and political science. But which over the years had also come to have as much to do with the natural human resources definitive to national character as do such Department of the Interior concerns as roads and bridges and waterways and mineral deposits and parks and wildlife have to do with national subsistence.

Not to mention the exercise of national power in international affairs, which include matters that you were to become increasingly aware of your personal involvement with as you advanced from the geographical descriptions of elementary and intermediate school studies to the awareness of historical causes and effects that high school and college courses and professional monographs were so much about.

The original out of doors benchmark and mercator projection school map triangulation point of all of which was the chinaberry spyglass tree in the front yard of that sawmill quarters shotgun house in Gasoline Point on the L & N Railroad outskirts of Mobile, Alabama, from which the North Pole was due north beyond the Chickasabogue horizon and Nashville, Tennessee, and Louisville, Kentucky, and Cincinnati, Ohio, and Chicago, Illinois. Which made Philamayork north by east up the Southern and Seaboard route to the Pennsylvania Railroad. So San Francisco, California, and Seattle, Washington, were north by west as the eagle flies, whereas Los Angeles, California, was west to the Pacific from New Orleans through the deserts and plains and across the mountains. Due south beyond Mobile Bay and the Gulf Coast was the old Spanish Main of the historical romances followed by the boy blue adventure stories about derring-do and the seven seas.

Zone of the interior, zone of the interior, zone of the interior, I said as I let the seat all the way back to the reclining position and closed my eyes. What the Marquis de Chaumienne may or may not have known was that you for one could have become as instantaneously nostalgic about the Mobile and Gulf Coast environs of the Alabama that was the wellspring of all of my sky blue aspirations when I heard "Back Home Again in Indiana" (for all its Hoosier connotations!) as when I heard "On Mobile Bay" or "Stars Fell on Alabama."

Nor could "The Star-Spangled Banner" take you more deeply, if as deeply, into your own personal zone of the interior than Louis Armstrong's rendition of "Sleepy Time Down South" always did. What "The Star-Spangled Banner" was most likely to take you back to were those Mobile County Training School flagpole ceremonies and assembly room periods that were so much a part of what being an all-American schoolboy was also about. As did "My Country 'Tis of Thee" and "America the Beautiful." Whereas Louis Armstrong's instrumental version of "Sleepy Time Down South" took you all the way back to the coziness of the chimney corner chair on winter nights and the breeziness of swing porch steps on summer evenings back in those ever so wee preschoolboy years when the yarn spinning used to begin as early as twilight time.

Return of the native born, I thought once more as the tires of the landing gear finally screeched, skipped, and settled ever so gently down onto the runway, and as we headed for the taxi lane and our parking berth, you felt the way you felt because you were rearriving in North America for the first time ever. *Commodious vicus of recirculation, indeed*, I reminded myself remembering the very first globe I ever saw and which Sunday school boy that I also was at that time I thought represented the whole universe above which was heaven and everlasting bliss and below which was hell and eternally infernal damnation.

Remembering also how it revolved on its tilted polar axis and how because of its position with reference to the sun, its revolutions made the difference between the nights and days that add up to weeks and months and years and so on to ages on the one hand and on the other hand could be subdivided into hours and minutes and even split seconds. Then later on there was also the equally important matter of the earth's orbit around the sun, which accounted for the seasons.

Which is why it was that even as I made my way through customs, I had already decided what I wanted to try to get set up to do in New York during the next fall term. And I had also already estimated that I could complete all of the advanced arrangements for matriculation and lodging in ten days or less. After which I would be heading south for the outskirts of Mobile. But only after the commuter flight from Atlanta to central Alabama by way of Montgomery at long last for the also and also of the reunion in the home place of Eunice Townsend.

Apropos of all of which was also the also and also of the encounter I had with a long forgotten hometown boy during the last three days of the stopover, who said what he said about his own obligations, aspirations, and expectations and who also said what he said about the way things turned out for him that Wednesday night.

I.

when I came out of the IRT subway on the uptown exit between Seventh Avenue and Broadway, I stopped at the newsstand and bought the *Times*, the *News*, and the *Post* and waited for the light to change looking at the traffic flowing along Broadway toward Times Square. The sidewalks were already thick with late morning sightseers and theater district people, performers with makeup kits, dancers with their rehearsal togs in shoulder bags, entertainment producer and agent types with briefcases.

across Broadway in the same block as Jack Dempsey's restaurant, which was a midtown sporting scene landmark in those days, there was the usual cluster of musicians on the corner near the Turf Club eatery and the Brill Building in which there were booking offices as well as rehearsal studios, and I was suddenly homesick again for my schoolboy status in the band, which I knew was doing one-nighters in the Midwest. I hadn't seen the Bossman Himself since California. I hadn't heard from Joe States since his letter responding to my card from Juan-les-Pins.

when I looked up Broadway toward Columbus Circle I checked my watch against the clock on the Mutual of New York insurance building and remembered that Carnegie Hall was on the southeast corner of 57th Street and Seventh Avenue. The traffic light was green again then, but as I started to cross the street a cab pulled up to the curb and I recognized the young man getting out as soon as the door opened although I hadn't seen him since he left Gasoline Point back when I was still in high school.

it all came back in a flash. He had gone to Chicago and I don't remember hearing or even thinking about him since I left town for college. He stood waiting while his companion closed the door and paid the fare. Then the two of them turned and started toward the newsstand. They were a perfect match for size and also seemed about the same age. Both were wearing gray turtleneck sweaters and identical safari jackets and tan water repellent porkpie golf hats, brims down.

hey, you're Marvin, I said. Marvin Upshaw!

and he saw me then and turned and came toward me calling my name as easily as I had called his. The last time I saw him he was fifteen. Now he was six feet tall and weighed at least one hundred and seventy pounds.

man, what you doing way up here, this far away from the L & N Railroad and the cypress swamp bottom? he said. And I said, Man, just dogging around, just dogging around. And he said, Hey, this is one of my old homeys, man. And as his companion, whose name was Ben Rutledge and who I could somehow tell was also a down-home boy although not a hometown boy, shook hands, he (Marvin Upshaw) said, Man, this is a hell of a long ways from Hog Bayou. Man, this is a thousand miles beyond Chickasabogue Bridge and Hog Bayou. Man, they don't have no fishhead stew up here.

and I said, Man, that's not what they told me. Man, they told me you can get that stuff anywhere these days and they were not lying because I had some of the best I ever tasted down in southern France. They called it bouillabaisse over there but they can't fool me, not about that kind of stuff. Which is not to say that they can't lay some of the greatest dishes in the world on you, I said. Man, they declare that that is the original gettin' place for fishhead stew, I said.

and he said, Hey, man, you too? Man, it didn't take me no time at all to find out that you can get black-eyed peas and collard greens in Chicago just like on the outskirts of Mobile, Alabama. And I'm talking about along with all that big city stuff to boot. Ben knows what I'm talking about. I know I don't have to tell you he's one of us. He's not a city, but he's a statie. Ben's from the Ham, man. And Ben Rutledge said, Bessmer.

and when I said, One of my very best older friends is from the Ham, thinking of Joe States, he winked and said, And I bet he intends to stay away from there too. I sure do. I intend to stay as far away as I can get. And the reason I ain't no further than I am now is that I really do believe the world is round so I'm subject to come around to it again if I go any further.

hey, Marvin Upshaw said, let's have a quick sip of something if you've got a couple of minutes. We have a few. Where you headed? And I said, Pork Chop Eddies. And he said, Too many people in there I don't want to have to talk to today.

so we stopped at the snack bar on the corner and they ordered hot tea with lemon and I ordered the same, but with sugar and remembered the two of us in Gasoline Point. He had never been one of my cut buddies, but at one time Little Buddy Marshall and I had been very friendly with him, and sometimes the three of us used to turn up at the same time to hang around to eavesdrop on the man among men conversations in Papa Gumbo Willie McWorthy's barbershop when old Cateyed Gander Gallagher the gallinipper had a shoeshine stand there, inside in the winter and out on the porch in the summer. And sometimes we also used to stand out on the sidewalks together waiting for the girls to come out of Alzenia Nettleton's cook shop at twilight on Saturday nights.

when he and his family moved up north to Chicago I knew about it, but only because I heard about it, and I didn't really miss him very much because he had dropped out of school and gotten a job first as a delivery boy for Stranahan's store and then in downtown Mobile, and all we had been doing the last year or so was waving and nodding at each other as we passed on the street. I don't remember anything that we actually stopped and talked about during that time.

from where we sat you could see across 50th Street and Broadway to the huge Roulette Records billboard. As I sipped my tea, he said, So, are you still into baseball as much as you and old Little Buddy Marshall used to be? You still walking in the footsteps of old Gator Gus? And I said, Man, I haven't played baseball since high school. And he said, Is that so? I was already gone before then. But that's right, I remember all that now. You were one of the smart ones in school. Man, me, I found out what that thing was about and that was the end of school.

and Ben Rutledge said, Man, that was the end of school for a lot of cats I know, including me. You know what I told them? I said, I got your conjugation. I told them, Man, while y'all conjugating all them verbs for class, me, I'm going to be doing my kind of conjugation even in the grass, if ain't nowhere else handy. And Marvin Upshaw said, Man, the goddamn grass is exactly where I started, playing hide and seek.

but now him, he said looking at Ben Rutledge but indicating me with his thumb. He was out there digging his toes in the grass, not just on picnics, but anywhere else just like he's one of the gang and all the time he was sneaking off not just con-jugating them verbs for class but reading every book he could get his hands on.

and when I said, Hey, man, they had girls in school too, he said, Man, I forgot all about them. Man, I guess I must have thought them girls up in Tin Top Alley and places like that were the only ones doing it. Man, I never thought about schoolgirls like that. Man, if I had known then what I found out later about how hip them girls were by the time they got to college I probably would have gone on and got myself a goddamn Ph.D. by now. Man, all that ladylike neatness, de-portment, and punctuality turned me off, man.

and when I said, What about Miss Lexine Metcalf? he said, Man, I was scared of that woman. Man, he said shaking his head in schoolboy bewilderment that many years later, I was scared to even think about Miss Lexine Metcalf.

and I said, Man, I never have been scared of anybody that good looking. Man, I couldn't keep myself from dreaming about her like I also used to dream about old Creola. And he said, Old Creola Calloway, Yeah. Everybody used to dream about old Creola. But that Miss Lexine Metcalf. Man, that was a mean and evil woman.

and I said, Not if you got her lessons.

which I damn sure didn't ever do, he said. Man, that woman was so mean and evil, she was downright ugly to me. Like them evil women in them nightmare movies. Man, as far as I was concerned Miss Lexine Metcalf was as ugly as any bear in the bottoms. Man, every time she crossed my mind, all I could see was that classroom and them blackboard problems, maps, and shit like that.

but hey, man, he said then looking at me with down-home affection and approval, what you been doing with yourself? I can see you've been doing all right whatever it is.

and I said, Man, you won't believe it and don't ask me to explain it. Man, I went on and finished high school and college and since then I've been knocking around as a musician. And now I'm right at the point where I'm about to decide what I'm going to do next.

that was when I told him about how I happened to go with the band and about being in Hollywood and about going to Europe. I didn't mention Jewel Templeton. But I did name some of the records I had made with the band. And he said, Hey, that's big league stuff, Scooter. Man, that is sure enough incredible. Man, when I think of you back when we were kids, what I remember didn't have nothing at all to do with being a musician. I mean what comes to my mind is school and sports. Man, I remember you being as crazy about sports especially baseball as about school. And here you come helping Joe States and Otis Sheppard lay down stuff for Herman Kemble and Scully Pittman to the specifications of the Bossman Himself.

Malachi Mobes, Ben Rutledge said, Mister Chandler, Ike Ellis, Osceola Menefee. Man, you turn up with a musical instrument around them thugs and ain't ready you'll get mugged not out in no back alley. Right up there in the spotlight! And Marvin Upshaw said, I can't get over this. But now that you're telling me what you're telling me I do remember that you did used to hang around Papa Gladstone's jump band even when they were just rehearsing. But a lot of baseball players were like that about music, just because they were so hip and so smooth with the chicks on the dance floor. But you, man, you were always such a schoolboy, I figured you were all set on being a doctor or lawyer or somebody who was going to break some new ground and open some doors in politics and stuff. Or maybe get into something sociological. Or maybe philosophical. Man, I never would have thought you'd be a musician of any kind, let alone a big league musician.

and I said, Man, me neither. Man, I just woke up one morning and I was on my way into the greatest band there ever was. And he said, Now that you tell me, I really shouldn't be surprised because you always did have that reputation for picking up on things. So now that I think about it, I bet you just automatically memorize every last note played by every last member of Papa Gladstone's band.

then for the benefit of Ben Rutledge he said, Old Papa Gladness. Man, the dances he used to play at the Boommenunion. The old Boommen's Union Hall Ballroom. The men who used to work in the log boom feeding time up the chute to the log carriage in the sawmills. Gasoline Point was a sawmill outskirts of Mobile long before they built the Gulf Refinery tank yards there.

it was part of a seaport area too, I said, with dry docks and a waterfront and longshoremen and all that with ships coming from all over the world. And Ben Rutledge said, Naturally we knew about Mobile being a banana and coconut town up in the Ham. And I said, And a railroad town too.

then Marvin Upshaw said, But old Papa Glad. He always did have a big league band. Did any of them big name bands mess with him except to try to steal away some of his musicians? Man, Papa Glad and them fools would tear you up. Tell them cats a band was coming through from somewhere up north and they'd start licking their chops before the word was out of your mouth.

we laughed remembering and then I said, What about you, Marvin? You used to try to box. And he said, Man, I'm still trying. And I looked at his face and hands more closely. Some prizefighters are really show biz personalities. They wear show biz clothes and have their hair taken care of like nightclub entertainers. But he looked like a cleanly scrubbed and massaged college athlete, a shifty halfback or a fancy dribbling basketball playmaker back in the days before it was unusual for basketball stars to be only six feet tall. Ben Rutledge was his trainer. You hardly noticed the scars on their faces and neither had cauliflower ears.

all I could say was that I had been out of touch with the fight game for a longer time than I realized. And he said, I fight under the name of Maddox. Then he said, I'm in this thing this Friday night. And Ben Rutledge said, It's in there, pointing to the newspaper at my elbow. And I said, Hey, let me see and opened the *Times* to the sports section. And there were waist-length bare-knuckled pictures of him and a fighter named Buddy McDaniels. The caption was, TITLE QUEST. The winner of the match at the Garden Friday night between contenders Marvin Maddox and Buddy McDaniels (a.k.a. Buddy Mack) will be the next challenger for the light-heavyweight crown currently worn by Freddie Hopkins. Queried as he broke camp in New Jersey yesterday, the ever cordial Maddox, who skips rope to Duke Ellington's "Mainstem" and whose graceful intercollegiate bearing belies the lethal power of his hands, admitted that he would be gunning for a quick KO and the odds are tipping in favor of his explosive right, which has dispatched his last three opponents within five rounds. Buddy Mack would say only that he was in excellent condition and expected—

there was Marvin Upshaw's voice again then, Hey, maybe you'd like to come, he was saying. And I said, You know something? I just might try to do that. And he said, Be my guest, and nudged Ben Rutledge, who reached into his bag and took out a breast pocket billfold and handed me a ringside ticket. And Marvin Upshaw said, Old home boy and all. Man, I haven't run across anybody from down the way since I don't know when.

we finished our tea and came on back out to the sidewalk again, then, and I said, Marvin Upshaw. Old badass Marvin Upshaw from Stranahan's Lane, which folks used to think was haunted because that was where Bea Ella Thornhill killed Beau Beau Weaver. You remember that? Ripped his bowels open with a switchblade. *Bea Ella with a switchblade!*

and he said, Man, I used to have to walk that lane to get home at night. But speaking of remembering Stranahan's Lane, how about that time when you went upside my head about them marbles. Then smiling at me ducking behind my elbow, he told Ben Rutledge, He tore me up.

and I said, Man, I forgot that. Man, I forgot all about that as soon as I saw how fast you were outgrowing me. Man, you just shot up overnight and I never did catch up.

that was when he said, Come on back to the dressing room afterward. Ben will let you in. And we shook hands, and as he turned to head for Eighth Avenue he said, Win, lose, or draw.

2.

he was wearing purple trunks and from the third row inside seat I could see the expression on his face as he danced up and down in his corner, touching his gloves together, his feet barely leaving the canvas, his head cocked to one side, the blue and gold robe draped around his shoulders. He looked ready and confident but I felt myself becoming tense. It was always easier for me to sweat out something I myself was getting ready to do than to watch as somebody else's time came nearer and nearer. When it was me, I was always busy thinking about what I was going to do, but when it was somebody else (whose side I was on) my best wishes were always mixed with misgivings.

around me amid the mounting excitement there was the up-tempo but detached and comfortable banter of sports reporters and old ringside hands. I looked across the ring at Buddy McDaniels, who stood shifting his feet out and back, his arms hanging casually at his side. And I wondered if he were moving his bandaged fingers inside his glove and that made me remember the Bossman Himself moving his fingers as he stood waiting to come on stage from the wings. He was wearing black and gold trunks, which made me remember the Bama State Hornets basketball team, many of whose games used to be followed by a dance played by the Bama State Collegians, the best college dance band ever. He rotated first one shoulder and then the other and then turned to his corner and began to do a slow shuffle, facing but probably not really seeing the dim rows of spectators.

when I looked across at Marvin Upshaw again, he seemed unconcerned enough, but I had never seen him fight as a professional and I didn't know what to expect. The last time I had seen him in a prize ring he was fighting in junior weight preliminaries and battle royals, and I had no idea that he had any serious notions about becoming a full time boxer. He was just old badass Marvin Upshaw from Stranahan's Lane who, come to think of it, sometimes did stand around going through symbolic motions of Jack Johnson's old notorious uppercut much the same as he used to imitate James Cagney hitching his waist with his elbows. As I looked at Buddy Mack and realized that he was probably one of Jack Johnson's boys too I remembered Royal Highness talking about himself and Jack Johnson and I also remembered my homemade cement sack punching bag under the chinaberry tree in the front yard of our old shotgun house on Dodge Mill Road, and then I also realized that even as I practiced my Jack Johnson moves I was wearing my money ball pitcher's blue baseball cap because I was also one of Gator Gus's boys.

then I remembered becoming an all around high school athlete. Plus lead-off orator and clean-up debater because I had also become one of Mr. B. Franklin Fisher's Early Bird boys headed for college, where my good old best of all possible roommates used to say, Yea, verily I say unto you my good fellow, such is the nature of true, which is to say functional ancestry that necessity is the mother of fathers. It's a matter of choice my good fellow, he always liked to say. It is a matter of incentive and depth of personal motivation—a matter of horizons of aspiration.

while the two fighters surrounded by their handlers continued their warmup routines, neither looking in the direction of the other, in the row in front of me the sports reporters went on comparing notes. I listened to them sizing up things according to the latest inside dope and it sounded mostly like the same old stuff sports reporters usually talk. I didn't read sports columns very much anymore. They're almost as bad as jazz columns. But not quite. Sportswriters know at least as much about the sporting event they cover as do most sports spectators, and their predictions are either borne out by the final score or they're not. Many jazz journalists, on the other hand, often write as if they have earned an authority that qualifies them to pronounce final decisions on the outcome of a jazz endeavor so much so that without knowing what a given jazz musician is trying to do (what raw material he's trying to stylize into aesthetic statement) too many jazz journalists presume to report and assess the outcome.

as I looked around the ringside I thought about the sportswriters dead and alive that I still liked. I still liked A. J. Liebling and Ring Lardner and Red Smith and some of the ones on *Sports Illustrated* when it was new. There were also famous sportswriters who couldn't tell the players without a scorecard, but at least they knew whether they were looking at baseball, basketball, football, tennis, track, golf, or boxing. The distance of jazz journalists from flesh and blood musicians was mostly such that they obviously relied on scorecards. In any case they were usually accurate about the names of the musicians that they bested in their perpetual game of one-upmanship.

the radio and TV crews were already on the airways with up to the minute prefight details, and as the cameramen focused on the preparations in the ring I thought about sports announcers and disc jockeys. There was no comparison. There was no way in the world for sports announcers to ignore athletic champions and record holders the way disc jockeys (and some ideological jazz journalists) ignore living master musicians in favor of the latest bad taste.

there was the ring announcer then and then the referee took over and the two sides were in the center of the ring, the fighters finally looking at each other when they touched gloves. Then they were back in their corners and then the gong sounded and they moved toward each other.

and as I leaned forward watching Marvin Upshaw I remembered what I had read about in the prefight buildup. I liked his stance and I was also watching reflexes, and as soon as the first punches were exchanged I could see that his hands were as fast as they had been reported to be. And he moved his feet like a welterweight. Buddy McDaniels was also fast and no less shifty. It was not easy to hit him and when you did he could take it, and he counterpunched so sharply and followed up so naturally that you forgot who actually started the exchange.

but Marvin Upshaw had his own bag of tricks, and the next time he led he knew exactly what to do. He jabbed, slipped a counterpunch, got his cross in, followed it with a right, and kept the initiative, forcing Buddy McDaniels backward. There was applause then and I felt easier about him in spite of myself.

he got the best two out the next three exchanges, and looked good in the clinches, and near the end of the round he scored on a combination that caught Buddy McDaniels by surprise and brought cheers from the crowd. Buddy McDaniels was not hurt but when the bell rang he knew that he had lost the round.

the second round began with Buddy McDaniels moving in, and I got a chance to see how good Marvin Upshaw was when he was forced to be on the defensive. He could block, roll, sidestep, counterpunch, and I especially liked the way he scored moving away. He did not try to take the initiative back until the round was half over and then he finished toe to toe and I thought he evened things up, but I wasn't sure enough not to feel a twinge of uneasiness.

they stepped up the pace in the third round and it seemed to me that Marvin Upshaw still had the edge and he was snapping and jabbing and increasing his lead all the time. But you could also see that he was not really trying to win on points. He was scoring effectively but he was really looking for an opening. Neither had tried a big punch yet.

at first Buddy McDaniels was going for the body, but near the end of the round he shifted and got in a sharp snapping left to the face and Marvin Upshaw tied him up in a clinch. But as they were separated, he got in two left jabs, which he followed with a hard right and a left hook that left a gash. And when the round ended, Marvin Upshaw's right eye was beginning to close.

they stopped the bleeding and put cold compresses on the swelling, and when round four began I knew that the exploratory phase was over. The pace picked up and the punches were harder. Buddy McDaniels switched back to the body attack but he got caught with a neatly executed combination and had to clinch, and when they broke there was a cut under his left eye.

they're gunning now, one of the sportswriters near me said. And the one next to him said, Smoking. Which was an old term I associated with the great Sugar Ray Robinson. Smoking, man, smoking. Man, these dudes can smoke.

which reminded me that whereas sportswriters not unlike jazz journalists have been picking jive language from athletes and musicians for years, athletes were now beginning to use sportscasters' lingo as a part of their idiom—for interview effect in any case. They now talk about holding their focus and concentration and developing a very fine ball club and so on, in accents straight out of the broadcast booths and editorial rooms.

this is anybody's fight, a third sportswriter said. And there was another tit for tat exchange of snapping lefts and Buddy McDaniels backed away with a cut under his eye and before he could get set, a right jolted his head back and I knew he was hurt. The crowd was in an uproar then, and I must have relaxed, or somebody must have jumped up and down in front of me, because the next thing I saw was Marvin Upshaw's knees buckling and Buddy McDaniels, one eye swollen shut, moving in on him.

the bell saved him. I watched them working on him in the corner and they had him on his feet before the fifth round again. Buddy McDaniels sat on his stool until the gong sounded. And then he moved in swinging. He knew he had him then and he was out to win big, to increase his bargaining power for the championship fight he was now next in line for.

but he couldn't knock him off his feet. The referee stopped it after a minute and forty-five seconds. It was nine-thirty.

3.

as I made my way toward the dressing room I was trying to think of what I was going to say. But when I got there and finally got inside, he was already in the shower. The doctor still wearing a stethoscope was talking to the handlers, who were waiting at the rubdown table. The manager stood off in the corner with two men I guessed were either his assistants or his business associates. I waited just inside the door near Ben Rutledge. Everybody was standing around in clusters, but nobody was saying anything about the fight. The manager was talking about airline tickets. The two handlers were telling the doctor about a forthcoming golf tournament.

he saw me and waved as soon as he came out of the shower. So all I had to do was wave back. I didn't have to say anything. He was cut and bruised and his right eye was still swollen but he looked as much like a getaway halfback as when I recognized him on Broadway. He had been banged up in that last round, but looking at him toweling himself you couldn't tell whether he had just won or lost.

hey, stick around, he said as he moved over to the rubdown table, I promised I'd bring you home with me. He put on his shorts and sat on the table and the doctor checked him over again. And then while one of the handlers worked on his face, the other gave him a massage. And when they were finished he sat up with one towel draped over his head and another around his shoulders and they let the reporters and photographers in.

he looked like a prizefighter again then, and as the photographers' lights began flashing I remembered Gasoline Point once more and how much I used to like the way the sports pages used to feature the faces of prizefighters and baseball players as cutouts on a white background.

there was always something about that which went with trophies and medals and citations with seals and ribbons. Sometimes a sports page cartoonist would sketch a crown at a jaunty angle on the head of the cutout of the champion and then sketch the rest of his body in miniature, one foot forward, gloves in position.

it was a great fight, man, a reporter said as they crowded around the table. And he said, Thanks, I hope everyone got their money's worth. And then he said, Man, the biggest drag is when they come out saying it was dull. And somebody said, Not this fight, Marvin. Never a dull split second with you in there. And he said, Well, I sure hope not. And when someone said, How do you feel, Marvin? he said, Surprised, shaking his head. And then he said, And hungry. And somebody said, Good sign, Marvin, good sign.

he took the edge, someone else said, but he couldn't put you away. So do you think he ever had a chance to throw his Sunday punch? And Marvin Upshaw said, Man, I honestly don't know. But I would say he must have got in most of the rest of the days of the week.

did he hurt you?

not really, but maybe I was too numb to know it. However, I won't deny that my feelings were hurt when I realized they were stopping it.

when did you begin to realize that you were in trouble?

when they stopped it and held up his hand.

not until then?

man, I was pretty busy up there before then. Or at least I thought I was.

what do you think of his chances with the champ?

he's a pretty rugged boy.

what are your own plans, Marv?

to get back in the top running as soon as possible, the manager said cutting in. That's all for now, fellows. Let's give him a rest. Thanks for coming by to see us. We really appreciate you not forgetting us on a night like this.

when we came outside most of the crowd was gone. The traffic along the avenue was normal again and as we stood waiting for Ben Rutledge, I looked up at the stars twinkling beyond the lights of the Manhattan skyscrapers and thought about the New York of the Hollywood cops and robbers melodramas and drawing room comedies of my early and middle teen years.

the dark aviator glasses that Marvin Upshaw was wearing covered most of the Band-Aid under his right eye. He turned up the collar of his trench coat and stood with his hands in his pockets. Behind us were the huge placards announcing the matchup of the two leading contenders for the light-heavyweight championship.

man, Estelle is really looking forward to meeting you, he said. I was telling her about you being a college boy and all that. She went to college for a while, too. And I said, You've been married five years. And he said, Six. They got it wrong in the paper. Man, I won the middleweight Golden Gloves, got married, and turned pro all in about eighteen months' time. And was on my way to being a father too. I'm actually a little older than you, but not as old as old gallinipper.

a black Cadillac with Ben Rutledge at the steering wheel pulled up to the curb then and we headed up Eighth Avenue the three of us sitting in the front seat listening to the radio. We were on our way to 730 Riverside Drive, which was at the end of West 155th Street overlooking the Hudson to Palisades Amusement Park. But at 58th Street they decided to take the long way around through Central Park. So we circled the statue of Christopher Columbus and passed through the portals at 59th Street where Eighth Avenue became Central Park West.

the record playing on the radio was a series of long-winded empty-headed fancy-fingered solos strung together by a piano pretending that what was being played was not the changes to "Please Don't Talk About Me (When I'm Gone)." It was all very hip, and each soloist knew exactly what he was doing because he knew precisely whose gimmicks he was stealing. And so did I. And the chase choruses went on and on and then finally as we came on toward the 72nd Street exit to the east side and the cross route to the west, there was a commercial.

they decided to continue on up to the 110th and Seventh Avenue exit and cross on over to Riverside Drive from there, and when the next number came it was the Bossman Himself. He was playing low register piano in unison with the bass with Joe States answering their call with his ride cymbal. They did sixteen. Then the piano called in the trombones and the whole band fell in growling and sounding almost sadly yearning at the same time.

hey, yeah, Marvin Upshaw said snapping his fingers and tilting his head to the right in time with the big stomping bass. Hey, is that you on that record?

not that one, I said. Because it was Scratchy McFatrick and he had it thumping. That's since my time, I said, missing them more than I could have brought myself to admit.

that's a good one, man, he said. And Ben Rutledge said, Listen to that goddamn Herman Kemble cutting them dots. And now here come old Wayman Ridgeway. That's when Marvin Upshaw said, I've got to get some of those records with you on them. And I said, I'll get some to you. And he said, You in there with the Bossman Himself. Boy, can't nobody say you ain't no big league musician. That smooth talking somitch has been the champion ever since I can remember.

ever since anybody can remember, Ben Rutledge said. Man, all that old jiveass bullshit is just to put people off because what he's hiding is the fact that he is as much an outright genius as any raving mad scientist you ever saw in any of them late-night movies.

and that was when Marvin Upshaw said what he said, as if he had forgotten that anybody else was present. Now that somitch is always in there winning because ain't nobody yet come up with nothing that he ain't got an answer for.

we were on the upper end of the park then and you could see the reflections of the lights in Harlem through the trees as you curved downhill and around the outdoor swimming pool and lake area. But instead of bearing a right and going up Lenox Avenue we went left to the Seventh Avenue exit. And nobody said anything about music or anything else until Ben Rutledge let us out in front of the apartment building.

man, this old lady of mine is a natural born stone fox, Marvin Upshaw said as the elevator started upward. If I do say so myself, man. He had buzzed the apartment as we came through the lobby and when we stepped out on the eighth floor she was waiting in the open door across the hall. She was wearing blue slacks and a gray V neck cashmere sweater with the sleeves pushed up and with a purple silk scarf knotted cowboy style. And I said, You said it, man.

we were there then and you were that close to that copper-brown, satin-smooth skin and her dimples went with the way the fullness of her hips matched the thinness of her waistline. The way her shade of brown skin complemented the glossy sheen of her jet black bangs and ponytail suggested down-home black Creek Indian relatives rather than the taste of curry sauce.

as she said, Estelle, and we shook hands and stepped inside the apartment, there was an after hours cocktail lounge organ, drums, and tenor sax combo recording of an ever so soft blues shout thumping ever so cozily on the sound system, the controls for which I spotted at the other end of the living room near the dining area. I didn't know whose group was playing it but I liked it. I also liked the apartment.

hey, sonny boy, Estelle said putting her hands on her hips and pretending to frown as she looked her husband up and down, You look like you went out somewhere and got into a fight or something. She kissed him then and Marvin Upshaw said, imitating Louis Armstrong, You hear this stuff, man? You see what Papa Gumbo and them were talking about when they used to be talking about them old battle-axes, bears, and bar-racudas? Man, he went on, You come home after a hard day's work and the very first thing you run into is some old bossy lady ready to turn salty on you.

boot chicks, man, he said as she gave him another squeeze and then a shove and headed for the kitchen.

she was born and raised in Savannah and had gone to Spelman for two years before her family moved to Chicago, where she began taking professional classes in music and drama and decided to go in for show business. She had been a nightclub entertainer in the Chicago area for several years when she met Marvin Upshaw and decided that they would be good for each other and also good parents.

man, I might as well tell you this too, Marvin Upshaw said, I'm all signed up with one of the sneakiest broads you ever came across. *Man, she was there tonight. She was there, man.* She was sitting way back up in there somewhere with them goddamn spyglasses. He pointed to the binoculars case on the shelf near the record player and said, That's supposed to be part of her racetrack equipment, but man, she was right up there zeroed in and trying to help me duck all that shit that somitch was throwing at me.

she came out of the kitchen and went into the dining area, and that was when I noticed that table places were already set up for three. The record player was still going with the same extended blues romp, which by that time I realized was intended to last an entire set and which I decided to pick up at a record shop before leaving town. But even so I couldn't help wondering if we wouldn't have been listening to Ellington's "Mainstem" if Marvin Upshaw had won.

you never know when she might be there, he said as she went to get Virgin Marys for the two of them sour mash on the rocks as a down-home gesture of welcome back stateside for me. Sometimes, he said, it's all straight and she'll be right there at ringside, but sometimes she'll be talking about promising to go somewhere to play cards, which takes care of having to bring in a baby-sitter and then she'll sneak up there somewhere with them glasses.

he shook his head and pretended that her concern added up to an unnecessary burden, but he couldn't quite hide the fact that he was as pleased as he could be because she tried so hard to hide whatever anxiety she may or may not have about any given fight. Sometimes she stayed away or pretended to stay away because she suspected he was too sure of himself, and sometimes she was there in the third row hoping that her presence would give him the additional confidence that she was afraid he very much needed.

you never know, man, he said. Then she came back with the drinks, flirting with him with her eyes and her walk and taking me into their orbit of affection with her smile. He said, Like I told you, home boy, she's a natural born stone fox. And I said, Hey, man, you remember that old one on the piano rolls when we were way back down in grade school? And he nodded and together we said, If you've never been vamped by brownskin, you've never been vamped at all.

and he said, Old Scooter, the same old Scooter. Always did have that special birthmark for remembering everything like a flesh and blood dictionary. No, wait a minute, like a walking encyclopedia of universal information. What did I tell you? Didn't I tell you that this cat is something else? That's what I remembered after all these years as soon as I realized who you were when you hailed me down on Broadway the other day.

you had to be flattered, but what coming up with James P. Johnson's old ragtime piano roll had also brought back to my mind was the fact that I was all set to go by and visit Royal Highness that next afternoon.

but Marvin Upshaw went on telling his wife about the old days. Old Scooter, he said as she moved back and forth between the dining room and kitchen, He always was one that was staying in school and also keeping tabs on all of that old street corner and honky-tonk jook joint jive at the same time. Without any of them bell ringing roll book wardens over at old man B. Franklin Fisher's county farm ever catching on. Old Scooter, he said. That's how deep you already were. Even back then. Like I say, psychological, philosophical.

all I could do was shake my head and laugh at his impression of me as I was that many years ago. Then as if he suddenly remembered that he himself was now the father of a little boy who would be scooting about on his own terms more and more every day, he said, What about Wendell? And his wife, who was just about ready for us to come to the table, said, He's okay. No sweat. I told him it wasn't your night.

he already knows that you don't win them all, he said. But he thinks you should always try. He's going to be the world's champion jet pilot or spaceman or something plus a TV detective. When he retires from being the world's champion shortstop after setting the record for double plays.

at the table my place was the one that faced the window and I could see the traffic lights along Riverside Drive and the Henry Hudson Parkway. And I guessed that if you moved close enough to look north from the window you could see at least the New Jersey side of the George Washington Bridge.

it was a down-home meal of baked rabbit with all the trimmings including sweet potatoes, turnips, and thin golden brown slices of corn bread. And as we sat down he said, Well it's about time. Man, this woman may be as ugly as homemade sin, but she sure can cook. That's one thing you got to give her. She can play natural dozens with a mixing bowl. Man, that'd be the last thing you ever thought about if you saw her on the stage, but man, this foxy lady can make a frying pan talk down-home talk with some of the best I can remember.

hey, you better let him taste some of this stuff first, honey, she said. After all, he's not just another hungry Alabama prizefighter. He's a big time musician. He's used to all kinds of good eating and all kinds of places that I'm not so sure we're going to be able to afford when you get to be champion. Light-heavyweight champion. Maybe heavyweight—

man, he said cutting in before she could finish, I'm telling you she's right up there with Miss Alzenia Nettleton and Aunt Nicey Tompkins. And as soon as I took my first mouthful I said, He's not bragging. He's just telling it like it is. And I stood up and said, My compliments to the chef, who gets four stars in my Michelin any day.

we started talking about restaurants then and neither one of them said anything else about the fight until we finished eating and were back in the drawing room area and she put on another blues organ combo record. We sat keeping time, me on the couch, him on the overstuffed leather chair, and her on a hassock with a cup of coffee on a stool beside her. We were just sitting listening together like that and I had decided that I would say good night in ten minutes.

but as soon as the combo hit the groove on the third number I saw him drop his head and begin staring at his hands. And she must have seen it at the same time because she stood up and went over and sat on his lap and put his arms around her and kissed him.

you had him, she said. He's good. Very good. But you can take him and you had him. I don't know what got into you. And he said, Me neither. He said, I thought I had him too. And when she said, I knew you had him, he said, Maybe that's what happened.

then very casually she said, How do you feel? And he said, Right now I feel fine. I really do. I started my left and it got all tangled up in a bunch of cobwebs. And before I could get it free and shoot my right the fight was all over.

still ever so casually she ever so gently touched the tape under his eye and said, How about this? And he said, Nothing to it. And when she said, That had me a little worried, he said, I figured that and that's why I got him back double. He cuts a lot easier than I do. But when she said, But seeing you getting carved up bothers me more than seeing you go down, he said, Maybe that's because you ain't never seen me not get up. And she said, That's true. I've been spared that so far. But I still don't like nobody carving on that pretty face.

she started kidding him again, then and he started talking like Louis Armstrong once more and I got up to leave. And she brought me my hat and at the elevator he said, Sure is good to come across an old home boy, Scooter. And don't forget, me and Ben Rutledge will be driving you to the airport Monday morning. Call me Sunday night.

XLVII

So it's back down home from up the country for you, hey, Scooter? Marvin Upshaw said as Ben Rutledge pulled on through the tollbooth between the Triborough Bridge and the Hellgate span to Long Island en route to LaGuardia and my flight to Alabama by way of Atlanta. On our right across the East River as we merged with the traffic coming down from the Bronx, there was that view of the Manhattan skyline that suddenly gave me a pang that I later realized always came back whenever I took that route on my way out of the New York area by air.

Back from up the country and elsewhere as well, he said. And I said what I said then because I had already been thinking about what I was going to be saying and repeating when I re-arrived in Gasoline Point from central Alabama and begin making the old rounds to Stranahan's store, Papa Gumbo Willie McWorthy's barbershop, Miss Alzenia Nettleton's cook shop, all on Buckshaw Mill Road now become the U.S. 90 approach to Cochran Bridge, and then on up to Shade's across from the old Boommen's Union Hall Ballroom up on Green's Avenue and also on over to the Mobile County Training School campus once more. I said, Back down the way from up the beanstalk.

I said, Back down the beanstalk that the chinaberry tree became, thinking: and Miss Lexine Metcalf's magic wand Windows on the World continued.

And Marvin Upshaw said, See what I mean? What did I tell you? Didn't I tell you that this cat has always been something else ever since I first knew him when we were kids in knee pants? Man, I remember you up there in that chinaberry tree using your cupped hands as make-believe binoculars and sometimes a long cardboard wrapping paper tube for a pilot's spyglass. Up there boxing the compass, man. And I'm not just talking about just some Boy Scout woodcraft stuff, man. This little rascal was already geographical even back then.

Old Scooter, he said. Man, me and old Ben here were talking about you yesterday and on the way over to pick you up just now. Old Scooter. Back down to Gasoline Point from points north and elsewhere.

And I said, Back to touch base before heading out again. I didn't do so after college. I joined the band in Cincinnati to pick up some cash I had to have to go with my graduate school scholarship, and one thing has led to another and another up to now. So now, I said, crossing my fingers, I got to go back and find out if I can pick up on some of the matters that have been on hold all this time, if you know what I mean.

And he said, I can guess. And man, if she's anything like that stone fox I lucked out with, which I have good reason to believe she could be, because I remember you and Charlene Wingate just like I remember you and that chinaberry tree and old Little Buddy Marshall. Take her with you this time. Maybe you don't know it yet, but you need her, man.

And I said, She was still in school when I graduated and there were also some hometown strings attached to her college scholarship, but she's supposed to be beyond all that by now. So what it really comes down to at this point is whether I get the benefit of the doubt, I said. And he said, Man, if she's the one, you will. And that's all you need.

We were out at LaGuardia in plenty of time for me to check in and also have breakfast with them in a concourse snack bar, and when we came on through the cafeteria line and found a table, he said, Man, I wouldn't take nothing for running into somebody from down home like this, especially somebody like you, Scooter. Because you remembered that I didn't have enough sense to want to hang on in school and get up there and be one of old man B. Franklin Fisher's Talented Tenth Early Bird boys like you did, and you were from even deeper down in the sawmill and L & N Railroad bottoms than any of us. But once I got up to Chicago and saw all them skyscrapers and plate glass windows and glittering lights, the bulbs in my dumbass head started lighting up and I got my stupidass ass back in school.

I earned myself a trade certificate first and along with it I also got the message of what schooling is truly all about if you really want to do something with your life. So that's when I made up my mind and went on back and got in night school and got my high school diploma. Because by that time I was saying to myself, Hell I could be my own kind of Early Bird. I told myself, If you buckle down and get to be good enough at doing something that amounts to something you can be somebody folks would be just as proud of as any other kind of Early Bird.

So that's my story, Scooter. And one of these days I hope to make old Mobile proud to claim me just like Chicago is going to be doing before I'm through. Man, like me and Estelle have already started telling Wendell, Whatever you do, if you do it with enough class, you can make your ancestors smile in their graves.

And I said, Hey, man, they smile in their graves whenever a contender sets his sights on the championship. I said, man, they start smiling in their graves the very minute they realize that you realize that nothing less than your personal best is good enough. I said, But man, what makes them turn over in their graves is a promising apprentice and journeyman who becomes a qualified but contented craftsman among other craftsmen instead of a contender to be reckoned with in the realm of mastercraftsmanship.

Man, I said as we headed for the departure gate, That's why I'm still trying to figure out what it is that I'd be best at trying to do.

And Marvin Upshaw said, Hey, look, Scooter, I'm just going to say this for what it's worth coming from somebody like me that's been out of Gasoline Point all these many years and wasn't ever all that close to you back then. And man, this ain't just because you told me you're coming back up to go to graduate school either.

Man, he went on then, My guess is that it's bound to be something psychological or philosophical because look, Scooter, just about everybody in Gasoline Point have always been knowing that something like that is what you have been about. Just like home folks can tell when somebody else is all about growing up to be a preacher or something. See, now that's how me and you are different. What I got is an undeniable obligation to try to be champion. But that's not a calling. That's just my obligation to do my best whatever it is I'm into. But a calling is for the rest of your life.

Like the Bossman Himself, Ben Rutledge said as I took my place in line with my boarding pass ready; and Marvin Upshaw said, That's exactly what I'm talking about. Man, when you told me you went straight out of college and into that band, I was really surprised at first. But then it hit me. Man, the Bossman Himself ain't the bossman just for nothing. He knew exactly what he was doing when he hired you right out of college with no professional experience and didn't even major in music.

Like wham, man, he said. And that's also the way it hit me too. So there you were, up there helping him and Joe States and old sporty-otie Otis Sheppard keep the beat and hold the time frame and boot the accents for that band of all-star musical thugs. Man, that's got to mean that he spotted something philosophical about you that you yourself didn't know you had yet, home boy.

And that was when Ben Rutledge got in the last word before we slapped and snatched palms and I headed for the gate. Man, he said, talking about philosophical. Man, it's exactly when that stuff of his hits that groove whether it's in a dance hall or anywhere else and that somitch starts siccing old Bloop and old Sir Wayman Ridgeway and old chickenbutt Ike Ellis and booty-butt Scully Pittman, the Gold Dust Twins, and old Malachi and that nasty talking plunger or any of them other laid-back ass-ripping tigers on you and you start snapping your fingers (and not just patting your feet) because your insides are already dancing, that's when he's laying his heaviest philosophical stuff on you. Man, but I don't have to tell you that that's when that stuff is really deep. What I'm talking about is some stuff just as deep as anything that ever made folks shout in church.

The also and also of all of which is also why, airborne and southbound to Alabama by way of Atlanta once more, I settled all the way back in my seat next to the window remembering yet again what Mr. B. Franklin Fisher always used to reiterate so strongly in his Principal's Farewell Remarks at the close of every commencement ceremony. As soon as he came to the part that you knew was going to be about faring forth, you knew he was also going to remind one and all once again that, along with literacy, the most important portable equipment that your MCTS diploma certified amounted to a compass, a spyglass for microscopic as well as long-distance inspection, skill with pencil and paper, and a knapsack for the other minimal personals. But no maps and mileage charts and timetables. Because pioneer pathfinders, trailblazers, early settlers, and frontiersmen must of necessity shoot their own azimuths, select their own triangulation points, and establish their own often tentative benchmarks.

So then with a smoothly droning Delta Air Lines jet cruising on southward above and beyond Maryland and Washington and on over Virginia and the Carolinas, there was also the also and also of my personal accountability to the ancestral imperatives again. *Not to the people of Gasoline Point, I said to myself. Not as such at any rate, I said. To the imperatives as such, I said. Your own azimuths, triangulation points, and benchmarks, indeed, I said. What are the expectations of a brownskin boy from the outskirts of Mobile, Alabama, when it comes to basic questions of the human proposition and the expansion and elevation of horizons of human aspiration? No less than is expected of any other boys elsewhere.*

Then there was the pilot's voice back on the intercom again announcing that the flight would soon be entering the Atlanta area approach and landing pattern, and I felt the way I felt because there was only that much more time before I would be back home again from college after that many years. *But only for the time being. Home again, home again, in again, out again. And do you come back bearing the Golden Fleece? The golden apples? The magic jewels? The magic wand? You do not. As Odysseus, most masterful of voyagers, did not. What he brought was that which he had acquired in experience in due course of his meandering: perhaps more pragmatic insight into his own identity and a deeper appreciation of chance, probability, and just plain lucking out. As for magic keys, are they not always a matter of the cryptographic information you acquire about combinations?*

The estimated time of arrival of the flight from Atlanta was only a matter of approximately thirty minutes once you take off and turn into your designated heading, and what I will probably always remember about that leg of the journey home is not so much what I was thinking as what I was wishing. *Rover boy, rover boy, where have you not been? Not yet to any castle with the true princess therein.*

Then, when the light propeller-driven short-range commuter craft touched down at last in central Alabama and came rumbling on along the taxiway to the two-story tri-city airport hangar where Eunice Townsend was waiting thinking whatever she was thinking, I uncrossed my fingers and crossed them again.

THE MAGIC KEYS

For Mozelle and our Michele

I

THE EARLY-MORNING walls and windows of the fourth-floor apartment were there once more even before you opened your eyes. And outside, the nightlong mid-September drizzle had finally stopped. So you already knew how the neighborhood streets of your part of Greenwich Village and what you would be able to see of the Manhattan skyline would look later on when you came along the sidewalk to the Sixth Avenue bus stop. With your eyes still closed you were also already aware of how the recently rented three-room apartment looked in the dim early-morning daylight.

But before any of that you were already also very much aware of the also and also of who was no longer in bed beside you because you could hear her moving about in the bathroom, and then there was the sound of the shower, which is why I crossed my fingers for good luck once more, thinking, *This many miles from Gasoline Point, this many miles along the way.*

(You do not wake up every morning actually saying or even consciously thinking: and one and one and two and three and four and one two three four/one two three four plus the also and also of the specific day of the week, month, and year once more. Not as a deliberate or even conscious routine. But the also and also continuity of the pulse of the conventional actuality of the workaday world of clocks and calendars and maps and mileage charts is there even so. As is also the awareness of local landmarks, and thus destinations and aspirations, however obscure, without which chronology itself may well be not only pointless but perhaps also even inconceivable.)

When I heard the softly padding footsteps heading back through the living room to the kitchenette, I still didn't open my eyes. So what was said was not good morning. What was said was seven o'clock. Which was also the way Mama used to say what she used to say to let you know that it was time to rise and wash up and brush up and shine up before breakfast and the first bell of school bell time. *September, September, and this time in New York. The Philamayork of the old Mother Goose mantelpiece clock fireside tell-me-tale times of the long-gone*

*boyhood nights on the outskirts of Mobile, the Alabama Bay city
gateway to the Spanish Main and the Seven Seas.*

*And also the New York City during the time of the central
Alabama college campus clock tower chimes as you heard them
through the shrubbery outside the ground-floor periodicals room
of the library and beyond the tip-tops of the poplar saplings outside
the long second-floor main reading room during study periods;
and also as you visualized it in the after-hours darkness of the
dormitory lounge when the radio announcers said it the way they
used to say it along with the sound of the station signal.*

*Nor was there anything more evocative of New York as bean-
stalk castle town of skyscrapers and patent-leather avenues and
taxicab horns and motors and subway trains than the* Street
Scene *score that so many sound tracks for drawing-room comedies used to begin with, the camera panning the skyline from
the air and then zooming in on the midtown traffic and people
along the sidewalks with the shopping district showcase windows
sparkling in the background, before settling on the swanky hotel,
apartment building, or town house where you picked up the story
line.*

September, September in New York City once more, and
this time also the also and also of Eunice née Townsend now
become Mrs. Me plus the also and also of my graduate school
course of study at New York University off Washington Square
and of hers at Teachers College, Columbia University, up on
Morningside Heights. Eunice Townsend, Eunice erstwhile
Townsend who was there because she was the one above all
others ever considered all the way back to the crepe myrtle
yard blossom and dog fennel meadow days of Charlene Wingate, who said, Not now, Scooter, and said, I'll tell you when,
Scooter, and finally did. But not for always.

Eunice Townsend, Eunice née but now erstwhile Townsend.
(And also no longer the Nona that she had been nicknamed
during her freshman year at State Normal Junior College.) She
did not say anything else to keep me from dozing back off to
sleep, because we had been married and living together for
many weeks then, and she knew that I was already sitting up.
Because she was also very much aware of the fact that I was the
way I was about never being late for anything, and also that
with me it had already become a matter of not being tardy for

school bell time long before it also became the basic principle of road band bus departure schedules and being dressed up and tuned up and onstage before curtain time.

Before I opened my eyes I was also aware of the sounds and aromas of breakfast preparations in the kitchen then. But then, as also used to happen during school bell days of the week when it was Mama in the kitchen, and the stove was a wood burner and the light was from an oil lamp, it was almost as if you were all alone. Because you had to prove to Eunice as you used to feel that you had to prove to Mama that you could go out and do whatever you were supposed to do. *Because then I was remembering what book I had been reading the night before and what references I was using and where I stopped and put in the page marker and turned off the light. Which is why I also already knew how the desk would look in the morning light before I opened my eyes and stood up and headed for the bathroom.*

Which is why what I began to think about then were the specific research materials needed for the term paper I was working on. And about how much I preferred looking things up in the New York Public Library up at Fifth Avenue and Forty-second Street to trying to use the crowded university campus library. *New York, New York.* So far the public library was never overcrowded in the mornings and as you worked on your academic exercises you were also aware of being in the midst of the comings and goings of professional scholars, authors, and journalists, many of whom you recognized at first sight. *New York, New York.*

When I stepped out of the shower and began getting dressed, there was the static blurred chatter that was the portable radio chatter that in those days was the equivalent of the New York tabloid newsprint, from which you could foretell the headlines and flash photos that you would see along with the bright covers of the weekly and monthly magazines on the sidewalk stalls on your way across Sheridan Square to the uptown Sixth Avenue bus stop.

We ate breakfast sitting on the high stool at the barlike sideboard shelf attached to the ledge of the wide window that overlooked the backyard patio four flights below and from which you could also see out across the rooftops of many of the old Federal period buildings in that part of town, which had turned out to be less than a ten-minute walk from the University Place and Washington Square corner of the campus.

All of the graduate school sessions for my course of study in the humanities were conducted in the evening in those days. And the special advanced seminars and laboratory sessions in Education for which Eunice had enrolled at Teachers College met in the afternoons. So there was no rush to be in place for morning roll checks, but we kept ourselves on a strict morning timetable anyway, precisely because of all the local attractions in New York City that were not there for you in any conventional university town, where campus activities were the main local attraction. Not that we passed up very many of the not-to-be-missed feature attractions that we could afford from time to time, but otherwise we followed our regular self-imposed Monday through Friday study schedule, even on the mornings we spent studying in the apartment and taking care of domestic chores.

Me and you, I said as I kissed her at the door on my way to the elevator, me and you, which she knew was a jive line that I had picked up from Joe States, the all-star drummer who was also from Alabama and who had become my self-elected mentor the day after I joined the band of the Bossman Himself as a temporary replacement bass player in Cincinnati the week after I graduated from college, because I had told her about him in the first letter I sent back to Alabama, and I began using it as a complimentary close before my initials on all of my letters and tourist postcards to her from then on. And her response when I finally came back south and said it in person was always a playful mock pucker as she kissed me back—as if to say, One jive gesture deserves another.

What she said this time was, See you back here for dinner at eight-thirty sharp, Rover Boy. Or for warmed overs if not too long thereafter. After which it's leftovers—but of course there's always the phone. And I said, Hey me, I did time helping to keep time for the Bossman Himself.

Which is why when I came on outside and headed for the bus that morning I was thinking about Joe States again. Good old Joe States from the 'Ham in the 'Bam. *Who was to say what he was to say when the band came back into Manhattan several weeks later, and I took her backstage that first time. Hey, here he is, he said, coming toward us. What did I tell you about this schoolboy statemate of mine! Check it out for yourself, fellows.*

And as I told her he would, the Bossman Himself said, He said you were most beautiful, but he didn't say that you were this *beautiful. And she smiled as he gave me an ever-so-father-caliber avuncular wink as he spoke and then he gave her the one for each cheek routine, and Joe States hooking his arm in hers took her in tow to introduce her to everybody else while I talked to the Bossman and then Old Pro, the chief arranger and straw boss in charge of rehearsals. Then there was Milo the road manager, also known as Milo the Navigator, who gave me the rehearsal schedule and address of the hall that they would be using before moving into the recording studio that next week.*

Eunice Townsend, Eunice Townsend, Eunice Townsend, Joe States said again at the stage door leading back out into the audience as he had said when he first heard her name when I mentioned her to him shortly after I joined the band in Ohio that June after graduation, which is when he also said, Eunice Townsend. Sounds like it goes with somebody come from a family that stands for something very special, Schoolboy.

And when I dropped in on them by myself two afternoons later he said, Hey, she's down home all right, Schoolboy. And Aladambama people to boot. How 'bout it, Bloop! And Herman Kemble the big-toned tenor saxophone player from Texas said, Hey, Schoolboy, when you come up with somebody like that, man, you make us all look good and feel good, too. Just like when one of us hits that right note that sounds like something we were all waiting to hear without realizing it before we hear it.

Which ought not to be no big surprise to anybody in this outfit, Osceola Menefee the trumpet player who sometimes doubled as vocalist said. I mean after all, it was just like he was raised to be one of us as soon as he came on board when Shag Phillips had to split. So now he can't help being one of us for the rest of his life, don't care where else he goes or what else he might end up doing for a living. Talking about keeping the right time with the right people, Schoolboy. That's the thing about life, just like it's the thing about music.

And that was when Joe States said, Hey yeah, man, but let me tell you something else. About what I'm talking about when I say what I say about being down-home people. I'm talking about somebody got all them knockout cover girl good looks and all that college girl class about her, who I bet you a hundred to one can also step into the kitchen and stir up a batch of some of them old-time Mobile tea cakes. Just like the ones that come from the old Rumford Baking Powder recipe, the ones your mama used to roll out like biscuit dough and cut out with a top of a baking powder can. Man, what I'm talking about is somebody that can do what your mama or your favorite aunt or even your grandma can do, because she's them kind of people along with everything else. Hey, and with them same honey brown fingers that make you realize what all that diamond and gold stuff in Tiffany's is really made for. One hundred to one, first come, first served, and I know my bet is safe because I know my main man here.

On the bus rolling uptown from Fourth Street along Sixth Avenue I began thinking about how Miss Lexine Metcalf would be most likely to feel when she found out that I was back in school again; and I was pretty certain that I knew what she would tell her present group of students at Mobile County Training School about me and I hoped that they felt the way I always felt about her because she was the one who made me realize that the also and also of school bell time was not as different from the also and also of Miss Tee's storybook times in Mama's rocking chair and yarn-spinning time in Papa Gumbo Willie McWorthy's barbershop as I and perhaps the majority of people had taken for granted because of the stern sound of period bells and harsh actuality of passing and failing grades.

As the bus rolled on toward Herald Square I was thinking about how Miss Lexine Metcalf was also the one who made it a point to keep reminding me every now and then even when I was still in junior high school that I should never forget that I just might be one of the very special ones who would have to travel far and wide to find out what it is that I may have been put here on earth to make of myself.

Which is why as we came on through the intersection of Broadway and Sixth Avenue at Thirty-fourth Street, I was also thinking about my old roguish-eyed freshman and sophomore roommate again who, when I told him about what Miss Lexine Metcalf used to say about faring forth, said, hithering, thithering, and yondering, picaresquely but not quixotically, one hopes. Because in quest and maybe even conquest rather than serendipity. Because such a quest is for clues, my good man. That Miss Lexine Metcalf of yours is right on target.

And so was my Miss Jewel Templeton of Hollywood, when she said what she said in the south of France about magic keys (some sharp, some flat, some natural; some solid gold, some sterling silver, some perhaps even platinum, or in fact of any other alloy, whether already in existence or yet to come).

And so also was my good old roommate himself with his yea, verily as he scribbled each entry in the notebook in which he recorded evidence that he called the goods that added up to his personal estimate of the situation for the time being. So was he on target, who was the one who said what he said about necessity being the mother of the invention of fathers and who was also to say what he said about the function of father figures as symbols of direction and thus also of detours.

At the Forty-second Street stop I used the rear exit, and as I came along the sidewalk past Bryant Park and up the steps to the side entrance to the library I was still thinking of my old roommate and I wondered how long it would take his next letter from wherever he was to get to me from the last forwarding address that I had sent to his last forwarding address, and I couldn't help guessing what he would say about my being back in school and about my new roommate.

I took the elevator up to the third floor and came around the corner and along the hall and turned into the old card index area. Then from the checkpoint for the south wing of the main reading room I could see that I had arrived in time to get the table and seat that I had already become used to settling into as if into my own private cubicle.

II

BY THE first week in October I began to feel that I was getting used to being back on an academic schedule once again without really missing a beat and that I was also beginning to be used to staying on in New York City longer than the three- to fourteen-day periods that I had spent working there from time to time when I was with the band. Because back then sometimes it would be on a three-day stopover for a dance and maybe a two-day recording session, or maybe one or two days for working over new material followed by one solid day of takes with very few retakes as insurance against studio equipment flaws. Or sometimes we would spend all three days in the studio because the Bossman and Old Pro would begin recording as soon as we got set up the first morning and keep on adding unscheduled old numbers because the new items had taken less time than they had estimated, and sometimes also because they both wanted to take advantage of the mood the band was in that day.

You could always count on that outfit rising to the occasion in response to an enthusiastic audience in a dance hall, in a first-run movie showcase theater or at an outdoor festival or picnic. But there were also times when they sounded extra special not in response to an extra-special reception but to show their supporters that they didn't take them for granted, indeed that they would come on just as strong for a midweek audience at a one-night stand in some obscure down-home roadside joint as they had been heard doing on records and live coast-to-coast radio broadcasts. But sometimes they would also hit a very special groove just because they were having such a good time listening to themselves. *You hear these thugs, Joe States would say to me at such times. Can you believe that this bunch of granny dodgers can really team up and get to you like this? Boy, this so-called Bossman of ours is a goddamn genius. Man, what can I tell you. Man, who else can take a bunch of splibs as mixed up as this crew we got and get them each to enjoy hearing themselves and then turn around and have everybody else do the same thing one by one. Man, my money says very few people have ever seen anything like these splibs this man has making his kind of music.*

All of which is to say that I had been to New York as many times as I had been there while I was with the band but never long enough for me to feel that it was home base, as I had thought it would be when I left Alabama to join the tour in Cincinnati. It was not a New York band as the Earl Hines band was a Chicago band and as Benny Moten and Andy Kirk had been Kansas City and Southwest Territory bands along with

Troy Floyd and Alphonso Trent, or as King Oliver's bands would always be remembered as New Orleans bands. It was not a regional band but a cosmopolitan band, and its home base was a city that was cosmopolitan rather than regional. As Paris and Rome and London were cosmopolitan rather than regional. You could feel it as soon as you arrived, just as you had anticipated you would. But before there was time to begin to really get with it, as you had gradually become used to being a college freshman and then sophomore and eventually an upperclassman on the campus down in central Alabama, you were back out on the road again, getting used to not being used to being somewhere else.

Not that I had ever actually decided that I was going to make New York City the place of my permanent and official residence one day. I had thought of being at home there as I had also come to think of the possibility of getting to feel at home in Los Angeles and Hollywood and then perhaps in Paris and on the Côte d'Azur and also in Rome and in London. But that was not at all the same as choosing the place where you would eventually settle down for good, which many, maybe most, people do years before their thirtieth birthday.

As a matter of fact, even as I used to listen and realize that it was the Philamayork of the blue steel, rawhide, and patent-leather yarns being unspooled once again during fireside and swing porch tell-me-tale-time sessions, I also realized that it was also yet another homespun version for the fairy-tale castles I already knew about from rocking-chair storybook times. And it now seems to me that on some subconscious level of awareness I also knew even then that sometimes a fairy-tale castle was no less a point of departure than a point of arrival. Which is precisely what I had found New York City to be when I was a member of the band, *the castle town from which the Bossman and his merrymakers like the dukes of derring-do of yestertimes were forever sallying forth to encounter and contend with the invisible and indestructible dragons of gloom and doom once again and again.*

I knew all that very well. And yet getting to feel like a New Yorker among other New Yorkers (a very significant number of whom had as I was also very much aware grown up elsewhere not only across the nation but also around the globe) was the main reason I had decided to come to do my graduate work in New York City and not in New England, the Midwest, or anywhere in the Far West or out on the Pacific coast.

And it was also why I did most of my library research for assignments at the public library rather than on the campus at Washington Square. In fact, I used the excellent university library only when certain references that professors had put on special reserve status were not also available in the public collection at Forty-second Street, which was not very often, the point not being that it was as if the New York Public Library was really a part of NYU but rather that it was not. Not to me, at any rate. To me it was to big-league research technicians and world-class scholars and intellectuals what Yankee Stadium and Madison Square Garden were to championship-caliber athletes.

There was, as I not only realize and acknowledge now but also as my old roommate and I were completely and admittedly aware from the outset and at every turn even then, an entirely obvious element of make-believe in a considerable amount in everything we did as undergraduate students. And we were also very much aware of the fact that our playing around with notions of medieval scholarship and the Renaissance workshops of the likes of Benvenuto Cellini, Michelangelo, and Leonardo da Vinci, the polymath, led other students to respect our sincerity and dedication. To them it was an act, a jive tune, a put-on.

And as for our identification with life in the grimy garrets of bohemian Paris, not with berets and goatees but with plain gray extra-large sweatshirts symbolizing smocks that made being in college on scholarship merit awards (but in my case mostly without pocket change or even bus fare for a two-hundred-mile trip to Mobile for Christmas) more a matter of bohemian glamour and vagabond adventure and romance than of the grinding poverty that it undeniably was.

But when I arrived in New York that September, being a graduate student was another matter altogether. So much so that the fact that I was now actually living in Greenwich Village, the legendary center for bohemian life in the United States, had much less to do with what I had read by and about the generation of Edna St. Vincent Millay, Maxwell Bodenheim, E. E. Cummings, Max Eastman, and the like than with New York friendships I had made backstage or in nightclubs when I was in town as a member of the band. And besides, along with the time that I had spent doing what I had been doing since leaving the campus in central Alabama, there was also the fact that I had now become a man with a wife.

Perhaps for some of those who go directly from the bachelor's degree to the master and sometimes the doctorate programs, often on the same campus and sometimes with some of the same professors, the break was not as obvious as it was for those who took time out to teach for a while or did something else, as I did before enrolling as a graduate student. In any case, I had decided that graduate-level academic work was really a special form of adult education, and as such there was something part-time about it even when you were enrolled in a full-time course of study that you were expected to complete in a scheduled (even though not strictly required) time frame.

What I really had in mind when I decided that the time had come for me to register for a graduate course of study that year was not a specific profession, but what Miss Lexine Metcalf had kept repeating to me when I reached senior high school because that was when you really began competing not only for college eligibility ranking, but also for scholarship grants, some special few of which were not only for tuition but also for room and board. And it was also at this point in the Mobile County Training School program for upward-bound early birds that vocational guidance sessions began to focus on individual career choices, which in due course also became a matter of the choice of your first, second, and third preference as to the college you hoped to attend, given your final grade-point average and your financial means. Which in my case was a matter of a high grade-point-average eligibility and high faculty recommendation and hardly any financial means whatsoever. As she well knew but only regarded as a challenge to my ingenuity and no great one at that. Certainly not for the sort of splendid young man that she herself always led me to believe that she thought I was, or that she was still counting on me to become, as she had begun doing when she became my homeroom teacher when I reached the third grade. Which was the beginning of geography books and maps and the globe and the sand table projects and windows on the world bulletin board displays of peoples and customs of many lands. That was where and when it had begun between her and me. And she was the one who even so early on as that had already earmarked me as a likely prospect for Mr. B. Franklin Fisher's early bird list of candidates for the Mobile County Training School extracurricular program for the talented tenth, who according to his doctrine of uplift and ancestral imperative were the hope and glory of the nation. It was the early birds from whom he expected the most immediate and consummate response to his exhortation to so conduct, *nay, acquit yourselves in all of your undertakings that generations yet unborn will rise at mention of your name and call you blesséd.*

Incidentally, it was Mr. B. Franklin Fisher, the principal and thus the *man* as in the *big man* and *bossman*, but who looked like a boy evangelist, who was the one who spoke of ancestral imperatives in national and also in ethnic terms, such as our nation and our people and our people in this nation, whereas Miss Lexine Metcalf never said who else among our people if not you, but who else in the whole wide world if not you. Which is why hers was the school bell time voice that I always found myself responding to even as I had always that of Miss Tee's rocking-chair storybook time voice and as I had also already been responding to the baby talk voice of Mama herself calling me her little mister scootabout man *out there among them*! Which is why Miss Tee also called me little mister man and then my mister. *Hello, my mister. You, too, my mister. You can, too, my mister.*

But it was when Mr. B. Franklin Fisher, whose pulpit eloquence with its reverberations of Henry Ward Beecher and Abraham Lincoln, Frederick Douglass, Booker T. Washington, and W. E. B. Du Bois and ranging from down-to-earth aphorism to silver-tongued oratory as the occasion required, delivered another one of his ancestral imperative pep talks that you heard the school bell time equivalent to the ethnic and political concerns that you had come to know about and identify with from all the talk and signifying that also went with all the tales, tall and otherwise, from the fireside, porch swing, and even on the front stoop and around the hot stove near the cracker barrel in Stranahan's General Merchandise Store on Buckshaw Mill Road.

All of that was what Mr. B. Franklin Fisher was best known and celebrated for. Whereas with Miss Lexine Metcalf, as with

Miss Tee and with Mama, you did what you had to do because that was what growing up into full manhood was all about. And yet even when she insisted that you had to go on beyond high school as she did when you were in the ninth grade, she never was to say which college or what for. Nor did Mr. B. Franklin Fisher himself, who after all was not only the ultimate approval authority on college eligibility and scholarship grants at Mobile County Training School, but also had a record as an expert on vocational guidance that was unchallenged. When he referred to himself as a fisher of humankind, a spotter of prospects, and a molder of heroes and nation-builders, nobody ever took issue, not even in private. In public, the response was always applause, which became a standing ovation.

Still, not even he, with whom my status as an early bird was second to none and who was forever predicting to the student body at large that I would become one who would accomplish something that would make me a credit to my people and the nation, acknowledged or not during my lifetime, but would enjoy the high regard of generations yet unborn even so. *All I ask of this one, he said on commencement day, as if keeping a promise to Miss Lexine Metcalf, is that he always do his best. Not even he ever gave the slightest hint of a suggestion as to what my career field would be.*

Meanwhile, Miss Lexine Metcalf was the one who never stopped reminding me that I might just be one of those whose destiny was to travel far and wide in order to find out what it was that I should try to make of myself in the first place. Which she had begun to do when I reached the third grade and the first-year geography book that you had to have for the homework to go along with the maps on the wall rack with the globe and the displays on the bulletin board better known as windows on the world, and also the sand-table cutout mock-up projects that made her classroom seem like a department store toyland from time to time.

That was where she began, and it was as if she were my own private Mobile County Training School guardian from then on, because all of my subsequent homeroom teachers and officially designated class sponsors deferred to her on all matters concerning me. As did Mr. B. Franklin Fisher himself. Or so it still seems to me. Because I still cannot remember any special project that he ever assigned me to be responsible for or any award that he recommended me for that had not already been discussed with her beforehand. But then I had been *her* special candidate for his early bird initiatives program in the first place.

Whatever she said to him, to me she always said, Who if not you? Who if not you, my splendid young man, who if not you? Who if not you may have to go where you will go and find out what you will find out, whatever you will find out? To me she also said, You will know you are where you should be by the way you feel, where you should be for the time being; at any rate she also said because such was the also and also of whatever you do wherever you are.

All of which is also why she had also come so immediately to mind along with Mama and Miss Tee when my old roommate read to me the passage from *Remembrance of Things Past* that he was recording in his notebook, the passage in which Marcel Proust has an artist tell the narrator that *we do not receive wisdom, we must discover it for ourselves, after a journey through the wilderness that no one else can make for us, that no one else can spare us, for our wisdom is the point of view from which we come at last to view the world.*

Which I also find to be entirely consistent with the behavior of Miss Tee toward me, especially as it struck me after I found out the secret about how she came to be in Gasoline Point that I didn't know about until the night I awoke on the front porch in Stranahan's Lane during Mr. Ike Meadow's wake and kept my head in Mama's lap as if I were still asleep.

So yes, on the outskirts of Mobile, Alabama, where I come from, you were indeed weaned from the home to be bottle-fed by teachers, but from these same teachers you also learned that you had to prepare and also condition yourself to assume total responsibility for yourself, *because once you graduated and went out into the world, you were on your own.* And who if not Mr. B. Franklin Fisher himself for all of his community uplift and vocational guidance expertise always ended his annual commencement address by reminding the graduating class that it was going out into the real world equipped with what really amounted to a compass, a knapsack, and a notebook or chapbook (*for what my old best of all possible college roommates was to call the goods*).

III

So YOU decided to get yourself back on some school bell time for a while, hey statemate, Joe States said as we waited for our orders to be served that afternoon of the day before the band headed back out west by way of upstate New York and a swing over into Canada to Montreal, Ottawa, and Toronto after its second trip back into town that fall.

I had come up from the Forty-second Street library and he had come across and down Sixth Avenue from the recording studio the band was using on Forty-eighth Street about halfway to Seventh Avenue and Times Square, and which was also only a few doors from the music store from which he had always bought most of his drum equipment over the years.

I can dig it, he said. And so can the boss and Old Pro and everybody else I spoke to. But what the hell, I don't have to enumerate and elaborate and all that because I'm satisfied that you really know more about them than they actually know about you. Because you came in with us already checked out on us all the way back to our first records and broadcasts. I just want you to know there's not just only me and the man and Old Pro. Because hey, man, these cats know a special thing when they see it and they pegged you special from day one. And the thing about how you laid that bass in there with us right from the get-go. That let everybody know that you had your own personal way of listening. Everybody in every section felt like you heard every note they were playing. Because you see, now, me, sometimes my job is to make them get to *me*. And the way you laid your thing in there helped them stay with the man and me. Man, you could have had that job for as long as you wanted it. I mean, even if Shag Phillips had wanted to come back we'd have had two basses. And if you'd wanted to come back we would have had two, you and Scratchy.

Hey, but the thing I'm really getting at, he said as the waiter served our orders, is not just how you fit in the band. I'm talking about how much these guys respect your judgment. Believe me, these cats will lay money on anything you decide to try. And of course that also means if you need some bills, get to us first. Don't hesitate. Get to us first. *Get to us fast.*

We were in a restaurant that he had first taken me to one night between shows back during the first week of the run we had had in that showcase theater in Times Square with Earlene Copeland as our featured vocalist. He used it when he wanted to get away from the showbiz crowd he ran into in the snack bars in or near Times Square and along Broadway up to Columbus Circle. We both had ordered oxtail soup and a mixed green salad and pumpernickel bread, which was still something of a New York City novelty for me in those days.

But now what I'm also to make sure you understand is that every cat in this crew knows exactly what the Bossman and Old Pro were talking about when they said what they said when you stayed behind in Hollywood. As we pulled on out to the end of the freeway and headed into the open country again I went up to talk to them and feel them out. And guess what? The goddamn Bossman sounded like he was more concerned about how much I was going to miss having you to be clucking at and carrying on over than the effect on the music. But finally he also said, You know something, Joe? As much as we all liked having him in here doing his special little thing with us, he just might turn out to be somebody that can do us even more good out there doing his thing on his own. And Old Pro said, Whatever his thing turns out to be, I'm sure that what we're trying to do in this outfit is going to be an important part of it. That's been my idea about him ever since he decided to put off going right on into graduate school at the end of that first summer. Mark my words.

Now me myself, Joe States said as we buttered our bread and started in on the thick, meaty oxtail soup, as far as I can figure it out I myself was put on this earth to make music. This music we play. So what else can I tell you, my man? I'm lucky. Hell, when you come right down to the facts of life, I really owe this band. And the only way I can pay my debt is by always giving the Bossman my best, and I'm also going to do what I can to have somebody else ready to fill my shoes when the time comes.

That was also the afternoon that he told me what he told me because he wanted to remind me of several other details of his special slant on the facts of life that he had begun clueing me in on as the band bus circled down into Kentucky and back up into Ohio, rolled on across to West Virginia, and Pennsylvania on the meandering route to the one-night dance stands we were booked for beginning the weeks following the June morning on which I arrived in Cincinnati.

One thing is for damn certain, Schoolboy, he had already gone on to say during one of those early-on open-road sessions, as far as I am concerned, I for one was definitely not put here on this planet among all these possibilities just to spend my time and whatever little talent I might have going around bellyaching because some paleface somich don't like me as much as I might think he ought to. Hell, me? If somebody don't like me, I don't like him right back, and if we tangle and the somich don't do me in for good, I'm sworn to get him back if it's the last thing I do. Me, I don't look for no trouble. And I don't run from it either, once I'm in it.

But what I'm really getting at, he had also made sure to remind me, is doing your thing. Look, here's what I'm really trying to tell you, my man. You're not out here to prove that some used-to-be little snotty-nosed kid from the outskirts of Mobile, Alabama, can impress some puffed-up somiches just on some old principles from back during slavery time and Reconstruction. You're out here to find out what you can make of yourself in this day and age. So don't give up until you make sure you're on the wrong track. And on the other hand, don't get faked out by a lot of applause too early on, either.

He let me think about that for a while as we went on enjoying our soup and salad. Then he said, So how you making out with these up here splibs, homeboy? You remember what I told you during those rookie sessions I made it my personal obligation to put you through?

And I said, Never is to forget any part of any days like that, Papa Joe. You being a statemate to boot and all. And even as I spoke I found myself remembering exactly how he had looked when he pushed his bus seat all the way back in reclining position. *Because it made him look exactly like a not-quite-middle-aged general merchandise storefront bench Uncle Bud, Doc, Mose, or Remus who might well have been taking a snooze in Mr. Slim Jim Perkins's vacant barber's chair number three in Papa Gumbo Willie McWorthy's Tonsorial Parlor up on Buckshaw Mill Road across the lane from Stranahan's General Merchandise Store on Mr. Slim Jim Perkins's day off.*

And as he went on saying what he was saying, I was aware once again of that ever so subtle wisp of his Yardley's English Lavender brilliantine and of the fact that he, like Jo Jones of Count Basie's band and Sonny Greer of Duke Ellington's, was an expert twenty-mule-team skinner who never seemed to work up a heavy sweat, which also reminded me of how redolent of bay rum and the aftershave talcum brush mist along with the cigar smoke and shoe polish the atmosphere in Papa Gumbo Willie McWorthy's used to be. Then by the time I was on my way through the last year of junior high school, there was the precollegiate atmosphere of Shade's up on Green's Avenue across from Boom Men's Union Hall Ballroom, where the hair and skin preparations came from the same downtown Mobile haberdasheries that carried the latest fashions you saw in Esquire *magazine, which by then had become the sartorial bible of the man about town.*

Man, these up here splibs, he had said one morning on the road. Man, them and us, and us and them. Man, especially when it comes to these up here jaspers. My experience is that as soon as they hear that you're from somewhere down home they're subject to come on like the fact that they're from somewhere up here automatically gives them some kind of status over you, especially if you ask them something about something, and I'm not talking about asking them *for* something. Boy, but as soon as they find out that there's a bunch of jaspers carrying on about you, man, that's another tune. Man, you go from cotton-chopping pickaninny to street-corner hangout buddy buddy just like that! But now, on the other hand, it looks like some of *their* jaspers might want to get next to *you*, watch out!

Because, you see, he had also said during another of one of our early-on sessions, speaking of these up here jaspers, man, the problem with *them folks* is how many of them can't tell one of us from the other after all. And these up here splibs figure we're bound to spot how easy it is for almost any old dog-ass splib to take them in like netting mullets in a goddamn barrel. That's the big secret. Ain't nothing a bigger mullethead than a benevolent up here jasper. Man, the hype they lay on these people is a sin and a shame. But the scandal of it is that it's mostly just about some chicken feed, or some goofy broad that don't even wear no drawers.

I dropped some pretty heavy stuff on you, right from the get-go, my man, he said as I chuckled to myself, remembering. You being a college boy and all, he said, and you listened like a bass player is supposed to listen. And I told the Bossman, I can see why we can hang this whole thing on a kid like him. I said he's not only a quick study, he's somebody that's been on his way to getting on our kind of time even before he was old enough to know that he could tell the difference between us and somebody else. Which was a hell of a long time before you realized that for us this stuff is not just a job but a calling. Which is another thing that makes for the great big difference between this man's band and all the others.

That was also when he began saying what he was to say about another thing that he along with a number of others, none of them schoolteachers as such, incidentally, used to re-mind you of in one way or another from time to time back in the days when I was coming of age but also stretching all the way back to as far as I can remember. Sometimes they called it quality. And sometimes they called it class.

What he had said about that back when he filled me in on "the character of the cast of characters in this man's lineup" was that it was something more than education, and not a mat-ter of birth and family background and how much money you could live on or get to to back you up. All of that might give you some clout of one kind or another. But class don't need clout. Class is its own clout, young fellow, and it's pretty much the same with hustle. Because you see the thing of it is that class and hustle don't really go together. It's a matter of being on the ball, on the money, on the minute without coming on like an eager beaver. Man, what I'm talking about is also being able to miss the cue, miss the mark, and still hold your own and not lose anybody's respect and faith in you. In school you've been thinking mostly in terms of passing or failing, but out here, in the everyday here and now, it's also very much a matter of whether you can also lose or fail and still have people betting on you on the next go-round.

Which reminds me that it was also during those initiation sessions he used to continue between naps as the bus zoomed on and on through the open country that he began telling about what he told me about the big con, which was his word for the confidence games that certain hustlers play. There were two main kinds of con artists or slickers, he said. Most people knew about the first kind. Now that somich is an acknowledged criminal and a cold pro. And when he takes risks, the odds are always in his favor, no blind bets, no coin flipping. The deck is always stacked. But now there is also that other kind of con man. Now this somich begins by conning himself into believing that he can con everybody else. All he's got to do is get up enough nerve to give it a try with a straight face. He's like a gate-crasher. In fact, he really *is* a gate-crasher and a self-effacing flatterer at the same time, and I mean to the point of begging and groveling. And the thing about a somich like that is that he really forgets that he's conned himself. That he's a lying phony. Because once he gets his lie started he gets so deep into it that he believes it himself. Which is why he can get all tangled up in contradictions. A cold-blooded somich never forgets he's lying. This cat just might.

Along with all of the bus sessions out on the open road during those first months, there had also been all of those backstage tips, and after-hours and off-day rounds of pop calls, introductions, and briefings for future personal as well as professional reference. Not to mention all of the ongoing fill-in data not only on each section, but also on each sideman's approach to every tune in the book for the current tour. There was also Old Pro's preliminary technical breakdowns, but once the number was kicked off onstage, he (Joe States), being the mule skinner, was no less responsible for locking things in as the Bossman wanted than the Bossman Himself. You know that old jive about his nose itching and me sneezing, well, you better believe it, Schoolboy, because when I sneeze from now on, you poot—not just by the numbers, my man, but by *my* numbers.

Ever so often when he was passing on another personal background clue for somebody's part on a tricky passage, he would wink and say, Of course you already know what every last one of these cats in this lineup is about speaking in just musical terms. But what we don't ever let any newcomer to this outfit forget is that we don't just play music in this man's band, we play life. L-I-F-E, as in flesh and blood. And me and you and old Spodeody and the man make the difference between metronome time and pulse. Like I told you. Metronome time is mathematics, Schoolboy. Pulse is *soul*. Talking about the rhythm and tempo of life as *the folks* came to know it and live it in *down-home* U.S. of A. Talking about stuff them other folks at first thought was just some more old countrified stuff like talking flat because you cain't spell and articulate and cain't write!

As we came back outside the restaurant and headed along the sidewalk to Sixth Avenue that autumn afternoon in New York, he said, So, now tell me how things are going with them fine people you're camping with, my man. And when I gave him the old OK fingers crossed sign, he said, The unanimous impression back on the old Greyhound is that she just might have what it takes to make a real man out of our schoolboy. Not that any of us think you don't know what you're doing. Man, we're just backing your solo like jamming on a tune you called. Because we figure it'll do you good to hear some amen corner backup every now and then. Especially coming from that bunch of thugs we got in that crew.

Then as we clasped shoulders and stepped back before he turned to head up along Sixth Avenue to Forty-eighth Street, he raised his hands as if about to whisper a last word in the italics of the ride cymbal and said, Daddy Royal, homeboy. Remember Daddy Royal. He's there for you, homeboy. Get to him fast. Get to him fast. Express time, Schoolboy.

IV

ON MY way up Fifth Avenue from the library to the Gotham Book Mart at 41 West 47th Street about a week and a half after the band had hit the road out of New York that mostly bright blue and mildly breezy autumn, I overtook somebody I had not seen since my freshman year in college. I had not really gotten to know him back then, because he was an upperclassman,

two years ahead of me, and had not come back to complete his
senior year, by which time I had come to be on fairly casual
speaking terms with most of the more advanced students that
I was most curious about. I did know that he was enrolled
in the school of music and that he often served as the student concertmaster who conducted the band when it backed
up the cheerleaders during athletic events in the campus bowl
and field house. But I recognized his walk as soon as I saw him
moving along up the sidewalk about ten yards ahead of me.

He was doing his own individual sporty-almost-limp variation of the marching band trumpet player's parade ground
strut. I still don't remember having thought or wondered
about him after I myself left the campus, but suddenly there he
was again, posture correct but shoulders a little less rigid than
an eager beaver infantry cadet, right leg with an ever so slightly
but unmistakable hint of a drag, which added up to not quite
the prance and not quite the lope that anticipate ponies posting on the right diagonal, so that in mufti the effect was that of
a civilian musician rather than a military band man.

As I picked up my stride to overtake him I realized that I
remembered his name from that long ago although I had never
used it to address him person to person. Because the only verbal encounters I ever had with him were when he was on duty
as a student assistant checking books in and out at the circulation desk in the main reading room of the library.

Each time, he looked at my name and stamped my slip and
filed the card and pushed the book gently toward me and said,
Handle with care. And all I said was, Thanks. Now as I came
up close enough behind him on Fifth Avenue that many school
terms later, I still didn't call him by name. What I said in my old
roommate's mock conspiratorial stage sotto voce was, *Hey, let
that goddamn bucket down right there where you at, old pardner.
You know what the man said!*

And as if we were rehearsing the sequence in a theater piece
he turned and looked at me, not in recognition, but as if more
amused than surprised and said, What say, man! How are
things down the way? And I said, Still in process, man, still in
process, and told him my name and my class years, and that
was when I said, Edison, Taft Edison. Taft Woodrow Edison.
And he shook his head and said, What can I tell you, man.

What can I tell you. My folks were big on newsworthy names. All I can do is try to make mine mean what I want it to mean so that when somebody drops it in there on me it sounds as if it belongs as much to me as to that son of a bitch Wilson, if you know what I mean.

And I said, I think so. And then, looking at the attaché case he was carrying, I said, Hey, but man, that don't really look like no bucket I ever did see either on land or at sea, and no trumpet case, either. Is that some sheet music and your batons or something in there?

And he said, Man, that trumpet stays in the same case I had back on the campus. Same trumpet, same case. And when I said, So what's up, man? He said, Man, I really don't think of myself as a musician anymore. My big thing now is trying to find out what my interest in composition and orchestration can do for me as an apprentice writer, man.

Which didn't really surprise me, since I for one had always seen him most often not in the music area of the campus but either in the library or on his way to or from Professor Carlton Poindexter's survey course in the novel. He had not been a member of either of the two student dance orchestras, but I did remember seeing him and hearing him from time to time in the brass section of the chapel orchestra. So not only was I not surprised but even before he said what he said I realized that he had been an upperclassman who had always come to mind above all others when I thought about advanced reading courses, even after he had left campus.

What did surprise me somewhat was the way he was dressed. I had also remembered him as one of the upperclassmen who, not unlike my roommate, dressed in the collegiate style that I most admired in the fashion magazines: three-button tweed jacket with patch pockets and welt-seamed lapels, usually with contrasting tan twill or gray flannel pleated slacks and no hat. You stopped wearing hats and caps at Mobile County Training School in those days by the time you became a junior, knowing, however, that if you went to college you were going to have to wear a beanie or "crab" cap during your freshman year.

Now on Fifth Avenue he was wearing a snap brim brown felt hat, a three-piece Brooks Brothers business suit, wing-tipped shoes (which brought back to mind the two-toned moccasins and plain-toed brown crepe sole shoes back on the campus), tattersall shirt with a solid tie. All of which along with the fine leather attaché case he was carrying gave him the look that I thought of as being post–Ivy League Madison Avenue and/or Wall Street. Not that there wasn't also an unmistakable touch of uptown hipness about the way he wore it all even so.

I said, Damn, man, that just might turn out to be old BTW's freshwater bucket after all. And that was when he said, Man, if I could bring this stuff off that I hope I've got coming along in this briefcase, it just might turn out to be not just a bucket of whatever it is but a whole keg of it. Maybe some dynamite, among other things. He chuckled as if to himself and I smiled and waited and then he said, Man, when them people find out what I think they're up to down there on that campus I just might have to carry myself some kind of automatic weapon around in this thing to protect myself from their network of fund-raisers.

I didn't say anything about that, because at that time I had never really concerned myself about the overall educational policies of any given college. Once I realized that Harvard, Yale, and Princeton were out of the question so far as my undergraduate student days were concerned, the main thing that mattered to me was what range of liberal arts courses would be available wherever I was able to go. My alternative undergraduate choices had been Morehouse, Talladega, and Fisk in that order, but once I was all signed up and beginning class sessions, especially with Mr. Carlton Poindexter, and settling in with my polymath of a roommate, I had been operating on the principle that everything was up to me and I was on my way.

He (Taft Edison) chuckled to himself again and then he said, But man, that's not really what this stuff in this bag is really about. Not really and certainly not only. In fact, only incidentally. When I cut out from down there that spring, I really intended to go back and finish. But by the end of that summer I had changed my mind not only about music but also about my whole outlook on life. And while I was trying to figure out what I really wanted to do with myself I fell back on a few things I used to play around with, beginning all the way back in my first classes in the general science laboratory. I guess you could say that I became a jack-legged gadgeteer who became good enough tinkering around with photography, radio and sound system repair to keep enough coming in for room and board and decent changes of clothes. And I've also shipped out with the merchant marine from time to time.

Meanwhile, he said after nodding to somebody waving to him from across the street, I've also been doing a little journalism, mostly freelance, that doesn't add up to enough to live on, but as of now I'm managing by hook or crook to bring in enough to allow me to spend more and more time playing around with notes and sketches I'm lugging around in this thing.

And as I looked at it again I decided that it was the same type of expensive attaché case that was used by globe-trotting diplomats and that it made him seem even farther ahead of me as an advanced Manhattanite than he had been as an upperclassman back on the campus down in central Alabama.

Then it seemed to me that when he said what he said next, it was as if he had decided to change the subject because what had suddenly come back to mind was a matter that he had been concerned with time and again and that was no less personal than it was intellectual. People, man, he said. They don't really see you. There you are, right there in front of them, or beside them and you think they're looking at you and they don't see you, close up, full view, multiple takes.

I was not sure that I knew what his point was, so all I said was, And they don't always hear you either, man. Then I said, Sometimes they do at least recognize you by name on sight. But let them repeat something you're supposed to have told them about something and you just might not recognize anything that you ever told anybody about anything at any time in your whole life.

I let it go at that because I decided that he was really only musing about some note he had made or was planning to make on one of the scratch pads that I assumed he always carried either in his jacket pocket or along with the other papers in his briefcase. I remember thinking that maybe it was somewhat like people translating what they think they are hearing when they listen to a foreign language. Their vocabulary reveals the limitations of their conception of things. (*Which suddenly reminded me of old Joe States looking at somebody out on the dance*

*floor and whispering, Man, don't tell that cat he ain't swinging,
He really feels like he's swinging his old butt off, and he can't
even stay in time with most of them other folks out there. It's all
in his own head, man, he said. And then when he said, You got a
textbook word for that kind of psychological jive, Schoolboy, and I
said, I don't know, maybe solipsism, he said, No better for him.*)

We were standing at the northwest corner of Fifth Avenue
and Forty-seventh Street. And when I stuck out my hand before heading for the bookstore, and he said, So what about
yourself?, I assumed he was asking more out of the good manners of his down-home upbringing than out of any genuinely
personal curiosity. So all I said was that I was checked into
graduate classes in the humanities at New York University after
two plus years of knocking around to accumulate a little graduate scholarship supplement, among other things.

At that time I didn't mention anything at all about the time I
had spent with the Bossman Himself. It crossed my mind, but
I decided against saying anything about it, not only because I
didn't remember him as having any special interest in that kind
of music back on the campus, but also because there was no
reason to expect him to have any special curiosity about any
particular details of my background. When I had mentioned
that I was from the outskirts of Mobile, for instance, he didn't
say anything about the marching bands of the Mardi Gras parades or about jook joint piano players or about itinerant guitar players. Which didn't surprise me because when I thought
about him and music I really thought of conservatory musicians who tended to regard road band and nightspot musicians
as being inadequately trained entertainers.

As he turned to continue his way on up along Fifth Avenue, he said, Well, welcome to the city of the fables and the
fleshpots, man. Then he said, Maybe we can get together and
swap some lies long and short about the old country. I'm in
the phone book.

And when I said I just might take you up on that, he said,
Some down-home lies in and out of school, foul mouth or
fancy tongue, about all this stuff. And I said, I'm for it, man.

On my way on along Forty-seventh Street, I suddenly realized what I could have said about my roommate whom Taft Edison probably would have remembered from the band cottage

during my freshman year, because from time to time my room-mate would rejoin the French horn section of the marching band because it was being expanded for some special upcoming event, such as a trip up to Chicago for the halftime show during the annual football game with Wilberforce at Soldier Field.

Which, however, was only partly the reason I arrived at 41 West 47th Street thinking of the one and only self-styled Jeronimo as in Geronimo and also Hieronymus as in Bosch whose real name was T. (for Thomas) Jerome Jefferson, also known on campus as The Snake, as in snake doctor and snake oil sales-man, because a tent show magician claiming a diabolical con-tract is what Herr Dr. Faustus came across as in a bull session in which I referred to him as the best of all possible roommates that first September. Of course, "best of all possible" was a phrase I got from him, who got it from Voltaire's "best of all possible worlds" in *Candide* and by which he assumed Voltaire meant things good and bad as they actually are because such is life in our time, but by which I meant and still mean that you couldn't have dreamed of having a better roommate if you had gone to Harvard, Yale, Princeton, Cambridge, or Oxford.

The brief encounter with Taft Edison was reason enough for my train of thought, but even so who else if not my old room-mate back in Atelier 359 would pop into mind as you stepped down from the sidewalk and into the entrance of Gotham Book Mart? Not even Miss Lexine Metcalf, who in this in-stance would come after Mr. Carlton Poindexter.

V

ONE LATE morning about a week after I overtook Taft Edison on the way up Fifth Avenue that afternoon, I looked up from my usual place in the south reading room in the library and saw him standing at the checkpoint on his way in. I stood up and raised my hand and he nodded and headed toward me, and when we met in the center aisle he said he had stopped in to double-check a few details in the Americana section, which was at the south end of the reading room in those days, and also to invite me out for a midday snack and chat if I could spare the time. And I said I could and ended up spending most of the afternoon with him.

That was when I found out that when we had parted at the corner of Forty-seventh Street the other time he had continued on up Fifth Avenue only as far as Forty-ninth Street. Because at that time that was where he did what he did from 9:00 A.M. to 6:00 P.M. every week Mondays through Fridays; because what he was using as his writing studio at that time was a book-lined back room of an exclusive jeweler's showroom on the eighth floor of the Swiss Building on the southwest corner of Forty-ninth Street.

I said, Hey, man, I said, Hey, *goddamn*, man! I said, This is some little cubbyhole you've got yourself up here, man. And he said, Man if I ever get enough of this stuff ready to start publishing it nobody's ever going to want to believe that I was up here cooking it up in a place like this. If they don't try to put me in the nuthouse.

And that was when he also said what he said about trying some of it out on me before long. Me being not only a down-home boy but also a graduate student in liberal arts by way of becoming a literary type myself.

And I said, Let me know and I'll find the time, and he said, Maybe during some weekend, and I said, Just let me know.

As I stood looking down through the window onto the low roof of the southeast corner building of Rockefeller Center, I saw that we were diagonally across Fifth Avenue and Forty-ninth Street from Saks and in the next block north was St. Patrick's Cathedral and as far as you could see in that direction in the hazy midafternoon light there were more yellow cabs than any other vehicles weaving in and out of the traffic southward from Fifty-ninth Street, and there was also a steady flow of city Transit Authority buses pulling over to the curb every several blocks.

He said, Man, I come down here on schedule every morning just like everybody else working in this part of town. I check in here just like punching the clock, he said. And I said that I had been surprised to find that he had given up the trumpet and music composition but was not at all surprised that he was working on a book, because I had kept coming across his name on the checkout slip in so many of the books I borrowed from the library, not only while he was there during my freshman year but also during the rest of the time I was in college.

That was when I said what I said about the morning my roommate and I had circled over to the library on our way to our early English class period and found him already there sitting on the steps with his trumpet case between his legs and with an open book on his knees. And when I said I remember the book and it was *The Autobiography of Benvenuto Cellini*, he said he remembered the book but not the encounter. And I said it was not a verbal encounter. I said I just happen to be the kind of freshman who was very curious about what kind of reading other than textbooks and reference assignments up-perclassmen were doing. And so was my roommate, I said, and he knew who you were by name because he had already started going over to the band cottage to practice with the French horn section because he wanted to make the free trip home with the band when it went along with the football team for the annual game against Wilberforce in Chicago. I knew that you were waiting on steps for the doors to open because I knew you worked in the library, I said. Because I had seen you working at the main circulation desk.

That's all I said about that at that time and that was when he told me what he told me about how he had come to have use of the Fifth Avenue workshop we were in. It was not really his, he said. It had been leased from the jewelry company by one of his very well-to-do friends, a writer who spent long periods away in Europe doing research for scholarly and criti-cal books and articles on French, Italian, and German writers and artists.

It turned out to be just what I needed to make me buckle down and really try to find out what I could do with some of this stuff I've been playing around with from time to time, he said. And then he said, Man, if I can get enough of this stuff to come off the way I think it should I just might be able to cause a few people to reconsider a few things they take too much for granted. It's not just a matter of saying this is my way of coming to terms with this stuff, it's more like saying Hey, this is another way that might be even better or at least a pretty good alternative. It really is a matter of trying to test the validity of one's own sense of things.

And, of course, you know I know that there are going to be some people out there who are going to think I'm out of my mind. Or wonder if I *have* a mind. But what the hell, man, that's a chance I'm willing to take. After all, trying to do what I'm trying to do with this stuff is exactly what I put the horn aside for. I didn't give up on that horn, man, he said. Hell, I can still make a living with it, but I'd rather be trying to do what I'm trying to do with this stuff, some of which I must admit sometimes sounds pretty wild, even to me. *But I'm afraid it really does represent my sense of what life in these United States is like.*

Then, while I was looking at titles on the bookshelves and thinking of what I was going to say about some of the books of contemporary poetry and fiction I knew he had read in college, he stepped back out into the showroom and said something to somebody there, and when he came back and said what he said about what I had told him in the snack bar about the courses I was taking, that was when he also said, Man, I sure hope your class work is not going to keep you so tied down that you won't have enough free time for us to get together from time to time when I get this stuff up to the point where I'm going to need to start running it by somebody.

Somebody not only from down the way but also somebody who spent even more time in that neck of the woods than I did. And you might just be the one I suddenly realized that I should have been looking for. Somebody from down the way who's also interested in what books are really about. Man, most of the grad students I run into up here seem to think of poetry and fiction mainly as raw material for research projects that will enhance their academic status.

I said, I know what you mean, I really do. I said, Man, I think that was the first big thing I realized when I got to college. Some courses were about grade-point averages, but some were about the nature of things, and I don't mean just geology, physics, and chemistry classes. All of that was obvious. I mean the way some of the liberal arts courses were taught. Man, I used to go to the library to work out academic assignments, but what I really did was get the class work out of the way so I would have more time free to get on with trying to find out what literary books were really all about, *without being concerned about answering test questions about them.*

Then I said, Hey, speaking about research and homework assignments, as things down in Washington Square are going now, I'm pretty sure I can find time to listen to whatever you decide you'd like to run by me from time to time some weekends. Just let me know ahead of time. Not that I can promise any editorial expertise, but that's not what you're looking for at this point, is it? Anyway, you're on.

And he said, The main thing is that you're not only somebody from down the way and was actually in that place part of the time I was there and even saw me there and actually knew about some of the books I was reading on my own along with all that music theory and all those required practice sessions, it's not just that. Man, what I'm hoping is that just the experience of hearing myself reading some of this crazy stuff I'm playing around with to somebody like you, just might be all I need to keep me going in the outrageous direction I'm going.

And that was when I also told him about how my roommate and I had started reading books on the reading list for the special elective course on the novel for upperclassmen because it was being taught by Carlton Poindexter, who also taught our section of freshman English. Then I said, As things turned out neither of us actually took that class in the novel because my roommate transferred to the Yale School of Architecture after his sophomore year and the course was not available during my junior year, because Mr. Poindexter was away in graduate school on a special fellowship grant, because he was going to be the new librarian.

And anyway, man, by that time the main thing for me was that other reading list that my old roommate and I had tacked on the wall of Atelier 359 by the end of our freshman year. And there was also all of those follow-up references in those wide-ranging anthologies and follow-up stuff to articles in current magazines.

And then I also said what I said about spending all three of my college summers on the campus working as a hospital kitchen helper the first summer, as a power plant engineer's unskilled assistant the second summer, and in the stacks of the library itself during the summer before my senior year.

And he said, You, too? Because it turned out that he had also spent the two summers of his three college years working

Which gave him a reputation that did him no harm whatsoever when he went cruising among the upperclass coeds during social events, I said, and when the elevator door opened, Taft Edison had said what he said about hearing talk in the band cottage about a freshman known as the Snake because he had a very special recipe for chem lab cocktails that some of the musicians in both student dance bands liked to sneak into the parties they played for on campus back in those Prohibition era days.

And before the door closed I said, Hey, but as for old high butt Thomas Wolfe, man, I don't remember all that time I spent and still spend in the library as any goddamn hunger to devour the whole goddamn earth at all. I can go along with the part about being somebody who reads whole libraries or at any rate whole collections as other people read books. Because, man, I don't think I ever thought of reading as acquisition as such, but rather as preparation. *Preparation for unknown, I thought, as the bus headed down Fifth Avenue toward Forty-second Street. Preparation by reducing the unknown. Be prepared. The Boy Scouts of America had already said that.*

VI

As THE fall term moved on into November of that first school year in New York, I began to feel that I had the preparation of all of my seminar discussion assignments and research reports well enough ahead of schedule so I could spend more and more time doing nonacademic things that made you feel that you were at last beginning to become another inhabitant of Manhattan at large as well as a student at the Washington Square campus.

Not that Manhattan or anywhere else could ever become another benchmark in the same sense as Gasoline Point on the outskirts of Mobile, Alabama, on the bay of the Gulf Coast had always been and indeed in the very nature of things, would also always be. As not even the campus in central Alabama for all its archival treasures could also be, being, after all, only a four-year stopover en route to other perhaps temporary destinations as yet as undecided upon as Hollywood had turned out to be (although

California, which was that many miles and travel days and nights west from Mobile by way of the L & N to the Southern Pacific from New Orleans and left on the wall map in Miss Lexine Metcalf's third-grade classroom, had once been a boy blue future point of arrival and at least somewhat like Philamayork itself).

Because as benchmark, Gasoline Point, Alabama, would always be that original of all fixed geographical spots (and temporal locations as well) from which (properly instructed as to its functional and thus tentative absoluteness) you measure distances, determine directions, and define destinations, all of which are never any less metaphorical than actual. And, of course, there is also the irradicable matter of the benchmarks of your original perception and conception of horizons and hence aspirations in terms of which everything else makes whatever sense it makes.

The also and also of all of which is, incidentally, why it is also in the very nature of things that even as you finally began to realize that you are beginning to feel about Manhattan as you had imagined you would as you began looking forward to your next return there back during your first year on the road with the band, you also realize that it would nevertheless remain the metaphorical Philamayork of the blue steel, rawhide, and patent-leather preschoolboy fireside aspirations you would always remember whenever you remembered the thin blue horizon skies fading away north by east beyond Chickasabogue Creek Bridge as you saw them from the chinaberry tree, south of which beyond the river and the bay and the old Spanish Main of buccaneer bayou times were the seven seas.

(Along with all of that, to be sure, there was also always that ever so indelible twelve-bar matter of old sporty limp-walking Luzana Cholly picking and plucking and knuckle knocking and strumming and drumming on his ultradeluxe twelve-string guitar singsongsaying, Anywhere I hang my hat, anywhere I prop my feet.)

Which is also why what it all really came down to was a matter of settling in for the time being whether for the duration of the courses at the university or for the duration plus whenever, whatever, wherever. In either case, beyond the immediately functional details of basic household and neighborhood routines that incidentally were no less directly geared to the academic schedule than was campus dormitory life, there was a snack before rambling on through part of the birdwatchers' sanctuary before continuing on north beyond the Great Lawn and the Metropolitan Museum of Art area to the reservoir, beyond which by late afternoon we had also come on between East and North Meadows to Harlem Mews, and finally there was 110th Street, which was also Cathedral Parkway in those days.

We came back downtown along Fifth Avenue on one of the open double-decker buses that used to be so much fun for New Yorkers and tourists back then. So on our left were the mansions and ultradeluxe apartment buildings facing out onto and over the east side of the park, and from time to time you could also see through open spaces all the way across the malls and meadows to the towers along and beyond Central Park West.

Then as you rolled on down below Seventy-second Street, there was the Central Park South skyline in the offing, and when you pulled on into the vicinity of the Hotel Pierre, Sherry Netherland, and the Plaza with Fifty-seventh Street and the great midtown Fifth Avenue shopping district coming up you were suddenly aware once more of being in the most cosmopolitan area in the entire Western Hemisphere. *New York, New York, I whispered, thinking, Philamayork indeed: to all intents and purposes the lodestone center of the twentieth-century universe and perhaps beyond. Philamayork, ultima Thule, capital of the world!*

As we crossed Fifty-seventh Street and came on beyond Tiffany's nudging each other and nodding at the glittering stretches of cosmopolitan shop windows, I was thinking what I was thinking about how this part of midtown Manhattan always made you feel and about how when you were in some neighborhoods, sections, and districts you forgot all about the fact that Manhattan was actually an island, even when you were overlooking the Hudson or the East River or even the Battery. And, of course, it was almost always as if the tunnels and bridges had nothing to do with going onto or going away from an island.

But as the bus moved on along in the canyonlike flow of the Fifth Avenue traffic toward Forty-second Street and the Empire State Building at Thirty-fourth Street, everything you saw,

including the ever so obvious variety of people of different na-
tionalities, most of whom seemed to be going about their daily
routine activities, reminded you of how directly this part of
Manhattan was related not only to Wall Street, the banks, and
rail and air terminals and not only to all of the neighborhoods
in all the boroughs, but also to the world at large.

*Capital of the world I thought again, remembering Ernest
Hemingway's short story about what happened to a young Spanish country boy's fantasies in a Madrid that was never the capital
of the world as Rome had been and Paris and London became.
Then there were also Balzac's young men from the provinces in
Paris of the nineteenth century. Philamayork, Philamayork, remembering how the old L & N Railroad porters used to call out
stations and say here it is, been long hear tell of it, and now here
it is. Take everything you brought with you, you'll need it!*

After Thirty-fourth Street there was mostly the sound of the
lower midtown Manhattan traffic of that late part of the day,
and as we snuggled closer and I kissed her cheek ever so softly
as she nodded off, the old sweet heartthrob pop song lyric that
I suddenly found myself trying to remember after all those
years stretching all the way back to how I was already beginning to feel about pretty girls and crepe myrtle blossoms even
before Charlene Wingate told me what she told me that spring
now long since once a upon a time was *if you go north or south
if you go east or west*. Because the refrain was *then I'll be happy*,
which was the title, and the first words of the chorus were *then
I'll be happy*. There may or may not have been a verse, but the
only thing that ever mattered to me was the chorus. *I want to
go where you go, do what you do, then I'll be happy, sigh when you
sigh, cry when you cry . . .*

The next big cross street coming up was Twenty-third, which
was still that many blocks away so what you would see first
in the distance would be the triangular Flatiron Building in
the point where Fifth Avenue crossed over to the west side of
Broadway, which came in diagonally from Herald Square and
continued on down beyond Union Square and on through
Greenwich Village and across Houston Street and Canal Street
on its way to City Hall, Wall Street, and the South Ferry.

After Twenty-third Street, Fifth Avenue would continue
on across Fourteenth Street and end at the Washington Arch

entrance to Washington Square and the New York University campus area. But the bus turned east on Eighth Street, so we got off and came west to Sixth Avenue and then down to Fourth and headed toward Sheridan Square and home that way.

It was not until we came back from our bus excursion to see the fall foliage up along the Hudson River countryside that following Saturday that we finally got around to tasting the roasted chestnuts from one of the sidewalk vendors between Eighth and Waverly on Sixth Avenue. And I said, OK, but I'll take chinquapins over these and she said, Me, too, and when we got home and looked up chinquapin in the dictionary and found out that the shrub we remembered from Alabama chinquapin thickets as we remembered huckleberry bushes from Alabama huckleberry thickets was actually a species of chestnut, and I said, bush nut rather than tree nut. And that's also when I said that the only taste of chestnuts I could remember was in a sauce for venison that I had at a big spread for the band one night in Beverly Hills.

I said, Me and you. I said, Me and you this many miles north by east from the chinquapin thickets off the blue poplar trail to Mobile County Training School, and she said, And the huckleberry thickets in the part of Alabama I come from. And I said, And the pecan orchards as you come out of Montgomery heading east on Route 80. And then there was the old crepe myrtle blossom pop tune again, but I didn't whistle it and I didn't hum it, but I did cross my fingers as I kissed her again.

VII

THE NEXT time Taft Edison and I got together again was when he came back by the library one late morning about two weeks following that afternoon in his workshop, and that was when he said what he said about getting together from time to time beginning even before he was ready to start reading parts of his manuscript to me. Just to keep in touch, he said. Because he had decided that being two book-loving down-home boys he and I had a lot to talk about, especially about the literary possibilities of the down-home idiom. Something beyond the same old overworked sociopolitical clichés about race and in-justice that had long since become so usual that they were also the expected and tolerated and indulged. Neither one of us said anything at all about the down-home music of the blues and jazz at that time, but when I got around to saying what I said about it sometime later on, he said I was on to something basic and that I should consider some sort of graduate school paper on it just for a start. No telling what else would turn up, he said. Just remember the old Hemingway principle and stick to what it has really meant to you over the years and not what somebody else thinks it should have meant. Hell, they were not there, you were.

I said I was all for his suggestion about getting together. And then I also said that I would also be ready for my noon break in about thirty minutes, and he said in that case he would wait in the periodicals room, which was downstairs on the first floor, if I had time to have a snack with him. And I said I would and when I came downstairs he was just putting a magazine back on the rack. And we came outside and east along Forty-second Street to Vanderbilt Avenue and the Oyster Bar down-stairs in Grand Central Station and ordered New England clam chowder, and what we talked about that time was what we both remembered about some of the students and members of the staff and faculty on the campus down in central Alabama. He began by asking about some of the old campus slickers who used to hang out in and around the main entrance to the very same upperclassmen's dormitory to which my roommate and I were assigned, in a somewhat atticlike fire-escape room on the third floor as freshmen and where I remained for all four years, two by myself after my roommate left for Yale.

Old Daddy Shakehouse, he began by saying. And I said, the Lord High Chancellor of the Outlying Regions of the after-hours juke joints. And he said, Did that old bear chaser finish whatever it was he was supposed to be taking down there in the trades school area? Hell, he must have already been down there on that campus at least three or four years before I got there. Man, he was a notorious campus operator of long stand-ing when I was trying to get used to being a freshman. And I said, He was there on one of the work-your-way programs and he finally did get his certificate in industrial arts at the same time that I got my degree in a course of study that amounted to liberal arts. And that he then got a job in the maintenance department and was probably still there. We were both aware that we were talking about a place with a standard of living that was much higher than what most of the student population was used to in those days and perhaps most would settle for as graduates, as most faculty and staff members obviously had.

Old Daddy Shakehouse, he said chuckling to himself as he ate several more spoonfuls of the Oyster Bar New England clam chowder that he had not only recommended over the Manhattan recipe but also as being unsurpassed by any other around town, including Gage and Tollner's over on Fulton Street over in Brooklyn. Old Daddy Shakehouse, he said again.

Then he said, What about old Jay Gould, old Jay Gould Weddington? Man, you had to know who old Jay Gould Weddington was. Everybody who was down there when I was there knew about him. And I said, old Jay Gould, old Jay P., John D. Weddington, the wolf of Wall Street. Business school. Man, when I graduated he was still running them floating card games and crap shoots, and was still the number one campus loan shark and pawnbroker. I think he must have hit that campus about the same number of years ahead of me as you did, but he was another one of those special work-plan students on a part-time academic schedule because his background in clerical work was such that he already could take care of several kinds of office jobs well enough so that sometimes he worked full-time during the day and took classes during the early-evening sessions and at other times he took a full class load during the day and did part-time office hours at the end of the day or for a few hours at night.

I didn't really know him, I said, but during my junior and senior years he did hire me to help him tidy up a term report and also to look up something in the library for him from time to time. And, of course, with him it was always cash on delivery. But as for borrowing money from him, man, not me. Man, that was for the ones who were getting those monthly or quarterly checks or money orders from home. Which old Jay was promptly collecting on because he had somebody in the campus post office keeping tabs on when each one of his debtors' letters from home arrived.

Which was when Taft Edison said, Well, I knew him well enough to bet that he wasn't going to finish all of his courses and end his student status until he had accumulated enough capital to go directly from college into business on his own. Because I did know that he already had enough money to take a regular four-year course of study and that he wasn't dependent upon any support from whatever family he had. Anyway, I wouldn't be surprised to find out that he's running his own business by now or even his own bank of some kind. Or that he actually is up here with something going on for him down on Wall Street.

And when I said, Where the hell was he from?, he said, Florida, boy, and then he said, Somebody else that everybody probably remembers from those old bull sessions is old Freeman Clark. And then I said, Better known as the ghost of Marcus Garvey. And old Marcus Garvey himself wasn't even dead yet, he said. And I said, Which is to say ghost as in Holy Ghost, man. Then I said, Zebra jockeys, man, zebra jockeys. I said, Man, Mr. B. Franklin Fisher had inoculated me and most of my classmates against all of that old zebra jockey hocky jive by the time we reached the ninth grade at Mobile County Training School.

That was when Taft Edison said what he said about not having much time to spend on the stem and in the stem lounge, what with working in the library and living in the band cottage, and with all the hours he was required to spend down in those old rehearsal cubicles in the basement of Harrison Hall plus the sheet music copy work and also the endless reading time involved in preparing for Mr. Carlton Poindexter's junior-year course in the novel.

But I did have one part-time buddy that I used to run with every now and then, he said. Old sleepy-eyed Sid Palmer. You must have known him. We were the same year but he was in the School of Education, majoring in science with a minor in math. He used to make it down to old Jay Gould's floating concerns pretty regularly. But when he'd get the urge to hit a few spots in the outlying regions he always checked to see if I could go along, and whenever I could I would, beginning back during that first summer that I spent down there. Man, I stuck pretty close to prescribed campus routine during my freshman year. So by that next summer I was beginning to figure that I knew enough about who was who and what was what and where on campus to do a little extracurricular exploration and by that time I also knew enough about old Sid Palmer to take him up on his invitation to come along on a few rounds in the outlying districts.

He went on eating his clam chowder, smiling to himself as he remembered his days on the campus again. And then he said, Old Sid Palmer, down there from Richmond, Virginia. Man, being a loner that I guess I've always tended to be, old Sid was about the nearest I ever came to having a running mate down there, not that the two of us actually had any common career objectives. He didn't seem to have any trouble getting passing grades in those School of Education courses he was taking, but my guess is that he was really interested in becoming some kind of school administrator, not a classroom teacher. Anyway, the only books he read were the ones required by his assignments, mostly chapter by chapter as assigned. But come to think of it, he was pretty keen on the statistics of tests and measurements, which he was taking during our junior year.

He shook his head still remembering, and then smiling he said, We did have fun hitting those joints together though, but that was about it. We liked the same joints, but we never really talked very much about barrelhouse, honky-tonk, and gutbucket music as such, except to mention the local guys that we liked or didn't really think very much of. Anyway, when I think about old Sid and all of that now, I give us both credit for realizing that it was something that we should stay in touch with in spite of the fact that most of our teachers seem to regard it as something beneath the taste of the kind of respectable people college-educated people were supposed to be.

I said I knew what he meant because I had gone to college not only from the Mobile County Training School of Miss Lexine Metcalf and Mr. B. Franklin Fisher, but also from the Gasoline Point of old Luzana Cholly and Stagolee Dupas fils and old Claiborne Williams of Joe Lockett's-in-the-Bottoms. And that is also when I went on to say what I said about the one and only Mrs. Abbie Langford, the legendary housemother of the upperclassmen's dormitories on the upper end of the campus who was actually employed as the supervisor of housekeeping and maintenance by the Buildings and Grounds Department but acted as if her authority came from the Dean of Men's Office and the Disciplinary Committee.

Man, I said, not that I have any plans to be heading back down in that direction anytime soon, but boy, just wait till I tell her that old Taft Woodrow Edison is up here in New York City and is still as quietly studious and as dapper as ever, but is carrying a Madison Avenue briefcase instead of a trumpet case.

And when he said, Man, how is that old battle-ax, I said, Still there as far as I know, still exactly the same, and still outraged at the slightest mention of your name.

Oh, boy, he said, shaking his head, and we both laughed and he said, Man, she had me all figured out and sized up on her own and she wouldn't let me tell her anything.

Everybody down there at that time knew the story about Taft Edison and Mrs. Abbie Langford. When he arrived on campus for his freshman year he was not only ten days early, but all he had with him was a state scholarship voucher and one extra shirt and a change of underwear and his toilet articles all folded up inside a twill topcoat, which he rolled so that he could carry it slung over his shoulder with a belt like a knapsack.

He had hoboed and hitchhiked all the way from Oklahoma City and had arrived so far ahead of time that he decided to look for a temporary job to pay for interim room and board until official check-in and registration day. And when the grand old gal heard this story from somebody she not only hired him for the time being, but she also started talking about how if he passed the promptness and precision work test on his temporary tasks as the indigent young Booker T. Washington had done so well to enter Hampton she might sponsor him; and for the next week and a half he had bunked in a basement room and helped the janitors and listened to her praise him for being another young Booker T. letting down his bucket and getting ready to be the next one to keep one foot on the trail between the farmland and shop or factory while he stretched the other all the way to tea in the White House and board meetings on Wall Street.

But behold! Outrage! Scandal! Flimflam!!!

His trunk arrived and it turned out that he not only had a trumpet that was more expensive than any brass instrument owned by anybody else on the campus, music school instructors included; but he also had a wardrobe that was as up-to-date as anything in the September issue of *Esquire*, the number one men's fashion magazine of the day. The twill topcoat that he had used as a knapsack and bedroll turned out to be the latest thing in what my roommate (who also had one) and I called cloak-and-dagger trench coats.

She was so outraged that she threatened to have him kicked off the campus as an impostor who had come not because he was seeking higher learning and the uplift of his people, but to take advantage of inexperienced younger students and well-meaning but unsuspecting staff and faculty members. She didn't follow through with her threat when he explained that he was there all on his own and with no family support whatsoever and that he had spent a whole year between finishing high school and his arrival on campus working in a haberdashery shop earning enough money to supplement his scholarship grant and also outfit himself (at employees' discount rate) in the attire of a self-respecting collegian.

Man, he said, I wasn't about to let anybody treat me like a charity case because I had to have a job to supplement my scholarship grant. Not that I had anything against that Booker T. Washington and Horatio Alger true uplift grit that they were forever evangelizing as the salvation of the masses, but it was just not for me. My mother had to help me to get that far and when I finished high school I was on my own because she had my younger brother to take care of and she said she was very confident that I could not only look out for myself from then on but would also find a way to make myself somebody special.

And that was also when he said what he said about finding his own way, which reminded me of what Miss Lexine Metcalf would say to me about how I was one who would have to go wherever I would go and do whatever I would do in order to find out for myself whatever I should try to make of myself. Miss Lexine Metcalf, who also said, Who if not you? and then always also called me her splendid young man. Who if not you?, my splendid young man. Which is also what Miss Tee, who almost always spoke as if for Mama herself, implied when she called me her mister. My mister. Here comes my mister. *Hello, my mister.* Because what Mama had always said from as early on as I ever remembered was, *Mamma's little scootabout man, that's what him is.*

But I didn't say anything about that at that time. I said what I said about Miss Abbie Langford. I said, Man, you know how some of these old house mothers are about some students that they always remember for one reason or another. Man, ten, fifteen, twenty, thirty years later, when certain ones come back for class reunion, old Abbie Langford is right there expecting them to come by to see her and be reminded of something she reprimanded them for doing however many years ago.

And before he said what he was going to say I said, Hey, but reunion or no reunion, man, you are still one of the ones she remembered every time she heard somebody mention your name while I was down there: *You all talking about Taft Edison? That old Taft Woodrow Edison could blow that horn like John Philip Sousa himself when he wanted to and he also could have become another R. Nathaniel Dett. So they used to say over in that music school. But with all them quiet manners and bow ties, and special tailor-made clothes, he was still tangled up with all that old low-life music, too, him and that old Nighthawk Palmer.*

As we came on outside again and headed back along Forty-second Street he shook his head chuckling and said, Well, the next time you're down that way and see that old battle-ax you can tell her you saw old Taft Edison up in New York City still messing around some more of that old back-alley stuff that she didn't report me and old Sid Palmer for. And tell her I'm not blowing any trumpet like John Philip Sousa or anybody else. Tell her I'm playing my riffs on a typewriter these days.

When we came to the corner of Fifth Avenue, he said what he said about being almost ready to start reading sequences of his manuscript to me, and then just before he turned to head back up to Forty-ninth Street he reached into his right hip pocket and pulled out a set of brass knuckles and said, That old battle-ax never suspected that I was packing these, but man, you never know when you might have to take emergency action on some incoherent fool.

VIII

IT WAS not until the night that I went up to his apartment at 749 St. Nicholas Avenue that I found out that Taft Edison was a longtime friend of Roland Beasley, the painter I had met in Paris before coming back to Alabama after the time I spent on the Côte d'Azur with Jewel Templeton.

I had come uptown that evening because Taft Edison was finally ready for me to listen to him read a few scenes and sequences from the manuscript of the novel I knew he had been working on for some time but that he had not yet discussed in terms of any overall narrative context. So I was looking forward to finding out what the basic story line was. My guess was that the scene of at least some of the action would be a college campus based on the one where I first saw him when I was a freshman and he was a junior. The only hint, however, was what he had said that first afternoon as we came along Fifth Avenue up to Forty-seventh Street, and I said what I said about his briefcase not being the trumpet case that he had in college.

When he called that morning and asked when I would have time to come by and listen to a few passages that he was thinking about selecting to fulfill requests for magazine publication, I got the impression that what he wanted first of all was my response to a narrator's voice on a page, his angle of observation and context of recollection. Then he would want my immediate opinion of the literary quality and orientation that the verbal texture suggested.

But when he opened the door for me to step down into the vestibule of his studio apartment, the first objects I noticed on the wall before following him through the door on the right were two watercolor abstractions mounted on pale blue mats and matching, rimlike maple frames. And when I said they reminded me of the matted tear sheets of abstract paintings with which my roommate had lined the wall from the head to the foot of his bed by the end of the fall term, he said they were the work of a friend of his.

I also said it was my old roommate who told me about what books to check out of the library if I wanted to find out what modern art was about. And when I said, The first book I checked out was *A Primer of Modern Art* by Sheldon Cheney,

Taft Edison said that it had to be the same copy he had checked out when he was a freshman because he worked in the library and there was only one copy of it in the collection.

That was when I said what I said about my roommate growing up going to exhibitions at the Art Institute of Chicago because Chicago was his hometown and also said that he was enrolled in the Department of Architecture, but he had a richer background in the humanities than all the students in the liberal arts courses that we took together. And Taft Edison said that the watercolor abstractions that I saw as I came in were the work of a friend of his who had gone to college to study mathematics but had become the painter whose work impressed him more than any other that he had seen by anybody else in Harlem.

Then when he said who the painter was I said what I said about meeting him in Paris and as I did I also realized that I had not called him since coming to New York and also that I had not told Royal Highness about how I had gone over and introduced myself to Roland Beasley at the Metropole in Paris that afternoon because I overheard him telling his companion about seeing the great Royal Highness onstage back during the heyday of the old Lafayette and Alhambra Theaters.

Old Rolly, Taft Edison said as we came on into the one-room plus bath plus stove and refrigerator nook apartment, and I saw the floor-to-ceiling bookshelves and other paintings, watercolors, drawing, and silk-screen reproductions. The furniture included his convertible couch and a coffee table that could be unfolded to become a six-place dining table.

Look him up, man, Taft Edison said, giving me time to glance around. I'm sure he was right at home over there trying to come to personal terms with all of that heritage of articulate mankind. So you already know that he's not just another one of these uptown provincials who have so few if any connections with the very things we went through what we went through to get up here to get next to. Look him up and go by and see some of his really ambitious pieces. I think he just might be the one to do for American painting what old Louie Armstrong and the Bossman are doing for American music.

And that was also what he went on to say what he said about how local or idiomatic variations sometimes become not only widespread but also nationwide, just as a local joke, saying, tall tale or legend may come to be regarded as everybody's common property. And then he also said, Look, as far as I'm concerned, if it's supposed to be American art and it doesn't have enough of our idiomatic stuff, by which I mean mostly down-home idiom, in there it may be some kind of artistic exercise or enterprise but it ain't really American.

I was ready for him to take my hat and trench coat then and when he hung them in the closet and came back saying what he said about what our old down-home stuff had done for church music not to mention pop tunes and ballroom music, I thought about Eric Threadcraft and the Marquis de Chaumienne but I did not mention them because I did not want to use too much of the time that he may have hoped that I would be able to spend listening and responding to what he had planned to read. Which is also why when he asked me if I wanted to sip something I said, Maybe later.

So, here we go, he said, pointing me to an overstuffed lounge chair as he turned and went over and sat in the swivel chair at his writing desk and began turning the pages of his manuscript, humming quietly to himself until he found the sequence he was looking for. Then he said, Let's see how this comes across without any introduction.

But then as he put on his reading glasses he smiled shaking his head and said, Look, I have just one restriction. I really want to know what you make of all this stuff. So I'm open to cross-examination. Except for one point. Man, don't ask me why I'm trying to do whatever this stuff is about. With a pencil and a typewriter and not with valves and keys.

Stipulated, my good fellow, I said, remembering my old roommate again, Stipulated. Then I said, But I must say this. What I remember about you down there on the campus I am surprised that you seem to have put that horn down altogether, but I'm not at all surprised that you are this serious about writing. After all, I was always more impressed with your interest in literature than with your special status as a scholarship student in the School of Music.

Then I went on to point out that I had always remembered seeing him in the library more often than I could recall seeing

him go to and from the School of Music or the band cottage. I also knew that he was an outstanding enough member of the band to be the student assistant who tuned the
band for the bandmaster and who led the band when they
played for the cheerleaders during football games in Alumni
Bowl. But I didn't mention that I couldn't remember how
he actually sounded on the trumpet. Nor could I remember
whether he was a regular member of either of the two student
dance bands. However, I did remember that he played with
the chapel orchestra.

On the other hand, however, I could also have pointed out
that I had always thought of him as being more involved with
becoming a composer and conductor than with becoming an
instrumental performer as such. Because that was what had
always come to mind when I had remembered seeing him in
the main reading room of the library when he was not on duty
at the circulation desk. Because he would always be sitting at a
table all by himself doing copy work of sheets of music.

When he began reading that night, it was very much as if I
were back down on the campus in central Alabama with my old
roommate again. Because it was during that first autumn term
that he said what he said about tune in the head and voice on
the page. He was not talking to me, he was talking to himself,
and he said it twice. We were sitting across the room at our
individual desks with our backs to each and we were working
on our first assignment in English Composition 101. You could
supply your own title, but the theme was first-person singular.
And the objective was to introduce yourself to your classmates.
So we did not discuss what we were going to write about ourselves, and I did not ask him what he was chuckling to himself
about from time to time.

But when his paper turned out to be the one Mr. Carlton
Poindexter chose to read aloud to the class as the best example
of what the assignment was supposed to do, I was not surprised. And I could still hear my roommate's voice on the page
even as Mr. Carlton Poindexter was reading it in his own voice.
And when I said what I said about it when we were back in the
dormitory that night, my roommate said, Tune in the head,

IX

So HERE she is at last, Royal Highness said, as Eunice and I
stepped out of the elevator and headed toward where he stood
waiting outside the open door to his apartment that evening.
I had told him about us when I had called him on the phone
shortly after we arrived in New York back in September. And I
had also called him from time to time just to keep in touch, but
this was our first trip up to Sugar Hill together.

Yeah, here she is at last. So this is the one that's really the
one, hey, young soldier, he said, putting his left arm around
her shoulder as he slapped right palms with me and said, Miss
Lady. Hey, what you talkin' 'bout, young fellow? Yes, indeed.
But now look here, Miss Lady. They all told me you were
good-looking but ain't none of them said a word about your
being *this* good-looking. And with the class to go with it. Well,
I guess they did mention something about class. But I guess
you had them all tongue-tied.

Then he said, Now see there, that's exactly what I'm talking
about. Just look at that brush-off she just gave me disguised as
a blush. You're something else, Miss Lady. Because, you see, I
know good and well you heard this old jive line before, but this
is the first time you've heard it from the *source*. And that goes
for this, too, he then said, and put both hands on her shoulder
and gave her four mock ceremonial kisses, and still holding her
shoulders at arm's length said, A smack for all four cheeks, Miss
Lady—if you get the implication of my latter clause.

Man, he then said as he hooked arms and guided us into his
living room, you got yourself some fine people here, young
soldier. So you all come on in this house and make yourself at
home. The rest of us will be out in a little while. I told them to
go on and finish what they were doing back there and let me
have you all to myself for a little while.

Then when we helped ourselves at the bar and took our seats
at the end of the couch nearest his favorite overstuffed chair,
he said, You know something, young soldier? I'm still getting
great reports about how you handled yourself out there when
you were on the road with the band.

It just keeps coming up, he said. Time and again. Even the
Silent Partner dropped in a good word about you. Hell, I

forget what the hell we were talking about, but at some point there he was asking me when I had heard from you and saying what he said about how everybody was betting on the school-boy without even knowing or even speculating about any profession or line of work in particular. He just struck everybody in that crew as somebody special, Miss Lady, a young fellow with a very high-class education that didn't put on no airs at all and could pick up on new things like he was born knowing.

Hell, they were not talking about getting along with him as a very young newcomer on his very first professional gig. There wouldn't be any problem with that at all, because the man wouldn't put you in there with all them thugs in the first place if that was going to be a problem. And then in the second place when he picks somebody they all know he already has plans for him because he represents something that he wants to fiddle (hey, dig that) fiddle around with at least for a while and ain't nobody in there ever question the Bossman on anything like that to my knowledge. Not in that band. Hell, in that band they never know what they themselves are going to have to adjust to next.

No, he said, looking at me while still talking to her but signifying at me even so. No, the way we all see this young soldier here is that he's one of the ones that was gifted and lucky enough to go to college. And serious enough to make the most of it. Now he has all kinds of options to pick and choose from.

So you see what you got yourself into, Miss Lady, he said as Stewart Anderson came in from the hallway that led to the dining room and kitchen. Eunice already knew that when Royal Highness had said what he said about the rest of us he was referring to Stewart Anderson, formerly of the old vaudeville comedy team known as Stewmeat and Small Change and his wife, Cherry Lee, née Cherie Bontemps, who were not only his business partners who ran a restaurant for him but also shared and took care of his extensive four-bedroom apartment.

Looka here, looka here, Stewmeat Anderson said, heading straight to Eunice, who stood up to greet him. Yes, indeed, he said. And then he said, I'm Uncle Stew, and I just want to say don't be no stranger up this way, and you don't have to wait for him to bring you back. And as for you, young fellow, what can I tell you? I'm not surprised.

His wife, Cherry Lee, had come in then and poured herself a glass of muscatel and she said what she said about us all being from down home and gave me a peck on the cheek on the way to lock arms with Eunice and take her outside to show her the twilight view of Manhattan from the terrace. It was as if she actually had known that it was something Eunice was expected to be shown because I had written to her about it after my first visit.

As I was saying, Stewmeat Anderson said, I'm not a bit surprised that you turned up with a solid stone fox that is also one more fine and I mean certified fine lady like this one, my man. Not after what everybody was saying about how impressed they were with the way you handled yourself in that department all across the country. But now let me tell you this. Man, every last one of them thugs would bet hard money on anything you decide to have a go at. Like when you decided to stay out in Hollywood for a while, for instance. So far as I know, not a single one of them accused you of being dazzled by all that hyped-up glamour and glitter out there. It was something you wanted to stick around and study for a while and that was that, and here you are to prove that they were right.

And as I said what I said about how in my case you had to learn how to tell the difference between good looks and well-stacked availability (even if coy-seeming) on the one hand and a truly certified stone fox on the other in order to make it out of Mobile County Training School let alone out of Mobile and into college, I was also remembering that nobody in the band knew anything at all about me and Jewel Templeton, not even Joe States. The only one I ever told anything about that was Gaynelle Whitlow.

The band had not swung back to the coast while I was out there on my own, but I wouldn't have ever mentioned Jewel Templeton if it had. Not even to Joe States. If somebody in the band had found out about us, that was another matter. But any mention of it by yourself would raise questions about whether you were taking all the make-believe in stride for what it is. After all, how could you ever forget what happened when you said what you said to Ross Peterkin about what happened with Fay Morgan after the Beverly Hills party following the opening night at the Palladium. I hadn't been taken in and exploited by Fay Morgan and I still think that Joe States knew as much but he still let Ross Peterkin lecture me as if I had allowed myself to be used, as if I were a horny greenhorn just to make sure and also to see if I would take the reprimand in my stride.

Now me myself now, Stewmeat Anderson said as we stood up but finished our drinks before following his wife out into the hall and into the dining room, I lucked out. But now, you see, showbiz was my biz in the first place, so what the audiences paid to come to see as something ever so glamorous, I knew damn well was always also a matter of greasepaint. I'm not going to try to tell you that what I saw across the footlights didn't have much to do with it, because it had a hell of a lot to do with me taking notice of her in the first place. But the girl I married is the one I met and got to know backstage.

The main course that night turned out to be possum with sweet potatoes plus side dishes of mustard greens and stir-fried medallions of okra with bits of steak of lean, which they decided would be a nice little down-home surprise for us after that many months of being primarily concerned with picking and choosing New York food markets as well as snack bars and restaurants, and they were right. And there was also corn bread that was crackling bread. Then, since sweet potatoes came with the gamy taste of the possum, there was pecan pie with dasher turned ice cream instead of sweet potato pie. We went on talking about down-home menus and recipes as we ate, and that was when they told us about the truck merchants who came up to Harlem, some from Virginia and the Carolinas and some from as far down the coast as Florida and could be found parked on certain corners and certain blocks displaying and selling whatever was in season, straight from the gardens, fields, orchards, and woods of their down-home localities.

Which is why I was not surprised when Stewmeat Anderson told us that their larder was also stocked with such other special down-home game meat as rabbit and squirrel and raccoon and even venison. But that was the first time I'd ever heard of down-home folks keeping a supply of frozen catfish fillet on hand for an occasion not unlike this one, when fish, not game, would be the pièce de résistance.

And guess what else besides?, Royal Highness said, when I said that I assumed that venison was no problem to come by in New York. He said, You're right. And then he said, I'm talking about turtle meat, underground turtle meat. Not the sea turtles, that's what they have down in them islands in the Gulf. But now talking about some meat that's kind of special down that way but ain't no problem in New York. There's goat meat. As I remember it, the main time for goat meat where I come from was when there was some kind of barbecue, especially a big holiday picnic barbecue or a church barbecue. But now up here some of these splibs from the islands are very big on goat meat with curry and fresh-grated coconut and stuff. And another thing some of those other island folks up here go for much more than I was ever used to down home is a whole pig pit roasted on a spit.

And those Cubans know what to do with chicken and rice, Stewmeat Anderson said. But speaking of them street-corner truck vendors from down home, when it's the right time of year I also know where to find some that bring up stalks of sugarcane and ever so often they might also bring along a few pecks of scuppernongs. Now that's something that really takes me back, Miss Lady, he said.

And I said, Me, too. I said, Not as far back as you're talking about. But not just back to the outskirts of Mobile as a place as such, either. But still back as long ago as those old unpaved streets with horse droppings along with those automobile tire ruts. Then I said what I said about remembering scuppernongs as yard arbor muscadine grapes and also about remembering fig trees as fruit-bearing yard trees. And about never having seen any orchards of fig trees anywhere in or near Gasoline Point.

Which is also when I said what I said about how during muscadine season we used to roam the woods on the slopes above the L & N Railroad bottom at Three-Mile Creek Swamp and sometimes also the slopes and woodlands above Chickasabogue Swamp and even as far as all the way up the AT & N Railroad to Bay Poplar woods. Which also led to what I said about how muscadine season being tree-climbing time because the muscadine vines I knew about entwined themselves around tree branches much the same as scuppernongs entangled themselves in the latticework of yard arbors.

As for vineyard grapes, in Gasoline Point in those days before the fully stocked supermarket chains replaced the old neighborhood grocery and general merchandise stores, like orchard fruits and other street-vendor produce, they came from elsewhere (which for oranges, grapefruit, and pineapples was as nearby as Florida; and for okra, butterbeans, scallions, lettuce, tomatoes, strawberries, cucumbers, new potatoes, and so on was only as far away as the truck gardens across Mobile Bay).

That brought us to what the two of us remembered about canning, pickling, jam, jelly, and winemaking season in our two sections of Alabama; and that was when Royal Highness said, What did I tell you? and nodded at Stewmeat Anderson, who got up and went through the door to the kitchen area and when he came back he was carrying two quart-size bell jars, one of green tomato chowchow relish and one of peach jam and two pint-sized glasses, one of blackberry jelly and one of pear preserves.

Folks down the way don't never let us run out of these kinds of good old goodies, Royal Highness said as Stewmeat Anderson put the jars and glasses in front of Eunice's place and gave me a playful jab and a mock conspiratorial wink on his way back to the kitchen to help Cherry Lee bring in the pecan pie and dasher turned ice cream that he himself had frozen and packed that afternoon.

Well now, seeing as how y'all already been through Christmas and New Year's up in this part of the country, Royal Highness said as Cherry Lee went back to the kitchen to bring in the coffee to go with the dessert, I'm satisfied that you got everything squared away in the chitlins, hogmaw, and trotters department, including all the trimmings. After all, young soldier, you were in that band long enough to pick and choose chitlin joints and barbecue pits from border to border and coast to coast. So I'm sure that old Joe States personally saw to it that you got checked out on the choice of trimmings in New York.

And when I said, Including a little ceremonial taste of moonshine as well as the big uptown, up north thing of champagne, he said, Hey, what you talking about, young soldier, whatyoutalkingabout?

It was a very fine old-time down-home dinner table gettogether like some of the very special ones for very special out-of-town company that you remember from childhood. And as Royal Highness and Stewmeat Anderson and I headed back to the drawing room to settle down and puff on the extra-special

Cuban cigars that Royal Highness would choose for us from his antique buccaneer humidor while Cherry Lee took Eunice on a tour of the apartment, the topic was the band again. And when Cherry Lee and Eunice rejoined us, I had been brought up-to-date on the band's current tour, and Royal Highness went on to say again what he had said early on about how pleased he was over the fact that I had decided to spend the time I had spent with the band between graduating from college and going on to graduate school.

That's something you'll never regret you decided to do, young soldier, he said. Then as he turned to Eunice he said what he said about having very special high hopes for me not because he thought I had all of the earmarks of a young man on his way to fame and fortune in the usual everyday sense of becoming a widely publicized celebrity with a big income and lots of expensive possessions, but because my earmarks were those of a young man who just might someday be able to fulfill the ambition I finally settled on. Whatever it was, he said. *And that was when he also said what he said about how it was perfectly normal for some people to make up their minds about their line of work way back in early childhood and about how some can remember exactly when, where, and why they did and others can't remember when they had not already done so. And then he said what he said about how it was also perfectly normal for some others, some very special ones, to spend a lot of time still trying to get themselves together and on to some definite course even after their formal schooling was well into the postgraduate level because they were the ones who saw themselves as having so many possibilities to pick and choose among.*

Anyway, he said, as he stroked Eunice's hand, what I'm talking about is what I saw when this one turned up here holding down old Shag Phillips's job like that, *mainly just because he needed a temporary gig for the summer after graduation from college.* When the Bossman brought him up here, the earmarks I saw belonged to a young fellow with as wide a range of eligibility and potential as I've ever come across. And I've covered some territory, Miss Lady.

Which was the very point he came back to at the end of the visit as we stood up to shake hands and head for the door. As he gave her his ceremonial four, one for each cheek, kisses, he said, I hope I didn't say anything to give you any notion that I think you didn't already know what you were letting yourself in for when you hooked up with my young soldier here. I just want to let you know what kind of impression he made on me and the Bossman and all them old thugs in the band, too. So I'll just say this. All of us think that maybe what he's still trying to figure out is how to do something that none of us even know we need him to try to be the one to try to do for us.

Then as we headed for the elevator he said, Now that you've been up here and seen us for yourself, don't be no stranger.

X

TAFT EDISON was the one who made sure that I was alert to the so-called revolutionary political recruitment operating procedures that you were likely to encounter in New York City in those days. But it was through Roland Beasley that I became more sensitive to New York City variations on old confidence games that he pointed out as having been a universal element of city life ever since the first trading and business settlements came into being and the first bargains and markdown sales were offered and special escort and guide services part-time or full-time became available for hire or for free.

Not that Roland Beasley thought that I needed any of the usual fundamental orientation to big-city life as such. After all, when he met me in Paris I was on my own after having been in most of the biggest cities in the United States. And as for my being a down-home boy, the fact that I was also a college boy who had worked with the band that I had worked with in order to go on to graduate school was not likely to be lost on him either, not to mention the fact that not a few of the most notorious big-city slickers in just about every region of the nation were once down-home boys.

I think Taft Edison may have assumed that the time I had spent in the band with Joe States looking after me had pretty much taken care of the big-city initiation part of my postgraduate orientation. But I also think that he may have felt that I probably did not know very much about political recruitment because the band never stayed in any one town long enough for any revolutionary political recruiters to make any effective follow-up on whatever may have been set up by any initial contact. And I also think that Taft Edison may have felt that I was a more attractive possibility to political recruiters because I was a graduate student than I had been when I was a musician who was not a headliner with a lot of worshipful fans. As a graduate student I was a potential revolutionary intellectual technician who could be especially useful in recruiting and/or indoctrinating the so-called masses in preparation for the rebellion that would overthrow the status quo.

But he actually told me what he told me when he told me to be me on immediate alert mainly because of what was happening to him, and which he thought might involve me simply because I was beginning to be in regular contact with him. Yet the way he said it also let you know that he did not expect you to be alarmed. It was as if he took it for granted that you would take it as yet another kind of thistle in the briar patch.

Which in effect was also what Roland Beasley expected of me when he explained what he explained to me about confidence games of the local city slickers as a routine part of my orientation as a newcomer settling down in New York for an extended or maybe permanent residency. But unlike Taft Edison, who was outraged by what struck him as the self-righteous gamesmanship of what he called revolutionary recruiters out to kidnap your mind, Roland Beasley almost always sounded as if he were sharing his curiosity about something rather than warning you about it.

He never sounded as if he thought you needed to be warned. It was always as if what he said about some example of the confidence game as he knew it was something that amused him and also something that you could probably match with some anecdote of your own. And whenever you did, he would say, Hey, old buddy, that's my good buddy. Man, you're as up with this stuff as old Rolo.

Even when he started breaking it all down in terms of variations on basic game patterns, it was still as if he were primarily concerned with your appreciation of his anecdotes, and it all came across as if it were more of a hobby, like cowboy and gangster movies and sea stories, than as a matter of serious concern.

But as is often the case with many people and their hobbies, his insights on procedures were no less precise or comprehensive for not being professional, and one day after we had been going to museums and galleries and bookstores together for several weeks after my first visit to his studio, we stopped in at Gotham Book Mart, and while I was browsing the shelves labeled We Moderns, he bought a book the clerk had been holding for him, and when we came back outside he handed it to me and said, Hey, man, I know you already have a good grip on this jive because you had some basic anthropology in college, so you know this stuff is not just a matter of classic pattern and variation, this stuff probably goes all the way back to primitive rituals of those early days when people first started using words to make deals with. Because I'm pretty damn sure that jiving and conniving are just about as old as language itself. Hell, even older. After all, there was a lot of bullshit gesticulating and face-making before they got around to using words.

And that was when he said, Anyway, this is something you might find very interesting when you can spare the time away from your academic assignments. I think you just might find this kind of journalistic writing amounts to something pretty close to anthropology.

It turned out to be as evocative of certain aspects of American city life during the first forty years of the twentieth century as such old Herbert Asbury books as *Gangs of New York*, *Ye Old Fire Laddies*, *The Barbary Coast*, *The French Quarter*, and *The Gem of the Prairie* (Chicago). But its specific focus was on the dynamics of the swindling racket known as the confidence game or the big con, which it described as being operated by one or more *grifters*, who choose and set up the prospective victim or *mark*, who is led to the *store*, which is operated by the often informally recruited but expertly coordinated *mob*, who set him up for the *kill* by allowing him to make an impressive amount of money by some means the *mark* knows is crooked. This gives *the mark* confidence and sets him up for *the kill*, which is the amount of money *the mark* is willing to risk on a sure but illegal bet or investment. *The grifter* then plays *the mark* against *the store*, which is immediately raided by the other members of *the mob* disguised as law-enforcement officers. This allows *the grifter* to *brush off the mark* by spiriting him away by pretending to be as vulnerable to the arrest as he is. The objective of the confidence game is not simply to take money from *the mark* but also to do so without allowing him to catch on to the fact that he has been taken.

Indeed, the book also makes much of the fact that *the mark* is not supposed to realize that he has been duped and thus lose confidence in himself. The very fact that his confidence remains high is what leaves him vulnerable for other grifters! Much is also made of the fact that many people become ideal marks who are roped, taken, and brushed off time and again because they have come to believe that the high social status they enjoy because of the money they inherited or married into is a result of some inherent special superiority. His unshakable confidence in his own keen business judgment is precisely what leads him to get roped into one con game after another.

I started reading it on the way home, and when we got together about ten days later I had checked back through *Suckers Progress* and *The Gem of the Prairie*, which was one of Joe States's favorite books on the subject. He had given me a copy of it that he had picked up in the Pickwick Bookstore in Hollywood several days after the visit to Ross Peterkin's apartment after I said what I said about the night I spent with Fay Morgan in Bel Air following the first Beverly Hills party I went to with them after the band opened at the Palladium. And the first thing I said was, Hey, man, anthropological is what it adds up to, all right. But come on now, man, this stuff is not only loaded with ritual patterns and variations. It is also just as full of visual patterns and variations. So don't tell me you haven't been noodling and doodling and vamping and riffing at least some sketches for some uptown takes and takeoffs on not only the likes of Daumier, Goya, and Hogarth. But what about Brueghel's *Revelers* and some uptown takeoffs on Hieronymus Bosch's *Garden of Delights*?

I said, Man, ain't no telling what some Beasley riffs could add up to. I said, Man, how about a series or sequence of *From Down-Home to Uptown Sketches, the Natural History of a Hipster*, or, say, *The Shady Side of the Stem* (as in mainstem), or *Slapping Seventh Avenue with the Sole of My Shoe*, or *The*

Rounder, or *The Sidewalk Pounder*? Man, I could go on and on and so could you. Me, I'm just running on and on about something I just thought of.

And he said, Hey, but you're on to something, man. And then he said, Did old Taft tell you that I took classes with George Grosz at the Art Students' League? And I said, *Ecce homo*. And he said, The same. And then said, I was very much into political and social cartoons at that time. But when I went to study with him, he turned out to be the one who really put me on to the fundamentals of serious craftsmanship, and he inspired me to study the world history of art and learn from the great masterpieces.

So like I said, he said, You're on to something, my man. Then he threw a playful left jab and clinched me and on the break he said, So didn't you tell me that old Joe States and the Bossman's wrecking crew called you Schoolboy? Well, that means that they really appreciated what you are really about, and just to show you that I do, too, I'm herewith designating you Chief Literary Consultant. But no kidding, my man, as soon as we got together in Paris, I realized that there were a million things I'd like to talk to you about.

In Paris he had told me that his studio was on 125th Street in Harlem, in the same building as the Apollo Theatre. But when he had answered the phone number that Taft Edison had given me, he said he had moved all the way down to Canal Street near Sixth Avenue, on the way to Chinatown. He had invited me to come down as soon as I could spare the time. But my first and only visit so far had been a very brief pop-in call one afternoon.

Not long after that was the first of the three times that he had stopped by the library to treat me to a snack on the way to the Museum of Modern Art, the Metropolitan Museum, and the galleries on Fifty-seventh Street and along Madison Avenue. This was before the Guggenheim was built, and the Whitney at that time was still down on Eighth Street between MacDougal and Fifth Avenue in Greenwich Village, near where most of the small galleries and studios were located in those days.

On my first trip down to the studio on Canal Street there had been only enough time for me to see the framed paintings, drawings, and sketches of his that were hanging on the walls, along with the framed works of other New York painters who were mostly close personal friends of his. And there were also a few of his framed and unframed and perhaps not quite finished canvases on the floor leaning against the wall, against a chair here and there and the worktable near the easel.

But when I went back the second time, he had brought out a number of framed and unframed but finished pieces from his storage area, and there were also several sketchbooks and folders of drawings and watercolors on the worktable. And when he said what he said about giving me some idea and concrete evidence of what he had been up to and what he was about, I said, It does, man, it does.

And I was impressed but not really surprised because by that time, his responses to what I had gone with him to see in the galleries and museums had given me what turned out to be a very reliable impression of his general aesthetic and intellectual orientation and also what his special individual emphasis was and how it fit into the comprehensive context of the role of art in human consciousness. In fact, at the time of that second visit I had already begun to think of him as someone who just might become my very special visual arts cut-buddy, as Taft Edison was becoming my literary cut-buddy, as my now far-away best of all possible roommates had become during my freshman and sophomore years in college.

Which is why when he said what he said about wanting me to give him my literary response to what he had done, was doing, and would be doing, I said, If you say so, man. Because by that time I also realized that he was as enthusiastic about popping into bookstores and browsing through the literary section with me as I always was about going to exhibitions with him whenever I could spare the time away from my academic assignments.

Man, he said, when I looked at my watch and stood up because it was time to go, I can't tell you how much I'm looking forward to what we are going to be doing about all this stuff. Man, I can't get over it. Man, see now that's that goddamn Paris for you and this goddamn New York. Where the hell else am I going to find just the right kind of down-home cat I didn't even know I was supposed to be looking for?

And that is when I said what I said about being like the
man in the frame shop. And he said, The literary man matting
and framing for the exhibition. That's it, man, that's it. You
already got it. The man in the frame shop is the one who is
most immediately involved with how I want this stuff seen.
The man in the frame shop. Hey, that's pretty good. That's
damn good. Context, man. But I said, Not just in the literary
sense of mythological or historical context. I said, That, too,
but we're also talking about a frame that functions like the
stage proscenium when the curtain opens. It makes the make-
believe believable and at the same time it reminds you that it is
all also a matter of artifice.

You got it, man, he said, you got it. Then he said, Man, that
goddamn Paris. Man, this goddamn New York. This goddamn
United States. We got to get with it, man. What does it all
mean? What are we going to do? He said, Get with it, man.
Me, I'm all about the figure in the fabric, and I think of you as
being about the angle of vision, the relativity and ambiguity of
it all. My man with the four dimensions of space which include
Proust's dimension of time. Plus *metaphor and syncopation*!

XI

TWO NIGHTS before the band came back into town that next
time, Joe States called from Richmond to give me the name
and address of the rehearsal studio they were going to be using
until they moved into the recording studio I remembered from
the last time. He sounded as fine as usual, and when I said so
he said what he always said, and I could see his eyes and his lips
and the tilt of his head and the angle of his neck, and the sound
of his voice made me feel the way it always made me feel.

Me and you, Schoolboy, me and you. Get to me fast. And
this time I'm also speaking for the Bossman, too. I just told
him I was on my way to make this call when I waved to him
over that crowd around him in his dressing room, and he said
for me to tell you that he hoped the two of you could work
out a little one-on-one checkup this time around. Like I keep
telling you, Schoolboy, you got yourself another alma mater,
of which he's the papa.

So there you go, statemate, he said, as if using the cymbals to bring you to the solo microphone. And then as if adding a light roll as segue, he said, And speaking of the Bam, give all of our best to them fine people you went and got yourself all married up with. And tell her we also hope that she can also make it by to give us another little peek. Tell her I know how busy she is with both of you all taking classes, but tell I say all she got to do is just pop by the recording studio for a couple of takes and I guarantee that our permanent acknowledgment will be right there on everything else we do for the rest of the session. But now you, he said then, you get to me fast and I know I don't have to tell you that the Bossman ain't shucking about something like this.

The first rehearsal session was from 2:00 P.M. to 6:00 P.M. that Tuesday. When I came into the studio he was all set up, adjusted and tuned, and so was everybody else. But there was time to make the rounds to each section and greet everybody one by one because the Bossman and Old Pro were still at the copy table deciding on the sequence of what they were going to run through.

Then shortly after I made it back to Joe States, I saw Old Pro begin to gather up the scores, and I moved on over to the copy table and said what I said to the Bossman first, and he waited while Old Pro and I said what we said to each other and I promised to call and find out about his free time.

Then I followed the Bossman on over to the piano, and as Scratchy McFatrick and I were slap-snatching palms again, the Bossman had already started playing around with a series of runs even before he sat down and adjusted his seat to the key-board. Then as I came on over to him he moved over so that I could sit on the seat beside him and went on vamping what he was vamping at the same time that he was saying what he was saying about letting me know when he would be free so that I could meet him somewhere for an update while the band was in town this time.

Not that we need to lose any sleep over the likes of you, he said, still running variations on the notion he had either made up or picked up. Sometimes it might begin as any old sound at all, just something he heard and decided to turn into music, or sometimes it would be a phrase he heard somebody using as a part of a warm-up exercise and when he decided which way he wanted it to go, he would say, Hey, Bloop, or Hey, Jomo, or Hey, Mobe, how about this, and perhaps more often than not whoever he had picked it up from would not recognize it. But from time to time somebody might also say, Yeah, that's a little run I picked up from old so-and-so back when I first started going to rehearsals trying to get in the high school dance band from the marching band. Or sometimes whoever it was would say, I still got the record that was on and I still remember all of it note for note, but that was the part I had to work on the hardest, so every now and then I use it to check up on myself.

Now you, he said, still doodling and noodling; I just don't want you to forget that my best wishes are just the same old conventional down-home ones handed down from generation to generation, beginning as far back as the time of the abolitionists and the Underground Railroad. All that is a part of it, too, as I'm sure you know, but what I want you to keep in mind is that with me it is also personal. Which means that I'm all for touching base in person from time to time, however briefly.

He went on noodling and doodling on the keyboard, pausing from time to time to make another notation on the fresh copy sheets on the top of the piano. The fact that he could say what he wanted to say to me while going on with what he was doodling on the piano (and with his pencil) was something I had become aware of the very first time I went to hear the band in person that night out at the Dolomite. I cut classes to go out there that day to watch and listen to them rehearse some new material for an upcoming recording session when they hit New York a few weeks later. So when I went back out to the dance that they were in town to play that night, I was already in a state of fairyland euphoria.

But not to such a degree that I would miss what happened when the band came back onstage for the second set. Hortense Hightower came up to say something to him from the dance floor, and he had her come on up to the bandstand and sit beside him. And since they were playing a dance and not a concert, he didn't announce the selections, he just vamped the signal for each number, sometimes bringing sections of the whole ensemble in on the first chorus as written or in any case as I remembered it from the recording; but at times he might segue to another chorus, even the out chorus as if it were the first chorus. And if you were out on the dance floor you would be so involved with what the music was stimulating you to do that you probably wouldn't have time to notice very closely what any individual musician's posture and gestures were as he played what you were responding to.

What you had to get out there and do from time to time, because how could you resist that part of being right there with them playing "live and in person"? But at the beginning of the second set that night out at the Dolomite I was as close to the bandstand as you could get, and that was where I was when I saw what I saw and realized that the Bossman could carry on what was obviously a serious, extended conversation while not only leading the band from the keyboard, but also keeping track of what everybody in each section was doing at the same time.

They were playing a number that was one of my favorite recordings, and I was keeping an eye on the trumpet section because I knew that there was a chorus coming up in which I wanted to see how the three horn men looked doing what they were about to do. So I was watching them and I saw old Osceola Menefee making signifying head gestures to Jomo Wilkins and Scully Pittman about how preoccupied the Bossman was with the conversation he had going with Hortense Hightower.

Then when they came to the part I was waiting for, the three of them stood up to hit one sharply percussive note in unison. But when they raised their sparkling silver horns to do so, old Osceola Menefee didn't put his mouthpiece to his lips, and the instant the rim shot–like note went *spat!*, the Bossman's head jerked up and he wagged his finger at Osceola Menefee, who grinned as if to say, Just checking, maestro, just checking, and saluted as the three of them sat back down.

And now, he said as we took the first sip of our wine after giving our waiter our short order that afternoon on which I had been able to make it up to the recording studio at Sixth Avenue and Forty-fourth Street in time to spend his snack break recess with him as I had promised through Milo the Navigator on the phone the night before.

The two-hour break for the rest of the band amounted to about an hour and a half for him. So he had taken me to a cozy little place two and a half blocks up Sixth Avenue where there was a table waiting for him. And when he gave the waiter his order I said I'd have the same, which is also what I had done when they brought him a glass of the wine that they already knew he wanted.

So now, he said as we put our glasses back on the table before taking a second sip, let's get personal. How are things going for my fine young all-purpose timekeeper? And I said, Still trying to keep it swinging, maestro. Still trying to keep as much of it together as I can, still trying to find out how much else I should be trying to get together. And he said, They get into some pretty tricky stuff in outfits like the one you're hooked up to these days, but of course you already knew all about that part of it before you made your move. I'm satisfied on that score. So I'm not asking because I have any doubts. I'm just keeping in touch.

And that was when he went on to tell me what he told me about what Hortense Hightower had told him about why she had given me the bass fiddle. She told me that it was the one basic instrument that even as a beginner you could play almost the same way you just naturally did whatever you just naturally did when you were just listening and responding to whatever you were hearing when you were listening and responding with nobody else around. Just think how different it would be if you were playing the same notes on a tuba.

That, he said, was a pet notion of hers, and I said it made a lot of sense to me, because it did. But when I called to tell her that I was thinking about sending for you as the stopgap replacement for Shag Phillips, she was all for it, but she still immediately reminded me of what she had told me about not mistaking your all too obvious love for music and close identification with musicians with any personal desire on your part to become a professional musician as such. Not as your life's work. Even though you hadn't yet settled on what you wanted to try to make of yourself.

Which I could also understand, he said, and I promised her, and I kept my word as you well know I did. And by the way in case you haven't already figured out why I picked an inexperienced youngster like yourself to fill in for Shag Phillips, what impressed me was how natural your sense of time seemed to be. *Because what it all added up to was pulse, which is not just metronomic precision but a matter of personal feeling, gut feeling. Technique is fine, but it doesn't always add up to music, not the kind of music I'm always trying to play. Not that you or anybody else were born with it, for Christ sake but you were conditioned to it early on.*

We were well into our snack by that time and he looked at his watch and said, I don't pick my musicians like anybody else anyway. With me it's not their expertise but their potential. So what happened with you was the way you locked in with old Joe and Otis and me was not just surprising, it was downright incredible. And so far as I was concerned it had to do with a lot more than execution. It had to do with feeling. Look, we could always improve your execution with practice. That's what the hell rehearsal is always about, but feeling is something else, and the texture of my music is always all tangled up with the blues.

Which I could have said was essentially a matter of idiomatic sensibility. But I didn't, because I didn't want to sound that much like a graduate school academic. So what I actually said was that I knew exactly what he meant. And even as I said it I was remembering those old long-ago summer twilight times on the steps of the swing porch, with the antimosquito smoke wafting and curling across the chinaberry yard, when old Luzana Cholly used to come sporty limping up along Dodge Mill Road from the L & N Railroad bottom, strumming his twelve-string guitar on his way to whichever honky-tonk or jook joint he was going to play in that night.

Not that it wasn't as if church music was also always there. But church music was about church service, which was about heaven and hell. Whereas the blues was about everyday good times as well as holiday good times. I don't really know which I heard first, but I do remember that Luzana Cholly with his guitar and sporty limp walk was there quite a while before old patent-leather-tipping, flashy-fingered-piano-playing Stagolee Dupas fils first came to town.

So I said what I said because suddenly all of that had come to mind. But what he was saying then was that as far as he was concerned, musicians should never become so preoccupied with what they were doing technically or theoretically—and certainly not with how their technique is impressing other musicians—that they forget that the truth of the matter is that the people in the real audience respond to what you make them *feel*.

So, he said, when we returned to that part of the conversation as we finished our dessert and stood up to leave, so what good is impressing other musicians with your virtuosity if nobody out there in the ballroom, the auditorium, and the record store is responding? *Which sometimes people do in spite of themselves.* In other words, describing and explaining how the sounds are made is elementary for musicians themselves, but all of that is only a matter of craft. But when my band plays something, I want the craft to add up to what good music is supposed to do for people who come to hear it and dance to it. Not because they understand it but because they feel it.

Then as we came on back along Sixth Avenue toward the studio, he said what he said about Hortense Hightower and that was when I said what I said about Luzana Cholly and Stagolee Dupas fils. That was when he went on to say what he said about what great but undefined expectations Hortense Hightower had told him she had for me. And I said what I said then because that was when he had gone on to say, As you already know I'm with her. And so is everybody in the band. And that was when he smiled his very pleased Bossman Himself smile and then raised one eyebrow and said, But I still can't help being curious about what you yourself think about how you happened to come by such an intimate identification and involvement with music without becoming a musician.

So that was when I said what I said about that and I don't remember having ever said it or even thought about like that before. *I said that there never was a time when I wanted to become a musician per se. I said as much as I always wanted to do things like Luzana Cholly, who was my very first legendary hero in the flesh, I don't remember ever wanting to become a guitar player, not to mention a twelve-string guitar player. I said old Luzana Cholly's sporty limp walk was in itself a downright epical statement but whenever I did it, the imaginary object that I would be pretending to be holding so expertly would not be a make-believe guitar but old Gator Gus's baseball pitching glove. I said, even when little Buddy Marshall and I tried to skip city by hopping a northbound freight train to follow him that time and he himself caught us and brought us back to Three-Mile Creek bridge, neither one of us had thought of ourselves as hitting the troubadour trail as an itinerant guitar player.*

And the same was true of old Stagolee Dupas fils, the flashy-fingered jook joint and honky-tonk piano player from down in New Orleans, the Creole and voodoo and steamboat city beyond the Gulf Coast Mississippi canebrakes and bayous where the L & N Railroad made its junction with the California-bound Southern Pacific and the Santa Fe. I used to spend hours just listening to him practicing, sometimes on the piano at home and sometimes all by himself some mornings in old Sodawater's empty honky-tonk, just practicing and playing for himself or making up new numbers or new twists to use on old numbers. But I didn't ever really want to become a piano player either. I just wanted to do whatever I decided to try to do like he did what he did playing the way he played the piano.

I said, With old Luzana Cholly what I heard was blue steel routes and destinations and what they required was rawhide-tough flexibility. I said, With old Stagolee Dupas fils and his custom-tailored big-city clothes and jewelry, it was the sights and sounds along patent-leather avenue canyons. I said, I told you that time about Papa Gladstone's band. But I must say, maestro, as many of those rehearsals as I used to go to and as many of his dance dates as I began listening to from outside the dance halls even before I was old enough to buy a ticket even if I had been able to afford one, I don't remember ever having any urge to play any instrument for him someday, even though I memorized and could hum and whistle just about every part of most of the numbers in his book and could spot any phrase that any newcomer didn't get right.

And that was when he said what he said about having not only the knowledge but also the feeling about how it all goes together and if the feeling comes first, so much the better. He said, Our friend Hortense knew exactly what she was doing when she gave you that bass. She knew good and well that a special scholarship college sharpie like you could and would pick up on the basic technical facilities in no time at all and that whatever skill you were capable of just naturally followed.

We came on across Forty-fourth Street and into the building where the studio was, and as the elevator started upward he said, So with that kind of background you actually came into our band knowing why I sometimes kept the fluffed notes in. And I said, Because if you like how it sounds, it becomes the right note. And that was when he said what he said about sheet music versus ear music. So far as his band was concerned, sheet music was there to remind you of ear music.

When we came on back into the studio where Old Pro was waiting for him at the piano, he gave me the old mock French military one for each cheek farewell for now routine and said, And incidentally for whatever it's worth, I also want you to know how pleased I am that you're still touching base with old Daddy Royal. Ain't but the one. As I'm sure you already know, and as I'm also sure you already know what it means to have somebody like that expecting something special from you, even before you yourself have settled on what you would really like to do with yourself.

When I went back to the studio at the end of the week for my this-time-around get-together with Joe States, the very first thing he said as we came on out onto the sidewalk en route to Sam's Musical Supply Shop on Forty-ninth Street between Sixth Avenue and Times Square was also about something that Royal Highness had said about me.

Well now, just let me say this, my man. Old Daddy Royal has got your number. So if the impression you're making on them profs down there at that university is anything like your hitting it off with him, you got this grad school gig off and popping like these old thugs in this outfit hitting when the Bossman sics them on with one of our old surefire getaway jump tunes. Man, talking about a bunch of jackrabbits! Man, when the Bossman sics them splibs in that outfit on a Broadway audience they hit like they got the lowdown on the mainstem of every metropolis there ever was.

XII

WHEN I finally told Taft Edison about the time I had spent on the road with the band, I said, Man, it began as an incredible summer transition job that I needed because I had to get enough cash from somewhere to supplement the graduate school fellowship grant that I had been awarded along with my B.A. degree at commencement that spring. I said, Man, nothing like that had ever crossed my mind before. I said, Man, when I left home for college my main musical involvement beyond listening and dancing to it was humming and whistling it.

That was my second visit to the writers' work space on Fifth Avenue at Fiftieth Street that he was still using five days a week, Monday through Friday, because the owner was still away on a biographical research project in France and Italy. He was sitting at the long heavy oak conference table that he used as a writing desk, and I was sitting across from him in a chair near the window through which I could look north beyond St. Patrick's Cathedral toward Fifty-seventh Street and Central Park South, and from that many floors up, the sound of the traffic was all a part of the midtown Manhattan hum and buzz as I already remembered it from movie sound tracks when I heard it on my other visit.

I said, Man, when Hortense Hightower told me what she told me about suggesting me as a stopgap replacement when the Bossman Himself called and just happened to mention in passing that Shag Phillips had given notice, I couldn't believe it. But she said, Don't worry about it because he doesn't go around looking for superstars. He makes his own. Not because it's a game or some kind of challenge to prove anything about his ingenuity as some kind of mentor either. She said, He hires his musicians because he has decided that he wants to find out what he can do with something he's heard them playing. And that is when she also said, Believe me when I tell you that the very fact that he remembered you as soon as I mentioned you is what counts, because that means that you did something that caught his ear—not necessarily something musically technical either, something that goes with something he's got filed away in that steel-trap mind of his. You've heard about those big-time college profs talking about those legendary linguistic experts that can listen to half a sentence and tell you where you come from? Well, that's him when it comes to music. And then she also said, One thing is for sure, you can't find a better way to spend a summer after four solid no-letup years on a college campus down here in central Alabama than hitting all those towns all across the country with those guys in that outfit. You just wait.

I said, Man, the thing about it is that I don't remember ever really touching, let alone trying to fool around with, the bass fiddle before Hortense Hightower gave me that one in the spring of my junior year. Man, or any other instrument, except for the toy snare drum I once got for Christmas because I wanted Santa Claus to bring me one like the ones in the Mardi Gras parade bands that I used to imitate on a tin bucket during my preschool days—and come to think of it, there was also a time when some of us, in spite of the fact that our main interests were cowboys and baseball and boxing, used to make ukuleles out of wooden Cuban cigar boxes, but I don't remember that as something that I still had very much interest in doing by the time I reached junior high school. By that time it was track and field events and the Boy Scouts.

I said, Man, the one who took me through my rudimentary exercises on that present from Hortense Hightower was a sophomore string major and chapel orchestra cellist from St. Augustine, Florida, named Willis Tucker and called what else but Pluck Tucker because he also played the string bass in one of the campus dance bands, whose fingers were even more nimble than those of old Tricky Lou Cartwright, the fanciest bull fiddle thumper I ever heard during all the time I was growing up on the outskirts of Mobile. I said, Now I'm pretty sure that old Tricky Lou started out on the tuba like the one I first heard him tooting in Papa Gladstone's marching band in the Mardi Gras parades long before I found out that old Papa Gladstone also had the number one (and sometimes also the number two) dance band in town.

Then I said, Which reminds me that Tricky Lou sometimes also used to play the tuba in the dance band, because I can still remember him tooting what I used to call the circus elephant parade tuba part in old Jelly Roll Morton's "Kansas City Stomp" when the dance band used to set up in the front rows

of the grandstand at the baseball field and play a few numbers to advertise the eight-o'clock dance that would follow the
game after supper that evening.

I said, But man, old Pluck Tucker was strictly a string man.
I said, He was in the freshman class that checked in for the fall
term of the year that you cut out. So my guess is that he's at
least about a year younger than I am, so he just might have
started out on a cigar box ukulele, the four strings of which
you tuned from top to bottom by playing the right tones for
"My Dog Has Fleas."

That was when Taft Edison said what he said about how
popular Hawaiian and Latin American music became for a
while back during the early days of radio when I was just getting up to junior high school level and he was on his way out
of it. And he said that was probably also when Spanish guitars,
which had been becoming more and more popular ever since
the Spanish-American War back in 1898 (and the Panama Canal project), became more widely used in dance bands than
banjos. And when I asked him if he had ever played around
with any of the south of the border high-note fiesta trumpet
stuff, which sometimes we also used to think of as being bull-
ring trumpet stuff, and also peanut vendor trumpet stuff, he
shook his head, chuckling to himself.

Then he said, Man, well do I remember when young trumpet players around my hometown used to find that stuff just
about irresistible. But man, some of the strictest musical teachers around my hometown were also the very ones who had
been directors and instrumentalists in military bands down in
Cuba during the Spanish-American War and in the cavalry on
the Mexican border in the teens.

I had never thought of him as having ever had any serious personal professional interest in dance bands as such. As far as I
knew, none of the music school courses of study had anything
whatsoever to do with becoming bandleaders and arrangers/
composers like the Bossman Himself. There was no school of
music as such at Alabama State Teachers College in Montgomery, but if you were mainly interested in becoming a dance
band musician, that was your best bet so far as college was
concerned in those days.

My impression of Taft Edison from the very outset was that his ambition was to create compositions based on down-home sacred and secular music, including workaday chants and hollers, that would be performed in concert halls by concert hall–type instrumental and vocal groups and philharmonic orchestras. Because when I arrived on the campus as a freshman that fall, he was a junior who impressed me more than anybody else in the School of Music because he was the student who conducted the school's widely popular college marching band when it took its place in the grandstand in Alumni Bowl to play for the cheerleaders during football games, and he also was the one who supervised the tune-up before the faculty bandmaster took over to direct the concerts in the bandstand on the promenade lawn across which the weather-green copper tower of the chime clock faced the rust red dome and the white Doric antebellum columns and eaves of the brick red dining hall, in the basement of which the student social center was located in those days.

I can still remember how special the musical insignia on his nattily tailored ROTC cadet uniform looked compared with the plainness of those worn by most other cadets who were infantry privates without cadet NCO stripes or the Sam Browne belts and rank insignia that cadet officers used to wear. So he was obviously a very outstanding student musician.

But although there were also two student-led dance bands on the campus at that time, I can't remember having ever seen him playing with either of them. Not that I ever got the impression that he disliked or had no interest in that kind of music, or that his attitude was one of condescension, as was the case of many conservatory-oriented students at the time. Not at all. Because when you saw him at seasonal and fraternity and sorority socials and at benefit dances, he was not only very much in circulation, as we used to say, but was also always up-to-date on all the latest steps. And also when he stopped by the Mainstem Lounge, where you used to listen to the late-night radio broadcasts from such then famous nightspots as the Savoy Ballroom and the Cotton Club in Harlem and the Grand Terrace on the South Side of Chicago in those days, he could identify as many bands and sidemen as instantaneously as any of the dance band musicians, record collectors, and patent-leather avenue sharpies as happened to be there at the time.

So when I told him what I told him about my stopgap gig with the band, I didn't know what his response would be, but I did so because I had decided that I had better mention it myself rather than running the risk of having him find out about it just incidentally somehow and wonder why I hadn't mentioned it on my own and why I hadn't yet said anything at all about ever having played any musical instrument, not even in junior high school. Not that I thought that he would think I was trying to impress him; however, I felt I was in an awkward position either way. And also what if he already knew about it?

But as I should have remembered from his completely un-surprised and ever so casual response when I introduced myself to him on Fifth Avenue that day, he didn't register any surprise at all. Not to avoid any embarrassing questions about my qual-ifications but because he also seemed to know almost as much about how the Bossman Himself picked musicians as Hortense Hightower did. Anyway, all he said was that he hadn't heard the band during the period between Shag Phillips and Scratchy McFatrick.

But, he said, I do remember hearing something about some college boy filling in for a while. So that was you! Which just goes to show you. If whoever it was that I heard it from had mentioned the name of the college boy's school, I probably would have asked you if you happened to know him when we met that day down in the Forties. I must say that must have been something. Man, as definite as I was about moving out of music as a profession by that time, I myself would have had a hard time turning down the chance to hit the trail with that fabulous crew of thugs for a while. Man, I can just imagine it. Man, when I woke up every morning and realized why I was wherever I was I would have had to pinch myself.

I didn't say anything about me crossing my fingers, because then he changed the subject to what he had been planning to talk about when he called me the night before and invited me to come by that afternoon, and that was when he said what he said about how much talk about political issues, movements, organizations, involvements, and affiliations you heard among the people in the academic and literary circles he had begun to move into shortly after he decided to settle in New York for at least a while instead of going back down to the campus for his senior year.

Look, man, he went on to say, I don't know how politically active you are, or what your political affiliations, if any, may happen to be, but I was wondering about how much of that sort of thing you might have run into by now. Because, man, one of the first things that struck me about this town when I arrived and first started making the rounds was all the political recruitment I was forever running into. Somebody was forever trying to get me to join some political group or other, all of them calling themselves either liberal, left-wing, or downright radical if not outright revolutionary.

Man, you'd see some very fly fay chippie and catch her eye or the sparkle that she's aiming at you and you move in on her or she might move in on you and take her to your place or perhaps more often to hers, and the next morning you'd find out what the game is. She was the one that had you in her sights as soon as you hit the scene. Not because of all that ever ready automatically syncopated action she says you inherited from your stud horse male ancestors she was thanking you all night for laying on her. Man, all of that hair-trigger ecstatic response is subject to be the standard prelude to a bunch of political pamphlets that she's going to lay on you. And if she doesn't quiz you about them on the next tête-à-tête she's definitely going to check you out on the third. Then if you become a recruit she might keep you in her stable for a while before passing you on to somebody closer to the inner circle.

SOP, man, he said, chuckling again. Standard operating procedure. *Standing revolutionary recruitment procedure for the ostracized minorities!* Man, you've got to watch that stuff, or you'll be well on your way to becoming a statistic on somebody's revolutionary agenda. Man, that stuff used to be downright evangelical. But of course I don't have to tell you that most down-home cats drop those pamphlets in the first trash can they come to en route to the subway. Man, you know as well as I do that what them down-home boots were out for was not some abstract political program but some unsegregated easily accessible living and breathing hot-to-trot body action for free, or at least for not more than a drink or two.

He said, Man, a few jive artists might have tried to fake and cross talk their way through some of that stuff if reading it was what you had to do to get to the sack in the first place. But my guess is that not many were likely to work their way through that kind of stuff to get back to the sack for a second go-round. Because all they were out for was a one-night pickup in the first place. Man, as far as they were concerned, it was not a matter of how many times with the same chicks but how many chicks.

But on the other hand, though, as you also know, there were and are also some splibs who figure that they have to read that stuff to prove that their formal education qualifies them to move in such exclusive, articulate and up-to-date company as they assume their present company represents—just in case there's any question of basic intellectual eligibility. *Hey, don't play me cheap, Miss Lady Blueblood playgirl. Some of us may be from across the tracks, but here's one who can dig this dialectic jive, too!* Now, man, that's a sitting duck.

Which brings me around to why I've been meaning to get around to this topic in the first place: so here comes old Taft Woodrow Edison with his high grade-point average flashing like stop-look-and-listen at an express crossing. Not to mention three years of college earned through meritorious scholarship! So what does he on whom little in the weekly, monthly, and quarterly journals and critical reviews in the periodicals room of the campus library was lost—man, what does he do with those evangelical pamphlets? *He reads them! Man, he reads them to satisfy his endemic Oklahoma suspicion that they are not worth reading. They are not worth the cornbread paper they are printed on. And then does he dump them in the nearest garbage drop? Absolutely not! Because he's made so many marginal notes that he wants to argue about that he calls up his recruiter for another date! And man, that call led me into some stuff that is a part of what I'm still trying to come to terms with on my own as a writer.*

Then he said, Of course when I think back on it now I see it as something that turned out to be a sort of catalytic agent. Or let's put it this way: I would not be going about this thing of being a writer in the way I'm going about it as of now if that encounter hadn't turned out to be one of those encounters.

That was why it was on the same afternoon that I told him about my time on the road with the band that I also told him what I told him about what happened when my roommate and I read André Malraux's *Man's Fate* during my sophomore year. I said, Man, the first thing I ever really heard about what that kind of recruitment was like was what my roommate told me about what he had already found out about the movement (meaning the underground movement) in Chicago by the time he finished junior high school. Before that the only kind of political recruitment I can remember hearing about was labor unionism, mainly the longshoremen's union strikes and picket lines and scabs down on the Mobile, Alabama, waterfront, where Uncle Jerome worked for the United Fruit Company. Man, what my roommate told me about the movement in Chicago made it all sound like joining a very strict church whose members were always on the lookout for transgressors.

I said, Incidentally, we also read Malraux's *The Conquerors*, but he had transferred before I read *Man's Hope*, and I didn't get around to Karl Marx until my senior year, and by that time not only did dialectic materialism sound as much like the gospel as something you were reading in a political bible, but man, that was also when I realized *that all political systems were run by politicians, just as all religions were run by preachers and preachers and deacons elected or self-designated.*

I said, Man, when I was a senior in high school, what I was mainly concerned with was getting to college. I said, Man, my preoccupation was not with changing the world. Man, I was still trying to find out what all this stuff was all about. And what I was eligible for. I said, Man, in the third grade there was geography along with all of those maps and the globe and the bulletin board windows on the world and peoples of many lands.

I said, Then when I got to senior high school and started spending more and more time in the library I discovered world history and anthropology. And that was when I began to realize that I was going to have to be a schoolboy for some time to come. So man, I guess that's where whatever immunity to political recruitment I've developed began. I said, Anyway, by the time I was halfway through college I was too wrapped up in doing what I was doing on my own to be recruited for any political movement. I said, Man, none of that theoretical stuff

I was also reading in those current political journals in the periodicals room added up to the magic keys I was looking for (*mentioning Miss Lexine Metcalf, who said some golden, some silver, some platinum, and maybe some of some as yet undiscovered alloy. But not mentioning Jewel Templeton, who said some sharp, some flat, and some natural*).

Then I said, But to answer your question, as yet I haven't run into the kind of recruitment you're talking about. Not since I've been here and not anywhere on the road with the band. Not even in Hollywood. I said, Man, now that you bring up the subject, come to think of it, I don't remember anybody in the band ever bringing up the subject of political recruitment at all. Maybe they thought that being a college boy I was already hip to all of that *theoretical* jive. But none of the fans I got to know in any of our stopping places ever asked me very much about anything except myself and my relationship to the band.

But I didn't go on to mention anything about people like the Marquis de Chaumienne and Jewel Templeton, and that was when he said what he said about down-home church folks and hypocrisy. There was all that Sunday church meeting singing and shouting and amen corner moaning and clapping. And for those who wished to express a more comprehensive devotion, there were midweek prayer meetings with hymn singing. But as often as not, when things came down to the nuts-and-bolts actualities of everyday goings-on and the situation added up to put up or shut up, you couldn't tell a spoonful of difference between the most righteous church members and just plain old everyday looking-out-for-number-one folks. So man, you get my point about the folks. Down home it's religious hypocrisy. Up here it's political hypocrisy, which just might turn out to be a very crucial saving grace indeed, given the political temper of the times.

XIII

AT THE end of the spring term I had completed all of the requirements for the Master of Arts degree except the thesis, on which (in addition to the other research reports) I had begun working during the Christmas holiday break and which I finished and submitted by the late-summer deadline. So I was eligible to enter the Ph.D. program that next September. But when I went to register and work out my course of study and request my choice of professors, I had already decided that I was going to spend only this consecutive year attending formal classroom lectures and seminars and doing academic research reports in preparation for the dissertation required for the doctorate in the field of humanities in those days.

One more consecutive year of academic gumshoe, I told Taft Edison the day after I was notified that my thesis had been approved. And when he asked what about the year after that, I told him about Eunice's plans and also about the letter back in June from the English Department down in central Alabama offering me a temporary position as an instructor of freshman and sophomore composition and introduction to literature.

You didn't have to explain that the offer did not imply that anybody down there assumed that I had decided to be a college professor and that it had been made only as a suggested option in the event I needed more cash to supplement my fellowship grant. Taft Edison already knew that because he already knew that the head of the English Department making the offer was Carlton Poindexter, whose junior-year class in the English novel he was enrolled in and who also was his informal extracurricular reading consultant when I was a freshman.

By that time Taft Edison also knew that I had not yet decided *not* to become a college teacher, because he knew that I had not yet finally made up my mind not to complete the Ph.D. program. But he did know that I was beginning to question the relevance of the Ph.D. degree to achievement in the arts. Because he was the one to whom I had said what I said about the difference between formal training in the arts and in the sciences and mathematics. I said if my main intellectual orientation had led me into science and mathematics I probably would have been aiming at a Ph.D. since junior high school. Because you had to work your way up to that academic level just to become involved with what had now become an indispensable part of the most elementary terminology, equipment, and procedure.

In the arts and the humanities, on the other hand, I said, you could actually come by all of the fundamentals by the time you could function on a senior level of an accredited high school. Because by then you would have been initiated into the realm of the great world masterpieces of literature, music, and history, and the ones you had not read as class assignments on your own initiative were part of the same universal context as the ones assigned. After all, it was not as if you had to go on beyond high school and then college and then graduate in order to read other masterworks by the same Homer, Virgil, Shakespeare, Balzac, or George Eliot, a sample of whose works you had already come to terms with in high school or even as a high school dropout.

Eunice, who had fulfilled all of the requirements for the M.S. degree in education at Teachers College, was looking forward to spending the next year in New York working as a part-time substitute elementary school teacher. But I knew that she felt that after that she should spend at least several terms working as a teacher, administrator, or supervisor down in central Alabama. She knew very well that the hometown benefactors who had provided the four-year college scholarship to earn her B.S. degree, without which she would not have been in position to win the fellowship for graduate study for the master's degree at Teachers College, would not feel that she had deserted them.

She knew as well as I did that their reaction would be exactly the same as when down-home folks have always celebrated local people who succeed elsewhere, especially up north in Philamayork. Who knows? Such down-home celebration of locals who make good elsewhere may have begun all the way back in the era of the fugitive slave, of whom those still down on the plantation most often said not that he or she ran away and left us, but rather *if he or she could do that, other folks down here can do it, too.*

I could already hear all sorts of variations on remarks like: Y'all remember little ol' frizzly-headed Eunice Whatshername that use to pass by here going to and from school? And went on through high school and got that big send-off to college? Well, they say when she finished up her college course she got another

*big send-off to New York. And when she passed some courses up
there they hired her. Everybody always did say that girl was going
places. I always liked the way she carried herself on the way to and
from school and anywhere else. Always neat as a pin whatever she
was wearing and never one to cash in on being that good-looking.
You can ask anybody and they'll tell you. Didn't go around with
her nose in the air neither. That child had her nose in them books
every chance she got. I always did say she could make it anywhere
doing anything she put her mind to.*

She was as aware of all that as any other scholarship student I ever met. So she also knew that her hometown folks,
like mine down in Gasoline Point and Mobile County Training School, wanted her to go wherever her quest for further
development led her. And she also knew that their trust of her
judgment was such that none of her down-home benefactors
had assumed that she had given up on her own professional
objectives to get married. After all, it was as if she had gotten
married and gone straight off to graduate school as if on an
extended honeymoon.

In any case, if I had said nothing about going back down
to central Alabama because I had decided to stay at New York
University for a third consecutive year as I had originally anticipated, she would not have said what she said about going
back when she did since she already knew that I had begun to
question the relevance of my academic research assignments
to the way I was beginning to want to come to my own terms
with things. When I showed her the letter with the offer from
central Alabama she said, Why not? She said, Meanwhile, I
have some unfinished business of my own down in those parts.

You didn't have to explain any of that to Taft Edison, and
when he said, Speaking of roommates, I've been making a few
cautious moves in that direction myself, and there is somebody
you'll be meeting soon, I knew that he was changing the subject. And I said, Whenever you say.

I knew that he had been married for a short time during his
second year in New York, and I also knew that former wife's
name and that she was a nightclub entertainer, but he never
discussed their relationship except to say that it was a mistake that was soon corrected and that there were no lingering

after-effects. That was all he said and I did not ask him anything else about her.

He said, Her name is Janice and we've been seeing each other for a few months now and have just about decided that we've got something going that should be continued at a closer range of involvement. So we're looking for a place. I must say, and as you probably guessed, this was not something I was looking for at this time. It just happened and I must tell you, man, as much as she has going for her, no small part of it is the fact she knows how I feel about this thing I'm tangled up with, this goddamn albatross of a manuscript of a homemade novel—*man, talking about mammy made!*

And that was when he also said what he said about what he was trying to do and also said that if he came anywhere close to what he had in mind he did not expect the sales to add up to enough to put it on the bestseller list and that if there were enough sales to encourage the publisher to offer him a contract for another book, he would consider himself as having been successfully launched on a career as a literary professional.

Man, he said, she knows that I have to try to see if I can do what I think I should be doing with a book.

And I said, She sounds like she's the one, all right. And he said, Could be and he said, So far, so good, I must say. So now we're going to find out if she can put up with the likes of me on a daily basis.

When he called again several weeks later, he said, Hey, man, looks like we have a change of address on our hands over here, and yes, that means that I've given you obvious reason to assume it implies. We've jumped the broom, tied the knot, and are about to give up my place on St. Nicholas and her place on Convent for a larger place over at 730 Riverside Drive, an eighth-floor place from which you can see directly across the Hudson River to Palisades Park and also a partial view of the George Washington Bridge! So, man, we're hoping to get it all presentable enough during the next few weeks to have you all and a few other friends over for an old down up plus "up here" New Year's Eve celebration. With pigs' feet, black-eyed peas, collard greens, okra, and corn bread, plus down-home bootleg white lightnin' as well as up-here champagne, and for dessert gingerbread muffins and/or sweet potato pie.

XIV

As FOR the one who was to be the one for the likes of me, when I got to college the main thing during those first two years was the necessity to maintain the grade-point average required for the renewal of my scholarship grant. Then there was also the no less urgent matter of coping with how my roommate was taking all of those college-level course requirements in stride as if they were as routine as current newspaper and magazine articles.

I was the one who was enrolled in the Department of Liberal Arts. He was in the Department of Architecture. But it was as if the main thing for him was the wide selection of the great books of world history, literature, philosophy, and science that he could check out of the library and read on his own.

Elementary, my dear Watson, he said when we came back from our first exploration of the card index in the main reading room and the racks and shelves of the periodicals room. Elementary. Name me *any* human concern that your qualified architect is not expected to know where to find the goods on. Context, my dear fellow, nor do I speak only of material surroundings and time frames.

Jerome Jefferson, polymath. T. Jerome Jefferson. Better known on campus as Geronimo from Chicago, and also as the Snake, as in snake in the grass, and as snake doctor as in snake-oil doctor. But only partly because the snake oil was actually the chemistry laboratory alcohol cocktail he used to concoct and bootleg from time to time, especially when there were campus socials.

Taft Edison, who was there only during that first year, now remembered him not only because his chem lab concoction had predance customers in the band cottage, but also because as a freshman he had joined the augmented French horn section that the band took to Chicago along with the football team for the annual game with Wilberforce University at Soldier Field.

Neither of us became involved in an ongoing relationship with a special on-campus girlfriend during those first two years. With me it was a matter of avoiding encounters that were not mutually casual, because I couldn't spare the extra money you had to have for regular dates, treats, and ceremonial gifts. But for him, it was a matter of choice. He could afford the extra spending change, but he preferred "freelancing" because it was consistent with the bohemian nature of college life that he had in mind for us when he labeled our room Atelier 359.

When classes began on the first day of my third fall day on campus, my roommate was no longer there, because he had transferred to the School of Architecture at Yale. And as much as I missed him, I was also pleased that, so far, nobody had been assigned to replace him because I was then twenty-one years old and I had never had a room all to myself before. Now I was twenty-one and also an upperclassman.

Then it was the first week of that third October, and there she was. I was on my way up the steps of the main entrance of the library and I overtook someone I had not seen on campus before and stopped to hold the door open for her to step past me into the lobby. And in that time frame of less than one bar of music it was as if I had stepped into that enchanted boy blue zone of crepe myrtle yard blossoms and dog fennel meadows again. And I had to say something more than just hello or good morning. So I said, How is freshman orientation coming along this year? And that is how I came to know that she was a sophomore who had transferred after spending her freshman year at State Normal. And I said, I hope you will be glad you did.

We came up the wide staircase side by side and step by step, but I didn't say anything else until we stepped onto the second-floor landing and then all I said before she turned left to go into the main reading room was, Well, good luck, and I hope you like it here enough to stick around.

And she said she already liked it very much and when I said, So we'll be seeing you around, meanwhile, best wishes, she said, Thank you again. So far everybody has been very understanding and very helpful, especially when they find out that I'm not a freshman.

That was all that happened. And I came on into the reference room and checked out the books I wanted from the special reserve list shelf and it was not until I sat down to open the first book that I realized that I had not asked her name and I had not given her mine. That was how it all began for me, because even as I realized that I could go into the main reading room and find her, I also realized that all I could do was just sit there with my fingers crossed and hope that she had not been on her way to join somebody. Maybe even somebody she had transferred from State Normal to join—or even more probably, someone she had met since arriving on the campus.

Which is why for the next week every time I went into the dining hall I crossed my fingers hoping that I would not see what I did not want to see. I came through the same side entrance that I always used because it was the one you came to first when you came along Campus Avenue from the dormitories on the upper end of the campus or across from the quadrangle, which included the library, the main academic building in those days, and the gymnasium, which included the main entertainment auditorium, beyond which were the tennis courts and the campus bowl. But instead of scanning the tables to locate who was already there and sitting with whom and where, I headed straight to and through the serving line and onto an empty table all the way at the back of the hall near a window through which you could look down the slope to the campus power plant and campus laundry area. And when I finished I left through the exit nearest that part of the building, which was also the shortest route back to Atelier 359.

So I didn't see what I didn't want to see and after four days I realized I hadn't seen what I really wanted to see either. And then I also realized that I was crossing my fingers again, not only because I wanted to see her all by herself again, but also because I was hoping that she had not decided to go back to State Normal or had transferred to Talladega or Fisk or Spelman. Or maybe she didn't eat in the cafeteria because she didn't live on campus. Maybe she had relatives or family friends with whom she was boarding on or off campus. *Or maybe she was living off campus because she was married to somebody who already lived off campus and that was why she had transferred from State Normal in the first place!*

Not that I was any more able to begin a steady on-campus relationship than I had been during my freshman or sophomore years. I could spare enough cash for an off-campus caper now and then, and I could also manage to keep enough petty cash on hand to go out to listen to the best of the topflight dance and variety orchestras when they included a one-night stand at the Dolomite on their annual coast-to-coast and border-to-border bus tour schedules.

So far this had happened only several times each year. But it was something I didn't intend to miss. Because although I never had any urge to become a musician myself, old Luzana Cholly and his twelve-string guitar, and old Stagolee Dupas fils and his honky-tonk gut bucket and patent leather avenue stride time piano and the sound of Bessie, Mamie, and Trixie Smith and also old Jelly Roll Morton and King Oliver and Louis Armstrong on Miss Blue Eula Bacoat's gramophone over in Gins Alley were already indispensable parts of what having a good time was all about that many years before I was to become the schoolboy that Miss Lexine Metcalf and Mr. B. Franklin Fisher wanted me to be.

So I felt the way I felt about the Dolomite because out there not only could you finally hear the actual bands playing the music they had made famous on recordings and radio, you could also get into personal contact with the musicians themselves.

So far, so good, I remember thinking as I moved along in the registration line for junior-year students that third September. So far, so very good. So far, so very, very good. I had not been able to go back home since I arrived on campus, but by taking a full-time on-campus job during the Christmas holidays and the summer vacation months I had been able to supplement my scholarship grant budget and provide myself with basic incidentals with just enough left over to get by on if you pinch pennies.

Indeed so far, better than ever because not only was I halfway to graduation but I was also enjoying the highest standard of living I had ever had access to. Nothing was hand-me-down or makeshift. On the contrary, dormitories were inspected daily and there were also summer entertainment features and campus recreational facilities plus the library and all that freedom from class assignment time for the extracurricular reading I had come to realize I needed to do. And besides, what would I do back in Gasoline Point, anyway? I had never had a job in Gasoline Point or in downtown Mobile either, and unskilled jobs were as scarce as ever.

So far, so good, yea verily. And after all, when I got on that Greyhound bus with my new gladstone bag and my scholarship award voucher and my one-way ticket, my intention was to be long gone and farther, and when I arrived on campus my question was not When do I return to Gasoline Point and Mobile? but Where do I go on to from here? Philamayork, Philamayork, the also and also of Philamayork, to be sure, which even before junior high school was already a fireside, tell-me-tale code name for the best of all possible places.

But even that early on you had also already come to realize that even if your Philamayork turned out to be Philadelphia or Pittsburgh, Pennsylvania, or New York City, New York, or Chicago, Illinois, or Detroit, Michigan, or Los Angeles or San Francisco, California, once you headed out from Gasoline Point toward the ever so Marco Polo blue horizon mists beyond Chickasabogue Bridge it would be as if your destination were wherever east of the sun and west of the moon was.

So far, so good. But what now? Because there I was with my fingers also crossed because this time I was wishing what I was wishing as if the crisp autumn green campus, lawn grass, and shrubbery and the bright blue silk and cotton white autumn sky made my circumstances no less fancy free than they had ever been back during the springtime elementary school bell days of honeysuckle thickets and dog fennel playhouse games. All I had to go on was that ever so polite exchange in the library. I didn't even know her name and was not even certain that she was still there. But by the middle of the next week, the very thought of her being on the campus had become as much a part of my speculations about what my junior year was going to be like as about any of the new electives on my academic course of study.

Then after that many days, there she was in person again, coming up the steps and into the library again all by herself again. And as I opened the door for her and said, Nice to see you're still here, she smiled but I couldn't really tell if she remembered me or was just being a nice, well-brought-up young lady who was not cynical and didn't consider herself vulnerable. So when I said what I said about becoming used to not being used to being at State Normal, she smiled again. And when she said what she said about becoming used to being a sophomore and that she had originally expected to be a freshman on this campus in the first place, all I could say was, Is that so? Because I couldn't say how glad I was that she had not arrived before now, not to mention my freshman year.

We stepped onto the second-floor landing again, then and to keep her from realizing how excited I was to see her again and how eagerly I was looking forward to seeing her as often as possible, I stepped in the direction of the reference room before turning to say, So nice to see that you're still here, and that was also when I finally said my name and where I was from and that I was getting used to not being used to being a junior in liberal arts.

And when she smiled and said her name and what part of central Alabama she was from, all I could say was, Well, hello again, statemate. And all I could do was tighten my fingers because they were already crossed.

That was how it all began with the one that I decided was the one for me, because, as luck would have it, when it was deep purple wisteria time on the campus again that next spring we had become as close as we had become because our self-imposed restrictions were as compatible as they were because it turned out that we both were there on renewable scholarship awards that had to be supplemented with what you could earn in cash or credit from jobs available through the student employment office.

So I had not seen her in the dining hall because she did not eat in the dining hall. She lived in the sophomore women's dormitory, but she ate all her meals in the visitors' guesthouse, where she worked when not in class or at the library and from the early-evening meal until seven-thirty, after which if she did not have to go back to the library, she did what she had to do back in the dormitory. As for nonacademic activities, she had decided to restrict herself to an occasional choice from the schedule of athletic events, movies, stage productions, and concerts covered by the prepaid incidental-fee admission coupon.

I didn't make my first obvious move until the fall dance gala on the night following the homecoming football game in November, the biggest social event of the fall term. During my freshman and sophomore years my old freelancing roommate and I went to such shindigs unattached and made our forays on targets of opportunity as we spotted them from the stag line (or "Murderers' Row") near the table of refreshments. But this time I was glad he was not there anymore, because I still had not seen what I had not wanted to see in the dining hall or anywhere else. And because I was still hoping what I could not keep myself from hoping since that midmorning when I first saw her on our way up the steps and into the library.

When I arrived, the band was already halfway into the first set, and the dance floor was already more than half full of couples, with a steady stream of others joining in, some directly from the coat-check windows. My old roommate and I had always stopped at the refreshment table for a waxed paper tumbler of student punch-bowl punch, which he always spiked— his, not mine—with his own chem lab cocktail concoction from his pewter hip pocket flask. But this time I took mine and sipped it as I slowly meandered my way toward the bandstand, because I still had no way of knowing whether I was going to see what I hoped I wouldn't see.

So she may have seen me before I saw her this time, because when I came within eight yards of the bandstand, there she was sitting at a front-row table in the waist-high spectators' gallery on my right. And with her were two other sophomore coeds whom I remembered from the year before but had not met. And when I was as sure as I could guess that I was in her line of sight, I waved and she waved back and when I held out my hand, she stood up and came down onto the dance floor. And when I said her name, she said mine.

XV

HI YA, fellow, the voice on the phone said. And I said, Eric von Threadcraft. And he said, Got you. He said, Got you in two rings. And I said, Hey, man, I said, What say, Mice? I said, Goddamn, man. How you been and what you been up to? And he said, A little of this and some of that plus the same old ongoing, but always on the afterbeat, man. You know me, fellow. And then he said, Hey, what this is about is that I caught the band in person out here tonight for the first time since you cut out, and naturally I went backstage to check with Papa Joe and he gave me your number and told me what you were up to and into these days. So how is school and how is family life?

And I said, Man, the thing about graduate school is that the more advanced the courses of study, the more basic the material and the more obvious the assumptions and the more relative and tentative the conclusions. So it's the also and also all over again, my man, the also and also and also, perhaps even as the also and also of arithmetic becomes the also and also of algebra, calculus, and trigonometry.

Then before he could say anything about that, I said, As for family life, affirmative by me, man. What can I tell you, man? *Je suis tout à fait en train d'être dans le vrai*, if you remember that old Flaubert riff you tried to sneak in there on me that time. Or should I say *heureusement en train*?

And that was when he said what he said about me spending the time I spent keeping the time as a bass player, and about how lucky I was to have come across that particular instrument of all musical instruments the way I did. Then he also said, Speaking of fundamentals, my man, that fabulous Miss Hortense Hightower you used to tell me about, had your number, fellow. Just think about it, Schoolboy, if you will pardon the expression. There you were up there in college because your Miss Lexine fairy-tale aunt Metcalf had earmarked you as early on as the third grade for some undefined something special requiring higher education. So there you are up there on the campus flat broke except for what little was left over from the fellowship grants, but determined to pass the academic equivalent of every obstacle that Jason the argonaut was supposed to pass to qualify himself for the ultimate boon of a golden fleece and here you come out of there on commencement day having earned yourself not only the magic sheepskin but also the bull fiddle, of all things. A goddamn completely unacademic jazz-anchoring bull fiddle!

That's something else, fellow, he said. That's something to think about. Because, man, are you sure that your Miss Hortense Hightower was not your Miss Lexine Metcalf in the disguise of an after-hours nightclub diva? And what about that roommate of yours that turned up down there from Chicago and stayed around just long enough to become in some ways even more and certainly no less indelible than your Mr. B. Franklin Fisher himself, without whom, after all, there would have been no Miss Lexine Metcalf in the first place? No him without her, but hey, no *her* without him to bring her there as if specifically to find the likes of you. Fairy-tale stuff U.S.A., fellow.

Just look at how it all hooks up, he said. It was Hortense Hightower who got you that incredible quantum leap of a break that didn't just land you a gig with the greatest band that ever was, but also meant that your *elementary*, repeat elementary, as in beginner's school music, faculty was made up of none other than Joe States, Old Pro, and the Bossman *Himself*! Incredible, fellow! *Incroyable!* Think about it, fellow, think about it.

And I said, I hear you, man. I really do hear you. But you feel like that because of what music means to you as a musician. But man, I was doing what I was doing because that was what came up for me that summer, and I've always done the best I could and once more it was good enough to get me by. Because they were not looking for an expert. You know the Bossman, Mice. Sometimes he just likes to find out what he can make of whatever turns up. You and I have been over that, I said, reminding him of references he and I had made from time to time to how visual artists sometimes used unaltered and somewhat altered found objects!

I said, man, they weren't even looking for an expert when they picked up Scratchy McFatrick. They were looking for a replacement for Jamison McLemore, who was only a temporary—no, interim—replacement for me. Because Jamie had no intention of staying away from L.A. and his family for more than a short period. So when old Scratchy Mac turned up with all of that virtuosity he also fell right into the Bossman's old utilization approach, but this time there was so much more there than anybody on that instrument had ever come in with from anywhere. Man, I like to think of old Scratchy as the Bossman's reward for the good deed he did for me.

I said, Man, as for me getting with cutting them dots, that was Old Pro's department and sometimes he used to call me up to sit with him on the bus as he checked through the score sheets and made sure that all of the Bossman's latest revisions were in place. That was something he used to do, especially during those long stretches when the landscape was the same old stuff mile after mile after mile and everybody else was nodding and I was awake and happened not to be reading.

And he said, See what I mean, man, that's precisely the kind of priceless stuff I'm talking about. But hey, look, I better cut this off so you can get back to your homework. Speaking of which, I must tell you this. Man, when Papa Joe States clued me in on your whereabouts these days I could just see you relaxing back in one of those comfortable, heavy-gauged oak New York University classroom chairs with your invisible bass fiddle sound box between your legs like a cello with your pizzicato fingers here and your fretting fingers up here and the ornate tuning pegs and scroll protruding above your head like some kind of regal decoration.

And then he said, Anyway, I just want you to know that I've missed you, fellow. As tied up as I've been since I came back from that deal in Europe not long after you cut out and also disconnected your answering service, I still kept expecting you to turn up any day. But hell, I guess you can tell I've been thinking about you. And oh, by the way, before I hang up I also want you to know that Felix has some loot for you. That movie thing didn't go through because something so much better turned up for me. But there was something up front for the preliminary work that we did and part of it is yours and we kept expecting to hear from you. So it will be on the way to you tomorrow.

So I really better get off the line now, he said then, but I just had to call and let you know how much I'd like for us to get together the next time I'm in New York. And naturally I'm just dying to meet that fine stone fox of a roommate of yours that Joe States was carrying on so about. He calls her some fine people, which just knocks me out, fellow. Because just leave it to old Papa Joe. Because I don't know whether he's riffing on our man James Joyce's Annalivia or not, but calling her some fine *people* brings back to this schoolboy's mind *Plurabelle*, which I distinctly remember you yourself using in a conversation we were having about "Sweet Georgia Brown" on the way back to Hollywood from a Central Avenue jam session one night. I kept talking about how those battling tenors kept leapfrogging each other and you said what you said as if any parody of James Joyce or Williams and Walker, or was it Miller and Lyles in a vaudeville skit? *Man talking about Annalivia, man, I could tell you something about Annalivia, about the plurabilities of Annalivia Plurabelle! Yeah, man, but what about this? Man, I know that, but let me tell you about the time when. Hey, yeah, man, but listen to this* . . . with the rhythm flowing like old James Joyce's river running all the way back to Eve and Adam.

I often think about how you used to come up with stuff like that, my man, he said then. Who knows? Old Joe States has a set of ears second to none. And a mind like a steel trap. If you ever started signifying about that tune like that anywhere near him he's subject to pick up on that Plurabelle part right away, and riff it back at you so fast you won't even recognize that you're the source. His source, in any case.

Then just before he actually did finally hang up he said, But hey, look. Speaking of Plurabelles and plurabilities, I must confess that there are perhaps some possibly significant reorientations in progress chez your old scene cruising friend Mice these days. But which I'm not going to tell you about until I get to New York before long or maybe even sooner. But definitely as soon as I can make it and that means the next time I call I just might already be there on my next as of now inevitable trip back east.

XVI

MAN, WHAT can I say? Roland Beasley said as we crossed Madison Avenue on our way along Fifty-seventh Street to Fifth Avenue and Rizzoli's Bookstore. We had spent the first part of the afternoon at an exhibition of Jacques Callot drawings, sketches, and etchings that Roland had invited me to come along and see at an upstairs gallery near Park Avenue.

I had told him what I had told him about how I had begun reading about the Commedia dell'Arte during the fall of my freshman year in college. And when he called he had also reminded me that I also said what I had said about Jacques Callot the first time we talked about the reproductions of the Harlequins and Saltimbancs in a book from the Museum of

Modern Art about the first fifty years of the paintings of Pablo Picasso.

I had become aware of the origin and existence of medieval miracle, morality, and passion plays by the time I finished junior high school at Mobile County Training School, where nobody who ever heard Mr. B. Franklin Fisher talk about how citizens of the German town of Oberammergau traditionally spent ten years developing the roles of the biblical characters they had been chosen to represent that many years ahead of the next periodic production, were ever likely to forget what a Passion play was about. And of course, that story was also related to what you already knew about Christmas and Easter pageants, not to mention class work that became a part of the history pageants presented as part of general assembly programs and graduation exercises. Not to mention the fact that Mobile being not only the pre–New Orleans French Gulf Coast settlement town that it was, I had grown up knowing about riverboat entertainers along with traveling tent shows and vaudeville acts as well as annual carnival costume masks and parades.

But before the fall term of my freshman year in college I had never become aware of anything at all about the Commedia dell'Arte as such, although I did know what Harlequin and Pantalone costumes looked like and that both represented stock characters like the stock characters in newspaper comic strips and also like Punchinello in the Punch and Judy puppet shows and like Charlie Chaplin and Buster Keaton of silent moving pictures.

As we stopped at the corner of Tiffany's and waited for the light to change so we could cross over to the west side of Fifth Avenue, Roland Beasley shook his head and clenched and rubbed his palms, saying, What can I say, my man? What can I tell you? I really do think that we just might be on our way to getting next to something that we can riff on for days, man, and I mean day and night.

And I said, You said it, old partner. I said, All you've got to do is start vamping and riffing around stuff like "Drop Me Off in Harlem" or "Echoes of Harlem" or "Slapping Seventh Avenue with the Sole of My Shoe," and what about stuff like

"Harlem Airshaft" and stuff like that. And just watch how variations on old Jacques Callot's and all that jiveass crew will start turning up stomping at the Savoy and jumping at the Woodside and cooling it at Connie's Inn just like they did in Picasso's Belle Epoque Montmartre, and just look at all of those theater and nightlife characters already there in Toulouse Lautrec. And don't forget Degas and all those dancing girls and scenes.

There we go, he said as we turned into the entrance to Rizzoli's, no doubt about it. Degas and Toulouse Lautrec and Picasso at Connie's Inn and Small's Paradise, at the Lafayette and at the Savoy, *the Home of Happy Feet*. You know what I mean? Not them, me. Old Rollo! *Old Rollo's visual echoes of Harlem.* Old Rollo. Not Miguel Covarrubias and all that old-trouble-I-seen-eyed blubber-lipped, blubber-butt, blubber-foot refugees from the goddamn cotton field out barrelhousing on Saturday night in their Montgomery Ward and Sears, Roebuck Sunday best. Man, talk about square. Man, even the goddamned drummers looked square in that goddamn Covarrubias stuff. I know better. Man, I was right up there. Man, I'm from North Carolina, but I grew up right around the corner from Connie's Inn and the old Lafayette Theater. Man, remember to remind me to tell you about Big John's, where they used to serve that Big John Special that Fletcher Henderson's band made that Big John Special record about. Boy, we used to live right off Seventh Avenue on 131st Street, and the Old Rhythm Club, where most of the uptown hoofers and keyboard ticklers used to hold those legendary cutting contests while waiting for gigs in between tours, was on 132nd Street, right down the block from the Lafayette going toward Lenox Avenue. Boy, if old Covarrubias was ever in there, he must have been blind as a bat and had plugs in his ears.

You got him, I said. And then I also said, He was OK on that stuff in the Balinese islands and the southern part of Mexico, because he was looking at it as something ceremonial, ritualistic, and anthropological. But his down-home, across-the-tracks stuff and uptown stuff is only ethnic caricature that gets swinging all mixed up with being wild and gets being cool all confused with being melancholy.

Then I said, OK, so we know very well that Callot's Commedia dell'Arte stuff is very much the same stock character
stuff as our old minstrels used to be based on. But hell, man,
for my money even old Roark Bradford understood the farcical and satirical dimensions and implications of that stuff far
better than Covarrubias, who gets it all tangled up with the
grotesque. Man, as that tongue-in-cheek director and cast of
Green Pastures knew, Old Roark was out to swing that stuff no
less elegantly than Old Rabelais.

We didn't spend the amount of time that we usually spent
browsing in Rizzoli's whenever we were in that part of town,
because it was already as late as it was when we got there that
afternoon, and I wanted to get on back down to Forty-second
Street to the library and the assignment I had planned to finish
before going down to Washington Square. And also even as
he went on talking about what we were talking about as we
came back outside and along Fifth Avenue, I knew that when
we came to Rockefeller Center he was going over to Sixth
Avenue to take the D train down to Canal Street because he
wanted to get back down to his studio and sketch pads as soon
as possible.

So when the phone rang as if on cue just as I was finishing my
homework that evening I knew exactly who was calling and I
picked up the receiver and said, Rollo, old Rollo. How about
that stuff, Rollo? And he said, Man, what can I tell you, man,
I'm off and running like a striped-assed ape. Man, I just had to
stop and buzz you before you got to bed.
    And when I said, I was expecting this call, man, he said, I'm
not going to keep you but a minute, but this stuff is coming
at me so fast that all of a sudden I was beginning to feel like
the man in that story about mounting a horse and dashing
off in all directions. So I'm calling this late because I wanted
to make sure to clue you to remind me to tell you about a
bunch of fellow teenagers I used to hang out and make the
scene in the after-hours rounds with, and how we used to
sneak out after bedtime because our turf also included eavesdropping whichever any of those old rent party piano ticklers
cutting contests and all-night jam sessions you could get close

enough to. And man, sometimes we also used to just trail along, just following our favorite stage show entertainers to their all-night hole-in-the-wall joints. Then we would have to sneak back home to bed before daybreak. But guess what we called our crew? The Dawn Patrol. You remember that silent movie, etc.?

When he came by the library to take me out to lunch that next Thursday, he was carrying a five-by-eight sketch pad in each of the two bottom pockets of his safari jacket. And as soon as he saw me spotting them, he smiled and patted the assortment of colored felt-tipped marking pens in the jacket's left chest pocket and said, What can I tell you, Hawk? I'm hooked. Like I told you. All directions, coming and going. Man, I don't dare get fifteen feet away from pen and paper. Man, I have to keep this stuff in reach, even in the bathroom.

So you and your after-hours cut buddies used to call yourselves the Dawn Patrol, I said as we came outside and down the steps to Fifth Avenue and headed south to Forty-first Street on the way over to a French bistro on Madison Avenue that he wanted me to check out. And he said, Making the rounds, man. Talking about making the rounds, and we also used to call ourselves the Rounders. Here come the old rounders, bounders, and sidewalk pounders, which meant that you had to be slick enough not to get spotted by the cops walking the beats and tapping the lampposts and curbs with their billy clubs in those days.

Then he went on to remember that the main avenues were Lenox and Seventh, and the cross streets were 125th, 135th, and 145th, with 125th Street just hitting its stride as he reached his mid-teenage years. And the Apollo was becoming as famous for having the music of the great bands onstage as the Savoy Ballroom up on Lenox was for dance dates and swing band battles. Down the block from the Apollo there was the Hotel Theresa, on the corner of 125th Street and Seventh Avenue. It was also during this time that the Hotel Theresa bar was just becoming the mainstem where most musicians, actors, entertainers, sportswriters, entertainment page columnists, politicians, pimps, gamblers, and racketeers popped in almost every day to keep current.

There was also the Woodside Hotel, up on Seventh Avenue and 142nd Street. It's a long block over from the Savoy on the east side of Lenox Avenue, stretching from 140th Street to 142nd Street. By the time I left town for my freshman year in college, the Theresa was the cornerstone of the mainstem and there were joints jumping in just about every block east to Park Avenue and west to Broadway and the Hudson River.

At the cozy little French restaurant, we were seated immediately, and as the waiter left with our orders, I said, Believe it or not, Rollo, but down in that sawmill and L & N section gang quarters settlement on the outskirts of Mobile that I come from, my running buddy and I began eavesdropping outside the old piano and/or guitar jook joints and honky-tonks and at about the same time that we were considered big enough to go to and from school on our own.

I said, We called ourselves the Rover Boys because we were also explorers and trailblazers. And then there was a classmate I started running around with as I moved on from junior to senior high school. We were the ones who eavesdropped on the admission fee dance hall dances, where the bands from downtown Mobile and New Orleans and other towns in the southeast territory used to play from time to time. We called ourselves the Night Owls. But actually we had to be home and in bed by midnight, because we were underage! And then we didn't have the price of admission anyway.

The latest thing we got a chance to stay up for back then was the radio, with those coast-to-coast network hookups. Back in those days they used to sign off at midnight, so eleven to midnight in New York was only ten to eleven in Mobile. So we knew about the Cotton Club in New York, the Grand Terrace in Chicago, and old Louis at Frank Sebastian's Cotton Club all the way out in California.

That was when we said what we said about listening to the sports announcers broadcasting the Rose Bowl games, the World Series, and the championship prizefights on radio. And he said, Look, man, we had a radio right there at home, but I'm sure you already know that the Dawn Patrol always had to get together somewhere for stuff like that even if it was in our own living room. Some things you might just take in on your own, but not stuff like that.

He had taken his work pads from the pockets of his safari jacket and I had just started looking at his sketches and doodles he had pushed across to me when I saw the waiter coming back with our orders. And I said, I can already see what you mean by all directions. You also mean panorama. So now you've got to look out for old Goya. Old Goya zooming in. Old Goya's microscope. Old Goya's X-ray. All become old Rollo's vamps, riffs, takeoffs, and getaways on Jacques Callot plus the Belle Epoque. We started in on our lunch as I was saying what I was saying, but before we were half finished, he opened the other work pad and started doodling and sketching again, moving back and forth from plate and fork to pen and pad as smoothly as if he were taking dictation on the phone while eating and talking about what we were talking about.

Then, when it was time for me to be on my way back across to Fifth Avenue and the library, I said, Man, you and old Taft Edison. You and the Bossman Himself, and Old Pro and old Joe States. I said, Here I am, doing what I'm doing on this goddamn schedule and there you guys are, doing what you're doing on your own. Because you want to and even as you're doing it for yourself, you're also doing it for others. Others here, there, and elsewhere. I said, One of these days, man. One of these days. But as of now I've got to be going back to the salt mines at Forty-second and Fifth.

XVII

THE NEXT time I had a midafternoon snack with Taft Edison our table was the same one at which I remembered finding Old Pro having breakfast and checking through the final morning editions of the newspapers as the two-way traffic outside along 125th Street rolled east and west between Seventh and St. Nicholas Avenues on that first day in New York. I was on my way with my guidebook to see as much of midtown Manhattan as I could find my way around to alone before coming back uptown by check-in time for rehearsal. So I had come in to have a very quick snack, but when I saw him there by himself I remembered what Joe States had said about getting to the one closest to the Bossman Himself as soon as I could catch him off-duty and alone, I cut back on my sightseeing plans and asked him if I could join him.

I didn't mention anything about any of this to Taft Edison as we settled into our seats and gave our orders to the waiter that afternoon. Because when he called me that night before about joining him to check out the matinee performance of the band being featured at the Apollo Theatre that week, he had also sounded urgent when he said that there was a personal matter that he wanted to tell me about, and I was still waiting for him to bring up whatever it was, because he had not yet given me any clue to what it was about. Not even during the set changes between the variety acts.

He hadn't brought it up on our way to the restaurant and as we waited for the drinks he began talking about the music we had just heard, and about the band, which had begun as one of those now-legendary "territory bands" like the old Oklahoma City Blue Devils that he had grown up hanging around, as I used to listen to Papa Gladstone's Dance and Mardi Gras Marching Band in Mobile and at the Boom Men's Union Hall Ballroom up on Green's Avenue in Plateau. The territory bands operated mainly out of Kansas City, which was where the Blue Devils became a part of the nucleus of the world famous Count Basie Band.

Those guys. That music, Taft Edison said as we finished our drinks and started on our snack. That's something I always have to keep in touch with. Hearing and seeing those guys riffing that stuff like that reinforces my connection with a lot of idiomatic fundamentals that I am not only trying to work in terms of as a writer, but also that I don't ever want to get too far away from as a person. Man, that stuff plus all of that old church stuff was my raw material even when the music I was trying to learn to compose was concert hall music. Which is why I was all the way down there in Alabama and not at Juilliard or the Boston Conservatory or even Oberlin in the first place.

And that is when he also said, Man, just the opposite of those folks taking owls to Athens, or coals to Newcastle, I'm trying to take chitlins to the Waldorf. And I suspect you're also up to the same caper. Otherwise why would a liberal arts major with a fellowship to graduate school spend as long as you spent on the road with a band that keeps dipping as deep down into that old gut bucket no matter what else he's up to. Anyway, the more I think about it the more I look forward to running some of my prose sequences by you even while I'm still fiddling around with them.

Look, he also said, I know quite a few literary experts up here who think they know where I'm trying to go. But I'm counting on you to spot where I'm coming from. After all, since you and I took going to college as seriously as the best of them did we don't need them to tell us what we're trying to do. We just want them to be un-condescending enough to acknowledge what we are doing when we do it.

It was not until we were almost through eating and ready to order coffee that he finally got around to bringing up the personal matter that he had mentioned on the phone the night before. And it turned out to be personal not in the sense that it was a very intimate private matter, but only in the fact that it concerned him as an individual. Which did not make it any less important or urgent, but it did make it less delicate and not embarrassing to talk about. But no less confidential—or maybe even more confidential because it was also potentially if not already a matter of personal security.

Because it was about politics. By which it immediately became clear that he meant political indoctrination and recruitment for international revolution, any involvement with which required a degree of loyalty that exceeded the strictest religious devotion known to most Americans, if you were not for the organization you couldn't possibly be neutral or politically uninvolved, you were against it and might even be a special espionage agent whose purpose was to collect names for some sort of blacklist for investigation by some wing of the federal government.

You remember me telling you about those party girls and those pamphlets? he said. And about how I got myself mistaken for a likely prospect, because instead of throwing that crap in the trash can en route to the subway the next morning, I read it?! I told you about that. Well man, I'm not sure that that crew don't have me tagged as an active enemy of the goddamn cause. I do think I have reason to believe that they are checking me out for some reason. Now it could be to find out whether or not I'm worth intensifying their drive to recruit me since I've published several little pieces of attempts at a few basic definitions, nothing polemical, no clear cut position taken or specific political alignment, just attempts at elementary clarification. But you never know what they might make of it. They might see it for what it is and write me off for an academic which I'm not. Or they might decide that it is some sort of cover device for my underground mission. Anyway I'm pretty damn sure they're checking me out, and I don't know what the hell they're up to.

Man, he said, if this sounds paranoid, hell, maybe I am paranoid. But damn if I'm hallucinating—as I think I'm going to be able to show you before you head back downtown. Maybe I'm exaggerating but not out of thin air I assure you. I'm a suspicious son of a bitch I admit, but I'm not that suspicious.

And that was when he said what he said about being more of a loner than anything else and reminded me that if I remembered anything about him from that year when we were on the campus down in Alabama at the same time, I couldn't possibly have missed noticing that he kept to himself most of the time when he was not with the band or in class. And I agreed. Not that he ever struck me as being out of touch with what the hip crowd was up to.

I made a reasonable share of the dance parties and the seasonal balls, he said. But I never was a joiner of any kind. Not even back in Oklahoma City. I had my contacts, but I didn't belong to any gang. My only club on campus was really a scholarship club that also had its own socials from time to time.

Then he got the waiter's attention, and as we were waiting for the tab he nudged me and nodded toward a pedestrian strolling along the sidewalk outside the plate glass window and said, Whether you noticed it or not he's been passing back and forth and looking in here ever since we came in. Sometimes on this side of the street and sometimes on the other, and I'm pretty sure that he's not going any further east than Seventh Avenue and no further west than St. Nicholas.

And I said, Now that you mention it. But after all I am not familiar enough with this part of town to make anything of what he might be up to. What do you make of it?

And that's when he said, Well now he could be a pimp keeping tab on his chippie or chippies. Or he could be in the numbers racket. Maybe. But I don't think so, unless they're just breaking him in, and I doubt that the numbers wheels would put a novice in this area. You earn your way up to territory like this. And of course he could be a greenhorn out on his own trying to peddle some cheap light stuff. But I don't think so. No, this just might be something else. I have my suspicions. The question is whether this guy is as obvious as I think he is because he's supposed to be obvious.

So let's find out, he said as we came outside and headed for the subway stop at 125th and St. Nicholas Avenue. He didn't look back to see if we were being followed but he steered me to the uptown entrance instead of the downtown side. He still didn't look back to see if we were being followed. But when we pulled into the 145th Street and St. Nicholas Avenue station, we crossed over to the downtown platform and took the express to Columbus Circle, from where he said he was taking the bus back uptown, and I continued on downtown on the express to West Fourth Street and Sixth Avenue.

Well, that was that, he said on the phone when he called after I came home from class that night. I think he may have given up on it when we switched over on 145th. Anyway, my guess as of now is that the organization is spot-checking me. They evidently think that this writing involvement makes me somewhat special. On the one hand it's something they can utilize in a number of ways in propaganda operations, not just as a journalist or a theorist working on one of their own publications, but as one of their agents working as a regular staffer on some establishment publications.

But the problem as he saw it was not a simple matter of saying yes or no. The problem was that they knew that he spent Mondays through Fridays writing whatever he was writing in an office on Fifth Avenue at Forty-ninth Street as if on an official schedule for which he was paid by the hour. So, as far as they were concerned, he could very well be an undercover agent of some kind on official payroll and yet as he explained it, it was not necessarily as simple as that either. Because in addition to having to be on the alert for counterrevolutionary agents they also had to be able to spot agents from their own internal security system.

I just called to fill you in, he said. That's what I had in mind when I called about meeting to catch the show, and then there it was. So now I just want you to know that I don't think it has anything to do with you personally. But if you notice anything like what happened today, let me know. I have my ways of dealing with invasions of my privacy. After all—or really first of all—I'm trying to write a goddamn novel, man, and, besides, I absolutely have no patience at all with any outfit that operates on the assumption that it has to enslave me in order to free me. Hell, I know something about military and also maritime discipline and these characters don't allow furlows or shore leave.

Later, he was also to begin filling me in on what he had been thinking about such matters beginning all the way back during his senior year in high school, when what it amounted to was applied civics. But for now he just wanted me to be on the alert to what you could be getting yourself involved with if you showed any sign of inclination to become affiliated with or even curious about a certain kind of political ideology.

As for myself, he said before hanging up, Man one of the very first things that I began to realize when I checked in on that campus down there in central Alabama was that I have to learn how to be a good man on my own, because I was the one and the only one who had to decide what kind of person I wanted to be. Which was exactly the same as choosing what I wanted to do with my life. The profs were there and the books and so were the laboratories and practice facilities, but as soon as I got there and began finding my way around the campus, I began to realize that for all the legitimate pride that the administration faculty and trustees took in the achievements of their alumni, I had not come down there to be turned into another one of any kind of any of the graduates that I knew anything about. That's when it hit me that you might think that you're already on your own in senior high school, but for me being away from home made all the difference in the world. Anyway that was when I actually began to realize that the one I had to answer to from then on was myself. Hell, I didn't even have to be down there in the first place if I didn't want to be. I had felt that I had to come, but once I got down there

I realized that I did not have to *stay* if I didn't *want* to. Hell, *I had forgotten all about truant officers after the ninth grade!*

But look man, he said as if suddenly realizing again how late the phone call was, I know you've got school work to get back to. I just wanted to give you a quick follow-up on what happened today. Not because I'm worried about you but just to let you know that I'm not. Man, I'm pretty sure that you're already as aware as I am that we're already one up on anybody that thinks that because we come from down the way and are impressed with New York City we are also impressed with them!

Man, I said just before hanging up, Most of the uptown splibs I've met so far couldn't care less about the New York I came up here to get next to.

XVIII

WHEN I PICKED up the phone and heard Eric Threadcraft's voice again, I said, What say, Mice? I said, So you're in town. I said, So can you look out and see old Sherman heading south even as we speak? And he said, Howya, fella? How'd you know? I mean, not only that I'm here but also where I'm calling from? And I said, Gotcha. But it was a dead giveaway, man. Damn, you sounded like you're already heading this way, very soon if not sooner, even as you hung up. And where else would a certified Hollywood maestro popping into New York be calling from if not the Plaza or the Sherry Netherland? Because we are talking about romance, aren't we? And I don't figure you for a Waldorf man. Anyway, if you hadn't sounded so much like you had your fingers crossed when you said what you said and didn't say what you didn't say I would have guessed that you were popping into the Algonquin on film score business as the saying goes, if I remember correctly.

And he said, Touché, fellow, touché. It's like our man Joe States clued me in on you at the outset. Bass fiddle time is your thing whatever the gig. Context, fellow. That's the Joe States thing about you. But listen, I'm calling you because I've been looking forward to this trip ever since old Joe gave me your number and told me about what you're into these days. But just a couple of days before I was to pull out, something came up that changed the whole nature of the trip, something that I've got to check into right away.

Then he said, Hey, fella, you said I sounded like I had my fingers crossed just before I hung up that last time. Man, that was humility before an incredible possibility of good fortune. What I'm into now is anxiety.

And when I said, Hey, man, next time around. After all, I plan to be here for at least two years, he said, Hey, but that's not what I really mean, fellow. This is something confidential that I really want to talk to you about as soon as we can find a corner to whisper in. Man, I'm calling to find out how fast I can get to you. This morning, if possible. I don't know what you can do about this new situation. But since I was already looking forward to touching base with you, I decided that you're the very one I should run this by. Even before I let anybody else know that I'm already in town.

So I said, Since I'm going to be up at the Forty-second Street library by midmorning, why not the Algonquin lounge at say ten-thirty? Not later than eleven.

And when I asked for a hint, he said, Hey come on, fellow. Why would I have my fingers crossed if it didn't have anything to do with a woman? We're talking heartthrobs here, fellow. Man, I don't think I ever crossed my fingers in a boardroom full of wheelers and dealers, or even out at the track, win, lose, or place, or else. But when it comes to what I'm into now, it's wishful thinking from the get-go.

Which was about as much of a hint as you could expect to get on the phone from somebody you already promised to meet as soon as you could get up to Forty-fourth Street from Eighth Street and Sixth Avenue by bus or subway. So I said, See you there, man.

And when I came in and spotted him in the lounge, before looking into the bar, he was at a table for two, being served coffee. He saw me and stood up and we slapped palms and bumped shoulders, and he said, Man, this is not quite the New York junket I had in mind when I said I'd probably already be in town when I called the next time.

So when I said, So what's up? he began at the beginning. Her name was Celeste Delauny (as in Sonia and Charles Delauny, but of another family), a French fashion designer from New York, and he had met her at a party in Beverly Hills while she was in Hollywood on special assignment as a costume designer and consultant for a production that was in its early planning phase and for which he had also been offered a position as a special music consultant, arranger, composer, and combo leader. What was being planned was a high-budget comedy of manners showcasing clever dialogue, state-of-the-art furnishings, and high fashions that would also include after-hours combo music as well as hotel ballroom production numbers.

And guess what, fellow? A high-fashion expert turns out to be not only a Parisian but she's also a jazz buff! Man, the very first thing she says when I'm taken over to be introduced was that she hopes that it won't be too much of a bother for a professional like me to suggest some truly authentic spots for her to check out during the ten days that she was scheduled to be in town during this preliminary stage of the film. *Which incidentally also just happens to be the biggest thing ever to come my way. I've been doing all right, but man, this is about as big as they come for this kind of slick flick.*

But the production as such and the big breakthrough it represented for his career as an arranger/conductor was only incidental to what he had come to the Algonquin to tell me about as soon as possible that morning. Because, as he went on to say, as important as all of that was, the minute the producer who was taking him around the room introduced him to the French fashion designer from New York and he saw how she responded when she was told that his main interest as an arranger/conductor was jazz, he could hardly wait to get through the rest of the introductions and figure out a casual way to get back to her before some big-time glamour boy zeroed in on her.

And what happened was absolutely the biggest surprise he had ever been taken by. He made his way to the bar, and as he turned to sip his margarita and figure out an excuse to go back and say something to her in French, if only *aimez-vous le* jazz hot? the very first person he saw less than twelve feet away was her, obviously heading directly toward him. And before he could get his tourist guide French together she was apologizing in British English for intruding and was asking him if he could spare a few minutes and give her the list she had mentioned.

Man, what can I tell you? he said taking another sip of his tea. I told her in English that out of my longtime awareness of and respect that I had for French taste in jazz, I would not only supply her with a list of the best spots in and around town but would also be only too happy to serve as her personal tour guide. And when I saw that she was going for it, I said, Beginning as soon as you think it's discreet to check out of the present festivities. To which she said, Fifteen minutes. So we separated to take leave of our host and acquaintances and then when we came outside, she said, My limousine or yours? I heard myself saying mine because that way I get to take you home.

Then he said, Now you know damn well that I don't have to tell you which way I told my driver to head. I'll just say that Jamison McLemore and all the rest of the cats really came through for me, inviting me to sit in for a couple of numbers that they knew very well would give me the opportunity to not only show off a few of my favorite licks, but also would vouch for my authenticity. As for old Papa Ford Shelby, he treated me like a member of the family, and to my classy-looking French stone fox he said, Hello there, Miss Lady. Come on in this house and make yourself at home. You've gotta be somebody special to come out here to this scene from Paris by way of New York and latch on to somebody as with it as my boy here on the first go-round. So just make yourself comfortable and familiar, because if you dig the music, like most folks who come in here from Paris, we'll be seeing you again and again.

Man, Eric Threadcraft said as the Algonquin waiter brought more tea, I never felt so lucky in all my life, and when I took her to her hotel just before dawn the next morning, all I could think of was that I was going to be with her again that very night, which, by the way, turned out to be no letdown whatsoever from the night before, and I was on cloud nine for the rest of her stay in Hollywood. And when she went back to New York that next week, I had just about decided that we were made for each other, although, by that time, she had mentioned the fact that she had been married some time ago. Man, all that mattered to me was her future availability, which I was hoping, really fantasizing, would be exclusive. And actually I had already followed up with a brief visit here as if on urgent music business just before Joe States gave me your number. Which is why I dropped that crack in there about some anticipated changes chez Mice, just before hanging up. And you picked right up on it, fellow, because I sure as hell did have my fingers, toes, and everything else crossed.

So anyway, he went on, when old Joe States gave me your number, the renewal of our friendship on purely personal, or in any case, nonbusiness or transactional terms, gave me another perfect means of making another pseudo-urgent visit to New York to see her seem somewhat incidental withal, if you get what I mean. Man, I was really looking forward to seeing you again, but I was absolutely dying to see that fantastic and unbelievably receptive woman again, and also as often as possible without seeming overeager.

Then he went on to explain why she was not making any return trips to California. First of all, his trips were not to be taken by her as visits, but pop-ins incidental to other very urgent matters, which, as luck would have it, coincided with his admitted desire to see her as often as possible, circumstances being what they were. Which was the fact that the big Hollywood production was already very much under way, as he very well knew. But she didn't have to leave her exclusive fashion enterprise in New York to come back out to California until time for the in-person cast fittings for the actual wardrobes.

Hey, man, Old Mice has been in there doing what he can to keep any possibility from fading—as coolly as possible, you understand. Which just about brings us up to why I am here talking to you about why I am here talking to you. Man, there I was with my hotel reservations all set and my airline ticket all laid out along with my all-purpose Manhattan-bound travel gear, and when I go out to the studio two days before I'm booked to leave, there are whispers about a security check on all new foreigners under contract, and on the list to be investigated is French high-fashion designer Celeste Delauny, known in the trade as Celeste. Man, I don't know what the hell any of this has to do with designing a chic wardrobe for a super-sleek drawing room comedy. But a routine background check seems to have turned up evidence that she's being blackmailed and they're going to be digging in to find out if there's any connection with any questionable political affiliation past or ongoing.

Man, he said, shaking his head, I never felt so much like I was one of those frail-looking kids wearing thick glasses and carrying a violin case. Man, I never felt so unhip and unwith-it since way back in my preteen days when I was a conservatory-bound piano prodigy and a scholarship shoo-in and heard my first jazz records on radio and snuck off to my first chitlin circuit theater to hear some musicians playing it in person in one of those matinee vaudeville variety shows. Man, I don't remember ever being so unwith-it about anything in my life before.

And when I said what I said about that kind of idiomatic initiation adding up to the maestro that Joe States put me in touch with in Hollywood, he said, Man, that was the music scene. Man, this stuff sounds like some international intrigue involvement that I never thought of as being related to me on any personal level. Man, the only personal concerns I ever really had about international relations have been with keeping my passport up to date and getting my stuff through customs, duty-free or not, it's all the same to me.

So here he was back in New York to see her again, but now the cover story about being in town to reestablish his special schoolboy-to-schoolboy relationship with me also covered the fact that he was also in town to get some expert advice from some of his old local show business contacts about hiring a reliable private investigator to fill him in on the political past of Celeste Delauny of the very exclusive Celeste haute couture line and boutique.

Look, fellow, I know you know damn well that I know how uncool this sounds, he said. But man, I'm also counting on you to realize that all of this is still very much in vamping phase. Which is why it's absolutely impossible for me to even hint that I question anything of any sort whatever about her. Man, I'm just trying to vamp this infatuation thing until she comes back out to the coast. What all this has been about all along is me vamping this thing until she comes back when the producers start pulling all the logistics together and now I've got to find out if it's worth it or if it's all going to go up in smoke.

XIX

WHEN HE finally called me from Hollywood to bring me up-to-date on the situation a week and a half later, as soon as I heard his voice I knew that whatever had happened during the rest of his trip to New York or after his return to the coast had changed his mood from shock and anxiety to an enthusiastic anticipation that I remembered always being there whenever we were doing whatever we had been doing in California.

So what can I tell you, my man? he said, before I could even say Hello. You already know that Hollywood is seventy-five percent if not ninety percent pop song romance, Sunset Boulevard and blue horizons indeed. So what can I tell you, fellow? Old Mice got it bad and gotta try to make it good. So I got over that attack of cornballitis.

Man, he went on, I realize what had hit me right after we came outside and you headed across the street to the arcade to Forty-third Street. Suddenly there was this irrepressible need to hear her voice again as soon as possible. So that I could be sure that I hadn't made the whole goddamn thing up. So I decided to call her up and ask if I could pop by the boutique.

Which he had done from the phone in the lobby of the bank at the corner of Fifth Avenue, and she had said yes and as he hung up he suddenly realized that the relationship he was trying to develop with her was only incidentally and at most only temporarily connected with the film production that neither of them had ever mentioned to each other. After all, her profession was high fashion as such, not costumes for show business, and she had come out to Hollywood only to look around, mainly because the producer had sent for her, hoping that the visit would change the "maybe" she had given them to a "yes."

Look, man, he said, I think I made it pretty clear that I got to meet her in the first place because she was more excited about the music she might be able to check out while out there than she was about the technical details in the production of what to her was only a sweet drawing room comedy that she was out there to decide whether she wanted to work on.

I grunted to let him know that I thought he was making his point, and that was when he went on to say, Now hey, fellow, you know as well as I do that a job as composer/consultant on a high-budget production like that was a pretty big break for Old Mice's status as a sound stage studio pop pro in this town, as far as that sort of thing goes around here. But although it was my new status that got me to that Beverly Hills production party where I met her, it was because of the music that I'm most serious about that I got to take her out that very first night.

You've got to believe me, fellow, he said, neither one of us mentioned anything at all about that goddamn sleek-ass production. Not even a word about when or if she might have to come back out for final fittings and the shooting. My guess was that she would take the script and do all the designs and sketches in New York and send them out for approval and suggestions and make whatever adjustments and revisions they requested and sew everything up in New York and come back out west to check things out when the actual shooting began.

Anyway, as he had come on along Forty-fourth Street and turned up Madison Avenue, the only thing that mattered was that she was waiting for him and he would be there in less than ten minutes and would see how her head tilted and her hair fell as her eyes sparkled when her Parisian lips moved as she said whatever she would say.

He had not taken a taxi because he needed that much walking distance to get himself back together after what he had put himself through. But every time he had to stop at a traffic light he realized he was struggling to keep himself from springing forward before the yellow light changed to green again.

Hey, man, when I stepped into that *endroit* of ultimate chic while the fragrance matched the background like music and a design on display seemed almost as much a part of nature as the flower arrangement and here's this stone fox of a Parisian high-fashion designer looking like she's one of her own models. Man, not just waiting for me to pop by for a brief arrival chat but also ready to turn me right around and head for a cozy, nearby bistro because it's lunchtime.

He then went on to say that by that time it was as if he had never ever heard of a private investigator or ever even seen the ones he grew up going to see in the movies. Then he also went on to tell me that even as I had disappeared into the arcade that it hit him. He was not going to hire a private investigator because he was not going to let this incredible prospect of a relationship that would fulfill so many of his adolescent and undergraduate fantasies get away whether she stayed on that movie production or not.

We're talking infatuation here, my man, he said. That's why it's taking me this long to call up and report. I was in bad shape when I called you that morning and I'm glad I did, but afterward I was so embarrassed because I must have sounded so unhip. But then I finally said what the hell, my man has got to meet this trillie. He's got to see for himself what made Old Mice hit the panic button like that.

Man, every time I think about how I must have sounded to you. All ready to plunge into class B movie international intrigue because a goddamn Hollywood studio that's running a routine background check on a classy Paris fashion designer who is already established in New York and who has no special interest in working on flicks in the first goddamn place.

Look pal, he said, the more I thought about that, the more embarrassed I became until this morning, when I finally said, Goddamn, here I go again. And that's when I said, What the hell is all this? I've gotta call him. That's my man and all I did after not seeing him for that long was to lay that on him. So here's Old Mice, pal. What can I tell you?

That's when I said, Ah, come on, Mice. You're the professional musician, not me. I'm just the schoolboy. You're not only an arranger, you also love to jam, catching as catch can. And when you hit a goddamn clinker, which everybody, including the Bossman Himself, does from time to time, you don't stop playing. You riff right on beyond it.

Hey, yes, he said, and I visualized him looking down at the keyboard because I already assumed that he was calling from the phone he kept on the piano, when you're rehearsing you can stop and hack at it until you make it something you feel you can live with, but when you're out there with a mike and footlights on, it's the real thing and the metronome is still clicking and clocking you. You've got to get with it.

And besides, I said, don't nobody know anything about this but you and me, man. The main person has no idea what you put yourself through. So come on, man.

And he said, Hey, fellow, you said it, man. That's exactly what this is all about. So look, the main reason I'm finally making this call is to get us back to what I thought my other trip to New York was going to be about. *I've got to get the four of us together.* Man, you've got to meet this lady, and my stock-in-trade with her will go up when she meets you. As for your fine people, as Joe States calls her, tell her how sorry I am that I got too tangled up to meet her on my last trip to town. But don't tell her why, as of course you wouldn't anyway. See you soon, fellow, real soon. As soon as I can get this recording studio backlog out of the way of that movie thing. So expect me, fellow. Any minute.

XX

GUESS WHO? Eric Threadcraft said as soon as he heard my voice answering the phone. And when I said, Maestro, what say, Mice? You back in town, Mice? He said, Just checked back in across Fifth from old you know who southbound. Haven't even unpacked yet. First item being your earliest availability for that too-long-overdue foursome for lunch or preferably dinner and music. Music afterward, that is. And then I said, Hey, sounds absolutely top-notch to me, Mice, and I myself happen to be fairly flexible this week, but I can't speak for the family. So call me back for the official estimate of the situation—say, round about midnight. Which he did and when he gave the date, time, and place he said, Celeste chose the restaurant and you and I will decide whose group to check out afterward.

Hey, man, he said then. This is great, fellow, just great. Not only am I finally going to meet Miss-All-Them-Fine-People rolled into one that old Papa Joe has made me so curious about. And not only are you going to see what the goddamn French hit Old Mice with right out there in the world's most over populated briar patch of starlets trying to become movie queens. And man, you yourself are just going to enhance the idiomatic authenticity of Old Mice's musicianship. Man, you know how the French are about the natural history of this stuff. Remember what I told you about taking her over to West L.A. that first night? Elementary, as your Sherlockian roommate used to say, elementary.

We saw them as soon as we came into the four-star midtown French restaurant that mild midspring Friday night. We were not quite ten minutes early, but they were already there waiting for us near the short line to the coat-check counter, and when he saw us coming he waved, and as we joined them he said, So here at long last is her fantastic self in person. And this is Celeste, also in person. But also a part of Old Mice's world of fantasy even so.

And I said, Who else, maestro, who else but, my man? Man, my confidence in your piano vamping applies to these matters, too.

From the very first time he mentioned her, he had been so busy telling me how he felt about her that he had never got around to describing any of her physical features at all, not even the color of her eyes and hair. But she looked just about like I expected her to look. Because she looked more like French women look in French movies and paintings and as you visualize them when you read about them in French novels than like pictures in the fashion magazines.

We checked our New York early-spring wraps and as we fell in behind the two of them following the maître d' leading us to our table, I was thinking that I also assumed that the way her eyes and lips moved as she spoke English with a throaty British-tinged Parisian accent would have a very similar effect on his U.S.A. schoolboy sensibility as it would have on mine.

So I nudged him and whispered, Hey, man, the way she gasps *oui*! is worth the whole price of the goddamn admission. To which he said, What can I tell you, fellow, what can I tell you?

He put his arm around my shoulder then and said, Look, I'm well aware that this thing of mine is only a matter of months, but even as ongoing as the excitement of the newness of it all, at this very moment I still have the feeling that this pas de quatre is long overdue. Which probably just goes to show what I've been putting myself through these last months.

Then when we were seated and Celeste had suggested choices from the menu, he turned to Eunice again and then turned to me and said, Incurable schoolboy as I myself also am I must point out a little academic detail that you and old Papa Joe left out: Nefertiti, fellow, Queen Nefertiti, sans the Egyptian headgear, of course.

Sans Egyptian headgear, to be sure, I said. And then I said, Because as my old roommate, who cut out before Miss You-Know-Who arrived, but who was the one who was reading the volume on art history in which I first saw a color photo of that famous bust, said, Who knows but the head beneath that ever so regal crown or whatever it is may be as hairless as a cue ball. So I concede the teacake tan skin, quibble the neck as artistic license, but no deal if Nefertiti's hair is not Creole or Latino frizzly.

And he said, Deal, fellow. I never would have guessed central Alabama if you hadn't already told me out in Hollywood when you first mentioned her. I would have guessed she was the one from Mobile and the Gulf Coast area and you were the one from central Alabama. But then your flesh-and-blood parents are from central Alabama, aren't they? See, I remember you telling me about that, too. But anyway, fellow, old Papa Joe got it right. She is fine people. Extra-fine people. Extra-superfine people.

He turned to get her attention then, but I didn't hear what he said because that was when Celeste asked me if a teacake was an American madeleine. And I said not really because it was really a very plain, not very sweet soft cookie, whereas a madeleine was very sweet like a down-home muffin and was baked in a muffin pan. You could bake teacakes on a cookie sheet, but since they were made from rolled dough like biscuits, a bread pan was better, but teacakes were not as spongy as biscuits.

When I paused I could follow what Eric was asking Eunice about campus life in central Alabama, but before he turned to me, our waiters arrived with our orders, and we all turned to Celeste, and Eric said having her as hostess was absolutely the next best thing to being in the region of France where each recipe came from.

When Eric asked me to tell Celeste about my trip to the Côte d'Azur and Paris and I mentioned Marquis de Chaumienne, she said she knew who he was but she had not become aware of his special interest in American music until she returned to Paris after her first trip to New York.

I was here on business, she said, an ambitious young upstart that I already was, I had spent all of my time in midtown on Fifth and Madison Avenues and down in the garment district. And at night there were the midtown restaurants, including this one. And also the Broadway and Times Square movie houses, which I'm afraid I had very little time for. But when I came back to Paris and said no when asked if I had been taken up to Harlem to hear American music not to mention dancing at its best and in unmatched variety, I was made to feel that I was deficient in an indispensable dimension of the spirit of the times. They were shocked. It was almost as if a supposedly sophisticated Englishman had come to Paris and remained oblivious to what Montmartre, Montparnasse, and St. Germain des Prés were all about!

Or so I felt, at any rate, she went on to say. And that was what led her to find out that the Hot Club of France was neither just another Parisian fad or cult, but included truly cosmopolitan people like the Marquis de Chaumienne, who regarded many of the jazz musicians they heard on recordings and in person, on tours that included Paris and other European capitals, as representative contemporary artists who transcended the context of popular show business entertainment that they most often worked in.

I've never met the marquis, she said, but I'm told that in addition to recordings, he also collects other American artifacts, especially of ranch life and the western frontier, which I'm told also includes paintings and bronzes by Frederic Remington.

To which I said I had also been told included a very special interest in quarter horse racing and rodeos, sporting events that required skills basic to cattle-herding. The quarter horse was a sporting version of the sprint-oriented, ever-so-maneuverable cow pony. And the rodeo also included such cowpuncher skills as roping, throwing, and binding calves for branding, as well as demonstrating the cowpuncher's ability to hang on to a

wildly bucking untamed horse, the first step in taming his own
mount.

I told her that it was said that there had been a time when he
came over for the quarter horse racing season every year, but
that he also had no special interest in western music beyond its
use in Hollywood movies about cowboys—nonsinging cowboys. And Eric pointed out that back during the days of silent
films, cowboy movies used to be called *horse operas*, because
the incidental music played along with them in the theaters
on an organ consisted of excerpts of classical compositions by
European composers.

That was, I also told her, what I had heard about when he
came over for the Thoroughbred races, his trips to the Kentucky Derby also included visits to hear music in New Orleans,
Memphis, and Chicago. And when Eric said, And New York
was his home base for the Preakness and the Belmont Stakes,
right? I said, So I've been told, but I've also been told that
there was a time when he used to spend the night before or after the Preakness in Baltimore because it was the hometown of
so many eastern ragtime piano players, especially Eubie Blake
and also Joe Turner, who was to spend a number of years touring in Europe, settling in Paris from time to time.

That was when Eric Threadcraft said what he said about his
trips to Paris, so I didn't say anything else about the Marquis
de Chaumienne and he went on to say what he said about not
having had a chance to see Paris and France with Celeste yet,
because she had not gone back since the two of them had met,
which, after all, had been a matter of several weeks rather than
months.

When the waiter cleared the table and left with our orders for
desserts, I asked how their production assignments were coming along, and Celeste said that her designs had been approved
and were in production and that she was not needed in Hollywood until time for the fittings for the actual filming.

And Eric said, Man, as you were out there long enough and
close enough to that operation to know, you're not through
with a film score and the final cutting operation until after
the previews or even after the official opening—while they're

holding up distribution. But as of now, I'm feeling pretty good about how things are coming along so far, and at least nobody is squawking yet.

The cab ride downtown to the nightclub took less than fifteen minutes, and we arrived in time to get seated and to order our after-dinner liqueurs and brandies before the second set began. And it began on time. The group was a five-piece combo led by a piano player and included a drummer, a bass player, trumpet, and tenor saxophone. None of them were famous, but all of them had played and recorded with well-known leaders. Eric was more familiar with all of them than I was. He was also more up-to-date on the latest musical fads and trends—that was an indispensable part of his job as a recording studio technician and conductor.

That was also why I had deferred to his choice of an after-dinner music spot without suggesting any alternative. And he had said, Hey, no big deal. Something OK, but won't get in the way. It's just a thing I have about coming back to New York, however briefly. You know me, fellow, missing out on this music in New York would be like not even getting a glimpse of the plage on a trip to the Côte d'Azur.

And that was also when he went on to say, Like I said, fellow, this pas de quatre has its own sound track. Man, I must confess: if the Bossman and old Papa Joe and that gang were here tonight, it would be *too much*, if you know what I mean. Later for nights like that. Too much for how I feel as of now. You know what I mean.

XXI

I DIDN'T HEAR very much of what Celeste and Eunice talked to each other about in the restaurant and between numbers at the nightclub that evening. But the last thing Eunice said when the cab let us out at our address before heading up to midtown was that she would call and confirm before Tuesday afternoon.

And Celeste said, *D'accord, merveilleux.*

And Eric and I slapped palms.

And the cab pulled off, and as Eunice and I headed across the sidewalk to our entrance, she said she had promised Celeste that she would let her know which day next week would be most convenient for the two of them to meet for lunch and for a visit to the boutique.

They spent most of that next Friday afternoon together. And it was when Eunice told me what she told that night at dinnertime that I found out what I found out about what her impression of him was when they were introduced to each other at that producer's party in Beverly Hills on her first trip to Hollywood.

Of all the artists and technicians involved in the production being initiated, the ones she had been most curious about were the composer and conductor of the incidental music score. She had already read the script and had already seen sketches and models for the settings. But she had no idea of what the incidental music would be like. The production was not a Hollywood musical, but she was hoping that the score would not be what she thought of as standard American drawing room comedy music featuring a light or semiclassical string orchestra playing the all-too-conventional pipe organ–derived urban soap opera variation of the old Wild West horse opera music.

She knew very well that designing a chic wardrobe for an American sitcom was not to be confused with designing costumes for an opera or ballet. Costumes could be obviously unrealistic, downright symbolic, or even outrageous. Sitcom wardrobes were perhaps not only au courant but perhaps most often dernier cri—indeed, as dernier cri as the current fashion magazines. Certainly that was what this script called for. So what she had been hoping was that her haute couture designs would be obviously consistent with, if not altogether emblematic of, the contemporary American spirit as it was expressed in the music and the dance movements that she had become so fascinated by.

So when she and Eric Threadcraft were introduced to each other and he turned out to be a young American professional recording studio arranger and conductor of jazz-based popular music, she was pleased because she felt that he would be responsive to her conception of how her wardrobe designs and his score would go together.

Not only was he sympathetic, his immediate response was to invite her to come along as he made the rounds, dropping in on several of his after-hours spots, beginning in West Los Angeles and including a cruise along Central Avenue, depending on who was where. After all, in addition to the headliners in the glittering addresses along Sunset Strip, there was always a wider choice of first-rate professionals from every section of the country playing somewhere in or around Los Angeles just about every night, and he kept tabs on most of the best.

That was when I told Eunice what I told her about what he told me when he called from the Plaza that first time, and I met him at the Algonquin that morning. I said that was not the first time he had mentioned Celeste Delauny, it was also the first time he had ever mentioned anything about any date he had ever had with anybody, not only in Hollywood but anywhere else. I said I knew he was single and that my impression was that he had never been married but had not mentioned having any special girlfriend even when I would say what I would say about Miss You-Know-Who from time to time when he and I made the rounds we used to make to nightspots from time to time. My impression on those occasions was that his interest was not social but musical, not with getting a date, but getting an invitation to sit in on piano during a jam session.

I said I had told him about us when I told him about the campus not long after Joe States had introduced us that night at the Palladium, but it was not until Joe States told him about me showing up with Miss Fine People Herself that he not only mentioned that he had met Celeste but also that he expected to see me soon because he was coming to New York to see her.

I didn't say anything at all to Eunice about how upset he was when he and I met at the Algonquin that morning because just before leaving Hollywood he had found out that the studio's background check report contained evidence that suggested that Celeste was being blackmailed by somebody in Paris.

I hadn't mentioned anything about it to her at the time, and I didn't say anything about it later on because he had not said anything else about it since he said what he said when he called when he got back to Hollywood. I wondered what happened between that call and the next, but I didn't ask and he didn't tell and I acted as if he hadn't told me anything except how much he liked everything about her.

She likes him very much, Eunice said when she came back from the luncheon date in midtown and the afternoon visit to the boutique on Madison Avenue in the Sixties. She kept saying how *très gentil* he is and freshly American, not fresh in the down-home sense, but in the sense of being enthusiastic instead of laid back. But as excited as she seemed about how things have been going for her in New York and now also Hollywood, and as enthusiastic as she seems about dating your friend Eric, not only because he is so nice, but also professionally involved with the movies he's involved with, I must say I don't think she's about to give up Paris for New York and/or Hollywood.

And I said, We shall see what we shall see. But as for him, I can see him giving up what he's doing in Hollywood to take a band out of New York on the road for a while, but I doubt he'll give up what he's into in Hollywood for what he's likely to be doing in Paris. But we shall see what we shall see about that, too, won't we?

XXII

WHEN JOE STATES called from Chicago that night and told me that the band would be back in New York that next week for a brief stopover en route to Europe, he said, Get to me fast, as he almost always did, but this time he also added, Even if you have to skip a class session or two. Details eye to eye. Just be ready to zip to me at the time and place I'll give you a lead on as soon as I arrive and schedule my pretakeoff errands.

They were due in at twilight that next Wednesday with time off until the night flight to Frankfurt Friday, to open in Berlin that Sunday for a week before going on to Paris, Amsterdam, Copenhagen, Stockholm, and back Stateside by way of Amsterdam and London.

I was to pick him up at Gabe's Barbershop up on Broadway between 151st and 152nd Streets, and when I got there he was in a barber's chair with his back to the entrance, but we saw each other in the mirror at the same time, and he said, Here's that schoolboy ahead of that tardy bell as always. What say, States? Hey, Gabe, this is my young statemate from the Beel I was telling you about.

And as Gabe, who was the barber serving him, turned the chair around and shook my hand, somebody in one of the other chairs near the magazine rack said, Mobile, old Cootie Williams used to play all that signifying trumpet with Duke was from Mobile. And somebody else said, old Satchel Paige. Old Satchel already had all of them fancy strikeout pitches, including the *fadeaway*, before he left Mobile and freelanced and barnstormed his way to the Kansas City Monarchs.

Joe States was standing up then and as Gabe went on to finish brushing and whisking him, he said, And don't forget the one and only Mr. James Reese Europe, the head honcho of the famous Clef Club back in the States when Hotel Marshall down on Seventh Avenue and Fifty-third Street was the main hip brownskin hangout in midtown. I'm talking about where you'd find all them old pioneering show cats like old Will Marion Cook and old Harry T. Burleigh and where Bert Williams and George Walker used to touch base regularly.

Old Jim Europe came to New York from D.C. but he got his start right down there in the Bay-City-on-the-way-to-the-Gulf-Coast-town of Mobile, Alabama. Yeah, old Jim Europe, Gabe said. Man, back during World War I old Jim Europe took a band of syncopating hellfighters from the old Harlem 369th to France and became the rage of Paris! And even before that he was the one that helped that classy ofay dance team of Vernon and Irene Castle establish the fox-trot. Good-bye, cakewalk, and look out, waltz! Here come the shout, the shimmie-she-wobble, the mess around, the stomp down, the Birmingham Breakdown, not to mention the Charleston and all them Lindy-hopping jitterbugs!

Nice to meet you, Mobile, Gabe said as he walked us to the door. Come on back and touch base with us from time to time. This a regular checkpoint for a lot of down-home cats, especially ones in showbiz and sports. Also a few grad students from Columbia. Now old Joe here usually pops in here when the band's in town long enough, but always whenever they're heading across the water. Got to get that fresh touch-up, boy, especially back in the old days when the conks were in. Them Euros dig our music and jive, but they're not quite down with our hair styling yet. Although they like what we do with it. They're coming along, but they ain't quite there yet and so far all them different kind of Africans over there speaking the hell out of all them European languages plus educated British English, don't add up to much help in the barbershop.

As Joe States and I came down along Broadway toward the subway station he said, Hell, let's walk a while. You know me. I've got to keep myself in shape for driving that twenty-mule team. As you well know, the goddamn Bossman expects me to be as ready as he always is, and I mean always is. So let's go see who's at the Y.

And when we came to 145th Street we turned east and headed toward Convent Avenue, which would run on past Hamilton Mews and into the campus of City College to the turnoff path that you could take downhill to St. Nicholas Avenue and 135th Street.

Now look, he said as we stopped for a red light at Amsterdam Avenue, all you've got to do is just say you already have enough plans of your own. This is just something we came up with when I heard what I heard from my man Eric and mentioned it to the Bossman and talked to Old Pro. My man Eric just happened to ask me if you had mentioned anything about getting away from that Ph.D. jive for a while and do some thinking and researching on your own while doing a little part-time college teaching back down on your old stomping ground.

Then as we came down the sloping sidewalk to the Convent Avenue turnoff he said, So the three of us put our heads together and the boss came up with something so fast that we realized that he already thought about it some time ago, and Old Pro and I said, Why not? This is just the thing! And I said, Let me be the one to take it up with him, because if the boss suggests it he'll say yes whether he really wants to do it or not. Because he feels he owes him anything he asks for and the same thing goes for you, Pro.

So here we go, he said, punching me playfully, And I can help you lie your way out of it if you'd just as soon not take it on. We could just say sometime later after you check out the routine down the way.

Then when I said, What's the proposition, Papa Joe? he said, First let me say this. Because this is not just some kind of stop-gap favor. This is foundation stuff, a real fundamental research and writing project and the thing about it is that the man had you pegged from the get-go. And I'm talking about all the way back to when he heard you in that combo with the one and only Miss Hortense Hightower. She wanted him to hear you in that combo in that lounge that night, not because she thought you might be on your way to becoming a musician, but she just wanted him to pick up on how you listen.

Man, he then went on to say, you may not have ever really thought about becoming a musician, but your ears are something else! So who the hell knows? Maybe it's a part of your gift as a storyteller and lie swapper like back in primitive times even before English was English or, hell, even Greek was Greek or the Bible was the Bible. I don't know, but I do know you've got the musical version of a photographic memory. You hear it, you've got it. And that includes absolute pitch, and along with all that, you hum everything like a conductor who knows how all the sections hook up.

Hey, but look, he said as we came along Convent Avenue to the 140th Street entrance to the campus, I know that I don't have to go into all this. You already know that you're as much our own special schoolboy as anybody else's, including who else but the one and only Miss Hortense Hightower, who sold you to the Bossman in the first place and is in on this, too. In case you haven't guessed.

Then he said, So here's the proposition. The Bossman wants you to write up Daddy Royal. When I told him what my boy Eric told me about you thinking about taking a term or so off to do some part-time teaching while deciding what you really want to do with all that big-league education besides teaching it, what he came up with was Daddy Royal and all them prizes and souvenirs and stuff that he's accumulated over all these years.

All I could think to say was, Hey, man, this is some pretty heavy stuff you guys want to lay on me. *But even as I said it I began to smile because it was as if I were all the way back in Miss Lexine Metcalf's third-grade classroom in Mobile County Training School again and she was going to say, "Who if not you, my splendid young man?"*

By which I knew she meant that I, who was only nine, was already her preteenage choice candidate for Mr. B. Franklin Fisher's Principal's Corps of Talented Tenth Early Birds.

So I also said, But after all, this is not the first time you guys would be taking a chance on a novice. And he said, Man, the boss already had your number months before Shag Phillips's emergency came up. Our Miss Hortense Hightower saw to that just out of Alabama pride because she herself was impressed.

Then when I said, What about Daddy Royal himself? he said, The boss is ahead of all of us on that, too. And I mean way out in front of everybody. Didn't he take time out to personally take you up to see him the first break he got on your first trip to New York? As busy as he always is when we're in town, he took time out to personally take you up there and introduce you to him. Not as a new sensational fiddle player, but as a schoolboy who was trying to learn how to fit a whole lot of stuff together.

As we left the CCNY campus to come down the steep slope and across St. Nicholas Avenue to 135th Street, he said, Now get to this: when we brought Scratchy Mac into New York with us that first time, the Bossman and Old Pro couldn't hardly wait to send a limousine up to the Hill so Daddy Royal could put on his light fantastic patent leather boots and come down and pat his feet and wiggle his toes while old Scratchy and me did what we did to Broadway. But he didn't take Scratchy up to Sugar Hill to go one on one with Daddy Royal.

On the way along 135th Street to cross Eighth Avenue all he said was, Of course you know good and well who the Bossman had called all the way down in Alabama, even when he and Old Pro and I were still talking about what my man Eric had told me. And she also thought that working down there was not only a good idea but also a lucky coincidence.

Then there was only the sound of the traffic and our footsteps as he let me think about what I was thinking about for a while.

But when we came on to the corner of Seventh Avenue and stood waiting for the green light with the Harlem YMCA pool-room now only half a block away, he said, So, what say, States? What do I tell the man and Old Pro? Check with Miss Fine People and buzz me anytime tonight or before ten in the morning and if I'm not in, I'll be buzzing you from wherever I am, because I'm buzzing the boss around ten, probably about lunch.

And I said, Me and you, Papa Joe.

And he said, Charm Miss Fine People for me, Old Pro, the Bossman Himself, and Daddy Royal. Not that I have my fingers crossed, because I know one when I see one. And she's for real.

XXIII

WELL, HERE'S that down-home johnny-right-on-the-dot school-boy, Royal Highness said as soon as he heard my voice saying hello into the telephone that Wednesday night. Then he said, What say, young soldier? Damn if I wasn't already thinking about you just before the phone rang because I was actually expecting to be hearing from you round about now. So, the Bossman and Old Pro sicced old Joe States on you.

And when I said, You know them, Daddy Royal, you know them better than anybody else I know, including everybody in the band, he said, Hell, I probably do at that. And as I'm sure you already found out before I said this the first time, that band is a family, and I guess I'm something like a godfather and grandfather or granduncle all rolled into one. I told you about me and the Bossman and me and Old Pro. And I'm absolutely certain that old tight-butt, trigger-footed Joe States clued you in on himself and the two of them as well, you coming right in there with him and the boss in the rhythm section plus also being from Alabama and all.

Then when I said what I said about what I would be doing on the campus back down in central Alabama, he said, So before you go down there, why don't you just come on back up here the first chance you get and let's see what the hell we can do about this thing while you're down there. You know you're long overdue on your next visit up here anyway.

And when I went back up to Sugar Hill to see him that next Saturday afternoon, he said, Let me tell you something, young soldier, this proposition don't really come as no big surprise to me at all. Hell, I know something extra special was up from the very get-go. Here you were on your very first trip to New York City and you're going to be here for only a few crowded days with the goddamn time clicking like a goddamn roller coaster, and here he come calling to tell me he's bringing Shag Phillips's *temporary* replacement by here to make my personal acquaintance! Some nice neat kid fresh out of college down in Alabama and on his way to work on his master's and Ph.D. as soon as he can come by enough cash to go with his college commencement grant for advanced study.

I remember, I said, and I see what you mean, but at the time I thought that visit was mainly about rhythm and tempo because he was getting me ready for my first recording session— and also because he probably knew that I grew up knowing about you from placards and also from pictures and articles in the *Chicago Defender* and the *Pittsburgh Courier*.

Yeah, that's a good point, all right, he said. But mark my words. If he had any doubts about you being ready to record you wouldn't have been heading for that studio in the first place. No, he had something else in mind, and this proposition just goes to bear out my hunch about what it was.

And when I said, You really think this goes back that far, Daddy Royal? He said, No doubt in my mind, now that I think about it. But here you come talking about a temporary replacement and anybody could see he was already treating you like you were his adopted son or at least some kind of newfound nephew or godchild or something, knowing full well that you are not about to give up going on to graduate school to get yourself at least a master's degree. In literature, not music, even when you stayed on beyond that first summer. I know he knew that because I know him. So I knew he had something else in mind other than keeping you out on the road with the band.

Look, he said, just think about it. This whole thing is as plain as day. All we've got to do now is just continue what we started the very first day he brought you up here and have continued off and on ever since you came back to go to the university.

I'm telling you, young soldier, he said, even when you left the band to stick around out there in Hollywood, he didn't give up on you. He just chalked it up as some more useful experience that went right along with what he had in mind for you when the time came. And he knew what he was doing because you didn't give up on school for them bright lights out there either.

We spent the rest of that afternoon looking at some of the items in his collection of show business memorabilia that he had not gotten around to bringing out for me to see before. But this time he limited his ongoing remarks to identification and chronology, saving all anecdotes for the actual work on the project.

And when I stood up to get ready to move toward the door, because it was time for me to head back downtown, he said, Of course you know good and well by now that all this about me and my story is just the beginning of this thing. What they got in mind for you goes a long way beyond me and this. As a matter of fact, as soon as I just said that, it put me in mind of something, some old professor in Germany or Switzerland or somewhere over there said to me when I was first touring over them countries across the water years ago. It just popped into my mind again after all these years. He said people started dancing before there was any music to dance to. So dance comes first and then music. Of course, you know as well as I do them professorial cats over there got theories about everything. But I bet you music follows dance *this* time, if you get my point.

He had come on along the hall to the elevator with me then, and just before I pushed the button, he put his hand on my shoulder and said, Of course, you also realize that this whole thing just might have got started with Hortense Hightower down there in Alabama in the first place. This could have been the deal from the very beginning. I wouldn't be a bit surprised if all of this wasn't the main point of the deal when she got the boss to let you fill in that summer when Shag Phillips had to check out. She knew the boss knew damn well she wouldn't be asking him to take somebody in there that couldn't cut the mustard. And you know as well as I do that she wouldn't even think about asking him to do something like that before checking it out with Joe States. No way she would ever go straight to the boss with something like that without first checking with old Joe.

XXIV

So THERE I was once more en route south and into the also and also of a very old place once more. *Me and all of the obligations, expectations, and ever-alluring and expanding horizons of personal aspirations that were already beginning to be part and parcel of those now ever so wee lullaby rocking chair storybook adventure times even before I was yet old enough to stay awake for the long winter night tell-me-tale-time semicircle around the red brick fireplace beneath the Mother Goose chime clock mantelpiece.*

Southbound once more by erstwhile thunderbird become at least for the time being Whisperjet. *Me and the one who was the one for me and would also go north or south and would go east or west and also east of the sun and also west of the moon even as she also fulfilled ancestral hometown expectations along with personal aspirations of her own.*

In those days you took the Delta Airlines Shuttle from LaGuardia in New York to Atlanta International. Then you transferred to the southwest-bound commuter flight to Montgomery and central Alabama and so on to Mississippi and Louisiana was only one more hour, departing Eastern Standard Time and arriving the same hour Central Standard Time. *And as our flight entered the landing approach pattern and we brought our seats upright, I said, Here we go, thinking, all the way back to within this many Alabama miles north by east from the outskirts of Mobile and the river and the canebrakes and cypress swamp moss and the state docks and the bay and the Gulf Coast beyond the storybook blue and storm gray horizons of which were the old Spanish Main and also the Seven Seas and the seven storybook wonders of the ancient world.*

As the airport limousine pulled on away from the city limits and settled into the thirty-mile interstate highway drive to the campus exit, we said what we said about the central Alabama preautumn countryside, and when she closed her eyes I went on remembering how uncertain everything had been for me that first September.

But I had said to myself what I had said to myself even so. Because I was there not only from Mobile County Training School and Miss Lexine Metcalf and her windows on the world and Mr. B. Franklin Fisher and the early birds, I was also there from Gasoline Point. So I said what I had already been saying long before school bell time became more urgent than train whistle and sawmill whistle time. I said, Destination Philamayork, remembering the comings and goings of old sporty-limp-walking Luzana Cholly with his blue steel .32-.20 in his underarm holster and the delicate touch and locomotive thunder of his rawhide tough twelve-string guitar fingers and what he said that time under the Three-Mile Creek L & N bridge. And there was also old patent-leather-footed, pigeon-toed-tipping Stagolee Dupas fils with his diamond-flashing piano fingers and tailored-to-measure jazz-backed suits, who did what he did that night at Joe Lockett's in the Bottoms and didn't skip city afterward. *Because Philamayork was not somewhere you escaped to. It was somewhere you earned your way to, your hithering and thithering way through, thick and thin and wherever and whatever to.*

I also said what I said when I arrived on campus that first September because my destination was already what it was long before I was aware of anything at all about what actually made Luzana Cholly Luzana Cholly and Stagolee Dupas fils the notorious Stagolee Dupas fils. Because for me it all had actually begun all the way back during the now only vaguely remembered time when Mama began calling me her little old scoot-about man, even before I had learned enough about words to know what scooter and scooting about actually meant.

But by the time I had arrived on campus as a college freshman that first September I had learned what I had learned from that many rockabye tale times and all the midwinter fireside times and summer night mosquito smoke times even before the day came when Mama let Miss Tee take me to be enrolled because my school bell time had come. And I was a schoolboy from then on and Mama said, That's Mama's little old Buster

Brown scootabout man over there scooting about that school-yard just like some little old cottontail jackrabbit scooting all over the briar patch.

So I said what I said about myself as I looked out on the part of the campus you could see from my dormitory room, and when my roommate arrived from Chicago, I said what I first said about him because his nickname was Geronimo, which I associated with the escapades of Reynard the Fox. But when class sessions began I said he was like a young Dr. Faustus, which earned him the campuswide nickname of the Snake, as if that made him a devil-ordained tent show and vaudeville magician or snake-oil con man, not to mention an ever so—and ever so lethal snake in the grass.

When the limousine stopped, I opened my eyes and realized I had dozed off and that we had taken our exit from the interstate highway and were waiting to pull into the local route into town. So I said what I said because I knew we would be rolling through the Court House Square area and on out by the old antebellum Strickland Place and into that end of the campus within the next twenty-plus minutes.

We signed in at the campus guesthouse, and when we came back downstairs after I called Mr. Poindexter and helped with the unpacking of what was needed from the luggage for the time being, it was not yet late afternoon. So we decided that there was enough time for a leisurely homecomng alumni stroll before changing clothes to join the Poindexters for dinner and information about a choice of a furnished apartment on or off campus.

Which was why we headed up the incline of Campus Avenue under the overhanging oaks and elms instead of popping across to the off-campus main drag for a drugstore fountain Coca-Cola, for a quick peek around in Red Gilmore's Varsity Threads Haberdashery, and the mandatory back-in-town-from-up-the-country-and-elsewhere round of palm slapsnatching and back patting in Deke Whatley's Barbershop.

So here we are once more, I said, as the upcurving side-walk leveled off and we came on by the concrete steps leading down to the main campus promenade lawn where the outdoor concert bandstand was and across which the three-story dormitory where the dean of women's office and the campus clock tower faced the white Doric columns and recently repainted dome of the antebellum-style brick red, white-trimmed dining hall. We came on past the main building of the School of Music and came to the turnoff to the dining hall, the building on our right was the one then known as the Office Building because at that time it not only included the president's office and registrar's office and those of the treasurer and the dean of men but also the post office and the bank.

The street you came to from the rear entrance of the office building was the thoroughfare that ran from town and on out past the residential neighborhoods where most faculty, staff, and other campus employees either owned or rented homes. So we had to stop for the fairly steady stream of traffic, and then we crossed over and came on along the hedge-lined walk to the wide quadrangle in which the gymnasium faced the open end and across which the library faced the Science Building.

As we passed the tall shrubbery framing the main entrance to the library we nudged each other without looking or saying anything. Then as we came on to the next open space, you could see the red clay tennis courts beyond the parking space reserved for the buses of visiting athletic teams. And up ahead near the side entrance to the gymnasium there was a traffic circle, beyond which were the ticket booth and entrance to the bowl down the steep hill directly behind the gymnasium.

We followed the curving walk on around past the box office and main entrance to the gymnasium that was not only the headquarters of the Department of Physical Education and the venue for the annual conference basketball tournament in those days, it was also where all of the big campus dances were held, weekly movies were shown, and where touring repertory theater companies and dance and musical groups performed in those days.

Off to our right as we came around the loop to the science building side of the quadrangle was the campus water tower, beyond which was the baseball field, which was up the steep wooded hill and on the other side of trees directly behind the covered student grandstand in the bowl.

When you reached the other end of the science building, you were back at the tree-lined throughway, and as we came on across to Campus Avenue, the dormitory on the right of the quadrangle you faced was the one that Atelier 359 overlooked, and suddenly I missed my old one and only and best of all possible roommates again. But as we came on back along the main stem past the dining hall, the bandstand and the clock tower again, all I said was "seven league boots, indeed."

XXV

THE POINDEXTERS lived in the first block of the faculty and staff off-campus housing area that began outside of the Emancipation Memorial Pillars of the main entrance to Campus Avenue. So it was only about a two and a half block stroll from the guesthouse, which also meant that they lived only about seven blocks along the municipal thoroughfare from the academic quadrangle where the office of the English Language and Literature Department was in those days.

When we arrived for dinner, our on-campus apartment assignment, and preliminary registration orientation that first Wednesday night, they both greeted us in the living room and there was now a second child, a boy, born during the term following my graduation. The first was a daughter, whom I remembered as having been in elementary school during my senior year.

I knew that Mrs. Poindexter, whose first name was Estelle, and who was just about the same shade of teacake tan as Eunice, but with freckles that you didn't see until you were close enough to shake hands, had been his hometown sweetheart when they were in high school in Washington and that they had married the year after he came back to Washington with his M.A. degree and then came down to central Alabama that following September. By the time I arrived on the campus he had not only been back to graduate school to finish his residence work toward his Ph.D., he had also become the chairman of the English Department, which always surprised visitors and newcomers to the campus because he could still be mistaken for an upperclassman.

The first time I had seen his wife was during the break between the winter and spring terms of my freshman year, when I was invited to come along to his residence with my roommate and several upperclassmen for an informal extracurricular discussion of current books, magazines, and quarterly literary reviews.

She didn't come in to say hello that time until we were all in the study, which was on the left as you entered the living room. We were still standing and moving around looking at the bookshelves and the diplomas and citations and also at the paintings, sketches, and photographs. She had come in, and he presented each one of us by name in class, and she served us tea and cookies and excused herself to do what she had to do as a young mother.

This time she left us in the living room with her husband and went to turn the children over to a babysitter and finished what she had to do in the kitchen and dining room before calling us in to dinner. So we were led into the study for a glass of dry sherry, and that was when the orientation session began. And the first item on his briefing agenda turned out to be a matter that was more personal than official.

Incidentally, he said, you probably haven't been back on campus long enough to have been cued in on one unmandated change in common student parlance since either one of you was last here. Your host this evening is no longer addressed or referred to by the official name you and your classmates used. He is now generally addressed and referred to even by faculty colleagues as Prof Dex.

So it was to be Prof Dex and Prof from then on. I never addressed him as Dex even when he and I became as casual with each other as my relationship with my old roommate and with Taft Edison had become. I would say, Hey, man, and hey, Prof, but never hey, Dex, and he never did call me Scooter. He called me Don. Because from our Composition 102 self-portrait paper he had found out that when my roommate and I were not make-believe Belle Epoque, Montmartre bohemian offspring the likes of François Villon, we were the local versions

of Oxford and/or Cambridge dons, which was not only appropriately academic but also had the titular ring of jazz, kings,
dukes, counts, earls, and barons as well as tongue-in-cheek
overtones of Don Juan and Don Quixote.

As for our on-campus apartment assignment, all he had to do
was name the address and give Eunice the keys. Neither she
nor I had ever been inside that particular faculty residence,
which was near the student nurses' dormitory area and not far
from the campus infirmary, but I was pleased because I liked
the cross-campus walk from there past the clock tower, the
bandstand on the campus promenade lawn, and through the
post office to the main academic area.

We had made no special requests other than for an on-
campus apartment for two, but both Eunice and I had hoped
that we would not have to be assigned to one of the duplex or
triplex units on the deans' and administrators' row along the
municipal thoroughfare between the main academic quadrangle and the block where the drugstore, Red Gilmore's Haberdashery, and Deke Whatley's Barbershop were.

Our on-campus quarters assignment turned out to be the
only official orientation item on the agenda for the evening,
because any detailed clarification of specific academic assignments and standard operation procedures in the orientation
material would be addressed during the preclass period depart-
mental meeting that first Monday morning and in one-on-one
appointments with the department head.

So I asked what I asked about faculty and staff changes since
my graduation, because the only officials I had seen since our
arrival that afternoon were the ones on duty at the guesthouse.
And that was when I found out which of the people I remembered were away in graduate school completing their time in
residence required of Ph.D. candidates. Then as we were taking our last sip of sherry we were called into the dining room
and as we settled into our first course I said that I had nothing
else to add to what I had said on the phone from New York
about the Bossman's Royal Highness proposition. So the main
thing we talked about was the work of fiction that Taft Edison
was already preoccupied with when I introduced myself to him
in New York and told him that I remembered him from my

freshman year on campus. Two of the sequences he had read to me sometime later had recently been published in current highly rated magazines, both of which placed more emphasis on literary quality than on social issues and political positions as such.

I've seen a few things he did for the sociopolitical corn-bread paper sheets a year or so ago, Prof Dex said, but these new pieces are impressively different, and I must also say that they represent not only a logical but also an astonishing development of the Taft Edison who was a student in the course in the English novel which, by the way, he was concurrently supplementing on his own initiative with works of Zola, Hugo, Tolstoy, and especially Dostoevsky.

As Jerome Jefferson and I were well aware, I said, and he also knew that he was reading a lot of twentieth-century poetry. You know, Pound, T. S. Eliot, E. E. Cummings, Wallace Stevens, Marianne Moore. Incidentally, I can also remember the copies of Thomas Hardy's *Return of the Native*, *Jude the Obscure*, and *Mayor of Casterbridge* on your bookshelves in the office of the English Department and also how old Jerome Jefferson, better known as Geronimo, used to sneer whenever he heard somebody saying, Beyond the maddening crowd. It's *madding crowd, my good fellow*. Hardy got it from Thomas Gray's poem, not from some goddamn sports column hack. *Madding*, my good man. You're on a college campus. *Faites attention*.

Then when I said, So you like what old Taft is by way of getting into these days, he said, If he can bring even most of it off as these two excerpts suggest, he just might be capable of doing. We just might have a quantum leap to reckon with.

And I said, Well, I'm ready to tell you that he just might do just that. I can personally vouch for the fact that there is more to come that is even more outrageous. Voltaire, Cervantes, Rabelais, none of that stuff was lost on our boy. I must say, though, that it surprised me because as much as I had come to know about the library books he had checked out, old Jerome Jefferson was the one I had associated with the outrageous adventures and misadventures and absurdities of Candide, Gargantua and Pantagruel, and Don Quixote.

My main concern is that the universality of the picaresque misadventures of Candide and Don Quixote may be mistaken for a fictionalized sociological documentation of yet another black boy being done in by his own incompetence or downright stupidity. Whereas nobody assumes that Candide stands for all Westphalians or Don Quixote represents the nuttiness of, say, Spanish idealism.

He's very much aware of all that I said. So he hopes to make some of it outrageous enough to offset at least some of the ever-ready condescending compassion of survey-addicted do-gooders. He has already concocted a hilarious takeoff on Don Quixote that I think he's really going to bring off. The draft he read me reminded me of some of the sneaky stuff that old Jerome Jefferson used to read to me from his sketch book, which he referred to as the goods as in the goods on.

That's good, he said. The idiomatic particulars should be as evocative as possible, but beware of fictionalized sociological findings. Remember the great allegories about "*everyman*" and *Pilgrim's Progress* is about everyman who—*who would become whatever*. Let us not forget *Rake's Progress*.

Anyway, he continued as we headed for the door, this is all good news, and I don't have to tell you how pleased I am to have had anything whatsoever to do with you two becoming the kind of, what shall I say, collegial friends you have become.

And when Estelle Poindexter, who was walking arm in arm with Eunice, said, Spoken in parchment with the Honors Day enthusiasm of a certified and formally berobed Prof Dex if I ever heard one, he said, So, flip your tassels across your mortarboards.

XXVI

WHEN WE came downstairs to the cafeteria for breakfast that next morning, the main item on our agenda was what we were going to have to do to get settled into our on-campus apartment by that next Monday morning. It was now Thursday. Freshman students were already arriving, and general registration would begin Friday and end Saturday.

At that time there were five academic class days per week, with some courses meeting on Mondays, Wednesdays, and

Fridays, and others on Tuesdays and Thursdays. My first classroom session would begin at eight o'clock on Monday. But on
that first Monday morning there would be a faculty orientation
session in the office of the English Department at seven-thirty.
That was when you picked up your roster of registration en-
rollees, your attendance and performance record book, along
with your first stack of publishers' promotion copies of new
and revised editions of textbooks and anthologies.

Meanwhile, the fall term of the county elementary school in
which Eunice was going to be teaching would not begin until
Monday of the week after the first week of classes on campus
were under way. So according to the instructions she had received in New York along with her contract and other orientation data, all she had to do to arrange for commuter pickup
transportation was call the telephone number provided along
with the class schedule and give her name, address, and phone
number, and the dispatcher would call her back and give the
time to be ready to be picked up.

Given the school's widely celebrated emphasis on good housekeeping and also as returning graduates, we were not surprised
to find that our on-campus apartment was as suitable and well
furnished as it was. All we had to do before that next Monday
was to arrange for the books and other items we had shipped
from New York to be delivered from local railway express, and
shop for provisions for the kitchen and items for the bathroom.

From the window at the end of the living room where the
executive-size desk was, you could see the valley and the trees,
beyond which were the clock tower, the promenade lawn, and
the dome of the dining hall, which you could not see. The
other end of the living room could be converted into a dining
area by expanding and raising the coffee table. And when you
stepped into the hallway from the living room, the bath and
bedroom were on your left, and the kitchen with a breakfast
nook was on your right.

Before sundown that Thursday we had received all of our
deliveries and also completed our shopping, so we checked
out of the guesthouse that Friday morning, and by noon we

felt that we were ready to take off and have a snack at the drugstore lunch counter on the off-campus main drag. And afterward, while Eunice went to look up some of her old instructors in the Department of Education, I would drop in on Red Gilmore in the Toggery and Deke Whatley in the barbershop to let them know that I was back in town for a year or maybe two.

Red Gilmore was busy with two customers, so all I did was slap palms with him and take a quick look around at his fall term display and point to the barbershop next door as I came back out onto the sidewalk.

Hey, here he is, Deke Whatley said as I came into the doorway and then into the lotion-, talcum-, and tobacco-scented ambience of the barbershop. He did not have a customer at the time, so he was sitting in his jacked-up chair facing the entrance with his legs crossed as he puffed and flourished his cigar exactly as I remembered him doing when I saw him for the first time during my freshman year.

Hey, what say there, young fella, he said, extending his hand. We've been hearing some pretty reliable rumors about you heading back down this way this term. Hey, y'all remember this boy. Came up here on one of them special scholarship deals from that school down around Mobile way. What say, my man? Look at him, y'all. Yeah, here he is.

They were all looking at me then, and when I pointed at Skeeter and said, Hey, I'll be seeing you again at least for a while, he said, Man, you've been to a lot of super hip experts since the last time you were in this chair: Hollywood, Chicago, New York, and even all the way over to Paris, France.

And I said, Man, all I was ever looking for wherever I was, was somebody to keep it looking like you had it looking when I left here.

Of course, Deke Whatley said then, You must know who the main ones keeping me up on your doings and whereabouts was. Giles Cunningham. Y'all know that. Old Giles and Miss Lady took a liking to him. She was the one spotted him out at the Dolomite one night. Not because he was a musician, but because he was such a good listener. She could tell how keen his ear for music was just by the way he listened. So she checked him out and she invited him over to her house and they started listening to her collection of records and she said, Deke, that boy heard everything. She said, He listened like an arranger! And that's what led to her giving him that bass fiddle she had fixed up for him. So he could get some student in the string section of the chapel orchestra to teach him to run scales. Not that she was trying to make a musician out of him or anything like that. She just liked the way he kept time when all he was doing was listening just to be enjoying himself. And I'm not talking about dancing in your seat or something like that. What I'm talking about is that you don't have to be a music mechanic to be musical. That's what she realized right away. Hell, when you come right down to it, a lot of big-time musicians turn out to be more mechanical than musical!

Yeah, yeah, I see your point, Skeeter said as he turned his chair for his next customer to be seated. Just listen to how musical all them church folks always been and most of them can't read no music even if it's in boxcar printing.

Anyway, Deke Whatley went on, I know Miss Tense well enough to know very well that she knew good and well that this boy hadn't come up here to college to learn how to be no musician. No question about that. Because that's just how hip she is. So even when it turned out that along with all that special talent for time that she spotted from the stage that night, he also had that magic gift of whatsitsname, whatchamacallit, absolute whatchamacallit, absolute pitch! That's it—absolute pitch! Tone-perfect. And also that other genius-gifted thing, whatsitsname—*total recall, photographic memory.* One go-around and this cat's got it cold! But you see now, that's the boss lady for you. Even when she decided that he was good enough on that thing to start earning a little emergency change gigging with her combo out at the Dole from time to time, she still wasn't trying to entice him away from whatever it was that he was trying to do with his life.

But hey, he said, interrupting himself as Red Gilmore came in from next door, as I expected him to. Here's old Red boy. He knows almost as much about Hortense and old Giles and all this as I myself do. Tell him about them and this boy, Red.

Then when Red Gilmore shrugged off the compliment and bowed, signaling for him to continue, he said, Like I said, when

she got to the big Bossman Himself to let him go fill in that
summer while they were looking for a replacement when old
Shag had to cut out and go back home. She said she was just
trying to help him pick up some summer cash and see some
more of the world on his way to graduate school. Right, Red?

Right, Red Gilmore said, and it was the same when he cut
out from the band to spend that time doing what he was
knocking around doing out there in Hollywood.

And, Deke Whatley said, as Red boy also remembers me telling him, it was old Giles himself that was the one that brought
me the word about his girlfriend graduating and him marrying
her that same summer in her hometown and taking her straight
on off to graduate school with him like it was the same as going
on their honeymoon.

Well, Deke, Skeeter said, since they both had them graduate
school fellowship awards or grants or whatever you call them,
it *was* a kind of honeymoon, a special kind of honeymoon,
wasn't it?

That's exactly what I'm saying, Deke Whatley said. Hell,
they both come through here on scholarship awards from high
school, him four years from that Mobile County school and
her three years when she transferred from State as a sophomore
when he was a junior.

So now here he is, gentlemen, Red Gilmore said, back down
here because they sent for him to come back and join the faculty, even before he finished his Ph.D. Nice going, Mobile.

Like old Giles said, Deke Whatley said, that just goes to
show you about this generation we got coming along down
here in this neck of the woods these days. And they fanning out
and making good in every section of the nation. Check it out.
Don't take my word for it. Check it out for yourself.

Well, heyo, there, young Mobile, old Showboat Parker said.
He had pulled up out front in his Cadillac taxi and had come
in and waved and waited while Deke Whatley and Red Gilmore
said what they were saying about Giles Cunningham.

What say, there, Mr. Globe-trotter? We been hearing that
you just might be heading back down this way for a while. So
when did you get in?

And I said, Number nine, number nine. Old getaway number nine. Yesterday afternoon, number nine. Number nine and old Floorboard whatshisname, or was it Dashboard?

Floorboard, Showboat Parker said. Because he was the one noted for stepping on the gas to get the chippies back on campus before library closing time during the old days of warden-strict deans of women, and herd-riding housemothers. Old Floorboard is taking it easy somewhere down in Florida these days, young . . . excuse me, young prof!

And speaking of Florida, Red Gilmore said, that's where old Giles and Miss Tense ought to be rolling back in here from, just about now, this being registration week and also season opening week out at the Dole. Old Wylie was in to see me yesterday. Everything is all set and ready. All Giles and Tense need to do is to get back in place in time to greet people.

Hey, Skeets, I said as I was about to leave, I think I can promise you that you can expect to see me more regularly than in the old days. And he said, At your service, young prof. At your service. I just want you to know how much I appreciate what you said about remembering me in all them different places. That's nice to know.

Now me, Deke Whatley said, uncrossing his legs and stepping down out of his chair to walk me out onto the sidewalk, I just want to make sure you know that the fact that you made a special stop in here just to let us know you're back in town, says a lot. That's a true down-home boy, Mobile. A true homeboy come back to tag up and get long gone again. And further. Some of these somiches come back through here just to show off like they escaped from something here, forgetting that it was what they took up there from down here that took them up there out there and over there or wherever they got come by whatever. But so much for that. Here's what I just want to say. Not that you don't know it already. Giles and Hortense talk about you like family. That's the kind of folks to have in our corner. But hell, I ain't telling you nothing you don't know already. I'm just saying amen!

But just let me say this. The main thing about education. No matter what kind of course you take, and how many degrees you get, The main thing is *knowing what to want*! You understand what I'm saying? Don't care what courses and how many degrees, the main thing is know what you really want for yourself. I'm not talking about self-indulgence. I'm talking about self-satisfaction. Knowing what to choose. Knowing how to pick and choose.

XXVII

WELL, HERE he is just like you said, Giles Cunningham said, as much to us as to Hortense Hightower, when Eunice and I arrived at the Pit at one-fifteen that next afternoon and headed for the table where the two of them were just pulling out their chairs to sit down for the light midday meal I had guessed they would be having at that time. We stepped down from the entrance level to the dining level and came on over to where they were, and when we all had gone through old Daddy Royal's jive time greeting routine and sat down, he said, Right on the money. Man, the boss lady is still right on your case. When old Deke called last night to see if we were back from Florida and told us you were already back on the scene and making the rounds, you know what she said? She said, Well, most likely he'll be dropping by the Pit to catch us on our lunch break. Man, what can I tell you? Didn't I tell you she don't miss? Here you are and there are those two extra place settings.

I didn't remind him that even before he had given me the part-time job that summer before my senior year I had already heard enough about him to know that he usually spent the first part of Monday through Friday mornings in his headquarters office at the Pit, where he had breakfast and worked until mid-morning. Then unless there were appointments elsewhere he usually drove on along the interstate highway to the off-campus settlement area where the Dolomite Club was, and where if he had no other errands he stayed until he came back to the Pit to have lunch and an updating session with Hortense, who usually slept late, had breakfast at home, and spent the rest of the morning working on her own agenda, which was usually domestic, but along with which there were also details involved in the operation of the after-hours lounge at the Dolomite, where she sang with her own pickup combos from time to time.

Sometimes she also went along with him on his afternoon trip out to the Plum to keep in touch with Flee Mosely, but the only time she took her combo out there to play was on special occasions during the mid- and late-summer picnic and barbecue season, mainly for afternoon sessions that did not conflict with her after-hours schedule at the Dolomite.

So here he is, Giles Cunningham said as we settled into our chairs and I picked up the menu. And look who he brought along with him this time. It's just like the Bossman Himself said when he called us from Ohio to let us know that he could use you to fill in for Shag Phillips. He said, This kid may be just a beginner but he's already pretty much free of clinkers both personwise and musicwise.

And when I said, Meet Miss You-Know-Who, Hortense Hightower said, Miss Who-Else-But. Hi, sweetie. I hear you're already beyond the main part of getting settled in on your own. But any more help you need for getting around picking up stuff or whatever, don't hesitate to call me. Don't worry about interrupting my schedule. And don't wait until you need something. After all, I'm always available for another one of those sprees-of-the-moment girlie shopping trips, whether downtown or out of town to Montgomery, Atlanta, or Birmingham.

And when Eunice said, I promise, Giles Cunningham said, There you go. What did I tell you? How the hell the boss lady going to miss out on somebody you pick out for a wife? They got your scholarship record up there on the campus, but she's got your number. And like I say, she don't miss. No doubt about it.

Then she said, old Deke Whatley and Red Gilmore were the ones who knew that you were the one up there on the campus. And whenever this fella's name came up, even when he left the Bossman and the band to stick around out there in Hollywood, they'd always say, He'll be back through here. Mark my words. He's still got some unfinished business that's still in the works right across the throughway and campus avenue.

And that was when Hortense Hightower said what she said about not trying to get in touch with Eunice because they hadn't been introduced by me. And a casual encounter had been just about out of the question because in those days nightspots like the Dolomite were strictly off-limits to young women who lived on the campus.

As for this weekend at the Dole, Hortense Hightower said then, there's nothing special, no big deal. Just this snappy, up-and-coming, Columbus–Phenix City combo for the upper-classmen, with local contacts and incoming hotshots out to survey the off-campus possibilities.

And that was when Giles Cunningham said, Actually, you won't be missing anything special out at the Dole between now and when the fall season road band booking schedule clicks in—say, about the middle of next month.

We came on outside then, and as we stood waiting for Hortense Hightower to come and drive us back to the campus, Eunice said, Who is Speck, and why do they call him that? And I said, He is the one who runs the Pit. Wiley Peyton runs the Dolomite, and Flee Mosely runs the Plum. They call him Speck because he has freckles. Speck is for Speckled Red, as in speckled chicken, and there are also some who just say old Florida Red—as in Tampa Red.

That was that Friday afternoon. I spent the first part of that Saturday morning unpacking and arranging my books and pho-nograph records on the waist-high shelves under the windows behind the desk in my work area off the living room. Then as I made my way across the campus to find out which work carrel in the stacks behind the circulation counter in the main reading room would be reserved for me, even as the sound of the clock tower chiming above the hum and buzz and honking traffic and the chatter of the students reminded me of my own arrival as a freshman, I crossed my fingers, because I suddenly realized that I was rearriving as a freshman, a freshman with a graduate degree plus further study from New York University, but a beginner once more even so.

XXVIII

As WE pulled on away from the campus avenue parking spot where she had told me she would be waiting when I came down the steps from the post office that next Wednesday after-noon, Hortense Hightower said, About this Daddy Royal proposition. Of course, you already know that Giles and I have been in on it all along. So I thought I might as well clue you in on how it all got started and what it's really all about.

So as we came on down along the early-fall tree-shaded mainstem to turn left at the traffic circle and head for the exit to the municipal throughway outbound, she said, The fact of the matter is that I'm really the one that's actually responsible for starting it, although I really had something else in mind when I came up with the idea that led to it.

What I really had in mind, she went on to say as we pulled on off the campus to head along the thoroughfare to the intersection with the interstate highway across which was the street that led to the Dolomite, what I had in mind from the very beginning was something that had to do with the Bossman Himself personally. Something that I had first spoken to him about some time ago, once I got to be close enough friends with him.

And to tell the truth, she said, that's what all this about Daddy Royal is still about. Because old Daddy Royal is a very important part of the big picture, to be sure. But the Bossman, like old Louis Armstrong, is one of the main ones that somebody is always coming up with when questions turn to achieving a place in the history of music in the United States.

And that was also when she also said, As soon as I felt that my friendship was close enough I started mentioning that it might be a good idea to get somebody to help him start compiling all of the stuff that's been accumulating about him over the years. I would mention it to him every now and then without pushing too hard, and since he didn't dismiss it, I figure he just might have been considering it.

So then, she said, I began to wonder about who was going to be the one or one of the ones from the life this music comes out of that's going to be helping him pull all this stuff together. And I also made a point of mentioning that to him as often as I could without making him feel like he was being rushed because we were worried about you know what. That's why I always made it a point to put the emphasis on volume and kept saying what I kept saying about his *future* output overwhelming the present, with the past getting dimmer and dimmer.

This had been going on for some time. Not that she had ever thought of herself adding her voice to a lot of others, because she knew he respected her opinion and would give some serious consideration to anything she suggested, and that was as far as she was personally involved. She just brought it up from time to time, sometimes jokingly, saying things like, You understand, of course, that I'm not talking about a biography. What I'm talking about is a memoir. That's about as far as it went.

And then you showed up, she said. Then she said, Let me tell you something. The very first time I laid eyes on you sitting back there, just sitting back there on that stool at the bar listening like that, I said to myself, This one ain't just another one of them campus hipsters out looking for the latest do to impress them other hipsters and squares. I said, This one is out here to hear some music to connect with something he came to college to learn about life. You just struck me right off as somebody who came to get a college education. Not just to learn how to make a living doing something above common labor, but also to learn as much as you can about how to appreciate what a full life is really all about.

And that was when she told me that she had been more impressed when I said my course of study was liberal arts than she would have been if I had said it was music. And that that was when she decided to invite me to come by her house and listen to whatever I selected from what turned out to be her very comprehensive collection of recordings. We were at the intersection then, and as we came on across the interstate highway and headed through that settlement to the Dolomite, she looked at me and said, Although I didn't mention anything about it at the time, that was the beginning of what led up to getting you that summer gig with the band was all about. That's why as soon as I heard that Shag Phillips was going to have to go home, I called old Joe and said, See what we can do to get our schoolboy in there as a stopgap for the summer, and Old Pro went along with old Joe on it.

So, she said, that's how I went from making a suggestion to being knee-deep in the whole thing. But anyway, I was pretty certain that he would give me the benefit of the doubt. And when I heard his voice on the phone when he called to tell me when and where to send you up to Cincinnati, I considered my scheme was already under way, even if you had gone on to do that grad school work at the end of that first summer. Because by that time he had you checked out. So even when you decided to stay out in Hollywood that next time around, he was just as confident as I was that you hadn't given up on grad school because you were starstruck or anything like that. On the contrary. And also by that time old Daddy Royal was in on the scheme, so when you made that trip to Europe and came back and got hitched and checked into NYU, everything was falling into place, with old Joe keeping tabs.

Come to think of it—she began, as we came up the incline to the Dolomite and pulled into her parking place at the side entrance. Then she went on, You know something? Everybody in that band knew more about why you were really in there with them than you did. Because I hadn't said a word to you about what that bull fiddle was leading up to until now. And that was when she said, This is not what I had in mind when I had it fixed up and gave it to you, but it sure did come in handy when old Shag had to go home. That's when it hit me. Because I remembered that I had invited the boss to hear you with the combo and right away he spotted you as being from Mobile or somewhere in old Daddy Gladstone's territory. That's when I decided on what I said when I called old Joe.

Then as we came on into her office and dressing room after she said what she said to Wiley Peyton in the main entrance lobby and also told him to send in two tall fountain Coca-Colas, she sat at her desk and had me pull up a chair, and as we waited for the Cokes she said, We got a call from the Bossman last night and from Daddy Royal this morning, and I told him that I thought you were pleased with your class schedule and I was expecting to pick you up on the campus this very afternoon.

Then she said, So here we are. Because as soon as old Joe found out that you were thinking about taking a break from grad school studies and had an offer to do some part-time teaching down here, we both said, Hey, this could be the time. And I said, Let me be the one, and when I called the Bossman he said, Why don't we start with Daddy Royal. So that's the proposition old Joe laid on you.

So here we are, she said again holding up her fountain Coke again, and isn't it just like the Bossman to set us up with a vamp? *The deal is on, but we vamp till he's ready.* And you know what old Daddy Royal said? He said, That just goes to show you. He said, Once you bring up something you want him to consider and give him a little time to get around to it, that's exactly what he'll do.

Then he said, Yeah, I'm the vamp. He said, Don't you always start patting your feet before you start the music? Patting your foot and sometimes also snapping your fingers? You're already dancing before the instruments come in. See what I mean? And you can always bet when he comes in with that segue he's ready. He's ready. Jam, scram, or straight-ahead chronogram.

Old Daddy Royal, I said, Old Daddy Royal. *Old Daddy Royal is always on the case, I said, remembering but not mentioning that already before any proposal of any kind had been brought up, he had begun showing me his memorabilia simply because he assumed that I was a special kind of schoolboy who was curious enough and hip enough to appreciate them. And when we came to the scrapbooks that included clippings and other souvenirs of his early tours in Europe he said, Now we're coming into a territory where they have another attitude about all this stuff. It's not just some kind of light entertainment to them. Like that old guy. Some old professor somebody over there told me one time. I can't call him by name right now and he's not in any of these clippings but I'm bound to have it around here stuck in somewhere and maybe a picture, too, and I'll recognize it as soon as I come across it. But anyway, he's the one that said dancing came before music as such. He was talking about way back there, if you know what I mean. All the way back in what they call prehistoric times. And he was also the one who also said that the first floor of the theater is called the orchestra because that used to be the word for dancing space. I don't remember exactly what he said about how that word got to be the word for a big band. Maybe because that's where they used to sit before somebody came up with the idea of the pit. But anyway, the main thing for me was that dancing came first. He said, Dancing came first, then music. So that's the boss for you, and that's why he's the emperor.*

I tell you what, Hortense Hightower said as we finished our fountain Cokes and stood up. Since this thing has come back around to me, and I'm the one that brought you into it in the first place, why don't you just go on and get your campus stuff in the groove and maybe by, say, Thanksgiving, you will have had enough time to think about how all this can really fit in with what you went on beyond college to graduate school to learn.

Believe me, honey pie, she said, the last thing I want is for you to feel that we are rushing you into this thing. I haven't forgotten and never will forget what you told me more than once about what they taught you and what they absolutely did not try to decide for you down there at that Mobile County Training School under your Mr. B. Franklin Fisher.

But even as she was saying what she was saying and did not say what she did not say, it was as if you were listening to, Miss Lexine Metcalf herself again in her school bell morning enchanted classroom through the wall-length windows of which you could see the Chickasabogue sky beyond Bay Poplar woods even before it was your turn to stand erect and make your way past the bulletin board, the globe stand, and the map rack to the blackboard realm of schoolboy verbal and numerical derring-do.

Miss Lexine Metcalf, Miss Lexine Metcalf, Miss Lexine Metcalf, I said, Mama, Miss Tee and Miss Lexine Metcalf who was the one Miss Tee took me to when Mama let her be the one to take me to the campus to be registered when the first day of my first school bell September morning arrived that year. And Miss Lexine Metcalf took us to Miss Cox in the primer grade room and said, I will be waiting for you when you reach the third grade.

Miss Lexine Metcalf, who would be the one who would say what she said about me to Mr. B. Franklin Fisher himself, who said of himself Fisher—yes, Fisher, as in fisherman. Fisher of men. Fisher of men of special promise. Men worthy of the women who bore them and nursed them. Who said, Many are called but few are chosen. And my question is, Who will be one in that number??

Then on the day he came back to add my name to that year's list of prospects selected for matriculation in the Early Bird Preparatory Program when you reached the ninth grade, she was the one who said, Who if not you, my splendid young man? Who if not you, my splendid young man, from all the way down in Meaher's Hummock on Dodge Shingle Mill Road near the cypress swamp by the bottoms and the L & N Railroad. Who if not also you, indeed.

As Hortense Hightower took me around to see the changes
that she and Giles Cunningham had made in the Dolomite
since I graduated and left en route to Cincinnati to try out
for the summer job with the band before going to graduate
school, every time she pointed out and explained another addition or renovation, you could see she was not only pleased
with what she and Giles Cunningham were doing but also with
where they had decided to do what they were doing.

Which meant she was also pleased with the choice she had
made when she decided to leave the band she had gone on the
road with when she finished her college courses at Alabama
State.

XXIX

REMEMBERING THE trip out to the Dolomite as I settled myself at the desk of my carrel in the arts and letters stacks of the
library that next afternoon, I suddenly found myself thinking
about old Deke Whatley saying what he said as we stood at the
curb outside his barbershop after I had popped in to say hello
that first Thursday afternoon.

I just wanted to thank you for dropping in on us like this so
soon after you got back in town. It tells me a lot. It tells me
you still the kind of homeboy I took you for when you just set
foot in there as a freshman. So I also just wanted to step out
here and tell you how much I appreciate the postcards from
some of the different places you got a chance to see for yourself
after reading about. That tells me something.

That tells me something about knowing what education is
really about, he said, and then he said what he said about education and self-satisfaction, and that was when he went on
to say, Man, I been seeing them coming in as freshmen and
checking them that come back for their class reunions over
the years all this time I've been right here on this block. And
you know what I think education is really about? I mean really
about adding up to? *Knowing what to want.*

That's the key, he said again. Man, that's the key to the whole
thing. Man, you miss that and you miss the main thing about
what book learning is all about, don't care which colleges and

universities you go to and how many degrees you come back with. Remember them gold watch chains and neck chains and graduation keys graduating classes used to buy to wear once they got their diplomas? What did they fit into? Nothing. No locks that your grade-point average hadn't qualified to open, by that time if you see what I mean. And even as I said I do, I really do, the very first person who had come to mind was Creola Calloway, not because she knew what to want but because she was somebody who knew what she did not want, no matter how many other people agreed with each other about what they thought she should want. The one and only Creola Calloway, who became notorious in Gasoline Point because it was as if she was just about the only one in town who did not think she should go into show business and become rich and famous because she was as good-looking as she was.

Not that she thought that being that good-looking was not supposed to be a special blessing and a God-given blessing at that, and therefore something to be grateful for and modest about. And the fact of the matter was that just about everybody seemed to be so impressed with how good-looking she was that it was also as if they regarded her as public property, and had no choice in the matter of what she should do with her own future.

As I sat musing in the library that afternoon that many years later, I suddenly realized that it had been as if just about everybody in Gasoline Point back during those days had been so dazzled by how she looked that it was as if they never paid any attention at all to how nice and friendly and just like another one of the folks she always was with everybody. Nobody ever accused her of being stuck up. On the contrary, what some people said about her implied that her big problem was that she was not as stuck up as people wanted her to be!

I hadn't mentioned anything about Creola Calloway to Deke Whatley as we stood at the curb outside the barbershop that first Thursday afternoon. All I said at first was what I said about Miss Lexine Metcalf warning me that I might be one of the splendid young men who might have to travel far and wide to find out what mission I was best suited to or called to fill, and that splendid young men were precisely those who qualified for their mission even as they searched for it.

To which he said, See what I mean? So take your time and go step by step and get it right. Right for you yourself, man. I know exactly where she's coming from. Right out of that old one about answered prayers bringing more tears or grief and stuff than unanswered ones. You heard what I said when I said what I said about knowing what to want, didn't you? Well, there it is.

So before starting in on the academic materials that I had come to start collecting in preparation for the winter term for the course I was teaching, I went on thinking about what Deke Whatley had said to how pleased Hortense Hightower was with what she decided to do after she had finished college and spent the time she had spent singing with a road band.

And then I went on remembering how when I graduated with a fellowship for advanced study she got me the job as summer substitute and how that led to the time I spent in California that led to what turned out to be my friendship with Gaynelle Whitlow in West Los Angeles, and my very special relationship with Jewel Templeton of Beverly Hills by way of Minnesota on the upper Mississippi.

To Gaynelle Whitlow, not unlike Joe States, Hollywood was really pretty much the same as a factory town where production companies made movies, just as Detroit was a motor town where motor companies made automobiles.

So to her, glamour in Hollywood was really a sales device, much the same as body and accessory design were in the automobile industry.

As for her current means of livelihood, she described herself as a freelance projects administrator and office manager. As for the future, I'm all for it, she liked to say, and then go to point out that sometimes it brought good luck and sometimes bad luck but it was always hard on good-looking women whose beauty was their stock-in-trade. Not that she herself did not have the kind of good looks you could trade on. She didn't take your breath away, as Creola Calloway did, but as soon as I saw her in that booth in the Home Plate I knew she could get along very well on her looks alone. But as that first evening got under way I found myself thinking that she was just the kind of bosom pal Creola Calloway needed when I was the boy becoming the schoolboy I was becoming in Gasoline Point.

When I met Jewel Templeton, she had just recently met and become a friend of the Marquis de Chaumienne and some of his French and Italian friends, and was more concerned with what to do with the success she had already achieved as featured leading lady and costar than with becoming a superstar.

In any case, I got the impression that what made her friendship with the Marquis de Chaumienne so important to her was not his rank and social status as such but his cosmopolitan interests and his *taste*, which, as my old roommate would surely have reminded me anew even if he didn't think I had forgotten, was not unlike haute cuisine, predicated on a fine appreciation and respect for the intrinsic quality of the basic ingredients. Elementary, my dear fellow. Nobody appreciates the elementary like the ones who know what is relevant beyond subsistence.

So, upper Mississippi River pragmatist that she still was indeed and withal, she no doubt thought of the people in his set, beginning that season at St. Moritz, as being *dans le vrai* precisely because they struck her as knowing so much more than she did about what to want.

Dans le vrai, dans le vrai, dans le vrai indeed, I went on thinking as I stood up and headed for the shelves and the books I needed for my winter term lesson plans. Wasn't that what she also had in mind when she said what she said about magic keys when we said good-bye at the autobus station in Nice that afternoon? Some gold, some silver, some platinum. Or how about some sharp, some flat, some natural?

Why not? After all, had I not arrived in Hollywood, the land of lotus eaters, as a neophyte timekeeper in a notorious band of syncopated calypso vagabonds? Why not indeed, since they were not only keys that gave access to enchanted castles but also served as talismen in the pernicious passageways to the chambers with the chests of infinite treasure therein.

Not that the true storybook hero's quest is ever likely to be for material riches as such except to pay off *somebody else's* debt, otherwise his quest is likely to be for some magic means, not unlike the seed that became the beanstalk or the sporty limp stride of the seven league boots.

But old Flaubert was not talking about castles and the treasures and pleasures of court life when he said what he said. He was talking about the pastoral life of peasants, the blisses of the commonplace.

Creola Calloway herself would not have put it that way, I thought as I came along the aisle to the shelves from which I would select the books to be transferred to the reserve book room for supplemental reading for term papers, but the new friend of the Marquis de Chaumienne would have no problems pointing out that the blisses of the commonplace were precisely what nobody in Gasoline Point seemed to want Creola Calloway to want.

XXX

WHEN I CALLED Taft Edison that next weekend and told him about my arrival and about my dinner and informal but official orientation session out at the Poindexters', he said, Man, as ready as I was to get the hell out of that goddamn place after the three years I spent down there, I have to admit that you make me realize that I do get little twitchings of nostalgia for the old place from time to time. After all, it was a beautiful campus, as I have had no trouble recording in print, and the standard of living in the surrounding neighborhood and even some of the outlying regions was also impressive. And as you know as well as my instructors down there did, I never had anything but enthusiasm for the library.

Me and you, man, I said, mimicking Joe States's old catchphrase. Me and you. And my old roommate and your old classmate Treemonisha Bradley. Which is when he also went on to say, Man, the truth of the matter is when I look back on the year-round time I spent down there maneuvering among that nationwide, and I mean coast-to-coast variety of thugs, in that student body in those days, I'm absolutely convinced that I was better prepared to cope with these Manhattan hip operators than I would have been had I come straight up here from my hometown, which, believe me, was no hick town by any measurement.

Then he said, So our very own bespoke Ivy League liberal arts–type professor is still also pulling his share of the mandatory freshman composition and intro lit courses required of ag and tech as well as gym and bowl types down there, is he?

And I said, As of old, and also as of now yclept campus-wide as Prof Dex. I don't know, man, maybe all those jocks don't mind flocking to his lit classes because they are sure to be outnumbered by all of these high-grade-point-average females whose help with term papers they can pretend to be in urgent need of, and also because if they earn the kind of money and celebrity status they're aiming at, a little spot of that belles lettres jive might come in handy in the high social circles they might move in. Not to mention jobs on a college coaching staff someday.

Then when I told him what Hortense Hightower had told me about her involvement in the Royal Highness proposal, he said, Man, like I told you when you told me what you told me when Joe States first brought up this thing in New York, bring this thing off and good-bye, academic gumshoe. Incidentally, the Pit and the Dolomite seem to have really come along since I was down there. But gigging in places like that as close to the campus as that was strictly off-limits for music majors in my day. The two campus dance bands used to play off-campus gigs, but that was mostly for high school hops and civic benefit socials. The Dolomite was off-limits for anything representing the school, especially music majors. Come to think of it, rules for members of the chapel orchestra and choir were pretty strict, too, even if you were a local resident. If you were a member of the chapel choir you had to get cleared by the dean of the Music Department to sing in the choir of your family church.

Man, he said, I think I told you about how old Sid and I used to hit those joints in the outlying regions and beyond every now and then. But nothing as close to the campus as the Dolomite, which, from what you tell me, must have really hit its stride during those three years you were down there after I took off. The only big outfits on tour that came through that way when I was there were booked in the gym on the campus by the recreation committee, and they played concerts in the gym, not dances. Of course, the Pit was a restaurant that started out as a barbecue pit stop out on the highway about a mile going west from Court House Square, where the old Confederate monument is.

Old man Johnny Reb, I said. And he said, Old man Johnny Reb Comesaw. Yeah, I can still see the old son of a bitch.

So anyway, like I said, he said then. In my opinion this could be just the thing you didn't realize you should have been hoping and looking for just about now. And, of course, another thing I like about the whole deal is that it means that you'll have to be making trips back up this way far more often as a routine part of the project than you'd get around to doing otherwise at your own personal expense. So I'm all for it, man, after all, as you know very well from firsthand road experience, travel expenses are just about the most routine budget item in the world these cats operate in. So take them up on it, man, and save yourself some round-trip expenses back up here and save me some long-distance phone calls.

So what did I tell you when you told me what you told me when this thing first came up, Roland Beasley said when I called him to bring him up-to-date on how things were getting under way. Didn't I tell you I was not surprised that the boss and Old Pro had spotted my framemaker? Because they know one when they see one. So when one turns up, zap! They got him pegged. They can tell when you know where you're coming from. Man, my guess is that old Joe States has known what this thing was leading up to all along.

And hey, man, he went on to add, from what you say about that Miss Hortense Hightower of yours just about takes the cake. That's them cakewalking babies from home for you. That's down home for you, all right. And there ain't no such thing as up home. There is Philamayork. But it takes a lot of down-home stuff to get you there.

Speaking of expectations, there were also those of Gaynelle Whitlow and Jewel Templeton out in California. And as for the one and only Miss Slick McGinnis, she was the flesh-and-blood dimension of the actuality of the fairy-tale aunt that the real flesh-and-blood Miss Tee could not become, and that the official actuality of Miss Lexine Metcalf made taboo (but that Deljean McRae may well have turned out to be had she still been there as she had been early on).

The next time I saw Jewel Templeton after we said what we said and didn't say what we didn't need to say on the Côte d'Azur was at a party in one of the ballrooms at the Pierre two weeks before I pulled out to come back to Alabama. I was there backstage because two days earlier Joe States had called to give me the date and time that the band would be back in town to play a one-night stand in one of the ballrooms.

Get to me fast, my man, he said with his usual mock conspiratorial urgency. Let's touch base before you split for the 'Bam. This thing we're booked into for just one night is a private shindig, and we expect you backstage as soon as you can get there because we'll be pulling in just in time to set up to hit as scheduled. And we'll be pulling out for Canada as soon as we can repack and hit the trail. So we expect to see you backstage as soon as you can make it after we pull in, if not before. Milo will have someone on the lookout for you.

That's why I happened to be where I was backstage when one of the ushers came calling for me to tell me that one of the guests would be waiting to speak to me at the backstage exit to the ballroom during the first break. I said OK without asking who the guest was because I was talking to Old Pro, and when the time came we were there before I could guess who it could be. Eric Threadcraft came to mind, but I knew if he were in town, not only would he have called me, but also he would have found a way to get backstage on his own.

We were there then, and when I saw who it was, I was surprised, but not as surprised as I would have been if she had called me on the phone or even sent a letter or a postcard. But I was almost as surprised as I had been that Sunday night outside the Keynote Lounge on Sunset Boulevard waiting with my bull fiddle to take a cab back to the Vine Lodge when she pulled to the curb and offered to give me a lift.

So there you are, she said, extending her arms and initiating the old one-for-each-cheek routine that we had never done in public except on the Côte d'Azur. Then holding me at arm's length she said, You look every bit as good as you should.

And I said, Hey, coming from a marquis-certified sparkling daughter, that's enough to make brown sugar bubble.

A waiter came by then and she ordered a spritzer for herself and a vermouth cassis for me. And I said, *Comme d'habitude.* And that was when she said, I must tell you I'm here because ever since we did what we did with the marquis in the south of

France, I come to listen to this band every time our paths cross, and I make a report to the marquis, which pleases him no end and me no less. Because in a way it is as if I've stumbled on my own version of Alexis de Tocqueville.

So this evening's encounter was bound to happen sooner or later, she said, especially in New York. But I must say I didn't expect to see you here tonight, although you do always come to mind whenever the band is mentioned. So you were part of the content of my consciousness all day today, even so. And then all of a sudden there you were.

I just happened to get a glimpse of you in the wings, she said, because the drummer kept winking and flashing his sticks and brushes at someone in the wings during the warm-up number before the great charmer himself came striding out to direct the festivities from the piano. That's when I called the maître d' and gave him your name and told him where I wanted him to ask you to let him come back during the first intermission and take you to where an old friend from California would be waiting to say a brief hello for old times' sake.

That was when I told her that I was getting ready to leave graduate school for a while to take a part-time teaching position at my old alma mater. And she said, Well, good for them. They appreciate their own product. That's a good sign. A very good sign. This is good news that I must pass on to the marquis right away, so he'll know where to find you on his next trip over here. Ever since he met you in person in the south of France he has been looking forward to seeing your part of the U.S.A. with you. So now that he will know where you are going to be, watch out.

So that was when I told her that I also had been asked to help Daddy Royal write his memoirs. And she said, Who else? You are precisely the one I would suggest that people with questions about him go to as I'm sure the marquis would agree. Indeed, the very first thing I'm going to do when I get back over to the Plaza would be to call the marquis and pass your news along to him. And by the way, when you get word on him heading back over here, be prepared for sessions about Norman Rockwell's year-round Fourth of July paintings and images of the U.S.A. in Hollywood musicals.

Then as the band filed back on the stage for the second set, she said, But I must not intrude on your backstage errand any longer, especially in view of the fantastic project you're involved in and that I'm certain that you're going to bring off brilliantly. So says the authority of my muddy water daughter intuition.

We went through the old one for each routine again, then, and I said what I said about her recent movies. And then when I said, And of course you will tell Maurice and Esther that I asked about them, she said, But of course. And when I tell them that you're heading back down to Alabama for a while and what you will be doing in addition to your part-time class-room schedule, they won't even try to hide their satisfaction. To them, education is what you're all about. Knowing what things are about and how they're related to each other. How about that? Remember what we said about the magic keys? Well, they think of you as forging the *skeleton key* that opens up all sorts of treasures.

So there you have it, I said, stepping back through the en-trance to the backstage passageway, fairy tales for the likes of me and you, but nuts and bolts for them without the likes of whom not!

Also before I left New York there had been a call from Gaynelle Whitlow, who had recently seen Joe States, who had told her about Miss Fine People and had given her my phone number to have somebody in her office to call me for her, and when whoever it was called and I answered there was a pause and the next voice was hers, saying, So the all-American schoolboy is, as the saying goes, by way of becoming the what shall we say?

And when I said, Journeyman, she said, That's you, all right. Still on your way wherever it is you're headed.

Then when I said, Hey, thanks again for rescuing me even before I needed to be rescued, she said, You know the old saying about an ounce of prevention. A smart boy like you I'm sure you know that first night was a setup. Joe and the man. I'm pretty sure old Joe would have brought you by on his own, but it was on the boss's agenda, and he sent me a bouquet plus that was waiting for me when I got home that next morning—or was it still morning? So anyway, since you said you were definitely going back to school, I figured they had other plans for you other than just plucking on that bass fiddle.

And I said, Hey, that part was all news to me, too.

As I think about it now, she said then, as good as I thought you sounded in there with them that night in the Palladium and also with old Radio Red and on those other things you did with Eric Threadcraft I never really thought of you as an all-out, full-time musician. I said, Hey, he's on it, all right, but there's something else to this cat. So when you stayed in town and got yourself hooked with the all-American Miss Blue Eyes, I kidded you. But you knew I knew you were still on course whatever it was, didn't you?

And I said, Hey, some kidding! And then I said, For which much thanks, and when she said, I just didn't want you to forget your down-home upbringing, I said, Not me. When they used to say if you could make it down there on the outskirts of Alabama you could make it anywhere else in the world, I believed them, especially one very special teacher once I got to the third grade.

Which I could tell as soon as old Joe left you with me, she said. Then she said, So let me let you go now. I just want you to know that I'm looking forward to what you're going to be doing with old Royal Highness. That's old Joe, Old Pro, and the man for you. And I also got a pretty good idea of what you might be following it up with. So if your research brings you back out this way, let me know if you can. And by the way, our Miss Jewel still has most if not quite all of her blue-eyed American sparkle.

XXXI

WHEN I CALLED Royal Highness that Saturday morning he said, Hey, here he is. Hey there, young soldier. What you say, young soldier? Things shaping up on schedule down there? You ready to lay that comp on me yet? And I said so far, so good in the English Department and that I was just about ready to find out if he thought I was ready yet.

And he said, OK. So let's see which way you think this thing should go. You know what I mean? Not just another record of the same old rags-to-riches and fame and fortune and comfort jive. I'm not saying that that's not a part of it. But the main part of it was that I was *dancing*. That's what I'm about. That's what I have always been about, and that's what this book's got to get across. Just like the Bossman's book's got to be about him and his music. With him it's food, clothing, shelter, and music. And with me it's food, clothing, shelter, and dancing, with or without music.

So me and you, young soldier, he said. You're the schoolboy and I'm the subject matter in person, talking about the natural-born flesh and blood. So let's figure out how you're going to get me to tell them in words what I've been *showing* them from up there on the stage in all these different ways over the span of all these years I've been up there in the spotlight. Because, hell, you know how folks are. You draw them a picture or show them an act and an imitation of a picture in the flesh and they want you to explain it with a legend or something. Or if you start out with a legend they're going to want to see it as a picture, and let me tell you something, young prof, being a schoolboy you know even better than I do that pictures were mostly about action long before moving pictures as such came along. Hell, all that was right there for you in primer grade readers and them Sunday school cards, and what about old Santa Claus and them reindeers in the sky? And don't let nobody tell you that them so-called still-life paintings can do without rhythm. I'm a dancer. What about when I hit them with a freeze? It's like a bolt of lightning! Wham! Take the breath out of the whole audience.

But you get my point, he said then. So you tell me what was on your mind about this thing when you decided to pick up the phone and call me this morning.

That was when I said that the theme that I had been playing around with was *the dancing of an attitude*, which I said was like saying dancing is what I'm all about because this is the way I deal with what life is all about, because what I'm doing when I'm dancing, it is like saying this is the way I see it, the way I feel it, and the way I feel about it. And this is the way I say what I have to say about it.

So then I said, What I jotted down was ROYAL HIGH-NESS, *The Dancing of an Attitude.*

And he said, Hey, *yeah*, young soldier! You really mean business, don't you. I can already see right down the road you've got me headed along. Boy, you already got me going back to the days when I first found out about this kind of music and this kind of dancing.

Because first there was the church and that kind of group clapping and strutting and shouting. And then there were also the jook joints, honky-tonks, barrelhouse dives, and all that shuffling and slow dragging and bumping and grinding and then the traveling tent shows and all that fancy solo stuff, and that was for me. And then somewhere along the line I realized that I was doing what I was doing the way I was doing it because the solo was like a sermon, a foot sermon in the spotlight. Like the spotlight was my pulpit.

And that was when I said, Hey, I think you just said it, Daddy Royal. Man, I think you just said it. So how about this?

The Dancing of an Attitude
The
Footnotes
of
the One and Only
ROYAL HIGHNESS

And he said, See there? There you go, right on the after-beat! Footnotes! Boy, you got it! Boy, you know something! Boy, them thugs in that band mean it when they call you our schoolboy. Notice they don't call you the Professor or young 'Fess or anything like that, because they know that the Boss-man and Old Pro wouldn't have had you in that band if that was the case. And hell, they could see for themselves that you as hip to what the band is about as you are deep in all that college and university jive.

Footnotes, he said again, then, footnotes on the afterbeat! That just about sets it up, young soldier. Hey, man, I'm beginning to see this whole thing already, but hell, I'm not surprised. Hell, I know good and well that if there was such a thing as a literary comp artist, the Bossman would spot him if he showed up. I bet it didn't take no time at all for him to realize that Hortense Hightower had sent him one.

Then he said, You noodle and doodle and jive and connive to my segue *and here I come with my rawhide stride and my sporty, syncopated limp walk just like along any patent-leather avenue mainstem anywhere on the circuit, chitlin or caviar, transcontinental or intercontinental.*

So there you go, young soldier, right on the money. The dancing of an attitude! Now, that's saying something. Talking about not just what you say, but what you do and how you do it. That's who you are. That's your personal fingerprint, no, *footprint,* how about that, *footprint* in the footlights (thanks to Hollywood). After you've gone.

So what's all this got to do with them blues you get in the planetarium? It's what you're stomping with, young soldier. And when you trip the light fantastic at them you really mess with them, because then you're carrying on just like they ain't even there. Hey, then the softer you tip, the faster they fade away! Man, that's worse than thumbing your nose at them, because then you're carrying on like they ain't even there.

Man, when you start riffing on them breaks like they're clause after clause and chapter and verse after chapter and verse of the Emancipation Proclamation, while treating all that border-to-border and coast-to-coast U.S.A. dissonance and cacophony like it's sweet honey in the rock, you're taking care of some business, *and I'm talking about taking care of the nitty-gritty like it's all fun and games and one feast day after another! What you talking about, young soldier, what you talking about?!*

Footnotes, he said again then, that's really pretty slick, young soldier. Footnotes! Right on the button from the get-go. Footnotes on insights and outlook. That's exactly what riffing the blues on the afterbeat is all about. Walking that walk, like talking that talk. Because walking that walk, which ain't straight and narrow, you've got to zig as well as zag. But don't zig when you're supposed to zag. And don't be tapping when you're supposed to be tipping, especially when you're supposed to be tipping on the q.t., which I don't have to tell you has as much to do with politics as poontang. Talking about signifying, young soldier. So let's tell them what I've been showing them lo these many years on the boards here, there, and elsewhere.

So let's roll, young soldier, he said.

Then before I could say what I was going to say about getting back to him as soon as I could spare the time, he said, So now just go on and find your classroom groove, and get back to me and let's see what we can do about your Thanksgiving and Christmas breaks. Hey, how about me getting you all up here for Christmas? Anyway, whatever schedule we come up with, as far as I'm concerned this thing is already under way. As I'm calling to tell the Bossman and Old Pro and old Joe as soon as we hang up.

Hey, now, talking about some terpsichorean riff signification. Man, we got it percolating on the afterbeat already.

XXXII

CASTLE OR city-state, my old long gone and now also long since last heard from but still best of all possible college freshman and sophomore year roommates imaginable used to say, Castle to castle, stone walls with or without moats (or beanstalk with or without keeps) no less than chapels whether perilous or beneficent, the second law of thermodynamics always applies. Entropy, my good man. There you have it. That's the goods, my fine fellow. My estimate of the situation, as any elementary school trip to the planetarium should have long since made all too obvious. Elementary, my dear Watson, elementary indeed. *Your notorious snark by any other terminology is still a bojum!*

Thus if you miss the fun of the safari as such, what with all the standard deluxe equipment and provisions, *sine qua non*, you've missed the point! You've missed the *metaphor*! There is *entropy*, my good fellow, and there is *metaphor*, and if you miss the implications of the metaphor, you're stuck with clichés, which most certainly should not be confused with the *blisses of the commonplace*! Which so often turns out to be precisely what luxury is really about after all—*nay, first of all!*

Moreover, he also used to like to say, arching his ever so subtly academic brow as he used the transitional device I never heard another freshman or sophomore use before or since.

Moreover, as our very own La Bohème of Greenwich Village, NYC, U.S.A., said long before the publication of her ever so fatal interviews, "*Whether or not we find what we are seeking is idle biologically speaking!*"

So heh, heh, haay, roommate, he would go on in his mock penny dreadful villain's voice once more, clasping his archcriminal hands and rubbing his insatiably avaricious pawnbroker's palms, his eyes and nostrils narrowing satanically as if he also had a satanic tail to wag as he pounced!

It was ever thus, roommate, and so it will ever be—not only biologically speaking, but also geologically speaking, not to mention speaking in terms of third-grade geography after that field trip to the planetarium.

Anyway, so much for the all-American pursuit of the all-American melodramatic climax. After all, there is also the no less American soap opera, with its movie star good looks across the board and deluxe fashion and shelter magazine perfect town and country settings and dernier cri haute couture, may be concerned with existential problems that are much more relevant to human actualities as such in the context of the planetarium. After all, they almost always seem to be very well off indeed, biologically speaking. *Their perpetual concern is with the ongoing problem of getting along with each other.*

There is no guaranteed all-American movie-concocted melodramatic resolution out there, my ever so appropriately ambitious and unimpeachably sincere young man from the northbound L & N Railroad outskirts of Mobile, Alabama. Take it from old Geronimo, your newfound fellow trailmate from the South Side of Chicago. There is only the ultimate actuality of the entropy (repeat, entropy) *of the void*, upon which we impose such metaphorical devices as AND, as in (andoneandtwoandthreeandfourand) and one, and two, and three, and four and so forth and so on and on, from which we also get "*and it came to pass and so on it went time after time after time*, as has been recorded here, there, and elsewhere.

Picaresque, my dear fellow journeyman, he also used to like to repeat from time to time. Don Quixote and Candide, each in his own way, equals *farce*, the dynamics of coping with chaos, slapstick for slapdash: Buster Keaton's deadpan, Charlie Chaplin's ever so elegant nonchalance.

In all events, however modest that garden Candide so earnestly
promises to cultivate, it had better include an adequate crop of
ever more elegantly refined or at any rate resilient pratfalls, if you
know what I mean.
    So there you go.

XXXIII

SO THERE you go, fellow, Eric Threadcraft said on the phone
from Hollywood. Man, old Papa Joe and the crew were in
town last night on a stopover on their way up the coast to
Monterey, and he gave me the double rundown on what you're
up to and also heading into. Fantastic, old buddy. Like I always
say, I'm still getting special kicks out of the fact that old Papa
Joe was the one who had the idea that the two of us should get
to know each other and stay in touch. Anyway, man, I must
say that campus gig couldn't have been more timely. And, of
course, you know that the Bossman's proposition knocks me
out. Man, who else but him would realize how slick it is to
begin with Royal Highness. Hey, that's just as slick as it is deep,
fellow, and so obvious that you hardly notice it.

Then before I could ask about Celeste, he said, And now
comes the update on the situation chez old Mice: *We are just*
about to do it, fellow. Man, I'm taking the plunge. So there it is,
old buddy. You're the first to know.

Then he said, Man, you remember that studio thing about
foreign employee clearance that had me so nervous about political intrigue and extortion and stuff that morning when I got
you to meet me at the Algonquin and then didn't bring it up
anymore because I was already so far gone on this lady that I
just decided to play it as it lays.

And guess what? It turns out that what those studio-foreign
background checks came across and mistook for some kind
of political extortion and payoff turns out to be a very personal family matter. Man, Celeste is a very young widow with
a daughter whose father was what she describes as a café au
lait painter from North Carolina, who was killed in a racing
car accident. So guess what all the suspicion about political
shakedown was about? Celeste didn't want her child to come

into this screwed-up racial situation over here until she's gone far enough in school in Paris to have become indelibly French. Anyway, fellow, the suspicious "extortion payoffs" were all for child care. It was as simple as that. No international political intrigue at all. Hell, fellow, not even a case of small-town family illegality.

Then before saying, Buzz you later, he said, Oh, by the way, I've done my etymological homework on your Miss Fine People. So Eunice means happy victory! So what can I tell you? She couldn't have happened to a more deserving person.

XXXIV

MY OLD roommate had already said what he said about whoever turned out to be the one who was the one for me, when he replied to the letter along with the snapshot of me and Eunice that I had sent to him at Yale to tell him about what had happened to me and her between that third September and wisteria blossom time that next spring.

Man, he responded within the same week, you make it all sound like it's those Gulf Coast area boy blue skies above those crepe myrtle yard tree blossoms and dog fennel meadows, not to mention those playhouse times all over again. But man, watch out this time around. We're talking castles and perhaps even chapels perilous again, my man, he wrote. Because this, after all, is about fairy-tale princesses in the first place, is it not—without whom your castle may not be any more than just another earlier version of Fort Apache, if you know what I mean. Man, I know good and well that I don't have to tell you that without a fairy-tale princess your castle is no more relevant than any old ultradeluxe wayside inn.

It is she, my good fellow, who is the embodiment of the quintessential. That fifth essence(!). Without her, there is only air, earth, water, and fire. She is the element, my man, that gets us back outside the soundless fury of the planetarium and into the realm of the blisses of the so-called commonplace!

Nor, as any competent student of architectural design and engineering should be able to testify, does the perception of the so-called blisses of the commonplace have any less to do with the dynamics of enchantment than do nursery rhymes, fables, and Mother Goose tales. After all, to us a multimillion-dollar mansion is no less a stage set for being registered as privately owned real estate!

So here again, it's the metaphor that generates either the bliss or the banality! Thus one person's restriction may be another person's incentive! What one person may perceive as the outer limits of all that really matters (as the Chinese once dismissed whatever was beyond the Great Wall), another group of people may regard as *the come-hither region of ever more promising horizons of aspiration.*

In all events, that certainly strikes me as the snapshot of a fairy-tale princess you sent along with your update, my all too obviously lucky old cut buddy. So cross your fingers and touch your talisman and polish your wiles to their highest sheen. Who ever said that romance was not a game of chance?

Nor should you ever be unmindful of any of those slapdash— slapstick, nay, downright farcical escapades and labyrinthine misadventures old ever so jam-riff-clever Odysseus himself had to maneuver his way out of and back on course to and through the gateway to the remembered hometown boy blue bliss with the one for whom he had forsaken all others not only in Ithaca but everywhere else.

CONJUGATIONS AND
REITERATIONS

To Mozelle and Michele

CONTENTS

I

AUBADES

*Epic Exits and Other
Twelve Bar Riffs*

early in the morning
  hear the rooster crow
early in the morning
  hear the rooster crow
hear the freight train coming
  whistle moaning low

———————

old grandpa stole away
  north by freedom train
old grandpa snagged
  that underground freedom train
booked his passage through the grapevine
  stashed his pack
and prayed for rain, I mean heavy rain

———————

once was the north star
  then it was the L and N
used to be the north star
  then it was the L and N
not talking about cincinnati
not telling nobody where or when

———————

going down to the railroad
   down to the railroad track
going down to the railroad
   down to the railroad track
grab me an arm full of freight train
   and ain't never ever coming back

———————

early in the morning
   hear the sawmill whistles blow
early in the morning
   hear the sawmill whistles blow
then when the school bells ring
   it's my time to be ready to go

———————

they used to call me schoolboy
   and I never did deny my name
when folks called me schoolboy
   I never would deny my name
I said you've got to be a schoolboy
   if preparation is your aim

———————

early in the morning
listening to the radio
early in the morning
listening to the radio
first week on the campus
four chime time years to go

———————

I can drink muddy water
sleep in a hollow log
yes, drink muddy water
sleep in a hollow log
but one of these days
I'll be back home walking the dog
along the avenue
arm in cozy arm with you

———————

I said what I said
and her smile said we shall see
I said what I said
and her smile said we shall see
ain't no line of jive gonna ever make a
fool of me

———————

get yourself together baby
and let's get on some time
get yourself together baby
and let's get on some time
this is the nitty gritty, baby
this ain't no pantomime

———————

some folks out here
trying to change things
some others just come
to have their say
some out here running risks
to change things
some others just saying
the same old say
takes more than huffing and puffing
to blow them jim crow blues away

———————

found no enchanted castles
so there were no magic keys
there were no enchanted castles
and there were no magic keys
nor was there anyplace on this planet
that was a realm of total ease

———————

the world ain't promised me nothing
so it don't owe me nothing at all
no, since the world ain't promised nothing
it don't owe nobody nothing at all
makes no difference to the universe
whether you walk, swim, fly or crawl

———————

II

Landscape with Figures

I

the thing about
scarecrow plug uglies
is that
everybody (and creature)
who does not ignore them in the first place
catches on to them sooner or later
indeed even before boogerbear-oriented children
grow up to construct fake monsters
of their own
there were already unimpressed crows
who had long since mistaken them for a perch
and endowed them with the patina
of public park monuments:
perhaps "three quarks for mr. marx"
but certainly "plip plop and spatter batter on you
mr. whoever or whatever the hell
you're supposed to be"

II

on the other hand
as municipal cleanup budgets
for red letter day celebrations
of legendary heroic actions
have always reflected
(no matter who is elected)
bird spatterings on the time-honored
stone, bronze or gold-gilded patina
of public monuments
are a serious matter
of respectful aesthetics
not just of vain
chamber of commerce cosmetics

---

mug ugly frogs
may sometimes be
princes in uncharming
disguise
the purpose of which
is to test
the future queen's
sense of ambiguity
remember, it's what
happened in the dark
that made the princess
light the candle

---

during an ivy league
pit stop:
overheard t.s. eliot
giving the lowdown
on the west forty
disguised as london town
fallen down
to the dongless ding
of the land of the fisher king!
wiping out the folklore
of white supremacy
with far more implications
immediate or long range
than jack johnson's jokey
demolishment of jack london's
ever so bright comeback hopes
for jim jeffries
the truth of fairy tales
    must be read as formulas are

by substituting for the x, y, zero
   situations of the hero
concrete details which represent
   daily circumstances
thus are all romances
   whether of people or of numbers
made to fulfill a social function
   beyond mere elementary survival
and entertainment
   ugly terrain and foul weather
(no less than fair)
   come-hither castles,
cozy coves and reclining nudes
   are required by narrative
as whatever is by mathematical convention

the dragons however in whichever image
   or embodiment of entropy
are not only actual
   but can wreak such devastation
as only combat experience
   quod erat demonstrandum
can cope with
   on the other hand
who knows how much luck (!) may always
   be involved in the outcome of anything

———

to new york then I came
and found picasso's demoiselles uptown
in cotton club honey brown
projecting black and tan
(expense account) fantasy figures
replacing the can can
with the shuffle, the shimmy
and the birmingham break down

to the also and also
　　of paris I also made my way
following jim europe's syncopated footsteps
　　and those of louis and duke,
of both of whom the french said
　　not what do they want
but what have they brought us this time

as for what I wanted:
　　a rage of paris
publicity springboard
　　to points thisaway
and thataway
　　u.s.a.

but that was long ago
　　when french word
was aesthetic law

one must measure
　　one's own plurabilities
these days

III

Fable in the Fabric

if you got to ass
what it is
honey, you ain't yet with it,
thus old gates armstrong
(louis, yclept satchmo, erstwhile
satchel mouth and before that
dipper mouth, from which dipper & dip
even as satchmo was to become
satch
as in satchel foot for old satchel paige)

thus old satch (who was finally to become old pops)
to some fay chick unnamed
but variously quoted e.g. time, the newsmagazine
once the self-styled coca-cola of u.s. journalism:
2/21/49 "when you got to ask [sic!] what it is,
you never get to know"
and so old pops
had himself another glory
though some say it was also old fats
waller said it
who damn well could've
item: **man, if you don't know**
what it is
best you don't be trying
to mess around with it
so old fats too
whose eyes were forever saying
one never knows,
not do one?
but do one!

but questions pursue
the musicians backstage
as if verbalization means more than their music
indeed such used to be the downtown uproar
over duke's uptown downbeat
ass they did
and urgently, suspiciously

as if life itself were questionable
as if questions must always have answers
as if answers don't have questions of their own

as if facts beget experience
and information flesh and blood
so with as much cosmic implication
as is available to your own perception
of the nuts and bolts actuality
of anything whatsoever
you say—remembering bubba and duke:
it don't mean a thing
if it ain't got that swing
so do what? do art!
do what?
do art! do art!

nevertheless
the questions pursue the performer
not only backstage
but also back uptown (or crosstown, or wherever)
only to get the same answers
do art! do art! do art! do art!
do art! do art! do art! do art!
do what?
do art! do art! do art! do art!
do art! do art! do art! do art!

KC 4/4
(I)

said the nothing if not pragmatic
william james
basie,
the trigger-fingered count from
edmund wilson's red bank, new jersey,
by way of kansas city
and by virtue

of a not un-walt whitmanesque
four/four,
"beat, bite and real guts
under a good old post-ragtime
syncopated shout
with trumpet and/or trombone mutes
plungers and aluminum, plastic, felt
derby fans
will always put the blues
deep down in the dozens
talking about playing the dirty dozens with the devil!
(and if you don't play them
just pat your foot whilst I play them)
talking about how like the
oklahoma city
blue devils used to stomp
the red devils down in
slaughters hall and ralph ellison's other
deep second joints,
and remember
nothing is ever too slow
or too fast
to swing!"

KC 4/4
(II)

eventually
along with the already
universally irresistible kansas city four/four
came charlie parker
shouting the blues
that many bird intervals higher
and thus
with an even more captivating
velocity of celebration

Pas de Deux
(I)

all art,
said old walter pater,
speaking of sandro botticelli,
constantly aspires
toward the condition
of music.
so it is swing
that is the supreme fiction,
madam,
for
(given the concreteness
of physical experience *per se*)
our primary concern
is the quality of our consciousness
(how we *feel* about it all)
and swing, which is movement
and countermovement
which is life itself,
is that elegant resilience
that poetry would reenact,
its verbalization being
aesthetic kinetics!
after all, madam
(or rather first of all),
is not the primordial function
of verbal enchantment
the refinement
of our physical responses?
the objective of poetry
is to be *moving*, madam,
poetry is the supreme effort
to make words *swing*.
but, according to vico,
(giambattista, 1668–1744),

before articulation
became narration
there was only exclamation
(onomatopoeia)
along with pantomime
yes, as jamesjoyce came to know
and kennethburke came to say,
poetry is symbolic action
and symbolic action,
madam,
is the *dancing* of an attitude,
and dance, madam,
don't mean a thing
minus that insouciant element
of swing
there's your supreme fiction, madam,
it ain't what you do
it's the way that you do it.

l'envoie:
it must never
be more gymnastic
than elegant

Pas de Deux
(II)

swinging is never uptight,
my good fellow,
no sweat, my man,
cool, old pardner,
up-tempo relaxation
as it were, moreover,
given the inevitability
of entropy
and the ineluctable modality
of perception
and thus conception

swinging is not only
the most elegant mathematical
solution
it is also
the best revenge

Q & A

do the mutes sublimate
underground grapevine whispers
do plungers compensate
childhood repressions
schoolyard frictions
or perhaps stool restrictions?

are juke joint piano sounds
your evocations of untold stories
of jim crow towns,
the black and white keyboard
suggesting segregation
your exclusion from paradise,
the black key minors
touched for tears?
not if they swing,
my man, miss lady,
not if they swing

IV

Profiles

Premier Cru U.S.A.

american social science survey technicians,
whose *modus operandi* (nay, *sine qua non!*)
is segregation,
continue to proliferate norms and deviations
that are invariably skewed
to support the folklore of white supremacy
and the fakelore of black pathology
but the anecdotes
that most immigrants find most representative
are those horatioalgerisms that relate and reiterate
how the white human trash of europe
interacting with other human trash
of west africa and elsewhere
in accomplishing what the redskin elite
of the forest primeval had no aztec, inca, mayan
or toltec plans for
became the demographic cream of the crop
that by mid twentieth century
had already rendered the almanach de gotha
obsolete:
who is due at the castle
for dinner and global negotiations
bearing non-greek appropriations?

the progeny of all that
mayflower, middle passage and steerage
flotsam and jetsam
your highness
that's who

Private Stock

thelonious
the syncopating monk
whose preferred cloistersphere
seemed to be the misty morning atmosphere
of the after hours joint
from which the last of the nightlong
merrymakers have departed.
in all events
he almost always used to seem
to be resampling his honky-tonk piano
meditations and up-tempo stride time études
as much for his own private edification
as for the programmed entertainment
of any paying audience
indeed thelonious made music
as some monks have always made
and shared wine:
here's something else to my taste
try this
how about this
or
this

from washington
   once a man
and now a town
   came ellington
once a man
   and now a sound
that is storiella americana
   as she is swyung
up and down
   and all around
the globe

William Faulkner Noun Place and Verb

memory he said believes he said
and himself did who was himself
memory and did himself believe
and then remember to recollect,
whose name was william faulkner
whose place was mississippi
and whose verb was tell.

memory he wrote believes before knowing
remembers. believes longer than recollects
longer than knowing even wonders
knows remembers believes, he himself said
believing himself and mississippi august skylight
mississippi thickets in september twilight,
believing the dry hysteria: *something
is going to happen I am going to do something
something is going to happen to me*

and memory no less in mississippi than elsewhere
believes knows tells this:
the mississippiness of ancient oracles
of albatross sins ancestral; recollects remembers this:
presummersmell of wisteria
oldentime ladies in rooms unsanctuary

amid mississippi gothic behind cottonwhite
totems doric corinthian scotch irish
(O clytemnestra my black one
  O my firstborn son and brother)

and this also believes: cypress and gum trees
beach, cane and briar and three-note birdsong
reflections in branch water; mississippi distant horns
and gas engine smells fading beyond now and fury.
and this recollects and knows the significance of:
black human blood red on butcher knives
white female blood on phallic corncobs

memory believing yoknapatawpha indian doom
did not mistake the wilderness for sanctuary
either but wished it so as huntsman
but wishing does not know
forgets and gallops confederate cavalry in gail (tone)
    hightower
sermons
wish-fulfilling knighthood (without negroes)
wish-forgiving arrogance and the outrage of human bondage
wish-denying antebellum insurrection nightmares
while celebrating those who could survive them
but wishing is believing too
because the bones remember
(O canaan look away from dixie
away from bedford forrest O railroads
underground freedom bound)

and memory knowing this
knows more (believes infers
more complications than even those
miss rosa coldfield's perhaps once glittering
eyes gave quentin compson, who said:
and wants it told!)

memory
believes knows recollects in him (*whose nouns*

were courage and honor and pride and
he says pity and love and even justice
and liberty) believes knows and wonders at:
wishing become man-horse-demon
with twenty negroes (shackled) begetting
with one french architect (shanghaied) sutpens
hundred (*without gentleness begot*, miss rosa
coldfield says); wonders remembers
aghast but knows: mississippi dynasties
of somewhat
oedipal innocence with black
queen mothers and half brothers
knows jefferson the man and town
and public confederation of decorum; and also knows
remembers eighty miles to memphis
and miss reba's sanctum sanctorum of law and order
and sportsmanship

believes remembers
recollects, records in commissary ledgers
pharaoh-tale-accounts compounded in confounding
convolutions of all-too-human-impacted
good intentions which at any rate
reveal (or partly unconceal) himself:
william faulkner hamlet-hounded master
of mulatto metaphors among macbeths
in county courthouse castles out-demographed
by ever in-creeping miscegenated thickets

nigger? the sheriff said in hot pursuit
of the inherently illusive mississippi christmas,
nigger? he said. maybe nigger, maybe not
they told him then
whose memory like theirs believed in shadows
as much as men

Inside Dopester

sigmund freud, whose ego-id (or jekyll-hyde) dialectics
have become the opiate of so many contemporary u.s.
   intellectuals
to whom most dreams, however (whether pipe or utopian),
are not nearly so revolutionary as pornographic—
whose positive contribution to the mental health
of twentieth century mankind is not altogether
unquestionable, but who gave to gossip (back fence or
   cocktail party)
a terminological refinement it never had before,
did not write oedipus rex, antigone and electra
nor was he ever near colonus,
not circa 442 b.c. at any rate or sophocles who, incidentally,
not only made less insistent speculations
about bow and arrow wounds, for instance,
but also never forgot that dream oracles, like fortune tellers
are seldom scientific.

herr doktor (which is to say wish doctor) freud was the
father matriarch not of ancient greek
but of modern viennese mythology
he now rests, however, not in that city of elegant dressage
   (tho minus syncopating sidewalks!)
but in london the anglo-saxon citadel of
stiff upper lips
a refugee from the nastiness
of teutonic gas holes but not always consistently pro-semitic
   himself
resenting (somewhat) his own mostly nice paterfamilias
rationalizing it away with a cock and bull formula:
*parental regard is to greek incest as filial disobedience
is to murder*
and then charging his confused and scandalized patients
with (and for) hating (or loving) theirs
revealing in the process his other psychosis

as occupational: *the fee he said*
was part of the therapy

a natty dresser, a strict big daddy
who confessed moses but never met him
he could with impeccable-seeming manners
turn leonardo da vinci's dream kite into an italian vulture
and then proceed to desecrate the bloomers
of middle-aged nannies,
a long black non-viennese stogie
erect between his pale bearded lips the while
but, whether or not he shared jung's
naughty notions of u.s. negroes,
freud could never have forgiven their jazzy unconcern
with his own hopelessly unbooted conjectures
about mama love inhibitions and phallic envy.

all too sexual about matters intellectual
but always intellectual about matters sexual
the categorical professor freud became
downright academic
about such simple and completely ordinary things
as his and hers, and astonishingly theoretical
about what after all is the most natural
and necessary difference in the world.
and, what is more, remained all those years
adamant in his suspicion of fun
and games, preferring the dream world of fears,
queers, valse triste rituals, midnight tears.

and, almost as bad, his incurable *freudianism*
spoiled most jokes, and he decried most pranks
as intended crimes and seemed compelled
to make the simplest mistakes more embarrassing
by explaining them. but perhaps worst of all
he encouraged bookworms, statisticians and lab technicians
to assume that data can exorcise all adventure
and monographs expose the innermost secrets of
     wonderlands.

motivational revelations by all means
and the light which he gaveth shineth in the darkness,
yea verily, for thinking is indeed
mostly wishing—*tant pis (though perhaps less often fish-wishy
than just plain wishy-washy)*

but for all his carefully compiled dope sheets
he was not unlike so many cocksure tipsters
always somehow suddenly shy of the pragmatic
hands on, chips down
flags down, eggs down advice
poor old humpty dumpty's king's horsemen
need most urgently at post time
(it being too late for such freudulent hindsight
as: you should have stood longer in bed)
nor, come to think of it, did he ever really
convince himself or any of the faithful
that wishing won't wash any real enemies away.

nevertheless dear doctor freud, along with dear doctor marx,
remains the master of machine age medicine patents
most self-indulged by devoted disciples
but in them it all too often seems that he has bequeathed to
    posterity
more wise guys perhaps than wise men

Poeta de Época
(I)

chez hemingway
the elemental is *per se*
and thus timeless
universal
indispensable
ergo his factuality and musicality
are inseparable
his conjugations therefore required
the cadence of process

become ritual
each episode being
a ceremonial reenactment
rendered on a rhetorical principle
preferring precision of syntax
to the elaboration of synonyms

Poeta de Época
(II)

sharks, he said,
do not share.
nor, he might have added,
do cowards dare.
they stare,
then cringe
and seek sneaky revenge
as if the blame
for their most precious shortcomings
were someone else's fame
the glitter of which
obscures who is fitter.
machismo,
he always insisted,
was never a matter of
flaunting arrogance
but of overcoming fear
grace under pressure indeed

Miss Hot Stuff

did any dancer
ever dance
more elegantly
than she used to
all but prance
along the sidewalk

her hips swinging
as if to silent fingersnapping singing,
her preemptive back-at-you smile flashing
like the midsummer fountain splashing
in the squirrel tree dappled shade
of old wrought iron mobile's
bienville square?

perhaps not
still she was no wet dream storybook creola
she was only a frisky gal
a wannabe femme fatale

V

Gospel Reverberations

told you once
done told you twice
you'll never get to heaven
shooting dice
ain't no glory
without sacrifice

I looked over my shoulder
  and what did I see
a band of red devils with pitchforks
  chasing after me

Jawbone Sermon

Amen brothers and sisters God said
(Amen!)
Said, now Gideon. Said oh Gideon
(Amen!)
Said listen to me Gideon
and hearken to what I'm trying to tell you
(Amen!)
Said I'm trying to tell you something, Gideon
(Amen!)
Said I'm trying to tell you something good
for your soul, Gideon
(Amen!)
Said I'm not just concerned with your body
of flesh and blood and sinews and sinfulness, Gideon
(Amen—ahah!)
I'm concerned
(ahah!) with your soul, Gideon
(Amen!)

God wants to save our souls brothers and sisters
(Amen!)

Said Gideon
(Amen!)
Said you asked me for a sign
(Amen!)
Said I'm going to give you a sign Gideon
(Amen!)
Said listen to me Gideon
(Amen!)
I'm going to give you a sign
because you asked me Gideon
(Amen!)

Because I said ask and it shall be given
(oyez!)
I said seek and you shall find.
And I said knock
and the door shall be opened unto you
(Amen!)
Brothers and sisters
unto all men that seek
after goodness and righteousness
(Glory hallelujah!!)
Said *(nahah!)* I'm going to give you a sign
but said *(nahah!)* I want you to trust in me too Gideon
(nahah!)
Amen brothers and sisters
said I'm going to give you a sign
because I know how you feel
Said don't think I don't know how you feel
(nahah!)
Because what I asked ain't easy
(Amen!)
Brothers and sisters
don't think God don't know how you feel
all bent down with the troubles of this world
But God's ways mysterious
because his will is divine.

Said
amen

Gideon.
Said I might be a jealous God,
but I know how you feel.
Said I might be a wrathful God
but I know how you feel
(nahah!)
Believe me I know how you feel.
Said *(nahah!)* yes and I might even be a vengeful God,
but that don't mean that I don't know
exactly how you feel.
(oh yes, amen and amen again!)
Because am I not also a MERCIFUL God
in all of my almightiness?
Amen!
Brothers and sisters.
Talking about FAITH
(Glory hallelujah!)
FAITH

Said Gideon
(Amen!)
Didn't I say I would take care of you
if you would only just believe in my holy word?
Said didn't I take care of the Hebrew children
in a Fiery Furnace
(nahah!)
Said *(nahah!)*
didn't I take care of Daniel in a lion's den?
And *(nahah!)*
didn't I take care of Jonah
in the belly of the whale?
And I drowned old Pharaoh's mighty army in the Red Sea
to save Moses and the Children of Israel *(Amen! nahah!)*

Said I'm going to give you a sign Gideon
because you got down on your bended knee
and asked me
like I myself told you to do
(nahah!)

because I know what you're doubting
is not me and my WORD
and my PROMISE and my GLORY, Gideon
but your own self. What you're doubting is not
(Amen!)
whether I am the one,
but whether you're the one.
And I understand that.
But
(Glory hallelujah!)
we're talking about FAITH this morning.
Because brothers and sisters,
that's what God ALWAYS talking about.

Said Gideon *(Amen!)*
I'm going to give you the sign
because maybe what you're doubting
is whether or not this is ME.
Said *(Amen!)*
I can understand that too, Gideon
and I'm going to give you a sign
so there can be no doubt about it.
Said I'm going to show you
two signs of the fleece.
And said if you trust in me
I'm going to tell you
how to hand-pick your soldiers
—and you don't need but just a few
as long as you've already got me by your side
—and then just to show the world
and confound the nation
I'm going to empower you
to annihilate your foes
and all their multitudes alike
with nothing more than the jawbone of an ass!

Cold Clay Coda for Old Man Whicker Bill Comesaw

will there be any
black brown or yaller folks
at your funeral
and if so
will they be there
to grieve their loss
or to
verify your departure?

OTHER POEMS

"A man of no fortune, and with a name to come"
—Pound, *Cantos* I

my nickname is scooter
　　my real name ain't never been told
my nickname is scooter
　　my real name ain't never been told
my home has been the briarpatch
　　since before I was nine months old

now some call me schoolboy
　　and I don't deny my name
some folks call me schoolboy
　　and I never did deny my name
see me riffing them pages
　　taking care of business is my game

———————

train coming to the station
　　hear that whistle blow
train pulling in the station
　　hear that whistle blow
I got my suitcase packed
　　but I don't know where I want to go

———————

I didn't say good-bye
*   I said count the days I'm gone*
I didn't say good-bye
*   I said count the days I'm gone*
I said next time you see me
*   I'll be heading back to a higher zone*

———————

went all the way up the country
*   like my teachers said I should*
roaming all across the nation
*   just like they said I would*
because one thing leads to another
*   just like they said it would*

———————

came back down home
*   but I didn't come to stay*
said I'm back down home
*   but I don't intend to stay*
just come to check how things been going
*   since I went away*

Note Bene

my literary verb voice
as often as possible
is
active
whereas
the ever so politically active
bitching, belly aching
pissed-off brigades
is
passive!
thus with me
(note the preposition)
it's I and we
with them it's
alas
me and alack us

————————

while some (circa 1940–45)
took actual flight training ranging from
piper cub solos through
BT-11's, AT-6's–P-40's to F-51's,
dizzy gillespie and charlie parker
developed make believe
bird wings
and when jets and space missiles eventually
arrived—we were ready for them!
it was only a matter
of *segue*!

The Magic Keys

some sharp
some flat
some natural
the readiness is all
some golden
some silver
some platinum
some of some as yet
undisclosed alloy

———————

there were
fifty roads to town
which was
seven blue miles away
seven or
seven times seven
(plus one mile creek)
seventy times seven
plus the
seven seas

———————

what can I do
and not do
about
the cosmic
implications of
the ancient roman
still-life exhibition
at vesuvius?
you can proceed
as if it all mattered but
so much for the seven
cardinal sins
so much for crime and punishment

———————

when tomorrow
  becomes today
  and also what is left
  of yesterday
    we say
    NOW
    which is the ongoing
    in which we live
    and without which
    there is no past
    and no future

APPENDIX

The Luzana Cholly Kick

L IL' BUDDY'S color was that sky blue in which hens cackled;
it was that smoke blue in which dogs barked and mosquito
hawks lit on barbed-wire fences. It was the color above meadows. It was my color too because it was a boy's color. It was
whistling blue and hunting blue, and it went with baseball, and
that was old Lil' Buddy again, and that blue beyond outfields
was exactly what we were singing about when we used to sing
that old one about it ain't gonna rain no more no more.

Steel blue was a man's color. That was the clean, oil-smelling
color of rifle barrels and railroad iron. That was the color that
went with Luzana Cholly, and he had a steel-blue .32-20 on
a 44 frame. His complexion was not steel blue but leather
brown like dark rawhide, but steel blue was the color that went
with what he was. His hands were just like rawhide, and when
he was not dressed up he smelled like green oak steam. He
had on slick starched blue denim overalls then, and when he
was dressed up he wore a black broadcloth box-back coat with
hickory striped peg-top pants, and he smelled like the barber
shop and new money.

Luzana Cholly was there in that time and place as far back
as I can remember, even before Lil' Buddy was. Because I can
remember when I didn't know Lil' Buddy at all. I can remember when that house they moved to was built (Lil' Buddy's
papa and mama were still living together when they came to
Gasoline Point from Choctaw County which was near the Mississippi line), and I can also remember when that street (which
was called Chattanooga Lookout Street) was pushed all the
way through to the AT&N cut. That was before I had ever
even heard of Lil' Buddy, and my buddy then was old Willie
Marlowe. Lil' Buddy didn't come until after Willie Marlowe
had gone to Detroit, Michigan, and that was not until after

"The Luzana Cholly Kick" was the first work Murray published. It appeared
in *New World Writing 4* in October 1953, pp. 228–43, and in 1966 began to
appear in anthologies. The action corresponds to pages 6–25 in this volume,
though there are significant differences between the texts.

Mister One-Arm Will had been dead and buried for about nine months.

I can remember him there in that wee time when I couldn't even follow the stories I knew later they were telling about him, when it was only just grown folks talking, and all I could make of it was *Luzana, they are talking something about old Luzana again, and I didn't know what, to say nothing of where Louisiana was.* But old Luze was there even then and I could see him very clearly when they said his name because I had already seen him coming up that road that came by that house with the chinaberry yard, coming from around the bend and down in the railroad bottom; and I had already heard whatever that was he was picking on his guitar and heard that holler too. That was always far away and long coming. It started low like it was going to be a song and then it jumped all the way to the very top of his voice and broke off, and then it started again, and this time was already at the top, and then it gave some quick jerking squalls and died away in the woods, the water, and the darkness (you always heard it at night), and Mama always said he was whooping and hollering like somebody back in the rosin-woods country, and Papa said it was one of them old Luzana swamp hollers. I myself always thought it was like a train, like a bad train saying look out this is me, and here I come, and I'm coming through.

That was even before I was big enough to climb the chinaberry tree. That was when they used to talk about the war and the Kaiser, and I can remember that there was a war book with Germans in it, and I used to see sure-enough soldiers marching in the Mardi Gras parades. Soldier Boy Crawford was still wearing his Army coat then, and he was the one who used to tell about how Luze used to play his guitar in France, telling about how they would be going through some French town like the ones called Nancy and Saint Die and old Luze would drop out of the company and go and play around in the underground wine shops until he got as much cognac and as many French Frogs as he wanted and then he would turn up in the company again and Capt'n would put him out by himself on the worst outpost he could find in No Man's Land and old Luze would stay out there sometimes for three or four days and nights knocking off patrol after patrol, and one time in another place, which was the Hindenburg Line, old Luze was out there again and there were a few shots late in the afternoon and then it was quiet until about three o'clock the next morning and then all hell broke loose, and the Capt'n thought that a whole German battalion was about to move in, and he sent five patrols out to find out what was happening, but when they got there all they found was old Luze all dug in and bristling with enough ammunition to blow up kingdom come; he had crawled around all during the afternoon collecting hand grenades and a mortar and two machine guns and even a light two-wheel cannon, and when they asked him what was going on he told them that he had fallen off to sleep and when he woke up he didn't know whether or not any Germans had snuck up so he thought he'd better lay himself down a little light barrage. The next morning they found out that old Luze had wiped out a whole German platoon but when the Capt'n sent for him to tell him he was going to give him a medal, old Luze had cut out and was off somewhere picking the guitar and drinking cognac and chasing the mademoiselles again. He went through the whole war like that and he came out of the Army without a single scratch, didn't even get flat feet.

I heard a lot of stories about the war and I used to draw pictures of them fighting with bayonets in the Argonne Forest, and Soldier Boy Crawford used to look at them and shake his head and give me a nickel and say that some day I was going to be a soldier too.

I used to draw automobiles too, especially the Hudson Super-Six, like old Long George Nisby had; he said it would do sixty on a straightaway, and he had a heavy blasting cut-out on it that jarred the ground. Old Man Perc Stranahan had a Studebaker but he was a white man and he didn't have a cut-out, and he drove as slow as a hearse. Old Gander said Old Man Perc always drove like he was trying to sneak up on something but he never was going to catch it like that. The cars I didn't like then were the flat-engine Buick and the old humpbacked Hupmobile. I liked the Maxwell and the Willys Knight and the Pierce Arrow.

I was playing train then too, and the trains were there before the automobiles were (there were many more horses and buggies in that part of town than there were automobiles then).

I couldn't sit up in my nest in the chinaberry tree and see the
trains yet, because I could not climb it yet, but I saw them
when Papa used to take me to the L&N bottom to see them
come by and I knew them all, and the Pan American was the
fastest and Number Four was the fastest that ran in the daytime. Old Luzana could tell you all about the Southern Pacific
and the Santa Fe, but that was later. But I already knew something about the Southern Pacific because Cousin Roberta had
already gone all the way to Los Angeles, California, on the
Sunset Limited.

I used to be in bed and hear the night trains coming by.
The Crescent came by at nine-thirty and if you woke up way
in the middle of the night you could hear Number Two. I was
in my warm bed in that house, and I could hear the whistle
coming even before it got to Chickasabogue Bridge and it had
a bayou sound then, and then I could hear the engine batting
it hell-for-leather on down the line bound for Mobile and New
Orleans, and the next time the whistle came it was for Three
Mile Creek. It was getting on into the beel then. I played train
by myself in the daytime then, looking out the window along
the side of the house like an engineer looking down along the
drivers.

I used to hear old Stagolee playing the piano over in Hot
Water Shorty's jook at night too, even then, especially on Saturday night. They rocked all night long, and I was lying in
my warm quilted bed by the window. Uncle Jimmy's bed was
by the window on the other side of the fireplace. When it was
cold, you could wake up way in the night and still see the red
embers in the ashes, and hear the wind whining outside, and
sometimes you could hear the boat whistles too, and I could
lie listening from where I was and tell you when it was a launch
pulling a log raft or a tugboat pulling a barge or a riverboat
like the *Nettie Queen*, and sometimes it was a big ship like the
Luchenback called the Looking Back, which was all the way
down at the city wharf at the foot of Government Street.

I knew a lot about the big ships because Uncle Jimmy worked
on the wharf. That was before the state docks were built and
the big Gulf-going and ocean-going ships didn't come on past
Mobile then unless they were going up to Chickasaw to be
overhauled, but I had already seen them and had been on ships

from England and France and Holland and naturally there were always ships from the Caribbean and South America because that was where the fruit boats came from.

All I could do was see old Luzana Cholly and hear him coming. I didn't really know him then, but I knew that he was blue steel and that he was always going and coming and that he had the best walk in the world, because I had learned how to do that walk and was already doing the stew out of it long before Lil' Buddy ever saw it. They were calling me Mister Man, and that was when somebody started calling me The Little Blister, because they said I was calling myself blister trying to say Mister. Aun Tee called me My Mister and Mama called me My Little Man, but she had to drop the little part off when Lil' Buddy came, and that was how everybody started calling me The Man, although I was still nothing but a boy, and I said to myself old Luzana is the man, old Luzana is the one I want to be like.

Then I was getting to be big enough to go everywhere by myself and I was going to school. That was when I knew about Dunkin's Hill and going up through Egerton Lane. That was the short way to school, because that was the way the bell sound came. Buddy Babe and Sister Babe and old double-jointed, ox-jawed Jack Johnson all went that way too, but when it rained you couldn't get across the bottom, and that was when everybody went the Shelton way, going through behind Stranahan's store and Good Hope Baptist to the old car line and then along that red clay road by the Hillside store.

Then Lil' Buddy was there and it was sky blue and we were blue hunters and every day was for whistling and going somewhere to do something you had to be rawhide to do, and some day we were going to live in times and places that were blue steel too. We found out a lot about old Luzana then, and then we not only knew him we knew how to talk to him.

The best time (except when he was just sitting somewhere strumming on his guitar) was when he was on his way to the Gambling Woods. (So far as anybody knew, gambling and guitar picking and grabbing freight trains were the only steady jobs he ever had or ever would have, except during the time he was in the Army and the times he was in jail—and he not only had been in jail, he had been in the penitentiary!) We were his good luck when he was headed for a skin game, and we always used to catch him late Saturday afternoon right out there where Gins Alley came into the oil-tank road, because he would be coming from Miss Pauline's cookshop then. The Gambling Woods trail started right out across from Sargin' Jeff's. Sometimes old Luze would have the guitar slung across his back even then, and naturally he had his famous .32-20 in the holster under his right arm.

"Say now hey Mister Luzana," I would holler at him.

"Mister Luzana Cholly one-time," Lil' Buddy always said, and he said that was what old Luze's swamp holler said too.

"Mister Luzana Cholly all night long," I would say then.

"Nobody else!" he would holler back at us then, "nobody else but."

"The one and only Mister Luzana Cholly from Booze Ana Bolly come Solly go Molly hit 'em with the fun folly."

"Talk to me, little ziggy, talk to me."

"Got the world in a jug," I might say then.

"And the stopper in your hand," old Lil' Buddy would say.

"You tell 'em, little crust busters, 'cause I ain't got the heart."

"He's a man among men."

"And Lord God among women!"

"Well tell the dy ya," old Luze would say then, standing wide-legged, laughing, holding a wad of Brown's Mule chewing tobacco in with his tongue at the same time. Then he would skeet a stream of amber juice to one side like a batter does when he steps up to the plate and then he would wipe the back of his leathery hand across his mouth and squint his eyes.

"Tell the dy-damn-ya!"

"Cain't tell no more," Lil' Buddy would say then, and old Luze would frown and wink at me.

"How come, little sooner, how goddam come?"

"Cause money talks."

"Well shut my mouth and call me suitcase."

"Ain't nobody can do that."

"I knowed you could tell 'em little ziggabo, I knowed good and damn well you could tell 'em."

"But we ain't gonna tell 'em no more."

"We sure ain't."

"Talk ain't no good if you ain't got nothing to back it up with."

Old Luze would laugh again and we would stand waiting and then he would run his hands deep down into his pockets and come out with two quarters between his fingers. He would throw them into the air and catch them again, one in each hand, and then he would cross his hands and flip one to me and one to Lil' Buddy.

"Now talk," he would say then. "Now talk, but don't say too much and don't talk too loud, and handle your money like the white folks does."

We were going to be like him even before we were going to be like cowboys. And we knew that blue steel was also root hog or die poor, which was what we were going to have to do whether we liked it or not. Lil' Buddy said it was not just how rough-and-ready old hard-cutting Luze was and how nobody, black or white, was going to do him any dirt and get away with it, and all that. It was that too, but it was also something else. It was also the way he could do whatever he was doing and make it look so easy that he didn't even seem to have to think about it, and once he did it, that seemed to be just about the only real way to do it.

Old Luze did everything his own way just like old Satch played baseball his way. But we knew that we wanted to be like him for more reasons than that too. Somehow or other just as he always seemed to be thirty-five years old and blue steel because he had already been so many places and done so many things you'd never heard of before, he also always seemed to be absolutely alone and not needing anybody else, self-sufficient, independent, dead sure, and at the same time so unconcerned.

Mama said he was don't-carified, and that was it too (if you know the full meaning of the Negro meaning of that expression). He was living in blue steel and his way was don't-carified, because he was blue steel too. Lil' Buddy said hellfied, and he didn't mean hell-defying either, you couldn't say he was hell-defying all the time, and you couldn't say he went for bad either, not even when he was doing that holler he was so notorious for. That *was* hell-defying in a way, but it was really I don't give a damn if I *am* hell-defying, and he was not going for bad because he didn't need to, since everybody, black and white, who knew anything about him at all already knew that when he made a promise it meant if it's the last thing I do, if it's the last thing I do on this earth—and they knew that could mean I'll kill you and pay for you as much as it meant anything else. Because the idea of going to jail didn't scare him at all, and the idea of getting shot at didn't seem to scare him either. *Because all he ever said about that was if they shoot at me they sure better not miss me, they sure better get me the first time.*

He was a Negro who was an out and out Nigger in the very best meaning of the word as Negroes use it among themselves (who are the only ones who can), and nobody in that time and that place seemed to know what to make of him. White folks said he was crazy, but what they really meant or should have meant was that he was confusing to them, because if they knew him well enough to say he was crazy they also had to know enough about him to know that he wasn't even foolhardy, not even careless, not even what they wanted to mean by biggity. The funny thing, as I remember it now, was how their confusion made them respect him in spite of themselves. Somehow or other it was as if they respected him precisely because he didn't care anything about them one way or the other. They certainly respected the fact that he wasn't going to take any foolishness off of them.

Negroes said he was crazy too, but they meant their own meaning. They did not know what to make of him, but when they said he was crazy they almost did, because when they said it they really meant something else. They were not talking so much about what he did, but how he was doing it. They were talking about something like poetic madness, and that was the way they had of saying that he was doing something unheard of, doing the hell out of it, and getting away with whatever it was. You could tell that was what they meant by the very way they said it, by the sound of it, and by the way they were shaking their heads and laughing when they said it.

The way he always operated as a lone wolf and the unconcerned-, not the Negro-ness as such, were the main things then. (Naturally Lil' Buddy and I knew about Negroes and white folks, and we knew that there was something generally wrong with white folks, but it didn't seem so very important then. We knew that if you hit a white boy he would turn red and call you nigger that did not sound like the Nigger the Negroes said and he would run and get as many other white boys as he could and come back at you, and we knew that a full-grown white had to get somebody to back him up too, but we didn't really think about it much, because there were so many other things we were doing then.)

Nobody ever said anything about old Luzana's papa and mama, and when you suddenly wondered about them you realized that he didn't seem to have or need any family at all, it really was as if he had come full-grown out of the swamp some-where. And he didn't seem to need a wife either. But that was because he was not going to settle down yet. Because he had lived with more women from time to time and place to place than the average man could even shake a stick at.

We knew somehow or other that the Negro-ness had some-thing to do with the way we felt about him too, but except for cowboys and the New York Yankees and one or two other things, almost everything was Negro then; that is, everything that mattered was. So the Negro part was only natural, al-though I can see something special about it too now.

When you boil it all down, I guess the main thing was how when you no more than just said his name, *Louisiana Charlie, old Luzana Cholly, old Luze,* that was enough to make you know not only him and how he looked and talked and walked that sporty limp walk, but his whole way of being, and how you knew right off the bat that he all alone and unconcerned in his sharp-edged and rough-backed steel had made it what it was himself.

That was what old Lil' Buddy and I were going to do too, make a name for ourselves. Because we knew even then (and I already knew it before he came) that doing that was exactly what made you the kind of man we wanted to be. Mama said I was her little man, and Aun Tee always called me her little mister, but I wasn't anybody's man and mister yet and I knew it, and when I heard the sound of the name that Mama taught me how to write I always felt funny, and I always jumped even when I didn't move. That was in school, and I wanted to hide, and I always said *they are looking for me, they are trying to see who I am,* and I had to answer because it would be the teacher calling the roll, and I said Present, and it sounded like somebody else.

And when I found out what I found out about me and Aun Tee and knew that she was my flesh and blood mama, I also found out that I didn't know my real name at all, because I didn't know who my true father was. So I said *My name is Reynard the Fox*, and Lil' Buddy said *My name is Jack the Rabbit and my home is in the briar patch*. That was old Luzana too, and when you heard that holler coming suddenly out of nowhere just as old Luze himself always seemed to come, it was just like it was coming from the briar patch.

So when Mama said what she said about me and Aun Tee at that wake that time and I heard it and had to believe it, I wished that old Luzana had been my real papa, but I didn't tell anybody that, not even Lil' Buddy although Lil' Buddy was almost in the same fix because he didn't have a mama any more and he didn't really love his papa because it was his papa that ran his mama away.

But we were buddies and we both did old Luzana's famous walk and we were going to be like him, and the big thing that you had to do to really get like him was to grab yourself a fast armful of fast freight train and get long gone from here. That was the real way to learn about the world, and we wanted to learn everything about it that we could. That was when we started practicing on the switch engine. That was down in the oilyards. You had to be slick to do even that because naturally your folks didn't want you doing stuff like that, because there was old Peg Leg Nat. Old Peg Leg butt-headed Nat could hop a freight almost as good as old Luzana could. He called himself mister-some-big-shit-on-a-stick. He spent most of his time fishing and sometimes he would come around pushing a wheelbarrow selling fresh fish, shrimps, and crabs, but every now and then he would strike out for somewhere on a freight just like old Luze did. Mama used to try to scare us with old Nat, telling us that a peg leg was just what messing around with freight trains would get you, and for a while she did scare us, but not for long, because then we found out that it never would have happened to old Nat if he hadn't been drunk and showing off. And anybody could see that getting his leg cut off hadn't stopped old Nat himself anyway since he could still beat any two-legged man we knew doing it except old Luze himself. Naturally we had to think about it, and naturally it did slow us up for a while, but it didn't really stop us. Because there was still old Luze, and that was who we were anyway, not old Peg Leg Nat.

Then that time when I found out all about me and Aun Tee, I was going to run away, and Lil' Buddy was ready too. Then old Lil' Buddy found out that old Luze was getting ready to get moving again and we were all set and just waiting and then it was the day itself.

I will always remember that one.

I had on my brogan shoes and I had on my corduroy pants under my overalls with my jumper tucked in. I had on my blue baseball cap too and my rawhide wristband and I had my pitching glove folded in my hip pocket. Lil' Buddy had on just about the same thing except that he was carrying his first-base pad instead of his catcher's mitt. We had our other things and some something to eat rolled up in our blanket rolls so that we could sling them over our shoulders and have our arms free.

Lil' Buddy had gotten his papa's pearl-handled .38 Smith & Wesson, and we both had good jackknives. We had some hooks and twine to fish with too, just in case, and of course we had our trusty old slingshots for birds.

It was May and school was not out yet, and so not only were we running away, we were playing hooky too. It was hot, and with that many clothes on we were sweating, but you had to have them, and that was the best way to carry them.

There was a thin breeze that came across the railroad from the river, the marsh, and Pole Cat Bay, but the sun was hot and bright, and you could see the rails downright shimmering under the high and wide open sky. We had always said that we were going to wait until school was out, but this was our chance now, and we didn't care about school much any more anyhow. This was going to be school now anyway, except it was going to be much better.

We were waiting in the thicket under the hill. That was between where the Dodge mill road came down and where the oil spur started, and from where we were, we could see up and down the clearing as far as we needed to, to the south all the way across Three Mile Creek bridge to the roundhouse, and where Mobile was, and to the north all the way up past that mill to the Chickasabogue bridge. We knew just about from where old Luzana was going to come running, because we had been watching him do it for a long time now. We had that part down pat.

I don't know how long we had been waiting because we didn't have a watch but it had been a long time, and there was nothing to do but wait then.

"I wish it would hurry up and come on," Lil' Buddy said.

"Me too," I said.

"Got to get to splitting."

We were squatting on the blanket rolls, and Lil' Buddy was smoking another Lucky Strike, smoking the way we both used to smoke them in those old days, letting it hang dangling in the corner of your mouth, and tilting your head to one side with one eye squinted up like a gambler.

"Goddam it, watch me nail that sapsucker," he said.

"Man, you watch me."

You could smell the May woods there then, the dogwood, the honeysuckle, and the warm smell of the undergrowth; and you could hear the birds too, the jays, the thrushes, and even a woodpecker somewhere on a dead tree. I felt how moist and cool the soft dark ground was there in the shade, and you could smell that smell too, and smell the river and the marsh too.

Lil' Buddy finished the cigarette and flipped it out into the sunshine, and then sat with his back against a sapling and sucked his teeth. I looked out across the railroad to where the gulls were circling over the marsh and the river.

"Goddam it, when I come back here to this burg, I'm goddam man and a half," Lil' Buddy said all of a sudden.

"And don't care who knows it," I said.

"Boy, Chicago."

"Man, Detroit."

"Man, Philadelphia."

"Man, New York."

"Boy, I kinda wish old Gander was going too."

"I kinda wish so too."

"Old cat-eyed Gander."

"Old big-toed Gander."

"Old Gander is all right."

"Man, who you telling."

"That son of a bitch know his natural stuff."

"That bastard can steal lightning if he have to."

"Boy how about that time."

"Man, hell yeah."

"Boy, but old Luze though."

"That Luze takes the cake for everything."

"Hot damn, boy we going!"

"It won't be long now."

"Boy, Los Angeles."

"Boy, St. Louis."

"Man, you know we going."

"Boy, you just watch me swing the sapsucker."

"Boy, snag it."

"Goddam."

"I'm going to natural-born kick that son of a bitch."

"Kick the living guts out of it."

"Boy and when we get back!" I said that and I could see it, coming back on the Pan American I would be carrying two suitcases and have a money belt and an underarm holster, and I would be dressed fit to kill.

"How long you think it will take us to get fixed to come back?" I said.

"Man I don't know and don't care."

"You coming back when old Luze come back?"

"I don't know."

I didn't say anything else then. Because I was trying to think about how it was really going to be then. Because what I had been thinking about before was how I wanted it to be. I didn't say anything because I was thinking about myself then, thinking: *I always said I was going but I don't really know whether I want to go or not now. I want to go and I don't want to go.* I tried to see what was really going to happen and I couldn't, and I tried to forget it and think about something else, but I couldn't do that either.

I looked over at Lil' Buddy again. Who was lying back against the tree with his hands behind his head and his eyes closed. Whose legs were crossed, and who was resting easy like a ballplayer rests before time for the game to start. I wondered what he was really thinking. Did he really mean it when he said he did not know and didn't care? You couldn't tell what he was thinking, but you could tell that he wasn't going to back out now, no matter how he was feeling about it.

So I said to myself goddam it if Lil' Buddy can make it I can too, and I had more reason to be going away than he did anyway. *I had forgotten about that. I had forgotten all about it. And then I knew that I still loved Papa and they had always loved me and they had always known about me and Aun Tee.*

But I couldn't back out then, because what I had found out wasn't the real reason for going anyway. Old Luze was really the reason, old Luze and blue steel, old Luze and rawhide, old Luze and ever-stretching India Rubber.

"Hey Lebud."

"Hey."

"Going to the big league."

"You said it."

"Skipping city."

"You tell 'em."

"Getting further."

"Ain't no lie."

"Long gone."

"No crap."

That was when Lil' Buddy said my home is in the briar patch. My name is Jack the Rabbit and my natural home is in the briar patch. And I said it too, and I said that was where I was bred and born.

"Goddam it to hell," Lil' Buddy said then, "why don't it come on?"

"Son of a bitch," I said.

Then I was leaning back against my tree looking out across the sandy clearing at the sky and there were clean white pieces of clouds that looked like balled-up sheets in a washtub, and the sky was blue like rinse water with bluing in it, and I was thinking about Mama again, and hoping that it was all a dream.

But then the train was really coming and it wasn't a dream at all, and Lil' Buddy jumped up.

"Come on."

"I'm here."

The engine went by, and we were running across the clearing. My ears were ringing and I was sweating, and my collar was hot and my pants felt as if the seat had been ripped away. There was nothing but the noise and we were running into it, and then we were climbing up the hill and running along the slag and cinders. We were trotting along in reach of it then. We remembered to let an empty boxcar go by, and when the next gondola came, Lil' Buddy grabbed the front end and I got the back. I hit the hotbox with my right foot and stepped onto the step and pulled up. The wind was in my ears then, but I knew about that from practicing. I climbed on up the ladder and got down on the inside, and there was Lil' Buddy coming back toward me.

"Man, what did I tell you!"

"Did you see me lam into that sucker?"

"Boy, we low more nailed it."

"I bet old Luze will be kicking it any minute now."

"Cool hanging it."

"Boy, yair," I said, but I was thinking I hope old Luze didn't change his mind. I hope we don't miss him. I hope we don't have to start out all by ourselves.

"Going boy."

"Yeah."

"Going,
don't know where I'm going
but I'm going
Say now I'm going
don't know when I'm going
but I'm going."

We crawled up into the left front corner out of the wind, and there was nothing to do but wait then. We knew that she was going to have to pull into the hole for Number Four when she got twelve miles out, and that was when we were going to get to the open boxcar.

We got the cigarettes out and lit up, and there was nothing but the rumbling noise that the wide-open car made then, and the faraway sound of the engine and the low-rolling smoke coming back. That was just sitting there, and after we got a little more used to the vibration, nothing at all was happening except being there. You couldn't even see the scenery going by.

It was just being there and being in that time, and you never really remember anything about things like that except the sameness and the way you felt, and all I can remember now about that part is the nothingness of doing nothing and the feeling not of going but of being taken.

All I could see after we went through the bridge was the sky and the bare floor and the sides of the gondola, and all I can remember about myself is how I wished that something would happen, because I definitely did not want to be going then, and I was lost even though I knew good and well that I was not even twelve miles from home yet. Because although we certainly had been many times farther away and stayed longer, this already seemed to be farther and longer than all the other times put together.

Then we could tell that it was beginning to slow down, and we stood up and started getting ready. And then it was stopping, and we were ready, and we climbed over and got down and started running for it. That was still in the bayou country and beyond the train smell there was the sour-sweet smell of the swamp. We were running on hard pounded slag then, and with the train quiet and waiting for Number Four, you could hear the double running of our feet echoing through the cypresses and the marshland.

The wide roadbed was almost half as high as the telegraph wires, and along the low right-of-way where the black creosote poles went along, you could see the blue and white lilies floating on the slimy green water. We came hustling hot to get to where we knew the empty car was, and then there we were.

And there old Luzana himself was.

He stood looking down at us from the door with an unlighted cigarette in his hand. We stopped dead in our tracks. I knew exactly what was going to happen then. It was suddenly so quiet that you could hear your heart pounding inside your head, and I was so embarrassed I didn't know what to do and I thought *now he's going to call us a name. Now he's never going to have anything to do with us any more.*

We were just standing there waiting and he just let us stand there and feel like two puppies with their tails tucked between their legs, and then he started talking.

"It ain't like that. It ain't like that. It just ain't like that, it just ain't."

And he was shaking his head not only as if we couldn't understand him but also as if we couldn't even hear him.

"It ain't. Oh, but it ain't."

We didn't move. Lil' Buddy didn't even dig his toe into the ground.

"So this is what y'all up to. Don't say a word, not a word. Don't open your mouth."

I could have sunk right on down into the ground.

"What the hell y'all think y'all doing? Tell me that. Tell me. Don't say a word. Don't say a goddam mumbling word to me."

We weren't even about to say anything.

"I got a good mind to whale the sawdust out of you both. That's just what I oughta do."

But he didn't move. He just stood looking down.

"Well, I'll be a son of a bitch."

That was all he said then, and then he jumped down, walked us back to where the switch frog was, and then there was nothing but just shamefaced waiting. Then Number Four came by and then finally we heard the next freight coming south and when it got there and slowed down for the switch he was standing waiting for a gondola and when it came he picked me up and put me on and then he picked Lil' Buddy up and put him on and then he caught the next car and came to where we were.

So we came slowpoking it right on back and got back in Gasoline Point before the whistles even started blowing for one o'clock. Imagine that. All of that had happened and it wasn't really afternoon yet. I could hardly believe it.

We came on until the train all but stopped for Three Mile Creek bridge and then he hopped down and took us off. He led us down the hill and went to a place the hobos used under the bridge. He sat down and lit another cigarette and flipped the match into the water and watched it float away and then he was looking at us and then he motioned for us to sit down too.

That was when he really told us what hitting the road was, and what blue steel was. He was talking evenly then, not scolding, just telling us man to boys, saying he was talking for our own good because doing what we were trying to do was more than a notion. He was talking quietly and evenly but you still couldn't face him, I know I couldn't and Lil' Buddy naturally couldn't because he never looked anybody straight in the eye anyway.

We were back and sitting under Three Mile Creek bridge and he was not really angry and then we were all eating our something-to-eat and then we could talk too, but we didn't have much to say that day. He was doing the talking and all we wanted to do was ask questions and listen.

That was when he told us all about the chain gang and the penitentiary and the white folks, and you could see everything he said and you were there too, but you were not really in it this time because it was happening to him, not you, and it was him and you were not him, you were you. You could be rawhide and you could be blue steel but you couldn't really be Luzana Cholly, because he himself was not going to let you.

Then he was talking about going to school and learning to use your head like the smart white folks. You had to be rawhide but you had to be patent leather too, then you would really be nimble, then you would really be not only a man but a big man. He said we had a lot of spunk and that was good but it wasn't good enough, it wasn't nearly enough.

And then he was talking about Negroes and white folks again, and he said the young generation of Negroes were supposed to be like Negroes and be like white folks too and still be Negroes. He sat looking out across the water then, and then we heard another freight coming and he got up and got ready and he said we could watch him but we'd better not try to follow him.

Then we were back up on the hill again and the train was coming and he stood looking at us with the guitar slung over his shoulder and then he put his hands on our shoulders and looked straight at us, and we had to look at him then, and we knew that we were not to be ashamed in front of him any more.

"Make old Luze proud of you," he said then, and he was almost pleading. "Make old Luze glad to take his hat off to you some of these days. You going further than old Luze ever even dreamed of. Old Luze ain't been nowhere. Old Luze don't know from nothing."

And then the train was there and we watched him snag it and then he was waving goodbye.

Manifest Destiny U.S.A.

IT WAS during those never to be forgotten midwinter night tell-me-tale times in the semicircle of miscellaneous chairs around the brick-red and mortar-gray fireplace beneath the Mother Goose chime-clock mantelpiece that old Uncle Jerome, the jackleg freelance preacher, who was once an Escambia County plough hand and then a Piney Woods rosin collector and was now a United Fruit Company banana stevedore, used to deliver more sermons than he ever preached in the pulpit of any actual bell-ringing-and-tolling stained-glass-plus-organ-harmonizing church.

Not that he actually thought of them as fireside sermons, even though he paused from time to time to acknowledge an *amen* here and a *tell the truth* and *spread the message* and *share the wisdom* there. What he actually called them was elucidations of the preordained. "Gentlemen sir! Talking about destiny. Talking about everything conceivable to the ever so fragile and ever prone human mind. Everything from the miraculous seven-day beginning and the void.

"Talking about destiny. Talking about preordination. Talking about manifest destiny! Yes, the Lord works in mysterious ways, his wonders to perform. His blessings to bestow. Talking 'bout manifest destiny, gentlemen sir, and we, everybody in this room, we're all here in this U.S. of A. today because God wanted us here! Because he had a mission for us here, A HOLY MISSION FOR US HERE. It's all right there in the Bible, which makes it a holy mission and also ironic if you get my latter clause. He had us shipped all the way across the Atlantic Ocean just like he sent old Jonah to Nineveh and the belly of a whale! It's all right there in the Bible to be sure. But is also right there in the encyclopedia, and the history books. The first thing the good Lord always does for people when he has some special precious mission for them to fulfill IS TO GET 'EM OUT OF AFRICA. Just like he got his especially precious

---

"Manifest Destiny U.S.A." was the last work of fiction Murray wrote. He wrote it in late 2004 and early 2005. It appears here for the first time.

Hebrew children out from down in old Pharaoh's Egypt land by parting a dust-dried trail right down to the Red Sea for them to walk across carrying whatever they could take with them to the Promised Land.

"And he got us bargained away from them old scar-faced black west coast African chiefs and brought us over here across the Atlantic Ocean in the bowels of them old slave schooners just like Jonah in the belly of the whale. Don't take my word for it. As for Unka Jo Jo, how he got all the way over here, this far from his home folks in Africa, and he'll tell you about how his tribe was raided by another African tribe with different scars on their face and sold him to the slave merchants that brought him and a hundred and some odd others all the way over here in that same old *Crowtillie* or *Flotilla* or whatever it was that you can see the ruins of right down there in the bogs and cane brakes just beyond the Chickasabogue L & N Bridge where Chickasabogue Creek flows out into the Mobile River on its way to the Alabama River.

"But my main point is this. God had a profound purpose for getting us over here. And that purpose is to save this very special nation. (Talking about the ideals and prospects it's based on.) So it can stand and light the way as man's last best hope on Earth. Then it was as if he also said but the story will also be ever so ironic and contradictory. Because my intention is for them to light up the nation and I'm putting 'em in a position of the lowest of the lowly so they are going to have to push the nation up rather than pull it up.

"So they brought boatload after boatload of us over as slaves and just look what it did to the white folks. Most of whom as the history books tells us were the lowest of the lowdown poor white trash of Europe. It just about drove them crazy with *phantasmagoria*. Our very presence gave them the notion that they were bred and born to be some kind of heavenly species that we were put on Earth to serve.

"So there's where old Abe Lincoln come in. The good Lord said I elected old Moses to get my special children out of old Pharaoh's Egypt land after all those many years of bondage. So now this time I'm designating old Abe. Because this time is not about getting to the Promised Land, this many people are already here, so it's my will be done amen.

"So here come the one and only Abraham Lincoln. Now you take old Abe. Now old Abe was a bred and born cracker if there ever was one. I'm talking 'bout a natural born raw-boned narrow-assed Kentucky hillbilly. But he was the one the good Lord picked out to give the mission to, and he was the one that sent for old Ulysses S. Grant, and old Grant knew exactly what the situation called for; and when he got ready to throw his knockout punch he sent for old Sherman, who was the one he had left in charge down south after they took Vicksburg.

"So when old Grant gave old Sherman the fire and brimstone orders for that march across from Mississippi and through Atlanta to the sea, before heading up the Atlantic coastline states in case he needed him to help take Richmond, that brought everything that many steps closer to the fulfillment of the good Lord's plans for bringing us all the way over here to this neck of this planet.

"Because he had a profound and indispensable purpose for us over here and that purpose was to help save the nation so it could become that last best hope of mankind on earth until Resurrection Day. Talking about manifest destiny that was already on the way even before old Jefferson pulled off that big Louisiana Purchase deal with old Napoleon. So, here come the Buffalo Soldiers, to make up for what old fancy-pants Custer couldn't do, soon as the army would let 'em join the cavalry.

"Not that any of our people thought that the Lord had anything against the Indians as such because we knew that he created them along with everybody else just like he made old Pharaoh and everybody else and everything else, it was just time to move on. It was just time to move on beyond bareback riding and them wigwam ways of living. Just like you move on when the lightning strikes all them square miles of virgin forest, and what about those tornadoes and earthquakes?

"And I never heard tell of our holding no grudge against the Indians, quite the contrary. All my life I've always heard about how them expert Indian trackers used to welcome our runaway ancestors into their territories and then misdirect them old cracker patrollers and runaway slave hunters as to which way they seen them heading.

"Talking about the good Lord's will and mysterious ways, that brought us to where we are today with all this work we still have left to do. Why do you reckon that free public school education didn't come along until old Abe got us freed from the status of bondage in slavery and into the human status of citizenship, which was supposed to carry along with it the right to express our will as citizens at the ballot box. Now just think about this, when these old millionaire's peckerwood crackers we got down here in this part of the nation most of us still living in got up the Ku Klux Klan to keep us from registering and voting, God's will be done they didn't worry much about our children learning their ABC's and numbers, so long as it didn't interfere too much with planting and harvest times, as a matter of fact, come to think of it, it was some of them same old mean white folks right here that helped us keep some of the little hooky playing rascals of ours from dropping out of school altogether by hounding them with threats, putting them in juvenile jails called reformatory school, or putting them out on one of those country farms until they came of age.

"I don't know maybe it was also a part of the good Lord's master plan that most of us didn't seem to take to the books right away, like they did to voting. Anyway, the white folks didn't seem to mind the few of them that did as long as they didn't go to the class in the same school along with white children, although they were supposed to be studying exactly the same books, prescribed by the same state board of education. Talking about the good Lord's mysterious ways.

"Come to think about it, maybe it was also a part of the good Lord's plan that the first free generations shouldn't show too much interest in school because look what happened when everywhere you look they were heading for the ballot box in such droves, scared to death a lot of these Dixieland die-hard Confederates and started them running around acting like even after all these years we've been over here helping them to build this land up to what it had become, acting like we didn't deserve our chance at having the same kind of life everybody else had a chance at. And I'm talking about the very ones that got where they got to be today at our expense.

"Of all the people from across the north waters of the Atlantic Ocean, here they come talking about some kind of predestined white supremacy, just like nobody don't know doodlysquat about how raggedy and hungry every last one of them was way back when they barely did manage to make it over here from. I'm not talking about the ones that spreaded themselves all over the earth exploring and discovering new lands and things to take back to them castles and cathedral towns back home.

"I'm talking about the ones that came over here because they figured they had a better chance over here over in the wilderness with the wild animals and all them Indian war tribes than they were ever gonna get back where they came from. As a matter of fact, the history book tells us that a lot of them got shipped over here right out of them stonewall prisons and dungeons. Maybe that was the good Lord's mysterious ways of taking care of them. And just look what they're doing with their good fortune.

"No, as the truth is the light, just about every last one of them, except maybe a few gypsies that don't ever intend to set-tle down anywhere, thought of themselves in flight, in a word escaping from somewhere, even though nobody was patrolling and pursuing them.

"Who knows what the good Lord has in store for this young generation we have coming up now. But as for myself, I wouldn't be a bit surprised if the arrival of that new principal over there at that school ain't a godsent token of things to come. He look like a boy, and he sound like one of them boy-evangelist preachers.

"As soon as he hit town he made the round of all the churches, and when the pastors introduced him and invited him to say a few words because it was just a week before the new school term he had the whole congregation saying amen to salvation through book learning. Like getting religion for soul salvation during revival time.

"I mean gentlemen sir, brothers and sisters, he was a pistol! Suffer little children to come unto me before the tardy bell rings. I mean one and all with hair combed, nails clipped, shoes shined, clothes cleaned and pressed, all assignments prepared for hands ready to raise for recitation and blackboard exemplifi-cation and sandtable demonstration. Dotting their I's, crossing their T's, and pronouncing their G's. Talking about godsend there it was because there it is right here amongst us, right over there near that part of Bay Poplar Woods. And talking about close to home, here's this little bright-eyed boy sitting right here amongst us, taking all this in from that chimney corner over there. He's already that kind of school pupil been getting attention since the third grade when his homeroom teacher put his name on the principal's early bird candidate list. Talking about Whit and Miss Melba's little old Scooter boy. Right now you can ask him about all this I'm talking about and he can go get a book and read it to you and show it to you on the map.

"Gentlemen sir I am a witness, talking about God's will and our mounting expectations, let us look at how our heavenly father hides his mysterious ways right out into plain sight. Professor B. Franklin Fisher, fisherman of boys and girls for his four-star recipe for all-American men and women.

"So I'm telling you like that other Ben Franklin way back when they first come up with the notion of writing down a document declaring their separation and total independence from old King George and England. Old Ben Franklin said put your name on the dotted line and support this thing because the fact of the matter is we're all in this together and if we don't keep on hanging together, we're gonna keep on being hung separately."

Then he said *gentlemen sir as I am a witness* and there was only the cozy midwinter night tocticulation of the Mother Goose mantelpiece clock as its minute hand moved on closer and closer to the chime time for leaving and when old Mr. Donohue who also worked on the waterfront near the foot of Government Street came by to shake hands on the way out the two of them also patted each other on the shoulder. Then instead of Mr. Donohue saying *amen* or *x on the dotted line*, he said *I done told you*.

CHRONOLOGY

NOTE ON THE TEXTS

NOTES

Chronology

1916   Born on May 12 in Nokomis, Alabama, to sixteen-year-old
        Sudie Graham, at the home of one of her relatives. Graham
        (b. circa 1900), a Nokomis-area native living in Tuskegee,
        Alabama, will in the fall enter the teacher training pro-
        gram at Tuskegee Institute. Father, John Lee Young
        (b. circa 1895), is one of a middle-class black family in
        Tuskegee; he had met Graham the year before, when she
        worked as an assistant in his aunt's real estate firm. To
        protect her educational prospects and the Young family
        name, Graham gives the infant to Hugh and Mattie Mur-
        ray (b. circa 1868 and 1882, respectively), a childless couple
        of her family's acquaintance, who legally adopt him as Al-
        bert Lee Murray. Hugh Murray, who appears Caucasian in
        a photograph and will be remembered by his adopted son
        as resembling William Faulkner, is identified as black ("B")
        on the U.S. Census. He is illiterate and works in a lumber-
        yard. Mattie Murray, who is black and literate, is a home-
        maker. By year's end the family will move to Magazine
        Point, Alabama, a suburb three miles north of Mobile and
        about forty-five miles southwest of Nokomis. Murray will
        remember Magazine Point as a rough, poor black neigh-
        borhood alive with music and "rife with juke joints." Adja-
        cent African Hill or Africatown is home to the survivors
        (and descendants of survivors) of the schooner *Clotilda*,
        the last U.S. ship to import slaves from Africa, in 1860.
        (Scooter, the protagonist-narrator of Murray's semi-
        autobiographical novel *Train Whistle Guitar*, recalls the
        rivalry between the neighborhoods as follows: "When
        somebody from up there used to call us them old sawmill
        quarters niggers, section gang niggers and foggy bottom
        niggers who didn't come from anywhere but from looking
        up a mule's ass back on the old plantations back in slavery
        times, all I thought was that they were trying to get even
        because we were also not only closer to all the best places
        for hunting both land game and water game, but we also
        had a baseball team that was in the same class as those
        from Chickasaw and Whistler and Maysville and Bayou La
        Batre and Biloxi.") The hulk of the *Clotilda*, which was

scuttled then burned by her legally embattled owner, can still be seen at the mouth of Chickasaw (Chickasawbogue) Creek throughout Murray's childhood. Murray's neighborhood was rezoned for industrial use and razed in mid-century, but nearby neighborhoods retain the look and winding streets of the area, as well as the sort of shotgun-style house in which Murray grew up.

1920   Appears in U.S. Census of 1920 as the son (not adopted) of Hugh and Mattie Murray. By this time the Murrays are also raising three other children, aged ten to eighteen (and all with the last name Leatherwood), whom they list as "adopted."

1927   Works intermittently as a gofer during construction of the Cochrane Bridge, spanning the Mobile River. (Will later recall twice meeting Zora Neale Hurston, once while she was collecting folklore from workmen during the construction of the bridge, and again while she was interviewing community elder Cudjo Lewis, one of the last survivors of the *Clotilda*. In Murray's first novel, *Train Whistle Guitar*, Lewis is the model for Unka Jo Jo.) Adoptive father Hugh Murray manages semipro baseball teams, some featuring Mobile native Satchel Paige (a model for Gator Gus in *Train Whistle Guitar*). Murray closely follows the 1927 New York Yankees via newspapers; recalls it as a watershed moment in personal literacy, a realization that he is able to read more than what he is assigned in elementary school. In fall begins fifth grade at Mobile County Training School, which he will attend through 1935.

1930   Sudie Graham, who had moved to Mobile years earlier to be near Murray and whom he calls his auntie (Miss Tee in *Train Whistle Guitar*), marries and has a son, Murray's half-brother James Burke. (Burke, who will have a career in the military, writes to Murray in 2002, "I remember the auntie bit, but she *always* told me you were my *brother*.")

1931–35   As student in high school program of Mobile County Training School, participates in theatrical productions, playing Aubrey Piper in *The Show-Off*, a comedy by George Kelly, and Thea Dugger in *Bad Man*, a Harlem Renaissance "folk play" by Randolph Edmonds. Appears in Negro History Week pageants, one time performing a juba dance to "Juba," from R. Nathaniel Dett's piano suite *In the Bottoms* (1913). Excels in French and Latin. Paints.

Plays baseball and basketball. In sophomore year is voted best all-around student by the faculty.

1935   In January travels to Tuskegee Institute for a regional high school basketball tournament. There, through arrangements made by Sudie Graham Burke, meets for the first time his biological father, John Young. (Young is now a foreman at the institute's power plant, where he has worked since returning from World War I, and the father of Murray's eleven-year-old half-sister, Rowena Young.) Graduates from Mobile County Training School and is granted full-tuition scholarship to Tuskegee. Picks cotton for a week ("It seemed heroic to me") to earn the bus fare to Tuskegee, 205 miles from Magazine Point. Matriculates at Tuskegee, where he lives with Young and his family.

1935–39   Studies education at Tuskegee. Takes four years of ROTC training. Studies military science and tactics under Benjamin O. Davis, Sr. (the first black general in the U.S. Army) during his freshman year, and under Benjamin O. Davis, Jr. during his senior year. Joins Alpha Phi Alpha fraternity. Becomes president of Tuskegee chapter of Alpha Kappa Mu honor society. Works in the power plant with John Young during the summers. Also works as a cook in the veterans' hospital in Tuskegee. Mentored in modern literature by English department chairman Morteza Drexel ("Mort") Sprague, a charismatic teacher still only in his twenties. Reads James Joyce, T. S. Eliot, Hemingway, Faulkner, Edna St. Vincent Millay, E. E. Cummings, Wallace Stevens, W. H. Auden, William Saroyan, Charles and Mary Beard, Sigrid Undset, Romain Rolland, Kenneth Burke, and many others. Notices that many of the books he has been borrowing from the library have also been checked out by upperclassman Ralph Ellison, a clerk at the library's circulation desk and a fellow protégé of Sprague. (Ellison and Murray have a few brief conversations in the library but will not become friends until the 1940s in New York City.) In junior year writes one-act play, *Odds and Ends*, which is staged by Tuskegee's Little Theater on the evening of April 28, 1938. The setting is a shoe store in Mobile and the play has seven characters, none played by Murray. (Only a program survives.) Pays close attention to contemporary theater through periodicals and anthologies. After reading Thomas Mann's essay "The Coming Humanism" in *The Nation* (December 10,

1938), seeks out the author's *The Coming Victory of Democracy* and *Joseph* novels.

1939   Graduates from Tuskegee with BS in education. Reads Joyce's *Finnegans Wake* when it is published in the spring. Takes job as principal of Damascus Junior High School in Damascus, Georgia (population 477). When he misses a bus connection en route to Damascus and is stranded at night in Columbus, Georgia, a fellow black traveler points him to Ma Rainey's house. Rainey lets him sleep on her couch. (He will write about this episode, and of Rainey's kindness, in *South to a Very Old Place*.) Reading includes Kierkegaard, Sir James George Frazer, Virginia Woolf, and John Dewey.

1940   Position in Damascus proves disappointing. In the 1940 Census is listed as again living in Mobile with Hugh and Mattie Murray. In summer begins graduate coursework in education at the University of Michigan, likely his first trip outside the South. Reading includes Marx and Nietzsche. Studies Thomas Mann's work in depth. Returns to Tuskegee in the fall to teach in the night school and direct the Little Theater company.

1941   On May 31 marries Mozelle Menefee (b. 1920), who grew up in Tuskegee and has just completed her sophomore year at the Institute. Postpones honeymoon, and spends summer doing graduate coursework on theories of reading instruction at the University of Chicago and at Northwestern University. Returns to Tuskegee in the fall. Begins to develop two signatures, one for official documents, with a circular A, the other for writing his name in books, with a stylized, pointy A. Will maintain this system, with few exceptions, for the rest of his life.

1942   Teaches English at Tuskegee and directs the Little Theater company. In summer takes honeymoon trip to New York with Mozelle; they stay at Hotel Theresa in Harlem, then the hotel of choice for black show business and sports figures. Renews acquaintance with Ralph Ellison.

1943   On January 5 enlists in U.S. Army, and reports for duty one week later. Sent to Utah for basic training. Attends Army Administration School at Atlanta University from March through May. Mozelle graduates from Tuskegee in the spring. Murray attends Officers Candidate School in

Miami Beach, Florida, from September through January 1944. Commissioned second lieutenant. Daughter, Michele Alberita Murray, born on October 3.

1944 Transferred in January to Tuskegee Army Air Field and soon becomes assistant training coordinator for the Tuskegee Airmen. Studies War Department Pamphlet 20-6, *Command of Negro Troops*, published in February. Reading includes Kafka, Arthur Koestler, Anaïs Nin, and the autobiography of Giambattista Vico. Enjoys discussing Faulkner's work with Colonel Noel F. Parrish, commander of Tuskegee Army Air Field.

1945 In April takes training-instructor course in San Antonio, Texas. Promoted to training coordinator at Tuskegee Army Air Field on June 25. On August 2 is transferred to Army Air Forces Camouflage School in Buckley, Colorado. (He will later say that this transfer had something to do with plans for an Allied invasion of Japan, and that he had expected to end up in the Pacific theater.) Promoted to first lieutenant on August 8. Japan surrenders on August 14. Camouflage School ends on August 18. Returns to Tuskegee Army Air Field. Mozelle begins teaching career in Alabama public schools.

1946 On January 4, through arrangements made by an Army buddy related to Ellington band member Harry Carney, has backstage meeting with Duke Ellington after Ellington's fourth annual concert at Carnegie Hall. In October applies to remain on active duty during demobilization of the U.S. armed forces then under way. Application is denied. On November 13 the Army determines Murray's position to be redundant. Instructed to use sixty days of accrued leave time before being demobilized.

1947 Officially placed on reserve duty on January 14. Returns to Tuskegee Institute as instructor of freshman and sophomore English. In the fall enters the master of arts program in English at New York University. Lives at 147 Bainbridge Street in Bedford-Stuyvesant, Brooklyn, with Mozelle and Michele. Takes courses with Margaret Schlauch (Chaucer) and Oscar Cargill (American literature). Pursues active social life in Greenwich Village. Forms friendships with Maya Deren, Joseph Campbell, Seymour Krim, and Anaïs Nin. Spends his days studying, writing, and researching at the Forty-second Street branch of the New York Public Library. Frequently meets Ellison for lunch. (Ellison is working on *Invisible Man* in an office on loan from Francis Steegmuller at Forty-ninth and Fifth Avenue.) After classes at NYU, Murray goes sometimes to the Fifty-second Street nightclubs to hear Charlie Parker, Dizzy Gillespie, and other jazz musicians, and sometimes to Ellison's Harlem apartment to listen to him read from *Invisible Man*. Attends New Year's Eve party at Ellison's. Reading includes Constance Rourke and art historian Heinrich Zimmer.

1948   Writes master's thesis, "*The Waste Land* and *The Sun Also Rises*: A Comparative Study." Returns to Tuskegee in the fall and begins two-year stint of teaching. Master's thesis approved in October.

1949   Works on a semi-autobiographical novel concerning the childhood and adolescence of Scooter, a poor Alabama-born "jack rabbit raised in the briarpatch" who, in the extant version, with the help of several larger-than-life mentors, passes all the tests of life to become, successively, an accomplished student, a jazz musician, and a writer.

1950   Begins ten-year correspondence with Ralph Ellison (which he will coedit, annotate, and in the year 2000 publish as *Trading Twelves: The Selected Letters of Ralph Ellison and Albert Murray*). Ellison reports on the progress of *Invisible Man*—"the goddamnedest experience of my life"—and encourages Murray to complete his *Bildungsroman*. In late spring sails to Paris to study French at the Sorbonne courtesy of the GI Bill. Receives $300 grant for the trip from Tuskegee, equivalent to five weeks' salary before taxes. Stops first in Lisbon, Genoa, and Venice. Arrives in Paris in mid-June and stays at the Hotel Londres. Meets and forms friendships with James Baldwin, Jean Hélion and Pegeen Guggenheim, René Liebowitz, and H. J. "Kappy" Kaplan, a diplomatic attaché and Paris correspondent for *Partisan Review*, whose apartment is a social and cultural center. Meets Sidney Bechet. Meets painter Romare Bearden, who will become a close friend and intellectual comrade. Reconnects with Duke Ellington. Meets Ollie Stewart, foreign correspondent of the *Baltimore Afro-American*, who will devote half of his July 1 "Report from Europe" column to Murray's presence in Paris and work on a novel. Worries about being recalled to active duty when Korean War begins on June 25. Writes to Mozelle for news of war preparation at Tuskegee. Kaplan takes his family to the United States for the summer in late June or early July, and Murray moves into his apartment at 132 boulevard du Montparnasse, one floor above Henri Matisse. (Murray will recall catching glimpses of Matisse at work from the open elevator.) In August visits Antibes with Baldwin, whom he teaches how to swim. Leaves Paris on August 29. Returns to Tuskegee via Montreal and New York.

1951   Recalled to active duty in U.S. Air Force on June 6. Assigned to Tuskegee Institute as assistant professor of air science and tactics and teaches courses in geopolitics as well. Takes course at Air University at Maxwell Air Force Base in Montgomery, Alabama. Buys lot number three on Hudson Street at the intersection of Bibb Street in Tuskegee. Hires architect Bill Mann, an old friend from Tuskegee, to design a house. Completes first draft of semi-autobiographical narrative, provisionally titled "Jack the Bear," that will eventually yield the novels *Train Whistle Guitar* (1974) and *The Spyglass Tree* (1991). Sends manuscript to Ellison late in the year. Interviews Duke Ellington on local radio show.

1952   Ellison provides detailed feedback on manuscript in February letter. Murray follows reviews of *Invisible Man* closely when Random House publishes novel in the spring. Receives mixed criticism of "Jack the Bear" from Ellison's editor, Albert Erskine, who feels that Murray is under the spell of Faulkner. Reads André Malraux on art.

1953   Takes course for Air Force instructors at Ohio State University. Visits Cuba and returns home with conga and bongo drums, which he takes up playing. Submits novel, now retitled "The Briarpatch," to Arabel J. Porter, editor of *New World Writing*, a recently launched "paperback magazine" published by New American Library. Porter excerpts a section of "The Briarpatch" as a short story, "The Luzana Cholly Kick," and, in October, publishes it in issue number four. In a biographical note preceding the story, Murray writes: "We all learn from Mann, Joyce, Hemingway, Eliot, and the rest, but I'm also trying to learn to write in terms of the tradition I grew up in, the Negro tradition of blues, stomps, ragtime, jumps, and swing. After all, very few writers have done as much with American experience as Jelly Roll Morton, Count Basie, and Duke Ellington." Writes to Porter that being included in the anthology (which also includes Jorge Luis Borges, Gore Vidal, Nadine Gordimer, Shelby Foote, Robert Motherwell, and others) was like being "in the World Series in your first season in organized baseball" and "just about the best thing that could happen to an apprentice."

1954   Promoted to captain in the U.S. Air Force on March 11. Helps arrange for Ellison to speak at Tuskegee.

1955   Construction of house in Tuskegee begins in April. The Murrays will never live in it. In August Murray is transferred to Nouasseur Air Base, just outside Casablanca, Morocco. Lives first in Casablanca and then on the base. Buys Leica M3 camera for $244 in the fall. Begins discussing photography with Ellison, who had worked as a professional photographer in the late 1940s.

1956   Serves as chief of military training at Nouasseur. Tuskegee house completed in March and rented out. Rent covers mortgage and yields a small profit (rent collection overseen by local bank). At the request of the U.S. Information Service, begins lecturing (in French) on jazz at various Moroccan venues, including the Maison d'Amérique in Casablanca and the U.S. embassy in Rabat. Receives commendations from American diplomats and superior officers. Visits Greece in May. In the summer drives with Mozelle and Michele from Spain to Italy. They then travel through Europe with Ellison (then in residence at the American Academy in Rome) and his wife Fanny.

1957   Vice President Richard Nixon visits Nouasseur in March. Murray writes to Ellison about the surprisingly large number of blacks in Nixon's entourage. Murray writes memo to Air Force superiors in April: "I am particularly interested in working in a position involving international relations, perhaps in conjunction with an Attaché, Mission, or Advisory Group type assignment." Suffers mild heart attack on May 18. Recuperates at base hospital. Visits West Germany in June and the Netherlands in October. Returns to duty on November 20.

1958   Visits West Germany in January. In April is transferred to Air Reserve Flying Center at Long Beach (California) Municipal Airport and is placed in charge of personnel. In July buys home at 1515 West 166th Street, Compton, for $13,500.

1959   In the spring is reassigned by Air Force from position as
            personnel specialist to that of supply officer. Writes ardent
            letter to superiors protesting his new assignment as be-
            neath his level of training, established skill set, and previ-
            ous achievements. Also argues that reassignment violates
            established protocol, as he was not briefed ahead of time.
            Letter is either ignored or not acted upon. Takes three-
            month supply management course for Air Force officers in
            Amarillo, Texas. Becomes officer accountable for air base
            property in Long Beach.

1960   On June 20 photographs Duke Ellington's recording ses-
            sions at the famed Radio Recorders studio in West Holly-
            wood. Travels in summer throughout California.

1961   In January, as base accountable officer, signs documents
            closing the Air Reserve Flying Center in Long Beach. Be-
            gins new assignment at Headquarters Air Base Wing, Air
            Force Systems Command, at Hanscom Field in Bedford,
            Massachusetts, twenty miles northwest of Boston. Placed
            in charge of Materiel Control Office, becoming responsi-
            ble for sixty-four aircraft, some experimental. Lives in base
            officers' quarters while Mozelle and Michele stay in
            Compton so that Michele can finish high school there.
            Promoted to major "as a Reserve of the Air Force" on
            March 11. Quickly becomes a friend of Charlie Davidson,
            proprietor of the Andover Shop in Cambridge and a tailor,
            jazz buff, reader, and raconteur. (The Murrays and the
            Davidsons will become lifelong friends, attending the
            Newport Jazz Festival and sometimes vacationing to-
            gether.) Begins attending Alpha Phi Alpha gatherings
            around Boston. In June sells home in Compton for $15,525.
            Moves with Mozelle and Michele to 54 High Road in
            Bedford following Michele's graduation. Becomes chief of
            logistic branch at Hanscom on September 16. Michele en-
            ters Juilliard in the fall to study dance and lives with Ralph
            and Fanny Ellison in New York City.

1962   Sells house in Tuskegee on March 19 for $9,500. (Cost of
            lot and construction was $11,500, but probably realizes a
            small profit after seven years of rent collections and tax
            deductions.) Approaching fifth anniversary of heart attack,
            receives extensive physical examination at Hanscom from
            May 1 to 4. On May 15 a panel of Air Force physicians at
            Andrews Air Force Base, in Washington, D.C., determines

that he be assigned early retirement due to arteriosclerotic heart disease. Glowing report of physician at Hanscom emphasizes Murray's otherwise excellent health, and notes that Murray has never been prescribed cardiovascular drugs, perhaps to leave the door open for an appeal. The doctor writes, toward the end of a long report, "Patient is a well-developed, well-nourished, middle-aged man who appears neither acutely nor chronically ill and who is in no acute distress. . . . At the present time I do not think he has any symptoms due to heart disease." Yet Murray accepts early retirement. Retires on June 29, with the permanent grade of major. Will live another fifty-one years and never suffer further heart problems. Stands five foot eight and weighs 168 pounds. Letter of appreciation from his commanding officer states that Murray is "the prototype of the military man whose leadership qualities, devoted service, military bearing, and desirable personal qualities motivate our younger personnel to emulation." Moves to New York and rents apartment 8P at 45 West 132nd Street in the Lenox Terrace Apartments complex in Harlem, a middle- and upper-middle-class residential development whose residents have included many distinguished Harlem professionals and politicians, such as congressman Charles Rangel, New York governor David Patterson, and Manhattan borough president Percy Sutton. The enclave of six large buildings between Lenox Avenue and Fifth Avenue is less than a decade old when the Murrays move in. Their eighth-floor corner apartment has two bedrooms, one and a half bathrooms, a balcony, and spectacular views of Harlem and midtown. The Murrays will live here for the rest of their lives. Renews friendship with Romare Bearden in Manhattan. (The view from Murray's balcony of the west side of Lenox Avenue between 132nd and 133rd Streets will be Bearden's vantage point for his giant collage *The Block* [1971], which will be acquired by the Metropolitan Museum of Art in 1978. Two photographs by Murray of that portion of Lenox Avenue, taken from his balcony circa 1971, are also part of the Metropolitan Museum of Art's permanent collection.) Tries to revive prospects of "The Briarpatch," unsuccessfully submitting it to editor Peter Davison at Atlantic Monthly Press.

1963   Works assiduously on an essay, begun years before, on what he calls the "blues idiom," a special character of expression born of a determination to achieve "elegance in the face of adversity." The essay, called "The Hero and the Blues," will soon grow into a book-length manuscript. Mozelle begins teaching in New York City preschools.

1964   On January 20 enjoys stint as on-camera theater critic, reviewing three plays in an arts segment of *The World at Ten* on WNDT, New York. Publishes first work of nonfiction in July 3 issue of *Life*, an omnibus review of what the editors bill as "seven new works on the racial crisis." At Ellison's suggestion, begins reviewing books for *The New Leader*, a biweekly magazine of politics and opinion edited in New York by Myron Kolatch. Michele begins work as a professional dancer at the World's Fair in Queens.

1965   Ellison brings Murray on board as a credited consultant for three documentaries for educational television (WNET, New York). (Ellison, through his work with the Carnegie Commission, had been lobbying for the creation of a public television network.) Two are on jazz (*Jazz Goes Intellectual: Bop!*, featuring Dizzy Gillespie, and *Jazz: The Experimenters*, featuring Charles Mingus and Cecil Taylor) and the other is on Ellison himself (*Ralph Ellison: Work in Progress*). Murray serves as "technical consultant" and may have done some script work as well. Michele begins dancing with the Alvin Ailey Company. (She will work with other companies as well, including the Lar Lubovitch Company, before becoming a featured dancer with Ailey circa 1968.) Around this time begins tradition of throwing downhome-style New Year's Day parties—pigs' feet, black-eyed peas, collard greens, cornbread, bourbon—which will continue for several decades.

1966   During the New York City transit strike in January, Murray chauffeurs Michele and her dancer-colleagues from Harlem to the Clark Center in midtown for Ailey Company rehearsals. (He will abandon car ownership within the next few years.) In February is invited by editor Kirkpatrick Sale of *The New York Times Magazine* to write an essay on current and historical relationships between blacks and Jews. (Essay is rejected, with apologies from Sale.) In April speaks at the Peace Corps Training Center in Arecibo, Puerto Rico. Mozelle begins teaching in New York City public schools. "The Luzana Cholly Kick" (1953) is reprinted, under revised title "Train Whistle Guitar," in

John Henrik Clarke's landmark anthology *American Negro Short Stories*, published by Hill and Wang. Murray's essay on James Baldwin is a frequently cited highlight of *Anger, and Beyond: The Negro Writer in the United States*, a wide-ranging anthology of previously unpublished writings edited by Herbert Hill and published by Harper & Row. Mort Sprague dies, at age fifty-seven, at the end of the year. Sprague, to whom Ellison dedicated his essay collection *Shadow and Act* (1964), had been paying close attention to Murray's magazine work and writing to him about it.

1967   In April, begins two-year involvement with New York's Center for Urban Education (CUE), a public-education policy institute funded from 1964 to 1973 by the U.S. Office of Education. Contributes essays to CUE periodicals (*The Urban Review*, a bimonthly journal, and *The Center Forum*, a monthly newsletter) and works as researcher and consultant on several of CUE's multimedia educational initiatives. Writes draft of essay that will become Part I of his collection *The Omni-Americans*. Publishes negative review of William Styron's novel *The Confessions of Nat Turner* in December 4 issue of *The New Leader*.

1968   For the Smithsonian Institution's Archives of American Art Oral History program, interviews painters Charles Alston (Bearden's older cousin), Emma Amos, Merton Simpson, and Hale Woodruff. Teaches course at Columbia University School of Journalism. "Train Whistle Guitar" is revised for inclusion in Theodore L. Gross and James A. Emanuel's anthology *Dark Symphony: Negro Literature in America,* published by Free Press. Editor Angus Cameron at Knopf, responding to a proposal from Murray, says that he is interested in publishing a collection of his essays and reviews but disagrees with him on a few points. Meanwhile, two of CUE's top editors, David E. Outerbridge and Harris Dienstfrey, leave the institute to establish their own book-publishing firm. They admire Murray's work, and invite him to contribute to their list.

1969   Second excerpt from "The Briarpatch" is published in February issue of *Harper's* as "Stonewall Jackson's Waterloo." The magazine's editor, Willie Morris, then sends Murray on an assignment to assess the South, especially his native Alabama, in the wake of desegregation. This long nonfiction piece, part personal memoir, part interview-based journalism, will be Murray's chief project over the next two years. (Murray's interview subjects include Robert Penn Warren, C. Vann Woodward, Walker Percy, and many southern newspaper editors and reporters.) On March 3, Outerbridge and Dienstfrey make a formal offer to publish Murray's collection of essays *The Omni-Americans.* Murray, his discussions with Knopf having reached an impasse, accepts. In October acquires James Oliver Brown as literary agent.

1970   *The Omni-Americans* is published by Outerbridge and Dienstfrey in March. A Book-of-the-Month Club alternate selection, the collection is widely and enthusiastically reviewed. (Robert Coles, in *The New Yorker*, writes that Murray "speaks for himself [and] as a man who is proud of his people and their considerable achievements. . . . His purpose [here] is to set forth those achievements and to warn against America's 'experts,' especially what he calls 'social survey technicians,' [who] do not see the richness, the complexity of the black man's experience in America; they merely contribute to the caricatures that so many of us cannot get out of our heads.") Takes two-week vacation with Mozelle to Sag Harbor, Long Island, in July. In August delivers first post-*Omni-Americans* lecture, "Beyond Separatism," to Brandeis University's Summer Adult Institute. Serves as O'Connor Professor of Literature at Colgate University in the fall. Duke Ellington, then in residency in Los Angeles, interviews Murray for job as co-author of his autobiography. (In the end Ellington will write *Music Is My Mistress* [1973] with longtime confidant Stanley Dance.)

1971   Brown sells book rights to *Harper's* article to Joyce Johnson, an editor at McGraw-Hill and an acquaintance of Murray since 1969. In March Willie Morris is fired from *Harper's* and magazine publication of the article, scheduled for the fall, is canceled. Murray serves as visiting professor of literature at the University of Massachusetts–Boston. "Train Whistle Guitar" is reprinted in his friend Toni Cade Bambara's anthology *Tales and Stories for Black Folks* and is admiringly quoted at length by Toni Morrison in *The New York Times.* Michele tours Soviet Union with Alvin Ailey company. In November *South to a Very Old Place* is published by McGraw-Hill to excellent reviews.

(Robert R. Gross, in *Saturday Review*, writes that Murray, by intermingling "reminiscences of youth with engaging conversation, cultural criticism, and comments on his folk heritage," has created "a disciplined work of art: a reflective and elegant rendering of one man's coming to terms with his roots.") *The Omni-Americans* is reprinted in paperback by Avon Books.

1972	In January Ruth Ellington (Duke's sister and music publishing manager) throws book party for *South to a Very Old Place* at 333 Riverside Drive (which is also Duke's mailing address). In February accepts invitation from the University of Missouri–Columbia to deliver the Paul Anthony Brick Lectures for fall 1972. Revisits "The Hero and the Blues," his essay on the blues idiom, and begins adapting the material for a series of three hour-long lectures. *South to a Very Old Place* named a finalist for the National Book Award in the Arts and Letters category. Jack Valenti, formerly a top aide to President Johnson, writes to Murray regarding how much LBJ appreciated *South to a Very Old Place*, especially Murray's account of a conversation among elderly Alabamians about Johnson's civil rights policies. Receives Alumni Merit Award from Tuskegee. Speaks at Southern University, in Baton Rouge, Louisiana. Correspondents around this time include Michael Harper, James Alan McPherson, Ernest J. Gaines, Robert Bone, Martin Williams, and Leon Forrest. Spanish translation of *The Omni-Americans* is published by Editorial Letras in Mexico City. On October 7, 8, and 9, delivers Paul Anthony Brick Lectures at the University of Missouri.

1973	Serves as O'Connor Visiting Lecturer at Colgate University. Speaks at Yale University. Elected to executive committee of American branch of PEN. In spring Harvard undergraduate Lewis P. Jones III, editor of "Black Odyssey; A Search for Home," a special issue of the *Harvard Advocate*, invites Murray to contribute to the publication. Instead of an article, Murray suggests that the issue's chief theme, "the role and responsibilities of black artists operating in the larger American context," be the subject of a Harvard symposium and that the transcript be published in the *Advocate*. The symposium, moderated by Dean of Students Archie Epps and featuring Murray, Ellison, Harold Cruse, and Nathan I.

Huggins, marks the beginning of Murray's decades-long friendship with Jones, who will later have a career in law, banking, and finance. Brick Lectures published as *The Hero and the Blues* by the University of Missouri Press. (An unsigned review in *The New Yorker* says that "[Murray] is succinct, funny, and marvelously original in defining what a hero is in fiction and drama—his reading of *Oedipus* is a knockout, and his comparison of Mann's Joseph to American black heroes is eye-opening.")

1974   Elected to membership in the Century Association, an exclusive club of writers, artists, musicians, and patrons of the arts in midtown Manhattan. Quickly becomes a regular for lunch and an active participant in club affairs. (The club will remain an important part of his life through 2005.) At St. Peter's Evangelical Lutheran Church in Manhattan (famous for its ministry to the jazz world) serves on committee (along with Ruth Ellington, Phoebe Jacobs, Stanley Dance, and others) that organizes seventy-fifth-birthday concert for Duke Ellington on April 29. (Ellington will die on May 24.) In early May *Train Whistle Guitar*, a novel of childhood fashioned from approximately the first half of "The Briarpatch," is published by McGraw-Hill. The book, which will later that year win the Lillian Smith Award for Fiction from the Southern Regional Council, is well and widely reviewed. (John Edgar Wideman, writing in *The New York Times Book Review*, says that "the only way to appreciate the music of Murray's prose is to immerse yourself in long passages of dialogue and monologue, the lyric descriptions of countryside and fireside, which are nothing so much as the riffs and choruses of a blues artist translated into speech and action. . . . [They tell us] the truth about black experience just as resolutely as the runaway, star-climbing notes of a Charlie Parker solo.") At the invitation of Martin Williams, teaches at Smithsonian Institute in Music Criticism, where Gary Giddins is among his students. Is a regular at Upper East Side restaurant Elaine's. Speaks at public schools in Sacramento. Receives contract from McGraw-Hill for sequel to *Train Whistle Guitar*.

1975   Receives honorary doctorate from Colgate University. Social circle at this time includes Mary Hemingway, Robert Penn Warren, Sidney Offit, Herbert Mitgang, Drew

Middleton, John Chancellor, Matt Clark, John Hammond, Romare Bearden, and Ralph Ellison. Michele, no longer with the Alvin Ailey company, teaches courses on dance and movement for actors at Howard University.

1976   In October *Stomping the Blues* is published by McGraw-Hill. A study of the history, aesthetics, rituals, and anthropology of jazz, focusing on its black derivation and affirmative disposition, the book is widely reviewed in both the mainstream and the music press. (Greil Marcus, writing in *Rolling Stone*, explains that for Murray blues music "is not involved with self-pity or resignation . . . but with affirmation and the act of creation. . . . *Stomping the Blues* is anything but the last word on the blues. It is, though, the best word anyone has offered in a long time.") For book party, McGraw-Hill throws a "Kansas City Jam Session" at its building on Sixth Avenue in midtown Manhattan, featuring jazz legends Budd Johnson, Eddie Durham, Buck Clayton, Oliver Jackson, Mary Lou Williams, Bill Pemberton, and Doc Cheatham. Murray's students and acolytes around this time include Gary Giddins, Henry Louis Gates, Jr., Charlayne Hunter-Gault, and Stanley Crouch. Murray writes catalogue essay for Bearden's exhibition *Of the Blues* at Cordier & Ekstrom Gallery in New York.

1977   Jason Berry's essay "Musical Literature," the first long-form critical appraisal of Murray's oeuvre, appears in the January 15 issue of *The Nation*. Murray travels to West Germany in June for the United States Information Agency, speaking at the Free University of Berlin, the University of Bonn, and the University of Bremen. *Stomping the Blues* wins ASCAP/Deems Taylor Award for Music Criticism. Approached by Willard Alexander, longtime booking agent for Count Basie, to act as Basie's co-writer on an as-told-to autobiography. Agrees. Travels with Basie on and off through 1983. Repeatedly interviews old acquaintance Jo Jones, the drummer for the Basie band during its first decade, originally for background for the Basie book and then for a possible book on Jones's life. Exhaustively corroborates Basie's memories by interviewing bandmates, including Eddie Durham, Budd Johnson, Dan Minor, and Buck Clayton, and by checking Basie's memories against newspaper stories and publicity materials. Is "Special Guest Speaker" at conference of African and African American Folklorists at Indiana University–Bloomington. Speaks at the Studio Museum in Harlem.

1978   In spring is writer-in-residence at Emory University, where Mike Sager, who will become a prominent journalist, is among his students. Befriends literary scholar and biographer Richard Ellmann, also teaching at Emory. Conducts several long interviews with Jo Jones in the summer and fall. Writes wall labels for Bearden's *Profiles* series, on view at Cordier & Ekstrom. Presents lectures at Morehouse College and Howard University. Attends concert at the White House celebrating the twenty-fifth anniversary of the Newport Jazz Festival. Speaks at Long Island University's C. W. Post campus on several occasions throughout the 1978–79 school year under auspices of the political science department. Interviewed at his apartment by Henry Louis Gates, Jr. and Robert G. O'Meally (who sets up the interview). The interview is transcribed but is then set aside. O'Meally will find the transcription on the morning of what would have been Murray's hundredth birthday, May 12, 2016, and through the efforts of Gates, it will be published in the Winter 2016 issue of *The Paris Review* in December 2016 (after having been prepared for publication by Paul Devlin). In December, filmmaker Nelson E. Breen records joint conversation of Murray, Bearden, Alvin Ailey, and James Baldwin for the documentary *Bearden Plays Bearden* (1980).

1979   Writes recommendation on behalf of Eleanor Traylor to the National Endowment for the Humanities in support of Traylor's proposal for a fellowship to write a study of Richard Wright's creative process. Smithsonian interview with Hale Woodruff (1968) is published in the catalogue to Woodruff's exhibition at the Studio Museum in Harlem. Herbert Mitgang interviews Murray about his collaboration with Count Basie for his Book Ends column in *The New York Times* on November 18. Murray tells Mitgang: "My job is to help him get his voice right so readers will say 'I know that's Count Basie talking; what did Albert Murray do to get his name on the book?'"

1980   Begins teaching creative writing at Barnard College as an adjunct associate professor. (He will continue on and off through 1983.) Declines Nathan I. Huggins's offer of a teaching position at Harvard University. Stanley Crouch's laudatory essay "Albert Murray's Gourmet Chitlins" appears in the March 3 issue of the *Village Voice*. Works with Bearden and the photographer and movie producer Sam Shaw on *Paris Blues*, a book based on Shaw's 1961 film of that title. (The book, commissioned by a French publisher but never realized, was to include photographs by Shaw, collages and other artworks by Bearden, and a text by Murray.) Writes catalogue essay for Bearden retrospective *Romare Bearden: 1970–1980* at the Mint Museum in Charlotte, North Carolina. Travels to Charlotte for the exhibition's opening. Appears in documentary *Bearden Plays Bearden*, several scenes of which are filmed on the balcony of Murray's apartment.

1981   Delivers lecture on Bearden at the Brooklyn Museum in October; a concert by Teddy Wilson follows Murray's presentation. Introduced by Stanley Crouch to nineteen-year-old Juilliard student Wynton Marsalis, a composer and trumpeter who will become Murray's most famous protégé in terms of thinking about culture.

1982   Serves as Colgate Professor of Humanities at Colgate in the fall, teaching junior-level course on regional writing and senior-level course "Implications of the Blues Idiom in Contemporary American Literature." Attends an "All-Star Jazz Program" at the White House on December 4. Fires his literary agent, James Oliver Brown, whose firm, James Brown Associates, had merged with the New York office of prominent British firm Curtis Brown, Ltd. in 1978. James Oliver Brown was serving as president of newly formed Curtis Brown Associates at the time, and Murray felt that his account was not receiving proper attention. *Stomping the Blues* reprinted by Vintage a few months after Nelson George's lament, in the *Village Voice*, that it had fallen out of print.

1983   Increases frequency of interviews with Count Basie. Makes several trips to Basie's home in Freeport, Bahamas. Speaks at Drew University. *The Omni-Americans* reprinted by Vintage. Speaks at the Jane Globus Seminar at Baruch College. Serves as judge of the Robert F. Kennedy Book Awards.

1984   Count Basie dies on April 26, just months after he and Murray had completed the first draft of his autobiography, *Good Morning Blues*. Speaks at Swarthmore College.

1985 Signs contract with Random House for *Good Morning Blues*. (Andrew Wylie, who represents him in the deal, will remain his agent for the rest of his life.) Book acquired by editor Erroll McDonald, who will publish all of Murray's future work, usually under Random House's Pantheon imprint. Collaborates with saxophonist David Murray (no relation) on musical stage adaptation of *Train Whistle Guitar*. (Producer Joseph Papp of the New York Shakespeare Festival shows serious interest in this work-in-progress, but the musical is never realized.) In July Murray conducts his last interview with Jo Jones, who dies, at age seventy-three, on September 3. Speaks at Harvard University in November.

1986 *Good Morning Blues: The Autobiography of Count Basie as told to Albert Murray* is published in early January. (By March twelve thousand copies are sold.) Black-tie book party for a thousand people at the Palladium in New York on January 17 is covered by national news media. Conducts long interview with Dizzy Gillespie, a truncated version of which appears in *Interview Magazine* for April. Murray is included in a fashion photo shoot in *New York* magazine. Receives award from literary journal *Callaloo*, which in December hosts a tribute to Murray at the convention of the Modern Language Association, featuring readings by Elizabeth Alexander, Thulani Davis, and Melvin Dixon. Joins board of directors of American Composers Orchestra, and will serve until 1989. Appears in "Black on White," episode five of Robert MacNeil's PBS documentary *The Story of English*.

1987 With Wynton Marsalis, Gordon Davis, and Stanley Crouch, Murray serves on committee that proposes the establishment of a classic jazz program at New York's Lincoln Center for the Performing Arts. (He will work closely with Crouch and Marsalis over the next several years on developing the project.) Delivers lecture to the Peter Rushton Seminars on Modern Literature at the University of Virginia. Speaks at Ohio University. German translation of *Good Morning Blues* published by Econ Verlag. Speaks at Dayton Art Institute, with concert by David Murray following presentation. Appears in documentary *Long Shadows: The Legacy of the American Civil War*. Interviewed twice at his apartment by V. S. Naipaul, in the spring and the fall. Helps make arrangements for Naipaul's visit to

Tuskegee for his book *A Turn in the South* (1989). Mozelle retires from teaching in June.

1988   Romare Bearden dies on March 12, at age seventy-six. Murray becomes involved in creation of Romare Bearden Foundation. French translation of *Good Morning Blues* published by Éditions Filipacchi.

1989   On June 17, in honor of Murray's work with Central Pennsylvania Friends of Jazz, "Albert Murray Day" proclaimed in Harrisburg by Governor Bob Casey, Sr. Speaks at the New School for Social Research alongside Wynton Marsalis and jazz composer/arranger David Berger. Paperback edition of *Train Whistle Guitar* issued by Northeastern University Press with a new foreword by Robert G. O'Meally. Paperback rights to *The Omni-Americans* and *Stomping the Blues* licensed by Wylie to Da Capo Press.

1990   Appears in documentary *Lady Day: The Many Faces of Billie Holiday*. In spring spends two weeks at Dillard University in New Orleans, as United Negro College Fund Distinguished Scholar. In October takes long vacation with Mozelle and Michele to England and France, traveling from London to Paris to the Côte d'Azur, visiting friends along the way.

1991   Group of friends throws surprise party for the Murrays on their fiftieth wedding anniversary. Second novel, *The Spyglass Tree*, originally under contract with McGraw-Hill, is published by Pantheon in the fall. A sequel to *Train Whistle Guitar*, it continues the adventures of Scooter, now a student at a black college based on the Tuskegee of the 1930s. Novel is well received by critics, including Michiko Kakutani, who writes in *The New York Times* that "the book, as a whole, works beautifully . . . Like all good *Bildungsromane*, it leaves the reader with a vivid portrait of a young man and his struggles to come to terms with his receding past and his beckoning future." In December receives Directors Emeriti Award from Lincoln Center for outstanding service to the institution in a volunteer capacity. Writes script for and appears in British television documentary *Count Basie: Swingin' the Blues*. *South to a Very Old Place* reprinted in paperback by Vintage.

1992   On his birthday has conversation with Wynton Marsalis onstage at Lincoln Center. Endures operation on back and neck, after which he will walk with a cane for several years, and later with a walker. Speaks at the Center for American Culture Studies at Columbia University. Writes captions for photographer Ming Smith's book *A Ming Breakfast: Grits and Scrambled Moments.*

1993   Serves as Du Pont Visiting Professor at Washington and Lee University in the fall. Appears as commentator, with blues scholar Robert Palmer, in documentary *Bluesland: A Portrait in American Music.*

1994   Attends eightieth birthday dinner for Ellison on March 1 at Le Périgord in New York. Ellison dies on April 16 after a brief illness. In April Murray is interviewed at his apartment by Wynton Marsalis, and in July is interviewed by Robert G. O'Meally for the Smithsonian's Jazz Oral History Project. (These wide-ranging discussions will appear, along with a much longer version of Murray's 1986 interview of Dizzy Gillespie, in *Murray Talks Music* [2016], edited by Paul Devlin.)

1995   *South to a Very Old Place* republished in hardcover by Modern Library. *The Hero and the Blues* reprinted in paperback by Vintage. Paperback edition of *Good Morning Blues* issued by Da Capo.

1996   In February Pantheon publishes two new books to an avalanche of attention: a third Scooter novel, *The Seven League Boots,* and an essay collection, *The Blue Devils of Nada.* (In the daily *New York Times,* Richard Bernstein calls the novel "a prose poem full of character and wisdom" in which Scooter, now a young man, "becomes part of a famous jazz band, travels the country, conquers Hollywood, goes to France, and is loved by several glamorous women, all the while reflecting on history and mythology, on Odysseus and Telemachus . . . and above all on the folks back in Alabama who sent him into the world to do great things." Charles Johnson, praising Murray's "wise and authoritative essays" in the Sunday *Book Review,* writes: "What deserves very close appraisal in *The Blue Devils of Nada* is Mr. Murray's acute awareness of how the 'on-going dialogue with tradition' across cultures, races, and countries forms the basis for the works—especially American ones—deservedly enshrined in the pantheon of world-class masterpieces.") Murray is profiled in February 22 issue of *Newsweek.* Receives National Book Critics Circle's Ivan Sandrof Award for outstanding contribution to American arts and letters. Profile by Henry Louis Gates,

Jr., entitled "King of Cats," appears in April 8 issue of *The New Yorker*. Murray participates in "An International Celebration of Southern Literature" at Agnes Scott College in June, a "Literary Olympiad" event affiliated with the Olympic Games in Atlanta. Receives honorary doctorate from Spring Hill College in Mobile. Speaks at Cornell University at invitation of Cornell's president. Interviewed by Brian Lamb on C-SPAN's *Booknotes* program and by Charlie Rose on his PBS talk show. Gives a reading, combined with a performance by Wynton Marsalis, at PEN/Faulkner event at the Folger Shakespeare Library in Washington, D.C., in November. In December speaks at MLA convention in Washington as part of panel celebrating release of *The Norton Anthology of African American Literature*, which includes an excerpt from *Train Whistle Guitar*. Jazz at Lincoln Center becomes full constituent of Lincoln Center for the Performing Arts, and is now on par with the New York Philharmonic, Metropolitan Opera, and New York City Ballet. Murray will be an active board member through mid-2005.

1997　　In January elected to membership in the American Academy of Arts and Letters. Receives lifetime achievement award from the Anisfield-Wolf Book Awards "for important contributions to our understanding of racism and our appreciation of the rich diversity of human cultures." *Conversations with Albert Murray*, a collection of new and selected interviews edited by Roberta S. Maguire, published by the University Press of Mississippi. Delivers lecture in "Eye of the Beholder" series at the Isabella Stewart Gardner Museum in Boston. Receives honorary doctorate from Hamilton College, alma mater of his Tuskegee mentor Morteza Drexel Sprague. Speaks at Vassar and at Yale. Reads from his fiction at the Unterberg Poetry Center of the 92nd Street Y with John Edgar Wideman. Reads at twenty-fourth annual Faulkner and Yoknapatawpha Conference at the University of Mississippi. Appears on cover of *The New York Times Magazine* for March 9 alongside George Plimpton, Geoffrey Beene, Ed Koch, Allen Ginsberg, Cynthia Ozick, Eartha Kitt, Brooke Astor, Uta Hagen, and others under the headline "Funny, We Don't Feel Old."

1998　　Participates in tribute to Ellison at the 92nd Street Y along with Saul Bellow, James Alan McPherson, John F. Callahan, and R.W.B. Lewis. Elected to membership in the

American Academy of Arts and Sciences. Serves on literature awards committee of the American Academy of Arts
and Letters with William Weaver, Charles Simic, Robert
Stone, Reynolds Price, Anne Tyler, and Anthony Hecht.
Receives inaugural Harper Lee Award from Alabama Writers' Forum. *Train Whistle Guitar* is reprinted by Vintage.
Two lectures from the 1980s appear in Robert G. O'Meally's compendious reader *The Jazz Cadence of American
Culture* from Columbia University Press.

1999   Receives honorary doctorate from Tuskegee University
(formerly Tuskegee Institute), with which he and Mozelle
have maintained many connections over the past six decades.
On June 18 participates in reading from Ellison's posthu-
mously published novel *Juneteenth* with Toni Morrison and
Peter Matthiessen at Barnes & Noble bookstore on Seven-
teenth Street in Manhattan. Speaks at Ellison symposium at
CUNY Graduate Center at the invitation of Morris Dick-
stein. Jazz at Lincoln Center staff presents him with an
enormous birthday card thanking him for being its "resident
scholar and guru of the blues." Presents lectures at Iowa
Writers' Workshop at the invitation of James Alan McPherson. Italian translation of *Stomping the Blues* published by
Cooperativa Libraria Universitaria Editrice Bologna.

2000   *Trading Twelves: The Selected Letters of Ralph Ellison and
Albert Murray* published by Modern Library. Receives
honorary doctorate from Stony Brook University, through
the efforts of philosophy professor Lorenzo Simpson.
Good friends around this time include Paul Resika, Ber-
nard Holland, Matt and Phyllis Clark, Sidney and Dr.
Avodah Offit, and John Hollander and Natalie Charkow.
Favorite restaurants include Daniel and Bistro du Nord.
Delivers keynote address to Ralph Ellison–Albert Murray
Symposium at Dallas Institute of Humanities and Culture.

2001   Appears in Ken Burns's documentary *Jazz* and in the
University of Alabama/Alabama Public Television's *Coat
of Many Colors: A Tapestry of Alabama Artists.* Speaks at
University of North Carolina–Chapel Hill in February. In
March receives Clarence Cason Award from the School of
Journalism at the University of Alabama–Tuscaloosa. Paul
Devlin, an undergraduate at St. John's University in
Queens, New York, sends letter to Murray expressing in-
terest in his work. Murray and Devlin meet on March 28,
beginning what will become a close friendship. (Devlin

will quickly become the latest of Murray's many intellectual apprentices, as well as his chauffeur and all-around assistant.) In May buys diamond and platinum ring for Mozelle from Tiffany & Co., a gift for their sixtieth wedding anniversary. On 9/11 Mozelle is in Rhode Island visiting friends as the attacks on New York and Washington unfold. (Murray is especially shocked by the attack on the Pentagon, calling it unthinkable from the perspective of a retired officer.) Appears in "Giants of Jazz" photo shoot in October issue of *Talk* magazine, alongside several musical legends and up-and-coming performers. *Talk* feature also includes a philosophical statement by Murray in response to 9/11. Pantheon publishes two new books in November: a volume of new and previously uncollected essays, *From the Briarpatch File*, and a collection of poems, *Conjugations and Reiterations*. Real estate developer Jack Rudin throws grand book party for Murray at the Four Seasons restaurant in the Seagram Building in Manhattan on December 5, with performance by Wynton Marsalis.

2002   Participates in Mobile's tricentennial celebration. Attends exhibition opening for painter Richard Mayhew in New York and renews old friendship with him. Maintains demanding schedule of working on fourth and final Scooter novel and judging student essays for Jazz at Lincoln Center's "Essentially Ellington" band competition. *Good Morning Blues* is reprinted by Da Capo with a new introduction by Dan Morgenstern.

2003   Receives award for literary achievement from the Alabama Council on the Arts in Montgomery in May. Visits Tuskegee for the last time. Loans one of several works he owns by Romare Bearden, the 1985 monotype *Celebrations: Trumpet Spot, Wynton*, to the National Gallery of Art's major retrospective traveling exhibition *The Art of Romare Bearden*, and attends the show's opening in Washington in September. Speaks at St. John's University on September 30. It will be his last lecture at a college or university.

2004   Attends numerous events throughout the fall celebrating the opening of the new home for Jazz at Lincoln Center in the Time Warner Center at Columbus Circle. Attends black-tie gala at Columbia University for Basie's centennial. *The Art of Romare Bearden* travels to the Whitney in New York and Murray appears on a panel to mark the exhibition's opening on October 14. "Jazz: Notes Toward a

Definition" published in the *New Republic* in October. It is the last piece of his nonfiction published during his lifetime. Attends book party for Dan Morgenstern's *Living with Jazz: A Reader* at Rutgers–Newark in November. With novel *The Magic Keys* delivered to Pantheon, begins to imagine a work focusing on several minor characters in the Scooter sequence.

2005   Spends long afternoon in January in the Bearden retrospective, now at the Whitney Museum. Excerpt from *Train Whistle Guitar* centering on Jack Johnson is read in Ken Burns's documentary on the boxer, *Unforgivable Blackness*. Interviewed on Bearden at the Metropolitan Museum of Art in February. Falls from chair at home on May 15 or 16 and injures his head, possibly sustaining a concussion. Refuses to go to the hospital, citing several important events on his calendar. *The Magic Keys* published on May 17 to generally warm reviews. Extraordinarily heavy traffic the following evening delays his arrival for Q&A with John Edgar Wideman at New York's Housing Works Bookstore, but even after an hour's wait the capacity crowd does not thin out. Private publication party held in the rare book room at the Strand Bookstore on May 19, with performance by a combo featuring Wycliffe Gordon, Kengo Nakamura, and Aaron Diehl, followed by a public Q&A and book signing. Pleased by review of new novel in the May issue of *Harper's*, in which John Leonard calls it "less kiss-kiss bang-bang . . . than elegy, reverie, memory book, and musical score, as well as thank-you note to the entire sustaining community of black America." (Leonard describes the Manhattan sections, which include an *à clef* rendering of Ralph Ellison, as "the creation myth of the postwar black intelligentsia.") By mid-June it becomes almost impossible for Murray to stand up without assistance. For past few years he has been able to walk short distances but has used a wheelchair for excursions in public places such as airports, museums, and Lincoln Center. Severe back pain becomes worse. Begins to lose control of legs in late June. In July, at Mozelle's insistence, is admitted to Lenox Hill Hospital in Manhattan for battery of tests; remains in hospital through late August. Upon discharge is attended by nurses twenty-four hours a day and will be for the rest of his life. Makes rebound toward the end of the year, regaining energy and liveliness missing since his fall in May. Reads newspapers every morning at kitchen table. Assigns power of attorney and executorship of his estate to Lewis P. Jones III, his good friend since the *Harvard Advocate* symposium of 1973. (Jones will oversee the Murray family's personal affairs and finances as their attorney-in-fact and executor.)

2006 Enjoys cheerful, crowded ninetieth birthday party at his apartment on afternoon of May 12, and receives numerous visitors over the course of birthday weekend. Encourages Paul Devlin to listen to his 1977–85 interviews with Jo Jones to see if they might be turned into a book.

2007 Awarded W.E.B. Du Bois Medal from Du Bois Institute at Harvard University. Henry Louis Gates, Jr. bestows medal at a packed-house ceremony in Murray's apartment on afternoon of June 3. In hospital again from mid-December through January 2008.

2008 In January Auburn University hosts "Albert Murray and the Aesthetic Imagination of a Nation," the first symposium on his work alone. Italian translation of *Good Morning Blues* published by Minimum Fax.

2009 In final public appearance (and his first since 2005), receives Ed Bradley Award for Leadership from Jazz at Lincoln Center at concert portion of its fall gala in November. Receives standing ovation from sold-out concert audience. His hearing, which has been worsening for years, is now almost completely gone. Visitors must talk into a microphone attached to a headset, speak almost at a shout, or write questions and comments on paper to be understood.

2010 Photographed by Jake Chessum for photo-essay "Nine Over 90" in September 26 issue of *New York* magazine. Fellow nonagenarians profiled in the essay include Robert Morgenthau, Carmen Herrera, Elliott Carter, George Avakian, Ruth Gruber, Andy Rooney, Zelda Kaplan, and Hugh Carey. Enjoys the attention and commotion of the elaborate photo shoot in his apartment. Papers from the Auburn symposium, along with other articles and interviews, published as a book by the University of Alabama Press in June.

2011 Commemorates seventieth wedding anniversary with a small party at home. *Rifftide: The Life and Opinions of Papa Jo Jones*, as told to Albert Murray, is published by University of Minnesota Press in September. (The book, edited by Paul Devlin, is well received: in *The New York Times Book Review*, Colin Fleming writes that it is "the kind of book that delights jazz fans: the straight-talking, defiantly espousing firsthand record. Anyone interested in authenticity of voice is going to be on the verge of fist-pumping the air throughout, or else exclaiming, 'You tell it like it is, baby,' as if partaking in a call-and-response with the book.") In October becomes Director Emeritus of Jazz at Lincoln Center. The board's citation honors him as "Jazz at Lincoln Center's guiding spirit, shaping its values with the lessons of jazz and providing the pedagogical foundation for all its programs." Continues to receive visitors, but decline is noticeable. Talks of Mobile often. Mozelle, too, begins to need around-the-clock nursing care.

2012   Selection of five works from Murray's art collection (three by Bearden, two by Norman Lewis) exhibited at D.C. Moore Gallery in New York; the show, with wall text by Paul Devlin, runs from January 6 through February 4. In June receives lifetime achievement award from the Jazz Journalists Association.

2013   Strength and energy, declining for some time, fade rapidly in the late spring. Loses what had been a handshake with a viselike grip. Eats less and less, and then stops completely for a period in May. Makes modest rebound through June and July, but stops eating again in August. Dies in his sleep at home on the evening of August 18, at age of ninety-seven. Cremated. He is survived by Mozelle, his wife of seventy-two years, and by their daughter, Michele, now sixty-nine. (Mozelle will die in her sleep at home on July 3, 2015.) Wynton Marsalis and Jazz at Lincoln Center host memorial service on September 13. About five hundred people attend the midday event in the Appel Room, facing Columbus Circle, with an overflow crowd of approximately one hundred watching on screens in an adjacent room. In November Henry Louis Gates, Jr. delivers a tribute at the American Academy of Arts and Letters. "This was Albert Murray's century," he remarks; "we just lived in it. And as we keep on living, we will never forget what he meant to our American story or the music animating it with a soul force he taught us to hear."

Note on the Texts

This volume contains all of the published fiction and most of the poetry written by Albert Murray throughout his career. It includes the texts of the novels *Train Whistle Guitar* (1974), *The Spyglass Tree* (1991), *The Seven League Boots* (1995), and *The Magic Keys* (2005); the poetry collection *Conjugations and Reiterations* (2001) and eleven previously unpublished poems; and, in an appendix, the short story "The Luzana Cholly Kick" (1953, related to *Train Whistle Guitar*) and the previously unpublished story "Manifest Destiny U.S.A." (c. 2004–5).

TRAIN WHISTLE GUITAR

In the late 1940s Murray began work on a semi-autobiographical novel. Given the working title "Jack the Bear," this ur-novel, which is not known to survive in complete manuscript or typescript, corresponded broadly to what became *Train Whistle Guitar* and *The Spyglass Tree*. On December 26, 1951, living in Alabama and teaching at the Tuskegee Institute, Murray completed a draft of "Jack the Bear." He soon mailed a typescript to his friend Ralph Ellison, who provided a long and substantial assessment in a letter dated February 4, 1952. The typescript was then sent to Ellison's editor at Random House, Albert Erskine, who responded that Murray's fiction seemed overly indebted to William Faulkner. (Erskine was also Faulkner's editor.) In the late spring of 1953, via Ellison, Murray submitted a typescript—a version of the 1951 novel broken up into short stories and entitled "The Briarpatch"—to Arabel J. Porter, an editor at the prominent periodical *New World Writing*. In a memo to her colleagues of July 6, 1953, Porter wrote, "I love this stuff. It isn't Dylan Thomas, but it is good Negro-American—funny, poetic and foxy." Her favorite chapter was called "Stomping Room Only." It is unclear which section of *Train Whistle Guitar* this might have become, or if a version was incorporated into the novel at all. Porter ultimately selected what became "The Luzana Cholly Kick" for *New World Writing 4*, which was published in September 1953 with an initial print run of 100,000 copies. In October, an additional 40,000 copies were printed. Murray wrote to Porter and to Ellison separately that he was pleased that "The Luzana Cholly Kick" was chosen, as it would have been the excerpt he would have selected. "The Luzana Cholly Kick" is printed in this volume in the appendix and corresponds approximately (though with significant changes) to pages 6–25 of *Train Whistle Guitar* in this volume; its text is taken from *New World Writing 4* (Fall 1953).

The story met with acclaim. Margaret Young Jackson, a classmate of Murray's at Tuskegee in the late 1930s and in 1954 a professor at Morris Brown College in Atlanta, wrote to Murray that the eminent poet Sterling Brown, while giving a lecture at Morris Brown, had read from "The Luzana Cholly Kick" and "seemed to be very much impressed with your ability." Nonetheless, Murray's book-length manuscript was not accepted for publication.

In the mid-1950s, an anonymous reader's report commissioned by either an agent or a publishing house declared "the fault of this novel is not only the inadequate telling of a young man's discovery of himself and his world, but also the inadequate telling of a young negro man's position in the United States and therelations [sic] betwen [sic] the two complexities." The reviewer wrote that "our real sympathy and interest lies" with "the victims of injustice based on race and those who perpetrate the injustice"—presumably referring to a version of the Will Spradley–Dudley Philpot episode in *The Spyglass Tree*. This patronizing and condescending report, which is almost completely hostile to Murray's project, led to at least one rejection and may have reflected broader concerns among agents and editors. A wide market for the kind of fiction Murray was writing did not emerge until the late 1960s and early 1970s. Even into the 1970s, some prominent white critics expressed reservations about Murray's positively drawn African American characters. In 1962, Murray sent "The Briarpatch" to the editor Peter Davison of Atlantic Monthly Press, which turned it down. In 1964, Ashbel Green, an editor at Alfred A. Knopf, wrote to Murray asking to see his novel, after seeing a book review Murray wrote. But despite this interest, "The Briarpatch" remained unpublished.

In the years that followed, the story "Train Whistle Guitar," the new title given to "The Luzana Cholly Kick," was widely anthologized. It was included in John Henrik Clarke, ed., *American Negro Short Stories* (New York: Hill and Wang, 1966), in an unrevised version of the story as it had been published in *New World Writing*; writing in *The New York Times Book Review*, the critic Robert Bone praised it as the collection's best story. Then, with considerable revisions, it was published in James A. Emanuel and Theodore G. Gross, eds., *Dark Symphony: Negro Writing in America* (New York: Free Press, 1968). The *Dark Symphony* version is close to the final version of the material that appears in *Train Whistle Guitar*. Next, it was included in Toni Cade Bambara's anthology *Tales and Stories for Black Folks* (New York: Doubleday, 1971), which was reviewed by Toni Morrison in *The New York Times*; she quoted a long passage from Murray's story in her review. "Train Whistle Guitar" then appeared in two college-market anthologies, *The Norton Introduction to Literature: Combined Shorter Edition* (1973) and Scribner's *The Short Story: Fiction in Transition*, ed. John Chesley Taylor (rev. ed., 1973), and in the middle-school literature textbook *Responding: Six* (Lexington, MA: Ginn, 1973). A second excerpt from the novel, under the title "Stonewall Jackson's Waterloo" (corresponding to pages 44–59 in this volume), was published in *Harper's Magazine* in February 1969 and in Edward Margolies, ed., *A Native Sons Reader* (Philadelphia: Lippincott, 1970).

It is unclear when Murray decided to divide the ur-novel into two novels, the first focusing on the youth of the protagonist, Scooter, in and around the Mobile, Alabama, neighborhood of Gasoline Point, and the second on his college experiences. Following the critical success of Murray's memoir *South to a Very Old Place* (1971), Murray's editor, Joyce Johnson of McGraw-Hill, offered him a contract for *Train Whistle Guitar* (along with another book, at first envisioned as a book on Africa, either undrafted or unsaved; ultimately Murray's 1976 book *Stomping the Blues* fulfilled the contract). *Train Whistle Guitar* was published by McGraw-Hill in New York in April 1974 in hardcover. The paperback version published the following year contains several minor emendations to the hardcover text. Further emendations, written in Murray's author's copy, were not adopted in the paperback version but are included here. As with the other books in this volume, Murray did not revise the text for later editions, and unlike some of his works of nonfiction, there were no separate British editions of his novels. The text printed here is the 1975 McGraw-Hill paperback edition of *Train Whistle Guitar*, incorporating the additional authorial emendations based on his author's copy, listed as follows:

Jerome nicknamed me] Jerome not so much nicknamed as ordained me [13.10]
sweet mama or] sweet mama every night or [124.1–2]
billy-smelling] *billygoat-smelling* [129.4]
the folks] the old folks [132.15]
curd] cud [133.8]

THE SPYGLASS TREE

In 1974, following the generally enthusiastic critical reception given to *Train Whistle Guitar* (especially among young African American writers and critics), Murray signed a contract for *The Spyglass Tree*. In a 1974 interview, he said, "Most of my next novel is finished and it carries Scooter (the boy-hero of *Train Whistle Guitar*) up through his college years. A third novel will take him to his maturity." He continued to work on it and revise it, albeit fitfully, over many years. Other projects, including *Good Morning Blues: The Autobiography of Count Basie as told to Albert Murray*, begun in 1976 and published in 1985 by Random House, took him away from the novel, and for reasons unclear, his contract with McGraw-Hill was canceled. On November 18, 1979, Herbert Mitgang, in his "Book Ends" column in *The New York Times*, wrote, in a short piece on Murray's work with Basie, that Murray was still working on *The Spyglass Tree*.

Good Morning Blues was acquired by Erroll McDonald, later the editor-in-chief of Pantheon Books (a subsidiary of Random House), which published the remaining three novels in Murray's tetralogy, along with two essay collections and his poetry volume *Conjugations and Reiterations* (discussed below). *The Spyglass Tree* was published by Pantheon Books in November 1991. After publication, Murray made several emendations to the text in his author's copy, all but one of which ("corn whiskey-cozy," at 287.7, for "corn-whiskey, cozy") were followed in the Vintage paperback edition in 1992. The text printed here is that of the 1992 Vintage paperback edition, incorporating Murray's additional emendation.

THE SEVEN LEAGUE BOOTS

In the late 1940s, while Murray was working on the ur-novel that became *Train Whistle Guitar* and *The Spyglass Tree*, he was imagining a separate novel that seems thematically to correspond to *The Seven League Boots*. No draft of this novel has survived, but it appears to have been the narrative "about modern swing music and the men who make it" mentioned by the journalist Ollie Stewart in his "Report from Paris" column (*Baltimore Afro-American*, July 1, 1950), which described Murray, recently arrived in France, as "living in the Latin Quarter and working on a novel." In a letter to Ellison dated February 9, 1952, responding to Ellison's critique of "Jack the Bear," Murray wrote, "I'm going to have to go on to novel #2 (it seems). I think it's that cross country jazz thing and I keep wanting to call it 'Black and Tan Fantasy' for some reason or other." Only several decades later, however, did *The Seven League Boots* take shape. The third of his Scooter novels, it was published in November 1995 by Pantheon Books. Murray made no emendations following publication. One obvious typographical error in the first edition ("togethePr") was corrected in the Vintage paperback edition published the following year. The text of the 1995 Pantheon edition is printed here, with the error corrected.

THE MAGIC KEYS

After the publication of *The Seven League Boots*, Murray did not know whether he would attempt a fourth volume, because he was working on other book projects and devoting much time and energy to the newly formed Jazz at Lincoln Center, which he had helped to found. Murray did not discuss or allude to the subject matter of *The Magic Keys* in interviews. Nonetheless, the novel was drafted by 2002 and was close to its finished form by late 2003. It was published by Pantheon Books in May 2005. Upon publication, the first chapter ran for several months as an excerpt on the website of *The New York Times Book Review*. A paperback edition was published by Vintage the following year. This volume prints the text of the 2005 Pantheon edition.

CONJUGATIONS AND REITERATIONS / OTHER POEMS

Murray began writing poetry in the 1950s but became more focused on it in the 1990s. A version of "Landscape with Figures," found among Murray's papers, may date from as early as the 1950s. An early version of "William Faulkner: Noun, Place, and Verb" seems to be the poem that Murray describes reading for Robert Penn Warren in 1969 in *South to a Very Old Place* (*Albert Murray: Collected Essays and Memoirs*, 213). Read at the twenty-fourth Faulkner and Yoknapatawpha Conference on July 29, 1997, in Oxford, Mississippi, the poem was first published in Donald M. Kartiganer and Ann J. Abadie, eds., *Faulkner at 100: Retrospect and Prospect* (Jackson: University Press of Mississippi, 2000), 245–47, and then in *The New Republic*, December 11, 2000, 35. Murray read "Private Stock" on the National Public Radio program *Jazz Set with Branford Marsalis* in October 2000 on an episode in honor of Thelonious Monk's birthday.

In November 2001, Pantheon Books published *Conjugations and Reiterations*, Murray's sole volume of poetry. The text of the Pantheon first edition, the only edition published in Murray's lifetime, contains the text printed here, with the use of lowercase for "u.s.a." throughout adopted for consistency, following a typescript in the Albert Murray Papers, housed on behalf of the Hutchins Center for African and African American Research in Houghton Library, Harvard University.

The previously unpublished poems collected in this volume were found in manuscript in Murray's notebooks (one entitled "Poetry Workbook") and on loose sheets of paper among his papers, and are now included in the Albert Murray Papers; they are housed on behalf of the Hutchins Center for African and African American Research in Houghton Library, Harvard University. The poem that begins "there were / fifty roads to town" is the oldest of the "Other Poems" and dates perhaps from the 1960s or 1970s. Some of the previously unpublished poems were written in the late 1990s through 2001, the time when most of the poems published in *Conjugations and Reiterations* were probably composed. Others were drafted after that book's publication. These poems were selected by the editors for inclusion in this volume and appear courtesy of Lewis P. Jones III, Murray's literary executor.

APPENDIX

The appendix includes Murray's first published work of fiction, "The Luzana Cholly Kick" (discussed above) as it appeared in *New World Writing* in 1953. It also includes the last work of fiction Murray composed, "Manifest Destiny U.S.A.," written in late 2004 and early 2005, which Murray never attempted to publish. It was imagined as part of a larger work, abandoned in 2005 after Murray became ill (see Chronology), focusing on the lives of the secondary characters in *Train Whistle Guitar*. "Manifest Destiny U.S.A." is the only portion of the project to be realized. It was drafted on a yellow legal pad and typed by Paul Devlin under Murray's supervision in 2004 and 2005. The typescript draft typed by Devlin contains the text printed here.

This volume presents the texts of the editions chosen as sources here but does not attempt to reproduce features of their typographic design. The texts are printed without alteration except for the changes previously discussed, some changes in headings, and the correction of typographical errors. Spelling, punctuation, and capitalization are often expressive features, and they are not altered, even when inconsistent or irregular. The following is a list of typographical errors corrected, cited by page and line number: 6.29, Stacey; 7.9, swing-porch; 13.15, lengends and would-be lengendary; 22.16 (and *passim*), aint; 23.20–21, Chickasaboque; 27.1, *Sidney,*; 27.4, *Muira*; 27.8–9, *Steve Ketchell*; 27.9, *Colmar,*; 54.2, whereever; 60.35 (and *passim*), *Dauphine*; 68.23, then not; 88.26, Spaulding; 97.11, Cholly,; 100.10, bootlegger,; 111.2, now his; 117.15, Ela; 131.40, nickles; 135.11, curd; 137.22, an't; 150.13, Spaulding; 160.37, grade-schools; 176.31, Wolf; 179.7, it; 189.15, manners Sarajean; 193.12, on on chain; 195.34, used to used to; 234.8, Payton; 237.23, rundown; 253.24, Clara, Smith; 255.28, Gipson; 258.29, want; 261.28, Greens; 280.6, Slapping'; 281.19, as also; 285.29, Stuart's; 288.36, man?"; 342.14, *Fashion*; 411.23, as it; 419.7, MacKinney; 422.29, tune; 442.32, Frederick; 474.20, Bules," The; 474.20, Mama"; 480.6, lettuce a; 507.36, seguing; 514.35, Skies," Tea; 529.29 (and *passim*), Gin's Alley; 556.10, *and*; 568.10, at yet; 568.37, earlier than (this change and others on 568–69 have been made so that the account of time zone differences is accurate); 570.10–11, Montpelier; 586.30, togethePr.; 605.28, *Fritzhugh*; 606.8, *Almanac*; 616.27, des; 638.12, Gater; 641.36, 643.17, left eye (change made based on description of the boxing injury at 640.24); 652.3–4, craftsman; 661.37, talking; 665.22–23, that the; 674.16, *Green*; 682.12, curiosity, So; 711.36, great; 736.4–5, find about; 737.32, you way; 737.36, came to; 754.19, service. I; 754.36, mind is *Plurabelle,*; 764.2, at few; 779.19 Près; 783.18, impresson; 792.22, La Guardia; 808.16 and 811.26, Payton; 872.5, Said I',; 909.7, over the in.

The map that appears on the endpapers is based on a map drawn by Albert Murray, in pencil, in the 1950s or 1960s, and is an approximate representation of the area where he grew up and which he represented in his fiction, encompassing the neighborhoods of Magazine Point ("Gasoline Point") and Plateau, northern sections of the city of Mobile, Alabama. Paul Devlin discovered the map among Murray's papers in 2015. Murray's map corresponds to an older version of *Train Whistle Guitar* than the published book, and possibly to "Jack the Bear" or "The Briarpatch" (see above). Some of the places that appear on the original map do not appear in the book, and some of the locations in the published version of the book are not indicated on the original map. The endpaper map was designed and redrawn by Donna G. Brown of the Library of America, with considerable input from Paul Devlin. It was checked against Murray's texts and against various maps. The map's features (including the oversized chinaberry tree) correspond closely to Murray's original map. Devlin shared Murray's original map (as a digital file) as part of a public lecture he gave at the Ben May Main Library branch of the Mobile Public Library on May 4, 2017 (sponsored by the Alabama Writers Hall of Fame and the Alabama Humanities Foundation). On this trip to Mobile Devlin also explored the parts of the neighborhood that remain residential in order to better understand the map's dimensions and to gain a sense of its distances at street level. The area between the AT&N and L&N railroads was rezoned for industrial use at some point between 1940 and 1969 (see *South to a Very Old Place* in *Albert Murray: Collected Essays and Memoirs*, The Library of America, pages 286–87).

Notes

In the notes below, the reference numbers denote page and line of this volume (line counts include headings, but not the rule lines). No note is made for material included in standard desk-reference books. Biblical quotations are keyed to the King James Version. Quotations from Shakespeare are keyed to G. Blakemore Evans, ed., *The Riverside Shakespeare* (Boston: Houghton Mifflin, 1974). For further biographical detail than is contained in the chronology, see Roberta S. Maguire, ed., *Conversations with Albert Murray* (Jackson: University Press of Mississippi, 1997); Albert Murray and John F. Callahan, eds., *Trading Twelves: The Selected Letters of Ralph Ellison and Albert Murray* (New York: Modern Library, 2000); and Paul Devlin, ed., *Murray Talks Music: Albert Murray on Jazz and Blues* (Minneapolis: University of Minnesota Press, 2016). The volume *Albert Murray and the Aesthetic Imagination of a Nation* (Tuscaloosa: University of Alabama Press, 2010), edited by Barbara A. Baker, collects essays, scholarly articles, interviews, and personal reminiscences, and includes works such as "King of Cats" (1996), a *New Yorker* profile by Henry Louis Gates, Jr.; "An Interview with Michele Murray," by Paul Devlin and Lauren Walsh; "Albert Murray and Visual Art," by Paul Devlin; "Albert Murray and Tuskegee Institute: Art as the Measure of Place," by Caroline Gebhard; "Wynton Marsalis on Albert Murray," by Roberta S. Maguire (2001); and "At the Bar and on the Avenue with My Pal Al Murray," by Sidney Offit. See also Robert G. O'Meally's Smithsonian Jazz Oral History Project interview with Murray (1994); Kurt Thometz's interview with Murray (c. 2001) for Thometz's "Private Library/The Well-Dressed Bibliophile" series at colophon.com; Brian Lamb's interview with Murray (1996) for C-SPAN's *Booknotes* program, available at booknotes.org; an untitled interview with Murray on William Faulkner (1997) in Donald M. Kartiganer and Anne J. Abadie, eds., *Faulkner at 100: Retrospect and Prospect* (Jackson: University Press of Mississippi, 2000); David A. Taylor, "Albert Murray's Magical Youth," in *Southern Cultures* 16.2 (Summer 2010); and "Art and Propaganda," an interview from 1978 by Henry Louis Gates, Jr. and Robert G. O'Meally, published in *The Paris Review* 219 (Winter 2016).

There is not an abundance of scholarship on Murray's fiction or on his poetry, but a few works to consider for further reading are Robert G. O'Meally's foreword to the 1989 Northeastern University Press edition of *Train Whistle Guitar*, Bernard W. Bell's chapter on Murray's fiction in his book *The Contemporary African American Novel: Its Folk Roots and Modern Literary Branches* (Amherst: University of Massachusetts Press, 2005), Michael Borshuk's chapter on *Train Whistle Guitar* in his book *Swinging the Vernacular: Jazz and African American Modernist Literature* (New York: Routledge, 2006), Emily Petermann's commentary on Murray's fiction in her book *The Musical Novel: Imitation of Musical Structure, Performance, and Reception in Contemporary Fiction* (Rochester, NY: Camden House, 2014), and two chapters in Paul Devlin's doctoral dissertation at Stony Brook University (2014). Murray's fiction has been discussed briefly in many scholarly books. At a symposium on Murray's work at Columbia University in 2016, several scholars shared works in progress on Murray's fiction.

Grateful acknowledgement is made to the Albert Murray Trust, Kevin Burke, Lee Daniels, Rosemary Devlin, Amy Gosdanian, Glenn Horowitz, Kristin Jones, Lewis P. Jones III, Donald Kartiganer, Erroll McDonald, Joel Wilson Motley III, David Murray, Michele Murray, Sidney Offit, Bernard Schwartz, Marial Iglesias Utset, and Abby Wolf for their assistance on this project.

TRAIN WHISTLE GUITAR

3.17 AT & N.] Alabama, Tennessee and Northern Railroad.

3.19 L & N] Louisville and Nashville Railroad.

3.28 Skin Game Jungle] Skin, sometimes called "Georgia Skin," was a popular card game among African Americans.

4.10–11 M & O . . . N] Mobile and Ohio Railroad; Gulf, Mobile and Ohio Railroad; and Gulf, Mobile and Northern Railroad.

5.16 *drink muddy water . . . hollow log.*] Cf. "I'd rather drink muddy water, sleep in a hollow log," phrase that appears in songs in the blues tradition and is based on a black vernacular expression. Also, see poem on p. 841 in this volume.

6.19 .32-20 on a .44 frame] A large-frame revolver chambered to fire .32-20 ammunition.

8.12 *fils*] French: son.

10.10 *Well tell the dy ya.*] "Hit the mark" or "hit the bull's-eye," according to Murray's note in his copy of *Train Whistle Guitar*. The phrase's origin is unclear. Ralph Ellison, in a 1952 letter in which he comments on an early version of the novel that became *Train Whistle Guitar*, asks Murray, "what the hell does 'tell the dya' mean?" (*Trading Twelves*, 27).

26.12–13 *Jack Johnson*] American boxer (1878–1946), the first African American heavyweight champion, 1908–15.

26.29 *Jim Jeffries*] American boxer (1875–1953), the heavyweight champion from 1899 to 1904. Touted as the "great white hope" when he fought Jack Johnson on July 4, 1910, he was defeated by a technical knockout in the fifteenth round.

26.36–27.1 *Tommy Burns . . . Australia*] Johnson defeated the Canadian boxer Tommy Burns (pseud. Noah Russo, 1881–1955) for the heavyweight title on December 26, 1908, in a widely publicized match in Sydney, Australia.

27.5 *Barney Oldfield*] Popular American auto racer (1878–1946) who set several speed records. Johnson challenged Oldfield to a race and lost two heats to him in Sheepshead Bay, Brooklyn, on October 25, 1910.

27.8–9 *Stanley Ketchel's front teeth*] Middleweight champion boxer Stanley Ketchel (1886–1910) was knocked out by Johnson in the twelfth round of a twenty-round exhibition match in Colma, California, on October 16, 1909. According to boxing lore (derived in part from Johnson's account of the match), Johnson knocked out Ketchel after the middleweight had knocked him down with a sneak punch, even though the men had agreed in advance to fight for the full twenty rounds. It was said that several of Ketchel's teeth were embedded in Johnson's glove after the devastating punch.

27.14–15 *John L. Sullivan's color line*] American heavyweight boxer (1858–1918), the last of the bare-knuckles prizefighting champions. Like other white boxers of his era, he refused to defend his championship titles against black challengers.

27.28 *Joe Bowman*] Major League pitcher (1910–1990) who played for the Philadelphia Phillies and Pittsburgh Pirates, among other teams.

27.31–32 *George Pipgras*] Major League pitcher (1899–1986) for the New York Yankees and the Boston Red Sox.

27.32–34 *the year the New York Yankees won the World Series . . . four straight games.*] 1927.

28.15–16 *"Sundown" or "Little White Lies" or "Precious Little Thing Called Love,"*] "At Sundown (When Love Is Calling Me Home)" (1927) and "Little White Lies" (1930), popular songs written by Walter Donaldson (1893–1947); "A Precious Little Thing Called Love" (1929), hit song written by Lou Davis (1881–1961) and J. Fred Coots (1897–1985).

28.28–29 *Brunswick stew.*] A thick stew of vegetables and meat, popular in the American South.

43.12–13 Seven League Boots] Magic items in folklore allowing the wearer to take strides of seven leagues (approximately twenty-one miles) at a time.

47.11 the fire next time] From a spiritual: "God gave Noah the rainbow sign, / No more water, the fire next time!"

49.2 bonjour come on tally voo] I.e., the French greeting *Bonjour, comment allez-vous*: "Hello, how are you."

49.3 sand meal killing my trees easy to Paree] Probably corresponding, roughly, to the French phrase for "it's a thousand kilometers to Paris."

49.3–4 donay me unbootay cornyak silver plate] I.e., *donnez-moi une bouteille de cognac s'il vous plait*: "give me a bottle of cognac please."

49.4–5 voo lay voo zig zig] Do you want to sleep with me.

49.9–10 Argonne Forest or the Hindenburg Line] The Argonne Forest in northeast France was the scene of intense fighting in World War I, especially during the American Meuse-Argonne offensive, September 26–November 11, 1918. American veterans referred to the Kriemhild Stellung, the main German defensive position in the Meuse-Argonne, as the Hindenburg Line.

49.39 German Luger] A 9mm semiautomatic pistol.

49.40 musette bag] A haversack.

50.9–10 Big Bertha . . . Chau-Chau automatic rifle] "Big Bertha" was the Allied name for the long-range artillery guns used by the Germans to shell Paris from a range of over seventy-five miles, March 23–August 12, 1918. The Chauchat was a French automatic rifle widely used by American soldiers in World War I.

50.23 old John Henry] Figure of African American folklore (perhaps based on a real person) and the hero of a ballad: a steel-driver who won a test of strength against a steam drill, but died from his exertions.

50.24 old John Hardy] The subject of a ballad with many variations, John Hardy (c. 1866–1894) killed a man in a dispute about a dice game or a woman in Eckman, West Virginia; he was convicted of the crime and executed.

50.26–27 Stagolee shot and killed Billy Lyons . . . famous trial.] The St. Louis underworld figure Lee Shelton (1865–1912), known as Stagolee (and several variations on the name), killed Billy Lyons in a saloon on Christmas night, 1895. After a first trial ended in a hung jury, he was convicted of second-degree murder in a second trial in 1897 and sentenced to twenty-five years in prison. A well-known song was composed about the episode, with variations spreading through African American communities and making their way into popular culture throughout the twentieth century. The scholar Lawrence W. Levine has called Stagolee "the most important and longest-lived bad man in black folklore." For a valuable history of the legend, song, and their iterations, see Levine's *Black Culture and Black Consciousness: Afro-American Folk Thought from Slavery to Freedom* (Oxford: Oxford University Press, 1977).

50.29–31 Robert Charles . . . homemade bullets.] In New Orleans on July 23, 1900, Robert Charles (1865–1900), sitting outside a doorway with another African American man, was shot at by one of three policemen who had accosted the men. Charles and the policeman then exchanged gunfire and both were wounded. Later, at Charles's home, he killed two of the policemen sent to arrest him before escaping. In riots over several days, white vigilantes killed black residents and destroyed their property; Charles himself, armed with a rifle and making his own ammunition out of lead pipe, holed up in a house on Saratoga Street, which was besieged by a large mob. Continuing to fight, he was fatally shot after the mob set fire to the building. His corpse was mutilated before being buried in an unmarked grave. See William Ivy Hair, *Carnival of Fury: Robert Charles and the New Orleans Race Riot of 1900* (Baton Rouge: Louisiana State University Press, 1976; updated edition, 2008).

50.33   Railroad Bill] Morris Slater (d. 1896), known as Railroad Bill, was an outlaw who traveled around the Gulf Coast, especially around Mobile, from 1893 to 1896. For a comprehensive article on his legend, see Burgin Mathews, "'Looking for Railroad Bill': On the Trail of an Alabama Badman," *Southern Cultures* 9.3 (Fall 2003): 66–88. See also Levine, *Black Culture and Black Consciousness.*

51.12–13   had caught old Pancho Villa . . . New Mexico] After supporters of the Mexican revolutionary military leader Pancho Villa (1878–1923) killed twenty-four Americans during a raid on Columbus, New Mexico, on March 9, 1916, a punitive expedition commanded by Brigadier General John J. Pershing entered Mexico on March 15, 1916. The unsuccessful nine-month campaign ended with Villa still at large. Villa was assassinated in 1923.

51.15–16   Jessie Willard . . . Havana that time!] American boxer Jess Willard (1881–1968) defeated Johnson for the heavyweight title in Havana, Cuba, on April 5, 1915.

51.20–22   married to a white woman . . . back in the USA] Johnson was hounded by the U.S. Department of Justice for possible violations of the Mann Act (1910), a law that prohibited travel across state lines with "any woman or girl for the purpose of prostitution or debauchery, or for any other immoral purpose." The department's first, unsuccessful attempt to prosecute the boxer under the act was based on Johnson's relationship with Lucille Cameron, a white woman whom Johnson married on December 4, 1912. The following year, after his personal life was intensely scrutinized by the department's Bureau of Investigation, Johnson was indicted and convicted by an all-white jury on seven counts of Mann Act violations. Fleeing the country, Johnson stayed abroad for seven years. Months after the match with Willard, Johnson sold a purported confession that claimed that he had thrown the fight in exchange for $50,000 and a promise to be able to return to the United States without having to serve time in prison. Johnson surrendered to U.S. officials in Tijuana in 1920 and served a yearlong sentence for his Mann Act convictions.

51.26–27   couldn't even stand up to Jack Dempsey] Willard lost his heavyweight title to Jack Dempsey (1895–1983) by a technical knockout in the third round of a match on July 4, 1919.

51.30   Sam Langford . . . Harry Wills] Langford (1883–1956), a Nova Scotia–born black boxer who fought professionally from 1902 to 1926 in several divisions, including heavyweight; Wills (1889–1958), known as "The

Black Panther," was three-time holder of the World Colored Heavyweight Championship.

53.2   Natchez Trace] An Indian trail later used by European explorers, pioneers, and bandits that runs six hundred miles from Nashville on the Cumberland River to Natchez on the Mississippi.

53.15   Jubilo] Variant of "jubilee."

53.20   walls of Jericho] In the Book of Joshua, the city of Jericho is besieged by the Israelites until the walls come tumbling down, whereupon Joshua curses the city (6:26).

53.27–28   *before I'd be a slave . . . grave*] From the spiritual "Oh Freedom."

54.20   James Otis] Massachusetts attorney, politician, and antislavery advocate (1725–1783) whose writings on taxation influenced the American Revolution.

56.7   Vardaman . . . Pitchfork Ben] James K. Vardaman (1861–1930), Democratic governor of Mississippi, 1904–8, and a U.S. senator, 1913–19; Benjamin Ryan Tillman (1847–1918), Democratic governor of South Carolina, 1890–94, and a senator, 1895–1918.

56.39   E. Berry Wall] American socialite, sportsman, and gambler (1860–1940).

62.4   what was left of the old *Clotilde*] The *Clotilda* (often spelled *Clotilde* in older sources) was the last ship on record to have transported enslaved Africans to the United States; its captain fearing prosecution under federal law, it was burned and sunk shortly after its arrival in Mobile Bay in 1860 (long thought to be 1859). Many descendants of its passengers lived in Plateau, the neighborhood adjacent to Murray's neighborhood, Magazine Point. Cudjo Lewis, a leader of the group and its last survivor, died in 1935 at approximately eighty-eight years old. The definitive source on the *Clotilda* and the descendants of its captive passengers is Sylviane Diouf, *Dreams of Africa in Alabama: The Slave Ship Clotilda and the Story of the Last Africans Brought to America* (Oxford: Oxford University Press, 2007). Diouf cites several historical sources attesting to the visibility of the ship's hull in the period when *Train Whistle Guitar* takes place.

65.4   the dozens] Ritualized insults and inventive rhetorical dueling, practiced for sport in African American communities. See Levine, *Black Culture and Black Consciousness*; Henry Louis Gates, Jr., *The Signifying Monkey: A Theory of African American Literary Criticism* (New York: Oxford University Press, 1988); and Elijah Wald, *The Dozens: A History of Rap's Mama* (New York: Oxford University Press, 2012).

67.3–4   manger . . . swattling clothes.] Cf. Luke 2:12.

67.9   Vanity of vanity all is vanity.] Cf. Ecclesiastes 1:2.

67.10–11   man born of a woman . . . trouble.] Cf. Job 14:1.

71.9–10   go to Heaven . . . Elijah] In 2 Kings 2, Elijah is taken up to heaven in a whirlwind.

72.15–16   Katzenjammer Kids] Long-running comic strip by Rudolph Dirks (1877–1968) first published in 1897.

72.20   Maggie and Jiggs] The two main characters of *Bringing Up Father*, comic strip created by George McManus (1884?–1954) that ran from 1913 to 2000.

72.20–21   Mutt and Jeff] Daily comic strip created in 1907 by Bud Fisher (1885–1954).

76.21   "Nearer My God to Thee."] Hymn (1841), with words by the English poet Sarah Fuller Adams (1805–1848); the musical setting referred to here is by the American composer Lowell Mason (1792–1872).

76.29   original Bad Man Stagolee] See note 50.26–27.

77.6   king of the signifying monkeys] The signifying monkey is a trickster figure in folklores of the African diaspora. See Gates, *The Signifying Monkey*.

86.33–34   Pig Alley which was in Paris, France] Place Pigalle in Paris.

88.26   Reach and Spalding guide books] Annual guides for the American and National Leagues in professional baseball, respectively, named for the businessmen Alfred J. Reach (1840–1928) and A. G. Spalding (1849–1915).

89.1   Brunswick stew] See note 28.28–29.

96.17–18   "Ain't She Sweet," . . . "My Blue Heaven,"] Popular songs: "Ain't She Sweet" (1927), with music by Milton Ager (1893–1979) and words by his frequent collaborator, lyricist Jack Yellem (1892–1991); "Three Little Words" (1930) by the songwriting team of Bert Kalmar (1884–1947) and Harry Ruby (1895–1974); "Jeannine, I Dream of Lilac Time" (1928), music by Nathaniel Shilkret (1889–1982), lyrics by L. Wolfe Gilbert (1886–1970); "My Blue Heaven" (1927), music by Walter Donaldson, lyrics by George A. Whiting (1884–1943).

96.19–20   "Sundown," . . . "Love,"] See note 28.15–16.

96.20–21   "Dream a Little Dream of Me"] Popular song (1931), music by Wilbur Schwandt (1904–1998) and Fabian Andre (1910–1960), lyrics by Gus Kahn (1886–1941).

96.36   "I'll See You in My Dreams"] Song (1924) by Chicago bandleader Isham Jones (1894–1956), words by Gus Kahn.

123.28   "Kansas City Stomp"] First recorded by the pianist and composer Jelly Roll Morton (1890–1941) with his band the Red Hot Peppers in 1923.

123.37   "How Come You Do Me Like You Do."] Song (1924) written by the singer and songwriter Gene Austin (1900–1972) and Roy Bergere (1899–1969).

124.1   "Ja-Da"] "Ja-Da (Ja Da, Ja Da, Jing, Jing, Jing!)" (1918), song written by the pianist Bob Carleton (c. 1894–1956).

124.1–2   You got to . . . at all.] From "You've Got to See Mamma Every Night (Or You Can't See Mama at All)" (1923), music by Con Conrad (1891–1938), words by the theater producer and lyricist Billy Rose (1899–1966).

129.25   "Squeeze Me."] Song (1925) with music by the jazz pianist and composer Thomas "Fats" Waller (1904–1943), words by the pianist and bandleader Clarence Williams (1893–1965), though Andy Razaf (1895–1973) also claimed authorship.

130.25   "Everlasting Arms,"] "Leaning on the Everlasting Arms" (1887), hymn with music by Anthony J. Showalter (1858–1924), words by Showalter and Elisha Hoffman (1839–1929).

130.26   "Get Right With God"] Hymn (1910) by Eliza E. Hewitt (1851–1920).

130.27–28   "The Blood Done Sign My Name,"] A spiritual.

131.11   Ship of Zion] "Old Ship of Zion" is an African American spiritual.

133.28   Poll Tax] A fixed tax levied on every person within a jurisdiction. In the South after Reconstruction, the payment of a poll tax was often made a requirement for voting as a means of disfranchising African Americans and, in some cases, poor whites. The ratification of the Twenty-fourth Amendment in 1964 made it unconstitutional to impose poll taxes in federal elections; the levying of poll taxes in state and local elections was deemed a violation of the Fourteenth Amendment's Equal Protection Clause by the U.S. Supreme Court in *Harper v. Virginia Board of Elections* (1966).

THE SPYGLASS TREE

148.27   the "talented tenth,"] Title and central idea of a 1903 essay by W.E.B. Du Bois (1868–1963): "The Negro race, like all races, is going to be saved by its exceptional men. The problem of education, then, among Negroes must first of all deal with the Talented Tenth."

149.16   *Nettie Queen riverboat*] The *Nettie Quill* was a steamboat in operation from 1880 to 1909, mostly on the Mobile and Alabama Rivers.

153.6–7   legendary Buffalo Soldiers from the old Tenth Cavalry Regiment] The Ninth and Tenth Cavalry Regiments were segregated African American regiments deployed by the U.S. Army in the post–Civil War West, and later in the Spanish-American War.

153.11   Jack Johnson] See note 26.12–13.

153.18   *Pittsburgh Courier* and the *Chicago Defender*] African American newspapers.

153.20   Joe Gans] African American boxer (1874–1910), lightweight champion, 1902–4 and 1906–8.

153.29–30 "Sleepy Time Down South"] "When It's Sleepy Time Down South" (1931), song written by the actor and composer Clarence Muse (1889–1979), Leon René (1902–1982), and Otis René (1898–1970); it was often recorded and performed by Louis Armstrong.

153.30 "(Up a) Lazy River"] Song (1931) by the composer and pianist Hoagy Carmichael (1899–1981) and the clarinetist Sidney Arodin (1901–1948).

169.33 old *Clotilde* in August of 1859.] See note 62.4.

170.21–22 Teddy Roosevelt's Rough Riders?] The 1st U.S. Volunteer Cavalry, led by future president Theodore Roosevelt (1858–1919), whose exploits at the Battle of San Juan Hill in Cuba, July 1, 1898, made them national heroes during the Spanish-American War.

170.23 the Tenth] See note 153.6–7.

170.34 AEF] American Expeditionary Force: the armed forces of the United States in Europe during World War I.

176.31 Nero Wolfe] Fictional detective created by Rex Stout (1886–1975), who appears in many novels and short stories beginning with *Fer-de-Lance* (1934).

176.36 Benvenuto Cellini] Italian painter, goldsmith, sculptor, and writer (1500–1571).

179.17 Ethel Waters] African American singer and actor (1896–1977).

190.17 *Josephine Baker*] African American dancer, singer, and actor (1906–1975) who was enormously popular in France, where she spent most of her career.

195.9 Ma Rainey] African American blues singer and entrepreneur (1886–1939). For Murray's meeting with her, see *South to a Very Old Place* in this book's companion volume, *Albert Murray: Essays and Memoirs*, 223–24.

202.13–14 William S. Hart . . . Ken Maynard] Stars of movie Westerns in the silent and early sound eras: William S. Hart (1870–1946), Tom Mix (1880–1940), Buck Jones (1891–1942), and Ken Maynard (1895–1973).

202.15 crooks like Bull Montana] Italian-born wrestler and movie actor (1897–1950) whose films included *When the Clouds Roll By* (1919) and *The Lost World* (1925).

204.10 Battle of Horseshoe Bend.] The defeat of the Creek Indians by U.S. forces led by Andrew Jackson, March 27, 1814.

210.26 "High Society"] Ragtime composition (1901) by Yale undergraduate Porter Steele (1880–1966) that in adapted form became part of the repertoire of New Orleans jazz ensembles.

211.14 three princes of Serendip] Persian fairy tale first known in the West through a sixteenth-century Italian translation; after reading the story, the

English writer and politician Horace Walpole (1717–1797) coined the word "serendipity." "Serendip" refers to present-day Sri Lanka.

212.30–31   *"Precious Little Thing Called Love"*] See note 28.15–16.

213.29–30   *"Cake Walking Babies from Home," . . . record*] Clarence Williams's ensemble made two recordings of this composition (written by Williams, Chris Smith, and Henry Troy) weeks apart in late 1924 and early 1925. The singer Eva Taylor (stage name of Irene Gibbons, 1895–1977), Williams's wife, appears only on the second recording.

213.37–38   *"Sugar Foot Stomp" and "Royal Garden Blues"*] 1925 arrangement of trumpeter and bandleader King Oliver's (1885–1938) "Dippermouth Blues" for Fletcher Henderson's (1897–1952) orchestra; song (1919) written by Clarence Williams and Spencer Williams (1889–1969).

214.10   *"Kansas City Stomp"*] See note 123.28.

214.12–13   *Duke Ellington's "Birmingham Breakdown" . . . his "Cotton Tail"*] Compositions by the jazz composer, bandleader, and pianist Duke Ellington (1899–1974) from 1926 and 1940, respectively.

236.31–33   Jack Johnson . . . Joe Gans] See notes 26.12–13 and 153.20.

238.23   Jimmie Lunceford] Bandleader and saxophonist (1902–1947).

238.25–26   Sunset Royals] Florida-based band led by the trombonist Doc Wheeler (stage name of Wheeler Morin, 1910–2005).

238.30–31   "My Blue Heaven," . . . "Exactly Like You"] "My Blue Heaven," see note 96.17–18; "I Can't Believe That You're in Love with Me" (1926), song written by Clarence Gaskill (1892–1948) and Jimmy McHugh (1894–1969); "Exactly Like You" (1930), song written by McHugh and Dorothy Fields (1905–1974).

238.39   "At Sundown,"] See note 28.15–16.

250.13   Paul Bascombe was to record] In a 1940 recording, Paul Bascombe (1912–1986) played saxophone with the band led by Erskine Hawkins (1914–1993), which had been called the 'Bama State Collegians during the 1930s.

250.25–26   Ma Rainey . . . Trixie?] Ma Rainey, see note 195.9; the blues singers Bessie Smith (1894–1937), Clara Smith (c. 1894–1935), Mamie Smith (1883–1946), and Trixie Smith (1895–1943).

250.26–27   Jelly Roll . . . young Satch] Jelly Roll Morton, see note 123.28; the cornetist and bandleader Joe "King" Oliver (1881–1938); the saxophonist and clarinetist Sidney Bechet (1897–1959); the cornetist Freddie Keppard (1889–1933); Satchmo, Louis Armstrong.

251.34   "Cavernism"] Composition (1933) by Jimmy Mundy (1907–1983), saxophone player and arranger for the band led by the pianist Earl Hines (1903–1983).

252.8–9 "Echoes of Harlem"] Composition (1936) by Duke Ellington.

252.9–10 Count Basie's "Moten Swing"] 1940 recording by the Count Basie Orchestra of a piece that originated with Bennie Moten and His Kansas City Orchestra, on which Basie played piano.

252.30–31 Fletcher Henderson playing "The Stampede."] On a recording made in 1926. "Big John's Special" (252.34), written by Henderson's brother Horace (1904–1988), was first recorded in 1934, as was Fletcher Henderson's composition "Wrapping It Up" (252.35).

252.39 "Back in Your Own Back Yard" . . . "Sing You Sinners,"] "Back in Your Own Back Yard" (1928), song written by Dave Dreyer (1894–1967) and Billy Rose, first sung by Al Jolson (1886–1950); Jelly Roll Morton's "King Porter Stomp" (c. 1905); Fletcher Henderson's "Stealing Apples" (1936); "Blue Lou" (1935), words and music by Irving Mills (1894–1985) and Edgar M. Sampson (1907–1973), recorded by Henderson in 1936; "Sing You Sinners" (1930), music by W. Franke Harling (1887–1958), words by Sam Coslow (1902–1982).

253.1 Bessie Smith's recording of "Moan You Mourners,"] From 1930; the song, in the style of a spiritual, was written by Spencer Williams.

253.20 Buster Bailey] Clarinetist and saxophone player (1902–1967).

255.27 Peter Jackson] Boxer (1861–1901) originally from the West Indies who moved to Australia and won the Australian heavyweight championship in 1886. For Gans and Langford, see notes 153.20 and 51.30.

255.28–29 Satchel Paige . . . Bell] Negro Leagues baseball stars: the pitcher Leroy Robert (Satchel) Paige (1906–1982), the catcher Josh Gibson (1911–1947), the first baseman Walter (Buck) Leonard (1907–1997), and the outfielder James (Cool Papa) Bell (1903–1991).

255.29 Bojangles Robinson] Tap dancer and vaudeville performer (1878–1949).

255.30 Bert Williams] Vaudeville comedian and recording star (1874–1922).

257.34 RFD] Rural Free Delivery, a postal-service acronym.

261.29–30 Reach and Spalding baseball guides] See note 88.26.

263.3–4 Just look at what they did to *Uncle Tom's Cabin*.] The stage adaptations of Harriet Beecher Stowe's novel *Uncle Tom's Cabin* (1852) often adopted aspects of minstrelsy. For more on the development of these stage versions, see the chapter "Tom Everywhere" in David S. Reynolds, *Mightier Than the Sword: Uncle Tom's Cabin and the Battle for America* (New York: Norton, 2011).

269.25 Jacques Callot] French artist (c. 1592–1635) celebrated for his prints, for which he would make numerous preparatory drawings.

269.32–33   blue and rose period Harlequin] Pablo Picasso painted the subject of Harlequin in both his pre-Cubist "blue" (1901–4) and "rose" (1904–6) periods.

271.29   T. S. Stribling] Tennessee-born writer (1881–1965), author of *Birthright* (1921) and winner of the 1933 Pulitzer Prize for *The Store*.

271.29–30   Erskine Caldwell] Prolific writer (1903–1987) best known for *Tobacco Road* (1932), a novel about Georgia tenant farmers.

271.33–35   Hercule Poirot . . . Wolfe] Fictional detectives created by, respectively, Agatha Christie (1890–1976) and Sapper (pseud. H. C. McNeile, 1888–1937); Ellery Queen, joint pseudonym of crime writers Fredric Dannay (1905–1982) and Manfred Bennington Lee (1905–1971); Sam Spade, detective who appears in *The Maltese Falcon* (1930) and stories by Dashiell Hammett (1894–1961); Nero Wolfe, see note 176.31.

272.2–3   *The Conquerors* and *The Royal Way.*] Novels published in 1928 and 1930, respectively, by the French writer André Malraux (1901–1976).

276.11–12   *No Pygmalion I and no Galatea she.*] In Greek myth, Pygmalion creates an ivory sculpture of a beautiful woman known as Galatea and falls in love with her; she comes to life.

276.12–14   *Herr Doktor Faustus and his snake-oil princess*] In German legend, the scholar Faustus, unsatisfied with mortal beauty, summons Helen from the underworld. The Faust story was the basis for Christopher Marlowe's *The Tragical History of Doctor Faustus* (1589–92) and Goethe's *Faust* (1808–32).

277.38   *The moving finger having writ moves on.*] Cf. Rubái 545 in *The Rubáiyát of Omar Khayyám*, translated (1859) from the eleventh-century Persian by Edward FitzGerald (1809–1883): "the moving finger writes; and, having writ, moves on."

279.37   Cootie Williams] Jazz trumpeter (1911–1985) who joined Duke Ellington's orchestra in 1928.

280.25   Never is to be no CPT for me] Widely employed abbreviation for African American slang phrase "colored people's time," which means a relaxed approach to punctuality. Often used ironically or sarcastically.

282.26   Consarn] Expletive used in place of and so as not to say "god damn."

290.1–20   *remember that time when a bunch of them Old Ku Kluxers . . . Let's get the hell out of here.*] Members of the Ku Klux Klan marched through the town of Tuskegee and on the road that runs through the campus of Tuskegee Institute on July 3, 1923. The march was meant to intimidate Tuskegee Institute's president, Robert Russa Moton, into abandoning plans to have the nation's first Veterans Hospital for African Americans (built for the most part on 316 acres donated by the Institute) staffed solely by African Americans. The Institute responded to the march by deploying its ROTC cadets, led by

Colonel William H. Wolcott, in strategic locations in preparation to defend the campus. African American volunteers from around the state also drove in to help. The Klan, upon seeing the Institute heavily defended, did not seek to engage the defenders, and went on to burn a cross on the outskirts of town. W.E.B. Du Bois, James Weldon Johnson, and Walter White (who spent the evening in Moton's home) all wrote about the incident. The most comprehensive account of the incident is Raymond Wolters, *The New Negro on Campus: Black College Rebellions of the 1920s* (Princeton, NJ: Princeton University Press, 1975), 167–91. See also Paul Devlin, "The Armed Defense of Tuskegee Institute in 1923 and Albert Murray's *The Spyglass Tree*," forthcoming in *African American Review* in 2018.

290.34 *Brownsville raid*] Incident in Brownsville, Texas, in August 1906 in which African American soldiers were blamed for the murder of a white man. One hundred sixty-seven soldiers were dishonorably discharged unfairly. They received honorable discharges (mostly posthumous) in 1972.

293.40 old James P's striding left hand.] Referring to the jazz pianist James P. Johnson (1894–1955), among the pioneers of stride piano playing, characterized by leaps in the left hand.

THE SEVEN LEAGUE BOOTS

312.1–3 The castle hill was hidden . . . castle was there.] The third sentence (with "Castle" capitalized) of Franz Kafka's the novel *The Castle* (1926), as translated by Willa and Edwin Muir (1930).

317.12–13 *Leadbelly . . . Robert Johnson*] Blues singers, guitar players, and songwriters: Leadbelly, as Huddie William Ledbetter (1888–1949) is widely known; Blind Lemon Jefferson (1893–1929); Big Bill Broonzy (1893–1958); and Robert Johnson (1911–1938).

322.24 *Art Tatum's*] Jazz pianist Art Tatum (1909–1956); see also note 293.40.

323.33–34 Sonny Greer . . . Jo Jones.] Jazz drummers: Greer (1903–1982) played from the 1920s through 1951 with Duke Ellington; Murray met Jo Jones (1911–1985) around 1950 and went on to do extensive taped interviews with him for an autobiography, which were edited by Paul Devlin into *Rifftide: The Life and Opinions of Papa Jo Jones* (Minneapolis: University of Minnesota Press, 2011). Incidentally, several commentators (Gary Giddins, for instance) have noted similarities between Joe States and Jo Jones. For a Murray-Ellison exchange on Jones, see *Trading Twelves*, 97–98, 100–101.

328.39 *The Sea Beast*] Silent film (1926) starring John Barrymore (1882–1942), a loose adaptation of Herman Melville's *Moby-Dick*.

329.9 Vitaphone] A patented process for synchronizing sound with images, developed by Western Electric in 1925.

329.19–20 swallows . . . Capistrano] Referring to the popular song "When the Swallows Come Back to Capistrano" (1940), written by Leon René.

333.19–20 *Bessie and all the rest of them red hot Smith mamas.*] See note 250.25–26.

335.2 *Chansons de Geste*] Heroic poems of medieval France.

339.23 "Alabamy Bound"] Popular song (1925), music by Ray Henderson (1896–1970), lyrics by Buddy DeSylva (1895–1950) and Bud Green (1897–1981).

339.23–24 "Banjo on My Knee"] "Oh! Susanna" (1848), song by Stephen Foster (1826–1864), with its repeated line "I come from Alabama with my banjo on my knee."

340.25 "Stardust."] Song (1927) by Hoagy Carmichael, first recorded as an instrumental; Mitchell Parrish (1900–1993) added lyrics in 1929.

341.20–21 old stride time piano sharks . . . Johnson] Jazz pianists and composers Willie "the Lion" Smith (1897–1973) and Luckey Roberts (1887–1968); Johnson, see note 293.40.

341.23 Cook . . . Burleigh] African American composers who wrote classical music: Will Marion Cook (1869–1944), also a violinist and a mentor to Duke Ellington (see also p. 437 in this volume); Harry T. Burleigh (1866–1949), also a singer, who became known for his arrangements of spirituals.

343.29 *Clarence Cameron White, and R. Nathaniel Dett*] Classical African American composers: Clarence Cameron White (1880–1960), also a violinist; Robert Nathaniel Dett (1882–1943), also a conductor and the musical director of the Hampton Institute. See also p. 433 in this volume. For Murray's involvement with Dett's music, see Chronology, 1931–35.

346.17–19 9th and 10th Cavalry . . . 24th Infantry] See note 153.6–7. The 24th Infantry was an African American infantry regiment organized after the Civil War; like the cavalry regiments, it was deployed in the West and in Cuba during the Spanish-American War.

346.29 settlement] Idiomatic term for African American neighborhood.

354.16–17 Ernest Hogan] Stage performer and composer (1860?–1909), who starred in Will Marion Cook and Paul Laurence Dunbar's musical *The Origin of the Cake; or, Clarindy* (1898), among many other roles.

354.17 Williams and Walker] Bert Williams (1876?–1922) and George Walker (d. 1911), vaudeville comedy team whose vehicles included *The Gold Bug* (1896), *In Dahomey* (1903), and *Abyssinia* (1906).

354.17 Miller and Lyles] Vaudeville comedy duo of Flournoy Miller (1885–1971) and Aubrey Lyles (1884–1932), authors of the book for the musical *Shuffle Along* (1921) and members of the show's cast.

354.17–18   Slow Kid Thompson] Ulysses "Slow Kid" Thompson (1888–1990), dancer and performer, a member of the cast of *Shuffle Along* and one half of a successful husband-and-wife duo with his second wife, Florence Mills (1896–1927).

354.18   King Rastus Brown] Tap dancer (fl. c. 1903–1920s).

354.18   Bojangles] Bill "Bojangles" Robinson (1878–1949), tap dancer and performer in vaudeville and in Broadway productions such as *Blackbirds of 1928* (1928) and *The Hot Mikado* (1939), as well as in movies.

355.40   Irving Mills . . . Joe Glaser.] Music impresario, publisher, and lyricist Irving Mills, who managed Duke Ellington's band in the 1920s and 1930s; manager Joe Glaser (1896–1969), who represented many prominent jazz musicians.

356.13–14   Jack Johnson . . . Wills] See notes 26.12–13, 153.20, and 51.30.

356.16   Rube Foster] Dominant right-handed pitcher (1879–1930) in black baseball, later a manager and Negro National League founder and executive; for Paige and Gibson, see note 255.28–29.

357.8–10   Cab Calloway . . . in a revue tune called "Underneath the Harlem Moon,"] Cab Calloway (1907–1994) was a jazz singer, songwriter, and bandleader. From the revue *Fast and Furious* (1931), written by Mack Gordon (1904–1959), which trafficked in stereotypes.

357.11–12   Alain Locke's book *The New Negro* . . . Harlem Renaissance.] In the introduction to the essay collection *The New Negro* (1925), an important book in what would later be called the Harlem Renaissance, the writer and philosopher Alain Locke (1885–1954) identified "prophetic" Harlem as the place where "Negro life is seizing upon its first chances for group expression and self-determination."

363.37   Will Vodery and Ford Dabney] Will Vodery (1885–1951) was a conductor, composer, and arranger, well-known for his work with the *Ziegfeld Follies*. Ford Dabney (1883–1958) was a conductor and composer.

364.1–2   J. Rosamond and James Weldon Johnson's "Lift Every Voice"] Musical setting (1905) by J. Rosamond Johnson (1873–1954) of his brother James Weldon Johnson's (1871–1938) poem "Lift Ev'ry Voice and Sing" (1899), which came to be known as the "Negro National Anthem." For Murray's explanation of the song's influence and importance, see *South to a Very Old Place* (*Albert Murray: Essays and Memoirs*, 250).

364.5–7   "Sweet and Low," . . . Sunrise."] "Sweet and Low" (1863), musical setting by Joseph Barnby (1838–1896) of a poem by Alfred, Lord Tennyson; "East of the Sun (and West of the Moon)" (1934), song written by the Princeton undergraduate Brooks Bowman (1913–1937); "California, Here I Come" (1921), song by Buddy DeSylva and Joseph Meyer (1894–1987), sung by Al Jolson in the musical *Bombo*; "Avalon" (1920), song by Al Jolson, Buddy DeSylva, and Vincent Rose (1880–1944); "The World Is Waiting for the Sunrise" (1918), music by Ernest Seitz (1892–1978), words by Gene Lockhart (1891–1957).

367.1 Br'er Rabbit] Trickster character in folklore popularized in *Uncle Remus, His Songs and Sayings: The Folklore of the Old Plantation* (1880) by Joel Chandler Harris (1848–1908).

368.27–28 *Chickamauga Thomas*] Union Major General George Henry Thomas (1816–1870), called "The Rock of Chickamauga" because of the defense he mounted in the Civil War battle fought near Chickamauga Creek in northwestern Georgia, September 19–20, 1863, a Confederate victory.

368.37–38 *Fare-thee-well, land of cotton, jump for joy.*] Cf. Duke Ellington's "Jump for Joy" (1941), the lyrics to which begin "Fare thee well, land of cotton / Cotton lisle is out of style, honey child / Jump for joy."

369.18 *Seesesh*] Slang for secession.

369.30–31 *Nathan Bedford Forrest*] Confederate brigadier general (1821–1877), cavalry division commander in the Army of Tennessee.

375.17 Unka Remus] Uncle Remus, see note 367.1.

380.35 TJ] Tijuana.

381.19 "9:20 Special"] Jazz composition (1941) by Earle Warren (1914–1994), who played saxophone with Count Basie; it was recorded by Count Basie and his Orchestra in 1941.

392.6 Gaston Lachaise] French-born American sculptor (1882–1935), best known for his large bronze sculptures of broad-hipped, voluptuous women.

392.30–31 That's my name for myself after dark] Morgana is the name of a sorceress in medieval Arthurian romances.

393.17–18 *A sunkissed missy don't be late.*] Cf. a line from the refrain of "California, Here I Come": "A sun-kissed miss said, 'Don't be late.'"

395.34–35 August Belmont . . . Fisk] American financiers: August Belmont (1813–1890); James Buchanan Brady (1856–1917), famous for his vast appetite and lavish lifestyle; James Fisk, Jr. (1834–1872), partner of Jay Gould, murdered by a business associate and rival for the affections of his mistress.

397.30–31 7000 Santa Monica Boulevard] Address of famed recording studio Radio Recorders, used by many prominent musicians from the 1940s through the 2000s. Duke Ellington allowed Murray to photograph his orchestra's recording session there on June 20, 1960. Some of these photographs appear in *Murray Talks Music: Albert Murray on Jazz and Blues*.

398.23 a jive quotation from the signifying monkey.] See note 77.6.

399.26 a poem] "The Emperor of Ice-Cream" (1923) by Wallace Stevens (1879–1955).

406.1–3 *All I wanted to know . . . what it was all about.*] From Ernest Hemingway's *The Sun Also Rises* (1926), ch. 14. In this passage Jake Barnes, the novel's narrator and protagonist, is not in Paris but Pamplona.

417.17 *Karamu Playhouse*] Theater in Cleveland, Ohio, well-known for staging plays by African American writers.

419.5–7 Ethel Waters . . . McKinney.] Ethel Waters, see note 179.17; Adelaide Hall (1901–1993), singer, dancer, and actor who performed in Harlem and on Broadway before spending most of her later career in England; jazz trumpeter, singer, dancer, and actor Valaida Snow (1904–1956); Nina Mae McKinney (1912–1967), stage and film actor, singer, and dancer.

421.24 Hotel Theresa] Thirteen-floor Harlem hotel (1912–67) that was the preferred choice of black celebrities in the 1940s and 1950s.

422.29 Horace's jump tunes] "Big John's Special" (1934) by Horace Henderson.

424.6 *Commodious vicus of recirculation*] From the first sentence of James Joyce's novel *Finnegans Wake* (1939).

425.1–2 after graduating from the Yale School of Architecture.] These notes have generally refrained from speculation about Murray's characters being modeled on his friends and associates, but here the noting of an obscure source may elucidate this aspect of the story and shed light on Murray's method. Murray based Thomas Jerome Jefferson largely on his Tuskegee classmate John Gerald "Jug" Hamilton, whom he writes about in *South to a Very Old Place* (*Albert Murray: Essays and Memoirs*, 260–61, 263–71, and elsewhere); Hamilton, who was acquainted with Ralph Ellison as well, appears in the historical record only through Murray's and Ellison's writings. The decision to make Thomas Jerome Jefferson into an architect may have another inspiration, namely Murray's friendship with the African American architect William Emmett Coleman, Jr. (1922–1987), whom Murray met, most likely, during World War II at Tuskegee, when they both were stationed there. Coleman transferred to Yale after two years at the University of Illinois, and graduated from the Yale School of Architecture in 1947. He soon settled in Paris and remained in France for the rest of his life. All that survives of the Murray-Coleman friendship is a long letter from Coleman to Murray, sent from Paris and dated November 20, 1948.

426.9–10 A Study in Scarlet, The Sign of Four] The first two of Arthur Conan Doyle's Sherlock Holmes novels, published in 1887 and 1890, respectively.

426.11–12 Sticks and Stones, The Golden Day] Two books (1924, 1926) by the American social and architecture critic Lewis Mumford (1895–1990).

427.37 *Earl Hines*] See note 251.34.

429.26–27 Emerson . . . infinite time,"] In his essay "The Poet," collected in *Essays: Second Series* (1844).

429.34–39 Walt Whitman . . . gentle wires."] From the opening of Whitman's "Passage to India" (1870).

430.21 *three princes of Serendip*] See note 211.14.

431.34–35 Augustus Saint-Gaudens Civil War memorial] A bronze relief sculpture (1897) by the Irish-born American artist Augustus Saint-Gaudens (1848–1907) honoring Robert Gould Shaw (1837–1863) and the African American men of the 54th Massachusetts Infantry under his command, installed across from the Massachusetts State House on Beacon Street in Boston.

435.22–23 *"let down your bucket where you are,"*] See Booker T. Washington's speech at the Atlanta Exposition in 1895: "To those of my race who depend upon bettering their condition in a foreign land, or who underestimate the importance of cultivating friendly relations with the Southern white man who is their next-door neighbor, I would say: 'Cast down your bucket where you are'—cast it down in making friends, in every manly way, of the people of all races by whom we are surrounded."

435.37–38 *prospering in proportion . . . occupations of life.*] Nearly verbatim quotation of a passage from Washington's Atlanta Exposition address, which was carved into the stone bench encircling the statue of Washington later erected at Tuskegee University.

438.27–28 Chacun selon sa faim . . . selon son goût.] Each according to his hunger, and after, perhaps, according to his taste.

439.5–6 *Erskine Hawkins . . . Collegians*] See note 250.13.

439.30 *pigfoot and a bottle . . . beer.*] Reference to "Gimme a Pigfoot and a Bottle of Beer," song by Wesley Wilson (1893–1958) that was recorded and popularized by Bessie Smith in 1933.

442.32 Frederic Remington] The painter, sculptor, and illustrator Frederic Remington (1861–1909), known for his western subjects.

444.39–40 *"My mother . . . begetting?"*] Translation by T. E. Lawrence (1932).

445.2 *the dozens*] See note 65.4.

450.20–21 what W. C. Handy calls a sidedoor Pullman car.] In "Yellow Dog Blues" (1915), by the Alabama-born musician and composer W. C. Handy (1873–1958). The phrase refers to a boxcar, comparing it ironically to the luxury Pullman car.

456.29 Paul Robeson] Stage and film actor, singer, and political activist (1898–1976).

463.7–8 "Royal Garden Blues"] See note 213.37–38.

469.29 *faites comme chez vous*] French: do as you would at home.

472.38 Musicians Local 627] Union of African American musicians founded in Kansas City in 1917, affiliated with the American Federation of Musicians.

472.38 Pete Johnson] Boogie-woogie pianist (1904–1967).

473.2 Joe Turner] Big Joe Turner (1911–1985), vocalist who sang with Pete Johnson and Count Basie.

473.4 Mary Lou Williams] Pianist, bandleader, composer, and arranger (1910–1981).

473.5 Andy Kirk's] Bandleader and musician (1898–1992).

473.8 Jimmy Rushing] Vocalist (1901–1972) who rose to prominence singing with Count Basie in the 1930s and 1940s.

482.28–29 Henry James had called "the heiress of all the ages,"] In *The Wings of the Dove* (1902), James refers to its protagonist Milly Theale as "the potential heiress of all the ages."

482.36 Anna Livia Plurabelle] Female figure associated with the River Liffey in James Joyce's *Finnegans Wake* (1939).

483.36 *dernier cri.*] French: the latest fashion.

486.19–20 Daisy Miller] Titular heroine of the novel (1879) by Henry James (1843–1916).

488.14–15 TOBA showcase theaters] Theaters of the black vaudeville circuit. TOBA: Theatre Owners Booking Association.

488.25 so-called jubilee singers] Fisk University's Jubilee Singers, or vocal ensembles modeled on them. The Fisk singers gained fame performing spirituals in concert tours in the United States and Europe in the 1870s.

490.31–32 as Ernest Hemingway had done] In "Monologue to the Maestro: A High Seas Letter," published in *Esquire* in October 1935.

492.25 twelve tones.] Reference to twelve-tone composition, a system of atonality pioneered by the Austrian-born composer Arnold Schoenberg (1874–1951) that became the dominant compositional mode in twentieth-century classical music.

498.5–6 Will Marion Cook, Bob Cole . . . Vodery] Robert Cole (1868–1911), composer and musician who partnered with J. Rosamond Johnson and James Weldon Johnson, with whom he wrote musicals and songs such as "Under the Bamboo Tree" (1901); for the other composers and performers, see notes 341.23, 354.17, and 363.37.

498.22–23 stomp . . . even before the Savoy.] Reference to Edgar Sampson's 1934 composition "Stompin' at the Savoy," a jazz standard with lyrics later added by Andy Razaf. The Savoy Ballroom was a dance hall in Harlem.

501.7 *El hombre de época*] Spanish: "man of the epoch" or, as Murray wrote in his essay "The Function of the Heroic Image" (included in Robert G. O'Meally, ed., *The Jazz Cadence of American Culture*, 1998), "the representative man of the period," who displays "the symbolic conduct that is most adequate to the problems of our time."

501.11 José Ortega y Gasset] Spanish philosopher and social critic (1883–1955), author of *The Revolt of the Masses* (1929) and many other books.

507.1–2 *vicus of recirculation*] See note 424.6.

514.33–34 "All of Me," . . . Brown,"] "All of Me" (1931), written by Gerald Marks (1900–1997) and Seymour Simons (1896–1949); "Blue Skies" (1926), written by Irving Berlin (1888–1989); "Tea for Two," song from the musical *No, No, Nanette* (1925), with music by Vincent Youmans (1898–1946) and lyrics by Irving Caesar (1895–1996); "Sweet Georgia Brown" (1925), music by Maceo Pinkard (1897–1962) and Ben Bernie (1891–1943), words by Kenneth Casey (1899–1965).

516.27 James Scott] Ragtime composer and pianist (1885–1938).

519.6 "Dream a Little Dream of Me."] See note 96.20–21.

520.15–16 "Three Little Words."] Hit song (1930) by the songwriting team of Bert Kalmar (1884–1947) and Harry Ruby (1895–1974).

524.32–33 fay boys . . . boot cats] "Fay" (short for ofay) is slang for white person. "Boot" is slang for black person. See *Trading Twelves* (2000) for examples of contemporaneous use.

525.3 hincties] Snobs.

528.13–14 banana skirt . . . Folies Bergère.] To great renown, Josephine Baker (see note 190.17) wore a skirt made of rubber bananas in productions at Paris's Folies Bergère music hall in the mid-1920s.

535.13 like the Swanee River.] Referring to the vision of the South in songs like Stephen Foster's "Swanee River" (or "The Old Folks at Home") (1851).

537.37 Scarlet Creeper] Character in the novel *Nigger Heaven* (1926) by Carl Van Vechten (1880–1964), set in Harlem.

543.10 "Blossoms on Broadway,"] Title song of movie musical (1937) written by Gordon Jenkins (1910–1984).

554.10 notorious Hayes-Tilden Compromise of 1877] The contested 1876 presidential election between Democrat Samuel Tilden (1814–1886) and Republican Rutherford B. Hayes (1822–1893) was resolved via a compromise that awarded twenty disputed electoral votes to Hayes in exchange for the withdrawal of federal support for Republican state governments in the South, effectively ending Reconstruction.

557.19–20 Sam Wooding, and Spencer Williams] Jazz pianist and bandleader Sam Wooding (1895–1985), who performed widely in Europe in the 1920s and 1930s; stage, film, and television actor, director, and producer Spencer Williams, who served in France during World War I.

558.31–32 *over there . . . war songs*] "Over There" (1917), words and music by George M. Cohan (1878–1942), was a popular patriotic song during World War I.

559.6 voulez-vous *zig zig.*] See note 49.4–5.

559.9 *sand meal killing my trees easy to Paris*] See note 49.3.

560.11–12 *Helen Waddell's novel*] *Peter Abelard* (1933) by the Irish writer Helen Waddell (1889–1965).

560.33–34 *the book's epigraph*] Gertrude Stein's remark "You are all a lost generation."

560.35–36 *Gerald Murphy said living well is the best revenge*] F. Scott Fitzgerald recalled that his friend Gerald Murphy (1888–1964), an expatriate living on the French Riviera, told him he admired the Spanish proverb "Living well is the best revenge"; the maxim was the title of a 1962 *New Yorker* magazine profile of Murphy and his wife Sara, and later a book, by Calvin Tompkins.

561.8 mon semblable, mon frère.] From the final line of "To the Reader," prefatory poem in *Flowers of Evil* (1857) by the French poet Charles Baudelaire (1821–1867): "Hypocrite lecteur—mon semblable—mon frère!" ("Hypocrite reader—my likeness—my brother!").

561.15–18 *"a monk by convenience . . . exuberance."*] From the introduction by Jacques Leclerq (1898–1972) to his 1936 translation of *Gargantua and Pantagruel* (1532–52) by François Rabelais (1494–1553).

563.30 *the Talented Tenth.*] See note 148.27.

571.20 *Gallia . . . divisa.*] Latin: "Gaul into three parts [was] divided." From *Bellum Gallicum* by Julius Caesar.

573.34 *Night Fishing at Antibes*] Painting (1939) by Pablo Picasso.

573.40–574.1 Rock Skipping at the Blue Note.] Composition (1951) by Duke Ellington.

574.23 côte de veau de la crème] Veal chops in cream sauce.

575.10 *Joie de Vivre.*] Painting (1946) by Pablo Picasso.

580.27 *L'Homme au Mouton*] Sculpture (1943) by Pablo Picasso.

584.17–18 very rich are different . . . Hemingway's quip] See early version of Hemingway's *The Snows of Kilimanjaro* published in *Esquire*, August 1936: "He remembered poor Scott Fitzgerald and his romantic awe of [the rich] and how he had started a story once that began, 'The very rich are different from you and me.' And how someone had said to Scott, Yes, they have more money." The reference is to the third paragraph of Fitzgerald's "The Rich Boy" (1926). Murray mentions this exchange and offers significant commentary on it in his essay on Hemingway in *The Blue Devils of Nada* (*Albert Murray: Essays and Memoirs*, 704).

586.16–17 Max Reinhardt, Norman Bel Geddes, Jo Mielziner, and Lee Simonson] Max Reinhardt (1873–1943), internationally renowned Austrian theater producer and director; Norman Bel Geddes (1893–1958), American stage designer, industrial designer, and architect; Jo Mielziner (1901–1976), American stage designer renowned for his work on Broadway; Lee Simonson (1888–1967), American architect and stage designer.

588.38 Denys Finch-Hatton] Denys Finch Hatton (1887–1931), British aristocrat, game hunter, and prominent member of the expatriate community in Britain's Kenya colony; he was a lover of the Danish writer Karen Blixen (1885–1962), as depicted in her book *Out of Africa* (1937), published under the pen name Isak Dinesen.

590.20 as it says in the song] In "Soon (Maybe Not Tomorrow)," sung by Bing Crosby in the movie musical *Mississippi* (1935), music by Richard Rodgers (1902–1979), words by Lorenz Hart (1895–1943).

595.1 "Indiana" (Back Home Again in)] "(Back Home Again in) Indiana" (1917), music by James F. Hanley (1892–1942), music by Ballard MacDonald (1882–1935).

595.29 *Count Basie's radio broadcasts from the Famous Door*] CBS radio broadcast performances by Basie and his orchestra during their residencies at New York's Famous Door nightclub on 52nd Street in 1938 and 1939.

595.31 *Lester Young*] Saxophonist (1909–1959) whose legendary career as a jazz musician began with the Count Basie Orchestra; with Basie on piano, his Lester Young Quintet recorded "Indiana" in 1944.

596.2 *ineluctable down-home plus uptown modality*] Cf. James Joyce's *Ulysses* (1922), ch. 3, in which Stephen Dedalus thinks of the "ineluctable modality of the visible" and then the "ineluctable modality of the audible." For Anna Livia Plurabelle, see note 482.36.

597.24–25 "Please Don't Talk About Me (When I'm Gone)"] Popular song (1930), music by Sam H. Stept (1897–1964), words by Sidney Clare (1892–1972).

597.29–30 *Bien sure*] Deliberate distortion of *bien sûr*, French for "of course."

601.35 *tercios*] Spanish: thirds, referring to the three stages of a bullfight.

603.34 *as Thomas Mann put it, "life's delicate child"*] In *The Magic Mountain* (1924) by Thomas Mann (1875–1955), referring to its protagonist, Hans Castorp.

605.12 *le vrai lapin agile*] French: the true nimble rabbit, a reference to the Paris cabaret Au Lapin Agile.

605.21–23 *as Edna St. Vincent Millay declares in that poem . . . speaking.*] See the final lines of the sonnet beginning "I shall forget you presently, my dear" (1920) by Edna St. Vincent Millay (1892–1950): "Whether or not we find what we are seeking / Is idle, biologically speaking."

605.27–29 *Lord Raglan . . . his book about the origins of civilization*] *How Came Civilization?* (1939) by Fitzroy Richard Somerset, 4th Baron Raglan (1885–1964).

606.7–8 *Burke's Peerage* or the *Almanach de Gotha*] Guides to British and European aristocracy, respectively.

607.17 Mont St. Victoire] Mountain in Provence that Cézanne painted repeatedly.

608.12–16 "an ethnological purpose . . . endeavors."] From *Life and Times of Frederick Douglass* (1881, rev. ed. 1892).

612.37–613.12 Flaubert's famous remark . . . *ils sont dans le vrai*] "They are in the truth," remark attributed to the French novelist Gustave Flaubert (1821–1880) by his niece, Caroline Commanville, in her *Souvenirs sur Gustave Flaubert* (1893), after they had encountered the "honest and good" family of one of her friends.

613.18–23 *William Empson . . . refinement and elegance!*] In *Some Versions of Pastoral* (1935) by the English literary critic and poet William Empson (1906–1984).

613.26 "blisses of the commonplace"] In Thomas Mann's novella *Tonio Kröger* (1903), the title character writes that "there is a kind of artist so profoundly, so primordially fated to be an artist that no longing seems sweeter or more precious to him than his longing for the bliss of the commonplace." Mann referred to this phrase from *Tonio Kröger* when he wrote that Franz Kafka sought the "blisses of the commonplace" in his "Homage" to Kafka included in the English translation of *The Castle*.

617.31 kikis of Montparnasse] A reference to the artist's model, singer, artist, and writer Alice Prin (1901–1953), called "Kiki of Montparnasse"; she is perhaps best known from a work by her lover Man Ray (1890–1976), *Le Violon d'Ingres* (1924), in which her back is made to look like the body of a violin.

617.35–36 Belle Époque] 1871–1914.

618.28–29 Josephine Baker . . . Bechet] Black performers and entrepreneurs who flourished in Paris: Josephine Baker, see note 190.17; Bricktop, stage name of the dancer, singer, and Parisian nightclub owner Ada Louise Smith (1894–1984); Frisco, the pianist and entertainer Jocelyn Augustus Bingham, who owned nightclubs first in London, then in Paris; Spencer Williams and Sydney Bechet, see notes 557.19–20 and 250.26–27.

618.35 Yvette Guilbert, Jane Avril, and La Goulue] Yvette Guilbert (1865–1944), fashionable French cabaret singer and performer painted by Henri Toulouse-Lautrec, as were the French dancers Jane Avril (1868–1943) and Louise Weber (1866–1929), known as La Goulue (The Glutton).

619.5–6 Don Byas and Kenny Clarke.] The saxophonist Don Byas (1912–1972), who played with Count Basie and spent his later years in Europe; Kenny Clarke (1914–1985), drummer and a founding member of the Modern Jazz Quartet, who expatriated to France in the 1950s.

623.15 *Chacun selon . . . sa faim.*] See note 438.27–28.

THE MAGIC KEYS

658.13–14 Street Scene *score*] Score by the composer Alfred Newman (1900–1970) written for *Street Scene* (1931), film adaptation of the 1929 play about New York tenement life by Elmer Rice (1892–1967).

666.38–39 Maxwell Bodenheim] Poet and novelist (1893–1954) whose books of verse included *Minna and Myself* (1918) and *Introducing Irony* (1922).

666.39 Max Eastman] Poet and translator (1883–1969), editor of the socialist magazines *The Masses* and *The Liberator*, 1918–22.

670.15–21 the passage from *Remembrance of Things Past . . . view the world.*] Excerpt from a long statement made by the painter Elstir toward the end of part two ("Place-Names: The Place") of Marcel Proust's *Within a Budding Grove* (French title, *À l'ombre des jeunes filles en fleur*, "In the shadow of young girls in flower"), volume two of the six-volume novel *À la recherche du temps perdu* ("In search of lost time"), published in French in 1918 and in English in 1924. The title of the first English translation, by C. K. Scott Moncrieff, is *Remembrance of Things Past*. The title of the Moncrieff translation revised by Terrence Kilmartin (1981), revised further by D. J. Enright, and published by Modern Library (1992), is *In Search of Lost Time*. The quoted passage, which comes from this later translation, is highlighted in Murray's copy of the Modern Library's *In Search of Lost Time* edition. *Remembrance of Things Past* would have been the only English title known to Scooter circa the 1940s. The quote in the Moncrieff translation is nearly the same, with the exception of the first clause: Moncrieff's reads, "We are not provided with wisdom."

677.31–32 Gotham Book Mart] Manhattan bookstore (1920–2007) frequented by Murray, located at 41 West 47th Street for most of its history.

678.31–33 *let down that goddamn bucket . . . You know what the man said!*] An allusion to Booker T. Washington's 1895 Atlanta Exposition address; see note 435.22–23.

678.39   Taft Edison] Ralph Ellison signed his letter to Murray of February 4, 1952, "Ralph Taft Edison Ellison." This is the letter containing Ellison's extended critique of Murray's first novel (see Note on the Texts). Murray replied in his letter of February 9, 1952, "Taft Edison = Taft Jordan plus Harry Edison equal a double-barreled trumpet player, plus Thomas Edison minus Wm. H. Taft equals light bringer equals shining trumpet." See *Trading Twelves*, 31–32. The description of Taft Edison in the subsequent pages closely corresponds to certain aspects of Ellison's life (for example, his time at Tuskegee, the way he dressed, and his office in the back of the jewelry store for a time).

689.13–14   *Of Time and the River*] Novel (1935) by the American writer Thomas Wolfe (1900–1938).

689.26   Gounod character] In *Faust* (1859), opera by the French composer Charles Gounod (1818–1893); see also note 276.12–14.

690.11–13   Thomas Wolfe . . . devour the whole goddamn earth] Cf. Wolfe, *Of Time and the River*, "Young Faustus": "He was driven by a hunger so literal, cruel and physical that it wanted to devour the earth and all the things and people in it, and when it failed in this attempt, his spirit would drown in an ocean of horror and desolation. [. . .] Now he would prowl the stacks of the library at night, pulling books out of a thousand shelves and reading in them like a madman. [. . .] Within a period of ten years he read at least 20,000 volumes."

694.25   *ultima Thule*] Medieval geographers' term for a place at the northernmost limit of the known world.

695.7–8   *Ernest Hemingway's short story*] "The Capital of the World," originally entitled "The Horns of the Bull" when it was first published in 1936.

695.24–30   *if you go north . . . cry*] From "(I Wanna Go Where You Go, Do What You Do) Then I'll Be Happy" (1925), music by Cliff Friend (1893–1974), words by Lew Brown (1893–1958) and Sidney Clare.

699.16   Marcus Garvey] Jamaican-born black nationalist, entrepreneur, and advocate for economic self-sufficiency for blacks (1887–1940), founder of the Universal Negro Improvement Association and the Black Star Shipping Line.

703.20   *R. Nathaniel Dett*] See note 343.29.

719.7–8   a book the clerk had been holding for him] The sociological study *The Big Con* (1940) by the linguistics professor David W. Maurer (1906–1981), as described in the pages that follow.

720.35   Bosch's *Garden of Delights*] *The Garden of Earthly Delights* (1490–1500), triptych by Netherlandish painter Hieronymus Bosch (1450–1516).

721.6   George Grosz at the Art Students' League] The German artist George Grosz (1893–1959) immigrated to the United States shortly before the Nazis came to power and taught at the Art Students League in New York City from the 1930s through the 1950s.

721.6–7   *Ecce homo*] The title of a satirical book (1922–23) of lithographs after drawings and watercolor reproductions by Grosz, for which the artist was put on trial for obscenity and fined. The title refers to "Behold the man," Pilate's words to Christ before the Crucifixion, from the Latin Vulgate.

752.12–15   *Je suis tout à fait en train . . . heureusement en train?*] Approximately "I am fully trying to be in the truth"; *heureusement*: "fortunately." See note 612.37–613.12.

755.2   Williams and Walker . . . Miller and Lyles] See note 354.17.

755.7–8   James Joyce's river running . . . Adam.] See the beginning of *Finnegans Wake*, which continues the sentence fragment that concludes the book.

757.13–14   *Harlem . . .* Miguel Covarrubias] The Mexican caricaturist, illustrator, and painter Miguel Covarrubias (1904–1957) lived in New York in the 1920s and 1930s; he depicted Harlem subjects in his *Negro Drawings* (1927) and other works.

757.24   Big John Special . . . Fletcher Henderson's band] See note 252.30–31.

758.4–8   Roark Bradford . . . *Green Pastures*] Journalist and writer (1896–1948) whose collection *Ol' Man Adam an' His Chillun* (1928), in which a black preacher retells stories from the Bible, was adapted for the stage in 1930 as *The Green Pastures* by Marc Connelly (1890–1980). A movie version was released in 1936.

768.40   Sonia and Charles Delauny] The Ukrainian-born French painter Sonia Delaunay (1885–1979) and her son Charles Delaunay (1911–1988), jazz authority and cofounder of *Le Jazz Hot* magazine and the Hot Club de France, organization devoted to jazz.

774.30   *endroit*] French: place.

785.16–22   James Reese Europe . . . Walker.] The bandleader and composer James Reese Europe (1880–1919), whose Clef Club played compositions by African American composers at Carnegie Hall and elsewhere. For Cook and Burleigh, see note 341.23. For Williams and Walker, see note 354.17.

785.27   syncopating hellfighters from the old Harlem 369th] Founded during World War I, the U.S. Army's 369th Infantry Regiment was known as the "Harlem Hellfighters"; the performances of the regimental band, led by James Reese Europe, were enthusiastically received by military and civilian audiences in 1918.

799.23   Thomas Gray's poem] "Elegy Written in a Country Churchyard" (1751) by the English poet Thomas Gray (1716–1771).

800.18 *Rake's Progress*] The English artist William Hogarth (1697–1764) painted a sequence of eight canvases, collectively entitled *A Rake's Progress* (1732–33), that were made into a portfolio of captioned engravings in 1735.

808.19 Tampa Red] Hudson Whittaker (1904–1981), blues slide guitarist and songwriter who spent most of his career in Chicago.

813.30 *Fisher of men.*] Cf. Matthew 4:19, Mark 1:17.

813.32–33 *Many are called but few are chosen.*] Matthew 22:14.

825.35 *the dancing of an attitude*] See *The Philosophy of Literary Form* (1957) by the American literary critic and poet Kenneth Burke (1897–1993): "The symbolic act is the *dancing of an attitude.*"

828.16 CASTLE OR city-state] When discussing Tuskegee Institute, Murray often compared it to a city-state.

828.26 *snark . . . bojum!*] Refers to the fictional creature hunted in Lewis Carroll's nonsense poem *The Hunting of the Snark* (1876) and its final line, "But the snark was a boojum, you see."

829.3–4 *"Whether or not . . . biologically speaking!"*] See note 605.21–23. "Fatal interviews" refers to Millay's collection *Fatal Interview* (1931).

830.1–2 *that garden Candide . . . cultivate*] See the final words of *Candide* (1759), by the French philosopher and man of letters Voltaire (1694–1778): "We must cultivate our garden."

832.22 the one for whom he had forsaken all others] Penelope.

CONJUGATIONS AND REITERATIONS

841.7–8 *muddy water . . . hollow log*] See note 5.16.

845.15 "three quarks for mr. marx"] Cf. Joyce, *Finnegans Wake*, the opening of Book II, ch. 4: "Three quarks for Muster Mark!"

846.15–21 overheard t.s. eliot . . . fisher king!] Murray here makes several allusions to *The Waste Land* (1922) by T. S. Eliot (1888–1965).

846.26–29 jack johnson's jokey . . . jim jeffries] See note 26.29. Jack London (1876–1916) covered Johnson's championship match with Tommy Burns (see note 26.36–27.1) and exhorted Jeffries to come out of retirement to fight Johnson, writing in the *New York Herald*: "Jeff, it's up to you. The White Man must be rescued."

847.26 to new york then I came] Cf. Eliot's *The Waste Land*, III, 307, which Eliot identifies as a quotation from Augustine, *Confessions*, bk. 3: "To Carthage then I came."

847.27 picasso's demoiselles] *Les demoiselles d'Avignon* (1907), painting of five nude prostitutes by Picasso, a breakthrough in Cubist painting. It is in the collection of the Museum of Modern Art in New York.

847.33   birmingham break down] After this line, which in this volume falls at the bottom of the page, there is a stanza break.

848.3   jim europe's syncopated footsteps] See note 785.27.

848.4   louis and duke] Louis Armstrong and Duke Ellington.

848.18   *plurabilities*] Reference to Anna Livia Plurabelle in Joyce's *Finnegans Wake* (see note 482.36), called the "Bringer of Plurabilities." Also an allusion to *The Waste Land*: "One must be so careful these days." See also *Albert Murray: Essays and Memoirs*, 115.

851.13–15   time . . . 2/21/49] The February 21, 1949, issue of *Time* magazine featured Armstrong on its cover and a lengthy profile, which included his retort to a socialite when asked what jazz was.

851.28–29   one never knows . . . one?] Cf. Waller's catchphrase "One never knows, do one?"

852.10–12   bubba and duke . . . *ain't got that swing*] Duke Ellington and James "Bubber" Miley (1903–1932), trumpet and cornet player who played in Ellington's orchestra and was renowned for his facility with the plunger mute. According to Ellington, writing in *Jazz Journal* (December 1965), he first heard the expression "It don't mean a thing if you ain't got that swing" from Miley. The phrase is the title of Ellington's 1932 composition, with lyrics by Irving Mills.

852.28–32   nothing if not pragmatic . . . red bank] Count Basie was born William James Basie (1904–1984) in Red Bank, New Jersey, also the birthplace of the American literary critic Edmund Wilson (1895–1972). William James (1842–1910) was an American pragmatist philosopher.

853.18–19   ralph ellison's other / deep second joints] Referring to a section of East Second Street in Oklahoma City. An African American business district in Ellison's youth, it was also the title and subject of a poem by Ellison included in a letter to Murray in *Trading Twelves*, 53–55.

854.3–8   *all art . . . of music.*] "All art constantly aspires towards the condition of music": from the essay "The School of Giorgione" (1877) by the English writer Walter Pater (1839–1894), collected in his book *The Renaissance* (1888). Pater's remark is not about Botticelli in particular, though there is a chapter on Botticelli in the book.

854.10–11   is the supreme fiction, / madam] Cf. the opening of Wallace Stevens's poem "A High-Toned Old Christian Woman" (1922): "Poetry is the supreme fiction, madame."

854.35   according to vico] Murray copied out the following passage from Isaiah Berlin's *Vico and Herder: Two Studies in the History of Ideas* (London: Hogarth, 1976), 48: "[Vico] says that first came onomatopoeic monosyllables, then polysyllables, followed by interjections, pronouns, prepositions, nouns, and finally verbs. This is not accidental but springs from the fact that the concepts of 'before' and 'after,' and of movement, which verbs convey, necessarily came later than the apprehension of things—lumps of material stuff—objects denoted by nouns, which in their turn came later than the sense of personal identity, or the states conveyed by primitive cries. He provides equally fanciful arguments for the view that the earliest forms of verbs must have been in the imperative."

855.7–11   kennethburke . . . *dancing* of an attitude] See note 825.35.

855.17–18   *it ain't what you do . . . do it.*] Cf. "'Tain't What You Do (It's the Way that You Do It)" (1939), words and music by Sy Oliver (1910–1988) and James Young (1912–1984), first a hit for Jimmie Lunceford and His Orchestra.

855.33   ineluctable modality] See note 596.2.

859.16   forest primeval] See first line of *Evangeline: A Tale of Acadie* (1847) by Henry Wadsworth Longfellow (1807–1882): "This is the forest primeval."

859.20   almanach de gotha] See note 606.7–8.

861.13   memory he said believes] Here and throughout the poem Murray is quoting a passage from William Faulkner's novel *Light in August* (1932), ch. 6: "Memory believes before knowing remembers. Believes longer than recollects, longer than knowing even wonders."

861.26–28   *something is going to happen . . . to me*] From the monologue of Joe Christmas, the black protagonist of *Light in August*, before he commits murder.

862.3   *clytemnestra my black one*] In Faulkner's *Absalom, Absalom!* (1936), Clytemnestra is the daughter of the landowner and slaveholder Thomas Sutpen and a slave.

862.10   *black human blood red on butcher knives*] In chapter 19 of *Light in August*, the white vigilante Percy Grimm murders Joe Christmas, then castrates him with a butcher knife.

862.11   *white female blood on phallic corncobs*] In Faulkner's novel *Sanctuary* (1931), the impotent criminal Popeye rapes Temple Drake, the daughter of a prominent judge, with a corncob.

862.12   yoknapatawpha] Fictional county in which much of William Faulkner's fiction takes place.

862.16–18   gallops confederate cavalry . . . hightower / sermons] In *Light in August*, the Presbyterian minister Gail Hightower could not "get religion and that galloping cavalry and his dead grandfather shot from the galloping horse untangled from each other, even in the pulpit."

862.26   *bedford forrest*] See note 369.30–31.

862.31–33 rosa coldfield's . . . *wants it told!*] At the beginning of *Absalom, Absalom!*, Quentin Compson is summoned by the elderly Rosa Coldfield because, he believes, "*she wants it told . . . so that people whom she will never see and whose names she will never hear and who have never heard her name nor seen her face will read it and know at last why God let us lose the War.*"

863.5–7 with twenty negroes (shackled) . . . sutpens / hundred] In *Absalom, Absalom!* Thomas Sutpen, having been an overseer in Haiti, brings twenty slaves and an anonymous French architect to Yoknapatawpha County, where the architect, working for Sutpen against his will, designs the plantation house, called Sutpen's Hundred.

863.16 miss reba's sanctum sanctorum of law and order] Memphis brothel in *Sanctuary* where Popeye brings Temple Drake (see note 862.11) after raping her, run by a madam named Reba Rivers.

863.25–27 macbeths . . . thickets] In Shakespeare's *Macbeth*, Macbeth is told by the Third Apparition that he will not be defeated until Birnam Wood comes to Dunsinane (IV.i.92–94). Macbeth takes this to mean that he will never be defeated. His enemies later disguise themselves as vegetation from the woods (V.iv.4–7) and advance on Dunsinane.

863.28–29 *in hot pursuit . . . illusive mississippi christmas*] See *Light in August*, ch. 6.

864.1 *Inside Dopester*] American sociologist David Riesman (1909–2002) coined the term "inside-dopester" in his book *The Lonely Crowd* (1950), to describe a savvy observer of politics. When once asked what the phrase meant, Murray replied it suggested someone at a racetrack who claimed to have inside information about horses, jockeys, and so on.

865.11–12 jung's / naughty notions of u.s. negroes] Carl Jung (1875–1961) published "Your Negroid and Indian Behavior" in *The Forum* 83, no. 4 (April 1930): 193–99. The essay reflects common racial stereotypes of the time. Nevertheless, it is perceptive about the mutually constitutive nature of black and white American ethnic identity. For instance: "Since the Negro lives within your cities and even within your houses, he also lives with your skin, subconsciously."

865.27 valse triste] Sad waltz.

866.2 light . . . shineth in the darkness] Cf. John 1:5.

866.4 *tant pis*] French: so much the worse.

866.24 *Poeta de Época*] Spanish: Poet of the Age.

868.9 storybook creola] Creola Calloway, character in *The Spyglass Tree*.

871.14 Gideon] Ancient Israelite military leader whose exploits are recounted in the Book of Judges.

873.24   Fiery Furnace] See Daniel 3:19–30, in which Shadrach, Meshach, and Abednego miraculously survive being thrown into a "fiery furnace" (3:23).

873.27   Daniel in a lion's den?] See Daniel 6:16–23.

873.29–30   Jonah / in the belly of the whale?] See Jonah 2:1–10.

873.31   drowned Pharaoh's mighty army] See Exodus 15:4.

874.23   signs of the fleece.] See Judges 6:36–40.

874.34   *jawbone of an ass!*] See Judges 15:15–16.

875.1   *Whicker Bill Comesaw*] See *South to a Very Old Place* in *Albert Murray: Essays and Memoirs*, 202, 204, 216.

OTHER POEMS

879.1   "A man of no fortune, and with a name to come"] From the first stanza of "Canto I" (1917) by Ezra Pound (1885–1972), later incorporated into his long poem *The Cantos*. Elpenor speaks the line to Odysseus, envisioning it as his epitaph.

882.5   the readiness is all] Shakespeare, *Hamlet*, V.ii.222.

882.12   fifty roads to town] Once imagined by Murray as a prospective title for a novel.

APPENDIX

887.1   *The Luzana Cholly Kick*] For an explanation of this story's relation to *Train Whistle Guitar*, see the Note on the Texts.

892.23   "Well tell the dy ya,"] See note 10.10.

906.14–15   *Crowtillie . . .* ruins of right down there] See note 62.4.

This book is set in 10 point ITC Galliard, a face designed for digital composition by Matthew Carter and based on the sixteenth-century face Granjon. The paper is acid-free lightweight opaque that will not turn yellow or brittle with age. The binding is sewn, which allows the book to open easily and lie flat. The binding board is covered in Brillianta, a woven rayon cloth made by Van Heek–Scholco Textielfabrieken, Holland. Composition by Dedicated Book Services. Printing and binding by Edwards Brothers Malloy, Ann Arbor. Designed by Bruce Campbell.